THE FRAILTY OF PERCEPTION

BOOK I
THE ASHER BLOOM
CHRONICLES

JOEY RAWLINGS

COPYRIGHT © 2012 JOEY RAWLINGS

Paperback Version 1.0
ISBN: 978-0-9873748-1-3

This book is a work of fiction. Names, characters, places, and incidents are either products of the author's imagination or are used fictitiously. Any resemblance to actual persons, living or dead, events, or locales is entirely coincidental.

STAY CONNECTED

www.asherbloom.com

www.facebook.com/asherbloom

Twitter: @authorjoeyraw

CONTRIBUTORS

Editor: Nathan Lawrence

Cover Illustration: Sheridan Johns

To my family and friends,
my cohort of guinea-pig readers
and all those I met along the way,
I owe you a debt of thanks
For your support and insight.

With special thanks to:
Liz, for her endless support and oversight
Nathan, for his unwavering editorial scruples
Dan, for the limitless font of imagination
Patrick, for his deathly imagination
Sam, for her eagle eyes of grammatical lore
Brett, for picking out the plot holes
Rose, for her patience and female insight
Penny, for the sagacious advice of a stranger

To everyone else,
I hope you enjoy the ride.

PROLOGUE

Silence enshrouded the cobbled streets like a womb as the two men approached the row of tenement houses. One man dwarfed the other by nearly half, both in height and width, yet the two were as inseparable as air and breath. They had been ever since the Mortis Skulk first waged their insidious war against the unsuspecting inhabitants of the Cruaar Nation.

Rumours of the giant man's passage through the city had spread fast. The streets were empty. Doors were locked and windows shuttered. Of course, such weak countermeasures, no matter how heavily they were auganically enhanced, would do little to protect anyone whose name he called.

No-one ever came forward willingly, not to the Red Scar Guards and certainly not to their enormous leader, the Scarlet Commander. Whether it was guilt or fear holding them back, it mattered not, all those whose names were read inevitably answered the call, by subjugation or, more commonly, by overwhelming force.

The Half-brute at his side was his right hand, but everyone knew him as the Red Scar spymaster. Long had his ferrets exposed the traitorous ilk the Red Scars had been charged to destroy by the Grand Chancellor. The Red Scars were his personal guard in times of peace, but in times of war, they became so much more. They had adapted to this rebellion like cockroaches to nuclear waste and had grown strong where others suffered and broke.

If there was even so much as a whisper of a traitor or traitorous act, the Half-brute would hear of it and bring it to his master, regardless of whether its legitimacy held merit. It was not his place to decide the fate of those names he received, it was the Scarlet Commander's, and the man knew death like the rise and fall of his own chest.

Whether the Half-brute was named as such because he was half the size of his towering counterpart, or because he only had one arm, no-one knew for sure, and none dared ask. But all knew his network spread far and wide. Some even rumoured that his spies had even infiltrated the ranks of the Mortis Skulk itself, which was an act beyond reproach, none but cultists would dare raise a hand against him.

The abject terror that had burrowed deep within the minds of Undergall's populace, those who had not already fled to The Blind, had cast a long shadow over this once great city. The Mortis Skulk deception and betrayals that had followed had left this city a broken shell, as it had the others. Those that had not already fallen were now subject to the purge, instigated and carried out by the Tribarion Cohort and Red Scar Guard. No-one that bore the taint would be left alive to tell the tale. Only the loyal would remain. Since the fall of Cerebule, the Mortis Skulk's reign of terror was coming to a well-deserved end.

The diminutive Half-brute walked purposefully a step behind his master, perpetually bathing in the shadow of the veritable giant. The Scarlet Commander was a monster, clad entirely in black, except for two scarlet scars marring the mask he wore over his face. One ran across his eyes, the other down the left side of his face from hairline to chin. Easily double the size of the Half-brute, the Scarlet Commander was the embodiment of terror.

He had been appointed by the Grand Chancellor as the weapon that would cut out the heart of the Mortis Skulk infestation. Countless hundreds had died by the Scarlet Commander's hand, and hundreds more would perish in his pursuit to rid the city of all those whose augers bore the vile taint.

Today, two more traitors would join those already purged.

The Half-brute's network had provided two names and the location of where they were in hiding. "The two we seek evaded their tests." The Half-brute whispered in a gruff guttural voice. "Their guilt is assured."

The Scarlet Commander said nothing, but acknowledged his spymaster's intelligence with a nod.

"This one," the Half-brute muttered and stopped, nodding his head ever so subtly at the nearest run-down house standing opposite him. Its walls were crumbling and its windows were shuttered, albeit poorly. It would provide no defence to anyone sheltering inside.

"Their names?" The Scarlet Commander's voice was deep and coarse. It boomed like the echo of an empty oil drum when he spoke, and when he shouted it cracked like the percussive snap of thunder.

The Half-brute whispered their names and moved away from his master. He had made the mistake of standing too close once before, but never again. The traitor's blood had fouled his clothing and he abhorred the stench it left behind. His master, however, never seemed bothered by it and he bathed in it much more frequently than the Half-brute ever had.

"Penkora! Adama!" His voice echoed off the tenement houses like the lingering reverberation of a heavy gong. "You are charged with treason. You have been called."

Only silence followed.

No-one ever came forward willingly.

The Scarlet Commander smiled cruelly beneath his mask and channelled his blood into his auger. The gemstone was hidden beneath his heavy cloak, lodged within a secret pouch that hung between his shoulder blades.

No-one, not even the Half-brute, had ever set eyes on the small gemstone, nor the battle mantle in which it was set, nor would anyone while the Scarlet Commander continued to draw breath. His auger held secrets that could be linked to his identity; to reveal such a thing would give his enemies power over him.

Such a thing could never be allowed.

He felt the gem warm as it came to life, power surging though its surface as he lifted his hand before him and opened his palm upwards. Focusing his mind, he probed and searched for the aura of the accused within the house. It took him a moment to recognise the shimmer and flux of a sophisticated auganic shield, which may have fooled a lesser foe, but not the Harbinger of Hearts. He pushed against the shield with his mind, increasing the pressure until he had stretched it to breaking point.

He felt it shatter.

Then he found them.

He felt them tremble, feebly huddling against each other, protecting themselves against their already sealed fates. He was about to realise his mind, when he felt the presence of a third, much younger entity. A child.

It mattered not. Witnesses that he permitted to survive, he did so to recount stories of the horror visited upon traitors, to sow fear into the hearts of his enemies. Besides, he needed only one to draw out the other.

Sensing a weaker aura, he raised two fingers and waited. Only when he heard the distraught sounds of choking inside the house did he rake his arm back towards his chest. The front window on the second floor of the house shattered in an explosion of glass and fragmented timber as a woman's body was hurled outwards and down into the street.

"Penkora!" a man shouted, emerging briefly within view of the gaping hole now marring the side of the building. He desperately reached for her body as it flew forward, but his attempts to catch her were in vain. He shot a venomous look at the Scarlet Commander and disappeared back out of view, cursing the man to the depths of hell as he went.

The woman's bloody body landed two feet away from the Scarlet Commander's boots with a sickening splat of broken bones and bruised flesh.

"Penkora," the Half-brute murmured, and noted something down in a ledger he kept at his waist.

The Scarlet Commander turned his wrist and watched as the woman's body spun on the floor. Dragging his fingers upwards through the air her body levitated and she clutched at her throat, gasping for air.

"Please," the woman gurgled as the Scarlet Commander floated her helpless body ever closer towards him. "Not here. Not like this."

"Your auger," he commanded, applying more pressure by clenching his fingers against his thumb. The effect was instantaneous. "Show me your auger."

Penkora's face started to turn blue. Speech was almost impossible, but still she choked out a plea of help with a weak trembling voice. "Adama…"

"He cannot save you." The Scarlet Commander backhanded the woman with a savage blow that knocked out two of her teeth and sent them sprawling across the cobbles in a shower of blood. "Your auger, or death. You choose."

Though the gurgling sounds of the woman choking now filled the streets, the Scarlet Commander's senses picked up another sound. The sound of running feet. It was faint, barely above a whisper, but whoever owned them was coming and coming fast.

Adama launched himself out of the window with a parashu battle-axe extended high above his head, ready to deliver a fatal blow to the man assaulting his wife. His body radiated with power. But nothing compared to the power exuded by the Scarlet Commander. To the giant, this man was no bigger threat than a mildly annoyed lapdog with blunt teeth.

The Half-brute did not move and merely shifted his attention upwards towards the image of a desperate man's last actions.

Adama had eyes only for the Scarlet Commander, but for all his rage and the adrenaline coursing through his veins, his choice of attack had been poor. He had no escape, and could not counter a secondary blow should the Scarlet Commander evade or block the first. Adama's fury, fuelled him forward. He wildly drew the axe forward through the air, levelling its ornate blade at his enemy's neck.

The Scarlet Commander didn't flinch, instead he stood motionless until the last possible moment before flicking his extended wrist in the direction of his attacker.

Penkora's suspended body jerked through the air into position like a marionette. Twirling his fingers in a circle, he spun her around just in time to face her husband. A moment later the blade struck home, biting deep into her neck, snapping her collarbone and severing half of her rib cage. Bluish blood spewed from the wound in large messy spurts, quickly covering her husband's face and chest in a morbid display of betrayal and treachery.

Lifting up his other hand, the Scarlet Commander caught Adama just as the weapon struck and suspended him opposite Penkora. Slowly raising the same hand, he lifted Adama upwards until he was at eye level with his dying wife.

The Scarlet Commander wanted him to watch.

He wanted him to learn how traitors die.

It was the final insult dealt to a traitor. He had betrayed and killed his own wife, however unwittingly he had performed the act. The two helpless fools remained suspended in the air, both sodden with her blood, both choking from the invisible force crushing their windpipes.

Penkora's heart pumped furiously as the blood drained from her veins and down onto the street below. When she drew her last breath, her eyes rolled back into her head and her body went limp.

Adama's face was a mess of bluish blood-stained tears when the Scarlet Commander flicked his wrist and discarded Penkora's dead body as he would an unwanted garment. The axe fell from her shoulder a few feet away from the Half-brute, who picked it up and examined it closely. Blood continued to pool on the ground around Penkora's body, further staining the once-white cobblestones with the death of yet another traitor.

"Your auger will seal your fate, traitor."

"I... am... no... traitor." The man choked and gurgled as he struggled against his oppressor's invisible iron grip.

The Half-brute walked towards them and held out Adama's parashu battle-axe for his master's inspection. A single blade sat opposite an ornately interwoven steel spike. Another spike sat atop the shaft, acting both as a housing and protector to a small blue gemstone, just above where the arced blade met its moorings.

"The test."

"It is already done," the Half-brute murmured.

"He has no taint?" the Scarlet Commander asked in surprise.

"I'm... no... traitor," Adama gurgled.

"No, you are not," the Scarlet Commander agreed and lowered the man until his feet were almost touching the ground. "But you are a murderer. And the punishment is the same."

Before the man could even contest the accusation. The Scarlet Commander swiped a clawed hand through the air and ripped out the man's throat, showering the Half-brute in the man's blood. When Adama's body went limp, he dropped it at the diminutive's man's feet in disgust and said only three words.

"You... were wrong."

As he turned to walk away, his eyes fell upon a young boy standing in the doorway of the now-ruined house. The child said nothing but, instead, held a look on his face that the Scarlet Commander would never forget.

It was not rage, nor hatred, but a strange look of curiosity as he gazed upwards at the enormous masked giant that had just murdered his parents.

Raising a finger he mutely pointed at the man until both the Scarlet Commander and the Half-brute had both vanished from sight. With a whisper he muttered a single word in their wake.

"Traitor."

PART I

THE VERACITY OF TRUTH

"A lie, even if told in kindness, is doomed.
Forever cursed to carve far greater wound
Than even the most brutal of truths."

Aoladaire Heerdeguul
Senior Custodian
Undergall Augestry
1736

CHAPTER 1

THE CALL OF FLAMES

Asher wasn't much to look at. Most people that passed him in the street didn't give him a second glance. His clothes were filthy, but no less than his hair, which was also tangled, uncut and in dire need of attention.

When the scraggly blond strands weren't stuffed beneath his scruffy black baseball cap, he purposefully wore them down over his face to his chin, hiding his features from anyone that might care to look. He'd even gotten used to the unpleasant smell radiating from his clothes. It was little wonder ordinary folk instinctively gave him a wide berth in the street; and the streets were by no means clean.

For as long as he could remember, he'd been considered a vagrant, a sewer rat or a street urchin by everyone that cared to look at him. But Asher liked to think of himself as an adventurer of alleyways.

Asher was by no means good looking, but he wasn't ugly, either. His looks were plain, although, from time to time, Raglan caught glimpses of the man he would someday become from his expressions and mannerisms.

A strong jawline had set under the teen's cheeks and the hint of broad shoulders gave a sense that Asher would grow much larger over the coming years. Sharp blue eyes were each flecked with a tiny spot of auburn that caught the light on occasion, lending Asher quite a distinctive and disarming gaze.

Asher was also quite tall, more so than a lot of the native Egyptian teenagers the same age. This fact alone didn't do him any favours when it came to keeping a low profile.

Many might think that such a bedraggled individual would live a pitiful existence at best, yet Asher was anything but pitiful. Raglan—Uncle Raglan to Asher—had made sure of that. Although they may not have had two coins to rub together between them at the best of times, it did little to stop the street-savvy duo from enjoying all the bounty life had to offer.

Rarely parted from each other's side, they always managed to find a way to satisfy their needs. They ate when they were hungry, slept when they were tired and laughed whenever something remotely humorous caught their eye. Whilst they heavily relied on each other's street-sharpened instincts to survive, there was little the two went without, despite their unconventional way of life.

Raglan was a master at blending into his environment. His ability to vanish within a sea of familiar-looking faces was uncanny. The remarkable skill had come in handy time after time, especially when a quick escape was needed to avoid the attention of their victims, or the authorities. After all, few knew the darkened corners of the central laneways and makeshift alley shortcuts as well as Raglan. Despite the fact they had not been in this city long, Raglan knew the streets as if they were the creases on the back of his time-weathered hands.

Strange as it might sound, Raglan's incessant need to keep on the move had been the only constant in Asher's life. They never stayed in the same place for more than a month or two, at most. Border crossings were always hardest, but Raglan always got them across safely and, for the most part, largely unnoticed.

He had no choice. He had to keep Asher safe.

The pair ambled along one of the main streets of Aswan's old quarter. It was abuzz with merchants, shop owners and stall keepers, all vying for the attention of semi-gullible customers. They sold everything from goat cheese to used car parts, to the very latest in technology, be it stolen, legitimate, or clever brand-name knock-offs.

"Asher," Raglan muttered under his breath in a raspy voice, nodding his head towards a nearby fruit stand. The owner was otherwise preoccupied, engaged in an argument with a quarrelsome customer and, as a result, conveniently had his back turned to the pair's approach.

"Way ahead of you," Asher whispered back, waiting for just the right moment to deftly flick his hand out a few inches from his waist as the two passed the stall. The stall owner continued to engage wholeheartedly in the argument, none the wiser his street-cart was two apples lighter than it had been moments before.

A few paces on, Asher flipped a juicy red apple to Raglan and smiled as he took a bite out of the one he'd snagged for himself, thinking about the possibilities of the night ahead. It was only a few hours until his found-day and, being his tenth found-day, Raglan had promised him something special.

Raglan had never known Asher's real birthday, or age for that matter, though he suspected it was somewhere close to fourteen. So, instead of an annual birthday celebration, he'd made a point of celebrating the day he first found Asher all those years ago.

Asher never had reason to argue otherwise and, even if he did, it wouldn't change the fact he would probably never know his actual birthdate. Besides, Raglan made sure his found-day celebrations were much better than any regular birthday could ever be.

Moments after they passed the stall, a sharp gust of hot wind swept across the vendor's apple cart. The owner briefly abandoned his argument and turned his head in the duo's direction, hand held against his face, shielding it from the wind.

His new perspective instantly locked on to the two vagrants meandering down the road gnawing on a couple of juicy red apples. He knew only too well his stall was the only one that sold red apples within five blocks. Angry at his momentary obliviousness to the theft, he called out after them, hurling abusive Egyptian curses at them and their ancestors.

Raglan and Asher heard the cry and glanced back to see the irate stall owner bellowing after them, his hands in the air making vile threats. Simultaneously, they knew it was time to make themselves scarce and promptly changed direction into a much busier street: one bustling with people and loud, obnoxious street vendors. It was the kind of street that made it easy to lose a pursuer amidst the crowd, before properly disappearing into one of the larger open-air squares.

The nearest open-air square was a central bazaar in old town. From there it would be easy to vanish from sight as they had done two days ago. Bordered on all sides by tightly packed buildings, a multitude of narrow alleyways fed into the square, each providing a perfect escape route that one could disappear into and lose any pursuer in the maze of Aswan's back alleys.

In the centre of the square, a large group of people were busy congregating around a street performer. His enticing and exotic accent somehow rose above the noisy commotion of the inane day-to-day chatter of a hundred different conversations.

"Coom one, coom all, to wiitnass dee seecrats daat time foogot."

Forever curious, Asher flicked Raglan a brief look of permission before running ahead to see what all the fuss was about. Narrowly ducking behind a passing car, Asher disappeared amidst the undulating sea of tanned faces.

Raglan apprehensively surveyed the scene. Despite his uncanny ability to vanish within them in seconds, he hated large crowds, especially ones in open areas. There were too many places for a threat to hide.

Ever since he had found Asher, he had been forever searching for even the smallest sign that their presence had been compromised. Up until now, his constant vigilance had proven unnecessary, a fact of which he was eternally thankful.

Raglan craned his neck, attempting to scan faces in the crowd for possible threats. It was little use. Each face flashed before him for less than a second before disappearing behind another. It wasn't enough time to gauge whether they were threats. Besides, judging a person's face was only half the battle; if the eyes didn't give away their intent, their body movement or what they held in their hands nearly always did, none of which he could see any from his current position.

Even though he couldn't see anything out of the ordinary, it was a big enough crowd to place doubt in his mind, and his instincts knew better than to trust first appearances. Too much was hidden from view. He needed a better angle.

He needed a higher vantage point.

Skirting around the edge of the crowd, mostly to avoid his hatred of the tightly packed mass of people congregating in its centre, Raglan spied a wooden ladder behind some commercial rubbish bins in a back alley. It looked worn and rickety, but it was leaning against the wall of a single-storey bakery. To Raglan, it might as well have been an open invitation to ascend to Aswan's rooftops. In no time at all, he nimbly climbed the ladder and was on the roof.

A memory ran through his mind as the cool night air washed over his face. It had not always been like this. The world he abandoned and the life he had left behind should have felt like a pleasant dream, but all he could remember were the terrors in the darkness that drove him out.

Now his world was one where electronic equipment flooded the pockets of the masses, gaudy neon signs littered every storefront and people shuffled around blind to the realities he knew existed, realities hiding in plain sight.

Looking over the edge of the roof, everyone seemed only too happy to mindlessly deafen themselves with overly loud music delivered through crisp white headphones or, worse still, deafen everyone else with inconsequential chatter about the mundane on their insufferable mobile phones. It was a far stretch from the peaceful and rewarding life he'd led decades ago in MaiSchloss. At least, before it came crashing down around him in a torrent of blood-strewn rubble.

Even to this day, memories he spent decades trying to forget still managed to resurface and haunt him in his sleep, turning his dreams into nightmares and plunging his body into a cold sweat. Those horrifying memories had made it impossible for him to want to face his own kind again. So he did the only thing he could and turned his back on them forever, even if that meant forgoing his birthright to lead a forsaken life in The Blind.

However, it was this decision that had inadvertently led him to Asher, a discovery for which he would be eternally thankful. Raglan had lived the life of a wandering nomad for almost thirty years in a world now dominated and ruled by technology. He never stayed in the same place for long for fear of being discovered. It had taken time to readjust and he'd made mistakes along the way, but he'd learnt how to stay off the grid in order to stay safe.

No phones, no banks, no IDs and no-one to betray him.

Haunted by his past and filled with regret, fear and shame, Raglan had lived by these rules for years after his exodus, unable and unwilling to trust a single person. For a decade, he had cared for no-one but himself. It was not until he found a small boy no more than four years of age, covered in ash with eyes full of tears, blindly stumbling through the outskirts of the Hoia-Baciu Forest, near the city of Cluj, that Raglan's wall of selfishness and regret came crashing down. Despite searching the town and nearby area for days, Raglan never found the fire responsible for the boy's covering of ash, so he named him for it: Asher. In Raglan's mind, it was as good a name as any and, better yet, the boy took to it like a duck to water.

Raglan only knew a few words in Romanian, and it instantly became clear Asher was already much more proficient in the language than he would ever be, so instead he taught him English. Day after day, week after week, the boy's knowledge grew and the two began to communicate more effectively. Over time, Raglan developed a strong affection for the boy.

Raglan could not explain why, but from the moment he first laid eyes on Asher, he had instantly felt a duty of care to the boy. Even though he secretly knew he would never be able to provide the necessary protection Asher would need in the years to come.

Raglan had given up his right to those abilities many years ago, when he decided to forsake his birthright and leave the old world behind forever. It was not long after he'd taken Asher under his wing that long forgotten memories of his past life came flooding back to the surface: wave after anguishing wave. Every time he looked at him, fragments of his tormented past became an all-too-frequent reality once more.

He scratched his chin as he perched on the bakery rooftop, scanning the crowd. He knew over the coming days he would have to explain everything to Asher. Why it was imperative that Asher understand the dangers of the world Raglan had left behind. The world that lay just out of sight, hidden from those that lived amidst The Blind: those who were oblivious to all things but their own short-sighted existence.

Still not high enough to properly survey the bazaar's centre, Raglan craned his neck and looked for a higher vantage point. Spying a few convenient and easy-to-scale balconies, he urged his weary bones onwards to even greater heights.

Once the clock struck midnight it would be Asher's tenth found-day. Now, more than ever, Raglan knew in his heart that Asher deserved an explanation. He'd wanted to tell him everything, he'd just never been able to find the right words, or the right time. Soon, however, Asher would see things that no amount of logic, reason or science would be able to explain. No matter how much Raglan wanted to keep such things hidden, he knew Asher's own curiosity would eventually drag him into the thick of the very world from which Raglan had long since estranged himself.

It was only a matter of time before someone would discover the teenager, especially one as unique as Asher. His fate was inescapable. His rare condition guaranteed that much. Worse still, Asher had no idea about any of it.

Raglan's feet came to rest on the flat roof of a third-storey building. From his new perch he could see every square inch of the old-town bazaar. Squatting down on his haunches behind a squat chimney stack to avoid detection, he eased himself into a watchful position and surveyed the scene below.

Letting his instincts take over, his mind processed the bazaar, section by section: the sounds, sights, smells, direction of the breeze, sway of the crowd and, most important of all, the performer at its centre.

His gaze drifted back and forth like a pendulum, constantly scanning and searching. Commoners swarmed this way and that like frenzied ants, the majority pausing at least a moment to admire the performer that swayed and danced before them in a rhythmic, almost hypnotic, fashion.

A kaleidoscope sky farewelled the setting sun, which was a relatively quick process in this part of the world. Although the sun set late in the day, the coming darkness would limit Raglan's ability to perceive and ward off danger. On the upside, though, the bazaar would be adequately lit with street lights soon enough and he still had Asher firmly in his sights.

Nothing seemed out of place.

Raglan looked down at Asher darting this way and that, slowly working his way through the enthralled masses. Despite his uncanny aptitude for survival in the streets, in this part of the world, Asher stood out like a shovel amongst spears. Forget the fact the lad had bright blond hair, albeit stuffed underneath a dirty baseball cap, his pale face was a beacon amidst the sea of tanned locals. It didn't even matter that his face and arms were covered in dirt and grit from roughhousing in the city streets.

Ultimately, it was Asher's unique condition that would see him ostracised and gawked at, irrespective of where he was. Because of this, Raglan had taken every precaution to keep Asher's secret hidden at every turn, instilling a deep-rooted need for Asher to do the same, though the boy didn't yet understand why.

More artificial light spilled across the square as oil lamps, streetlights and torches sprang to life, each vainly attempting to ward off night's lingering darkness. Raglan's eyes preyed upon the crowd for any hint of danger, but failed to see anything out of the ordinary.

Over the years, he'd fervently insisted on teaching Asher a multitude of different ways to mask his most obvious characteristic from public view. In a city such as this it was relatively easy. People rarely gave any notice to a street rat. Fewer still looked at Asher for more than a second before dismissing him, despite his noticeably foreign looks, so long as he kept his distance. In another world, one hidden from untrained eyes, Raglan knew all too well the thin veil of a common bandage would do little to hide Asher's condition from anyone that laid eyes on him.

Normally, Raglan would have insisted Asher wear a leather glove, but Egypt's unrelenting sun made wearing such an item horrendously uncomfortable. So, instead, Asher replaced it with a crisp white bandage, at least, it had been when Raglan stole it for him in the first place.

So it was since Asher's found-day that his right hand remained concealed at all times. Whether wrapped in bandages, snug in a glove, or stuffed inside his pocket, the skin of Asher's right hand rarely saw the light of day or, worse yet, the dark of night.

Asher's condition was their secret, and Raglan had worked hard ever since he'd first found the boy to ensure it stayed that way. Growing up, Asher had never really asked too much about the secret they shared or his condition, despite his obvious discomfort and insatiable curiosity. Though when he did, he always received the same answer, accompanied by the same disconcerting look.

"You're too young to understand just yet, but one day, you'll know as much as I do." Raglan had used this line often. Knowledge of the truth would've done Asher no favours, past or present. But, in all honesty, nothing about the boy's condition would ever do him any favours.

In the centre of the square, the performer retrieved two waist-high chains from his violin case on the ground and twirled them in a dangerous but alluring fashion. His erratic twirls and spins made it hard for Raglan to focus on his actions or get a clear picture of the man, but fire-twirling street performers were as common as heatstroke in these parts.

Strangely enough, it was not the fire-twirling or the man's erratic actions that bothered Raglan: it was the violin case on the ground. It could just be a coincidence, but Raglan knew better than to place his trust in ideas as fallible as happenstance.

Musicians carrying instrument cases were rarely given a second thought by those in The Blind. Their eclectic and eccentric wardrobes helped them blend into the stereotype that allowed them free access to wander wherever they pleased; unnoticed, unapproached and, for the most part, unchecked.

A few of the streetlights flickered briefly at the edge of the square, but that was nothing new in this section of the city. Bad wiring and old transformers often faltered during the night as more and more lights came on, draining additional power from the decades-old electricity grid. A momentary flicker of light was not enough for Raglan's suspicions to surface just yet; but a nagging unease was growing deep in his gut.

The crowd clapped and cheered as the performer executed a series of dazzling spins and twirls.

A sharp pain ignited in Raglan's upper thighs as his muscles cramped. He shifted position in order to stretch and alleviate the oncoming pain, when an entire alleyway, off in the distance, descended into darkness. Raglan's eyes snapped to attention, instantly locking on to the alley, trying to pierce the darkness. For a second he thought he saw a blur of motion from within the shadows, but it was too dark to be sure.

He couldn't be certain his eyes weren't just playing tricks on him, or whether his pessimism was simply getting the better of him. However, the nagging unease spread to his bones. Between the violin case, the flickering streetlights and the sudden darkness in the alley, coincidence now seemed the least likely explanation. Or was he just being paranoid? Raglan retrieved a small looking glass from his pocket, closed one eye and peered through it, blocking out everything but the darkened alley. His growing sense of unease rapidly transformed into fear.

After much hustling and squirming, Asher made his way towards the front of the densely packed crowd. He was only able to catch glimpses of the street performer and only because the crowd's mass heaved and shifted to and fro with excitement at the man's dare-defying actions.

Around him, the crowd held up mobile phones and cameras, all pointed at the performer, hoping to record his entertaining fire-twirling antics. Asher brushed past a fat tourist banging the side of his camera as its screen started flickering until it showed nothing but black and white static.

"What the hell, I just bought this!" The fat tourist's shrill voice was laced with annoyance.

Another fool parted from his money by sweet-talking merchants. Asher smiled, knowing that he wasn't the only thief in the night stalking the streets of Aswan. He pushed past the tourist and several others in the crowd in order to get a better look at the performer. Strangely enough, they were all experiencing similar digital interference with their devices.

That's weird. Thief or not, no salesman is that good. Asher watched at least ten different screens flickering with static; their owners turning them this way and that, all searching for an apparent cause or fault, but finding none.

The performer twirled and spun, oblivious to the technological interference his audience was encountering. He wildly laced the air with blazing arcs of fire in a mesmerising display of power over the elements as he danced and spun.

Asher couldn't be sure whether the performer was foreign or native by looking at him. His skin was as black as coal, but that was nothing strange in these parts. His clothes were vastly different to the local attire: they seemed older, more worn; but, then again, street performers usually had strange outfits to distinguish them from the common beggars that infested the streets.

Asher only knew for sure when he heard the performer speak. Even though the man mostly spoke in Egyptian Arabic, which Asher couldn't understand, when he slipped in the occasional sentence of broken English, Asher found his accent wildly exotic.

They had not been in Egypt long enough for Asher to learn even basic Arabic. Short of the Arabic equivalent of hello and goodbye, the language just didn't make sense to him. Raglan had only ever spoken to him in English and he'd made damn sure Asher rarely spoke to anyone else.

"Hello? Hello? John, are you there? No, I can't hear you… Hello?" A loud foreign businessman stared at his phone as his connection faltered, before disconnecting entirely.

Asher shot the man a dark look, attempting to shut him up, but the businessman remained oblivious, attempting instead to redial the number without success. Asher turned back, released his frown and gazed upon the mysterious performer.

His dark skin glistened with sweat, each bead glimmering as it caught the light of the twirling fire, while his eyes shone a brilliant white. He addressed the crowd loudly, in Egyptian.

Even though Asher didn't speak it well, he could tell some of the locals were having trouble understanding the man's heavy accent. Regardless, everyone seemed to appreciate the man's mastery over fire and were all too happy to indulge him and cheer on his performance; even if they were unable to record it on their digital devices.

Close by, on an apartment building's rooftop, Raglan's eye was still locked to his looking glass. He'd seen neither hide nor hair of anything move within the darkness.

"Damn eyes playing tricks on me," he muttered to himself, before lowering the looking glass and returning his gaze to the centre of the bazaar. His eyes were instantly met by a hodgepodge of flickering digital screens that sparkled amidst the crowd like wavering stars.

Raglan knew in that instant that something was definitely

wrong. His instincts kicked into gear as a multitude of questions burst into his mind. *Where is the threat? Have they seen Asher? Can I get to them first?*

"In dee faar faar plaace, I laarn mee soom vaast fiiyah triiks."

Amidst the man's various twirls and spins, each laced with blinding streaks of fire, the performer repeated each sentence twice, once in Egyptian Arabic and again in his heavily accented, broken English.

Although both sounded unnaturally foreign to Asher, he quickly became adept at picking out the broken English and reinterpreting it in his mind to better understand what the performer was actually saying.

Asher looked around for Raglan, but couldn't see past the taller people behind him, so he turned his attention back to the performer who had just laid eyes on him for the first time.

The performer's eyes narrowed as he inspected the boy. A bedraggled teen with fair skin and messy blond hair stuffed beneath a raggedy baseball cap was an unusual sight in these parts. Even if he was filthier than a street rat.

Raglan squinted his untrusting eyes, peering again through his looking glass, focusing on the man that held the crowd's attention. This time he kept his left eye open and for good reason. Seconds later, he caught another glimpse of blurred movement deep within the darkness of the same alleyway as before. Swinging around his looking glass again, he peered at the black entrance of the alley. There was definitely something, just out of sight, hiding within the darkness, surrounded in shadow, but Raglan's eyes had caught it.

Raglan knew it was there.

Lowering the looking glass, his eyes flicked to Asher. He was still half a football field away in the centre of the bazaar, shielded by the crowd.

Raglan still had time; there was no way that whatever was

lurking in the darkness had seen Asher with so many people between them. Staying out of sight, he nimbly made his way from rooftop to rooftop, slowly moving towards the top of the darkened alleyway. Raglan felt his pulse intensify inside his chest, just like the fear creeping up his throat.

In the centre of the bazaar, the performer's tirade continued and the crowd responded to each fire trick with a vigorous bout of clapping, cheering louder for greater and even more daring feats. The performer spun on his heels slowly, scanning the faces of the crowd until once again his eyes came to a stop on Asher.

"Doos aanyoon heer stiill baaleeve iin dee oold waayz?"

To Asher, the question felt electric. The man's voice made the hairs on the back of his neck stand up on end. A tingling, shivering sensation ran down his spine, but that was not the most frightening thing that consumed Asher's mind. For the first time ever, his secret, wedged deep within a sea of scarred flesh within his palm, wrapped within a heavy bandage and stuffed deep inside his pocket, grew warm.

The heat emanating from his palm tingled as it spread up his arm. Asher clenched his fist and gripped his fingers into a fist, hoping to squash the sensation altogether, but the action only served to unleash even more narrow slivers of pain through his nerve endings.

Asher's eyes remained locked on the man before him, enraptured by his spellbinding voice and the fire he mystically twirled in his hands. As much as he knew he should, Asher couldn't look away. He was transfixed by the man's captivating movements as he laced the air with wild streaks of fire.

The man's black skin and wiry body stuck out of his layered robes like a spider's legs emerging from a web. His sandals looked as if they had grown out of his feet and his large brown eyes were tinged with the smallest fleck of emerald green.

For a brief second, Asher spied an unusual bulge beneath the robes on the man's chest. An instant later the bulge revealed

25

itself. A large medallion hung around the performer's neck. It momentarily swung into view, just long enough for Asher to see, before once again sliding back beneath the man's robes.

The vine-like chain holding the medallion in place looped around the man's neck, but most interesting of all was the gemstone that lay embedded in its centre amidst the thorns, leaves, roots and bark. A dark green stone the size of an acorn, shone with intense brilliance from within, igniting its core with light like a stained-glass bauble toying with rays of light. Asher had seen it's like before, but never like this.

Raglan slowed as he neared the rooftop that overlooked the alley where he'd seen a shadow shift and blur in the darkness. With short breath and a pounding heart, inch by inch he leaned out towards the edge.

Peering over the brink, Raglan waited: a motionless gargoyle perched above the alley below, his silhouette all but invisible against the inky black ocean of Egypt's night sky. With bated breath and tempered patience, Raglan waited for whomever, or whatever, was beneath him, to move, to make a mistake.

Show yourself! Raglan cursed at them in his mind.

"I diink daat soomoon heer haas muuch oof dee oold waayz iin deem veens."

The performer lowered his blazing chains to the ground, letting them fall in a heap on either side of his body. He muttered something inaudible and, with finger outstretched, proceeded to point at the floor just before the foot of the crowd.

He dragged his ebony index finger around his body in a wide circle, a simple copper ring catching the light as his digit spun. It seemed relatively plain and sat squarely below his knuckle, but it was too far away for Asher to see clearly. Flames rose from the clumped burning mass of chains and writhed about, dancing along the route carved out by his long finger.

Amazed, Asher completely forgot about the throbbing pain in

26

his bandaged hand, withdrawing it from his pocket and rubbing it against the back of his neck to scratch an itch.

Tiny figures appeared in the flames, as clear as day before Asher's eyes. Asher peered closer, his eyes focusing intently on the small animals taking shape amidst the fire. The smallest ones shuffled forward a few inches, then vanished in a spray of burning embers, larger creatures taking their place moments later.

Asher had never seen anything like it in his life. Everyone else in the crowd seemed oblivious to the creatures in the flames and gawped at the man's tricks. Asher could see those opposite him trying to figure out how the performer was making the fire follow his finger, some still wondering why their cameras and phones had failed for no discernible reason.

A flame-engulfed rat popped into view and stood to attention on its hind legs, pawing at its whiskers, only to transform into a rabbit, which bounded into the shape of a cat. Meanwhile, a burning heat in Asher's palm intensified, searing the skin of his neck with pangs of scorching discomfort.

Raglan refused to let loose even so much as an audible exhalation, so intent was his fixation on the darkness below. He remained a lifeless statue, perched atop the ledge: a grim spectre in the night, haunting the darkness in the alleyway from above.

Silently waiting.

Silently watching.

Every few seconds, more of the alley below came into view as his eyes adjusted to the lingering darkness. The blur of a shadowy outline emerged in the shadows, lurking a few steps back from the last remnants of light filtering into the alley's entrance.

Raglan narrowed his eyes and squinted even harder, but still couldn't make out its shape. Its shadow seemed to sway and heave in the darkness, reminiscent of a terrifying memory he'd tried long and hard to forget. Raglan shook the thought free from his mind. It was impossible. It couldn't be. There was no way.

They were all dead.

"Dee oold waayz bee loong foogotten, buut noow iim sees deem wiit iis oown twoo eeyes."

The man's eyes bored into the young teen in front of him. The heat from Asher's palm was unbearable, but still he found himself entranced by the man in front of him, unable to look away.

The performer, still with one hand outstretched, continued to draw an invisible line that the creatures in the fire obediently followed. Slowly, he unfurled his other hand towards Asher, beckoning him to do the same.

Asher tried to fight the urge but, before he knew it, his arm had left his neck and was stretching out before him. Instantly, the creatures in the fire vanished from sight, but Asher had more pressing concerns. He was no longer in control of his own body, and the realisation terrified him.

Inch by inch his arm extended farther away from his body. Within seconds, it was fully outstretched, his bandaged hand held upright, still clenched in a tight fist.

The performer clicked his fingers at Asher, which instantly sent a sharp pain echoing from his palm and up his arm. Asher winced, but the pain only lasted a moment. His fear, however, felt like it would last a lifetime.

Raglan hadn't moved a muscle. Barely breathing, his focus remained fixated on the alley below, but he soon felt the familiar bite of an oncoming cramp in his leg. He silently swore and shifted his legs, accidentally dislodging a small stone, sending it flying down into the depths of the alley below. It barely made a sound, but when it landed it might as well have been an avalanche.

A pair of malevolent blood-red eyes spun around in the darkness, searching for the source of the noise. Finding nothing, they shot upwards.

Raglan froze.

Fear gripped him and it gripped him hard. Even though his

silhouette was lost amidst the darkness, the blood-red eyes found him instantly. When their eyes locked together, Raglan's body froze with fear. The day he'd been dreading for the last decade had finally arrived and, worse yet, he had been wrong.

They aren't all dead.

The performer raised a finger of his outstretched right hand and pointed at Asher, copper ring glinting in the light of the dancing flames. Instantly, the patch of fire leaped from the ground and shot through the air, coming to rest millimetres above Asher's fist.

The crowd roared with excitement as the spluttering blaze became suspended above the quivering clenched fist of the teenager, who looked equally as gobsmacked as they were, albeit slightly more terrified than anyone else.

Asher's arm was ablaze with a searing intensity, but not from the fire dancing atop his tightly clenched knuckles. His palm ignited with pain, bursting to life underneath the burning wisps of flames. His face remained calm, his passive features lying to all those around him about the intense agony coursing through his veins. The bandages wrapped around his palm, caught alight and began to burn away.

Asher started to panic.

He couldn't let anyone see his secret.

Asher's pure terror at being discovered somehow broke him free of the performer's control, forcing his lungs to expel a violent gust of air. Two words sang out across the square.

"Raglan! Help!"

The lurking figure violently launched something at Raglan, before fleeing the alleyway and disappearing around the edges of the bazaar. A cloud of darkness engulfed the air around it as it fled, masking its escape. The fragile masonry beneath Raglan's feet erupted. He barely managed to avoid the blast as it exploded. It shattered the stone lip of the roof, showering the air with large chunks of bricks and mortar.

Raglan quickly regained his footing and looked in the direction of the crowd, just in time to hear the lingering sounds of Asher's cry for help. It only took a split-second for his eyes to lock on to a figure at the heart of the crowd, one hand ablaze with fire: Asher. Without thinking, Raglan withdrew something from his pocket and lit its fuse.

It was an impossible throw, especially for a man his age, but something inside Raglan had snapped. A ferocious cocktail of fear, adrenaline and rage was erupting in his veins, poisoning his better judgement with base instinct. He had only seconds to act. Any longer and it would be too late. There was one chance to save him, but Raglan was not thinking clearly and any mistake now would only have one outcome.

Asher would die.

The fuse sizzled and crackled. Sparks hissed furiously as they unceremoniously flared into existence, fizzling out an instant later, their purpose in life fulfilled.

Before Raglan even realised what he'd done, his eyes locked on to the small cylinder hurtling through the cool evening air, its tiny fuse little more than a flicker of light against the dark of the night sky. It arced upwards over the heads of the crowd, before losing momentum and spiralling downwards, tumbling down towards the centre of the square and the throng of unsuspecting innocents below. Down towards Asher.

Raglan's eyes went wide as the cylinder disappeared within the bustling bodies of the gathered crowd. He instinctively swallowed down his rising fear. A dry mouthful of air crept into his lungs as his heart leaped into his throat.

He hadn't thrown it hard enough.

The cylinder had landed ten feet short of its mark. Asher would have to save himself. Raglan desperately filled the rest of his lungs with the coarse dry air and threw his hands up around his mouth. He bellowed the only thing he had time to shout.

"Asher! Run!"

CHAPTER 2

The Face Of Evil

Distracted by the distant explosion near the edge of the square, the performer momentarily lost his focus on Asher. His eyes darted over the heads of the crowd, refocusing on a small cloud of debris as it erupted up into the night air. He heard a voice bellow out high above the bazaar. It echoed down a frightened warning above the din of the crowd and the crackle of his own flames.

"Asher! Run!"

Moments later, a tiny cylinder clattered down clumsily on the ground and exploded in a series of sharp bangs, sending fiery whizzes of smoke and light in every direction. The performer cursed under his breath. He'd not expected either distraction. Both had cost him his focus and control over the teenager.

Asher, momentarily free from the performer's control, needed no invitation to disappear. The performer spun around and lunged for the teen's hand, but Asher was already gone.

Most of the crowd assumed that the exploding spectacle of light, dancing and spluttering on the ground at their feet, was simply part of the performer's bag of tricks. They gave it a small berth and wildly applauded each new bang and whizz as they crackled and popped. Those closest to Asher, however, became anxious when he had turned and fled, retreating through their ranks and disappearing within the assembled crowd.

Asher looked down at the bandages covering his hand as he ducked and weaved his way through the crowd. They were in tatters, burned beyond recognition. The remaining blackened threads hung loosely from his hand, which still ached with a dull burning sensation. Rewrapping what was left of the burned bandages over his palm, he gripped their charred remains in a fist and ran. He had to protect his secret.

Now more than ever.

The crowd's unease grew when the performer's actions became more erratic and chaotic. When he tried to follow after the teenager, the crowd knew something was definitely wrong, but being much larger than Asher, his movement was blocked by the very people gathered to watch him. Some of those who'd watched Asher flee even attempted to hold back the performer. He viciously threw one man to the ground and pushed another aside. But it was no use. He'd never be able to catch the boy with so many people in his way. Infuriated, he roared at the top of his lungs and spun around to face the lingering flames on the ground. Raking his hands upwards through the air, he bellowed a single command at the dying embers.

"Pavora!"

An enormous pillar of flame erupted in the centre of the square, sparking instantaneous widespread panic throughout the huddled masses.

The bazaar exploded into pandemonium as terrified feet pounded the cobbles, everyone scrambling to get away from the blazing inferno at their backs. Arms, legs and torsos collided heavily with one another as people knocked each other over. Hysteria set in and gripped the minds of the terrified crowd. Frenzied hands, fists and shoulders lashed out, everyone vying for their own personal escape route out of the bazaar.

Asher found himself enveloped in a wave of panic, as the crowd around him spooked and tried to take flight from the pillar of fire behind them. He had no idea that, amidst the hysterical shrieks and cries ringing out around him, the race for survival was already well and truly underway and he was losing.

Loud screams echoed in his ear, much louder than before, as a brilliant yellow light burst into his periphery. Glancing back over his shoulder, he saw a column of flame rise high into the air. Silhouettes of alarmed citizens screamed in terror as the blaze intensified and Asher soon found himself struggling to keep ahead of the surging sea of panic that had been unleashed on the unsuspecting crowd.

"Come here, boy!" the performer bellowed at Asher in perfect English. The sound carried over the shrieks and cries of the frightened crowd, but his words were lost on Asher. He was too busy running for his life.

Raglan was already halfway down from the rooftops when the centre of the square erupted in a sea of fire. He swore under his breath but didn't dare stop. There was a far greater threat at hand than the fire-wielder assailant, even one as close as this.

He cursed himself for his short sightedness.

He should have better investigated the performer. He should have never let Asher out of his sight. He'd seen the violin case, the flicker of street lights, the malfunctioning digital screens, and still had failed to act. Bounding from rooftop to terrace to awning and finally to the unforgiving cobblestones of the street, Raglan landed heavily in the square with a loud grunt.

Ignoring the sharp stabs of pain shooting up his legs as they pounded against the pavement, he careened as best he could against the surge of the terrified crowd. Raglan knew where Asher was headed. Even in a state of pure terror, Asher's instincts were uncannily reliable. He'd head to a safe location. The closest was a secret basement in a nearby derelict warehouse they'd used last week to lay low and hide out when the streets had become untenable.

It wasn't far, but Raglan knew he'd never be able to catch Asher on foot heading directly across the square, the teeming mass of the crowd had made sure of that. However, Raglan knew a few shortcuts of his own. He silently hoped Asher would be able to outrun his pursuer but, more importantly, that the figure lurking in the shadows was still unaware of Asher's existence.

Slipping through a gap in the crowd, Raglan cut down a side alley to escape the maelstrom of panic in the bazaar. He put his head down and sprinted as fast as his legs would carry him.

Something exploded violently next to Asher's head as he raced down an alley, filling the air with flying chunks of stone and debris from a nearby wall. In the seconds it took him to turn the corner, Asher caught a glimpse of the performer racing after him, violin case in hand, pushing aside people as he ran.

Asher only saw him for a moment, but that was all it took to recognise the fierce look of determination branded upon his face. He shouted something at Asher, but whatever he said was inaudible. Asher's ears were deafened by the lingering screams echoing from the bazaar, the rush of the wind over his ears, and his own breathless gasps for air.

His instincts kicked into overdrive as he sped along the cobblestones. Without trying, Asher drew a map of the streets in his mind, plotting an escape route. He mechanically cut down a narrow service alley at the last second and slammed into the wall, but it didn't slow him down. He needed to put as much distance between his pursuer and the heels of his boots as possible.

Deafening booms and flashes of light echoed from the streets behind him as he rounded another corner. It sounded as if a war was being waged on the cobblestones, but Asher could not afford to waste time finding out who was waging it. He nimbly ducked through the open doorway of a house and out a window on the opposite side, then into a disused back alley. Dodging piles of rubbish and discarded junk, he bounded down a narrow set of stairs, ducked around a corner and sprinted headlong towards one of his more recently discovered hiding spots.

The rooftops loomed over the narrow city streets like prison watchtowers, looking down on him as he ducked and weaved through a myriad of deserted lanes, alleys and lesser-known passageways. The streets were mostly silent now, but Asher could still hear the distant furore of the panicked masses fleeing the bazaar. But it was not the cries of the frightened masses that scared him. Even with the wind rushing over his ears, Asher could distinctively make out another far more terrifying sound.

His legs fired away underneath him, but the sounds of heavy footsteps slapping against the cobblestones behind him reverberated in his mind like the rhythmic beat of a war drum. Ever relentless, their sound grew louder with every step.

In that moment Asher realised the performer was gaining on him and he couldn't outrun his pursuer. However, there was a chance he could turn his strength, size and speed against him. Following the escape route in his mind, Asher's feet pelted down against the uneven cobblestones like a jackrabbit in heat.

He rounded another bend, narrowly avoiding a homeless man pushing a fully laden cart of precious junk. Hurling a slew of curses in Egyptian at Asher as he sped off, the old man's cries were silenced as he and his cart were viciously knocked to the ground by a tremendous force.

Asher's pursuer was closing the gap between them.

The bells of a nearby church chimed loudly, signalling that the hour was midnight, but the sound was of little comfort to Asher. He knew the next passage was tricky to navigate at the best of times, more than that, it was life-endingly narrow if misjudged. But it was also narrow enough that his pursuer wouldn't be able to follow him. Asher had trouble fitting through the tight gap in the wall himself. The long-limbed performer would stand no chance, especially at speed.

Asher fled headlong towards the corner and launched his body off the ground. Grabbing an upright signpost with both hands, he swung himself around the bend, lifting his legs up to his waist. When his body was almost around the corner, he released the signpost and straightened his legs, threw his arms back above his head and exhaled.

His momentum propelled his body through a tiny gap in the opposite wall, missing the unforgiving jagged edges of the opening by a fraction of an inch. Landing clear on the other side of the wall, he skidded to a stop and breathlessly peered back through the gap.

The world around him turned black.

A deathly figure, shrouded in darkness glared back at him, held at bay only by the small gap in the wall. A floating veil of darkness emanated from the creature's body, staining the air around it with oppressive obscurity, hiding the creature's true form from view. A pair of blood-red eyes, full of malice, hovered amidst the impenetrable black cloud.

Asher tried to shuffle backwards, but his back was already hard up against the wall. The darkness ebbed and pulsated, staining the air around it like dye spreading through water.

A low hiss crept through the gap, followed by a stream of the shadowy black shroud. It poured into the alleyway and spread. A sea of shadow slowly surrounded Asher on both sides and his world became a claustrophobic nightmare.

Asher made sure to keep his aching hand out of view. With pupils fully dilated, he stared directly forward, absolutely terrified. He found himself unable to look away from the demonic red eyes that hung and swayed in the void beyond the gap.

When the cloud of darkness had nearly enveloped the entire alleyway around Asher, the red eyes crept forward: passing through the hole in the wall and inching closer by the second. A maniacal laughter choked Asher's ears, filling his head with thoughts of unspeakable and insatiable hatred.

The blurred outline of a hand, engulfed in thick black tendrils of smoke and shadow, extended out towards him. Cruel talons bent and flexed, scratching the air in anticipation. Inch by inch they got closer, desperately trying to clutch at his clothes, skin and flesh. A whisper came at him in the darkness. Its voice sparked terror in Asher's heart like the sharp cut of a knife as the creature's tormented voice eviscerated his sense of safety.

"Vox Vita..."

The words hung in the air as the wraith-like claw lunged at him. Asher slammed his eyes shut and instinctively held up his hand in front of him. The remnants of his tattered, burned bandage fell away as a sharp stab of pain shot up his arm, nearly crippling it.

Asher cried out in pain.

It felt like the creature's talons had ripped the flesh of his forearm from his bones. A second passed, and then another, but the pain did not subside, nor did it grow any worse. It was a constant, yet bearable, agony.

Asher slowly opened his eyes.

To his utter amazement, his arm was not the bloody stump he thought it would be; he didn't even see any blood. Instead, a blinding golden beam of light splintered outwards from his palm in every direction, simultaneously halting the advance of the wavering cloud of darkness and the creature's shadowy talons.

A wretched ear-splitting shriek tore through the alley as the creature drained its lungs of breath, venting its anger at Asher. The sound sliced through Asher's eardrums like an oar through water, shredding his consciousness and threatening to break his mind in two.

The only thought Asher could piece together devastated him far more than the pain ripping through his mind. *My secret is exposed. Everything Raglan has taught me about keeping it hidden— keeping it safe—is dead and gone. I have broken my promise to the one man who has always looked after me. I have failed Raglan and now he might die because of it.*

Worse yet, the foul beast that thrashed wildly before him had borne witness to what he had kept hidden for over a decade, and there was nothing Asher could do about it.

He struggled to his knees, using one hand to keep the other propped up in front of him. The golden gemstone—marred by an ink-black streak that hovered and swayed beneath its surface like suspended oil—was exposed. Blood oozed from the sea of scarred flesh of his palm surrounding the gem as a prism of light poured out of its centre. It burned with a ferocity that sent Asher's mind into excruciating spasms as an indescribable power tore through his body, up the length of his extended arm and through the gemstone's face.

Despite the physical torment raging across his body and the sheer madness waging war within his mind, he held his hand high and kept it there. He had to. It was the only thing keeping the monster at bay. He watched on in an agonised daze as the creature bucked and writhed within its own shroud of darkness, flinching backwards every time it got too close to the golden shards of light.

Its blood-red eyes jerked out of view and the shroud of darkness was yanked back through the gap. Its talons clawed at the edges of the stonework as its arm retreated, leaving four gouges an inch deep on the edges of the gap.

Asher lowered his aching arm. The protective golden light disappeared, letting the natural light of the moon filter down into the alley once more. But the battle beyond the wall had only just begun. Howls of anger and shrieks of pain ripped through the alley as a blinding flash of green fire streaked the air beyond the wall, engulfing the right side of the beast's darkened flank in flames.

Clutching his throbbing hand, Asher watched as the lanky frame of the performer stepped into view, hurling brilliant arcs of green elemental flame with his hands at the shroud of darkness. He cursed and shouted at the creature in a foreign language Asher did not understand.

Immediately after releasing each blast of green fire, another emerald ball of flame sprang to life in his hands, each giving off more raw power than the last. He marched steadily forward, forcing the creature back, green explosions unleashing a barrage of savage elemental heat against the beast.

Asher watched on in awe as the performer waged an unearthly war beyond the wall. The man's layered robes had fallen from his shoulders and now hung loosely across his waist, exposing a powerfully muscled and heavily scarred torso. His glowing medallion sat squarely on his chest, pulsating with chaotic bursts of emerald light as he flared his emerald flames to even greater intensities.

His skin glistened with sweat, each bead reflecting the flickering green light. They dribbled down his face as he gritted his teeth, throwing all of his strength into every attack; but it was not enough.

He'd caught the creature by surprise, but his advantage was long since lost. The retaliatory onslaught the creature hurled back at him was brutal and unforgiving. Dark streaks of energy whipped at his flesh, two wounds appeared as the skin above the performer's ribs was sliced open. With each blow, splashes of green-tinged blood splattered on the man's clothes and surrounding walls. Without looking at Asher, he commanded him to flee in plain unbroken English.

"Run Vita-born. I will hold the Skulk for as long as I am able."

His accent was gone.

His voice was clear.

His instructions were simple.

Asher couldn't believe his own eyes. The performer's words had been lost on him; he was still in a state of shock. He crept forward, angling his head to better peer through the gap. Placing his hands on either side of the hole next to his head, he saw creatures appear within the green flames: viscous beasts, savage-looking and fearsome.

Wolves and vultures materialised and attacked in a devastating swarm of fire, only to be replaced by more fearsome-looking creatures that Asher couldn't have imagined in his wildest dreams. The man's hands were stained with his own green-tinged blood. Vicious wounds had appeared on his arms, chest and legs.

The performer flicked Asher a spine-chilling look, his eyes luminous emeralds in the darkness, ablaze with the blood lust of battle. "Run, damn you!" he bellowed and flicked his wrist at Asher.

A few droplets of the man's green-tinged blood landed on Asher's clothes as a force threw him backwards, away from the gap. Clenching one hand at the bricks above the hole, the performer wrenched it down through the air towards the ground.

Asher saw the medallion on his chest erupt with a flare of green light just before the wall collapsed in on itself in a shower of shattered stonework, crushed mortar and bursts of green flames.

Asher cowered on the other side of the alley as a large cloud of dust and soot exploded over him. His world became a haze-filled cloud, penetrated only by the cold blue light of the moon, until the damp florescent glow of nearby streetlights permeated the mist.

Partially blinded by the residue of dust and soot caught in his eyes, Asher heard the ferocious sounds of battle echoing from beyond the collapsed wall. He wiped his eyes as best he could on his filthy sleeve, picked himself up and ran. A fine shroud of dust fell from his clothes as he sprinted down the alley, but his mind was clear and filled with questions.

"What was going on? Where was Raglan? Who was the fire wielder? Why did he call me 'Vita-born'? What were those creatures in the fire? What was that thing in the darkness?"

His hand throbbed with pain. In his amazement at what had just occurred, he'd almost totally forgotten about the pain. He winced again as slivers of agony shot up his arm.

What was the golden light? The question burned in Asher's mind as he ran down the street. Stealing a glance down at his aching palm he instantly noticed there was dried blood all encasing the scarred skin around the gem: his blood. Slowing down to search his palm for a wound, he held it up to his face. To his astonishment there was even blood inside the gem, swirling amidst its core like drops of crimson oil.

Amongst the blackened streak that stained the luminous golden centre of the gem, he watched his blood fuse and disappear, merging into oblivion within the core gem as it pulsed with unnatural energy.

More diabolical screams sang out against the stillness of the night behind him as wild bursts of green flame and ink-black darkness billowed up into the sky.

Forgetting the discomfort of his hand, he clenched it back into a tight fist and raced down the few remaining streets that would lead him to the hide-out, blindly following a path his feet knew all too well. He rounded one last corner and entered a deserted alcove. He ducked his head outside to ensure he hadn't been followed.

The coast was clear.

He pulled apart some loose sheet metal on the wall of the alcove, slipped through the gap and disappeared off the streets.

His legs were shaking.

His breath, short and sharp.

His hand, bloody and aching.

The room Asher entered was pitch black. He grabbed a half-melted candle from its usual hiding place, struck a match and shielded the flame with his good hand. The candle wick caught and flickered to life, dimly illuminating his surroundings. Hot wax ran down the length of the candle and dripped onto his palm. The warm sting of the wax felt good next to the lingering pain that had recently taken up residence in the skin around the gemstone.

The candle was not bright, but even in next-to-near darkness Asher knew this room well enough. Moving away from the doorway, he crossed the empty space and kneeled down beside some debris hiding a hole in the floor in the corner of the room.

The empty silence of the room was rudely interrupted as he pushed aside a large wooden packing pallet, revealing a ladder leading down to a subterranean basement. He nimbly descended and dragged the pallet back over his head in one swift movement. But before his feet could hit the floor, he was pulled from the ladder and down into the void by rough hands.

The candle fell through the air and extinguished.

Asher felt the air rush from his lungs as a vice-like grip closed around his body and tightened, squeezing the life out of him.

CHAPTER 3

REVELATIONS OF BLOOD

Asher's body did not hit the ground. Instead, he found himself suspended in the air, a set of familiar arms encircling his body in a relieved bear hug.

"Raglan?" he tentatively whispered.

"Asher, thank the stars you made it." Raglan's smile beamed out amidst the darkness.

"Raglan," Asher sighed heavily in relief and wholeheartedly returned the embrace as best he could. Raglan put Asher down and lit a fresh candle on the wall. He instantly caught a glimpse of the panic caught in the teenager's eyes.

"Asher," he said awkwardly, "there is much you must know and even more I would tell you." Working quickly, Raglan lit a number of candles around the room and looked at an old rusty clock on the wall.

It read 12.05.

With a sly smile, Raglan looked at the young teenager he'd grown to love. "First things first, happy found-day." He removed a tiny package wrapped in newspaper from his clothes and held it out to Asher. Asher snatched the present, clenching it in his fist and allowing his anger to surge to the surface.

"Forget my found-day; I nearly died out there! What the hell's going on? Who was the man that made the creatures dance in the fire? What was that thing in the darkness? Why is the gem in my hand glowing? And, more importantly, why's my blood in it?"

Raglan grabbed Asher's hand and examined the gemstone. A confused look spread across his face.

"You used your auger, but..." he mumbled to himself, "you aren't even aligned."

"What's an auger?" Asher yanked away his hand. Raglan's face

42

betrayed his confusion, a faraway look echoing in his eyes.

"Raglan, answer me."

"Hmm. Sorry." Raglan's mind snapped back into focus, his eyes betraying the shame he felt in his heart at the thought of letting down Asher. "Sorry, I thought I'd be able to keep you from all of this. I thought we'd have more time."

"All of what?"

"Your heritage, Asher. Your past." He paused and took a deep breath. "Your future."

"I don't understand," Asher looked up at his uncle, his innocence beguiling his ignorance all the more.

"Of course you don't, because I have shielded you from it your entire life. But not anymore." He took another deep breath, steadied himself and uttered the words he'd been dreading for years. Raglan motioned Asher to sit and groaned as he eased himself down on the floor.

"You're a Vox Cruaar, Asher."

"I'm a what?"

"There is no easy explanation. Your blood is unique. Within each and every drop lies a power imbued within your bloodline, passed down from generation to generation. You are the embodiment of that power; you are the voice that allows it to be heard."

Asher sat in silence for a moment, allowing what he'd just heard to sink in, repeating the phrases in his mind. *Unique blood, power and bloodlines? Passed down from generation to generation? The voice that allows it to be heard?* None of it made sense. It sounded like nonsense. He had so many questions, but one question rang out in his mind above all others. "My bloodline?" he paused lowering his voice to a whisper. "But you said you never knew my family."

Raglan sighed, Asher had always been curious about his past: curious about the family he had never known. Raglan had never known what to say. "And I never did, but you are a Vox Cruaar. That much is certain." Raglan looked as if he was holding back something, but Asher couldn't be sure. "It is as much a part of you, as once… as once it was a part of me."

"You're a Vox Cruer as well?"

"Cruaar," Raglan bluntly corrected, "and, yes, a long time ago I was one of the many Cruaar within this world."

"There are others?"

"Thousands. Tens of thousands. An entire nation, although none quite like yourself." Raglan nodded to Asher's palm before placing it in his own. "You're unique, Asher. One of a kind."

Asher looked more confused than ever.

"I don't understand. The performer in the square, was he a Vox Cruaar? And the creature in the darkness that spoke to me?"

Raglan tightened his grip on Asher's hand, his tone of voice rising in urgency, "the creature in the darkness followed you? It spoke to you? Did it see your hand?"

"I tried to keep it hidden, but the wrappings were burned," Asher stammered.

"Think carefully, Asher, what did it say?" Raglan gripped him with both hands, his face a mask of worry and fear.

"I don't know, 'Vox' something… 'Vox Vita', I think," Asher trembled, the confusion in his eyes escalating by the second. Raglan's face drained of colour. His face was a ghost, pale and drawn. A single tear rolled down his cheek.

"They know. How could they know?"

"Is it because I held the fire creature in my hand?" Asher asked nervously. "I didn't mean to. It just happened. It's not my fault. I couldn't control it. It just took over. First the fire, then the golden light that held the darkness at bay."

Raglan looked at him in disbelief, Asher's words barely registering as a fresh wave of fear washed over the old man's mind. "I've failed…" he whispered under his breath.

"Raglan," Asher pleaded.

"I can no longer protect you."

"Raglan, please," Asher begged, gently shaking Raglan by the shoulders to snap him out of his daze.

"All these years for nothing," Raglan slumped against the cold wall behind him.

"Raglan!" Asher shouted, unable to rouse him from his stupor. Finally, he slapped the old man hard across the face. The cold slap broke Raglan from his daze. Raglan's face was a mixture of wonder, amazement and fear as he looked up at Asher's confused and frightened expression.

"We must leave. It's no longer safe for us here." *It is no longer safe for us anywhere.* Colour flowed back into Raglan's face, his cheek marred with the bright red outline of Asher's palm. He looked at Asher apologetically. "I'm so sorry, Asher. I should've better prepared you."

Asher dragged Raglan to his feet as best he could, but froze as a loud groan pierced the silence of the room above. Someone had pulled back the rusty sheet metal from the outside wall. Silently, they listened as a soft footstep scratched against the ground above their heads.

Raglan motioned Asher to remain completely still. He quickly doused the candles, plunging the room in darkness. They heard the scrape of another footstep displace a loose can above their heads, sending it rattling across the room.

The two stood motionless, waiting for the next sound to betray the exact location of the intruder above. Another soft scrape echoed from above, followed by a more prominent footstep, much closer towards the hidden ladder. The darkness was suffocating, made worse by the fact that neither Asher nor Raglan could do anything without giving away their position.

Like living statues they waited in silence—motionless—not game to move. A small amount of illumination pierced the gaps between the slats of wood of the packing pallet drawn across the hole in the roof.

Raglan scoured the floor at his feet. It was covered in dirt, dust, refuse and broken glass. There was no way they could escape without being heard. He silently cursed his own foolishness again for not being better prepared, when his eyes caught on something in the darkness.

A spec of glowing green had stained Asher's rags. Raglan reached out and collected it on the tip of his finger. Most of the performer's blood came off at his touch, the rest had already sunk in and stained the material below. The damage was already done. Their pursuer had marked Asher and tracked them. *Now there really is no escape.*

The light grew brighter above them. Streaks of yellow luminance permeated through the gaps in the wooden pallet hiding the hole to the basement. Without warning, white hot sand floated down through the hole in the ceiling, followed by a small patch of green fire blazing brightly on the floor.

Raglan and Asher's anxious faces were instantly illuminated by the flickering emerald flames. Forgoing all manner of stealth, Raglan grabbed Asher by the shoulder and moved him forward. An avalanche of noise erupted amidst the silence as dirt, glass and garbage crunched and scattered under their heels.

Silence didn't matter anymore. Only escape.

The cacophony of their plight prompted a loud and instantaneous response from above. "Fear not, progeny of the Cruaar. I mean you no harm," a deep voice boomed downwards through the gap, increasing the intensity of the fire as each word struck home. Raglan stopped in his tracks and peered up at the ceiling.

Briefly stealing a glance at Asher, he whispered, "whatever happens, keep your wits about you and be ready to run." Rising upright, he directed a surprisingly strong and authoritative voice at the gap in the ceiling. "My name is Raglan, formerly of MaiSchloss. Declare yourself."

"And the boy?" the voice asked from above.

"A youth in my charge."

The covering of the ladder shifted aside and Asher watched the performer climb down its protesting rungs. Each undutifully moaned as they took his weight.

"I think we both know," the man continued as he climbed down and placed his feet upon the cold hard floor, "that he is much more than that."

Asher looked at the man who had saved him from the shadowy creature. The wounds on his arms and chest had partially healed and he'd reshouldered his robes. He somehow looked much more dignified than the foreign fire twirler he'd masqueraded as in the square, even though his clothing was now torn and ripped in places.

His head was clean shaven and his jawline strong, enhanced all the more by his rough acne-scarred skin. He was not a handsome man by any means, but he exuded a confidence and authoritative power that lent him a charismatic aura, even if most of it was lost in the near darkness of the small space. He held the leather-bound violin case in one hand and extended his free hand outwards, palm up, in a gesture of peace as he approached.

"I have no desire to see things turn uncivilised. My name is Braak Saada, Vox Natura, Second Edict, Warder of Undergall." He spoke with quiet confidence. Asher felt Raglan breathe a small sigh of relief.

"Raglan, formerly of MaiSchloss, has been kind enough to lend me his name, but yours, young man, remains a mystery." Braak shifted his gaze to Asher. Without waiting for Raglan's approval, Asher brokered a shy response.

"I'm Asher. Asher Bloom."

"Hmm," Braak stroked his chin thoughtfully, "it suits you. Here I find you covered in ash and dust and yet here you are, alive and well, after a Mortis Skulk attack no less. Bloom you do; not many could survive such an attack, let alone emerge unscathed to tell the tale."

Asher nimbly stepped to the side of Raglan to better view the man. "Your voice is different. What happened to your accent?"

The man smiled and laughed, revealing a mouthful of bright white teeth.

"Waat? Yuu meen diis oon?" Braak slipped back into his guttural foreign tone for a moment, causing a numbness to wash over Asher's limbs.

"The easiest way to control a crowd is to control their minds. A common enough trick," Braak slipped back into his guttural language, "iif yuu knoow hoow."

Asher felt his mind instantly put at ease as the man's foreign garbled tongue invaded his eardrums.

"Enough of that." Raglan shook his head clear of the man's persuasive hold over him. "I would have words with you, Warder."

"Very well," Braak nodded, and allowed Raglan to approach.

Raglan gingerly stepped towards the man and whispered something in his ear. Asher strained to overhear what was said, but the sound refused to carry. Moments passed as the whispering continued, Braak's eyes growing wider with unabashed disbelief at each new utterance. Raglan finished with a nod and stepped aside, motioning Asher forward with a wave of his arm.

"Show him your hand, Asher," he commanded.

"But you said—"

"I know what I said," Raglan interjected, "but you will be able to trust him."

Asher was barely higher than Braak's massive chest, but he cautiously held up his hand to the man who had only minutes before saved him from the darkness. The light that had previously radiated from within his gem was now dull, but still glimmered amidst the darkness. Dried blood surrounded its edge, but all traces of blood had vanished from within its core. The blackened streak across its face was unmistakable, the importance of which was not lost on the tall warder from Undergall.

Braak gently took Asher's hand and cradled it in his own, a look of concern crossing his face when he realised what he was looking at.

"Vox Vita… or just another traitor with the taint?" Braak clenched his fist around Asher's hand. Asher felt the cold bite of the man's copper ring press into his skin. The fearsome look in his eyes betrayed the man's uncontrollable disgust and distrust.

No sooner had the words left his lips than Braak felt the cool touch of steel press against the nape of his neck. The jagged tip of a dagger up against his flesh, directly in line with his spinal column.

Raglan held the blade with deft precision, puncturing the man's flesh with the tip of the dagger to press the point of his precarious situation. "One wrong move and your bloodline ends with you."

"Raglan, what are you doing? You said we can trust him," Asher stammered, his hand still in the grip of the performer.

"And you will, as soon as he performs the rite of bonded blood." Raglan's face displayed an emotion of inarguable countenance.

"You ask me to bond myself with one bearing the taint?" Braak started to sweat, his eyes looking around the room judging his situation. He saw no opportunity for escape. "I'll not willingly sign my own death warrant."

"The mark you see is not the taint." Raglan pressed the knife into the back of Braak's neck a little harder. "He has carried it as long as I have known him."

"Even if I believe your lies, you know the Rite of Bonded Blood requires his auger to first be aligned."

"Look at his auger, Warder. It needs no alignment. It has already tasted his blood."

Braak looked at the teenager again, then down at the gemstone embedded in his hand. His eyes grew wider in disbelief. "But how is that possible?"

"How is not important. Time is a liberty we lack. I can no longer keep him safe," he paused, "especially where you must take him."

"Take me?" Asher faltered. "Take me where?"

Raglan ignored him. "Swear on your bloodline you'll keep him safe where I cannot," Raglan's hand tightened on the dagger, "or you'll taste my blade and welcome death as a brother."

Raglan increased the pressure of his dagger on the man's neck, digging the tip deeper into Braak's neck until it punctured his flesh. A trickle of blood oozed out from under the metal tip and ran down Braak's back.

"What say you, Warder?"

Braak paused to consider his options. He saw none. "You swear he has born the mark for as long as you have known him?"

"I swear it on my bloodline."

"The blood lineage of a coward means nothing to me, Augmad," Braak spat.

"And yet I can claim no other." Raglan replied coldly.

Braak's eyes met with Asher's, their gaze locked. It seemed as if the man was judging Asher's soul in the back of his mind. After a long pause he spoke. "Very well, I will perform the rite."

With one hand Braak reached down into his violin case, pulling out the medallion Asher had spied around his neck earlier. It was even more impressive up close. A tangled combination of thorns, bark, roots, leaves and sap acted as a chain, holding the medallion in place. The stone sitting in the centre resembled a large emerald. It came alive at the man's touch, pulsating with wild streaks of light.

Braak held his auger above the gemstone in Asher's hand and mumbled something incoherent in a foreign language. Braak's gemstone grew brighter and brighter, radiating a rich shade of green. The whites of his eyes glazed over with a murky green haze as his chanting intensified, until both eyes became vibrant pools of emerald light. Asher watched in amazement as the medallion sprang to life, sending brilliant green shards of luminescent light cascading across the room. The chanting ended abruptly, then silence. Braak eventually broke the eerie quiet and spoke aloud in a clear voice. It faintly echoed in the small space.

"Bond thee this life to mine, auger to auger, blood to blood."

A vortex of coloured gas swirled within Braak's medallion, moving faster and faster until small droplets of blood formed on the outside of the gem. He let the blood drip from its surface onto Asher's palm and over the embedded gemstone, watching each droplet as it was drawn into its golden centre.

Asher looked down at his palm. A raging torrent of gold and black surged within the gemstone's walls as it fed upon Braak's green-tinged blood. Moments later, a gold-tinged steam rose from Asher's auger and slowly fused within Braak's auger above.

Asher felt weak at the knees, as though a small part of his life had been stolen from him. He wanted to collapse, but Braak's iron grip held him in place, until a single drop of blood fell from Braak's auger just as another rose from Asher's. The two met, colliding and fusing together, suspended in space.

Asher felt his mind plunge into a haze of mindless images.

A loud clap resounded about the room as the merged blood particles exploded in a blinding burst of green and gold beams of light.

"It is done, Augmad. Release me!" Braak commanded, feeling the pressure of the knife ease from his neck. Raglan breathed a sigh of relief as Braak examined his own auger for something. When he was satisfied with his inspection, he released Asher.

Asher's body slumped to the ground, his energy sapped. He lost consciousness just as his head came to rest on the floor, one hand throbbing with pain, the other clenched in a fist, still clutching Raglan's unopened birthday gift.

CHAPTER 4

PLIGHT TO PABLO'S

Asher's ears started working long before his eyes. His mind was a murky haze—strange thoughts—each more bewildering than the last. Ambient sounds filtered in and disrupted the blur of confusion plaguing Asher's subconscious. He heard the scurry of tiny claws on stone and an owl hoot in the distance.

It was still night-time.

The sounds of shuffling feet scraping across cobblestones invaded his eardrums.

We are moving.

He could feel his body shifting weightlessly this way and that, cradled within two muscular arms.

I am being carried.

Raglan's voice spoke in hushed whispers from somewhere ahead in the darkness. His voice was noticeably anxious. "Asher knows nothing of our world, or of his ability. He will need guidance and instruction above all else."

"Don't presume to tell me what the he requires, Augmad." Braak spat the last word at the man, "I may now be bonded to him by blood, but you and I share no such allegiance. Once he is safely in Undergall, you will be held accountable for your actions. On this I swear."

"I did what I had to, Warder. The consequences of my actions are of no concern, as long as he survives the night," Raglan wheezed. His breath reeked of dismay and failure. "Now that his presence is known to the Mortis Skulk, I can no longer keep him hidden... or safe."

Raglan paused, his voice growing louder and closer to Asher's ears. The two men must have been standing mere inches from each other. Raglan spoke with unmistakable certainty.

"You know full well they'll come for him, and when they do

he must be ready." Asher felt a familiar hand gently grip his own. "He must be able to defend himself." The warmth Asher felt on his hand lasted only a second before his body jolted forward once more.

Braak's deep voice hissed back at Raglan. "You were a fool to attempt to keep him hidden in the first place, especially without the power of your blood to call upon. His fate will be left in the hands of the council. Now, how far to the nearest networked vertistrand?"

"There are no networked vertistrands here," Raglan snapped back. "Why do you think I hid him here in the first place?"

Asher's mind reeled with unanswered questions. He tried to open his eyes, but they refused to cooperate. Braak muttered something sharply under his breath, and Asher's mind lurched upwards as his body was thrown into the air. He landed rather heavily on what he assumed was Braak's shoulder. His eyes snapped open as air exploded from his lungs. He desperately gasped for breath, but found himself struggling to breathe.

"Asher?" Raglan's voice came to him in the darkness. Asher couldn't answer. His lungs were empty. Braak slowly lowered his body to the ground and Asher felt the cool chill of the night spill into his throat, precious oxygen filling his chest.

"Asher, dear boy, answer me."

"What's a vertistrand?" Asher gargled back.

"The way to Undergall," Raglan's face smiled down at him, "the oldest of all Cruaar cities."

"I have already sent word via the sands. The council are awaiting his arrival." Braak's deep voice loomed from overhead.

"What? How? There is no herald here." Raglan's confusion was evident. Asher's face betrayed his obvious bewilderment, but the two men paid him no notice.

"Herald?" Asher saw Braak stifle a look of disdain as he removed something from his robe. "Heralds have been obsolete for decades. Did you think the progress would stand still in your absence, Augmad?"

Raglan ignored the jibe and gently took the object in his hands and inspected it, eyes full of intrigue. A small shard of mirrored glass had been set within an ornate carving of ivory.

"A portable herald. Extraordinary."

"It's a crier." Braak continued, snatching the object back from Raglan, "council issued. Every warder is given one so they can report in from The Blind."

"What council? What's Undergall? Where are we?" Asher rubbed his eyes as he rose up on shaky feet. Raglan soothed Asher's questions with the stroke of his hand down the side of his face.

"In time, my boy," he placed his hands either side of Asher's face. "We're safe for now. We're in Lightfoot Tunnel."

Asher looked around in the dim light and finally recognised his surroundings. He knew Lightfoot Tunnel well. Raglan had named it after Asher had begrudgingly shown it to him a few days earlier. In recent weeks, it was where Asher would go to escape the world and, as such, he was very reluctant to offer up its existence. Since its discovery, it became clear that it was not habitable or welcoming to humans. Asher was the only person to use it on a daily basis.

After much gentle persuasion from Raglan, Asher had finally given in and showed the old man where he would disappear for hours at a time and how he'd managed to escape so many angry stall owners after an interlude of thievery.

The tunnel was actually an underground maze, honeycombed across the underbelly of the city. It offered a multitude of secret access points if you knew where to look, but few knew and fewer still wandered into them because of the fear of becoming lost.

Asher, however, had come to learn the majority of entrances and exits and could traverse the tunnel system without problem. Lightfoot Tunnel was his.

Raglan had been amazed at Asher's innate ability to navigate the length of the tunnel system without making a sound. Dodging puddles and skipping over debris and rubbish, Asher moved through the labyrinth of interlocking tunnels like a sure-footed alley cat. Raglan, on the other hand, whilst able to traverse the system given enough time, had never been able to match his partner in crime's knowledge and speed. Asher looked around, but already knew where they were.

They were at the third landing of Fishgutter's Gap.

Asher had created names for every section of the tunnel. It was a method he had taught himself to better navigate the twists and turns of the tunnel in the dark. He could smell the nauseating bile of rotting fish carcasses from one of the many pits littering this section of the tunnel, all fed from drop-shafts above.

They were close to the Nile's fishing district, where the local fish merchants would sell only the freshest fish and were only too happy to discard the rest. The whole place stunk to high hell, but not to Asher.

"So where are we headed then? Can you at least answer me that much?" Asher asked.

"Hanafi Bazaar." Raglan looked at the young man in front of him, clearly thankful he would not have to lead the way through the maze of tunnels. "We need to get to Pablo's, and if we do it without being seen, all the better."

Braak's eyes narrowed at the name, but he said nothing. Asher, on the other hand, quickly mapped out a route in his head. They were about four hundred metres from the bazaar, most of which could be traversed in safety within the tunnel system. There was, however, a significant gap where they'd need to go above ground and travel the length of a street, and of course, cross the bazaar itself. The street would most likely be deserted at this time, but the bazaar was anyone's guess.

Asher quickly explained the route.

"I don't like it." Raglan rubbed the back of his neck worriedly.

Braak scoffed at Raglan's fears. "We have little choice, Augmad. Asher, lead the way. From here on in we should travel in silence. I doubt we have lost our pursuer so easily."

"At least we can agree upon that." Raglan beckoned for Asher to take the lead and the trio set off. Asher had forgotten all about his unopened found-day present, which Raglan had stuffed deep inside Asher's pants pocket.

The tunnel was dark and dank. Faint reflections of light glinted off pools of stagnant water littering the slimy moss-covered floor. As the trio moved forward, Asher in the lead, they were met with a rank odour rising from the decomposing piles of waste. The smell was so bad it forced Asher's companions to hold their hands over their noses and mouths, in an attempt to choke back the urge to gag. Asher picked up the pace, hoping to move past the unpleasant smell, motioning the others to follow his footsteps precisely.

Traversing the narrow tunnel-system was much easier for a fourteen year old. Asher's taller and bulkier companions grunted awkwardly as their extremities collided with walls and became lodged awkwardly in piles of rubbish. Raglan had lost count how many times he'd bumped his head against the unforgiving ceiling.

Asher turned a corner and hugged the wall, placing both feet on a raised gutter, carefully avoiding a rather large pool of water which ran the length of the tunnel's shaft. He turned around just in time to see Braak nearly step into the water.

Asher's hand lashed out, hitting him hard in the chest.

With bent back, Braak looked at him with his head tilted in confusion. Asher pointed to the body of water, then drew a single finger across his throat. He remembered the first time he'd nearly fallen into the submerged hole. The still face of the water was as deceiving as it was black. Beneath the calm glassy surface lurked a gaping drop-shaft, the bottom of which was pummelled by a relentless undercurrent passing through two drainage grates positioned opposite each other.

Asher only knew as much because a rabid dog had chased him into the tunnel system and had fallen victim to the watery trap mid-pursuit. A raging torrent of water had careened over the dog's body and pinned it against one of the submerged metal grates.

Asher had returned months later to see the pit uncovered, a canine skull and a pile of bones resting at the bottom. Even now, he shuddered to think what had eaten the rest of the dog's carcass.

Braak edged up onto the raised gutter.

Raglan did the same and the trio resumed their journey through the darkened crawl space of Lightfoot Tunnel. Moving ever closer to the bazaar, their passage through the remainder of the subterranean tunnel system proved uneventful. The only exceptions were a few instances when the two larger men became stuck in spaces that even Asher struggled to fit through.

Shafts of moonlight filtered down randomly into the tunnel system through drains overhead. Asher stopped in a slightly larger section of tunnel and waited for his companions to catch up.

Braak emerged first and stepped to one side whilst he readjusted his robe. His medallion clung unnaturally to his chest, but was devoid of any sign of internal luminance or life.

Upon catching sight of Braak's medallion, Asher checked his own gemstone. It too was dark and lifeless, the pain and throbbing gone.

Braak's dark skin made him the perfect ally when alone in a dark space. He was practically invisible until he passed under a shaft of moonlight, the light reflecting off his sweaty skin.

"What's with the violin case anyway?"

Braak looked at Asher with a strange expression, as if the question was idiotic. "It acts both as a disguise and a shield to stop our augers from being detected."

"From who?"

"Humans, mostly, and those that seek to expose us, but also certain creatures that are attracted to the power of our blood."

"Won't they be able to find us if you have it out like that?"

"It's not my scent they track," Braak said solemnly, his words weighing heavy on Asher's nerves. Asher gulped back his fear as Raglan emerged from the darkness, his greying hair and clothes drenched in sweat. Asher knew negotiating the tunnels was not easy for his uncle, but, like Braak, Raglan offered no word of complaint.

The three came together in the small space so they could talk. Asher spoke in hushed whispers, but even whispers no louder than the flap of a sparrow's wings sung out like a choir in the confined space.

"Our exit's up ahead. The last stretch to Pablo's is in the open, down this street and across the bazaar."

"How far?" Braak asked.

"A hundred steps to the bazaar and then another forty to Pablo's front door, give or take," Asher guessed. Braak nodded, but was not entirely happy with Asher's reply.

"The vertistrand's at the back of the shop, but it's ancient," Raglan wheezed, "and I have no idea where it leads. But the less time we spend exposed in the bazaar the better, so it would be better if we didn't have to pick the lock."

"Leave the lock to me." Braak replied curtly. "Just pray the vertistrand works, old man, for all our sakes. There is no telling where we will end up after we go through, so stay close." He uttered the warning specifically at Asher. Moving forward towards the concealed exit from the tunnel system, he surveyed the deserted street looking for any signs of an ambush.

"Asher, listen to me," Raglan whispered, "I know there is much you do not understand, but you must trust this man. Your lives are bound together in blood and he will protect you." Raglan looked at Braak's darkened silhouette that stood crouched just out of view from the street. *He must.*

"Whatever happens, you must stay alive." Raglan took Asher's face in his hands. "Do not stop. Not for me. Not for anything."

"What?" Asher exclaimed in surprise. "No."

"Promise me." Raglan insisted, "promise me you'll save yourself."

"I…" Asher stammered.

"Swear it." Raglan commanded.

"I…"

"Dear boy, you must promise me this."

"I promise." The words fell from Asher's lips as his eyes brimmed with tears.

"Good lad." Raglan looked lovingly upon Asher, soaking up his features in an unwavering gaze before hugging him and ushering him towards the exit. "Now you must focus, we still have a ways to go."

"Ready?" Braak asked the two behind him without turning around.

"On your word," Raglan replied. Asher said nothing.

"Asher, you go first. I will be right behind you." Braak swung open the rusty sewer gate and the three emerged into the brisk Egyptian night.

The street was deserted and dimly lit, mostly by pale moonlight and the golden glow of a few streetlights that lazily hummed. Long shadows crept over the cobblestones on either side of the street like lurking death, but the coast was clear.

Asher crawled behind a parked car and jumped to his feet. A second later, Braak and Raglan stood on either side, each peering off into the distance, scanning for signs of danger.

"Stick to the light of the moon. Go!" Braak murmured at them both. Asher did not need to be told twice. He dug his feet into a groove and spurred his legs into action. It only took four steps before adrenaline was coursing through his veins. Another four steps and Asher was nearing full speed.

Even as a child he'd always been a quick runner, but Braak was faster. His long legs were easily able to keep pace. He remained two steps behind Asher at all times, eyes darting this way and that, analysing every shape and shadow for signs of danger.

Raglan followed the pair no more than three steps behind Braak's muscled form at all times. He may have been much older than the two, but his lean body showed little sign of ageing.

Asher put his head down and ran for his life. Wind rushed

through his hair as his lead increased. His legs burned with every step as he flew past a series of wooden doors on his left and a slew of parked cars in an alleyway on his right. The only sounds were their footsteps slapping against the pavement, Braak's louder than both Raglan's and Asher's combined.

A stray dog barked in the distance.

All else was still.

Asher was still thirty yards from the end of the street. With every step more of the bazaar came into view. Closed vendor stalls littered the area like a poorly constructed obstacle course, shoddily attached wind shades and drapes writhed about in the unnatural tempest, casting shadows in every direction, all dancing in tune with the chaos.

Asher hadn't noticed the gale-force winds that had seemingly sprang out of nowhere as he sprinted down the deserted street. But, as he neared the entrance to the bazaar, the unnatural raw power of an elemental force became instantly evident. His eyes scanned the bazaar's deserted marketplace as best they could in the dim light. Shadows twisted and shifted like tortured demons, each writhing about more violently than the last.

Asher glanced back over his shoulder.

Braak and Raglan were still hot on his heels and moving fast. Returning his gaze on the bazaar, he slowed his pace, ready to navigate the hard corners of the many market stalls. A chilling cold instantly stung his face and made his eyes water. Blinking them clear, he swerved to the left of one stall and veered to the right, crisscrossing his way towards Pablo's Antique Store.

He could still hear Braak's heavy footsteps behind him, but the hodgepodge of market stalls and flailing material made keeping sight of his two companions almost impossible after he'd rounded the first two corners. A loud bang rang out somewhere behind him. Then only the sound of the wailing wind met his ears. The heavy clunk of Braak's footsteps had ceased.

Asher slowed his pace and spun around. There was no-one behind him. He was alone, lost amidst the twisting shadows and deafening winds ravaging everything in their path.

Another loud bang rang out, somewhere above and in front of him. A transformer box exploded in an electric shower of sparks. The few working lights that still glimmered around the bazaar simultaneously blinked out. Two more explosive booms rang over the roar of the wind, this time somewhere to his right, but it was a far more terrifying sound that grabbed his attention. Frenzied footsteps, moving too fast to belong to any human, scraped against the ground, racing towards him.

"Raglan?" he whispered at the wild shadows that terrorised the gaps between the closed stalls. He heard nothing but the silent shriek of the wind. "Braak?"

Fear reared its ugly head inside Asher's conscious. He felt his chest constrict and his breath shorten. A nearby coup of chickens went berserk, squawking and clucking in hysteria as a hulking form swept by them in a burst.

"Run, damn you!" Braak commanded as he violently grabbed Asher and forced him into a headlong sprint.

"We must rid ourselves from this place."

CHAPTER 5

A HARROWING EXODUS

Half stumbling and half dragged by Braak's powerful arm, Asher broke into a desperate run. He dove down a gap between two rows of market stalls before changing direction down another, weaving his way closer to the edge of the bazaar. Braak was hot on his heels, not willing to lose sight of Asher again.

Rounding the corner of a final set of stalls, he finally laid eyes on the door of Pablo's Antique Store. It was old and wooden, an antique in itself. Its heavy iron hinges stretched across the width of the door, bracing it against any unwelcome attempts to force it open.

"There it is," he called to Braak, who lifted up his hand and shouted something at the door, but most of what he said was lost to the wailing wind. The door's iron locking plate incinerated and exploded inwards, leaving a gaping hole in one side of the door as it swung ajar. Asher ducked inside and spun around, just in time to see Braak close the remnants of the door behind him.

Blocking the door with the weight of his body, Braak peered through the newly create gap for any sign of Raglan. All manner of shadows swayed and thrashed in the moonlight, but Raglan was nowhere to be seen.

"Raglan?" Asher murmured, looking at Braak.

Braak said nothing, his gaze locked on the limited view of the bazaar outside. Asher peered around at his surroundings: a dull nightlight had been left on in the front windows, which spilled over the front half of the store. There was only one room: it was long, narrow and crammed full of old furniture piled high on top of one another.

The more valuable showpiece items had been prominently displayed at the front of the store, most likely to act as bait, in the hopes of luring customers into the store to be preyed upon by salesmen. He glanced over a matching set of vintage, high-back, pin-cushioned velvet chairs standing neatly beside a series of hand-carved camphor chests and smaller jewellery boxes.

Directly opposite them, a large blue-and-white mosaic-topped table rested underneath a magnificent chandelier made of pearl, ivory and glass. The rest of the store was filled with furniture of a much lower quality. Run-down cabinets stood firm in their place next to ageing chests of drawers and hall tables.

A few more tired chandeliers and antique light fixtures from a bygone era hung dangerously from the roof, threatening to free themselves from their locking bolts at a moment's notice. At the rear of the store, a series of old wardrobes resided against the wall. Many of their hand-carved veneers concealed beneath heavy sheets, covered in a decade's worth of undisturbed dust.

Asher looked for anything that might resemble a vertistrand, but he had no idea what he was looking for so instead turned to face Braak. The man's fierce gaze was still locked to the shopfront windows, peering outside into the shadowy maelstrom overwhelming the bazaar.

"Where is it?" Asher whispered anxiously. "The thing. Where is it?"

Braak turned for an instant and scoured the back of the store, eyeing off the long row of dusty sheets. He pointed to one particularly thin object in the back with a finger.

"There."

Braak refocused his gaze outside, his eyes searching for any hint of Raglan, whilst Asher ran to the indicated item. Pulling on the heavy and dusty sheet covering it, he gingerly tried to free it from its cover.

Nothing happened.

He pulled a little harder.

Still nothing.

Mustering up all his strength, he yanked the sheet with everything he had. Years of settled dust exploded around him showering Asher in a fine grey film. The heavy sheet flew off the object and came to settle on the floor in front of him in a heap.

Asher coughed and wiped the dust from his face. Through watery eyes Asher saw his own startled, dust-smeared expression staring back at him. A full-length mirror, encased in an ornately sculptured bronze frame, stood before him.

"There's some kind of mistake. It's just a mirror." Asher called out, but Braak ignored him. "Did you hear me? A mirror!"

"Keep your voice down," Braak hissed at him, wedging an oversized cast-iron paperweight in the shape of Anubis under the gap in the door. Retrieving a small leather pouch from his waist, he quickly opened its draw strings as he retreated to the rear of the store. He took a moment to inspect the carvings on the mirror's bronze frame, running his fingers over every groove.

The vertistrand was older than any he'd ever seen. The mirrored glass was badly scratched in the centre. The edges of the frame, however, were under siege by an infestation of a thick black mould that was deteriorating its once lustrous surface.

"The glass is still intact. It will serve."

Reaching into his pouch he drew out a pinch of white sand and held his fingers against his medallion. An eerie green light filtered throughout the room as the sand turned iridescent. Braak threw the sand against the face of the mirror, but the grains did not fall, instead, they floated and spread.

The reflection in the mirror churned and transformed into an image of a sandstone wall, ablaze with daylight. The rear of the store became awash with natural light as it streamed through the shimmering face of the vertistrand. Braak mumbled his immediate displeasure at the blinding light.

There was no hiding now.

An agonising wail sung out above the terror of the wind outside. It had come from just beyond the first line of stalls.

"Raglan has fallen. We must escape. Now!" Braak's voice boomed out over the cry throughout the tiny room, all pretence for silence gone.

"You don't know that for sure. He could still be out there. He could need our help. We have to help him. We can't leave him." Asher adamantly refused to believe his friend was dead. "Raglan! Raglan we're coming for you!" Asher's hoarse voice pierced the night as he lunged towards the door.

Braak caught him with one arm and dragged him towards the glimmering vertistrand.

Asher's eyes looked at Braak, desperately seeking the slightest sign of sympathy.

None came.

Braak didn't even look at him.

Asher struggled against Braak's powerful hold, desperately looking back at the entrance for any sign of Raglan. The only thing he saw through the shopfront windows, was row upon row of closed market stalls vanish, as a tidal wave of darkness washed over them.

Braak sensed the impending attack and spun around. His medallion surged to life as he channelled his blood into it, but it was already too late. The entire storefront exploded inwards in a violent eruption of glass.

Asher was knocked off his feet, but shielded behind Braak's body as the man bore the full brunt of the explosion's wrath. Fragments of splintered wood and shattered glass bit into his flesh, tearing skin from muscle in the blink of an eye.

Darkness flowed into the store like a tidal wave, enveloping the front row of antiques in mere moments. It surged forward relentlessly, spilling over tall cabinets and low chairs. Within seconds, the entire front half of the antiques store had become an undulating sea of nightmares. In its centre, two blood-red eyes glared at them triumphantly.

Asher met its stare the same way he had done the first time: eyes wide with terror. Even with Braak in front guarding him, he felt his blood turn cold in his veins and the air in his lungs become clammy and suffocating.

Despite his wounds, Braak stood his ground valiantly against the surging darkness. Blood flowed into his medallion, igniting his palms with brilliant pendulums of green flame. He tried to launch a counterattack at the spectre, but his efforts were in vain.

His wounds were too great.

A sliver of darkness shot out from within the shroud and struck Braak square in the chest, rending skin from muscle and tendon from bone. Maniacal laughter echoed around the room as Braak wailed in agony.

"Bow before the Mortis Skulk, Warder," a sinister voice echoed in the gloom, before another debilitating attack hit Braak across the knees.

Braak's legs collapsed under him, forcing him to kneel before the darkness. With his last vestige of strength, Braak reached back and extended his hand defiantly at the dazzling vertistrand, amplifying the blazing light shining through its shimmering face.

For a moment it almost looked as if the act might hold the sinister creature at bay; but Braak's strength was waning. The light briefly flickered, its intensity fluctuating as Braak's energy waned.

The spectre tried to launch something dark and shrouded at the mirror's face, but Braak's free hand shot up and deflected the blow. The sliver of darkness combusted into a spatter of bright green flame as it passed over Braak's head.

"Asher!" Braak yelled between attacks. "Through the vertistrand boy, go!"

Asher ignored his command.

The thought of Raglan flickered through his mind. The man had been his one and only friend, his protector and mentor, and now he was gone: most likely killed at the hands of this shadowy beast. The thought fuelled his body with a venomous rage. Dark emotions manifested deep within him, twisting any thoughts of survival into a need for vengeance. He felt his gemstone spark to life in his palm. It burned as it fed on bitter blood coursing with the ravenous hunger for revenge.

He rose from the floor and stood behind Braak's crumpled

form. Braak was holding on, his defences barely able to withstand the hailstorm of dark energy raining down upon him. Each attack exploded in dazzling bursts of green flame, creating a shimmering umbrella of emerald in front of them.

Asher raised his hand in defiance, blood-drunk auger outfaced, ready to kill. Relinquishing control over his body to base instinct, he surrendered his sanity to the vengeful thirst within.

"Join me, Vita," a garbled voice hissed at him, taunting him with its depraved insidious laughter.

"No!" Asher's resolute answer resounded in the dark space like the blast from a horn of war. He felt the sharp jab of pain in his palm. It shot up his arm and into his chest as a golden light spewed forth from his gem. His felt his eyes glaze over with an insatiable fury as he watched the spectre's advance falter. The onslaught of radiance intensified as Asher channelled more and more blood into his gem. Wild streaks of light shot forth into the void like gilded lances, piercing the darkness. It wailed like a wounded animal, retreating away from the perilous attack, back through the store, its back to the door.

The darkness had nowhere to hide. The blood-red eyes bucked and swayed as long black tendrils, lashed out, ripping antiques in two and tossing furniture about the room like confetti. Its cover of darkness had been almost completely negated by Asher's merciless assault.

Asher saw nothing but a blur of golden light.

The poisonous rage swelling inside him filled his veins with bitterness and a savage bloodlust he had never felt before. The spectre's attacks ceased altogether as it found itself struggling to maintain the upper hand.

The shroud had completely receded, clinging to the creature's humanoid shape in the doorway of the store. A sickening half-human, half-demonic wail screeched at the prospect of defeat, but Asher didn't hear it, nor did the figure that launched itself at the creature from behind.

A bloody arm slid around the beast's neck in a chokehold as

two gangly legs wrapped around the beast's waist, locking together. A momentary flash of silver cut through the shroud as a metal dagger plunged into the beast's shoulder. Raglan grinned as he felt the knife hit home.

"Did you forget about me, Skulk?"

The sound of Raglan's voice snapped Asher out of his rage. Surprise and relief swarmed over him as his eyesight returned. The golden light spewing from his gem faltered, then disappeared, leaving Asher utterly exhausted, his entire arm and blood-soaked hand throbbing in agony.

Braak, still crippled by his wounds, struggled to his feet as best he could, all the while watching Raglan battle a demon shrouded in shadow. Raglan tried to plunge the dagger down again, but a darkened claw, engulfed in black tendrils of smoke, caught his hand before the steel could bite. Raglan's eyes locked with Braak's, a ferocity burning behind his eyes.

"Run."

Braak turned and grabbed Asher by the waist and swept him off his feet. He groaned as Asher fought back. His wounds were far graver even he cared to admit.

"Raglan!" Asher cried out, kicking and screaming as Braak stumbled forward. Half-carrying half-dragging the boy towards the vertistrand, Braak could only shuffle forward two steps at a time: it was all his injuries could bear.

"Raglan! No!" Asher's wails only seemed to further empower the old man. He increased the ferocity of his attack against the spectre, tightening his grip on the shadowy figure, refusing to give the creature once ounce of quarter.

The blood-red eyes thrashed viciously from side to side, bucking in the shroud of darkness. A chilling howl echoed as Raglan bit into the creature with his bare teeth. Braak chanced a look back and nodded a silent goodbye to the man sacrificing his life for theirs. He wasn't even sure if Raglan saw it or not, but they couldn't wait. He threw Asher through the vertistrand and stumbled through its shimmering face moments after.

Raglan caught a fleeting glimpse of the two as they disappeared. The spectre screamed in anger and bucked Raglan from its shoulders, lunging after them. Raglan fell hard against the floor as the creature surged towards the shining light. Raglan rose to his knees, exhaled and raised his dagger. He took aim and hurled it with all his might towards the mirror's brittle frame.

The knife sliced through the air with expert aim, racing past the spectre's head and its shadowy talons as it tried to catch the blade. With a heavy thud and a dull shudder, the dagger struck home. The sharp metal bit deep into the heart of the mirror's bronze frame, shattering it.

The image of Braak's haggard form cracked and splintered like a spider web before exploding outwards in a blinding eruption of light. The blast showered everything in the rear of the store with a thousand shards of mirrored glass, most of which had hit and lodged within the hollow frame of the spectre.

It shrieked in pain as its shrouded body was cut to ribbons, its eyes twisting back on themselves in the darkness, glaring furiously at Raglan. Raglan calmly spat out a mouthful of blood and smirked. "Do your worst, Skulk!"

Raglan coughed, choking on another mouthful of blood as the beast lunged towards him with venomous intent. Its shadowy talons pierced the skin on Raglan's arms and wrapped around the bones beneath his biceps. Despite the mind-tormenting agony, Raglan refused to give his assailant the satisfaction of drinking in his fear. His voice was weak and his mouth was bloody, but his words were unmistakable.

"Asher Bloom will live."

CHAPTER 6

THE FALL OF FOREGUARD

Asher experienced a brief moment of weightlessness as a faraway scream echoed through his mind. When he finally passed through the vertistrand, his momentum sent his body crashing down hard.

Braak followed him through moments later, just as the vertistrand shattered behind him. He collapsed in a heap on the sand, his injuries making it impossible for him to stand any longer.

Asher felt sick, like his insides had been twisted inside out. He spun around to look for Raglan, but saw only the broken shards of mirror and the brittle fragments of the bronze frame heaped upon the ground. The urge to vomit magnified until he could no longer contain it. He threw up on the ground as a single thought ripped through his conscious.

Raglan is gone.

Tears streamed down Asher's face as he fought back the urge to be sick again. His stomach was a series of knots, his mouth unable to find the words to express his momentous sense of loss.

Raglan had sacrificed himself, so he might live.

"We have to go back." Asher choked out in a raspy voice. "We have to help him." He ran his hands over the wall where the bronze frame of the vertistrand had stood, frantically searching for a way back, but his efforts were futile. The vertistrand was broken beyond repair. Its shattered remnants lay on the sand, multiplying the reflections of Asher's tears tenfold, all of them staring directly back at him.

"We can't," Braak's voice was barely a whisper. His body was a broken mess of hewn flesh, covered in a thick layer of green-tinged blood. Scraps of skin hung from his chest and arms like butchered meat.

"We can't leave…" Asher's words trailed off when he spun around and saw the extent of Braak's wounds. Bloody and broken, Braak was agonisingly trying to raise his ravaged body off the sand. Braak's unbreakable expression betrayed his determination not to yield to the mortal agony threatening to drown him.

Swaying unsteadily, his balance waivered to and fro like a drunken sailor. Slowly, one motion at a time, he managed to force himself upright. Heavy knees displaced mounds of sand as he pushed fragile limbs down into the treacherous sand for support.

"We can't go back," Braak coughed, blood spattering against his teeth as he spoke. His solemn expression would be forever etched into Asher's memory. "He sacrificed all he had to save you. Never forget that."

Asher broke down in a slump on the sand, unable to speak, tears streaming down his face. His only friend in the whole world was gone. He'd never see the old man's kind face gazing down at him again. He hadn't even been able to say goodbye.

"Your tears honour his memory," Braak winced, but even his heartfelt words served only to worsen the feeling of loss in Asher's heart, "but they will do you no good here. Strike them from your eyes." Braak looked away from Asher, arched his back and strained his legs for all they were worth. Struggling through the anguish the movement unleashed, he forced his spine upright. Small fragments of glass and splinters of metal riddled his flesh, releasing fresh spurts of blood with every movement.

Asher's hesitance to accept the man vanished. He was in complete awe that Braak had managed to maintain consciousness throughout the ordeal, let alone had the strength to force himself to his feet. Asher's hesitance was replaced by a small measure of respect, in time it might even transform into admiration.

Even so, Asher found it near impossible to hold back his tears. He dried his eyes on his sleeve in an attempt to hide his crying from Braak and mimic the man's limitless fortitude.

"Lambosulus eluo." In barely audible guttural tones Braak chanted the same strange sounding words over and over again.

A small viper of brilliant white fire emerged from Braak's medallion. Licking the warder's skin with a tongue of flames it slithered up over his shoulders and around his body. Braak closed his eyes and winced as it crawled over his skin, its tongue flicking out every few inches, feeding on his blood as it slid over his open wounds. Braak's body trembled. He clenched his jaw to stifle a moan as he struggled to control the excruciating pain.

Every time the snake's body slid over a sliver of glass, a splinter of wood, or a shard of metal, the fiery serpent erupted in a shower of sparks, eradicating the protruding fragments, cauterising the wound in the process.

The fiery serpent grew larger with each lick of blood it fed upon. It devoured everything in its path, blood and debris alike, leaving Braak's skin healed, but covered in a new set of fresh scars. When its work was done, it slithered back into Braak's medallion. The last remnants of its white flames flickering out as its tail disappeared inside his auger.

Braak's contracted muscles instantly relaxed.

He took three deep breaths and sighed loudly, before gingerly flexing his legs, arms and chest. Wounds that had been dripping with blood mere moments ago now resembled well-earned and honourable battle scars.

"Are you hurt?" Braak's voice had returned to its normal, stoic demeanour. Asher's shook his head.

"How did you do that?" Asher whispered, amazed.

Braak checked his body for further lacerations before answering. Not finding any, he unlooped his medallion from his neck and held it out for Asher to inspect. Asher watched as the core of the gem pulsated with an unnatural green life force.

"The gem is called an auger. It allows a Vox Cruaar to augment their blood into something much more powerful. This is its mantle." The man ran a finger over the rest of the medallion.

Large thorns pierced strips of bark, whilst small roots had

entwined themselves around colourful living leaves. Everything was bonded together by small globules of orange sap, whilst beneath it all a moulded stone frame encased the edges of his auger. "A mantle is made up of many different elements, seven in total. Each acts as a focusing agent, allowing us to better channel our blood and gain even greater mastery over our abilities."

Braak rehung his auger around his neck; once again it unnaturally stuck against his chest. "Do you understand?"

Asher shook his head. Braak looked like he was about to continue his explanation, but then changed his mind.

"It is not my place to teach you of such things. I will try to explain what you bear witness to while in my company but, beyond that, your education is best left in the hands of those better suited to the task."

"Like who?" Asher asked, looking around anxiously.

"Enough." Braak looked around, but saw only mountains of sand and a large sandstone wall protruding from the side of a dune. "We must work out where we are." He turned and set off, following the wall in the direction of the highest rise, leaving behind the shattered remnants of the vertistrand. "Come, we do ourselves no favours lingering in this place."

"Where is here exactly?" Asher asked, dropping in behind Braak, his feet struggling in the sand as it sunk and shifted under his weight.

"I'm not entirely sure, but I believe we are somewhere near..." Braak stopped in his tracks as he crested the rise, gazing out over the horizon, "the Fall of Foreguard."

"I've never heard of any Fore..." Asher trailed off as he joined Braak on the ridge. The spectacular ruins of what was once a mighty city lay strewn on the horizon, creating a broken haphazard landscape, besieged by the devastation of war and ravages of time.

The ruins looked much older than they were in Braak's eyes. The remaining intact buildings were worn: punished beyond measure by an unnatural force. Everywhere Asher looked, ugly mutated weeds and vines had done their best to reclaim the city, growing over any building with enough shade to weather the blazing heat of the desert sun.

It was obvious, even to Asher, that the city had not been abandoned. It had been razed to the ground and left to rot under the burning sun. High above the city, a swirling maelstrom of purple, black and orange storm clouds loomed over the city like the chaotic gates of hell. Towers that had once stretched high into the sky lay toppled on their side, wasting away beneath mountainous dunes of black sand. The blight sat like a pestilence over the city. It covered everything, shifting every few moments as a torturous wind tossed it back and forth, shifting the decrepit dunes atop yet another ruined building.

An entire row of what once must have been grand halls and stately buildings had been reduced to rubble. A series of broken pillars were all that was left of the colossal bridges that once spanned a giant ravine that had weaved throughout the city like a splendid silk scarf. Now only a dry gorge remained: a choking collar, squeezing the city of whatever life remained. The streets were barely recognisable. Only the widest and sun-exposed thoroughfares remained untouched from Foreguard's decaying blight.

Asher had never seen so much devastation in a single place. "How can you possibly keep a whole city hidden?"

"Just because we keep those in The Blind ignorant to our existence, it does not mean we remain invisible to those that know how to look."

"Don't you mean where to look?" Asher attempted to correct him. Braak did not even glance at Asher before answering, responding to him as he would a subordinate.

"It is exactly that misguided and ignorant mindset that keeps the humans blind to us and places such as this."

Asher frowned, he was not used to having his intelligence insulted. Braak walked along the crest of the dune scanning the horizon, displacing large amounts of sand with every step, revealing even more of the cursed black blight underneath.

"The Cruaar have been discovered many times before, mostly by the illegitimate offspring of a Cruaar and human coupling. Those gifted with the natural ability to see past our projections."

"What projections?"

"Everything you see here remains hidden to those in The Blind because we wish it and they do not know how to look. A human would only see this entire area as a barren desert and feel an instinctive need to steer clear long before they ever got this close."

"Right," Asher scoffed dubiously.

"Call it what you will. Illusions, magic, miracles, acts of God; humans love to mislabel things they do not understand. In any case, those that are able to see the truth of such things have always struggled to adapt, so we dispose of them for the greater good."

"You mean kill them," Asher accused him blatantly.

"Do not be so quick to cast judgement on things you do not understand. The truth is far less barbaric, at least on our part. Throughout the centuries, we have merely preyed on the human's natural fear of things they do not understand. In ancient times, we simply made sure these people were branded as witches and sorcerers. The humans took care of the rest.

"Then religion and kingdoms structured their world, and their understanding of such things changed. So we simply named them heretics, heathens and false prophets. Again, human fanatics and those in positions of power did the rest.

"Next came the centuries ruled by medicine, governments, and the spread of information, manufacturing and technology. Each time the humans made it easier and easier to label them insane: enemies of the state, anarchists and terrorists, amongst countless other titles.

"Each generation is ultimately the same. The smarter the humans become the easier it is for us to coexist among them, because the simple fact is, they don't want to see the truth."

"That's horrible."

"And yet still better than a bloody and brutal war between our two races. Look around you, this desolate wasteland is all that is left of the once great Foreguard. It was once the mightiest city of our people, a haven for all Vox Cruaar... until it fell during the Guillotine Rebellion." An immense expression of sadness crept across Braak's face; the unmistakable sense of loss Braak felt in his heart shone through his eyes.

"We did this to ourselves," he cast his eyes out over the ruins of the city. A single tear glistened in the corner of his eye, before he buried the thought deep down and blinked away the memory altogether.

"What do you mean?" Asher repeated, soaking in the unsettling reality of the evidence that lay before him.

"The Mortis Skulk ensured this city tore itself limb from limb, from the inside out. Hundreds of thousands murdering one another in cold blood: anyone they could not trust, all at the whim of the Cerebule and the vile traitor, Pracca," Braak spat on the ground at the mere mention of their names.

"Cerebule?" Asher repeated, letting the name sink in to his memory.

With a sharp wave of his hand Braak cut off Asher's line of questioning. "We dishonour the dead by uttering his name in this wretched place. Come, we have much ground to cover and we must be wary. Much life remains amidst these ruins and none of it welcoming, especially with that unshielded auger of yours leaking the scent of your blood everywhere."

Asher glanced down at his auger, before stuffing his hand back in his pocket as Braak set off at a brisk pace towards the heart of the city, violin case in hand. His newly-forged scars were a distant memory as he navigated his way down the sandy embankment. The sun was high in the sky and largely hidden by the swirling storm-clouds in the centre of the city, but still Asher felt its heat beat down on his neck and face.

"How is it light right now? It was midnight in Aswan." Asher questioned the man whilst trying to stay in the shade of his shadow.

"Ah, the ignorance of innocence," Braak mumbled condescendingly. "What I would give to be in your shoes, child."

"I'm not a child," Asher said indignantly, "and my name's Asher."

"Very well, Asher." Braak turned and held up a hand at the panorama of destruction around them. "It is daylight because we've just travelled halfway around the world."

"What?"

"I think you can agree, we are not in Aswan anymore. The vertistrand we passed through is a gateway. A gateway activated by augmented sand. We call it the shifting sands." He tapped the pouch Asher had seen him reach into earlier.

"Most vertistrands are connected via a central network called the strand. They allow passage between one another to any desired location. However, there are older variants with only a single fixed connection, which is precisely why we find ourselves lost amidst Foreguard, instead of the council halls of Earthreach Spire."

"But it was just a mirror," Asher replied, his mind trying to make sense of it all.

"To anyone that does not know how to look upon such things, perhaps; but once our blood fuses with our auger, it alters our perception. We see more of the world around us than our human counterparts. Which is why they have never discovered these ruins, nor will they."

"How can they not see it? You can't hide a whole city. What about satellites? Or planes? Or other human tech? Surely something must see it even if the humans can't."

"You do not see the wind, yet it exists, does it not?"

"That's hardly the same," Asher tried to argue.

"And ultraviolet light, it too lies beyond your vision but human science has proven it to be real."

"Yes, but—"

"What of a memory, an instinct, the ozone? Do not be so foolish to think that because you fail to see something with your own eyes it does not exist." Braak said bluntly, insulting Asher's naivety in an attempt to make the boy open his eyes. "Remember when you first saw me in the square? Think back, what was it you saw that no-one else could?"

Asher's mind flicked back to his first glimpse of Braak. He'd been dressed in his strange robes, hypnotically twirling fire in wild arcs as he danced rhythmically in the square. Then his memory jumped to the small animals and creature immersed in the flames.

"The fire... there were creatures in the fire."

"Did you not think it strange nobody else could see the creatures that were as clear as day to you?"

"I, er..."Asher stammered, "I never really thought about it."

"The crowd saw only a street performer with clever fire tricks. Exactly what I wanted them to see. It is our blood that allows us to see what those in The Blind cannot. And your blood is rarer still."

"What do you mean?"

"You saw the fire creatures and called upon your blood before your auger was aligned. Such a thing has never happened."

"Never?"

"No," Braak replied sharply.

"What does that mean? Why does my auger need to be aligned?"

"It doesn't. That's the problem. I'd wager it has something to do with the fact that it's fused within your skin. Another thing that has never happened before."

Asher looked down at his hand, inspecting the gemstone nestled in a bed of scarred flesh. "Never?"

"No. Nor has anyone borne the deathly taint without first swearing allegiance to the Mortis Skulk or corrupting their bloodline with the necrotic arts."

"The deathly what?" Asher gasped, gazing down at his auger. The black streak swayed back and forth within the gem, more prominent than ever in the blazing sunlight. Braak picked his next words carefully. He'd already overstepped his boundaries once before, he would be remiss to do so again. He took Asher's hand in his own and ran a finger over the black streak.

"This black scar in your auger will only ever be seen as the taint by those who look upon it–"

"But I've never killed anyone," Asher interrupted, "or sworn any sort of allegiance. I don't even know what a blood art is."

Braak looked at him curiously, eyes warily judging Asher's claims of innocence; but regardless of whatever he thought to himself, he said nothing.

"So what does it mean?" Asher persisted, his tone becoming more agitated as Braak's uncomfortable silence extended. "What happens to those with the taint?"

Braak maintained his silence. Turning away from the agitated concerns of the teenager, he briefly lost himself in his own thoughts. Braak's mind flittered back to a much darker time in his life as he drowned out Asher's questions. When he resumed his trudge through the sand towards the city, it was at a slower pace than before. The mindless action helped clear his mind.

"During the Guillotine Rebellion, there were those that proved to be unworthy of the gift of Cruaar blood in their veins. Traitorous cultists, devoted to a madman, willing to kill all who opposed him."

"Cerebule?"

Braak shot Asher a dark look at the mention of the man's name. "At first the council thought a plague had spread through our nation, afflicting those weakest among us. Many disappeared for days on end, only to return later with no memory of where they had been, if they returned at all. Soon it became clear the only plague on our nation were the traitors that sought to destroy it. It was not until much later, when a lone warder managed to uncover a secret meeting of the cultists that we began to understand the truth. He followed them and watched as they pledged their life to the practise and worship of the necrotic blood arts." Braak sighed as his memory skipped to a bleak and dreary time he'd tried long and hard to forget.

"Unfortunately, the warder was discovered and ambushed before he could ever tell the council of the cultists' existence." A momentary shudder washed over Braak's face. "His body was found by his son, drained of blood and left to rot on the doorstep of his ancestral home. The Mortis Skulk had all the time they needed to plan their next attack and make their presence known to the Cruaar Nation by the public slaughter of the daughter of a lowly councillor.

"By the time the council recognised the threat, we were already at war. We just didn't know it yet. All those who had gone missing and mysteriously reappeared, turned on their own overnight. The slaughter was unimaginable.

"The Mortis Skulk successfully orchestrated the greatest massacre in our history, and nobody saw it coming. In the span of one night, the council was destroyed, murdered at the hands of their own families. With the council members dead, or unable to function, war spilled out into the streets.

"The three largest of our cities fell within weeks of one another, leaving our race on the very brink of extinction. Only two smaller cities survived."

"Undergall," Asher murmured under his breath.

"And Hollow's Rest," Braak added. "After the first city fell, the surviving men and women at arms rallied under the leadership of the only man willing to fight back: the newly self-proclaimed grand chancellor, Valderook Wrakburn.

"With the cities in lockdown, the tide of the war turned in our favour briefly. We managed to hold back the threat, but we were still losing the war.

"It was not until a lowly custodian came to him with an answer that we are able to fight back against the cultist scourge. He had devised a test of blood that could identify the corrupted necrotic blood of the cultists. Failing the test would unleash a permanent black scar upon their augers."

Braak ran his finger down the length of Asher's auger.

"The cultists had nowhere to hide. Anyone identified with the taint was sentenced to death on the spot, without trial, and the Legion of Auger Regulation was established. Every auger was checked, every traitor exposed. They were beheaded and leeched of their blood in front of everyone, all at the command and merciless eye of Grand Chancellor Wrakburn."

"The Guillotine Rebellion," Asher whispered. Finally everything he had heard since this ordeal had finally begun to make sense.

"Yes."

"Wait," Asher paused as a realisation clicked in his mind. He immediately backed away from Braak, "so I'm going to be beheaded?"

Braak turned, his gaze catching on something over Asher's shoulder. He slowly raised his arms in front of him and whispered, "Asher, don't move."

"Like hell! You're taking me to be beheaded," Asher's voice grew louder with every step as he continued to back away. Braak's expression was one of wild lucidity, his gaze locked on the beast slinking up behind Asher.

"Raglan said I could trust you. You promised. You performed that blood rite thing."

"I said don't move!" Braak snarled at him through clenched teeth as a demonic growl purred ominously behind Asher.

Asher froze as the loud snap of jaws bit the air somewhere behind him. The possibility of being beheaded was now the least worrying thing on his mind.

CHAPTER 7

YOUR LIFE TO MINE

"Listen to me," Braak hissed as he inched forward, arms raised in front of him. His auger was ablaze with a luminous emerald light. "I need you to very slowly lie down on the ground."

Asher couldn't. He had to know what was behind him. He twisted his head and hesitantly peered over his shoulder. The snarling jaws of a monster stared back at him no more than three feet away. Thick gooey saliva drooled down four elongated fangs and swayed in the breeze.

A savage canine monster, larger in size than a wolf by half, bared its fangs at its newly found prey and snarled. Its head and back were covered in wiry red fur, whilst a spattering of dried blood had stained the fur on its chest and throat a mottled black and brown. An enormous maw, overflowing with jagged teeth, salivated in eager anticipation of a fresh kill. Asher was close enough to see the hair on the back of its neck standing on end, tingling with excitement.

"Braak!" Asher's voice was shrill, his body frozen in place.

"Dammit, boy," Braak whispered, slowly lowering his hands to the ground until his wrists were buried beneath the sand. "Lie down."

The beast took a step forward and snapped at the air. Bending its head upwards, it sniffed the air again and let loose a wailing cry into the air.

Asher seized the opportunity and ran.

"Asher! No!" Braak cursed under his breath, but it was too late.

The creature sensed Asher's movement and pounced. Powerful hind legs propelled its hairy bulk forward as its claws raked back the black sand. A massive paw landed heavily behind

Asher's heels, hot in pursuit. One more lunge and its enormous jaws would taste Asher's flesh, thick fangs burying into the boy's thigh or calf muscles, injecting venom and immobilising its prey to feast upon.

Asher scrambled forward over the loose sand like a man possessed, but his feet were no match for the traction offered by a set of four massive paws. He could feel the warmth of the beast's breath on the back of his legs.

A vicious triumphant snarl transformed into a cringing yelp as thick black vines shot out of the ground, entangling the beast's legs. They grew thicker and stronger with every passing second, wrapping themselves around the bulk of its body, legs and neck until the beast was caged inside a living prison.

It thrashed about wildly, trying to free itself from its incarceration, but the vines held firm, responding in kind, by growing large thorns, which painfully dug into its hide. The more it struggled, the more the vines constricted and the deeper the thorns buried themselves until, one by one, they punctured its tough leathery skin.

The beast thrashed its head around until the vines closed in around its neck and snout, then movement became impossible. Its hind legs slumped to the ground. Panting heavily, it glared in the direction of its prey; its eyes were only just visible through the black vines, but still ablaze with indignant fury. Even with its mouth clamped shut, it still managed to bare its elongated fangs at Asher in defiance.

Braak regained his composure and channelled a second blood calling through the sands. A small flower blossomed in front of the creature's nose and released a powerful nerve toxin in a puff of spores.

The creature snorted violently. Its front legs faltered then collapsed completely. Its chest hit the sand with a loud thud, the growth encasing its body doing little to cushion its collapse. The thorn-covered vines around its chest and throat eased their torturous hold, allowing the creature to breathe more easily. Loud guttural snores soon followed as the spores' toxin did their work, sending the beast into a deep drug-induced slumber.

"What the hell is that?" Asher panted, dusting the sand from his clothes. Braak steadied himself and withdrew his hands from the sand. He glanced down at Asher as he stood up.

"A gavrin. He was drawn to the scent of your auger. The males are aggressive, but little more than deaf and blind brutes," Braak frowned at Asher disapprovingly, "unless you move… loudly."

"Good to know," Asher whispered in response.

"Had you stayed still, or remained silent, you would be as invisible to him as the humans are to…"

Another beast's head came into view on top of the rise. This one, however, was grey and larger again by half than the one entangled in vines. A large plate of bone crested the top of its head like an armoured helm fit for war.

Braak's eyes grew a wider and his voice lowered to a whisper. "Female gavrins, on the other hand, are decidedly more complicated." A second head immediately popped above the rise, followed by a third and fourth. Braak's voice faltered. "Especially when they hunt in packs."

Braak backed away, hands igniting with wild green flames.

Asher stayed behind him, edging backwards over loose sand. "Are these deaf and blind as well?"

"No. Females have excellent hearing, better eyesight and are immune to nerve toxins." Braak's eyes flittered back and forth between the dunes and the city as he formulated a plan in his mind. "I need you to run. Fast as you can. Head to the broken building behind us."

Asher nervously glanced behind him. All the buildings were broken, but he didn't dare argue or ask Braak to clarify. "When?"

"Now." Braak commanded in a whisper, simultaneously launched a large green ball of flame into the sand. An enormous eruption exploded between them and the gavrin pack, masking them behind a cloud of debris, dust and black sand.

A large green shape emerged through the debris and lumbered away boisterously, breaking into a wild gallop as it streaked past the pack of hungry gavrins. When the cloud of debris cleared, a large black camel with streaks of emerald green glowing from its hindquarters galloped across the dunes like a demon escaping the gates of hell. The gavrin pack gave chase, following the camel's trail. Small wisps of green fire continued to burn in the grooves its footsteps left in the sand.

Asher and Braak ran like a pair of thieves in the opposite direction, sprinting towards the ruins of Foreguard as fast as their legs would carry them.

All but one of the hungry gavrins had taken the bait, lunging after the fiery camel. Their jaws snapping savagely at the heels of their luminous prey as they gave chase.

One gavrin remained on the crest of the hill, however: the alpha. It watched the camel gallop away, eyes lingering on the small patches of fire sizzling on the sand after every footstep, when it caught a blur of movement in the corner of its eye. Swinging its snout around, two large pupils contracted, focusing on two rippling shadows striking out across the black dunes. It lifted up its snout and drew in a deep breath through its nostrils.

The burning camel's scent was non-existent, but a faint lingering smell in the air sent a ravenous chill down the alpha gavrin's spine: Asher's auger. The alpha howled loudly, ordering its pack to cease their pursuit. They had a new foe to chase.

The alpha gavrin took off, bounding down the embankment, breaking out into full stride once it hit the flats, its nostrils drinking in the sweet aroma of Asher's auger as it charged forward.

Asher and Braak sprinted past a multitude of collapsed buildings and piles of rubble as they entered Foreguard's desolated streets. Their target was the nearest still-standing building. The outer shell of the structure that had once stood four stories tall was now lucky to boast a second storey.

"Up there." Braak pointed to a half collapsed wall, half

crushed beneath a toppled column. A large sandstone pillar now lay diagonally across its face.

Braak glanced over his shoulder to assess the threat. The alpha gavrin had already halved the distance between them and was closing fast. Its massive paws sprayed hot sand into the air as its legs thundered over the sand. The wide pads of its feet were surprisingly nimble and effective on the treacherous surface.

The scent of Asher's auger on the wind only grew stronger with every passing step, fuelling the beast's desire to kill like a drug-induced stimulant.

"Climb!" Braak shouted, helping Asher scramble up the sandstone column's diagonal face. Asher's heart pounded as he scurried up the column and leaped up and over the wall it had crushed. He landed on his feet this time, safe within the second floor of the building's decaying entrance hall.

Braak waited until Asher had made the jump before following. Surging up the sharp incline, he shouted a command, channelling blood into his auger. His footsteps became powerful shock waves, reverberating down through the brittle sandstone and intensifying with every step. The column splintered, then cracked, then ruptured; an enormous fissure appearing that split open the middle of the stone. It buckled, but did not break.

Braak vaulted over the broken wall as the column broke apart under its own weight. It dropped a foot down the exterior of the wall as a large chunk fell away from its centre, but still stubbornly refused to collapse.

The alpha gavrin howled and snorted as it reached the base of the building, pacing and sniffing the ground until it could track Asher's odour to the decaying sandstone column.

"Come on, boy, run!" Braak commanded, pulling Asher along by his shirt. They raced along the balcony of the entrance hall, their frenzied footsteps leaving shallow imprints in the black sand. Bypassing a collapsed stairwell, they rushed to the end of the hall and burst through a heavy wooden door.

A cloud of dust exploded as the two fell through the doorway.

The small room looked as if it hadn't been disturbed in decades.

Braak slammed the door shut behind them and bolted its heavy iron latch.

Asher warily edged away from Braak, a rising fear evident in his eyes as his lungs heaved in his chest.

"Really? Still you do not trust me?"

Asher didn't. He backed away farther as Braak braced the door with his weight.

"Asher, we are bound by blood. You heard me swear the oath. You watched our bloods fuse."

Asher took another step away.

"Whatever happens to you happens to me."

Asher's backward steps faltered.

"Praccing hell, boy! If you die, I die!"

Braak's words hit him like a slap in the face. Asher's fear was instantly replaced by confusion. "What?"

"The Rite of Bonded Blood. It links your life to mine. You die, I die. I would never willingly walk you into certain death."

"So if you die, I die?" Asher gulped.

"No, I swore the oath, not you. The bond only extends one way. My life is bound to yours, but not yours to mine. If I am killed you'll surely feel it, but you'll live."

Outside, the alpha gavrin had grown tired of waiting for its pack and launched itself up the column, its paws loosely scrambling for a foothold on the crumbling stonework.

The added weight of the alpha gavrin's bulk tore the fissure into an enormous seam which split the middle of the column like a streak of lightning. Its claws frantically scratched and tore their way up the pillar as it finally shuddered and collapsed. The alpha gavrin launched itself towards the broken wall at the very last second. It pawed and clawed at the wall's crumbling edges for a foothold, hind legs first dangling, then scrambling, until it had all four paws on solid ground inside the decaying entrance hall.

The column shattered into pieces and broke apart even more as it collapsed against the building's exterior. Chunks of stone rained down, crashing into the sand and pelting the rest of the freshly arrived gavrin pack with debris and mortar. One was caught beneath a falling boulder and died instantly. The others scattered around the base of the building, howling loudly as they searched for another way in.

"Why didn't you do something?" Asher questioned. "Burn them with your fire, or summon those vines again?"

"Their hides are resistant to fire and they are much too strong for the vines or their toxin." Braak answered, bracing his shoulder against the door and listening to the hall beyond.

Asher gave the room a quick once-over, looking for anything that might help. The room was large enough but offered little in the way of escape routes. There were only two small windows, mere slits in the stone, that provided little more than glimpses of the outside world. A small measure of light permeated through the slits: just enough to keep the looming dark of the room at bay. It was immediately clear to both of them that there was only one entrance or exit to the room. The door they just came through.

They were trapped.

Before either had a chance to admit as much, a colossal force collided with the other side of the door with a tremendous thud. The whole room shook with the impact. A series of small cracks spread across the ceiling, raining down dust as chunks of mortar dislodged from the stonework bracing the door and fell to the floor. The thin layer of sand covering the floor vibrated and resettled, before it was rattled again by another mammoth crash. The wood between the heavy iron bars bracing the width of the door splintered and buckled.

Braak winced as the force of the blow slammed heavily against his shoulder. "This door will not hold for long, and I'd rather not be here when it breaks."

"So break a hole through the wall already."

"And bring the roof down on our heads?" Braak dismissed the idea, bracing his full weight hard against the door, waiting for the next attack. The beast snarled and howled on the other side of the door. Its attacks were becoming more violent and more ferocious as the door warped and broke.

Asher was frantic, desperately scampering over to each of the four corners of the room, looking for anything they could use, but the only furniture was a large heavy oak desk in the centre of the room. Its drawers were either empty or missing entirely and it was far too heavy for Asher to move by himself. Just the smallest patches of a rug could be seen hiding underneath its legs, but the patterned fibres were completely smothered by the desolate layer of black sand covering the vast majority of the floor.

"We need to barricade the door, can you move that desk?" Braak's voice was strained.

Asher scrambled over to the desk, but already knew he wouldn't be able to move it. The desk budged a little, but the fibres of the rug bit into the sand beneath it, holding it firmly in place. "It's too heavy."

Another almighty crash deafened the small space. The door slammed against its hinges, ripping them out an inch from the wall. More wood splintered in the centre of the door where the beast's bone-crested skull had rammed into it.

Braak seized the moment and lunged for the desk, pitting his weight behind the heavy oak. "Push!"

Their combined strength made the desk give way against the rug's stubborn sand traction and slide forward, dragging the rug with it.

A devastating crash and the sickening sound of splintering wood filled their ears as the centre of the door exploded inwards in a shower of wooden shards. A large four-clawed paw ripped at the newly created hole until the gavrin could fit its large snout and salivating fangs through the gap, snorting loudly.

The rusty iron brackets bracing the door made it impossible for the beast to squeeze its bone-crowned head through the gap. Its fangs and snout disappeared back through the hole, replaced instead by an enormous dilated eye, brimming with unbridled savagery as it glowered at its prey.

An instant later the eye was gone along with the vicious snarling on the other side of the door. Asher heard the sounds of heavy paws scattering sand as the gavrin retreated along the balcony in preparation for another attack.

"Push, damn you!"

The desk lurched forward, dragging the half-buried rug across the sandy floor. The heavy oak table slid across the room in one fluid movement, displacing piles of sand as it went, uncovering stonework that hadn't been exposed in decades. As the two heaved their weight against the rigid frame of the heavy desk, the sound of the gavrin's massive paws charging towards them in the corridor outside intensified. Then the sound ceased.

For an instant, the only noise that met their ears was the shuddering reverberation of the desk's groans as they pushed it across the floor.

A second eruption of wooden shards exploded into the room. The gavrin's thunderous collision with the door was brutal. The impact shook the four walls around them and threatened to bring the roof down on their heads. A large stone brick fell from above and landed square on the desk with a heavy thud, mere inches from Asher's fingers.

The hole in the door doubled in size. The top iron bracket ripped from the wood's surface, tearing away the bolts holding it in place as it cruelly warped out of shape. The door was now little more than a pathetic assortment of tattered wooden fragments held together by bent and broken iron brackets.

With a final effort, they pushed the desk into place, wedging it firmly against the doorway with a heavy thump. The walls and roof shuddered again as it slid home, a spray of powdered mortar the only warning as a brick crashed down from the roof behind them.

The roof was failing rapidly, but at least now a third of the hole in the door was now blocked by the desk. Even so, the beast still managed to shove its gaping muzzle through the gap to snap at them. It clawed at the desk's solid edges as it barked, spluttered and hissed at the two, furious it could not land its fangs on flesh.

Safe for the moment, Braak spun on his heels and examined the room. The path of the displaced black sand the rug had dragged across the room revealed a solid stone floor, but little else, certainly no escape route. He scanned the floor, but only layer upon layer of monotonous black sand stared back at him.

Seeing no alternative, he reached two fingers into his waist pouch and grabbed a pinch of white sand. Dropping it in the palm of his hand, he closed his fingers around it and raised it to his medallion.

His auger flared with emerald light, igniting the sand with an iridescent life of its own. Clenching the glowing grains in his fist, he raised it to his mouth and blew. The sand flew from his fist and scattered, floating upon invisible airways, each grain seeking out a different exit from the room. Tiny particles of white sand flooded the room, working their way over every inch of the walls, floor and roof, searching for any structural weakness that could be exploited.

Another deafening crash made the walls and roof shudder violently, sending even more wood splintering away from the door. The beast's snarls and howls became sharper, cutting through the air and breaking Asher's resolve.

"It's breaking through," Asher warned, attempting to ignore the alpha's savage howls.

Braak did not acknowledge the beast's torturous wails, or respond to Asher's warning. Instead, he carefully watched the iridescent floating sand as it explored every inch of the room for an escape. Four small lines of glowing sand converged on the rearmost corner of the room and erupted in a mad dance, their vibrations shaking apart their hold over the floor the black sand had claimed dominion over for all these years. Up and down they bounced and shook, causing the lifeless black sandy blanket to shift and part.

Another gut-wrenching crash echoed behind the duo. Only

two wooden slats remained, the bulk of the door had been ripped apart and now lay on the floor. The enraged gavrin tore at the last remaining shreds of timber, ripping the wood apart with its sharp claws and vicious fangs.

With a few quick swipes from his hand, Braak managed to dislodge the remaining sand in the corner of the room, uncovering a trapdoor with a heavy iron ring. He wrenched it open and peered down into the hole. The broken remains of an old wooden ladder, no more than two rungs high, descended into the darkness below.

He flicked three quick bursts of fire down into the hole. Each plunged past the collapsed foundations of the level below, briefly illuminating the jagged edges of rotting floorboards as the flames rocketed down into the darkness. Each flame came to rest a few feet from one another in a cavernous void. The flickering flames burned brightly against the oppressive darkness consuming everything below.

Braak eyes shot towards their rapidly failing barricade. The gavrin had almost torn the last wooden slat away from the door and was trying to clamber through the gap. "What are you waiting for? Jump!"

Asher's momentary pause left Braak with little option. He grabbed Asher by the shoulders and threw him headfirst down into the hole. Braak's battle-scarred muscular body followed moments after.

The gavrin stopped struggling and watched as its prey escaped for a second time. It howled in frustration and rammed the last wooden slat with its heavy boned skull in defiance until the wood shattered and splintered into shards.

Asher tumbled head over heels as he fell, plummeting into the darkness towards the three blotches of fire. He was given no reprieve when his shoulders collided with a mountain of sand. He was already sliding down the sharp incline when Braak's feet landed heavily behind him. Almost instantly Braak lost his balance and fell forward, barrel-rolling down the hill, losing his grip on his violin case in the process.

There was no telling how big the chamber actually was. The two had stopped trying to estimate its size as they sped down the slope, disappearing deeper and deeper into the darkness. A distant furious howl echoed down after them, but it sounded as if it was miles away.

Using his arms to steady himself, Braak managed to fling himself on his back and angled his descent down the sandy slope. Sliding towards Asher, he felt his speed slowing, until finally it stopped altogether.

Whilst Braak's body had slid to a relatively gentle stop, Asher's stop was decidedly more abrupt. He slid down the incline on his chest, face first into a low dune, leaving him with a sore face and a mouth full of sand.

Braak wasted no time before he was on his feet again, green flame ablaze in hand, working his way towards Asher whilst awkwardly trying to find stable footing in the deluge of still-moving sand coming to rest around him. His violin case skidded to a stop a few feet away. Braak scooped it up without a second thought and made his way to Asher's side. "Are you alright?"

"I've been better." Asher spat the sand from his mouth and scraped his tongue with a finger. "Where are we?"

"Nowhere good." Even in the darkness of the chamber, Asher could see the concern in Braak's large brown eyes.

High above them Braak's fires fizzled out, their light fading into oblivion once more as the last embers died. Neither of them saw the dark blur drop down into the shadows high above on the mountainous dune as the last glimmer of light faded away.

CHAPTER 8

GIBRALTAIR PRIVVYBELL REINE

The cavern was immense. An enormous wall stretched out of sight high into the darkness above them and to either side. Behind them lay the base of the great black sandy mountain that had just spat them out. The air was still and silent, like death leaking from a tomb. Its solitude interrupted only by the faint sounds of moving sand whispering down the mountain and the hiss and crackle of the flames in Braak's hand.

"Come. We must go." Braak increased the intensity of the fire in his palm, basking their surroundings with a dim olive glow.

"Where?"

Braak's keen eyes picked up much more in the darkness than Asher's. His years of combat and survival training in light-deprived situations had increased his ocular ability in the dark. His irises flickered with recognition, reflecting the glimmer of emerald green flames as they danced across his retinas.

His eyes latched on to an absence of light in the distance, against the base of the enormous stone wall. Narrowing his eyes to inspect it further, he recognised it for what it actually was: a man-made doorway cut neatly into the stone. "There. Come."

The pair set off under the guiding light of Braak's flames, warily making their way along the base of the massive wall. Small trickles of sand slid down the mountain at random intervals, but neither of them paid much attention.

Darkness reclaimed the forgotten tomb as Braak entered the small passageway, shrinking the flames to a more appropriate size for the confined corridor. Asher followed him inside and thought he heard something move in the darkness behind him but, when he turned to look, saw nothing.

"I don't think we're alone down here," he whispered to Braak.

Braak paused a moment in the passageway and listened. Hearing nothing, he decided to set the doorway of the passageway ablaze with an impassable waterfall of flames, just in case. "Steel your nerves. We have a long way to go yet."

Asher wondered for a moment if everyone in Undergall spoke in the same abrupt manner as Braak, or whether the man had other reasons for his curt manner. Braak gave him no time to dwell on the matter. The man turned his back on the raging fire and advanced down the corridor.

Asher and Braak walked on for some time in silence, both content they were no longer running from danger. Minutes passed by as the two continued deeper into the abandoned intestines of Foreguard. Asher tried to examine the stonework for any sign of where they were, but each square stone was as dull as the last. "What's that?" Asher's voice broke the eerie silence. "There, in the distance."

A black hole engulfed the sides and roof of the passageway not far from where they stood. Without a word in response, Braak edged forward, one hand holding his violin case, the other a dazzling ball of emerald flames, his medallion pulsating wildly on his chest.

Wary feet crept forward as they approached the black gap in the walls and roof. Asher quickly realised it was not a hole at all, but an open doorway into a much larger room. The light from Braak's flames spilled outwards onto the stone tiles and into the chamber as they approached. As they stepped into the room, its majesty was fully revealed. They saw row upon row of enormous stone statues, each at least three times the size of a man. The stone sculptures towered over them, but did not depict any creature with which Asher was familiar.

"A construct factory," Braak exclaimed with a mixture of wonder and surprise. "I thought them all destroyed."

Asher gazed up at the enormous statues. Their frightening gargoyle-like heads were almost hidden in the darkness. The light from Braak's flames was barely able to reach their ghoulish features, making them all the more frightening. Braak walked between the legs of one of the giant figures, running his hands over its coarse surface. "They were our builders, our machines, long before mechanaugs came along. Each was attuned with the partial life-force of a single Vox Scienta."

Asher looked back at him blankly, clearly not understanding the terminology.

"Semi-intelligent entities, neither alive nor dead. Created by the augineers of old and powered by their blood to be the building tools of our civilisation." He ran a hand over one of the mammoth stone legs. "Except the creators are all long dead."

Without warning an enormous hand reached down out of the darkness and snatched Braak off his feet, encircling both his arms and chest in a massive stone fist. Asher cried out as he too was trapped and swept off the ground. Braak's fire immediately went out, plunging the room into darkness.

"You'd think that, wouldn't you?" A voice ruminated from the darkness. "Fortunately, my great, great grand-pappy had the foresight to realise he wouldn't live forever but his creation might. Imagine my surprise when I stumbled across this burly old chap rotting away down here in this vapid tomb."

Asher and Braak struggled against the stone fists encasing their bodies. It was no use.

"Majestic aren't they? Granted, they're a little crude and rudimentary, but obstinately strong."

A dazzling blue light blinked into existence, blinding the trapped duo to the man sauntering towards them. After a moment, the light dipped and Asher's eyes were able to readjust.

A tall, elegantly dressed figure came into view, a walking cane resting on his shoulder, the tip of which emitted a brilliant blue light that doused the room in a cool artificial glow. More constant than the flicker of Braak's emerald flames, the light spilled across the darkened crevices of the factory floor; old shadows retreated and new ones emerged between the legs of the giant stone statues as he marched steadily forward.

Asher looked closely at the man as he approached. His opulent clothing was clearly intended for more lavish and pristine surroundings than the dusty forgotten factory buried beneath a ruined city.

The man's large-rimmed glasses had radiant orange lenses that seemed to adapt and change hue as the light shifted in the room. Asher couldn't see his eyes beyond the tinted lenses, but watched as the man casually dusted off his shoulders and chest before flicking the tip of his cane at Braak.

With the blinding blue light pointed directly at Braak's face, he reached out and lifted the medallion from around Braak's neck in one fluid stroke. Catching it as it slid down the length of the cane, the man turned it over in his hand and reshouldered his cane. Judging from his casual mannerisms, he held firm in the belief his captives offered no threat whatsoever.

"Now, my dear mysterious compatriots of crime, I must enquire as to who you are and what you're doing here." He looked up at Braak, before shifting his gaze to Asher. "You're clearly not augmads, judging by that horrendously primitive fire I saw you wielding moments ago. Nor do you seem devious enough to be a member of the Mortis Skulk." He inspected Braak's auger closely. "Nor do you bear their mark, which leaves only one conclusion."

His eyes flicked back and forth between the two carefully as he attempted to deduce an explanation for the pair suspended before him. "You have the look of a council whelp." He nodded at Braak. "Surely not a tribarion, or even a bireem for that matter, or we'd be having a much less civilised conversation."

Asher didn't understand either term, but said nothing.

"I thought not, which would make you a warder... and a rather poor one, judging by the number of scars you bear so proudly. Second Edict, I'd wager." His eyes swung to Asher. "Which brings our discourse to you, young man."

With a flick of his cane, the man motioned the construct to

lower Asher for closer inspection. Asher's body lurched towards the floor, stopping only a foot away from the man's face.

He was roguishly handsome. Long blond locks adorned the man's head, all drawn back over his ears and hidden under a white bowler hat. His jaw was chiselled and lined with day-old stubble, as was his dimpled chin. His clothes, however, were of the finest materials. Impeccably blue silks and delicate white satin trims adorned his tunic, pants and coat. All were inexplicably clean, even amidst the dusty atmosphere of the desolate chamber.

The man's cavalier attitude was unexpected, especially considering his current surroundings, but he pulled it off effortlessly, as though he'd been doing it all his life. His brow furrowed as he turned his head from side to side hoping to see something that would make sense of the young man before him. "You remain somewhat of a mystery. So what, pray tell, brings you deep within the intestines of this fetid ruinous beast?" He held up his hands and motioned to their surroundings.

Asher began, "we were atta—"

The man ended Asher's answer with a wave of his hand. "Dear boy, where are your manners? Never steal a mystery from an augiologist before he's had a chance to unravel it. Every intrigue must be satiated in the natural order, by deduction alone." He paused for a moment, inspecting Asher's blank expression.

"Your lack of recognition would have me believe you're not used to such terms or ideas, which would indicatively rule you out as an apprentice," the man continued to guess, gauging and measuring Asher's facial reactions as he spoke. "A sentinaug's ward perhaps... no, no, you radiate far too much power. Oh, you do present a challenge, don't you? A delightful conundrum." The man turned, stepped back and spun on his heels. "Let's start with names, then, shall we? Perhaps a title will allow me to glean an insight into your reason for being here."

"Enough. Let us down," Braak ordered, still struggling and visibly fuming at his imprisonment within the statue's grip.

The man held up a finger and hissed at him for silence. "Your name, young master; what is your name?"

"Asher Bloom."

"What an exotically plain and underwhelming appellation. And you my rude miscreant of fire and wrath?" He swung his cane to point at Braak without bothering to look at him, his focus fixated on Asher.

"Braak Saada, Warder of Undergall."

"Oh yes, yes, do not feel the need to repeat what I've already ascertained." His voice betrayed his boredom with Braak's answer. He whispered his next line to Asher whilst hiding a large smile behind his hand, "I've always had a knack for sniffing out the stench of a council lackey."

"Let us down," Braak barked, before he was sharply cut off.

"Tsk, tsk, Master Saada, the game is still afoot. But where are my manners? Allow me to introduce myself. I, gentlemen and ruffians of the ball, am…" he announced, "Gibraltair Privvybell Reine. Famed explorer and augiologist of the civilised, though more commonly uncivilised world."

He finished his introduction with an eccentric wave of his hand and a deep bow. Braak recognised the name, but had never met the man in person before.

"Who?" Asher asked, dumbfounded.

"Dear boy, is your head as dense as the stone that holds you? I shudder to think you've not heard of the exploits of Gibraltair Privvybell Reine," he repeated his name, still with the same theatrical enunciation. "I discovered the Shroud of Salvation and unearthed the Horn of Goopler's Cradle. Surely you've heard of them?"

Asher looked at him blankly.

"Perhaps hearing the Shroud's Truth will jog your memory." In an attempt to impress upon Asher the importance of his discoveries, Gibraltair recited the words that had made him famous. "To Vita true, I leave to you, the fate of our nation. Behold at first, a father's thirst, and life for our salvation."

99

Gibraltair, slightly flustered at Asher's lack of response to his exploits and fame, turned his attention to Braak's struggling.

"One might think it rude to interrupt prose with naught but moans and groans. Struggle and you'll only make it worse for yourself." Gibraltair waved his wand at the giant stone figure.

Braak gasped as the pressure on his rib cage increased, forcing the air from his lungs.

"Now, where were we?"

"Let us down." Asher's level of discomfort was obviously somewhat less than Braak's, but even he was tiring of the man's mind games. "Please."

"You see," Gibraltair smiled widely, his eyes shooting dark looks at Braak. "Manners cost nothing. But not just yet. A mystery must unfold in its proper order if we are to be illuminated by the perception of truth." His voice had an air of grandeur about it, spoken with perfect diction and articulation, even if a bit exaggerated at times. "Now to unfold the enigma that stands imprisoned before me. You're definitely a Cruaar, though you may not know it. I can positively smell the stench of your bloodline from here."

He scratched his chin, somewhat perplexed, as he pondered his thoughts out loud. "A trait that is singularly more impressive than any other you seem to possess. This leads me to believe that your bloodline is one of legends and heroes, undoubtedly passed to you by your father, who was?" Gibraltair paused, waiting for a response.

"I never knew him," Asher replied, managing to free one arm from the construct's grip.

"Add a pinch of tragedy to the pot to thicken the boil." The man stirred his cane through the air in a circular fashion as if he were stirring an overly large cauldron. "Mother?"

Asher shook his head.

"So the age-old song of a child abandoned plays once more. A recipe as complicated as it is ripe with scandal." Gibraltair paced the floor before his captives. "Orphaned in the rebellion like myself, perhaps? No, no, you're far too young for that. Perhaps you're the illegitimate offspring of a union between worlds, suffering through life amidst the visionless barrens."

Asher stared at him blankly.

Gibraltair shook his head and tossed away the thought, "no, far too common a tale for one so enigmatic." He turned around and waved his finger in the air. "Then, possibly, you stand as the begotten son of an augisarry, tracked down by said malcontent discourteous warder, to rejoin the depleted ranks of the Vox Cruaar war machine."

He waited for Asher's response. Asher had no idea what an augisarry was, but was quickly growing impatient of the man's questions and nodded his head, if only to shut him up.

"Less than entrancing, but adequately stimulating nonetheless," Gibraltair giddily clapped his hand together, his face glowing with satisfaction. "Yet it still doesn't explain your presence here."

Braak attempted to speak, but Gibraltair silenced him with a sharp wave of his cane before he even uttered a word. "Shh, can't you see young Master Bloom has the floor."

Asher began again, "we were attacked."

"Mercy no, not amidst the Fall of Foreguard?" Gibraltair bit one of his fingers in a mock look of shock.

"No, before that. A Mortis Skulk attacked me in the street and again in the antique store."

Gibraltair's cheery demeanour instantly dropped a notch.

"But we escaped through a vertistrand…"

Gibraltair's smile returned wider than ever, his hands rubbing together in anticipation of the next piece of the story.

"How thrilling."

"…only to be attacked again by a pack of savage beasts."

"Gavrins," Braak added only to have Gibraltair angrily shush him to silence once more.

"Which brought us here," Asher finished. "Wherever here is."

"Augisarries, Skulks, vertistrands and gavrins. My, my, you

have been busy and still alive to tell the tale. Who knows, you may have the blood of an augiologist running through your veins." He scratched his left ear with the handle of his cane, deep in thought.

Asher looked over at Braak, who remained powerless to help their predicament.

"A less-than-exquisite narrative, but then you are young and unwittingly dense." Gibraltair continued, waving a hand in a sweeping motion across the room. "Very well, Asher Bloom, your story has softened my resolve and, as such, warrants an end to your incarceration. So I humbly release you."

Asher breathed a sigh of relief.

"After you answer me a final question." Gibraltair leaned in close to Asher.

Asher was close enough to see the fine whiskers on his cheeks and smell a strong perfume rising from his body. The scent was intoxicating. It almost overwhelmed his senses, trying hard to send them reeling into a dizzy, thought-confusing spin.

"How is it your auger happens to be embedded within your skin?"

Braak shot a look of concern at Asher and frantically tried once more to escape the clutches of the construct, but his limbs were stuck, firmly wedged between the enormous fingers of the stone fist.

Asher reactively looked down at his exposed hand.

Gibraltair could only see the side of the gem from his position on the ground. Asher had forgotten all about his hand and the exposed auger, the black taint wavering against the gold of the gem, just out of sight from his inquisitor.

Clenching his fist even tighter to hide his auger from view, Asher heard the distinctively familiar sounds of paws sprinting on sand.

"Watch out!" Asher barked in warning.

Gibraltair instinctively stepped to his left in a single fluid motion, maintaining his impeccable form and composure, a split-second before a massive gavrin, mouth agape, lunged at his body.

Gibraltair spun on his heels and stabbed the tip of his cane into the alpha gavrin's furry hide, its gaping jaws missing his arm by mere inches. The glowing tip of the cane penetrated its rough hide easily, dislodging in its hairy flank amidst sizzling embers of green fire.

The light from the cane was now firmly embedded deep within the beast's side sending wild shadows scattering about the room. The beast's lunge ended as it slammed head first with a sickening thud into the construct's fist imprisoning Asher.

The smell of burning hair made Asher want to retch. The mammoth stone construct stood resolute against the attack and lifted its captors out of harm's way, launching Asher upwards into the darkness. Asher watched below as Gibraltair sauntered away from the beast, looking back at it over his shoulder with distaste.

The gavrin regained its footing and squared off against its newest opponent. It paused and lowered itself on all fours before pouncing again. Gibraltair nimbly dodged the attack swatting the backside of the beast with his cane.

"I bore of this encounter," he said loudly and rapped his cane against the ground.

Asher watched as a gem sitting atop Gibraltair's cane radiated a bright blue. Asher had not seen it before because the augiologist's hands had been clasped over it.

The glowing metallic tip of Gibraltair's cane, now lodged in the gavrin's flank, sucked the light back in on itself, transforming into a silvery liquid. The liquid expanded from the wound and spread over the beast's rugged hide.

At first the gavrin didn't notice, but soon the metallic liquid covered one of its rear legs, solidifying as it went. The gavrin's muscles cramped in pain as it limped towards Gibraltair, its shiny metallic leg tapping against the floor as it struggled forward.

Soon the liquid-like substance had completely covered its hind legs and the gavrin was unable to walk. As the liquefied metal spread and hardened, the gavrin's expression changed from one of raw anger to one of pure fear.

It tried to bite and claw away the substance, but that only served to hasten its spread over the beast's body. The liquid oozed into the gavrin's mouth and over its eyes as a horrified gurgling howl spilled from its lips. Within the space of a minute, its entire body was covered in the rapidly solidifying metal, leaving behind a metallic statue stuck in a panicked pose.

"That was awesome!" Asher yelled from the safety of his stone prison, high above the commotion.

Gibraltair bowed elegantly upon hearing the compliment. "Appreciation not withstanding Master Bloom, without warning it would not have been such an elegant encounter." Gibraltair tapped his cane against the ground and brought the head of it to rest against the side of his head. "Gentlemen, you have proven your resolve, both in story and in action. Please join me on a more level existence, so we may continue this discourse in a manner more civilised."

The construct lowered its captives to the ground and released them, before resuming its watchful position back in the ranks of the other solemn statues. Glad to be free of his stony embrace, Braak dusted himself off and shot dark looks at Gibraltair, before snatching back his auger and looping it around his neck.

Gibraltair took no notice of Braak's angry glare and casually approached Asher. As he sauntered forward he squeezed the handle of his cane and, without a sound, a shiny new metal tip appeared at its base, replacing the one lost in the fight just moments before. "Now, as for that auger, my dear fellow…"

But Asher had already hidden his hand deep within his pocket, his fingers wrapping around a hard object. Raglan's found-day present. The sides of Asher's mouth curled up for the briefest of moments, before the memory of his uncle's demise drew him back to reality.

Braak stepped between the two, blocking Asher with his body, and holding up his right hand at Gibraltair, palm outstretched.

Braak's loud voice firmly put an end to Gibraltair's line of questioning before it had even begun. "His auger is a matter for the council and it's in your best interests to recognise as much."

Gibraltair looked at Asher and then at Braak, this time noticing the menace behind the large man's eyes. He promptly decided it was indeed in his best interests to drop the issue entirely. "Right you are, good warder," Gibraltair's agreed quietly, his voice turning suspicious after spying something strange in Braak's hand. He quizzically tilted his head in order to get a better look at it.

"What?" Braak eyed the man off untrustingly, sensing the sudden shift in his attention.

"A ring, such as that, is not often seen these days, especially on the hand of a mere warder. Where did you get it?"

The bottom half of the ring was silver and much larger than the simple copper band stretching over the top of Braak's index finger. Asher's eyes only caught a glimpse of the ring's detail before Braak's fingers clenched, concealing it from view. It was all he needed to commit it to memory. Its design was circular, made from polished silver. It remained unblemished, which Asher guessed was by unnatural means. Seven raised lines extending outwards from a central tiny black polished pebble on its face.

"It was my father's. A dying gift, and is of no concern of yours," Braak said gruffly, killing the conversation in its tracks.

Gibraltair cast a sly glance at Asher before stamping a foot on the ground and flamboyantly spinning around. "Very well, then. Follow me, my enigmatic charlatans of mystery. If it's the council you seek, let's not tarry any longer. The strand is not far, though in recompense for escorting you, I will have to demand one small boon of you both."

"What might that be?" Braak called out irritably through gritted teeth at Gibraltair, who'd already set off at a brisk pace, theatrically weaving his way through the legs of the stone giants.

"When retelling this dreadfully dreary adventure to your

masters, could you, if it's not too much to ask, leave me out of it? They take a dim view of those that meddle amidst these ruins without the proper authority, which is not to say I do not have as much, but it'd be in my best interests, and yours, to leave such matters unsaid. Unspoken. Unmentioned. Comprende?"

Braak shot the man a chilling look. "Lead us to the strand and with any luck I'll never willingly have to lay eyes on you again."

Gibraltair paused to consider his offer. "Then we have an accord." He tapped his nose twice, "sally forth my inept wayfarers, this way," his voice trailed back at them as he set off down the enormous factory floor, the cane over his shoulder lighting the way.

"Is that normal behaviour in Undergall?" Asher asked as they followed the impeccably dressed man farther into the darkened ruins. Despite Gibraltair's guiding light, Braak summoned a bright green flame in his palm and made sure to keep the elegant augiologist in front of him at all times.

"Hardly," Braak said curtly. "Stranger yet is the motive behind his presence here."

Gibraltair slowed until the two caught up and then proceeded to regale Asher with his augiological exploits as they navigated their way through Foreguard's ruins towards the strand.

Time was meaningless amidst the countless subterranean corridors. Each new turn spawned yet another tale of herald and woe from the overly animated Gibraltair, most stemming from his prior noteworthy augiological achievements. After what seemed like hours they finally reached an unusually large passageway.

Gibraltair stopped short and turned to face the pair. "Well you've made tolerable journeying companions, but even our tale, short as it is, must draw to an end. At the end of this dimly lit concourse you'll find your exit and coincidentally the excavated remains of Foreguard's last remaining networked strand.

"A tribarion guards the gateway so you'll understand that this must be where our paths diverge. Fare thee well Master Bloom and council whelp Saada. Who knows, perhaps we shall meet again."

"I hope not," Braak muttered under his breath.

Without another word, Gibraltair twirled on his toes and marched back into the darkness, his cane tapping against the sand-covered stone as he went.

"Come, Asher, we've wasted too much time already." Braak urged Asher along the passageway until they rounded a corner and were instantly blinded by the blazing sunlight reflecting off the sand outside the corridor's exit. With both hands up, shielding their eyes, it took a moment for their retinas to slowly readjust to the abundance of light. When they had, the pair walked outside into the base of a colossal crater. A seamless combination of excavated ruins and mountainous black sand dunes stretched high above them in every direction.

No more than fifty feet away stood the remnants of a gigantic mirror that, in its prime, must have stood a hundred feet across. Now more than half of it was missing, the rest broken beyond repair or missing entirely.

The outline of a lone figure stood at its base, silhouette rippling in the midday heat. A voice boomed across the crater. "Stand and attest before the Tribarion Cohort."

Braak filled his lungs with air and shouted back, "Braak Saada Warder of Undergall."

"Warder Saada," the man repeated the name as he approached. "It is not often one randomly meets his best friend's son amid the Fall of Foreguard. Especially when he guards the lad that has the whole of the Cruaar Nation abuzz with villainous rumour."

Braak recognised the voice instantly, but yet could not see the man's face due to the sun's blinding glare. "Opspray?" Braak called out. "You old salted crumb, whose daughter did you lay hands on to be placed in this wretched post?"

A loud booming laugh resounded from the approaching tribarion as he came into focus amidst the rippling heat. Dressed from head to toe in heavily inscribed gilded armour, the man looked nothing short of magnificent. The sun bounced off his heavy gilded breastplate and the metallic helm he carried under one arm, but the heat did not seem to affect him, nor did the sun's blinding rays.

His other hand rested on his hips, just above a long golden chain with barbed ends that swung lazily as he walked. A large guitar case lay propped up against a low wall behind him. His feet carved a swathe through the sand as he approached, sending it flying up in the air around him with every step.

Braak and Opspray embraced each other with open arms like age-old war veterans. The tribarion looked no older than Braak; in fact, he almost looked younger, which thoroughly confused Asher as he could've sworn he heard the man refer to Braak as his best friend's son.

"How in Prac's unholy name did you end up here? The last I heard you were on the other side of the world, in The Blind of all places, traipsing after a Skulk sighting." Opspray smacked Braak heartily on the shoulder.

"Trust me, old friend, it is a long story, best told over an even longer drink."

"One we shall share soon enough, but not today. The Overseer has sent word. Your orders are to report in person at Earthreach Spire. The council has already convened and you know how impatient those bastards get in that stuffy old gallery, especially when you delay in bringing them a new toy to play with." Opspray smiled at Asher and gave him a sly wink. His eyes were warm and welcoming. There was something comforting in his demeanour that instantly put Asher at ease.

The tribarion turned and walked towards what was left of the great mirrored vertistrand. "She may not look like much, but the old girl has life in her yet." He delicately reached into a pouch hanging on his belt and withdrew a pinch of sand. Approaching the last remaining man-sized shard of mirrored glass, he swung his hand past the golden chain hanging on his belt and threw the iridescent sand at the face of the strand. The mirror's reflection swirled and fizzed as the sand fell through its face; their reflections rapidly transformed into one of a cold grey stone floor surrounded by curved walls.

"The first barrel is on me after you've fed the vultures," the tribarion grinned heartily at Braak, "you'll find me at the Swaying Tribarion soon enough. And you," the man switched his gaze to Asher and raised his voice, stepping forward to purposely tower over the young teen. "Don't let those council bastards get you down." The man laughed loudly, slapping Asher hard on the back and winking at him again before stepping aside to allow the two to disappear through the vertistrand's shimmering surface.

The entirety of the council watched two bedraggled figures emerge through the grand auditorium's private vertistrand.

Asher was again disorientated by the passage through the strand and struggled to maintain his balance, swaying heavily on his feet on arrival. He was in a large circular room, with layer upon layer of tiers that stretched higher than he thought possible. The centre of the room was engulfed in a pillar of light, illuminated as if it was directly lit by the sun itself.

A hundred heads or more sat silently behind their respective tiers and balconies. Each was draped with one of four large coloured banners—gold, green, blue or black—a unique coat of arms proudly emblazoned on the material.

One balcony in particular was larger than all the others and protruded directly opposite Asher three tiers up. It was adorned with a red-and-black striped banner with a unique insignia; but Asher could not see who resided behind it due to his diminutive position on the floor.

It was instantly obvious to Asher that the entirety of Undergall's council had been convened.

What was even more worrying was that he knew they'd been convened because of him. He felt the weight of a hundred pairs of eyes bearing down on him and, as far as he could tell, none of them were pleased to see him.

CHAPTER 9

AN UNKNOWN FATE

Hushed whispers reverberated around the circular tiers above Asher's head like a wheezing pipe organ. Each tier was filled with men and women of all ages and ethnicities, all of them leaning forward to better examine the small boy in the centre of the room. Their painted robes and dyed tunics created a kaleidoscope of colours against the gull grey of the stonework: a veritable peacock's tail amidst the otherwise drab fixtures of the towering gallery.

Asher could hear only snippets of conversations above, as prejudice and bias swirled around the room. Nothing he heard gave him any indication that the outcome of these proceedings would be tilted in his favour. Braak ushered Asher gently towards a large backless chair with high arms that sat a few paces from the centre of the auditorium's floor. It was completely immersed within the bright beam of light that shone down from above like the eye of a god.

Before Asher was able to sit down, an enormous man in heavy armour, made mostly of leather and resin, emerged behind him and marched across the floor. Asher glanced nervously at Braak, who gave him a reassuring nod in return before stepping aside. Without saying a word, the armoured man motioned for Asher to hold up his hands.

Asher did so obediently.

The bireem retrieved a large silver ankh from his waist and held it in front of Asher's face. Asher had seen many ankhs during his time in Egypt—mostly in paintings, drawings or knick-knacks that peddlers sold to tourists—but he had never seen one of this size, at least not up close and not being wielded like a weapon.

The man's hand wrapped around the shaft of a cross, whilst two perpendicular arms and a large oblong sat above his fingers. A large blue auger in the centre of the circle's hole warmed in colour and came alive under the man's will, an ocean-blue radiance growing faintly from within.

Asher saw a single drop of blood seep into the gem's centre and disappear as the enormous man waved the ankh up and down methodically over Asher's body. Moving it over the length of Asher's torso and finding nothing, he moved on to his legs, first checking the left, then the right.

Hushed whispers echoed down from the tiers above when a shaft of bright blue light erupted from the bireem's auger. His ankh was hovering over the pants pocket on his right leg. Asher felt a small bulge push against the confines of his pants, as if desperately yearning to escape.

Asher's mind flicked to Raglan's found-day present. With everything that had happened he'd forgotten all about it. With rough hands, the man reached into Asher's pocket and removed the item, still wrapped in cloth. Asher tried to cry out but couldn't. Nor could he reach for the man's arm to attempt to stop him. His arms were locked in place. He had become a prisoner in his own body without even realising. The armoured bireem placed the item on a nearby empty tabletop and returned to his duties, scanning Asher's body for more contraband.

Skirting around Asher, he resumed his search and waved the ankh over Asher's back, neck and head, the weapon mere inches from Asher's skin. Asher tried to gasp when his arms involuntarily shot up perpendicular to his sides, but even gasping was out of his control. All whispers ceased as the man moved the ankh over Asher's arms and down to his hands. Finding nothing on his left arm, he moved to the right.

Asher's fist had been clenched since he first arrived, but now he clenched his fingers even tighter, or at least he thought he did; he couldn't be sure anymore.

The ankh slowed to a stop over his hand and, once again, a

bright blue beam of light burst forth from the bireem's auger before spiralling into a mottled red as it bounced off the back of his hand. Asher felt the skin in his palm burn. The assembly of council members gasped and murmured loudly, a hundred voices muttering their opinions, surprise and fear all at once. Conjecture spread like a sickness amongst the tiers above until a single man raised his hands for silence. It did little to stifle the behaviour of the crowd.

"Enough!" a voice boomed. The murmuring instantaneously ceased. "Despite this display, I think we can all agree our guest is quite harmless in his current state. Bireem, please show him a seat."

Asher couldn't see who owned the voice, but it definitely came from the largest balcony in the room.

As the bireem walked forward, Asher felt an invisible force pushing him into the ornately carved bench. He blinked momentarily and shut his eyes as he passed into the blinding beam of white light. When they opened again, he was already seated on the bench, both arms locked into place on the armrests at his sides. From where he was, it was near impossible to see the darkened tiers beyond the wall of light.

A perfect interrogation room.

Asher made sure his fingers were still firmly clenched around his auger. If they wanted to see his secret, they would have to force him.

"Thank you, Bireem." The same voice spoke again. Atop the largest balcony in the room, an older man that looked to be in his mid-sixties rose to his feet and addressed the assembled members of the council.

"Undoubtedly, over the last few hours you've all been discussing the rumours that have spread like a pandemic through our great nation, namely that a Warder of Undergall had discovered someone in The Blind with an auger for a hand.

"I understand how such a rumour could be extremely disturbing, however, I find the matter of how Warder Saada's confidential report was leaked in the first place a much more disturbing factor here and, mark my words, it will be thoroughly investigated and the culprit brought to answer for their treason." The man's threat silenced the few people still murmuring amidst the higher tiers.

Silence descended over the gallery as he swept a hand out towards Asher. "Now, as to the matter at hand. I think we can all plainly see that our guest's hand is indeed just that, a hand. Whatever secrets the boy's palm may hold will be revealed in due time. So let us start first with the facts so we might uncover the truth as it is, and not as it is rumoured to be." He turned his head towards Braak and opened his palm, motioning him to take the floor. "Warder Saada, if you would."

"Grand Chancellor, councillors, auglorians, bireems, tribarions and custodians of the Augestry," Braak stepped forward a few paces into the beam of light to formally present himself to the assembly. "I come to you today with a strange story, indeed. It already appears that many of you have heard of the report I sent via crier some time ago of a very real Mortis Skulk attack on my person."

"How do you know it was a true Mortis Skulk attack and not an elaborate hoax?" a snide voice shot out from a balcony close to the auditorium floor.

Without saying a word, Braak calmly left the beam of light and walked to his right. He slowed as he approached a large circular table, three feet wide. A pile of white sand sat lifelessly on its surface. "I may only be a Second Edict Warder, but I alone looked my enemy in the eyes. They were as real as the scars it left upon my body. Yet if you still doubt my ability to discern fact from fiction, perhaps the echo of my auger will suffice as proof enough."

Braak's response was laced with just the slightest hint of contempt as he waved his auger over a large glass orb on the side of the table and stood back. The dormant sand sprang to life, building into a two-foot high miniature replica of the alleyway where Asher had first seen the red eyes peering at him from within its black floating veil.

Two figures emerged in the miniature alley of sand. Braak was instantly recognisable as he hurled powerful blood callings at the cloud hovering opposite him. The council members gasped as they watched the warder's memories spill onto the sand platform. A large cloud of white sand hovered opposite Braak's miniature, casting large blasts back against his body.

"How can we be sure what you encountered was not simply a wandering dark?" another anxious voice called out.

Braak looked to the direction of the voice. "Because it was intelligent. Because it fought with both cunning and power. Because it called upon blood callings of Decisus Umbra, but beyond all this," Braak punctuated his last remark one word at a time in an attempt to drive home the seriousness of his argument, "because. It. Spoke!"

Violent disbelief leaped around the auditorium amidst a hundred exhalations.

Braak held up his hands, motioning for quiet. All eyes in the room fell on Braak's austere dark features. "At the time I believed I was the Skulk's intended target, but soon I realised it was after another: the boy that sits before you now, Asher Bloom. The Skulk attacked him, not once, but twice in rapid succession."

"What interest would the Mortis Skulk have with a random from The Blind?" a pompous voice boomed out from an upper tier.

Braak steeled himself for his next sentence. "This I cannot possibly answer with certainty, but the boy is Vita born, that much is certain."

The auditorium erupted in loud cries and wild calls of disbelief. "There hasn't been a Vox Vita birthed outside the three cities in the last thirty years," an indignant voice bellowed from behind him, high up in the tiers.

"I am well aware of the statistics," Braak retorted and waited for the disbelieving cries to die down, "and yet the proof sits before you. However, there is yet more to this story, Asher was being cared for by an augmad, formerly of MaiSchloss, that went by the name of Raglan."

Asher winced at the mention of his fallen friend, but the name didn't seem to register with anyone else.

"The augmad raised him in secret and kept him hidden from us his whole life, for good reason."

"What reason?" a voice from a mid-tier balcony called out.

This voice was immediately followed by another from a balcony directly opposite Braak on the auditorium floor. "Why would an augmad attempt to hide a Vox Vita? That's a fool's errand, especially in The Blind."

Asher wanted to defend Raglan but he was unable to speak. The armoured bireem stood at his side, holding him in place, ankh locked in his hand, his auger still faintly glowing in its centre.

"Foolish or not, Asher is not just a Vita born. He is…" Braak selected his next words very carefully, "he is unique."

"What lunacy is this? Unique? Unique how?" a voice laced with authority and contempt shouted down from a tier adjacent to the largest balcony that loomed overhead.

"That, I fear, is a matter for the Elder Council, and the Elder Council alone. As warder and loyal servant of the Cruaar Nation, I hereby formerly invoke the right of Elder Mandate."

Outrage burst across the room as hundreds of insulted voices rained down their abuse at Braak. The warder had single-handedly stripped them of their right to vote over the case by the cunning manipulation of a single archaic law.

"Silence!" a voice roared over the din of the enraged council members' cries. An old thin man stood and stormed out of the main balcony, sweeping past the red-and-black draped banners, emerging seconds later through the vertistrand on the auditorium floor. A long tailed tunic billowed in his wake as he marched forward, legs filled with purpose.

Braak turned and kneeled before him. The man had a stern

facade, his face thin, aged and lined with fine wrinkles, all of it bordered by a sharp grey goatee and close-cropped hair. His hands were thin and impeccably manicured with a single ring on each index finger. His outward demeanour reeked of authority, almost to the point of arrogance, as he leered at Braak.

"You assume much, Warder. Pray what you have to say is worth the insult it wagered." Leaning in close he whispered in Braak's ear, "knowledge of Cruaar Law can just as easily break a man as it can save one."

The man turned, looked up at the tiers of assembled council members, many of whom had risen from their seats and stood at the edge of the balconies, still visibly fuming at the sudden turn of events. "The Elder Council shall continue this matter in private. We will resume in an hour when Elder Mandate is decided."

The council members subdued their outbursts in respect for the Grand Chancellor, but their faces betrayed their contemptuous outrage.

Three men and two women appeared through the vertistrand on the auditorium floor. All were noticeably old, though none had the sagacious look of scholars and academics. All bore the hardened faces of warriors. A powerfully built man with a thick two-inch beard picked up the cloth-wrapped item that had been taken from Asher as swept past the table.

Asher was forced back to his feet by the bireem and pushed towards the vertistrand. He felt the control of his arms and legs return to him, but his mouth was still firmly clamped shut and his actions heavily influenced to follow a certain set of instructions that weren't his own.

The Grand Chancellor ignited a pinch of sand and cast it into the face of the vertistrand. The five members of the Elder Council strode through the mirror without a second thought. Braak waited for the bireem to usher Asher through before following. He inhaled deeply before stepping through the glimmering vertistrand towards an unknown fate.

CHAPTER 10
ELDER MANDATE

When Braak emerged through the strand, the Elder Council had already convened and were seated around the curve of an immense arched oaken table.

Asher stood before the Elder Council, limbs trembling beneath his tattered clothing, eyes wandering from one face to the next. Five elderly Cruaar and a much younger-looking woman stared back at him, each contemplating what possible reason could possibly warrant the invocation of Elder Mandate.

"Warder Saada," the austere Grand Chancellor said with resolute clarity.

It was clear to Asher this man was in charge. His red-and-black attire was strictly formal, but when pitted against the otherwise intimate decor of the small chamber it looked almost tyrannical.

"The Elder Council has convened at your request," the Grand Chancellor continued. "We certainly hope, for your sake, your motive warrants the undertaking."

Asher couldn't help but notice that his jowls sagged slightly underneath his neatly trimmed beard as he spoke.

"Yes, Grand Chancellor," Braak stole a breath to help steel his nerves. "I believe it does. But first, please forgive my impudence, but I am not aware of the identity of the sixth person assembled here." Braak eyes shot to the face of the youngest woman that stood to the side of the great table.

"The new legate is here under my instruction, Warder. That is all you need know," the Grand Chancellor replied abruptly.

The young woman narrowed her eyes at Braak, but dutifully said nothing.

Braak bowed his head in compliance before continuing. "As you all know, there has not been a case of the taint within the three cities since the end of the Guillotine Rebellion."

The Elder Council nodded in agreement with the statement.

"Nor has there ever been an instance where an auger has fused with blood before first undergoing the ceremony of align–"

"We are well aware of our nation's history, Warder," Grand Chancellor Wrakburn cut him off. "Those that sit before you shaped much of it. We need no help recollecting common facts known to all Cruaar. Speed yourself to the point."

"Yes, Chancellor," Braak nodded, choosing his next words carefully. "I thought it best to present Asher's… unique condition in private, before rumours are mistaken as fact." Braak motioned to the teenager standing next to him. "His name is Asher Bloom."

"We know his name, Warder; what of him?" the Chancellor demanded, his patience running thin.

Braak swallowed nervously and steadied himself for what he was about to say. "Asher's auger has been embedded in the skin of his right palm. How? I do not know."

The council members sat up in their chairs, their interest piqued.

Asher clenched his fist tighter.

"After discovering the boy's condition, I was ambushed by the augmad and forced, at knife point, to perform the rite of bonded blood; such was the measure of the augmad's resolve to protect the boy."

"A severe conviction indeed," muttered the lady on the Chancellor's left.

Her face was bordered by the finest of wrinkles, but Asher couldn't help focus on the stunning dark green locks of hair that flowed down over her left shoulder. The style of her hair left her right ear exposed. It was pierced with no less than seven distinct earthen rings, green clasps and floral studs with a large ornate hair clasp and green gem tying her hair back on one side.

"Yes, Lady Mosslay, and I fear, one well warranted." Braak looked down at Asher, "Asher has already called upon his blood without the need of a mantle or alignment."

Three of the council members gasped. The largest and most brutish-looking member gazed at Asher under furrowed brow as his hands fiddled with something beneath the table.

The Chancellor, however, stood up from his chair in a rush, knocking it backwards across the floor. "Preposterous! What proof do you have of this?"

"Merely the echoes of my auger," Braak replied and walked over to a small table, waving his auger over the gem inset on the table's surface. "This is the second Skulk attack we encountered. If it were not for Asher's intervention, I doubt either of us would be standing here to answer your questions."

The Elder Council remained silent as they watched the miniature scene played out amidst the sand. The Chancellor looked on in astonishment as the sand re-enacted a miniature battle between Asher and the attack of the Mortis Skulk inside Pablo's antique store.

A volley of glittering sand hung midair, extending from Asher's miniature hand the exact same way Asher's blinding light had emerged during the encounter. The council members muttered under their breath, each as amazed as one another by what they were witnessing.

The legate's grip on her belt tightened as she watched, but her face was an impenetrable mask. She was all too aware that any outward portrayal of emotion would betray what she was thinking.

When the scene ended and the sand fell back into a lifeless heap on the table's surface all eyes behind the oaked table stared curiously at the teenager whose actions and very existence defied explanation.

The only person whose eyes did not burn holes into Asher's soul was that of the burly brute who sat calmly in his seat, gazing down at something in his hands beneath the table.

"How is this possible?" The echoes of Braak's auger had done little to shake the resolve of the Grand Chancellor.

Braak walked back to the centre of the room and stood by Asher's side. "This was the second time Asher called upon his blood during our escape. I was later told by the augmad that Asher had already called upon his blood earlier to escape the Skulk, though I did not see it with my own eyes."

The council studied Asher intently, their respective minds abuzz with unanswered questions.

"I think you'll all agree the boy's ability to call forth the Blood Nitor, not once but twice, confirms he hails from one of the strongest Vita bloodlines, but…" Braak readied himself for the moment he'd secretly been dreading, "his auger is scarred."

"What kind of scar?" a portly older man with a long grey beard that had the slightest tinges of blue asked gruffly, slapping the table hard with his hand.

"I…" Braak's words failed him.

Grand Chancellor Wrakburn frowned deeply and put two hands on the desk, leaning forward menacingly. "Does he, or does he not, bear the vile mark?"

Braak looked down at Asher. The boy's fear was evident. Braak gently placed his hands over Asher's fist, turned it over and motioned for him to release his fingers.

Asher had no desire to reveal his secret before the menacing faces of the Elder Council, but Braak's reassuring look compelled him to unfurl his fingers and present his auger for all to see.

At the first glimpse of the black scar that marred Asher's auger, the Chancellor had his hands around his throat and lifted him off the ground.

Asher had no idea how the old man had moved so fast. In the blink of an eye, the Chancellor had materialised through the table and was upon him before he even knew what happened. The man's cold clammy hands closed around the soft flesh of Asher's throat, his impeccably manicured fingernails digging roughly into the teenager's skin.

The Chancellor's face was mere inches from his own. Asher could feel the hatred that burned deep within the man's heart with every exhalation, even more so when their eyes met and locked together.

Asher's world blurred as he felt his life being choked out of him. He had not even noticed Braak drop to his knees beside him, hands at his throat, desperately gasping for breath.

The faces of the council members expressed mixed emotions. Lady Mosslay's face tried to hide her sympathy for the teenager in front of her. The portly man raised his eyebrows and ran a hand roughly over his chin. His emotions were obviously mixed about what was transpiring, yet he said nothing.

"Chancellor."

The vicious old man ignored the plea for restraint, eyes awash with cruelty as he felt the life drain away from the boy caught between his locked hands.

"Valderook!"

The enormous warrior gently placed his arm on the Chancellor's shoulder. For an instant the Chancellor redirected his rage, grabbing the man's giant hand in his own and twisting.

The burly man's enormous hand didn't so much as flinch under the assault. "You act before fact warrants judgement. Let us first find the truth before a traitor's death is imposed upon our guests."

The Chancellor's pupils dilated for a moment before his mind returned to its senses. His deathly grip around Asher's soft flesh eased as it did so.

Asher and Braak fell to the floor, desperately gasping for air; Asher's hand clenched in a fist to hide his auger from view. The brawny man released his grip on the Chancellor's shoulder and watched as he spun around to face the only member of the Elder Council that had remained silent throughout the entire proceedings.

"Finneus, extract the truth from this traitor so we can put an end to this charade." The Chancellor returned to his seat behind the table, a venomous anger still bubbling in his veins.

A thin man with gaunt features and a snide expression nodded obediently before rising from his seat. The sides of his head were shaven. A long silver plaited band of hair arched over his head and halfway down his back.

He'd forgone wearing his ceremonial attire, instead wearing a simple tunic of black with a fine bone trim. He prowled across the floor around the table's arch towards Asher's crumpled form on the ground and mercilessly placed a foot on Asher's wrist, pinning it to the ground.

Applying more pressure, he twisted his heel until Asher could no longer bear the pain and had no choice but to unfurl his fingers, exposing his auger. Peering down through black beady eyes, the corners of Finneus's mouth cringed as his mind registered what it saw.

Unlike everyone else in the room, the giant standing next to Finneus did not look at Asher's auger at all. Instead, he kneeled down and sought out Asher's focus on the floor, hoping to catch his gaze. The muscular man's face was tired, but despite the scars and blotched skin, it was his striking white eyes that endeared him with a wise and compassionate sense of lucidity.

Finneus, on the other hand, was anything but rational or compassionate. "Hide your secrets from me and I will rip them out."

"Explore the very depths of his soul, Finneus. Tear the truth from his treacherous mind," the Grand Chancellor scowled.

Finneus curtly nodded his gaunt head. His skin was paler than a corpse, like it had never once seen a ray of sunlight. His harrowing appearance was enhanced all the more by the long plait of silver hair that fell down over his shoulder like a barbed tail. He flipped it back over his bent spine and lowered his gaze until both of his deep sunken eyes were staring intently at the face of his prey. A bare hand disappeared inside his robes, returning moments later, fully enclosed inside a thick black glove.

A series of bones stretched over the exterior and down along each of his fingers, whilst a large black auger had been set within an interlocking prison of bones on the back of his hand. Finneus reached out and closed his gloved fingers over Asher's temple. Instantly, his auger turned a deathly purple, spewing forth a noxious haze over Asher's face, which flooded into the teenager's nose, mouth, throat and lungs.

Asher felt his mind cloud over; thick fumes clogged his thoughts as Finneus probed every inch of his consciousness. Asher could feel the man clawing at the faintest memories of his past, searching for anything that might link Asher with agents of the Mortis Skulk.

The deeper the man burrowed into Asher's past, the weaker Asher's consciousness became.

Even Braak suffered from the effects of the man's intrusion and, for a moment, their minds were linked.

Asher saw a small child weeping on a doorstop, cradling a dead man in his hands. Then the vision swayed and altered into the face of the angry merchant he had stolen an apple from. Asher's mind slipped deeper inside itself until he became lost and frightened: alone, wandering aimlessly through the murky daze of his own subconscious. The further Finneus plumbed, the only thing that remained constant in Asher's mind was the memory of a man, a friend: Raglan.

Finneus refocused his efforts to uncover more about this mysterious augmad that consumed much of Asher's thoughts and memories.

Asher tried to resist—to fight back against the man's incursion—but it was no use. No matter how hard he tried, he couldn't muster any sort of defence against the mind-rending invasion. Only when he felt his memories of Raglan under assault did Asher's indigent fury finally allow him to momentarily focus, his lips parting to release a single sentence.

"Get out of my head!"

Finneus faltered, his hand wavering momentarily.

The remaining council members were startled by the outburst.

"Finneus! How is he able to speak? Is he not under your control?" the Grand Chancellor demanded, his voice laced with indignant abrasiveness.

"He was…" Finneus stalled, "he is." The man faltered as he tried to comprehend how the teenager had broken through his paralysis bind.

"Whatever you think I am, I'm not!" Asher's mind rallied against the man's momentary lapse of control over him. The Chancellor slammed his fist hard on the table.

"Silence! You have no voice in this." The Grand Chancellor's anger intensified as his patience grew thin. "Finneus, what did you find?"

"Chancellor…" Finneus removed his foot from Asher's wrist and turned to face the old man, allowing Asher to sit up and nurse his sore wrist. "It is not the taint."

"What?" the Chancellor roared, furious at Finneus's explanation.

"He has been exposed to death. That much is certain, but his mind has little to no knowledge of the Cruaar Nation beyond what he has learnt since the attack. His older memories are hazy and fragmented, but such is the way with all youths that have encountered some form of trauma early in life."

"Speak clearly, Finneus." Lady Mosslay leaned forward and drew a finger back through her hair over her left ear. "If it is not the taint, then what is the mark he bears?"

"His blood is free of corruption. Whatever scars his auger, it is something else. Something I've never seen before."

"It's a trick. A new type of Skulk deception." The Chancellor leaned back in his chair, clearly unwilling to yield his position on the matter.

"You claim more knowledge about death and the Mortis bloodline than even I possess. Am I to understand you are, in fact, a master of the necrotic blood arts, Chancellor?" Finneus scowled.

A loud voice from the side of the room interrupted the two before a bitter argument could break out. His words rumbled around the room like a drum, causing Finneus and the Chancellor to stop and turn their attention towards him.

"Far be it from me to correct the master of Mortis and the Grand Chancellor within this sacred chamber," he respectfully directed his comment at the two men locked in a deathly gaze with each other.

"But as the Overseer of Undergall and High Cleric Pluwarie's replacement, while he's overseeing the defensive upgrades of Oakrim, I believe I might be able to shed some light on Asher's history without the need for bickering."

"His mind is fractured, Lobrolo; how is it you intend to enlighten us?" Finneus challenged the man's reasoning.

"With this," Lobrolo held up a miniature statuette of a wooden ibis between his two fingers.

Asher instantly recognised the bird. He had always been fascinated by their white feathers and black beaks. Raglan had told him they were once considered a sacred bird and were worthy of every man's respect, though few gave it these days. On Asher's second found-day, Raglan had taken him to the canals and had given him bread to feed them, in honour of their revered past. It was one of Asher's very first and favourite memories.

A memory he cherished and one he would not easily forget.

The Overseer's voice broke Asher's train of thought as his consciousness snapped back to the present. "It was the only possession the boy carried when he arrived here. I believe it to be a rudimentary pyxis." Noticing Asher's confused expression he paused to better explain the meaning of the word, "a messenger of sorts."

With resigned grace he pushed himself off the wall, crossed the floor and held out a hand for Asher. His enormous frame engulfed the light behind him as he approached, stepping forward with the abysmal grace of a top-heavy lumberjack.

Asher knew, from his life on the streets, this man was perhaps the most dangerous in the room, at least in terms of raw physical power. He accepted the man's outstretched hand and was effortlessly jerked to his feet.

Braak stood nearby, rubbing the lingering discomfort from his own wrist and shaking his head free of the dulling haze, dealing with the pain as a disciplined soldier should: in silence.

"You must pardon our barbaric ways. Old habits die hard... Traitors, harder." He held out the small carving for Asher to see. "Who gave you this?"

Asher stared at him blankly, unable to answer. He'd never seen the item before. Lobrolo clarified, "It was wrapped in cloth and hidden in your pocket when it was taken from you in the auditorium."

"It was a found-day present from Raglan."

"Found-day?"

"It's like a birthday, only not." Asher didn't feel the need to explain the tradition to the man. "Never mind, it's not important."

"Traditions are always important, especially ones that bind

us to one another. May I ask how old you are, Asher?"

"Fourteen, I think. Give or take a year."

"Fourteen, you say. A good age." Lobrolo shot a cautionary glance at the younger woman standing still near the edge of the table. "Allow me to be the first to bid you a happy found-day on behalf of the Cruaar Nation."

"Get on with it Lobrolo," Grand Chancellor Wrakburn's voice snapped across the room.

The man ignored the comment and comforted Asher with the delicate touch of his hand on his shoulder. "Raglan, he was the augmad that raised you?"

"I don't know what an augmad is but, yes, Raglan raised me," Asher nodded.

"An augmad is someone that chooses to forgo the calling of blood and life within our great Cruaar Nation, choosing instead to live out their remaining days in The Blind."

Asher didn't quite understand everything the enormous man said, but somehow it seemed to make sense when he thought back to Raglan's crazed ramblings. A sadness swept across his face at the memory of the loss of his uncle.

"I believe your found-day present may offer a clue to your past. If you'll allow me?"

Asher didn't quite understand what the man was asking. The object looked like an ordinary hand-carved wooden figurine. He nodded anyway.

Lobrolo removed a large pin from his coat and held it above Asher's hand. "May I?"

Asher nodded and Lobrolo jabbed the pin into Asher's fingertip, drawing forth a tiny drop of blood on the tip of its point. Asher winced in surprise but offered no complaint. The pain was fleeting.

Lobrolo quickly moved the pin over to the base of the figurine and turned the statue over in his hand. A small recessed metallic circle lay in the centre of its base. Lobrolo let the drop of blood drip onto its surface.

Nothing happened.

Then, slowly, the blood seeped into the metallic centre until it had vanished entirely from view. Lobrolo gingerly placed the figurine's base on top of Asher's outstretched auger and took a step back.

The instant the figurine's metallic surface connected with Asher's gem, the small carving of the ibis sprang to life and flapped its miniature wings. The top half of the pyxis shook off a layer of dust and coughed as if trying to clear its miniature throat, before a loud voice, familiar only to Braak and Asher, sprang to life from its tiny beak.

"Asher," Raglan's voice rumbled out of the figurine's mouth from beyond the grave, the little ibis replicating Raglan's intonation flawlessly.

"By now I hope you are safe in Undergall. Do not be afraid. I have kept much from you over the years and prayed you would never have to deal with the burden you bear under your hidden hand. If you are hearing this now, then I have failed you and am no longer able to keep you safe." The voice trailed off a little and became hard to hear.

"You will never know how that fact will torment me long into the afterlife. You must be strong, now more than ever. No matter what people call you, you are a Vox Cruaar… like no other I have ever met. I am, and forever will be, proud that my life was spent securing the safety of yours."

Asher wiped back tears from his eyes before any could stain his cheeks.

"To any other ears my voice falls upon, I pray my final message does not go unheeded. Asher has never known anything of our world, let alone anything of the mark on his auger which will be mistaken as the taint. I always feared if he were discovered, his condition would not be understood, which is why I kept him hidden, to keep him safe." Raglan's voice became strained, as if he was fighting back the urge to weep.

"It was my fear and my fear alone that kept him from the world to which he rightly belongs. I beg you not to punish him for my failings. He is unique and worthy of a life I could not provide him.

"His condition has plagued him ever since I found him. You must not judge or punish him for it. I swear this on my family's bloodline and my oath as a former prelate of the MaiSchloss Augestry, Turag Landry."

Asher had never heard Raglan's real name before.

All eyes turned to the Grand Chancellor, his eyes narrowed at the name resonating around the room.

"Asher, may this world offer you what I never could: a home. Remember the values an old man once taught you. Life above all else…" The ibis fizzled out and slowly resumed its statuesque pose atop Asher's hand.

Asher blinked away tears and tried to maintain a brave face. He never thought he would hear Raglan's voice again. The sadness it churned up inside of him was almost too much to bear.

"To my ears you've now heard from both Finneus and a former prelate of the MaiSchloss Augestry that Asher Bloom poses no threat to our nation," Lobrolo spoke with supreme clarity and distinction so as not to be misheard. "The mark he bears, while mysterious and worthy of investigation, is not the taint. Nor does it bear any allegiance to the Mortis Skulk.

"By all outward appearances Asher seems utterly clueless as to our society. He is as far detached as one could be from the mastery of Mortis, let alone the necrotic blood arts of Decisus Umbra. Nor does he outwardly bear any direct affiliation with the Mortis Skulk, other than being attacked by them twice."

"Your words are not lost on me, Overseer," the Grand Chancellor slumped back in his chair, scowling.

Braak breathed a sigh of relief as his heart descended from

his throat and back into his chest, just as the old man with the blue-tinged beard rapped one of his solid rings heavily on the table.

"The question remains, what do we do with him? We can't very well have him wandering the commons. That would set a dangerous precedent this city can ill afford."

Lady Mosslay was first to answer, her eyes locked on the mysterious teenager before her. "As always, Agnus, your forethought is a blessing. However, we must consider the fact that so rarely is a Vox Vita born without... aid, these days. It would be remiss of us to not think of the possibilities that might arise in the future of an erred decision made in haste.

"Perhaps Mantlecrest is a viable option, under watchful eye of course, until we discover what the mark is that his auger bears. What do you think, Legate? Could one such as this be any use to you?" Lady Mosslay directed the question at the youngest woman in the room who, up until this point, had remained entirely silent throughout the proceedings.

Overseer Lobrolo turned and studied the young woman's face carefully as she pondered her decision.

Legate Seville walked around the large table quietly, her eyes inspecting every inch of Asher as if he were a prize bull at a fair. Her body was impeccably taut. Underneath a tight-fitting white leather tunic, Asher could see a reservoir of strength packed into her slender frame.

"It is hard to say. I did however have the foresight to delay the Mantlecrest's latest intake on the off chance that I might be presented with such an opportunity. It would be a shame to waste someone already so instinctive in calling forth the blood-arts of Vita."

Lobrolo looked sternly at the woman. "Seville," Lobrolo barked, purposefully addressing the woman by her last name and not by her title, "if Asher is to be placed within Mantlecrest, he will be treated as any other apprentice, not some experiment for your amusement. Is that understood?"

It was instantly clear to everyone in the room, including Asher, his question was not a question at all, but an order.

The young woman's eyes narrowed, as though she was not used to having orders dictated orders to her in such a way. "While I may be new to the position of legate, do not think I am unaware of your objections to my acceptance of the role, Lobrolo." The woman squared off against the enormous man in the centre of the room, returning the insult by refusing to address him by his title of Overseer and using his first name instead.

Asher couldn't help but get the distinct impression they were not on a first name basis.

"I have always served the council's will and to a far greater degree than even you can boast. So, rest assured, I will continue to do so, even when governing your brother's precious Mantlecrest."

"This is a discussion the boy should not be privy to," Lady Mosslay interrupted, stopping the rising tension in the room from escalating any further.

Asher was about to say something when Braak shook his head at him in warning, indicating it wouldn't do him any favours.

"Warder Saada, see him to Ancestor's Hall until we have agreed upon a suitable mandate for his future." The Grand Chancellor's order gave Asher little hope for his future.

Braak nodded subserviently, briskly leading Asher towards the vertistrand. Casting a pinch of sand at the mirror's surface, he whispered in Asher's ear. "The worst is now behind us. Stay strong." With that he gently pushed Asher through the rippling surface of the shimmering vertistrand.

Asher emerged on the other side of the vertistrand in Ancestor's Hall and realised he was completely alone. Finally free of anyone else's control over his limbs, he scratched an itch on his neck and inspected his surroundings. The room could hardly be described as a hall, but it was grand.

There was virtually nothing in the space except three chest-high pillars, each with a unique artistic theme carefully etched into the smooth stonework in an array of beautiful patterns and crowned with a different granite bust. A faded stain on the floor indicated there had once been four pillars, but the fourth had evidently been removed a long time ago.

All the walls of the hall were all uniquely adorned with vivid tapestries depicting wild, bloody and brutal historical scenes. They hung on large metal poles fixed to a similar level of masterwork masonry Asher had seen in the council chambers.

Various paintings adorned the walls in the bare spaces, whilst a multitude of sculptures had been carved into the stonework of the walls themselves above and below the paintings. The room shimmered with a rich and dangerous history, none of which meant anything to Asher.

A recessed ledge high above him extended along the walls and around the four corners of the room, spilling a bright white radiance down over the artworks and tapestries to illuminate their distinguishing features. A large set of double wooden doors stood at the end of the chamber, partially hidden behind a thick red velvet curtain draped from floor to ceiling.

Asher took his time to inspect the bountiful artwork, before instinctively being drawn to one of the granite busts in the centre of the room. He gently ran his hand over the etchings on the face of the column, letting his fingers follow the cut and weave of the shallow grooves in the stone. He noticed all the markings were of a similar nature. It then became obvious he was looking at a foreign language, though he had no idea what any of it meant.

He ran his hand to the top of the column, accidentally

rubbing his exposed auger across a small onyx-like bauble he had previously missed. The bust crumbled and broke apart into a lifeless pile of sand.

Asher panicked and feebly tried to stop the bust from disintegrating with his hands, but it fell through his fingers in a heap. Most of it came to rest on top of the stone column in a lifeless pile, though some spilled over the edges and fell to the floor.

Asher backed away from the platform as the miniature shape of a hulking brute clawed his way out of the sand. Slowly, the miniature thug freed itself of its sandy embrace and stood upright, brushing the dust from its shoulders before opening a small book made of sand.

Asher had no idea what creature it was meant to be; it looked completely alien to him. Before he had any time to properly investigate, the tiny creature recited a poetic verse.

Its voice was aged and crackled intermittently between words, but as each slipped past its sandy lips, they became emblazoned on the column beneath in fine gold lettering.

In hallowed halls slumbers shattered mind,
Sensing six, not seven, gifts of life entwined,
Across plains and seas and mountains steep,
Ill-gotten ilk my heart does naught but weep.
Seek me out not for false desire,
Erred pursuit swells only black blood's ire,
Shield gilded virtue against last dark,
Trust first in blood and hope and heart.

"He always was painfully mysterious, forever riddling those around him with verse. At least, that's if you believe the Annals, in any case." Lobrolo's rugged voice interrupted Asher's concentration. "Strange, I must have stood here deciphering his riddles a hundred times, but I've never once heard that one before."

Asher hadn't noticed the large man step noiselessly through the vertistrand, which spoke just as much of Asher's amazement as it did Lobrolo's ability to mask even the smallest of movements of his imposing bulk with cat-like grace. "I'm sorry, I didn't mean to–"

Lobrolo raised a hand and cut him off mid-sentence. "You needn't worry. You'd need much more than a gentle touch to break the spirit of Vitalsior from beyond the grave."

"Who?"

"High Cleric Herion Friatt Vitalsior. He's one of the first families that founded Undergall. He's also the forefather of the Vox Vita bloodline. Your bloodline. I knew him only through my great grandmother's over-exaggerated bed time tales. Slightly mad old coot she was, but then again so was he towards the end, by all accounts."

"Why do you say that?"

"Many reasons, but most famously because he cut off several fingers and toes, a different one in every city he visited before his last known sighting right here in Undergall."

"What happened to him?"

"No-one knows for sure. One day he just disappeared and was never seen or heard from again." Lobrolo placed a powerful hand over Asher's shoulder and walked towards the large curtained doors at the end of the room. "But, I'm afraid we have slightly more pressing matters at hand than historical tales of our forefathers."

"What did the council decide?" Asher's heart leaped into his throat. "What will happen to me?"

"The Elder Council has voted. The decision was tied, which left the deciding vote to me."

"And?"

The burly man paused and looked down into Asher's eyes. "Asher, when I first laid eyes on you I did not see evil, malice or treachery. I saw frightened eyes that had never known safety, happiness or purpose. I would never deny a Cruaar these things before they first had a chance to seek them out them self."

"So…"

"I voted in your favour, Asher. You are free to become an apprentice at Mantlecrest, if you so wish. There you will learn to wield and control your blood callings as would any other young Cruaar in our nation." Lobrolo stopped walking and turned Asher around, placing both of his arms on his shoulders.

"Be warned, the path ahead you must carve yourself. It will be far from easy, with many dangers and it will undoubtedly leave you forever changed as a result."

"You mean, I could be like you, like Braak and everyone else?" Asher's eyes lit up with possibilities.

"If that is your wish, but you must understand many Cruaar still fear and distrust the mark you bear. You will have many enemies, but also, with any luck, some trusted friends. But you must not mistake the two. Trust must always be earned before it is given."

Lobrolo turned and walked Asher towards the end of the hall, stopping just short of the double doors. His bulk dwarfed Asher's small frame against the backdrop of the solid double doors. "Do you take the charge of apprentice, knowing full well the difficult road ahead?"

Asher didn't need to give it a second thought, as he nodded vigorously.

"Very well, then." Lobrolo reached for the door, but Asher's words stopped him.

"Wait, what would have happened if I'd said no?"

"You would have been banished from this world forever, your mind stripped of all memory and your hand severed from your body."

Asher grabbed his hand and gulped.

"But I had a strong feeling you'd say yes," Lobrolo said with a wink and opened the doors behind the curtain. The two walked out onto a large balcony and Asher's eyes widened in amazement.

Far below their lofty perch on one of the balconies in Earthreach Spire sprawled an entire city, blinking with mystical light and humming with vibrant activity. Asher could barely see the city's distant edges but what he could see astonished him. The entire city was awash with a strange luminous light that shone down from above. Asher held up his hand against it and saw the entire sky was in fact not a sky at all, but a cavernous roof illuminated with an artificial central light source that doubled as the sun.

Lobrolo rested his hands upon the worn stone balustrade and looked out over his city. He switched his gaze to Asher for a moment and smiled, noticing the expression of wonder and excitement on Asher's face.

"Welcome to Undergall, Asher Bloom." Placing one giant hand behind Asher's back, he looked out over the majesty of everything before them.

"Welcome home."

PART II

HEREDITARY HAZARDS

"Too much stock is placed upon the merit of honour.
The dead care not for such idiotic whims of the living
And their reign is eternal."

Last words of Lowquai Trittleflor
Executed taint bearer
Undergall execution gibbet
1952

CHAPTER 11

MANTLECREST

Lem had always been a little awkward around girls. He tended to overcompensate for his diminutive height with an overbearing bravado that his stature just couldn't pull off. So when he was paired with Lorrelli Wittlearch at Mantlecrest, he found himself at a bit of a loss.

It wasn't that she was rude, obnoxious or even stuck up; it was the fact she already had two older brothers and refused to take any nonsense whatsoever from males, in general. This meant that even his most ingeniously constructed stories, which fooled more-gullible girls, were rebutted and ignored faster than his tongue could deliver them. In less than half an hour in her presence, he'd already nearly exhausted every subject he knew girls commonly found interesting.

Granted, this list wasn't as extensive as Lem thought it was. It was mostly comprised of the current augmented fashion trends, or the latest gossip surrounding the more-attractive players of the Undergall Hopralas, but somehow, in the past, he'd always managed to get by with basic conversation with the fairer sex.

Rapidly running out of things to say, he looked around the room for inspiration. Spying an apprentice pair as equally odd-looking as their own matching, he gave Lorrelli a nudge and pointed at them with his chin. "So what do you think they'll end up as?" he nodded towards a chubby teenager and a slender girl of average looks standing across the room.

Lorrelli said nothing, but turned her head in the direction he was indicating, a long thin plait of hair on the left side of her head falling from behind her ear as she did so. She instinctively swept it back into place, habitually twisting the end of it with her fingers before releasing it.

"I mean, sometimes you can just tell by looking at someone what alignment they'll be. It's an odd pairing to say the least, but he is dead-set Scienta," Lem nodded his chin towards the chubby male apprentice before shifting his attention to the slender female next to him. "Whereas she looks like a born-in-the-wool Natura. What do you reckon? I know it's only a fifty-fifty chance either way, but come on, look at them."

Lorrelli looked at the pair and then disdainfully back at Lem. "What makes you so quick to judge? How do you know what you're going to be?"

Lem looked down at his own colourless auger that blankly hung on the first-year amulet around his neck. "Scienta, of course, maybe even a bireem one day. That'd be sweet," he said dramatically striking an action pose and grinning idiotically.

Lorrelli rolled her eyes at him. "And what's wrong with Natura?" she asked indignantly, if only to keep the awkward silence from creeping over the conversation for the fourth time in as many minutes.

"Nothing, but come on. What could be better than being the first Cruaar to invent and augineer a new device, or command a mechanaug?"

"My parents, sister and two brothers are Natura, and we get along just fine."

Lorrelli's annoyed tone indicated to Lem it was time for a new topic. Luckily for him the doors to the room had just flung open, providing him a new talking point. "Look, it's the new legate," Lem nodded towards a group of adults filing into the room, a young, fierce-looking woman in the lead. An unfamiliar teenager remained no more than two steps behind her at all times as her taught frame marched into the room. Lem edged around the other apprentices to get a better look at the procession at the front of the room.

Lorrelli dutifully followed, knowing that apprentice pairs were not to be separated until after the ceremony had concluded, but she wasn't happy about it.

"Do you think that's the one everyone's been talking about?" Lem whispered under his breath. "You know, the one with the auger for a hand?"

Lem was obviously not the only one who was thinking as much. Twelve other pairs of prospective apprentices turned their gaze and murmured in hushed tones, all staring at the teenager behind the legate.

"You're annoying, you know that, right? I can't even imagine what I could've done in a past life to deserve being paired up with you." Lorrelli exhaled, shaking her head, then sauntered off towards the front of the crowd in the opposite direction.

Lem begrudgingly followed three steps behind, none too happy about standing directly before the gaze of the new legate at the front of the room.

Lorrelli didn't seem to mind, taking great pleasure in her partner's obvious discomfort.

Legate Seville marched across the room towards its centre, a handful of adults filing into the room after her, riding her wake like a flock of birds. When they had all arrived and settled on the podium, she beckoned the young adults filling the room to gather closer together in front of her.

Asher remained completely silent behind her, his hand hidden from public view, eyes alight with excitement, but also wary with apprehension.

The legate's white leather outfit stood out against the grey backdrop of the stone surroundings like a swan on a stagnant pond. She surveyed the assortment of teenagers standing before her. Each looked up at her with a mixture of fear, excitement and anxiety. It was clear none of them knew exactly what to expect.

The female apprentices all wore their hair pulled back into a single ponytail, neatly plaited, whilst each of the male apprentices had one side of their heads shaved clean and the rest of their hair neatly cropped. Historic customs dictated the hair styles, but it definitely suited some teenagers more than others.

Lorrelli was the only female apprentice that had shirked

tradition, wearing a second thin plait of hair down the left side of her temple tucked away behind an ear. No-one had said anything, or even seemed to notice when she had arrived, so she'd kept it. "Gotta break at least three laws a day, right?" was the first thing she had said to Lem, when he questioned her about it.

Asher, on the other hand, had protested bitterly at the first sight of the razor, and fought tooth and nail as an elderly cleric attempted to give him the customary cleansing cut. Eventually, a bireem was called to hold him in place whilst his long blond locks were lopped off.

All the apprentices were dressed in customary plain white tunics and basic reagent pants, which would remain light grey until their augers had been aligned to a specific blood calling.

Asher thought the outfit looked completely ridiculous when he'd first put it on. Gazing at his reflection in the mirror, he couldn't help but think he looked like he belonged to some sort of weird cult. Upon seeing the rest of the assembled apprentices, however, he no longer felt as strange, even though his pants were golden and everyone else's were a dull grey.

In any case, his clothes had been cut from far better cloth than he'd ever worn before. He'd never known what it was like to wear tailor-made clothes. He'd long been accustomed to wearing a dirty assortment of rags, unwanted garments and items he had stolen from street vendors when their backs were turned. His mind was snapped back to the present by the legate's sharp and commanding voice.

It resonated around the room as she addressed the assembled group of apprentices before her. "Prospective apprentices, this day is a turning point in your lives. Some of you hail from rich and powerful Cruaar families and, as such, are well versed in the laws and rites of our culture. Some of you have had a…" she chose her next words carefully, "less-fortunate upbringing, while others amongst you hail from The Blind and know little, or nothing, of our ways.

"Irrespective of your past, today your life is no longer your own, but joined to the lives of the brothers and sisters standing beside you. Beyond those doors is your future," she raised one arm and pointed to the double doors to her right.

"Whether you survive, perish, or thrive within Mantlecrest and the world thereafter, will solely depend on what you learn during your time here." She lowered her hand and took a step forward. "We will be watching, forever and always." She placed both hands behind her back and calmly inspected the faces of the apprentices before her. Each was visibly filled with a deluge of apprehension and fear.

Although everything around Asher was new and strange, something deeply unsettled him about the legate's supercilious demeanour. There was something discomforting about the way she put emphasis on the wrong part of her sentences and never betrayed any hint of emotion. It was unnatural.

The leather-clad woman's eyes darted towards the rear of the room, searching for someone in particular. Her gaze stopped on the muscular form of a much older apprentice at the back of the room. "Bison, step forward."

A large figure that Asher had previously missed, casually sauntered forward, skirting the group of teenagers to stand before the legate's raised podium. He was tall, dark and powerfully built. He was closer in age to a man than any of the other apprentices, thick stubble lined his face, yet a wisp of youthfulness remained around his heavy-set eyes. Upon one arm he wore an enormous handcrafted gauntlet that stretched from fingers to elbow. It had been inlaid with precious metals, ivory and the talons of an enormous claw, strategically positioned in a line down his forearm like a mystical totem.

Asher couldn't imagine what kind of animal could sport talons that big, but the distinct scratches on their surface led Asher to believe the claws had been hacked from a kill as a trophy.

"Due to the long-standing service of the DeGrulz's family to the Cruaar Nation, his bloodline's unblemished record and his own control over the three distinct bloodlines, Bison DeGrulz will serve as Mantlecrest's tribune this year." The legate extended her arm and motioned for the tribune to join her. Touching him lightly on the shoulder of his black tunic, a large T-shaped white-hot fire blazed on its front. An instant later it was gone, but a white T remained, stretching across his chest and down his abdomen.

"He will act as my eyes and ears when the masters are absent and will be responsible for the continued operation and administration of this facility during the midnight hours. Should you have a problem you cannot solve yourself, Tribune DeGrulz will make himself available to you. Tribune, I trust I will not hear about any of the pranks or blood feuds from you that made your brother so notorious during his time here."

The tribune's mouth twisted into a strange smirk as he shook his head from side to side although, to Asher, the smirk looked like a malicious scowl hardened into his features.

"Of course not, Legate," replied the tribune.

She nodded and turned her attention back to the gathered apprentices, although the look on her face hardly acknowledged that she was satisfied with the authenticity of the tribune's answer. "Tribune, I'll leave the introductions to you." She motioned to the row of adults standing behind her before she turned and, without saying as much as a goodbye, left the room via the rear door. Asher made an attempt to follow, but one stern look from the tribune stopped him in his tracks.

Gusts of wind buffeted the room as she stepped through the heavy door as it swung shut behind her under its own weight.

"Listen up, apprentices," said Bison. "These men and women are the Masters of Mantlecrest, your masters, and you will treat them with respect, or you will answer to me. Master McGoven is reprising his role this year as the chief instructor of the Natura blood arts."

A large chubby man nodded his head, his double chin wobbling slightly with the effort.

"Mistress Catterfract is once again taking the reins of all

training relating to the Scienta bloodline."

An angelic beauty curtsied and smiled wildly at her introduction. All the male apprentices were instantly enraptured by her flawless appearance and smiled back idiotically.

"First Order Tribarion Karbosch will be assuming the dominion over all aspects of the Vita bloodline, although prior obligations keep him from attendance this day. And last, but not least, Master Slink, as always, will be the one and only Master of Mortis."

Finneus Slink didn't nod or even so much as acknowledge the apprentices as their eyes fell on him. His pale features and dead eyes betrayed no hint of amusement or interest in the proceedings to which he was bearing witness.

Asher didn't understand any of the titles or what they meant. The term Vita did register, but did him little good. Tribarion Karbosch, as the tribune had said, was mysteriously absent.

"During the ceremony, you will remember your duties to your partner; does anyone not remember what they are?"

After a second, a short teen at the front of the room timidly raised his hand. He was promptly rewarded with an unyielding gaze of disgust from the tribune.

"For all those not as brave as the pitiful Apprentice Slew here to raise their hand, allow me to reiterate what you should already know. All apprentices are to assist their partner with the blood offering. Only a drop of blood is needed; anyone spilling more than that will answer to me in kind.

"After the blood offering has been made and your alignment ascertained, you will join the rest of the apprentices in the Auxilia Amphitheatre and remain there, seated in silence until the ceremony concludes." Surveying the faces of the apprentices again, the tribune's expression hardened and his tone grew even more serious.

"If your auger cannot be attuned with a specific alignment, control your emotions. Panicking will serve no-one but your own illusion of fear." Turning around, he leaned over and hissed at

Asher. "You will wait until the end of the ceremony, freak, until I announce you. Understood?"

Asher nodded as a loud bell chimed four times and a riotous flurry of gushing air billowed under the doors of the next room. Without another word, or so much as a glance in the direction of the apprentices, the tribune turned and walked to the door and opened it, waiting for the masters of Mantlecrest to exit.

They silently filed out of the room, one by one, powerful gusts of wind billowing through the open doorway. Closing the door after them, the tribune marched back towards Asher, grabbed him by the arm and yanked him off the podium, throwing him down into the group of gathered apprentices.

A large fat apprentice groaned loudly when Asher collided with his ribs, but the sound was silenced by a loud boom that echoed around the room when the tribune slammed a clenched fist into the palm of his gauntlet.

"Know this. I am not here to help you, you will learn to fight your own battles and if you do, you might survive the year. Should you wish to speak to me, you'll address me by title and name only, Tribune DeGrulz.

"Insult me, or any other elder apprentice, regardless of reason, and I'll ensure your stay here will be grossly unpleasant and short. I don't care who your parents are or were, the alignment of your auger, or how many of your bloodline have passed through these hallowed halls.

"You'll train hard, obey the legate and, above all else, stay out of the way of the elder apprentices. Curfew is at nine. All apprentices will be in their racks, or approved training rooms, or I'll make you wish you were." He let the threat openly hang in the air, casting his eyes over the silent room. A small apprentice coughed to Bison's left, resulting in a villainous glare from the newly appointed tribune.

"Understand this. Mantlecrest always has and forever will, chew up and spit out the weak. Do not think, because it is your first year, it will be an easy one. Only the strong survive here. You have been warned."

Bison turned and walked towards the exit, his dark blue pants and black tunic cutting an impressive sight against the aged wood of the door. "I will be watching." He shot Asher a dark look before vanishing into the next room amidst a gust of turbulent air and the sounds of swirling wind. A mixture of relief, nervous exhales of breath and murmuring followed his departure.

Asher stepped away from the fat apprentice who had borne the brunt of his fall and murmured an apology before moving away from the group.

Almost immediately, two loud voices sung out from behind them, one male and the other female. When the apprentices turned to stare at the two statues on either side of the door the voices had come from, Asher was the only one who looked surprised when he saw the lifeless stone come alive and speak.

"Apprentice Gullybore and Apprentice Fillpot." The busts of a man and a woman were looking at two of the apprentices in particular as they nervously gripped their augers and left through the doors, before casting their gaze over the rest of the apprentices.

An anxious quiet returned as the doors swung shut and the wind died down again. The entire room stood apart from Asher, singling him out as a stranger in their midst. Asher desperately wanted to ask about the statues that had come to life, but wasn't going to be the first one to speak.

Lem, on the other hand, had no qualms about breaking the awkward silence. "Wow, I knew tribunes were usually hard-asses, but what a woody blanker," Lem said with a smirk. He crossed the floor and held out his hand to Asher. "I'm Lem, short for Bedlem."

"Asher," he shook it awkwardly, unable to stop himself repeating the odd phrase questioningly. "Woody blanker?"

"Bloody wanker," Lem grinned deviously and waved his hand in mock disdain at the shaking doors. "With any luck, we won't see too much of him. Tribunes are always busy doing something," he lowered his voice and raised his eyebrows. "Besides, just between you and me, if I do make trouble, I never get caught."

Asher smiled awkwardly, not knowing whether he was being serious, though he assumed not. The rest of the gathered apprentices settled down a little and talked amongst themselves, everyone except Lem giving him a wide berth.

"Have you met Lorrelli? Lem asked bluntly, reaching back and roughly pulling Lorrelli over from the crowd with one hand.

Asher looked at the girl to Lem's left and awkwardly shook her hand. She was pretty in a tomboy kind of way, but Asher's mind was too full of questions to focus on his mild attraction to her. "Hi, I'm Asher."

"Asher," Lorrelli repeated softly before introducing herself formally, "Lorrelli Wittlearch."

"Oh, didn't realise we were being all proper and such. Bedlem Bruwell." Lem bowed deeply in an exaggerated manner.

Lorrelli rolled her eyes at him again and shook her head. "Tribune or not, I don't want to be on the bad side of DeGrulz," Lorrelli said casually, glancing back at the door.

"You're from The Blind, right? Prac knows what you must think of us all by now. We're not all spoons just so you know."

Lem's laugh was infectious, causing a large smirk to appear on Asher's face even though he didn't understand half of the terminology he used. "Spoons?" Asher repeated trying hard to get up to speed with Lem's strange idioms.

"Yeah, spoons, you know, bent in the middle and blunt on all sides. Not like you and me, though, we're proper forked," Lem laughed out loud and slapped his thigh several times at the hilarity of his own joke.

Asher couldn't help but smirk at the ridiculous pun.

Lorrelli didn't laugh; instead, she looked Asher up and down, inspecting him closely, gathering as much information to make her own opinions. He didn't look like much, but there was something about him that piqued her interest and nagged at the back of her mind. She just couldn't nail down exactly what it was. "So this is all wildly strange for you, huh?" Lorrelli said unsympathetically.

Asher merely nodded in agreement, his eyes zipping around the room taking in as much detail as they could. There were sixteen apprentices in all, excluding himself and his two new acquaintances. It was a relatively small number considering the size of the city he'd seen. Each wore the same outfit he had on, minus the golden pants, but they also all sported a fine silver necklace with a colourless auger set in the centre.

Another pair of names was loudly announced, as two more apprentices shuffled anxiously through the windy doorway and into the next room; the eyes of the statues watched them intently as they left.

Lorrelli continued to stare at Asher, obviously awaiting a proper response to her statement. Her gaze was disarming and compelled him to share more than he would have liked.

"To be honest, before yesterday I never knew the Vox Cruaar even existed, let alone I was one of them… err, you. Us." He clenched his hand and gingerly touched the surface of his auger with his fingertips, making sure to keep it out of sight. "Everything since then has been like one long nightmare."

"Vox! What are you, ancient?" Lorrelli had to fight to supress a mocking laugh. "Just Cruaar, Asher, nobody says Vox anymore."

Lem couldn't help but laugh at Asher's expense. "She's got a point there. Only my step-dad and his bouche-dag friends still say Vox and they're well-old, and stiffer than the pole lodged up the tribune's rectal passage."

"I bet the new legate still uses it. 'Vox,' she tried to mimic the legate's voice, but failed horribly. "She looks righteously formal." Lorrelli shot a glance towards the vibrating doors, unconsciously twirling the end of her thin braided ponytail between two of her fingers.

"Don't get me started on her," Lem whispered under his

breath. "My mum told me the Chancellor overruled Lobrolo's choice for legate and appointed her himself."

"Why is that strange?" Asher asked, not understanding what he was getting at.

"Because, normally, a retiring legate gets to pick his successor," said Lem. "At least they used to. So what's your story anyway?"

Asher didn't answer. He remembered the Overseer's warning about being wary of whom to trust. He let the conversation lapse momentarily and, soon enough, another set of names were read out. Two more apprentices disappeared through the doors.

"Err, so what's all this anyway?" Asher asked.

"What? Oh right, you don't know anything," Lem said happily, slapping him on the shoulder, glad someone had broken the semi-awkward silence.

"Ease up," Lorrelli threw a moderately annoyed look at Lem.

"What? It's not my fault he doesn't."

"Beyond those doors is Mantlecrest's ceremonial well-shaft where the Ceremony of Alignment takes place," Lorrelli explained. "How much do you know about augers?"

"Practically nothing."

"Well, every Cruaar is partially attuned to an auger at birth. The Ceremony of Alignment completes the bond between our auger and our blood."

"Why aren't they fully attuned at birth?" asked Asher.

"A baby can't handle the bond," Lem laughed as if it was the most common thing in the world to know. "They'd die," he snapped his fingers together loudly, "just like that."

Lorrelli lazily swatted at him with her hand, but he merely grinned and evaded the blow. "Augers must be fully aligned either during or just after puberty, or the bond cannot be completed–"

"And we wouldn't be able to channel any of our blood callings," Lem interrupted her again, pulling a grim face and shaking his hands about in an absurdly scary manner.

Lorrelli rolled her eyes and lashed out at him again.

"What do you mean 'aligned'?" Asher asked, as Lem rubbed the back of his stinging scalp.

"Everyone's blood is naturally attuned to a specific bloodline, like Natura or Scienta. For some of us, more than one; although one bloodline usually ends up being more dominant," Lem casually scratched the back of his ear as he explained. "Bloodlines are passed down from generation to generation, so it's common for families to share the same alignment as one another."

Stepping to the side of Lorrelli, Lem raised his eyebrows in the direction of the heavy rattling doors. "The great big scary swirling vortex in the next room will complete the bond between our augers and our blood, aligning them to the bloodline we are most attuned to."

Lorrelli held up the chain around her neck, exposing her colourless auger. "And turn this clear little gem into a pretty green emerald." The sarcasm in her voice was evident, as if she already knew what she was going to become and the whole spectacle was an overly theatrical formality.

"Green, pfft… Natura's get green, I'm going to get a bad-ass blue. Scienta, baby. Where's you auger, anyway?" Lem asked, looking at Asher's neck and not seeing one.

Another set of names rung out across the room, but Asher ignored them and Lem's question, shrugging mindlessly.

"But sometimes, the alignment ceremony fails and an apprentice's auger can't be aligned." Lorrelli held up her auger and shook her head from side to side.

"Heinous, right? But it hasn't happened in a mawblink's age."

"Not since the vortex was re-augineered by Craftpaw Industries anyways," Lem added, then continued his history on the ceremony much to Asher's delight and Lorrelli's boredom. Soon, only Asher, Lem and Lorrelli remained in the room.

"So are you really a Vita born?" Lorrelli interrupted Lem's rant, gazing down at Asher's golden pants.

"Yeah, I guess so. That's what everyone keeps calling me,

anyway," Asher said plainly, grabbing the side of his pants to illustrate the point.

"Apprentice Bruwell and Apprentice Wittlearch," both their names echoed out from the room next door.

"That's what everyone keeps calling me." Lem laughed and mimicked Asher's expression. "Praccing classic."

Lorrelli slapped Lem hard this time, before casting one last lingering smile at Asher. "Righteous, more like. I hope we'll be seeing more of you, Asher..." she said and raised her eyebrows expectantly.

"Bloom, my last name is Bloom."

"Bloom? What are you, a flower?" Lem laughed and dragged a smiling Lorrelli out through the rattling doors, leaving Asher alone with his thoughts.

CHAPTER 12

THE CEREMONY OF ALIGNMENT

Asher found himself alone staring at the door Lem and Lorrelli had disappeared through. With nothing else to do and his interest piqued, he crept forward and pushed it ajar, just enough to peer through.

Seated around a small circular chamber sat a row of official-looking adults dressed in distinctive ceremonial attire, each seemingly more elaborate than the last. They maintained calm and austere expressions with no hint of surprise as though they had witnessed what was happening a hundred times before.

Lem and Lorrelli slowly walked forward, approached the centre of the well, and stepped just outside of Asher's field of view. He nudged the door open a little farther and witnessed one of the most incredible sights upon which he'd ever laid eyes.

A monstrous swirling vortex rose from a tiny hole in the bottom of the sunken floor and disappeared out of sight into an enormous well-shaft. The swirling maelstrom shook the room with violent gusts of wind as mystical forces twirled and spun in a savage elemental dance.

Asher watched with mouth ajar as Lem and Lorrelli approached the base of the giant swirling twister in the centre of the room, which threatened to spin out of control, yet somehow remained miraculously pinned to a small hole in the floor. A thin metal pole stood two-feet high, extending up out of the floor one foot away from the small hole that locked the base of the twisting vortex in place. A tiny, empty clasp was affixed to its top.

On the other side of the room, opposite the silent row of officials, two tall wooden posts, roughly two metres apart, loomed over the apprentice's heads against the far wall. A heavy iron chain hung down from each post, both of which rattled loudly as the frenzy battered their iron links against the steadfast timber struts. On the bottoms of each chain, a leather wrist-strap flapped wildly in the buffeting wind.

"Apprentice Wittlearch, you are called first." The legate's voice was barely audible over the churning winds.

Lorrelli turned to face Lem and anxiously nodded, more to reassure her own rattled nerves than his.

He responded in kind and smiled supportively, but was secretly thankful she was going first as he watched her walk towards the centre of the well.

She stepped forward carefully, holding up a hand to shelter her eyes from the ferocious gusts of wind. Several seconds later, she kneeled down and placed her auger firmly in the clasp affixed atop the metal pole. Instantly, the swirling turbulence funnelled down through her auger, wildly surging through the core of the gem. The tail of the tornado had become much more subdued, yet still spun madly, disappearing into the small hole in floor.

Lorrelli walked nervously over to the two wooden posts, turned and stood between them. Her eyes sought out each of the faces of the officials sitting opposite her in the viewing gallery before she willingly held up her arms for Lem to lock into the straps.

Lem dashed across the floor and secured her wrists in place within the leather straps. Making sure the bonds were fastened, he looked over his shoulder and glanced at the legate.

She nodded her approval and motioned for him to continue.

Lem nodded apprehensively and took a small pin from his pocket. Looking into Lorrelli's eyes, he silently wished her good luck. Holding back her tunic just enough to uncover her chest-bone, he jabbed the pin into her exposed flesh and watched as a small drop of blood seeped through the wound.

Lem caught the drop of blood on the tip of the pin and cradled it in cupped hands. Turning to face the centre of the room, his eyes narrowed against the gale-force winds buffeting the room. He approached Lorrelli's auger through the windstorm. Somehow the drop of blood had miraculously held firm on the tip of the pin. He took a deep breath and lowered his hands closer to the colourless gem holding the vortex in place. In one fluid motion, he brushed the tip of the pin against the top of her auger and immediately stepped back to watch.

Despite the battering of the tornado's fury, the droplet of blood sunk inside the walls of the gem and disappeared. As the blood faded away, the bottom of the vortex slowly raised up from the floor, retreating from the gem up into the well-shaft, until a single storm cloud raged high above them. The cloud grew dark and flickered with wild flashes of light. Violently, it changed colour in the blink of an eye, first from blue to violet, then to red and black, then to an ominous luminescent green and deep purple.

All the while, Lorrelli stood stock still, arms lashed between the wooden posts, silently waiting, bravely staring upwards. A bright flash of lightning struck down from the ceiling and engulfed her auger in a burst of sparks and energy.

Lorrelli screamed as the vortex re-emerged from the deadly lightning-scarred cloud and surged down towards her; but any noise she made was instantly cut off as the funnel poured through her open mouth and out of the pinprick on her chest, spilling towards her auger.

Lorrelli's face was torn between pure terror and unmitigated pain as the vortex coursed through her body, dragging wisps of blood from her chest and transporting them into her auger, which was now ablaze with blinding flashes of emerald light.

Lorrelli didn't cry out.

She didn't make a sound.

She couldn't.

Her lungs were filled with air, but her throat was choked by the rage of the tornado. Then, as soon as it had come, the light was gone. The vortex left her mouth and body, its tail returning to the hole in the floor, leaving Lorrelli and her auger alone.

Lorrelli closed her mouth and slumped down, letting her restraints take her weight as exhausted eyes gazed longingly toward her auger in the centre of the room. Much to her delight, the most brilliant shade of green emanated from deep within the gemstone.

"Vox Natura!" Legate Seville announced to the row of officials, each annotating the recorded outcome in several different archives held on their laps.

Lem untied Lorrelli and swapped out his auger for hers atop the metal pole. Returning to her side, he switched positions and stood between the posts, placing Lorrelli's auger in her outstretched hand.

The vortex continued to churn away, funnelling its way through Lem's auger as it had done to Lorrelli's, spinning away, lashing the room with sharp gusts of air.

"I told you she'd say Vox." Lorrelli smiled weakly as she strapped Lem in the leather restraints.

Lem smirked, but hid his anxiousness poorly. His worried eyes watching carefully as Lorrelli punctured the skin on his chest and repeated the actions he'd performed on her moments earlier.

Crossing the floor, she wiped Lem's droplet of blood on his auger and stepped away, proudly inspecting her newly transformed emerald auger in her hands. Just like before, the vortex raised up into the well-shaft, drawing itself higher and higher until, once again, the heaving mass of clouds built into a heaving storm front.

Lem closed his eyes and waited for the inevitable.

The storm-cloud gushed and swarmed high in the well-shaft. Flashes of light exploded and zigzagged across the storm's exterior. To Asher, it look like it was behaving differently than it had mere moments ago, but his view was extremely limited. He was not alone in his thoughts, however; soon the row of officials murmured amongst themselves.

Lem looked up at the violent surging cloud above him, an expression of fear creeping over his face. Minutes passed and still nothing happened. There was no crack of lightning. The vortex didn't descend. There was nothing except the concentrated swirling maelstrom that had stalled high above them.

Asher saw Legate Seville whisper something to Finneus Slink, who promptly stood up and left the viewing gallery. Lem was visibly worried now, his eyes gazing out at the row of officials staring back at him with disappointment in their eyes.

Finally, a tiny spark of lightning shot down from the roof. A sliver of light hit Lem's auger with a pathetic amount of force. But the vortex did not descend.

Lem leaned forward and stared down at his auger, as did the officials from the viewing gallery. For a second it seemed like Lem was going to break down in front of the entire room, until the legate appeared at his side and unbound his restraints. She promptly ushered both Lorrelli and Lem off the floor, grabbing his auger in her free hand before they left.

Asher caught a glimpse of Lem's gemstone before it disappeared in her hand. It remained devoid of colour.

It had failed to be aligned.

Asher looked at Lem as he was being led away. His face was a ghostly colour, a heartbroken expression smeared across it. Lorrelli tried to comfort him, but her words fell on deaf ears. The legate said nothing as she walked them out. One by one, the officials followed them out through a set of double doors and into the Auxilia Amphitheatre.

After everyone else had left the room, Legate Seville re-emerged and waved her hand at the vortex. It ceased its relentless churning and descended into the small hole in the sunken floor of the well-shaft.

The room fell strangely quiet.

Asher let the door close and listened to the legate's approaching footsteps. The door swung inwards towards her in a rush, but her face remained as emotionless as always.

"Come with me." The legate did not wait to see if Asher was following; instead, she spun and strode across the floor of the well-shaft and into the viewing gallery.

Asher dutifully followed, but she stopped him at the door.

"Wait here. You can watch the proceedings through the porthole." With that, she promptly disappeared through the door and walked onto the stage of the Auxilia Amphitheatre.

Asher peered through the window and marvelled at the mass of apprentices seated within the grand amphitheatre. Around a hundred young adults sat in uniform silence and awaited instruction from the legate. They ranged in age from a little older than Asher, to those in their late teens, and even their early twenties. The newest apprentices sat closest to Asher on the lowest tier, each still paired up with their alignment-ceremony partners.

Their pants were no longer a dull grey. They were now a mixture of either pale blue or dull green, much like the rest of the gathered apprentices. Their tunics, however, were distinctly colour-coded and ordered in several different rows. A rainbow extended up beyond the white-clad first-year apprentices. Their row of white was dwarfed by a row of violet, then navy, orange, purple, brown and, finally, black, each row growing smaller in number.

Asher suspected the tunic colour depicted the apprentice's year, but he didn't have time to dwell on the matter before Legate Seville's voice sang out within the amphitheatre, the room's natural acoustics amplifying it with ease.

"Apprentices, I do not care to waste time on the pleasantries of the day. You all know why you are here. Those in their first year, welcome to Mantlecrest. Treat her with respect, learn from those wiser than you, adapt to your surroundings and you will overcome any weakness you currently bear.

"This is my first year as legate, but do not for a second underestimate my resolve, or dedication, to your proper instruction and training. I dislike surprises like I dislike failure and yet today I have received two such surprises that I must announce to you. The first is that one of our newest apprentice's augers has failed to be aligned."

A few hushed murmurs and smirks broke out across the room, mostly from the older apprentices in the higher tiers of the amphitheatre.

"You will treat him with the same respect as any other apprentice, or the tribune will be only too happy to instil respect in you by any way he sees fit."

The corners of Tribune DeGrulz's mouth curled upwards slightly as the fingers of his open-gauntleted hand clenched into a fist by his side, illustrating the point. The murmurs ceased as sly smirks transformed into furrowed brows of subjugated silence.

"Secondly, it is my duty to inform you another apprentice will be joining your ranks. Not long ago, a young man was discovered by one of Undergall's warders, living in secret within The Blind. All of his life he has been shielded from our world and knows nothing of our ways. Regardless, he is as much a Vox Cruaar as any of you who sits here today."

The legate scanned the faces of the room; all eyes were upon her. "It has been decreed, by Elder Mandate, he is to sit his apprenticeship here at Mantlecrest."

The crowd let forth one short loud cheer in unison before falling back into silence.

Legate Seville lowered her voice and her tone took on a serious note. She briskly motioned to someone out of Asher's line of sight.

Asher heard footsteps coming towards him and slowly backed away from the porthole in the door.

"I feel it only fair to tell you the complete truth in this matter as this particular apprentice is, for lack of a better word, unique. To our knowledge, he is the first Vox Vita born outside the three cities since the rebellion. His auger is unregistered and his origins and lineage remain a mystery."

The amphitheatre's apprentices looked at one another in apprehension, most with disconcerting frowns plastered across their faces.

"You also have the right to know he was attacked by a Mortis Skulk cultist and survived. Not once, but twice."

A few of the elder apprentices nodded their heads and slapped their hands against their chests in approval.

"Not only was he able to fight off his attacker, he did so by calling upon the Blood Nitor, long before his auger was aligned, or he'd been trained to do so. I don't think I need to explain to you the significance of this remarkable occurrence, or the bearing it has upon the magnitude of what this Vita-born may offer."

The crowd of apprentices sat spellbound, hanging off her every word, each slowly turning their heads towards the entrance of the ceremonial well-shaft, not exactly sure what to expect of the apprentice about to enter the amphitheatre.

"Apprentices of Mantlecrest," she motioned an instruction for the man to open the door, "may I present Vox Vita, Asher Bloom."

At first there was silence. Stunned faces looked at the slight sandy-haired teen with a mixture of reverence and disbelief as he anxiously stepped forward. Asher paused and again felt the pressure of a hundred judgemental eyes bearing down upon him.

"Apprentice Bloom, I present to you, Mantlecrest."

The crowd erupted in a cacophony of cheers, although Asher couldn't help but feel they were not raucously applauding him, but rather his impressive list of feats the legate had just announced.

Asher didn't care.

He smiled widely for the first time he could remember. It was an arrival he had never expected, nor imagined.

The crowd continued to carry on and cheer until the legate held up a hand. "Asher's arrival at Mantlecrest was no easy feat. Not only did he survive two Mortis Skulk attacks, he also had to navigate through the decrepit tombs of Foreguard and escape a pack of gavrins."

A few of the older apprentices scoffed and smirked at the last claim, as though it was the easiest thing in the world to accomplish.

"Asher has experienced things that most of you can only dream of. So it is with this in mind that I demand your understanding on the unique condition he bears. Many of you are too young to understand the significance of what I am about to show you; others will know full well the ramifications." She silently gestured for Asher to hold out his hand.

Asher was clearly reluctant but did so: palm down, fingers clenched in a tight fist.

"Asher has not yet required a mantle to call upon his blood. His auger has been somehow set—burned, if you will, into his palm. How or why, we do not yet know or understand."

Many of the apprentices rose to their feet and leaned forward to get a better view.

"Not only this, but it bears a mark you will instantly recognise and fear. It is this mark that I demand your tolerance and understanding, for it is not what it appears to be."

Asher's trepidation was evident. At the legate's request he slowly unfurled his fingers and turned his hand over, exposing his auger for the entirety of Mantlecrest to see.

A violent outburst of shock echoed across the room. A few older apprentices spat on the floor and shot looks of hatred at Asher. Others called out insults.

Asher heard himself being called a traitor no less than five times within a second. Unabashed accusations and curses flew about the room like burning embers on the wind.

"Silence!" the legate's voice boomed throughout the Auxilia Amphitheatre. "What you see has yet no explanation, but it is not the taint. There is no evidence linking him to Cerebule, Shyloft Pracca or the Mortis Skulk."

The angry murmurs of the assembled apprentices died down, but their frowns and scowls remained.

"As apprentices of Mantlecrest, you will obey the wishes of the Grand Chancellor and treat him as one of your own or, should you find yourself unable, with blind indifference. Those who cannot, will answer directly to me." She said the last so quietly that the threat washed over the crowd like a soft breeze.

When her words landed, their scowls receded, but Asher knew all too well their resentment remained.

Legate Seville finally turned to Asher, who stood transfixed at the centre of the room.

His homecoming had turned into yet another sordid nightmare, from which he was unable to wake.

"Apprentice Bloom, join the apprentice ranks."

Asher really only knew two apprentices in the room, so his choice was an easy one. He approached a silent Lorrelli, who welcomed him by softly squeezing his forearm.

Lem, on the other hand, said nothing. His mind was still lost within the reality of his own predicament.

Asher wasn't even sure if he'd heard a single word the legate had said in the last five minutes. He sat down beside Lem and tried to avoid the venomous glares of apprentices bearing down from behind him in the higher tiers.

"As always, access to Undergall is off limits to all first-year apprentices," the legate continued, finishing off her address. "The exception, of course, is when visiting Ermalt Dopplebock's Mantle Emporium, in which case you will be accompanied by your relevant master.

"As a sign of goodwill towards you, I hereby change the laws regarding second- and third-year's access to the commons which, for the first time, will be allowed if accompanied by an elder apprentice."

A small portion of the crowd cheered and clapped, although they were mostly the younger apprentices in the two rows behind Asher. The older members of the crowd folded their arms and frowned as if they had been cheated out of something.

"My last announcement to you all is in regard to Mantlecrest's Undercellars, which have come under attack from a rather nasty outbreak of creeping mould. I have personally employed a specialist to look into the matter but, until such a time as we have the situation under control, the Undercellars are strictly out of bounds.

"Train well, apprentices. I hereby pass the floor to the visiting instructors of the elder apprentices, Montrook Ignaroff of the Undergall Hopralas and First Order Tribarion Roolta, here on loan courtesy of Oakrim's Tribarion Cohort."

Two adults—one in a rather roguish multicoloured outfit, the other in resplendent battle-ready gilded armour—rose from their seats and made their way to the centre podium. Legate Seville moved aside and swept across the room towards Lem, Lorrelli and Asher. "You three, with me."

Lorrelli pulled Lem to his feet and the trio fell in line behind the legate, quickly exiting the Auxilia Amphitheatre.

Asher was only too happy to leave behind the condemnatory glares boring into the back of his head like a woodpecker hammering against his skull. As the door closed behind him, Asher felt the looks of disgust, amazement and hatred melt away.

He breathed a sigh of relief, but the sensation only lasted a moment before a new wave of anxiety lapped at his consciousness. This time he was not the only one who felt it. He felt the cold touch of Lorrelli's fingers wrap around his forearm and squeeze. He couldn't be sure if it was for his reassurance or hers. When his gaze met hers, it was blatantly obvious she didn't know, either.

CHAPTER 13

RUMOURS FROM AFAR

The legate said nothing as she marched through the halls of Mantlecrest, leading the trio past a series of rooms, each adorned with simple yet elegant murals and artworks. The rooms' floors were predominately empty, free of clutter and furniture, but keeping up with the legate's speed made it hard for the trio to get more than a glance into each.

The din of the amphitheatre had subsided after the first stairwell, and soon they were deep within Mantlecrest's maze-like passageways, the three apprentices thoroughly disorientated and lost. The only sounds that reached their ears were their own muffled footsteps on the cold stone floors.

The silence only served to amplify the growing sense of paranoia in the back of Asher's mind. He was sure Lorrelli felt it, too. She kept casting anxious looks his way, poorly disguised behind a nonchalant smile. Lem stumbled along behind them blindly, dejected eyes glumly downcast on his colourless auger for the majority of their trip.

After what seemed like an eternity, the legate finally stopped and peered in every direction before deciding to speak. "Do not think these walls guarantee your safety," her words cut the air like a scythe through wheat. "An entire city looms just beyond our gate. Its heart beats, but is still fragile from the Guillotine Rebellion, not to mention other more recent events. Continued caution and vigilance must be paramount above all else.

"Asher, your…" she searched for the right words, "unfortunate condition bears with it a curse of hatred. There will be many Cruaar, apprentice and adult alike, who cannot put the past to rest and will seek to condemn you unjustly.

"You cannot change what life has dealt you, which means

your instinctual connection with Apprentice Wittlearch and Apprentice Bruwell will also see them singled out as targets for those who would do you harm."

"But I never meant–"

The legate held up her hand to cut Asher off. "Your heart speaks volumes for your innocence, but fear and ignorance blinds people to fact. The two of you," she looked hard at Lorrelli and Lem, "whether it is simple bad luck, or something greater at work, you have both been put into Asher's path for a reason." She gazed into each of the eyes of the trio to ensure she had their undivided attention.

"Asher will need strong allies if he is to weather the growing storm that moves against him. To this end I must now ask you both to take an oath."

Lem and Lorrelli stared back at the legate with a false sense of bravado, obviously confused and a little bit terrified by everything she was saying.

"Will you, above all others, stand by Asher's side against all guilt, trickery, deception and malice thrown against you?"

Lem looked at Lorrelli and then at Asher. He was obviously lost for words.

Lorrelli didn't blink at the question and replied off the cuff. "I suppose."

Asher threw her a thankful look, even if her answer wasn't as steadfast as he would've liked.

Legate Seville nodded once at Lorrelli before turning her attention to Lem.

He blinked away his momentary confusion and responded in kind, albeit somewhat more timidly. "I'm the first unaligned Cruaar since the Overseer. I'll need all the friends I can get," he said dismally, doing little to hide his obvious disillusionment with the outcome of the alignment ceremony.

"Good. Now hold out your augers. All of you."

The three did so, Lem and Lorrelli extending each of their augers outwards; Asher extended his hand, palm upturned.

The legate pushed their hands together and held her own hands over the three gems. Her eyes narrowed and her cheeks tensed as she concentrated. Slowly, faint wisps of light rose from each stone. Three different-coloured streams mixed together in the air between her hands and their augers: one gold, one green and one grey. A single cloud of swirling colour descended and split, sinking into each of their augers, until every fragment of light had disappeared.

"Then it's settled. Whatever drew you three together, your trust in each other will see you stay that way. The veritusk bind will ensure as much."

Lem looked more confused than ever, but the legate merely glanced at the partially open door to her left, opening it all the way with a prod of her finger. "I have an urgent matter to attend to. These are your racks. Rest well." With that she was gone, leaving the trio alone in an empty hall outside a row of doorways.

"I don't know about you, but I love being pressured into the path of danger," Lem muttered sarcastically as he stepped into the room. "What the ruddy prac is a veritusk bind, anyway?"

Asher shrugged and Lorrelli scowled in response, both following Lem into the spartanly furnished room. Four single beds lined each corner of the room with large trunks at their feet. Three had hot meals laid out upon them, steam still rising from the plate. Lem rushed towards the nearest meal and tore into a roasted chicken leg.

"You need to stop using that word," Lorrelli said to Lem and sat on the bed opposite, leaving Asher to take his pick of either of the two spare beds, in the corners of the room.

"What? Prac?" Lem repeated.

"Yeah, that one."

"What's prac?" Asher asked.

"Prac. You know, prac…" Lem looked at him bluntly, "as in Pracca, as in Shyloft Pracca. Infamous traitor, Cerebule's right hand and all that. My step-dad uses it all the time. Heard heaps of his friends use it, too. I guess it's the Cruaar equivalent of a curse word, you know like f–"

"It's offensive! Cut it out," Lorrelli snapped.

"Sorry." Lem looked away sheepishly after seeing the look on Lorrelli's face.

Asher sat down on the bed and looked at his two new friends. "I'm really sorry I got you two mixed up in all this," Asher said quietly.

"Hardly your fault," Lorrelli said casually, "besides, everything happens for a reason."

"Don't worry about it," Lem blurted out, spraying a mouth full of chicken all over his bed and Lorrelli's lap, and waving his colourless auger in the air. "It's not like it can get much worse than it already is."

"So glad I get to have you around all the time," Lorrelli looked angrily at him as she wiped chunks of chicken off her lap.

"Yeah, well, better the enemy you know, right?" Lem smiled at her, chicken still stuck in his teeth. Noticing the concerned look on Asher's face as he looked around the room, Lem swallowed the rest of his chicken and pointed at the door. "Well, at least we're safe in here. The security systems Craftpaw installed in this place are ridonculous."

"And how would you know about that?" Lorrelli said, taking a bite out of her own plate of steaming chicken.

"'Cause my step-father works there. Craftpaw was responsible for the security update for every square inch of Mantlecrest and nothing, I repeat nothing, gets past a Craftpaw secureaug system."

"Secureaug?" Asher repeated between mouthfuls of food.

"Oh, that's right!" Lorrelli exclaimed between mouthfuls. "I completely forgot. They refurbished the entire place after..."

Lem shot her a dark look and shook his head, raising his eyebrows and nodding at Asher.

Lorrelli looked instantly sheepish at her slip.

"After what?" Asher asked, suspiciously looking at the two, instantly picking up on their awkwardness.

"After Lobrolo replaced the old legate a couple of years back," Lem said quickly. "It was the most extensive security upgrade of any structure in all of Undergall, short of Earthreach Spire, that is. I snuck a peek at the plans when they were still in the design phase. They thought of everything."

"That's right. I remember reading about it in the Undergall Testament." Lorrelli snapped her fingers, silently thanking Lem for saving what could have been an awkward conversation.

Asher narrowed his eyebrows at the two of them, his suspicion of what they weren't saying amplifying in the back of his mind.

"It's kind of like a newspaper." Lorrelli spied something across the room and ran across to retrieve it.

Lem shot her a curious look with an eyebrow raised.

"What? My family holidays in The Blind. I'm allowed to know what a newspaper is, jackass." She returned with a solid tablet of smooth polished glass in her hand and handed it out to Asher. "Here you go."

The tablet was virtually weightless in Asher's hand, its face flawless. The entire tablet was without blemish, except for a small stained-glass dome at the bottom and an even smaller black pearl embedded in the top right of the tablet.

"I don't get it," Asher said blankly.

Lem, who had finished eating his chicken by this time, laughed and pointed at the glass dome. "Here, watch." Lem waved his auger over the dome, sparking the tablet to life. Tiny particles of coloured sand spewed from the stained-glass dome and formed words, paragraphs, headlines and images within the glass of the tablet until finally the words 'Undergall Testament' took prominent position at the top.

Asher looked up and smiled at the pair in amazement.

"Simple things, eh, Asher?" Lem snorted at Asher's expense.

Lorrelli and Asher ignored him, both eagerly looking down at the tablet as the day's headlines formed.

"It's updated in real time, so you're always up to date with what's going on. The news we get inside Mantlecrest is hugely censored, but it's better than nothing."

"At least it gives us the Utor Alea match results," Lem said happily.

Asher was about to ask what Utor Alea was when an article caught his eye.

'Council investigations persist as the Tribarion Cohort continues its search for fugitive Przra Laxo in conjunction with the murder of...'

The words faded and disappeared, rearranging themselves into new paragraphs before Asher had the chance to finish reading the sentence. "Hey, I was reading that!"

"Don't worry about it, that's old news," Lem said, hastily pointing a finger at the newly forming words in the centre of the tablet. "Look, a new story is breaking."

Asher watched as the text of the main story changed. A large picture took shape and the title reformed. Asher could only watch in awe as the stained-glass face of Gibraltair Privvybell Reine stared up at him.

"Well read it out, already."

"Right, sorry." Asher eyes sped from left to right as he read the story aloud. "Recent unauthorised discovery blows Foreguard myth out of the sands."

Lem's eyes lit up excitedly. "Hit the audio, Asher."

"Audio?"

"Here, I'll do it," Lorrelli said, taking the tablet and waving her auger over the black pearl. It instantly rippled to life, producing a crisp clear audio track. A man's voice instantly picked up where Asher left off, reading the story line by line.

"Rumours abound today amidst the latest unconfirmed discovery by the highly famed and sought-after augiologist, Gibraltair Privvybell Reine."

"Gibraltair, he's wicked," Lem blurted out in admiration,

snatching the tablet out of Lorrelli's hands.

"Today Gibraltair announced to the Cruaar Nation that the commonly accepted belief that certain augiologically significant mechanaugs, previously believed to be completely destroyed during the Fall of Foreguard, are, in fact, intact. It is a belief he claims was propagated by the council to bury the truth about a dark secret embedded within Foreguard's ruins.

"While augiological experts have yet to confirm or refute his claims, his unauthorised expedition into the Fall of Foreguard is now under investigation by sentinaugs of Oakrim and Undergall.

"Grand Chancellor Valderook Wrakburn refused comment today, instead issuing a statement of condemnation for the unauthorised incursion into Foreguard, calling the act, 'a vile invasion of our nation's tortured past.' Deriat Ungeltread reporting."

"Gibraltair," Asher murmured to himself, looking at the picture of the man etched into the stone tablet. "I met him."

"No, you didn't. No way. He's way too famous," Lem scoffed.

"I did, I swear. When we were escaping through Foreguard. He rescued us... well, sort of."

"Shh, not so loud." Lorrelli stood and waved her auger at a small glass dome beside the door. The door instantly swung shut and locked.

Lem rolled his eyes at her in an exaggerated movement.

"What? You heard the legate, who knows who could be listening."

Asher pointed at the door. "How did you?"

"Secureaug doors are attuned to certain augers," Lem answered impatiently, eager to hear more about Gibraltair.

"No-one can open that door but us and the masters of the Mantlecrest," Lorrelli finished as Lem shushed her and focused on Asher.

"Okay, so you met him, then. What's he like?"

"Strange is the first word that comes to mind, although insane is prob–"

169

"Wait," Lem cut him off as something clicked in the back of his mind. "A dark secret, you don't think they're talking about the Vitalsior Heart, do you?"

"So you're not willing to believe Asher met Gibraltair, but you are willing to believe Gibraltair's found a mythological object," Lorrelli scoffed disdainfully, shaking her head at him. "Did he mention what he was looking for, Asher?"

"Well, no. I mean, we didn't really talk all that much. He mostly talked at us, after he trapped us with an enormous stone statue."

"You mean a construct?" Lorrelli tilted her head and looked at him quizzically. "I thought they were all destroyed."

"The bruises on my ribs beg to differ."

"What bruises?" Lem said, inspecting Asher's ribs after lifting up his tunic.

"That's weird," Asher looked down where the bruises had been, but his flesh was clear and without blemish.

Lorrelli looked like she was about to say something but then thought better of it.

"Anyway, so what do you reckon, Asher? Do you think it's the heart?"

"What heart?"

"The Vitalsior Heart, of course; what other heart is there?" Lem raised his eyebrows twice excitedly at Asher, but only received a blank look in return. "Oh, right, you would've never heard of it. Well, legend has it High Cleric Herion Friatt Vitalsior lived for over five-thousand years."

"What? That's not possible?" Asher interjected. Asher missed the angry glare Lorrelli shot at Lem, but did notice Lem stumble over his next words as if he'd mentioned something he shouldn't have.

"Well, that part may have been exaggerated, but the Annals tell us that towards the end of his life his body absorbed his entire mantle, which was predominantly made of pure gold. Upon his death, his skin turned to dust and all that remained was his skeleton. His skeleton and an enormous heart, encased in augmented gold."

"Yet, amazingly enough, no-one ever actually found his body," Lorrelli mocked sceptically. "It's a myth, Lem, nothing more. Don't let this gullible dolt delude you with his nonsense, Asher. I'm sure Gibraltair will simply reveal the rediscovery of the giant constructs. That's still a great augiological discovery."

"Not half as exciting as finding the Vitalsior Heart would've been," Lem muttered under his breath dejectedly.

"I guess we'll find out soon enough. If he's being investigated by the council, he's bound to end up in Undergall at some point. Now we'd better get some sleep," she yawned deeply, "I'm wrecked. That alignment ceremony was brutal."

She instantly knew how careless the statement was as soon as she said it. She cast one sympathetic look at Lem to say sorry before waving her auger at the auglight by her bed, dousing its illumination and shrouding her side of the room in darkness.

She rolled over in her bed, distancing herself from any further conversation, leaving Lem and Asher to think about everything that had happened.

"I still can't believe I wasn't aligned. What am I going to tell my parents? My mother will disown me." He lay down on his bed, but knew he was unlikely to get much sleep. His mind was awash with the reality of his abysmal situation.

Asher sat on his bed alone, his mind still racing from everything that had happened in the past twenty-four hours. He waved his hand at the auglight by his bed in the same manner as Lorrelli, making darkness descend over the room.

Just before he closed his eyes and let sleep overwhelm his exhausted body, Asher thought he saw the briefest flicker of Raglan's face in the darkness. He tried to cry out, but he was already asleep; his dreams plagued by dark memories.

CHAPTER 14

WELTICRUM ROUSSO

Asher slept so deeply that when he awoke, Lem and Lorrelli had already left the room; yet he still didn't feel fully rested. Blinking away the sleep from his eyes, he looked around, but could find no way to tell what time it was. The entire area was artificially lit via auglights on the ceiling and walls, all of which had reignited and now illuminated the room in such a way that it looked as though it was immersed in broad daylight.

He found a fresh plain white tunic and another set of golden pants laid out at the foot of his bed. Changing into clean clothes, he stumbled outside his room and into a man half his size, knocking him over and awkwardly falling into the wall.

"Steady on, I may be small, but I'm still here," the man said abrasively as he and Asher collected themselves.

"Sorry. I wasn't looking," Asher glanced up and down the corridor.

"Don't worry yourself. I've taken bigger knocks than that in my time. No harm, no foul. The name's Gobbler and unless my eyes deceive me, you must be the infamous Asher Bloom I've been hearing so much about." Mason stared lazily at Asher's hand. It was hard for him not to; it was almost at the same level as his eyes.

Asher instinctively hid his hand behind him.

"Never mind all that nonsense, I'm in no position to judge anyone on looks," Mason held out his hand in greeting.

Asher shook it awkwardly, only just realising what the man meant. Mason stood no higher than four feet on a good day. He had long strands of brilliant white hair, but only down one side of his head, which he'd smoothed down over the other side of his bald scalp in a ridiculous attempt at a comb over. He wore an elegant green tunic, embroidered with ornamental badges and medallions that weighed down one side of his tunic, causing it to sag lopsidedly. He was a comical mess and drastically out of proportion, but it didn't seem to bother him.

"What are you doing here?" Asher asked curiously.

"Hmm? Oh, right. You're probably not used to seeing masters flittering about these hallowed halls, especially ones as dashing and striking as myself." He smiled slyly and slipped Asher a wink.

"Legate Seville contracted me to get to the bottom of the sodding green malarkey that's been plaguing the Undercellars of late. I was just checking to see if it had reached this level." He clicked the fingers of one hand and slapped Asher hard on the thigh. "You're safe for now, Goldilocks."

Asher only then realised they were completely alone in the hall. All the rooms up and down the hall were silent and presumably vacant. "Err, where is everyone?"

"I'd expect they're all probably on Mess Hill stuffing their gobs."

Asher looked at him blankly.

Mason pointed to a stairwell at the end of the corridor using the same hand with which he'd slapped Asher. The other he kept by his side, palm hidden from Asher's view. "Two floors up, second door on your right; just follow your nose."

"Thanks," Asher said awkwardly as he headed off towards the stairwell. Something about the unusually small man gave him an unsettled and suspicious feeling he couldn't put his finger on.

"Enjoy the view," Mason called after him as he left, his eyes watching Asher suspiciously as he deviously twirled a few strands of Asher's hair between his thumb and forefinger. He waited until Asher was out of sight before carefully placing them inside a glass vial for safekeeping and smirked to himself.

Asher followed Mason's directions, and smelled the sweet fragrances of cooked meat and spiced porridge long before he reached the doorway to Mess Hill. He stopped as he crossed through the massive double-door threshold and stepped out on the hill's grass landing. He'd seen Mantlecrest before, albeit briefly from balcony adjoining Ancestor's Hall, but the view from Mess Hill was equally as magnificent. As always, he didn't have enough time to properly enjoy its majesty before the attention of those nearby were alerted to his presence.

"Asher. Over here," Lorrelli called out from across the grassy lawn.

A lot of heads turned at the sound of his name and gawked at him with a mixture of emotionally charged stares as Asher nervously crossed the hill towards his two new friends. Whispers, rumours and conjecture flooded down its slope as Asher passed various groups of apprentices.

Everyone had stopped eating their breakfasts and whispered to one another in hushed tones, none willing to take their eyes off him until he'd moved past them. Some spat their food on the ground and moved to the other side of the hill to get away from him, others simply stared and shot him dark looks, their mouths firmly shut with either indifference or disgust.

Asher guessed that, for the majority of them, it was disgust. "I suppose I'd better get used to that kind of behaviour," Asher said quietly as he approached.

"Never mind those ignorant poss tots. Here, I grabbed you some grub." Lem held out a plate full of food as Asher sat down.

"Toss pots?" Asher reinterpreted Lem's backwards phrase.

Lem winked back at him. "You're not as dumb as you look."

Lorrelli and Lem were dressed in the same plain white tunic as Asher, as were many other apprentices on Mess Hill, but Lorrelli's pants were a light green colour and Lem's were a dull grey. His were also the only pair on the entire hill that were this shade. Just like the Auxilia Amphitheatre, a host of different-coloured tunics flooded the hill.

Most groups tended to be made up of the same colour, although Asher noticed a few groups that had multiple coloured tunics and pants worn by apprentices of various ages. "So what's with the different colours?"

"The colours? Oh, that's simple." Lorrelli answered. "The colour of your tunic denotes your apprentice year."

"White is first-year apprentices," Lem butted in, "AKA washouts, then you got violet for readers, navy for bruisers, orange for bleeders, purple for wielders, brown for duellers and black for the draft." The words fell from Lem's lips one after the other. It was almost as if he'd practised and rehearsed the phrase for perfect delivery. He finished his monologue by raising his eyebrows once quickly and gnawing into a freshly peeled banana.

Asher couldn't help but be impressed, even if he had absolutely no idea what Lem was on about.

"Don't worry about all that, all you need to know is that the colour of an apprentice's pants shows their alignment. The deeper the colour, the stronger their blood is attuned to the bloodline. Green for Natura, blue for Scienta, gold for Vita, black for Mortis and grey for–" Lorrelli stopped herself a second too late.

"Yeah, yeah, he gets the picture," Lem responded in a huff and returned the stern look she'd just given him.

"Sorry," Lorrelli apologized bashfully.

Asher decided it was probably a good opportunity to change the subject. "I can't believe this view, it's amazing," Asher's wide eyes gazed out over the sprawling rooftops of Undergall as he tucked into his breakfast.

"You can pretty much see the whole city from here," Lorrelli said as she too looked out over the city.

"Here comes the tour," Lem smirked.

Lorrelli made a point of ignoring him before pointing out different sections of the city. "That's the Forgotten Gardens over there, just outside Mantlecrest's walls." She pointed towards a large forest, too dense with trees and vines to properly see through. A flock of brightly coloured birds sprang into the air from the branches and adopted a circular holding pattern high above the forest.

"Wonder what's spooked them. Rarely see moonkites take

flight during the day," Lem pondered out loud to no-one in particular as he arched his neck back to watch the birds soar.

Lorrelli ignored Lem's question and swung her arm across the city to a large central mass of elegant sandstone buildings bordering a large central square.

A large statue sat in the centre of the square, but Asher couldn't quite make out what it was from this distance.

"Mastonon Commons is in the centre of town, and way in the back you'll find Fathomdeep Lake, but you can probably only see the Azuretop Falls from here."

Asher could only see glimpses of the lake through gaps in the buildings, but it was hard to miss the sheer magnitude of the massive plume of vibrant blue water cascading down from the roof of the cavern far in the distance. It dispersed into a mist of white towards the bottom, before its view was blocked by a row of buildings lining the banks of the lake.

"Where does all the water go?" Asher's asked curiously.

"Don't know, it probably just seeps into some underground reservoir or river," Lem speculated. "The Lake never seems to get any fuller."

"Okay, err, what's that?" Asher pointed out a darker section of the city with a mass of black and grey buildings set upon the side of a large rise, pockmarked with a series of caves that disappeared into the side of Undergall's giant cavern.

"Black Ingot Warrens." Lorrelli changed her gaze to the considerably older and more decrepit looking part of the city.

"Well dodgy they are. I went there with my step-dad once and it gave me the willies." Lem anxiously rubbed the back of his neck.

Asher's and Lorrelli's augers flared brightly all of a sudden, sending a warm sensation up Asher's arm causing him to grimace, whilst Lorrelli looked at her auger in confusion.

"Strange, it's never done that before."

"What now?" Lem asked, oblivious to what had just happened.

"Still getting used to everything, I guess," Asher shrugged. "So what's that?" Asher asked, pointing at an enormous spire looming over the city; the shadow it cast enveloped the vast majority of the Black Ingot Warrens.

"Earthreach Spire. It's where the council's chambers are, amongst the other things they wished we didn't know about."

The resplendent tower gleamed in the light, ornate statues and intricate carvings made its presence all the more majestic in Asher's mind. He held up his hand to block the light from his face as his eyes climbed higher up the giant tower. A multitude of balconies and stained-glass windows marked its exterior and reflected a thousand coloured beams of light down over the city like a magnificent prism.

He stretched back his neck, but had trouble looking at the topmost spire as it was almost totally immersed in light. He eventually gave up and looked away. "Where is the light coming from? I thought the whole city was underground." Asher rubbed his eyes to clear them from the dazzling spots of light forming on the back of his retinas.

"Auglights, the entire city runs off them. We've had them for generations. That one's the central auglight," Lem pointed skyward to the blinding light source that blocked Asher's view of the spire's top.

"And what's with all the steam?" Asher asked curiously as his eyes peered out at the hundred different columns of vapour, which drifted lazily above the rooftops of the city and slowly dissipated into shimmering pockets of hot air.

"They're from the massive geothermal vent deep beneath the city. They're also what keep this place roasty toasty all year round. Even Mantlecrest uses them. There's a central boiler room somewhere in the lower levels that captures it all and redistributes it around Mantlecrest," Lem answered with a slurp, midway through a mouthful of steamy porridge, "or so I've been told, anyway."

"Come on, you two, enough about your boring auglights and

steam vents, we've got to get to our first training session," Lorrelli interjected and jumped to her feet.

Many of the other apprentices had already begun to leave Mess Hill and were making their way towards the main doors.

As the trio made to leave, Asher noticed a line of towering columns that sat high on top of Mess Hill's summit. Each acted as the base for a series of large statues that depicted some strange creature as they stood vigil over the apprentices below. Asher wanted more time to inspect them properly, but Lem yanked him hard on the arm.

"What's the rush, anyway?" Asher asked, annoyed, and freed his arm from Lem's grip.

"'Cause you don't want to be late for training on your first day, that's why," Lem warned.

"But how do we know what training we have?"

"Look in your tunic pocket," Lem coughed loudly, effectively dislodging a bit of food in his throat, as he increased his speed to catch up to Lorrelli who was powering ahead.

Asher felt around inside his tunic pocket and found a small tablet of stone half as thick as his smallest finger. It looked very much like a miniature stone version of the Undergall Testament, except its face held a list of training times, names and locations.

"All first-year apprentices have the same training schedule. Our first one is Lore and Augers on the rooftop observatory with Master Rousso in five minutes."

Asher and Lem left the magnificent view of Mess Hill behind, following Lorrelli to the roof. By the time they arrived, most of the other apprentices had already gathered around a frail old man.

He stood stock-still and in total silence, resting one arm on the parapet as he waited for the apprentices to find a space and settle down. He looked visibly older than any man Asher had ever seen in his life. His tunic was shabby and hung drably around his ageing frame. After a few moments of awkward silence, some apprentices lost interest in him and let their eyes wander out over the panoramic view of the city.

"Profitant de la vue?" The old man's voice hung on the last syllable, his intonation rising to indicate he was asking a question, even though clearly nobody spoke his language or, if they did, they weren't game to answer. His voice echoed with intense clarity and distinction, despite his outwardly frail appearance. He directed the question at those nearest him who had let their gaze wander over Undergall's rooftops. Staring out at the confused faces before him, he repeated his question, this time in English.

"I asked if you were enjoying the view." The old man's voice was laced with a thick nasal accent and had a tendency to roll his r's and extend his e's.

"Distraction never plays its hand when something more interesting presents itself, which would lead me to believe some of you do not find me interesting, or, as interesting as I am, I cannot compete with a rooftop view of Undergall." Silence descended over the observatory as the old man paced about, warily eyeing off the newest intake of apprentices.

"Perhaps a demonstration of the blood callings I might impart to you will grant me your undivided attention." With cat-like grace, he flicked his wrist at the edge of the tower and a creeping darkness enveloped the rooftop, blocking out all views of the city until an impenetrable black dome encircled the rooftop observatory. Calmly looking at the faces of his apprentices, he waited for the auglights mounted on the parapets of the tower to ignite with light before continuing.

"Perhaps intrigue alone is not enough," he said as a few apprentices reached out to try and touch the darkness. "Perhaps, then, a reward will satisfy your attention. A horn's worth of whirlpool clarity to anyone that can explain what I just did."

A chime of answers volleyed back at him at once.

"A barrier of concealment," one apprentice answered.

"A good guess, but no."

"A blinding malady?" another offered.

"I may be old, but blindness has not found me yet. Search beyond the obvious and the answer may surprise you."

"A mesmerising chant."

"A solid hypothesis, but no invocation left my lips." He scanned their excited faces searching for a specific response.

"You're probably First Edict, you wouldn't need to say anything," another offered.

Asher didn't understand the reference but, then again, there was a lot going on around him he didn't understand and nobody seemed inclined overly inclined to enlighten him.

"I am, and I don't, but that has nothing to do with the right answer." He paced around a few seconds more, patiently waiting for any more attempts. "Anyone? No-one? As I expected, but you must not feel bad, no-one has been able to answer me that question in over twenty years. My offer of refreshment holds until you are dismissed, should anyone realise upon an epiphany."

He walked towards the centre of the tower, parting the crowd of apprentices as he went, motioning them to make a wide circle around him. "My name is Welticrum Rousso, La Tête Auglorian of the Undergall Annals. It is my job to impart the wisdom and lore of our turbulent blood-soaked history upon you all. Also, to explain how and why your augers will change the way you interact and, indeed, perceive the world around you.

"But first things first, I do not care for conventional training methodology, nor do I care for books, criers, parchment or heralds. I do not repeat myself so, should you seek enlightenment, listen once and listen well. The only thing I require is your attention and your aptitude to learn.

"Also, you should know that I never conduct my training sessions in the same location twice. It will be your duty to decode the clues I give you to work out where your next instruction will be. Miss an instruction, and ignorance will be your only reward.

"I shall grant another horn's worth of whirlpool clarity to any apprentice that manages to attend all my training sessions at the end of the year, but I warn you that hasn't happened in over thirty years. Now we've wasted enough time, let's begin."

He tapped a haggard-looking wooden cane to his temple. It

had a dual interwoven shaft completely covered in runes and carvings, all of which were completely foreign to Asher. "Not all our power stems from blood and augers."

"Not that mine would do any good," Lem muttered under his breath.

"Mutter not Monsieur Bruwell. If you've something to say, speak your mind," Welticrum chastised.

Lem instantly fell silent, a gloomy look marring his face. Welticrum tapped his cane once loudly on the ground.

"Now, what is an auger?"

CHAPTER 15

THE CHILD WITH FOUR SHADOWS

Welticrum looked around at the hesitant faces gathered before him, patiently awaiting a response.

"A means to channel the power of our blood," a female apprentice answered gingerly.

"True, Mademoiselle Percotty, but it is more than just that. Without a mantle, your auger is little more than a shiny gemstone, or so it would seem in most cases." The old man stole a glance at Asher for the briefest of moments before letting his gaze wander over the others in the room. "Your auger is an extension of your body. It has a profound symbiotic existence with your blood, but both are controlled by your mind, by your will."

Welticrum slammed the tip of his cane on the ground, which made the entire rooftop shake violently. "Even the deadliest augineered weapon pales in significance against the strength of will and a single drop of blood. Master your auger and control it always, each and every moment, lest it master you and the drain claims you."

He slowly twirled on the spot and raised his cane for all to see. Amidst the top of the interwoven wooden staves, a small gem brightened as a dull light radiated outwards from the inside.

"Your power comes at the sacrifice of blood. Channel too much of it, without the proper control, and your auger will leech the life right out of you. Use too little and you'll not be able to protect yourself against those who stand against you.

"Most of you will never succumb to the drain, if you are careful. Some of you, however, will be foolish and not only succumb to it, but be consumed by it. Hope that you do not fall into the latter category."

Holding his cane aloft, a small hole pierced the darkened shroud covering the observatory. He looked up towards the roof of the great cavern and asked another question. "Why is it we choose to live in cities, segregated and concealed from our blind brothers above?"

"They do not understand us," a small black-haired girl answered quickly.

"Wrong!" he rapped his cane on the ground.

"We are more evolved."

"Au contraire, Monsieur Mofarder. Humans have long since held both the power and means to wipe us from the face of existence, had they any inclination we existed or posed a threat."

"Their technology," Lorrelli answered.

"How so, Apprenti Wittlearch?" he asked, pointing the tip of his cane at her.

"Calling upon our blood causes their machines to malfunction. It sends their electronics haywire and ultimately breaks them."

"Go on…"

"Technology drives and sustains their world, their very existence. Break enough of it and it would cripple them."

"Très bien, Mademoiselle, although I think you'll find them a touch more resilient than you would give them credit. The simple act of calling forth the power of our blood does disrupt and damage the technology that drives their world.

"Why? We have never been fully able to understand. Although, many of you will be surprised to learn that much of the innovation and advancement of our augiological and mechanaug devices are, in fact, reverse augineered from advances in human technology.

"Much like how our augers are symbiotically paired with our blood, so too is our existence symbiotically paired with the existence of humans. That being the case, when we choose to walk among them, we do so with great care and use every caution to ensure our worlds are kept apart. Of course, there have been those in the past that have thought otherwise."

The briefest flash of a memory crossed his face as he aimed his crooked wooden cane at the floor in front of him and backed away towards the edge of the open circle. "Many of you are probably well versed in the historic Cruaar fables, likely told to you through the embellished bedtime stories of an augwife when you were but babes in a crib. For others, this particular tale will fall upon fresh ears. Hands up, who here knows The Child with Four Shadows?"

Most of the apprentices raised their hands.

Asher did not.

The old man nodded in satisfaction, the wrinkles in his face crinkling with the effort. "This tale, above all others, is one of the most important of our nation's history if you can decipher its true meaning." His eyes darted around the room as he snapped his cane on the floor once more, dispelling the small hole in the black dome instantaneously. "So pay attention."

Almost immediately the auglights around the tower top dimmed to a low glow. A faint light emerged in the centre of the floor and took the shape of a baby. "A long time ago, a child was born. A unique child, unlike any other born before it. He was the apple of his parents' eyes, but it was not long before they both grew ill and could no longer care for him. He became lonely and neglected, so he spoke and played with his shadow, the only company he had.

"The sicker his parents became, the longer he would spend conversing with his shadow. As a result, the shadow grew in both size and intelligence. It soon became curious and mischievous. When the child wasn't looking, it would search out the darkness and hide from him." The shadow grew in size and stature on the floor, before vanishing into the dark corners of the room whenever the child's back was turned.

"Finally, his parents succumbed to their illnesses and passed away, leaving the child completely alone with his shadow. By this stage the shadow had turned a malignant black and grown so large and intelligent, it had outgrown the child.

"The shadow wanted nothing more than to disappear amidst the darkness forever, so it began acting out, desperate to break free of the child's mastery over it." The shadow on the floor turned completely black and violently thrashed about, fighting back against the child's every movement like a caged animal.

"As time went on, the shadow's actions grew worse and worse, until one day its rage finally allowed it to breach the barrier between worlds. It lashed out and scratched the child's skin, drawing forth a single droplet of blood, taking it back into the shadow realm as a prize.

"The shadow had never tasted blood before and became drunk with desire, finally realising the untold power and knowledge that the child had purposely kept hidden. Never before had the child felt such betrayal and pain at the hands of his shadow. The child's fear consumed his every thought and he subsequently banished the black shadow from his side once and for all. He cast it out to live all eternity amidst the desolate darkness it craved so desperately."

Asher watched as the shadow disappeared from the child's side, its maniacal laughter echoing in their ears as it went.

"Lonely without his shadow, the child decided to make new shadows out of the things he cherished most dearly: the bark of his favourite tree, the leg of his favourite toy, and the light of the morning sun." Three new colourful shadows—one green, one gold and one blue—emerged by the child's side.

"The three new shadows lived in harmony, helping their creator whenever they could. The child welcomed them and cherished them dearly, conversing and playing with them always. He imparted the knowledge and power of everything he had learnt since the black shadow's departure. Their intelligence and power grew more each day as a result, but it soon became obvious that the golden shadow, made from the morning sun, was the child's favourite.

"He spent more time with it than any of the others, and it

became more powerful than the other two shadows combined, perhaps even stronger than the black shadow. It rewarded the child's attention by bathing him in eternal light, forming a barrier of illumination for all eternity to ward off the one thing the child feared most: the black shadow."

In the centre of the rooftop observatory, the child became immersed in a beam of light. Its brilliance fought back against the encroaching veil of darkness, forcing the blackness back to the far recesses of the room.

"The black shadow had flourished and thrived in its time living free in the darkness, but the light of its golden brother was now encroaching on its darkened domain. Angered by this invasion, the black shadow sought revenge. Fuelled by the lingering memory of the sweet taste of power stored within every drop of the child's blood, the black shadow became consumed by the thought of enacting vengeance. It began stalking the child and its three brothers, plotting and planning vile things from its sinister enclave."

Asher looked down at his feet and saw the black shadowy silhouette return, stalking around the edges of the darkness, circling the child's protective barrier of illumination.

"The black shadow realised the only way to extinguish the light was to destroy his brothers one by one and devour every last drop of the child's blood. Mustering all its strength, the black shadow enacted its plan in the dead of night, when the golden shadow's light was weakest. The black shadow, arrogant in his abilities, carelessly woke its brethren during the attack and was met with violent opposition.

"The three shadows banded together and warred against their darkened brother in order to protect the child. No matter how hard it tried, or what foul tricks it used, the black shadow could never get close enough to the child to fulfil its murderous plan.

"The shadow war waged on for what seemed like an eternity until the child could take no more. Appalled by the constant fighting, the child searched for a solution. He knew he could not destroy the black shadow without also destroying his cherished other shadows in the process. Instead, he chose the only option left available to him and decided to live apart from all his shadows once and for all.

"With the help of the golden shadow, the child fortified the protective barrier of light so it was, and forever would be, indestructible. Inside it, he knew no shadow would be able to follow and, without his presence and the temptation of his blood, the war would end. Or so he thought."

Asher watched as the child became barely distinguishable amidst a pillar of light. All four of his shadows faded away towards the edge of the clearing until they were barely visible.

"And so it was the child and his four shadows parted ways. After a time, the child grew up and forgot about his shadows altogether. So much so, even when he wandered from his sanctuary of light, he could no longer see them, or feel their presence next to him.

"He had become blind to the very shadows he once cherished, and lived out the remainder of his days in blissful ignorance, oblivious of the shadow war raging on around him."

Asher brought up his hand to scratch his head in confusion. As he did so, the darkened dome covering the tower top dissipated and cleared. He nervously glanced around and unwittingly dropped his hand to his side. The darkness quickly returned. Raising his auger back to his head, he turned to look back at the shadows on the floor before him. However, he did not see shadows anymore, he saw a solitary man and four exact replicas standing opposite him, each with a different coloured hue to their skin.

"Do you see that?" Asher whispered to Lem and Lorrelli.

"See what?" Lem whispered back.

"The men."

"What men?" Lorrelli asked, not seeing anything of the sort.

"The shadow-men," Asher whispered, pointing at them with his free hand. "They're standing right there." The four ghostly apparitions seemed oblivious to their recognition, Welticrum however did not.

"Très bonne, Monsieur…" he rested his withered cane against his head, "Bloom. It has been a long time indeed since I have had the distinct pleasure of discovering an apprenti with Deus Ocularis, but the majority of you would probably recognise it by its less formal name: the divine eye. How extraordinary."

Apprentices around the room gasped and swore, murmuring all the more at Welticrum's revelation.

Asher tore his gaze away from the ghostly apparitions and turned to face the old man's voice. The face that looked back at him was not that of Welticrum Rousso.

The haggard old man dressed in dull rags that had stood before him moments ago was gone. A diminutive creature with greyish pale skin stood in his place. His ears almost seemed moulded on the side of his head and a series of curved bones protruded above the visible skin of his exposed, overly long forearms.

"And so you see me clearly, piercing even my most complex projection; though I suspect it's not the first time you've seen through the truth in the world around you." The creature's large black glassy retinas studied Asher carefully. "Strange, is it not, how an altered perception of the world can change everything."

The other apprentices looked about awkwardly until Welticrum, who they could still only see as an old man, addressed them.

"Raise your augers to your head in the same manner as young master Bloom, and do not think about what you see. Instead, focus on what you do not. Should you complete your apprenticeships, you may even be lucky enough to chance a glimpse or two of the apparitions standing here before you, amongst the countless others masking the truth of our world." The man silently chuckled to himself.

"Although the majority of you, much like our human counterparts, will never glimpse what lies beyond our inherent frailty of perception." He dismissed the apparitions in the middle of the room with a wave of his hand, but only Asher actually saw them disappear. Everyone else saw only four shadows and a beam of light fade away into nothingness.

Tapping his cane on the ground, Welticrum also dismissed the darkened dome. It blinked out of existence and the view of Undergall's rooftops returned, much to the relieved delight of the apprentices.

"Harness greater control over your auger, and your ability to see the truth will increase tenfold. Harness it not, and remain blind to the world's hidden wonders, which, by the way, is the clue for the location of our next rendezvous. Adieu."

Many of the apprentices stood scratching their heads in confusion, obviously unaccustomed to such an abrupt end to their instruction.

"Out, out, out." He shooed them away with a bony old hand. "Apprenti Bloom, stay a minute, if you will."

One by one, the apprentices filed out and down the stairwell of the observatory, each casting astonished and fearful glances at Asher, who anxiously remained behind.

Asher lowered his hand to his side as they passed and watched as Welticrum reverted back into the image of the old man, covering his true demonic features.

"So, Monsieur Bloom, care to hazard a guess as to how I managed to pull off this delightfully dark and mysterious parlour trick?" Welticrum Rousso asked with a large smile on his face, as he pointed his weathered cane at the dome of darkness hanging over them.

Asher waited for the last sounds of the apprentices to fade away as they descended down the stairs. "What are you?" Asher could only murmur in reply.

Welticrum chuckled and nodded towards the direction of Lem and Lorrelli who had chosen to stay by Asher's side. "Direct and to the point, I see. I believe your young friend here can answer that particular question and, in doing so, answer mine."

Asher looked at Lorrelli, who could only shrug back at him. Welticrum coughed and nodded towards Lem.

Lem stepped forward and raised his auger to his head. Peering at Welticrum, he looked him up and down, trying desperately to see what Asher did. His eyes were met by the simple sight of an old man, nothing more; his visage didn't even flicker.

"Think back, young master, not all tales told to us by our parents are fiction."

"Papa," Lem paused, remembering an old story once told to him as a young boy by his father. "My father, my real father, told me he once worked with a man that could mask his environment with projections... illusions."

"What else did he tell you?" Welticrum leaned forward and raised a hand behind his ear.

"That only those with the divine eye could see him as he truly was," Lem shyly answered. "He confided his true identity to my biological father after he saved his life during the rebellion."

"And what type of being can do such a feat?"

"A Chromfaddar," Lem whispered under his breath. "But I thought they were a myth."

"Mythology often starts out as fact; but even facts as hard as stone can be diluted and transformed over time. Given enough time, and mythology now stands where facts once held so firmly in mind. A few of us managed to survive the war of false faces, although the vast majority of the Cruaar Nation would never know as much."

"So I'm not going mad," Asher said quietly, "I'm just seeing you as you truly are."

"Such is the blessing, and curse, of Deus Ocularis. I expect you only see the truth when you raise your auger to that rattled noggin of yours, correct?"

Asher nodded as he tested out the theory several times.

"Over time, your sight will strengthen as your ability to control it increases. Then you will begin to see the truth without the need of such an obvious action." Welticrum raised his cane and touched it to Asher's raised hand, lowering it to his side.

Lem and Lorrelli gazed at Asher with amazement, each wondering how one person could be so blessed and cursed at the same time.

"By the way, I was sorry to hear about your father's disappearance, Lem." Rousso nodded his heartfelt condolences. "He was always a loyal friend, ever since he hid me from the Red Scar Guards. He was but a child himself at the time."

"You're the man he saved?" Lem asked incredulously.

Welticrum nodded. "He was also one of the few that knew my secret long before it was safe to be branded Chromfaddar and live to tell the tale."

Lem smiled at the knowledge and the memory of his father.

"So none of this is real?" Lorrelli asked, looking around at the darkened dome.

"Reality is defined by your ability to interpret it. Asher here will be able to interpret a very different reality than the two of you with the gift of the divine eye. Truth is a valuable commodity in a world filled with deceptive falsehoods." He cast Asher a sly wink.

"But where are my manners?" He retrieved a small bottle with a horned top from within his shabby tunic pocket and held it out to Lem. "A horn's worth of whirlpool clarity, well earned."

Lem's face lit up as he received the flask and ran his fingers over the horn.

"Be mindful of its effects, they can be turbulent," Welticrum smiled, winking again.

"Righteous work," Lorrelli smiled and congratulated Lem, slapping him hard on the back with one hand as she twisted the ends of her thin plait with the other.

Lem's fingers briefly fumbled the flask, catching it a split-second later. He stashed it inside his tunic pocket for safekeeping.

"Not a word of this to any other masters or it'll be my head. Not that it is a particularly good-looking head, but I have become quite attached to it," Welticrum smiled and tapped his cane against his temple.

"Sorry, Master Rousso, but we have to get to our next training," Lorrelli apologised as she briefly examined her training session tablet. She dragged Asher and Lem towards the observatory stairwell.

They were already running late.

Welticrum nodded his understanding and let his voice trail after them down the stairwell. "Perception is a frail thing. Trust first in your heart and not what your eyes perceive, apprenti Cruaar… apart from you, of course, Asher Bloom."

CHAPTER 16

A SYMBOL TRAPPED IN STONE

Lorrelli briskly led the way through Mantlecrest's maze of corridors. Faded paintings, ornate statues and wall-length murals decorated a multitude of hallways, corridors and stairwells along the way, but they didn't have the time to inspect them properly.

"I can't believe you have the divine eye, Asher. You know it's one of rarest blood traits in existence, right?" Lem left the question hanging in the air as if he didn't really expect a response.

"I can barely believe it, either. Although it does explain a lot of what I've been seeing," Asher said after a few moments whilst raising his hand to his head and looking around.

"You see anything different now?" Lorrelli asked, looking around the corridor as they walked. Asher shook his head, still trying to test out his newfound ability.

"The divine eye only perceives the truth behind augmented illusions of reality. So unless someone has had a reason to hoodwink this hallway, I doubt that you will see anything different." Lem smirked, shaking his head.

"And how do you know so much about the divine eye?" Lorrelli asked, sceptical of Lem's claim.

"My grandmother was a phantom seer during the Guillotine Rebellion. She told me stories of how the Mortis Skulk would augment their appearance and adopt the face of another to hide in plain sight. At least, she did before she died." Lem's tone became very solemn at the mention of his grandmother's death.

"So it's not genetic or hereditary?" Asher asked, somewhat insensitively.

"Not by a long shot. No-one's ever been able to figure out what causes it, as far as I know," Lorrelli responded. Seeing

Lem's poorly disguised distress at the recollection of his grandmother, she quickly decided to change the subject. "Come on, you two, we've got Basic Augestry with Mistress Catterfract up next, and we're already late," Lorrelli said looking at the small tablet in her hands, snapping Lem out of his train of thought and returning him to reality.

Lem waited for Lorrelli to move ahead before slipping Asher a sly wink and whispering something under his breath so Lorrelli wouldn't hear. "I've heard she's the kind of instructor you want to arrive early for." Rounding a series of corners somewhat hastily, Lem collided with a small man rather heavily and tumbled head over heels. The diminutive man, who had previously been inspecting something on the walls close to the floor, was sent sprawling onto the floor alongside Lem like a rag doll.

"Why do people never watch where they're going?" the man exclaimed gruffly as he picked himself up off the cold stone floor.

"Sorry, I–" Lem stuttered.

"Didn't see you there!" the diminutive man angrily finished Lem's sentence. He turned to look at the three apprentices whilst dusting off his tunic. "Apprentice Bloom, I hope this is not going to be a regular habit of yours."

"Sorry, Master Gobbler, we weren't looking. We just didn't want to be late for Basic Augestry."

"We, is it? And who might this clumsy lout be?" Mason asked as he eyed off Lem and Lorrelli as best he could from his miniature position.

"Sorry," Asher apologised. "This is Lem Bruwell and Lorrelli Wittlearch. Lem, Lorrelli, this is Master Gobbler."

"Mason," the diminutive man corrected, "I am no more your master than he is a tribarion." His waved a hand at Lem, but his eyes lingered for an uncomfortably long time on Asher. When his gaze finally shifted towards Lem's awkward expression, he narrowed his eyes. "Judging from that dumb look strapped to your dial, I take it you've not encountered too many pint-sized encumbrances in your time?"

"Not exactly. Not that you're one, Master… Mason." Lem stammered awkwardly, still embarrassed about his fall.

Mason laughed and slapped his thigh twice, clearly enjoying pushing Lem's uneasiness to new levels. "Damn awkward little git, aren't you? Don't worry. I can't very well blame you for my lack of stature. After all, I do tend to put the Undergall in, well, pretty much everything around here." The small man let out a loud infectious laugh, which caused the trio to chuckle, albeit awkwardly.

"Sorry, sir, but we really must be going," Asher said quickly, making an attempt to leave.

"Nonsense," Mason swatted his leg with a hand, "I happen to know for a fact the Mistress Catterfract is running late admitting a new apprentice.

"How did you…" Lorrelli began, wondering how he knew where they were off to.

Mason ignored her. "Apparently she's a little like you, Master Bloom: rescued from The Blind, and all. So you three are all mine for the next few minutes. Besides, I could use a fresh set of eyes on this infernal slimy mess," he said loudly as his eyes unsettlingly focused on Asher once again.

"Err, what mess?" Lorrelli looked around but could not see to what he was referring.

"Well, you're not likely to see anything from up there, are you?"

Asher, Lem and Lorrelli looked at one another and shrugged, one by one dropping to their knees so they were at Mason's eye level.

"Look closely now and tell me what you see," Mason instructed the trio and rudely kicked the very bottom stone on the wall nearest to the floor. Slowly, all three dropped to all fours and inspected where Mason was indicating. They still couldn't see anything. Mason cleared his throat and nodded his head to the left, indicating a brick next to the one at which they were all looking. Almost instantly, they all saw trace amounts of a damp greenish mould that had broken out along the fine lines of mortar between the stones. "Granted, it's a small outbreak, but explain to me how it is that this darned mould can skip five floors and wind up here with no apparent reason or cause?"

All three apprentices looked at Mason rather awkwardly and shrugged their shoulders.

"Precisely. It baffles the breadcrumbs out of me, too. To make matters worse, there's another petulant outbreak of the gumball-green blighted stuff in the next corridor, as well."

Lem and Lorrelli stumbled to their feet and followed Mason as he quickly pattered off around the corner.

Asher lingered behind for a moment and looked again at the mould, this time raising his auger to his head.

His vision flickered for a moment, and then a small glowing symbol emerged in the corner of one of the stones on the wall. Upon further investigation it became apparent the spread of mould was growing directly outwards in all directions from the strange marking. Asher did his best to memorise the symbol and was in the process of slowly clambering to his feet when he felt a cold clammy hand land on his shoulder. A single icy finger scraped against the skin of his neck. Its touch sent chills up and down his spine.

"I thought it would take you at least a week before your first transgression," the voice paused mid-sentence, and Asher felt a sudden chill running down his spine, "Apprentice Bloom."

The monotonous undertones of Finneus Slink's voice bounced off the walls like a wet drum as he tightened his grip on Asher's shoulder.

Asher slowly turned to face Finneus, bending away from his grip as best he could. "I was—" Finneus cut him off with a wave of his auger, purple and black smoke oozed from its core.

Asher felt his mouth clamp shut.

"You may have tricked your way past my tests, but I alone have seen what lies deep in your soul," Finneus sneered as he snatched Asher's wrist and glared down at his auger. "You're a liar and a thief, Asher Bloom."

He leaned in close, so close that Asher saw every single pore littering the man's deathly pale complexion.

Finneus drew in a deep breath and seemed to revel in the sensation. "And you cannot hide the truth forever."

Asher's auger burned against his skin and the blackened strip that marred his golden gem grew larger under the strain of Finneus's grip. Asher winced in pain and inadvertently narrowed his eyes, as the faintest of smiles twisted upwards in the corner of Finneus's mouth just before he released his grip.

"Ah, Finneus," Mason's loud cheery voice interrupted them.

Asher felt Finneus's deathly pull on his auger ease. "These apprentices were helping me get to the bottom of the wretched mould."

"These apprentices are late for their training, Gobbler," Finneus snapped back at him. "Apprentice Bruwell, get that finger out of your mouth, fool of a boy."

Lorrelli and Asher shot him queer looks, but Lem merely shrugged and sheepishly removed his finger from his mouth; but his teeth still felt furry.

"Hmm, yes, perhaps you are right." Mason made an effort to make it look as if he'd lost track of time. "My mistake, I assure you. It seems I've stalled them here longer than intended. I'm sure I can manage here well enough without you all. Run along now."

Asher needed no invitation to leave. Briskly turning his back on the Master of Mortis, he sped off down the hall with his two friends in tow, leaving a glaring Finneus turning his attention on the diminutive man standing beneath his gaze.

"What was all that about?" Lem asked, rubbing his teeth once more in an attempt to rid himself of their furry sensation.

"Never mind," Asher whispered. "It's nothing."

Lorrelli's and Lem's augers instantly flared brightly with streaks of light, but both were in too much of a hurry to get away from the thought of Finneus Slink's disturbing glare to notice.

CHAPTER 17

BLOOD AND AUGERS

When they finally stumbled into one of Mantlecrest's largest instruction chambers, all the other apprentices had already arrived. The loud murmuring of unsupervised conversation had spread throughout the room and continued until a tall, elegant woman swept through the doorway, her long blonde locks flowing divinely behind her.

She was one of the most beautiful women Asher had ever laid eyes on. A single wave of perfectly straight blonde hair, with auburn-flecked tips, ran down her back to her waist, stopping at a beaded metallic belt that chimed softly as she walked. She seemed to possess an ethereal grace, making her outward appearance almost angelic. Asher raised his auger to his head to see if his eyes were being tricked by an illusion, but her heavenly looks did not diminish or change in the slightest.

A small apprentice followed her in. She was a frail little thing, with shoulder-length black hair cascading down over the left half of her face. Visibly shy, her thin arms, narrow waist and sunken cheeks made her look as if she hadn't eaten in weeks. She kept her hands in her pockets at all times and didn't raise her eyes to look at the other apprentices, despite their curious stares.

"All right, my darlings, settle yourselves." Penveli Catterfract's voice gently carried across the room like the soft strum of a harp, causing all murmur of conversation to fade away. Every pair of eyes in the room was entranced by the rare beauty standing before them.

"I apologise for my tardiness, but my duties to Apprentice Fitch delayed me longer than expected. Morreby, why don't you join the other apprentices?" she asked caringly as she ushered the small girl towards them with the lightest of touches on her shoulder. The small girl shuffled forwards, joining the group that vigorously slapped her on the back and tried to shake her hand. She didn't smile once. Both her hands remained wedged inside her pockets as she shrunk away from the enthusiastic welcoming slaps landing on her back and shoulders.

"The ones from The Blind get weirder every year." Lem whispered in Lorrelli's ear.

Lorrelli frowned and elbowed him hard in the ribs, nodding at Asher.

"He knows what I mean," Lem said defiantly, casting an unsubtle wink of reassurance at Asher.

"Now, my precious young Cruaar, as you may or may not know, my name is Penveli Catterfract, but you may call me Mistress Penny." She gave the nearest girl a warm smile and beamed at everyone else, instantly putting them at ease.

"I heard they started your teachings with Lore and Augers this year. Master Rousso likely knows more about the history of our nation than any other; but history will be of little help without first understanding the circumstances of your present.

"Namely, understanding the precious gift that is your birthright, the same gift you all so graciously adorn yourselves with today." She held up her own auger. It was set in a series of metal swirls interwoven with green vine and floral fixtures.

"One day, soon enough, your auger will be your most valued asset, your deadliest weapon and your most trusted method of defence. Hold them up, if you will."

One by the one the apprentices held up their augers. Asher and Morreby were the last to do so and held their augers half as high as everyone else.

Mistress Penny did not seem to notice. "You should all have an apprentice mantle by now. Understanding how they work is your first step towards achieving more and more powerful blood callings through your augers, so that none of that precious blood of yours is needlessly wasted. Is anyone here without a mantle?"

Only Morreby and Asher raised their hands. Asher raised his

left hand, his normal hand so as not to draw any more attention than necessary.

Mistress Penny held out a fine silver chain to Morreby, similar to the mantles everyone else had hanging from their necks.

Morreby quickly stuffed the chain inside her pocket.

Turning to Asher, Mistress Penny reached into her tunic and pulled out a small box. "I have a special gift for you, Apprentice Bloom, received only moments ago. A unique mantle to suit your unique auger, fashioned by none other than Craftpaw himself at the bequest of Overseer Altier."

The apprentices gasped and scowled at Asher. To own anything handcrafted by the father of all augmented devices was a prize in itself, let alone to have an augineered mantle specifically crafted for you.

Mistress Penny seemed oblivious to the other apprentices' scowls and stood waiting for Asher to open the box. Inside was a small elliptical circlet of gold, crafted in the most intricate of fashions. Several individual bands of gold had been woven around one another in an exotic free-flowing pattern. It was about the size and width of his palm, but Asher didn't quite know what to do with it.

Mistress Penny took the band in her fingers and tenderly reached for Asher's hand.

He was hesitant at first, but his resolve instantly melted at the slightest touch of her skin. She looped one of the circlet's swirls over his thumb, manoeuvred the large interwoven loop over the back of his hand and positioned the open eyelet over his auger. Gently releasing him, she took a step backwards and allowed him to test out his new gilded mantle.

It fitted within his palm perfectly and didn't constrict the movement of his hand at all. If anything, it almost hid the black scar staining the centre of his auger. Asher's smile said it all. For once, he was oblivious to the jealousy and angry looks that most of the other apprentices shot towards him.

Mistress Penny smiled at him warmly before shifting her

attention back towards the rest of the disgruntled apprentices. "Now, who here knows the difference between the four bloodlines: Vita, Scienta, Natura and Mortis?"

A volley of hands shot up.

"Yes, Apprentice Uller?" She pointed to a slightly chubby apprentice near the front.

"Each alignment allows a greater control over the blood callings best attuned to a certain bloodline."

"Absolutely correct, and so well spoken."

The apprentice's cheeks turned a bright shade of red.

"Each of the four alignments is unique. Each has their own purpose, place and use. Each has their own advantages and limitations. Blood callings, on the other hand, are how we call our blood to action. The more basic of which, like turning off an auglight, or commanding the shifting sands of a vertistrand, are common to all bloodlines."

She waved her hand at an auglight, dousing its light, then reigniting it moments later to illustrate the point. She peered around the room to ensure all the apprentices understood her. Not seeing any confused faces staring back, she continued. "However, it takes a more-focused mantle, one that's been precisely imbued with alignment-specific elements, to master the more complex and powerful blood callings."

A small redheaded apprentice raised his hand. "Do bloodlines grow stronger throughout a family over different generations?"

"They can do, yes. Although, there are very few families today that can claim an undiluted lineage. More commonly, bloodlines become altered and mixed through marriages, and other less-condoned practices."

Asher thought he saw her brow droop a little at the last remark, but a second later it was gone. The radiance of her perfect smile, combined with the lustrous shine of her golden, auburn-flecked locks made her positively glow in the centre of the room, as though she'd never known an ounce of unhappiness.

"Of course, there are those among us whose blood will share an affinity with two or more bloodlines. Blessed by what some may call a fortuitous blood anomaly. Bireems are able to call upon the blood arts from the two most common alignments: Natura and Scienta.

"I discovered myself capable of dual blood callings during the sixth year of my apprenticeship. I'm what you might call a late bloomer, but can now harness the blood callings of both bloodlines equally."

The same redheaded apprentice raised his hand again. "Is it true bireems do not live as long as other Cruaar?"

"Yes, Apprentice Rydecky. Sadly, yes. Our bodies are genetically incapable of coping with the debilitating toll that mastery over both bloodlines exacts. Needless to say, the small sacrifice of life is not without its perks."

She produced a seed from within her palm and gracefully placed it on the floor. With auger outstretched, she brought it to life with a dazzling green and blue shafts of light. A stalk sprouted from the seed and grew. It turned into a stem, then split off into a multitude of branches, each sprouting leaves, until finally a flourishing rosebush stood before them. Within seconds the bush was in full bloom, luscious plump roses blooming and releasing their sweet fragrance across the room.

"Each alignment is unique and will grant you mastery over a single domain. Natura will grant you the power over all things natural. Master it and you'll be able to control the smallest of vines to the oldest of oaks."

The rosebush caught alight and burned with a furious blue flame. "It will allow you to harness the weakest of sparks," the rosebush blazed into a towering firestorm, "to the most insatiable of infernos."

When the heat became unbearable, she waved her auger at the air above the highest tips of the flames, causing a small cloud to form. Tiny droplets of water rained down against the oppressive heat, dousing the flames, leaving the bush a smouldering pile of ash. "Natura will allow you to harness the gentlest or most ferocious of natural elements, should you have the strength to master your blood callings and properly focus your mantle with the right elements."

Lorrelli was spellbound by the beauty of it all, as were most of the other apprentices, although some seemed more entranced by Mistress Penny's beauty than the wonder unfolding before them.

"Who here was aligned to the Scienta bloodline? Raise your hands."

Half a dozen or so apprentices did so eagerly, clearly unable to contain their excitement at the prospect of what would happen next.

"Scienta is Natura's modern brother and has been vital to the evolution of our nation, as well as that of mankind when it needed a gentle push in the right direction. It allows one mastery over the unnatural world, namely all things Cruaar and man-made." With a flick of her wrist she produced a large rock from beneath her tunic and placed it on the ground.

"Everything you see within Undergall was first hypothesised, invented and crafted by the finest augineers that have ever lived. From the tool that enabled the seamless cut of stone in the walls, to the auglights that shine down upon them. Our own natural desire to innovate and create has seen Scienta's rise to prominence within the Cruaar Nation, rendering their mechanaug devices a systemic necessity to our everyday survival."

She gently tapped her finger against the rectangular outline of the training-session tablet hidden beneath an apprentice's robes standing nearest her. "Craftpaw Industries is now one of the largest producers of mechanaug devices and is forever blending the boundaries of imagination and reality. However, even the most advanced devices must first be built from raw materials."

She returned her gaze to the stone on the floor. Ever so slowly, tiny droplets of liquid metal wept from the surface of the stone. The rock rapidly halved in size, leaving four distinctive metallic pools on the floor around it. The pools slowly bubbled and solidified, hardening into various objects, each one different to the last. A rough iron pole formed in one pool, whilst various copper cogs and gears emerged in the others.

A third metal pool spun wildly on the floor, eventually crystallising in the shape of a diamond. A forth metallic pool crept over and coated the outside of the iron pole with a strange liquefied metallic substance that glimmered in the light. The original rock from which all pools of liquid had come had long since vanished, the precious ore depleted from its core.

The small collection of copper gears was magnetically drawn inside the hollow of the pole and the diamond-like crystal summoned to its peak. The metallic liquid quickly spread across the outside of the pole and hardened, locking every piece in place. Soon after, the pole's diamond tip grew in luminosity, illuminating the floor around it and causing some of the more excitable apprentices to burst out in a round of applause.

Mistress Penny walked over to the newly created auglight, picked it up and placed it on an empty wall fixture on the side of the room. "The Scienta bloodline has a pivotal role in the reinvention and evolution of our nation. Some of you may even go on to invent something truly breathtaking in your time that will change the way we live. Are there any questions, my lovelies?"

Asher raised his hand and blushed awkwardly when she turned her gaze upon him. "When I first saw a Cruaar in battle his blood was green. Why?"

A few apprentices around the room laughed at the idiocy of the question, but the smile she returned to Asher was almost as disarming as it was reassuring, instantly putting his anxiousness at ease.

"Such an interesting question for one so young and handsome. The physical properties of our blood will change over the course of our lifetimes. It's just one of the mysteriously delightful effects augers have on our body; but you'll learn more about that next year in Auganic Advancements." She held up her hands to her sides, palms outstretched and turned slowly in a circle.

"At the moment you'll all undoubtedly have the most lustrous crimson-coloured blood, as your augers have not yet begun your blood's metamorphosis into a more conducive state," she trailed off, her gaze drawn above the crowd of apprentices. "But this subject will have to wait. It would seem our surprise guest instructor has arrived." Mistress Penny held out her hand to an armour-clad woman who had somehow managed to enter the room without arousing any attention.

She stood in a militaristic pose surveying the small group of apprentices gathered before her. Her face lacked kindness and her skin looked as thick as leather, hardened by decades of warfare, the horrors of which Asher couldn't even begin to imagine. Taking a single step forward, she watched the apprentices closest to her instinctively back away. The look on her face at their natural reaction to her presence could only be described as one of pure revulsion.

Mistress Penny walked calmly across the room to greet her guest. She moved with all the grace and ease of a soft breeze as she glided between the assembled apprentices. Calmly extending her arm towards the silent armour-clad woman, whose eyes were strategically surveying those in the room, Mistress Penny introduced her. "Apprentices, please make welcome Oakrim's First Order Tribarion Roolta."

CHAPTER 18

A ROSE REBORN

"A Tribarion of the First Order is the highest military rank a Cruaar can ever attain," Lem whispered in Asher's ear. "Since the rebellion, there are only ever three of them in existence at any one time: one to command the Tribarion Cohort of each city."

"And she's a woman," Lorrelli interjected with a big smile on her face. "How righteous is that?"

"Penveli, you look lovelier than ever. I wish I could say the same about the spineless herd the legate has passed off as apprentices this year."

Mistress Penny laughed off the remark and stepped aside to allow the visually striking yet fearsome tribarion to take control of the room.

The tribarion marched forward, poking the sides of a rather pudgy apprentice with the tip of her scabbard as she went. "Stand up straight, your swollen gluttony dishonours the insignia stretched upon your breast."

The pudgy apprentice's face went bright red as he puffed out his chest and sucked in his gut.

Asher looked down at his own tunic. Sure enough, a large embroidered symbol of Mantlecrest's coat of arms sat prominently on his chest. The two creatures holding up the shield were completely foreign to Asher, but underneath them was a large banner, inscribed with a single phrase.

Elucidatus Introrsus, Expertis. Asher read the phrase over in his mind a couple of times, but had no idea what it meant. His question was answered for him as his attention was swiftly drawn back to the armoured tribarion at the front of the room.

"Enlighten Within, Without." The woman stood in a relaxed pose with one hand braced on her hip, her crooked elbow wedging an ornate golden helm in place, which was heavily inlaid with ivory. "Decipher its meaning, and you will understand much more than the words can describe." The woman's voice was confident, as was the way she held herself. Her free hand rested comfortably on the hilt of a sheathed sword hanging at her waist. Its scabbard was relatively plain in comparison to the sight of her sculptured golden breastplate, greaves, pauldrons and vambraces shielding the rest of her body.

The gilded armour and militaristic regalia of the Tribarion Cohort was as impressive as it was fearsome, but Asher couldn't help but wonder why the woman needed so much armour.

"Tribarion Roolta has kindly offered to demonstrate the power of the Vita alignment," Mistress Penny's voice chimed out from the rear of the room, "in order to give you an insight into what is required of the guardians that loyally serve our great nation."

The tribarion nodded once to signify she was capable of taking things from here. Her eyes busily scanned the faces of those before her, instinctively taking in every small facet and detail and committing them to memory.

"The insignia I wear proudly on my chest is not one easily attained. It can only ever be earned, never given, and only borne by those worthy of bearing it. If you can prove that you can put the needs of the Cruaar Nation before your own; prove that you are willing to sacrifice; prove you are willing to bleed and, if need be, die in order to protect those who cannot protect themselves, then maybe one day you might wear it, too.

"But be warned, it is not something we wear lightly. So strong and unyielding is a tribarion's devotion, all who join the Cohort do so willingly until death claims them.

"Once the tribarion's oath has been taken, a tribarion relinquishes all ties to their former identity, including friends and family, to become one with the brothers and sisters of the Cohort. Only our last name is preserved to act as a constant reminder of what we have sacrificed in order to serve."

Removing the hand from her scabbard, she struck her fist on the insignia of her breastplate with a loud metallic thud. "To become a tribarion, a Cruaar must be able to master three of the four alignments. Before the Guillotine Rebellion, one could choose any three of the four." A dark expression came over her face.

"But ever since the heinous betrayal of those that chose to follow the Mortis Skulk, led by the power-corrupt murderer Cerebule, tribarion's are now strictly limited to the mastery of Natura, Scienta and Vita." The tribarion's eyes scanned the room as if searching for a specific something, or someone. As her eyes passed over Asher, they narrowed and she frowned; but she said nothing and soon moved on.

Asher didn't realise Morreby Fitch had stepped behind him to hide from the tribarion's gaze.

"The most powerful alignment is Vita, stemming from Vitalsior's own bloodline. To call upon its power is to call upon the very lifeblood of the world that flows through all living things." She held up her hand and drew her sword. Drawing it across her forearm, she sliced a thin cut into her flesh. Blood tinged with gold seeped from the wound, dribbling down her arm and onto the ground.

Without even so much as taking a breath, the auger set within the hilt of her sword radiated with an unnaturally golden reserve of power. Almost instantly the wound closed in on itself, leaving no trace of its existence. "Those that can truly master the blood arts of Vita, and there have been very few in my lifetime, will have access to the most powerful and most elusive of all blood callings." She stepped forward to the pile of ash that had moments before been a flourishing rosebush and let a single droplet of her blood fall atop the burned mound.

After a few seconds, a single sprout grew up from within the mound of ash and germinated. Within seconds the bush had regrown its first leaf, then its first flower until, once again, a brilliant rosebush stood within the centre of the room.

The crowd of apprentices watched the display in awe.

"All life—even life prolonged from death's hand by our blood—is fleeting. Mastery over the forces of life does not, cannot and will not provide its wielder mastery over the inevitability of death." The tribarion let another droplet of blood fall upon the petals of a single rose. Asher watched as the rest of the plant withered and died around it.

A flawless red rose was left sitting amidst the mottled decaying bush. When the droplet of blood rolled off the last of the petal, the rose withered and died alongside the rest of the bush.

"The hand of life is forever balanced by the heavier hand of death. Only one born of the Vita bloodline can sustain, revive, and in certain circumstances elongate life, but even they cannot bring back something claimed by death. Even the greatest Cruaar, who have mastered the Vita bloodline and prolonged the hand of death from claiming them, have not been able to stop its tyrannical hold entirely, although many have tried. In the end, everyone dies."

A loud applause accompanied the end of the tribarion's speech. "Bravo, Tribarion Roolta. Oh, how I do so love a theatrical presentation," Mistress Penny exclaimed.

The tribarion merely nodded before she sheathed her sword and strode out of the room.

As she left, Asher felt her eyes turn towards him, penetrating the depths of his soul, as if she could see right through him. He shuddered and shook himself free of the alienating feeling. Whilst Mistress Penny was busy answering questions at the front of the room, the trio moved to the side of the space to talk in private.

"She gave me the absolute creeps. If that's what all tribarions are like, count me out," Lem shuddered.

"Agreed," seconded Asher.

"Trust you two to be intimidated by a powerful woman. She was righteous," Lorrelli mocked, still slightly enamoured with the powerful tribarion.

Mistress Penny's voice gently sung out, interrupting their hushed conversation. "Now, apprentices, by the door you will find a pile of seeds and rocks. I suggest you pair up: Natura with Scienta, and so forth. If there are any leftovers or double-ups, never mind, just grab whoever is closest and try to mimic the blood callings you have just witnessed in your allocated training rooms later. Apart from the tribarion's demonstration, what you have seen here are two of the most basic of power exertions. Both you should all be able to master by the next time we meet. Now, off you go, my darlings."

"We'd probably best stick together," Lorrelli said.

"Yeah, like anyone else is going to pair up with us," Lem mockingly agreed.

"Err, who wants the rock and who wants the seed?" Asher asked.

"I'm Natura, so I should take the seed," Lorrelli said quickly, scooping up the seed with a cheeky smile across her face before anyone could object.

"Naturally," Lem said mockingly as he picked up the rather heavy stone and stashed it in his pocket, causing one side of his tunic to sag.

Just as they were leaving, Asher caught a glimpse of Mistress Penny kneeling down in front of Morreby Fitch and whispering something in her ear. "What do you think that's about?" Asher asked the other two.

"No idea, but there is definitely something off about her," Lem answered, looking at the pair suspiciously.

Surprisingly, even Lorrelli agreed. "I thought I was the only one to notice."

Asher felt strangely drawn to the girl for some reason, but chose not to share this feeling with the others.

"Hurry up, you two," Lem piped up, "we've got Mortis and Mortality next with Finneus Slink and if there is one training I am not going to be late for, it's his."

Asher lost sight of Morreby Fitch as they left the room, but he just couldn't shake a bad feeling from the back of his mind about the small black-haired girl that kept stealing odd glances at him.

CHAPTER 19

THE CATACOMB CATHEDRAL

"So where is Slink's training held then?" Asher asked.

Lorrelli pulled out her schedule stone and scanned down the inscriptions until she reached 'Mortis and Mortality'. She stopped short in her tracks.

"What's wrong?" Lem asked impatiently with his back to them, his mood darkening for no apparent reason as he turned around.

"It's in the Catacomb Cathedral."

"Oh haccing prell," Lem swore.

"What's the Catacomb Cathedral?" Asher asked, a little lost.

"It's, err…" Lorrelli fumbled over her words, searching for the best way to put things.

"It's where we keep our dead," Lem said bluntly, almost to the point of indifference, "or, at least, where Mantlecrest keeps theirs."

"What, like a tomb?" Asher asked, trying to better understand.

"Tombs have doors, vaults and coffins; the Cathedral splays out the dead like they're decorations!" Lorrelli blurted out, trying to cover her obvious anxiety in a false show of anger.

"Whoa, alright," Asher held up his hands and backed away.

"I'm sorry. It's not you, Asher. It's…" Lorrelli choked up and could barely get out a word.

"Where you're from, it's customary to bury your dead, right?" Lem yawned unceremoniously.

"Or cremate them." Asher nodded, he wasn't quite sure where this exchange was headed.

"We, the Cruaar, see burial after death as a great dishonour. It's only done for those deemed traitors by the council and, even then, only after they've been bled dry and decapitated."

"I don't understand. What's that got to do with anything?"

"Well, our dead are laid to rest in their ancestral catacombs, either under their own home or that of the city they served. The Catacomb Cathedral holds the remains of all the apprentices and masters that have died here, or those that have a lasting connection to Mantlecrest. There they remain, underneath the protection of a Tutela Sky, until they are nothing more than dust and ash."

"What's a Tutela Sky?" The name meant nothing to Asher, but he could see Lorrelli visibly shudder at its mere mention.

Lem, on the other hand, smiled widely and shook his head ever so slightly. "One of the coolest and creepiest things you'll ever see. Come on," Lem's momentary indifference shifted into a grin as he took the lead from Lorrelli, navigating ever deeper into the maze-like entrails of Mantlecrest, whispering a warning over his shoulder as he went. "I hope you have a strong stomach, I've heard that if you're not used to... well, death, the Catacomb Cathedral can be praccing hard to handle."

"Are you?" Asher asked curiously.

"Am I what?" Lem replied merrily, not understanding the question.

"Used to death?" Asher clarified, unsure of why Lem would be used to such a morbid thing.

"I've been inside our ancestral bloodline's tomb. Saw heaps of the dead in there, so I guess I'm more used to it than some," Lem answered, after giving it a moment's thought.

Asher winced as a momentary stab of pain flared up his arm, sparking from his auger. Lorrelli's auger flashed with light, too, but it was out of sight, buried beneath her tunic. Asher gripped his hand into a fist and waited until the pain passed.

Lorrelli silently shot him a brief 'are you okay?' look, but he shook his head at her to dismiss her concern. She put a hand on Asher's shoulder anyway. "None of us are used to dealing with death," Lorrelli said, forcing the words through quivering lips.

"We were too young to experience what it was like during the Rebellion; but from the stories I've heard, the dead were everywhere. The Mortis Skulk and their conspirators were strung up in cages in the streets, their arteries severed, left to bleed out and rot. The bodies were only buried after every single drop of blood had drained from their limbs, pooling and stagnating in the streets, staining the cobblestones black."

"A constant reminder of the evil that our nation faced," Lem quoted part of a speech he had heard as a boy, deepening his voice to add a greater effect to his haunting words.

"I was only a baby when the last of the Mortis Skulk were hunted down and executed," Lorrelli whispered. Her face echoed the grave memory plaguing her mind. "But I can still remember the stench of their blood on the cobblestones."

"But why hold our training in such a horrible place if it causes so much pain?" Asher shook his head, unable to grasp why anyone would want to subject themselves to that sort of environment.

Lem answered first. "The council decided the ever-present reminder of death would keep us vigilant against the threat that the Mortis Skulk might rise again one day."

"That's barbaric," Asher exclaimed.

Lem and Lorrelli just looked at him, unable to understand what point he was trying to make. Lorrelli looked as if she was about to say something when Lem continued his explanation.

"Asher, the Overseer himself instigated the new regime Mantlecrest follows. It was his decree that even apprentices must be able to handle themselves in the face of death. That way, if the Mortis Skulk ever surface again, we wouldn't be struck dumb by the sight of death and would be properly able to protect ourselves."

Asher said nothing, but swallowed hard. He'd never seen a dead body before, let alone been close enough to touch one. He was about to enquire further about what Lem meant by 'new regime', but Lem was already on the move, ushering Lorrelli along.

"Come on, then, time's a-wasting, and the dead wait for no man."

The three rapidly descended down the spiral stairwell into the depths of Mantlecrest's catacombs. Soon enough, the passageways grew narrower and the stonework became noticeably older than any other Asher had seen. A strong stale smell hung in the air like a fetid blanket, but Asher couldn't place the hostile odour, nor was he entirely sure he wanted to.

"How exactly do you two know where to go all the time, anyway?" Asher asked as they hurried along a dimly lit corridor.

"Oh, right," Lem mumbled over his shoulder, he had his finger in his mouth again, rubbing the back of his teeth. He withdrew it with a loud slurp. "Think I still got some chicken in there from last night." Asher's auger flared again, but he ignored it as Lem grabbed him by the shoulder and apologised.

"Sorry, we should have said earlier. Your auger can lead you to anywhere you want to go if you can provide it with a suitable reference point."

"Reference point?"

"Just think about where you want to go and touch your auger to a relevant reference point." Lorrelli interjected, which seemed to ease her agitation slightly. "In this case, our training tablet acts as such, but a reference point can be anything linked with a location, an object, a memory... Then simply hold up your auger and watch to see what direction it indicates. It can't lead you to a specific person or a faraway location, but it works a treat if you are looking for an object or someplace nearby."

Asher watched as Lorrelli enacted her instructions to the letter. Her auger changed from a dull green to a bright lime colour when she passed it over one of the passageways.

"Is there anything they can't do?" Asher smiled as he repeated the act with his own auger. It sprang to life, sending a dull warmth up his arm as he mimicked Lorrelli's actions.

"Don't get too excited. It's still leading us to the Catacomb

Cathedral," Lem reminded him glumly, his mood once again shifting for the worse.

"What's going on with you, anyway?" Asher asked him. "You're all over the shop."

"Whatever," Lem sniggered. "You try dealing with this and then come speak to me." He held up his dull grey auger and marched off.

Lorrelli shrugged at Asher but said nothing. Finally, as they entered the last hall before the Cathedral's only entrance, dimly lit augers outstretched before them, Asher wondered why he hadn't seen any dead bodies. He took another few hesitant paces, keeping his curiosity to himself as his eyes wandered over the ornately carved indentations on either side of the hall.

"Oh my–" Lorrelli clasped a hand over her mouth and nose.

Lem was already bent over double, with both hands over his face when Asher ran past the column to their aid.

"What is it?" Asher didn't need them to answer. Immediately after stepping past the column, he felt a cold shiver pass over his skin. He was hit in the face by an oppressively rank odour.

It overwhelmed his senses.

Coughing and gagging he tried to cover his mouth and nose as best he could, but the smell was too much. He clamped his eyes shut and had to struggle to fight off the urge to retch at the repellent smell.

Battling against teary eyes himself, Lem grabbed Asher's free hand and placed it on his shoulder, motioning for him to do the same for Lorrelli. He then led them towards the last narrow doorway before the main hall.

Stepping under the doorway's arch, Asher peered around for the source of the repulsive scent. Inhaling the smallest of breaths through his mouth, he clamped his nose shut with two fingers and blinked his eyes repeatedly before looking around.

They were inside a large, hollow hall, edged with high stone colonnades. The room extended into the darkness. The arched entrances to a series of adjoining wings disappeared down either side of the hall's wide space.

Asher had no idea how far back the hall actually extended, but as his eyes adjusted to the light, he found something else far more horrific on which to focus: the strewn remnants of human remains were everywhere. Something snapped under his feet as he walked. Looking down, he saw the entire floor was covered in bones, some noticeably older and more brittle than others. Rib cages, pelvises and skulls littered the floor in every direction; in some areas bone piles had been stacked high upon the ground.

Some parts of the room were so densely covered in bones and rotting sinew that the stone pillars and alcoves seemed almost entirely constructed from the rotting remains of the dead. Perhaps they were.

Bones, however, were not the only thing that lined the walls. More recently deceased bodies had been laid to rest in large recesses around the walls. Decaying flesh slowly deteriorated against skeletal frames, bedraggled hair overgrew mottled faces, with teeth bared against the damp cold's bite. Whilst each corpse had been placed to rest in what looked like a peaceful pose, the flickering of nearby candles made their gaunt features all the more haunting.

In a small wing off the main hall, a crowd of apprentices were gathered around a large altar. It appeared to be constructed predominantly of human skulls haphazardly stacked upon one another with harrowing skeletal fingers of gruesome hands mortaring them in place.

A few of the more punctual apprentices had already vomited on the floor. Others were dry retching and gagging, trying to cover their mouths and noses with their tunics as best they could. There was no furniture in the wing, nor were there as nearly as many bones littering the floor as in the main hall. The large skull altar stood watch over a wide depression in the floor.

To Asher, the entire wing and lower circular floor looked very much a like a cultist's ritual circle. Its recessed centre had been paved with an ancient selection of stone, intricately inlaid with fragments of bone creating a concentric mosaic of death on the floor. The mosaic's design sat directly under a large chandelier made entirely of rib cages and strangely shaped skulls, all of which were illuminated by the firelight of candles nestled deep within the hollow cores of the skulls.

Asher gasped in surprise as his eyes travelled higher again. He saw a floating, rippling liquid that covered the entire roof. The dark substance swirled and undulated on the ceiling like a calm sea, occasionally flashing with flares of green and blue as if it something was living within the flood.

"The Tutela Sky," Lem said under his breath after looking at his friend's gobsmacked face.

"What is it?" Asher wondered out loud. As his eyes adjusted to the dimly lit ceiling, he noticed small droplets of different-coloured liquids suspended within the air beneath it, all slowly rising up only to disappear within the sea bed enveloping the roof. Looking around the gruesome wing, he saw more of the tiny droplets, all suspended in space slowly levitating upwards. His eyes worked their way down the room, until they saw a small droplet of bluish liquid escape from the decaying corpse to the side of the room.

In that moment, Asher realised the Tutela Sky was made entirely of blood leached from the countless dead bodies entombed within the harrowing cathedral. He instantly had to fight back another violent urge to be sick.

Lorrelli watched Asher's features as the horrid realisation washed over his face. "It guards the blood of the dead from the living." Lorrelli trembled, obviously terrified. "Some say it enslaves the souls of all those under it."

"Such farcical lies dishonour the dead," a harsh and unforgiving voice bellowed from the darkness, interrupting Lorrelli and effectively silencing the room.

"And the dead never respond well to insult."

CHAPTER 20

THE TUTELA SKY

The menacing form of Finneus Slink stood as still as the legions of the dead around him. His glum figure loomed behind the altar like a shade of the underworld. It was clear that he relished the dank environment, as he basked in the obvious terror of those around him.

His eyes were dark opals of despair. Looking at his face in the flickering candlelight was like looking at the face of the Grim Reaper itself. From within their sunken trenches, his eyes watched the living cower away from the dead as the apprentices latched on to one another's hands in a feeble attempt at reaffirmation of life.

Nobody spoke. No-one even so much as uttered a sound. Somehow, Asher felt strangely relieved. For once there was something more powerful than his presence on which people could focus. He felt Lorrelli's fingernails dig into the skin of his hand. Her body was visibly shaking and her fingers trembled. Her terrified expression barely even conveyed the depths of fear terrorising her mind.

Asher and Lem tightened their grip on her hands in an attempt to comfort Lorrelli, but their efforts did very little to aid her. Even Asher had to swallow down a small amount of fear as his senses dealt with the vast medley of death around him.

Finneus Slink's raspy voice echoed out across the room, causing trace amounts of settled dust to dislodge from the surface of the chandelier ominously hanging above the centre of the deathly mosaic. "Each and every Tutela Sky has been fashioned by a master of Mortis. Created out of necessity during the rebellion, it serves a single purpose: to protect the blood of the dead from the necrotic corruption of the living: the corruption of

Decisus Umbra."

Finneus leaned against the altar of bone as he would a dining table, as if it was the most common thing in the world. His gaunt cheeks exhaled stale air from his lungs and drew in yet another mouthful of the fetid stench. Picking up the skull of a small child in his hands, he gently stroked it with his fingertips as someone would a newborn babe.

"This place will evoke many emotions. The mere smell alone will instil sensations of revulsion, disgust and despair." He walked around the altar stroking the skull in his hands, the fingertips of his bone-embraced glove scraping over the skull with a coarse scratching sound.

"The power that death holds over the living is unpredictable. It weighs differently on us all. It is this fact alone that provided the Mortis Skulk with their greatest weapon of all: fear." Finneus spat the remark at the group of apprentices and meandered around the wing. Weaving his way between the various pillars of bone, his sinister features caught the light of the flickering candlelight, making his gaunt face even more unearthly.

"You must learn to master any fear your heart bears towards death. Your emotions will betray you if not controlled." He surveyed the group of frightened apprentices visibly trembling before him, hands and tunics pulled over their mouths and noses.

"The putrid smell gagging your airways cripples your ability to think and act. However, counter the smell of death and you will no longer be held hostage by it. Now do as I do." He raised his auger to his nose and muttered a single word: "Anoksium."

Instantly, his auger flared a brilliant purple and his nostrils clamped shut, only to slowly reopen with a fine veil of translucent skin covering both holes.

Apprentices everywhere attempted to do the same, some succeeding on the first try, others managing a single nostril, but for most nothing happened. One apprentice, who did not have his auger correctly positioned, started to panic when his mouth refused to open.

Asher followed Finneus's instruction to a tee and was breathing easier moments later. It took Lorrelli a little longer, but she eventually succeeded as well. Lem, on the other hand, failed miserably to master the blood calling. After an initial objection when Asher attempted to aid him in the task, the smell became too much to deal with and he finally conceded to Asher's help.

Finneus worked the room like a seasoned instructor, correcting the mistakes of those that failed with a flippant wave of his hand.

"I can't smell anything," Apprentice Slew declared happily after Finneus fixed his bungled attempt.

"Remove the sensory advantage the dead hold over the living and you may live long enough to muster a proper defence." Finneus stopped cradling the skull for a moment and set it down upon a nearby ledge, before slowly walking back into the centre of the room. Raising his auger above him, he ever so slowly drew forth a floating trickle of bluish blood from somewhere within the Tutela Sky rippling overhead. The blood dripped down onto the chandelier, inching its way down over a multitude of hanging bones. "The Mortis Skulk are undoubtedly the greatest threat the Cruaar Nation has ever faced. They existed and thrived without our knowledge, recruiting and swelling their ranks for many years before they were first discovered.

"They were masters of deception and held their secrets tight, behind locked lips. They masked themselves from detection using the very gravest and insidious subset of blood callings: Decisus Umbra."

"I've heard that term before. What's Decisus Umbra?" Asher whispered.

Lem was about to mutter a response when Finneus Slink's disquieting gaze swung around, levelling his black sunken eyes at them both. "Do not confuse the mastery of Mortis with the corrupted sickness that is Decisus Umbra. Where Mortis is the counterpoint calling of Vita, Decisus Umbra is a dark and twisted subset of the Mortis bloodline. It alone is responsible for the vile and forsaken necrotic blood arts that violate the blood of the dead."

Finneus stared intently at one set of remains in particular, lying just within the edges of his sight. Lowering his gaze to the floor, he turned his back on the remains and clicked his fingers, igniting a series of once-unlit candles intermittently strewn amongst the bones around the edges of the room. "It was not until one group of cultists in particular decided to kidnap, torture and mutilate the daughter of a lowly Cruaar official that suspicion was first cast upon their murderous world of deceit and atrocity.

"In retaliation, the council launched an investigatory task force—what you so commonly know now as the Tribarion Cohort—to uncover those responsible. It was not long before they discovered the blighted existence of the Decisus Umbra cultists and their conspirators within our society.

"As their investigation continued, more and more murders and disappearances were linked to the cultists. Many hundreds more went missing without a trace, victims of their sordid necrotic rituals."

Lorrelli and several other apprentices stifled back obvious signs of discomfort, but Finneus paid their fractured emotions no heed. "While their numbers were many, their sects were as divided as the human nations above. Eventually, the bloodshed, disappearances and murders reached a point where the council was forced to act.

"They outlawed the practice of Decisus Umbra, branding any and all Cruaar that practiced it traitors and kin-slayers. Their punishment? Blood leeching and beheading in the streets." Finneus drew a finger across both his wrists and then his neck.

"The first public beheading of an entire cultist group fell on what is now referred to as the Mortis Dawn, but the council was ill prepared for the aftermath that followed. It served as a catalyst, sparking the start of a vicious rebellion that brought our nation to its knees." Finneus spun on his heels, his sunken hawk-like eyes conveying the tortured agony of the past.

His skin was pale and his body bent, but somehow Asher could sense that a dark power lay dormant within: a sleeping malevolence yearning to wake. He got chills just looking at the man, as did many others, judging by the looks on their frightened faces.

"The cultists were infuriated at the slaughter of their ilk and retaliated in kind. At first, the attacks were manageable and the might of the newly assembled Tribarion Cohort was able to hold them at bay, but even they could not imagine the magnitude of the storm building against them.

"In the face of a much more powerful enemy, the cultist sects unified behind the sadistic leadership of one man—Cerebule—a vile tyrant that unified their splintered ranks into one united army of death and shadow."

A few apprentices mumbled muffled prayers to their ancestors at the mention of Cerebule's name.

"Soon, all but the rarest and most obscure sects were under his command. A dark army rose from the shadows and waged their war against us. There were more of them then the council ever thought possible. They were everywhere.

"Somehow, they'd managed to infiltrate every business, every house, even the council itself. Masking their identities with their foul blood arts, they would walk among us. Their true allegiance unknown and unseen, until the moment they betrayed their own bloodline to slaughter.

"Our cities became locked in an endless cycle of treachery, deceit and horror. No-one knew who to trust. The very fabric that held our society together was shredded into non-existence.

"Neighbours turned on neighbours, brothers on sisters, mothers on sons. Darkness and death swept through our cities like a plague."

An apprentice from the back of the room timidly raised her hand. "How did they stop it?"

"When hope was almost lost, a single man came up with a solution: one that would turn the tide against the Skulk pandemic.

Tyranus Ranpumk was only a lowly custodian of the Augestry when he first set out—into The Blind of all places—in search of a way to unveil the traitors so we might stand a chance of survival.

"By the time he returned, two cities had already fallen, and another was on the brink of collapse. His ingenuity in reverse-augineering the science behind human-genome sequencing unveiled what our greatest minds had overlooked: a simple test of blood that could not be corrupted or masked by augmentation, trickery or deception.

"A test that revealed any traitor whose blood had been corrupted by the necrotic practices of Decisus Umbra by scarring their auger with the taint. A single black scar that revealed the necrotic allegiance infecting their souls, much like the one Apprentice Bloom's auger bears today."

All eyes in the room swung to Asher. He kept his auger tightly clenched and hidden within the palm of his hand.

"Fortunately, you have all been tested and cleared of the taint. The test has been built into our Ceremony of Alignment and I have even have a test up my sleeve for Apprentice Bloom, which will prove he is no more a Mortis Skulk cultist than Overseer Altier." Finneus paused and raised a single eyebrow, then lowered the other, one beady eye scanning the room.

Asher swallowed in trepidation; he didn't think he was going to like Finneus's test.

Lem reassuringly bumped shoulders with him and nodded his support, but said nothing.

"But we'll get to that. Needless to say, the greatest threat our nation's ever known was not the evil that walked amongst it, but our ignorance of it." From somewhere within his tunic, Finneus drew a glossy black orb about the width of his palm. Its surface had been ornately inlaid with gilded fragments of bone and etched with archaic symbols that glimmered as they caught the candlelight. "Does anyone know what this is?" Finneus asked holding forth the object in question.

At first nobody said anything. A few seconds passed until Morreby Fitch raised her hand. Finneus leered at the gaunt black-haired girl and sharply nodded his head.

"A carcerion," Morreby's feeble voiced spluttered. Even in the claustrophobic silence of the cathedral wing, her frail voice was barely audible.

"Correct. Carcerions were the council's initial answer to the Skulk pandemic. A portable prison fashioned by the Elder Council from the very bones of our most powerful fallen tribarions.

"Easy to carry, easy enough to conceal, each carcerion was designed to ensnare and imprison a single traitorous entity. Protected by three individual seals—a seal of bone, a seal of blood and a seal of judgement—it was near impossible for any skulk cultist to free their captured brethren once imprisoned.

"Imprisonment within a carcerion is a more horrid fate than even I could inflict upon my enemies. It is an eternal sentence, unless someone is able to break all three seals." Finneus swung the ball around the room, holding it high for all to see.

"This particular carcerion houses a traitorous Skulk cultist captured at the very beginning of the rebellion. After imprisonment for such an extended period of time, this soulless turncoat will now hold but a shadow of his former strength and will have undoubtedly lost his mind. Even so, he'd still be able to kill every one of you, should you prove unable to defend against his attacks."

Finneus tapped the side of the orb with a single finger three times. "To release an imprisoned entity from a carcerion you must break the three seals. Only a unique keystone will unlock the seal of bone. Only the blood of the one who imprisoned it will break the seal of blood and, finally, only a Cruaar free of Decisus Umbra corruption will shatter the seal of judgement."

Finneus sneered wickedly as his beady eyes flashed with excitement around the room. "Normally, these three things would never be permitted to come together in the same room as the carcerion itself, but normality is sorely lacking in the minds of anyone who would see such a soul freed."

In a blur of motion his hand lashed out from his side, his bone-embraced auger igniting with purple brilliance at his unspoken command. The skull he'd set down earlier flew through the air and into his outstretched hand.

"In this case, the keystone happens to be set inside the skull of this unfortunate whelp." He yanked a tooth from its jaw and callously discarded the skull on the floor. Calmly inserting the tooth into a small depression in the carcerion's side, a loud whirring sound filled the room, followed by an abrupt click. The gilded fragments of bone that had lain flush on the carcerion's surface sprang outwards and locked into place like a set of jagged teeth.

Nearly all of the apprentices took a step backwards, edging away from Finneus's bent figure in the centre of the deathly mosaic. Before Asher had time to react or step away, Finneus was on him in the blink of an eye, dragging him by the arm into the centre of the room.

Lem and Lorrelli's jaws dropped as their surprise overwhelmed their senses, watching on powerlessly as Asher was thrust into the limelight again.

"Apprentice Bloom claims to be free from all Decisus Umbra corruption and will therefore break the judgement seal." Finneus paused a moment before plunging the glossy black carcerion with the gilded spike exterior into Asher's palm.

"Should he not, however…" Finneus left the threat hanging in the dead air. The inky substance just beneath the surface of the carcerion churned. The swirling darkness inside slowly fading, dissolving entirely within the glass, leaving nothing behind but a clear crystal orb and golden fragments of bone.

Asher felt compelled to peer inside the glass of the spiked orb, searching its depths for the soul imprisoned inside. Lifting the orb closer to his face, he made out a shape growing in size deep within centre of the orb, until a haggard and distorted face rushed towards the glass and mouthed a silent tormented scream against the surface.

The circle of startled apprentices swore and backed away even farther at the sight, but Asher couldn't.

Finneus's hold over him made it impossible to do anything. "And so the judgement seal is broken, as is any wavering doubt about your allegiances, Apprentice Bloom. Congratulations."

Asher wanted to be relieved, but he felt anything but. Finneus's iron grip on his arm refused to let him drop the carcerion or back away, so he did the only thing he could and stared back at the unnaturally gaunt face of madness. Its venomous gaze sneered back at him maliciously, locked inside the orb.

"As for the seal of blood," Finneus craned his neck and searched above him for the trickle of blood he'd summoned from within the Tutela Sky earlier. His eyes latched on to it just as it was about to fall from the bottom of a rib cage on the underside of the chandelier. "It was none other than Tribarion Tetrom that incarcerated this pathetic cultist all those years ago."

A single drop of blue-tinged blood fell from the bottom of the bone chandelier. Finneus swung Asher's hand holding the carcerion beneath the path of the falling droplet of blood. Asher couldn't have resisted against the man's strength if he wanted to. Despite his gaunt appearance, Finneus was as strong as an ox.

Lem and Lorrelli could only watch on in abject horror as the scene unfolded before them.

Through Asher's eyes, however, the world moved in slow motion. His breath caught in his chest. His heartbeat faltered. He could even feel the dribble of sweat, sliding along the crease of his brow, stop in its tracks. His terrified eyes watched on as the drop of blood sped through the air towards the outstretched carcerion. Asher's mind silently prayed it would miss, though his heart knew it wouldn't.

The disfigured face of the cultist raged with murderous excitement and shook wildly inside the orb as it watched the droplet of blood race towards him. Though no-one could hear his poisonous screams, Asher could feel the cultist's homicidal energy intensify in the palm of his hand.

After what seemed like an eternity, the droplet of blood splashed down on the topmost surface of the carcerion. It did not bounce or splatter, but fell through the glass and disappeared inside the orb, rapidly diffusing until no trace of it remained.

"So breaks the blood seal."

Even though Finneus's voice was calm beyond measure, his words pierced Asher like a poisoned arrow. He released his unbreakable grip on Asher's wrist and the apprentice let go of the orb as he stumbled backwards, falling over his own heels in a terrified attempt to get away.

The orb pulsated and smoked as it fell to the floor. A maniacal face cackled and howled insanely every inch of the way down. This time everyone heard his screams. The carcerion collided with the deathly mosaic on the floor with such force it shattered on contact, its contents exploding outwards in a cloud of dust, flames and smoke.

A deafening bang filled the room and the air was filled with the sounds of wild, bloodthirsty laughter. The silhouette of a small, shrivelled man stood in the centre of the debris cloud, laughing wildly and howling upwards in lunacy like an animal. He flexed his fragile limbs for a second and tensed his aching muscles.

The apprentices in front of him scattered away from his wild gaze.

Asher instinctively scrambled backwards, flinging small fragments of bone in every direction as his feet struggled for traction, his eyes locked on the shrivelled man stretching his muscles, his head jerking manically from side to side.

In an instant, the behaviour of the cultist changed. His body stopped moving entirely, as if his senses had just been alerted to something important: something dangerous. His head twisted around over his left shoulder, until Asher could see the creases in one of his closed eyes and the quiver if his nostrils as they drank in the scent of death.

He sniffed the air like a feral dog, his senses honing in on one scent in particular. Finally, his feet shuffled around until he was directly in front of Asher. His face was skeletal and harrowing, almost like the more recent of corpses lining the walls around him. One tooth was permanently locked over a deformed bottom lip, whilst a large iron spike pierced the bridge of his nose and extruded to the edges of his eyes. A revolting black tattoo ran down the left side of his face, its pattern extending over disfiguring scars that ensured his left eye would never open again. With one final deep inhalation, his good eye blinked open.

Asher felt the fear bubbling away in his stomach leap up to his chest.

The cultist's depraved cycloptic gaze had eyes only for him. A large gob of saliva dribbled down the man's chin as his lips parted, his garbled voice barely audible as it escape his throat.

"Hello, Vita…"

In the blink of an eye, an enormous black shadow erupted from the man's chest. It quickly engulfed both the cultist and the deathly mosaic in an impenetrable nightmarish cloud. The cultist's maniacal laughter and high-pitch wails echoed around the cathedral's side wing, spreading chaos and fear amongst the apprentices.

A single blood-red eye ignited into existence and Asher heard the cultist's lungs rattle as it drank in the fetid smell of the dead polluting the air. The glowing eye arched back and black tendrils stretched ominously outwards, preparing to attack. A horrendous bone-chilling laughter resonated from within the veiled darkness, bouncing back and forth off the bodies of the dead as the cultist worked himself up into a homicidal frenzy.

A hellish red glow popped back into view amidst the hovering darkness as the cultist's head snapped downwards, claws outstretched, ready to kill.

Then it lunged.

PART III

AUGEFACTS AND INFILTRATORS

"Mastering fear is only the first step
In the very tall stairwell of survival.
Regrettably, and often,
Leeches are carried to heights undeserved
On the back of heroes and villains alike."

Anonymous
Prison cell wall-etching
Foreguard excavation site no.73
Date unknown

CHAPTER 21

A NIGHTMARE RELIVED

Apprentices everywhere screamed and tumbled backwards over one another, all desperately scrambling to get away from the surging black cloud engulfing the insane cultist.

The cultist, completely immersed in a billowing black-blood veil, laughed maniacally as he lunged at Asher.

Asher instinctively raised his hand and auger in self-defence, when Finneus held up his hand at the shadowy wraith, his auger pulsing wildly with violent bursts of purple light, its core fuelled by the power of his blood. Instantly, the wavering shade stopped in its tracks, imprisoned by Finneus's auger.

"Fear is a Skulk's primary weapon, so yours must be controlled at all times. Embrace it and it will be the last thing you ever do," Finneus Slink's merciless voice cut through the cultist's insane howls like a bandsaw.

Asher was the only one still within the cultist's reach. His instinct to attempt to defend himself had negated his opportunity to retreat to the far walls where all the other apprentices watched on in terror.

Some even pressed themselves hard up against the decaying corpses rather than be any closer to the cultist's wavering black shroud than they had to be.

"What you see before you is the wretched form of a Cruaar corrupted by Decisus Umbra. At the centre of this vile shroud of necrotic blood lies nothing more than the pitiful body of the Mortis Skulk cultist you saw moments ago. Only true cultists, well versed in the arts of Decisus Umbra, can project their corrupted blood in such a way and maintain a wraith-like state.

"The more powerful the cultist's mastery over the necrotic arts, the more control they have whilst enveloped in the shroud. The less powerful they are, the less control they have over their own mind. Even now, his mind rots, his own corrupted blood eating away at his body and will eventually turn him into little more than a feral beast: a wandering dark, his mind forever lost in shadow, consumed by corrupted blood."

Finneus approached the glowering blood-red eye of the wraith and smiled evilly. Leaning in closer, he returned the cultist's hatred with a glare of contempt.

"Wandering darks are desolate and dangerous creatures, incapable of reason. They know only violence. They are mindless, forsaken souls, forever cursed to wander the darkness without thought, feeling or remorse. They feed on whatever they can, but are never able to satisfy the ravenous hunger of their own corrupted blood until, eventually, their bodies wither and die."

The shadowy figure bucked under the control of Finneus's bone-embraced auger, testing the strength of the man keeping him from his kill. Finneus paid it no attention, his strength more than a match for the weakened wraith thrashing about violently under his yoke. "Luckily, we have someone here, other than myself, who has weathered the unadulterated wrath of a Mortis Skulk attack and survived to tell the tale."

Finneus swung around until his eyes came to rest on Asher's terrified form on the cathedral floor. "Perhaps a demonstration of how he managed such a feat will show you that even darkness can bleed."

Asher had absolutely no inclination of reliving that particular nightmare again and scurried backwards, shaking his head, until his back was stopped by a large pillar.

"Cowardice will not stave off death from seeking you out," Finneus furrowed his brow and lowered his tone, delivering each word with a venomous bite. "Stand your ground."

Asher refused, shaking his head at the man who held the wraith at bay. Finneus Slink's frown deepened, his patience waning with each passing second. Releasing the beast, he flicked his auger at something behind Asher's head. The beast lunged at his captor, but it was not quick enough. Finneus imprisoned it again, without even so much as a glance in its direction.

Asher looked at Finneus with a mixture of fear and hatred, when he felt something scrape unnaturally against the back of his neck. One by one, the dead bodies behind him sprang to life and clawed at him, each trying to secure a grip on their living prey.

Haggard hands of bone scratched his shoulders and tore at his tunic. Several of the girls screamed as the walls around the room came to life from beyond the grave, until Finneus shot them a deafening look to silence their wails.

Asher pulled and yanked at the hands gripping his clothes and struggled to get away from the pillar. Finally breaking free, he fell to his knees in front of the spectre looming over him in the void.

Finneus turned his head to face the wavering blood shroud enveloping the cultist. Raising his free arm, he dragged his fingers upwards through the air like a claw.

Asher watched on in panic as the wraith did the same. Inch by inch, a shadowy limb engulfed in dark tendrils and menacing claws emerged out of the veil of darkness.

"Through the countless thousands he killed, Cerebule was the one and only Cruaar to ever truly Master the blood arts of Decisus Umbra. With the corrupted blood of those he killed, he discovered a thousand vile ways to disfigure the world and bring death to all who opposed him. One such disfiguration was the unnatural corruption of his own blood into this wicked wraith-like state.

"Only in this state can the Mortis Skulk enact the blood-leech embrace: the vilest and most deadly of all Mortis Skulk attacks. The slightest touch will allow them to drain the blood from your veins. Allow them to find flesh, and death will be the least of your problems, as Apprentice Bloom will demonstrate if he is unable to defend himself."

"What?" Asher exclaimed.

Lem nearly swallowed his own tongue as Finneus's words hit home.

"Asher," Lorrelli whispered timidly under her breath, her body racked with fear.

"Pay attention, should you ever wish to survive such an encounter!" Finneus snapped his fingers and raised the level of his voice, so no-one misheard him. "The blood leech embrace seeks to weaken and subdue its prey by draining its blood and, in turn, your ability to call upon your auger." The expression of Finneus's face was grave, his features unyielding.

"With every drop it feeds upon, it grows stronger, and you weaker. Allow it to syphon enough blood and you will be paralysed. Then the cultist will drain you, turn you, or kill you at its leisure." Finneus stalked around the room with his arm outstretched, continuing to enslave the creature behind an invisible prison. His auger throbbed violently, emitting a noxious purple haze as he fuelled it with more of his blood.

"For the blood leech embrace to be effective, they first need to be close enough to lay hands on you. Now," his voice snapped across the chamber, "there are many defences against such an attack, the most basic of which is a physical defence." Finneus walked around the room and kicked away the random bones between Asher and the wraith.

"Apprentice Bloom, you are the only Vita here. The cultist will naturally abhor and fear you, but it is weak and starving. Draining even a pittance of your blood would give it the strength it needs to escape. You must defend yourself. Defend your blood."

"What? How? I don't even know how to use my auger!"

"Your auger is but a tool. Simply command it to your bidding, by will of mind and blood."

"I don't understa…" Asher words failed him as Finneus released his control over the spectre, dropping his hand to his side. The wraith let loose a defiant deafening wail that echoed around the cathedral and stung Asher's eardrums.

Flaring its shadow even larger, it slowly advanced on Asher, blood-red eye blazing with hatred in the centre of its viscid black veil. With every step, its tendrils stretched out from within the black shroud even farther, like the hand of death itself.

Asher held up his auger in front of him.

Nothing happened.

The creature drew another step closer.

Asher desperately tried to focus his mind on what he wanted to happen, but it was blank, completely overrun by the terror creeping over his chest.

"Focus, Bloom," Finneus's raspy voice commanded from the side of the room. "The beast hungers for blood. It has not fed in decades."

"I'm trying," Asher shouted.

"Do not let its touch reach your skin. Find a way to keep it from you," Finneus roared, eyes wide with exhilaration. It had been too long since he'd been so close to the presence of death.

Asher's mind ran riot, awash with a barrage of thoughts.

A shield? No, too big.

The wraith inched closer.

A sword? No, too heavy.

Asher felt the air around him grow cold.

A door? No, there are no walls.

The creature's talons stretched out, closing the gap between them.

A wall?

Asher closed his eyes and thought as hard as he could about the strongest wall he could imagine. His auger burned and a deafening rumble engulfed the room, causing the floor to shake and tremble beneath his feet.

Asher opened his eyes to see a hail of dust rain down from four enormous walls of bone, sinew and flesh. A morbid prison encased the cultist and its black shroud of blood. Asher let loose a single incredulous laugh, clearly unable to believe his eyes at what he'd just accomplished.

A series of cheers and claps flooded the room from those apprentices not utterly petrified by what was happening.

"How adept you are at controlling the dead. Dangerous, though, you never know how the dead will take to instruction,"

Finneus warned, his face marred with a perplexed frown. Raising his auger, he enslaved the cultist again behind the walls of bone.

"Only a fool neglects their surroundings when in combat," his eyes shot back to Asher and burned a brilliant black. "But a true Mortis Skulk cultist will never be stopped by a wall of death. If anything, it will be strengthened by the remnants of blood it holds." Finneus lurked around the wall of bone, before releasing the creature from its imprisonment. "Raise your auger. It comes at you again."

Darkness spewed through the wall of bone like water through cloth. It crumbled and collapsed on the ground, scattering fragments of bone in every direction. An infuriated blood-red eye continued its steady advance towards Asher.

"The Mortis Skulk thrives in darkness. Remove such sensory advantage and see it weakened," Finneus's voice cut through the din like a cleaver through bone.

Asher desperately searched the room for inspiration. There was none, simply terrified faces dimly lit by candlelight staring back at him, glad they were not in his shoes. *Candlelight. Candles. Fire.* He held out his hand towards one of the candles and willed its flames into his hand.

Nothing happened.

The cultist's blood veil advanced another step.

Asher strained his hand towards another candle on the other side of the room. Ever so slowly, the candles flame flickered and swayed as if caught in a draft. A second later, it sprang free of its waxy fixture and rocketed through the air towards Asher's outstretched palm.

A black tendril burst out from the cloud of black blood, dousing the tiny glimmer of flame before it could reach Asher's hand. Asher tried repeatedly with other candles around the room, but the creature was cunning, foiling each attempt with its tendrils of darkness. Asher heard a small frail voice echo out from behind the creature.

"An auglight, you need an augli—"

Finneus drowned out the voice with a murderous growl. "Weaker Mortis Skulk and their conspirators will not attack groups stronger than themselves. They will isolate an individual and attack when their prey is at its weakest. Trust not in others for salvation. You will be alone when attacked."

Lorrelli shook herself free from her frightened stupor and hit Lem hard in the side with her elbow.

"Ow! What the prac do you want me to do?" he shot back at her through clenched teeth, eyes locked on the cloud of black blood advancing towards Asher.

"The rock, throw him the rock."

Lem's face lit up with understanding and he quickly reached into his tunic.

Without warning, a heavy rock flew from the darkness and bounced its way across the ground, landing at Asher's feet.

The creature shrieked with rage and lashed out in the direction it came from, only to be stopped short by Finneus's pulsating auger, which redirected the beast back to the centre of the room. Furious at the manipulation, the cultist redoubled its rage on the young apprentice cowering on the ground, advancing even more ferociously than before.

Asher didn't think twice.

Dodging a swiping tendril, he warily circled the floating black shroud, swinging his palm towards the rock as he did so, levelling his auger at its core.

He felt a familiar sting shoot up his arm as blood infused with his auger. The more he concentrated, the more the sensation stung, and he winced hard as the pain hit home. His mind skipped back to earlier in the day, and he willed the rock with all his might to disintegrate and transform into an auglight.

At first, the rock did nothing. Then it vibrated and shook, spilling pools of liquid from its centre in wild bursts, each coagulating together to form crude shapes on the ground.

The cultist closed the final gap between Asher and descended on him with claws outstretched swiping the air furiously.

Asher ducked, but not quickly enough.

He felt the tip of its talons scrape against his arm. Its touch sent a cold, incapacitating wave of pain through his body. The blood rushed from his auger as he snatched his hand away and frantically tried to grab whatever he could off the floor. His hands fumbled over the crumbling brittle remnants of bone until they felt the cold touch of metal. His fingers wrapped around a crudely formed copper pole. It was no auglight, but it was strong and it was heavy.

Asher swung it as hard as he could at the creature's gaping tendrils. The jagged metal bit deep in the cultist's withered arm. Asher felt the pole connect heavily against its flesh and the sharp snap of bone underneath.

The cultist let loose a horrifying wounded shriek of agony.

Snatching back its arm, the cultist halted its advance and retreated a few steps. As it nursed its broken limb, hatred and hesitation seethed through the blood shroud as it eyed off its prey.

The apprentices around the room cheered wildly, but not loudly enough to warrant any attention from the cultist.

Finneus held up his bone-cradled auger and locked the cultist in place. "Even the most powerful Decisus Umbra practitioners can be hurt by the simplest of means. See now how this pathetic example of a cultist bleeds." Finneus circled around the mosaic of death, pointing at the floor where droplets of black blood spattered and bubbled furiously.

"It is wounded. It has tasted pain at your hands. Now it must know fear. You now hold the advantage. Press the attack. Call upon the gilded bloodline that flows through your veins and end this fool's suffering once and for all."

Finneus kneeled down beside Asher, who was slumped against a pillar of bone, visibly exhausted and dripping with sweat. Finneus whispered in his ear, loud enough that the other apprentices might have heard, but the directions seemed to be for the benefit of Asher alone. "An enemy is most dangerous when it fights for its life. Show it no clemency. It would give you none if the roles were reversed."

Asher was tired beyond belief. Sparks of pain shot up his arm every few seconds, but he forced himself to his feet, knowing full well a mistake now would mean his life.

"A strong will to live is your best weapon against the Mortis Skulk," Finneus's voice echoed around the claustrophobic wing of the Catacomb Cathedral.

"Channel your life force into your auger. Dredge your inner strength from your subconscious. Let it envelop you. Let it wash over you. Let it free your mind. Harness it. Focus it. Force it upon your enemy."

Asher rose to his feet and awkwardly attacked the cultist, wildly swinging the pole with one arm, auger held firmly against the metal. The creature was caught off-guard by Asher's ferocity and was hesitant to retaliate, but it was obvious that Asher was beginning to tire.

Asher tried to think of something, anything, that gave him strength and hope, but all he knew had been ripped away from him. Even Raglan, his one and only true friend was gone, dead at the hands of one of these cultist fiends. The thought of his mentor and friend being savaged by one of these shadowy ghouls caused a rage to swell inside his veins.

A dormant power sparked to life and churned inside, fuelling his body with energy and adrenaline at the thought of revenge. Asher felt his eyes glaze over, blocking out all else but the darkness from his view.

"Yes, that's it."

Finneus's words were lost on Asher.

"Embrace your inner power."

Blood boiled and churned inside his veins. He felt wild lashes of power surge through his limbs, longing to be released.

The cultist sensed it, too, its blood shroud wavering in hesitation. With nothing to lose, it desperately lunged at Asher. A blackened tendril shot forth, talons rushing to land a shadow-claw on Asher's exposed flesh.

Asher swung at the arm as it came, grazing it with the pole's jagged edges. But the cultist was relentless. It came at Asher again and again, every attack more ferocious than the last.

Asher wasn't prepared.

He wasn't strong enough.

Asher swung too late, leaving himself exposed, allowing the cultist the opportunity it needed to sink it claws deep within the flesh of his forearm.

The other apprentices screamed and turned their heads away as the shroud of darkness converged on Asher and enveloped him, the cultist's insidious voice wailing in victorious defiance.

Those apprentices closest to Finneus begged him to help.

Finneus did not move.

He didn't make a sound.

He gave no indication whatsoever that he would even consider helping Asher. He remained motionless, a gaunt look of disapproval plastered across his face.

Asher felt the creature's talons bite deep, tearing into his muscles beneath his ruptured skin. He felt his blood spill from his veins as it was slowly drained from his body.

Surprisingly, he felt no pain.

Surrounded in a veil of darkness and shadow, Asher somehow only saw light that burned from within.

Lem lurched forward and raised his auger at the beast. Despite all his efforts, he could not channel anything from his auger. It remained lifeless and blank. "Somebody help him!" he desperately pleaded, looking around the room for help.

A series of mortified and frightened faces looked back at him helplessly.

Finneus merely scowled his contempt at the plea and turned his head back to the shadowy beast.

Realising the futility in asking anyone else for help, Lem grabbed a jagged bone off the floor and lunged again, adrenaline filling his veins. He ran at the beast headfirst, arm raised, jagged bone outstretched like a dagger. He didn't even realise what happened when he collided with an almighty invisible force. It knocked him to the floor, repelling his pitiful attack effortlessly.

Lorrelli stepped over Lem and summoned something bright and green from her auger, hurling it at the shadowy cloud, but it too was stopped short of its target.

A large transparent barrier shimmered and rippled around the two figures. More apprentices stepped forward and hurled whatever attacks they knew, which were few and far between, but none even came close to hurting the cultist.

Finneus stepped forward and ran his hand a finger's width away from the rippling edge of the transparent barrier.

"Once the blood leech embrace has taken hold, an umbraghaam is unleashed—a powerful shadow barrier—fuelled by the victim's own blood. It will protect the cultist until the subject is entirely drained, turned or dead."

"You can't let this happen," Lorrelli screamed at Finneus, her eyes brimming over with tears. "It's killing him. Do something!"

"Your tears only fuel its power. It feeds off your fear. There is nothing I can do. Apprentice Bloom must save himself."

Inside the barrier Asher's mind and body felt detached. He knew the cultist had its hooks sunk deep into his flesh, draining his blood away, and that it was growing stronger every minute. But Asher felt no pain.

He felt no fear, either.

He felt the remnants of a dormant power trying to wake deep inside his veins. His eyes became golden beacons embedded in his skull. He felt the creature's talons tremble slightly. The power ruminating deep within his blood, surged into his heart, across his chest and down his arm. He tried to channel it into his auger, but nothing happened, no matter how hard he willed it. The blood-leech embrace was too strong. Somewhere deep in the darkness of his mind, a guttural voice grumbled at him through insane bouts of laughter.

Mine, Vita! Your blood is mine!

The loss of blood made it hard to breathe. Asher's senses became overwhelmed and the power he'd felt so prominently flow through his veins mere moments before was now withered beyond reach. He desperately tried to hold onto it. But with each passing moment, it grew weaker and harder to focus on.

Amidst everything, he almost thought he heard the sounds of heavy footsteps, but they seemed an eternity away, if they were real at all; or perhaps they were merely figments of his imagination.

Just before his mind lapsed into unconsciousness, Asher could have sworn he caught a glimpse of a gilded sword arc towards him, slicing through the cultist's all-consuming veil of black blood like butter, before a blinding white light careened his mind into oblivion.

Finneus sneered a final insult at Asher's crumpled body as it collapsed into a heap on the cold damp of the cathedral's floor.

"How disappointing."

CHAPTER 22

THE BURDEN OF HOPE

"Are you out of your mind, Slink? What did you think would happen: unleashing a cultist upon a first-year apprentice?" Tribarion Roolta's gilded armour glinted as she furiously stormed back and forth across the legate's office.

"Do you have any idea of the precedent you've set? How could you be so praccing reckless? You know better than anyone, that all of this," she held up her hands at the walls around her, "balances on a thread: a thread already strained to breaking point."

"I had the situation well in hand," Finneus glared at the woman, casually dismissing her accusations and infuriating her with his outwardly dour demeanour.

"In hand?" Tribarion Roolta couldn't contain her astonishment. "In hand? A Vita-born, the first natural Vita-born since the rebellion, was nearly drained to death by a Skulk cultist."

Finneus Slink's sunken eyes glared at the armour-clad woman accusing him. With arms defiantly folded behind his back, he spat only one word in response. "Hardly."

The remark sparked the tribarion's anger to breaking point. She proceeded to barrage the room with a long list of how Finneus's actions had crossed the line, not to mention adversely affected the apprentices left in his charge.

Legate Seville sat quietly in the corner of her office watching the argument unfold, slowly piecing together the truth behind what had transpired within the Catacomb Cathedral.

When the tribarion's verbal bombardment had subsided, Finneus turned to the legate, ignoring Tribarion Roolta altogether. "Apprentice Bloom has reputedly defended himself

242

against a Mortis Skulk attack without a mantle, alignment, or previous training, not once but twice. Yet, when asked to re-enact the feat against a much weaker foe, he was found sorely lacking."

"Hardly surprising seeing as the attack was the initiative of a Master he was told he could trust," Tribarion Roolta snapped viciously.

Finneus ignored the remark and moved a step closer to the legate. "His story has been laden with falsehoods from the very moment he arrived."

"Apprentice Bloom was cleared of all charges. You looked into his mind yourself and found nothing."

"I was given but seconds to plumb the fractured recesses of his consciousness. I had to be sure. His ability to break the judgement seal has cleared him of Skulk allegiance beyond all doubt."

"It is not your place to question, Elder Mandate," Tribarion Roolta barked.

The remark broke Finneus's last ounce of patience with the woman hurling accusations at him. He spun around to face her, a ferocious undercurrent of anger burning behind his black sunken eyes. "You dare lecture me on Elder Mandate, Tribarion? I am one of the Elder Five, or have you forgotten?"

"And your vote to refuse Asher entrance into Mantlecrest was overruled Finneus," Overseer Lobrolo's voice resonated around the room, cutting short the war of words before it escalated further.

The heated quarrel had blinded those in the room to Lobrolo's silent entrance through the vertistrand. Both Tribarion Roolta and Finneus Slink turned in silence to face the Overseer.

He gazed back at each of them in turn, tempered patience weighing heavily on his brow. "It is not your place to lecture Finneus on how he chooses to train his apprentices, Tribarion Roolta."

"Thank you, Lobrolo," Finneus bowed his head towards the Overseer in appreciation.

"Nor is it yours to pit a first-year apprentice against an entombed Skulk war criminal, regardless of reason or suspicion!" Lobrolo barked fiercely at Finneus, a look of staunch disapproval evident on his face. "Seville, what do you make of this debacle?"

Legate Seville narrowed her eyes at the Overseer. The fact the man refused to address her by her title infuriated her now more than ever. Sitting in the legate's chair, behind the legate's desk, in the legate's office, as the Legate of Mantlecrest, she deserved respect, even if he was not willing to give it. Taking a moment to swallow her pride, she buried her resentment towards the Overseer behind emotionless features before offering a response.

"This incident," she said slowly, heavily downplaying the significance of the event, "left no-one gravely injured. If anything, it served as a reminder of the threat that once stood against us. I believe Finneus would never have let it go further than it did," Legate Seville said calmly, drawing a firm line in the sand as to where she stood on the matter.

"Of course not," Finneus replied and shot a dark look at the glowering tribarion next to him.

"So then, let what's done, be done and mention it no further."

Lobrolo paused for a moment, considering her words and the implications of what would happen if he sought to contradict her ruling on the matter. By law, the legate's decision was final for all decisions for all matters within Mantlecrest's hallowed halls. As Overseer, he did have the power to overrule her, but it would do little else than make another enemy he could ill afford.

Witnessing the Overseer's hesitation to act, Tribarion Roolta voiced her own steadfast objection. "Overseer, you can't seriously be thinking of letting this pass."

Lobrolo exhaled deeply and placed both hands on his hips, his decision already made. From across the room he thought he saw the corners of the legate's lips twinge upwards, marring her otherwise austere features with a victorious self-indulgent smile.

"This lies on your shoulders, Seville. You will bear the wrath of the council when it gets out; and it will get out."

Finneus and Tribarion Roolta said nothing, watching the tense power-play unfold between two of the most powerful people in Undergall.

"You leave the council and their Red Scar inquisitions to me," Seville jibed sharply.

Lobrolo narrowed his eyes at the mention of the council's elite guard, but chose to say nothing. Finneus stepped forward to offer explanation, but Lobrolo tersely cut him off with a sharp wave of his hand before he could utter a single word.

"Leave us. Seville will deal with you later." Lobrolo waited for Finneus to bow and retreat out of the room. The man's bitter frustration stayed in the air until the door swung shut behind him.

Lobrolo sighed deeply, crossed the floor and turned, leaning his weight against the legate's desk and settling in as though he had done so many times before. "You would think a Master of Mortis would be better able to mask his emotions." He shook his head ever so slightly and raised an eyebrow at the armoured woman standing in front of him. Her gilded armour glittered intermittently as it reflected the flickering auglights. "Thank you for bringing this sordid fiasco to my attention, Tribarion. How fares Apprentice Bloom?"

The tribarion attempted to hand Lobrolo a tablet showing Asher's recuperation report, but the legate appeared from around the desk and snatched it from her, reading select snippets of the report aloud. "All wounds and sustained blood loss were superficial … no lasting damage … any lasting illness or adverse effects unlikely."

"Good," Lobrolo said, relieved, as he and nodded his head, "though I fear it will be the only good news that comes of this. Seville, you had best go and prepare a report for the council. Better you bring this matter to their attention before half-truths and rumours flood the commons."

"Your will, Altier," the legate offered him a false smile, making it blatantly obvious that she understood she was no longer welcome in her own office. She bowed condescendingly, cast a pinch of sand into the vertistrand and disappeared through its shimmering gate.

Lobrolo Altier watched her go, his eyes burdened with troubled thoughts. "Tribarion, I understand your presence will be needed back in Oakrim to help oversee the installation of the latest defences but, while we have the chance to speak, I would ask of you a special request. A favour."

"Anything, Overseer, you have but to ask."

"Undergall's First Order Tribarion is away on special assignment and is unlikely to return anytime soon, but I would have you take a vested interest in Apprentice Bloom."

"Vested interest?" Tribarion Roolta repeated.

"Train him, personally. Guide him towards the mastery of the Vita bloodline. Too few Vita-born remain and those are already stretched too thin to focus on Asher's development."

"Forgive me, Overseer, but—"

The Overseer held up his hand, "Lobrolo."

"Very well, Lobrolo. I've never trained an apprentice before. Isn't there someone better suited to the role?"

Lobrolo looked deep into her eyes, his mind trying to discern whether to tell her something of vital importance. After a few moments, his tone lowered and he spoke in no uncertain terms. "What I am about to tell you does not leave this room."

Tribarion Roolta nodded.

"I'll need more than just a nod. You must swear an oath on your bloodline before I can entrust you with this."

Without blinking, the tribarion withdrew her sword from its scabbard and offered it hilt first to Lobrolo.

He stood fully upright and removed his own auger from within his tunic. A long dagger-like spike extended down from a fine chain of silver, a faded grey gemstone set within an ornate iron-and-platinum interwoven fixture below its hilt.

Tribarion Roolta inhaled a silent gasp at the sight of Lobrolo's greying auger, realising the implications of the gem's colour, but said nothing out of respect.

Sparks of power shot from Lobrolo's auger, until a long burst of raw energy surged forth and connected his auger with hers. Releasing the connection, he looked beyond the woman to the door at the end of the room. When he was satisfied they would not be overheard, his voice lowered. "It should be no surprise when I say that these are bleak days we bear witness to. The council fought me tooth and nail to keep Mantlecrest open, after what happened to my—"

Tribarion Roolta saved him having to say anything further by nodding her head in understanding.

He smiled at her grimly in return, his way of thanking her for her empathy in the matter. "They agreed to do so only under the promise of reform, but too many Cruaar cannot forget what happened here... what happened in the city during the rebellion. The mere sight of the stained cobbles is more than enough reminder to spark ill memories back to life that are best left forgotten.

"Mantlecrest's numbers dwindle further every year, despite my best efforts. Many prefer the more conservative methods of Oakrim's Featherpeak Conservatory, or the more archaic that have made Hollow's Rest Havenhaus Institute so prestigious." Lobrolo pushed himself upright and slowly paced around the desk, pausing to stare at the walls for a moment, a troubled expression crossing over his face.

"We have not had a true Vita-born come through these halls in over three decades. Any apprentice that has previously shown any affinity for the gilded bloodline has been instructed by First Order Tribarion Karbosch, but the painful reality stands: Undergall has not had a Master of Vita for some time now, nor are we likely to anytime soon."

"What of High Cleric Pluwarie?"

Lobrolo wiped his sleeve over his perspiring brow and gazed at the statues lining the walls of the legate's office. Austere faces carved into stone stared back at him, reflecting a more fortuitous time in Mantlecrest's history. He gingerly walked towards one of the granite busts and ran his fingers over the cool grooves in the stone.

"Pluwarie's extended absence in Oakrim has left Undergall and, in turn, Mantlecrest with a gaping hole that's not easily filled. I fear the lure of Oakrim's prestige is too great for one as fickle as Pluwarie. He will likely never stay in Undergall longer than it takes him to dirty his soles upon the cobbles."

"I did not realise," Tribarion Roolta sympathised.

"Though the rebellion never managed to topple Undergall, Cerebule and his minions left it crippled nonetheless. There is an undercurrent of futility instilled in the hearts of those who remained. The rare few who can see the depressing truth have already left, seeking sanctuary in Hollow's Rest or sheltering within Oakrim's impregnable bastion.

"Some even prefer to risk discovery and live in The Blind rather than abide another night, resting head on pillow in this accursed city."

Tribarion Roolta said nothing, unsure of how to respond.

"Make no mistake, Tribarion, Undergall is rotting. The Skulk attack on Apprentice Bloom in The Blind has unleashed a renewed shockwave of fear across our nation, reigniting sleeping terrors that should never have been allowed to wake."

"You believe they will return, don't you?" The tribarion's grip on the hilt of her sword tightened at the thought. Lobrolo's head snapped around at the question, his eyes carefully measuring the resolve of the woman before him.

"I don't know what to believe, but if they are brazen enough to openly attack a warder in The Blind, then Mantlecrest and the whole of Undergall finds itself atop a precipice. The survival of this city depends on the strength of its foundations, both Earthreach Spire and Mantlecrest. Should either fall, Undergall will crumble before the coming storm."

Lobrolo put both of his enormous hands upon the desk, drawing his fingers back into fists and flexing his muscular forearms. "Events like this only hasten the decay that eats away at this city: my city."

"What can be done?" Tribarion Roolta asked softly, not wanting to overstep her boundaries upon hearing the heavy revelations Lobrolo had bestowed upon her.

"Asher Bloom is much more than just a Vita-born. He is a symbol, a beacon of hope," Lobrolo's eyes flared wide as he spoke. "Hope begotten at the prospect of change."

"Forgive me, Overseer, granted he is a Vita-born, but is he not just a boy?"

"He is what I will make him!" Lobrolo banged his fists hard on the desk, causing its heavy wooden frame to shudder and groan. He pointed a finger at the tribarion with eyes wide open. "And what you will mould him to be."

The tribarion stared back at the Overseer, taken aback. His aged face was swollen with determination, his hand levelled at her face unwavering, impressing the depths of his resolve. "What are my orders, Overseer?"

"Help me give this city back its hope. Train him. Teach him how to protect himself. Help him realise his full potential. The odds against him are enormous, but without him my plan cannot succeed and all this will come crashing down on our heads."

Lobrolo gazed down at the desk as he used to when he held the title of legate and placed a large hand on the cool surface of the wood.

The tribarion came to attention and saluted, raising her fist up to her chest, then to her forehead, before cutting it downwards and away to her side. "I will do all I am able."

"I do not need able, I need exceptional. I need results!" Lobrolo barked, eyes betraying his exhaustion. Sinking back into the legate's chair, he fished a small metallic ellipse out of his pocket and threw it over the desk.

She caught it easily in one hand.

"An old friend from Craftpaw has lent me a prototype edurus herald and I now give it to you. Use it to train Asher, without restriction, beyond the reach of your natural abilities. Do you understand?"

She nodded once in acknowledgement as Lobrolo stood and turned away from her. He slowly walked towards the balcony of the legate's office and gazed out at Undergall through the glass.

Tribarion Roolta, sensing the conversation had finished, retreated to the end of the room to see herself out.

Lobrolo called out a final command as she was about to close the door behind her. "No-one must ever know what was said here this day, least of all Asher. The burden resting on his shoulders is already far too great."

CHAPTER 23

THE ENIGMA OF SURIO LETIFER

When Asher awoke he felt his legs, arms and torso immersed in a clammy substance. It felt unearthly, like an enormous slug was slithering over his skin. He blinked his eyes a couple of times just to make sure he was alive before he heard Lorrelli's voice ringing in his ears.

"Asher, you're awake!"

Asher rolled his head to one side and saw her blurred face. Blinking away the haze, half of Lorrelli was blocked by a large copper wall directly in line with his head. Twisting his head around, he saw another copper wall on the other side. Shifting his focus downwards, he saw that his body had been submerged in a strange greenish-yellow ooze that left nothing but his head exposed. A gentle warmth shifted upwards from his feet through the gelatinous substance, spreading up around his chest and head.

Returning his head upright, he gazed up at the roof and saw the trunk of a large tree extended upwards, the copper walls on either side of him cutting into its trunk. The same greenish-yellow substance oozed down its trunk around his head as large metallic pumps milked it from the tree.

"'Bout time, you kept us all waiting long enough," Lem joked as he gripped Asher's shoulder in a heartily way, wiping away the ooze on the side of the copper pipe in disgust. "Yuck, better you than me; that stuff's revolting."

"Augalyptus sap is not famous for its comforting feel, Apprentice, but for its regenerative properties," a neatly dressed man said without looking up from his clear-glass tablet. "How do you feel, Asher?"

Asher had never seen the man before and certainly didn't

recognise him. He was dressed in a crisp green tunic with a single stripe of gold running down its centre.

"Fine, I think. Who are you?"

"Cleric Riffenbon. You lost some blood, but nothing to be overly concerned about. Do me a favour and lift up your arms for me."

Asher tried to do as he was instructed but felt the strange liquid pull against his muscles. Straining a little harder, he felt his fingers break free from the clammy ooze, followed soon after by his hands and arms.

Soon, both arms were either resting, or perhaps floating, on top of the gelatinous ooze encasing his body; Asher couldn't be sure which sensation was more accurate. Clumps of the sweet-smelling substance clung to his skin like a sticky paste.

The Cleric waved his auger over the tablet in his hands and made a notation, presumably about Asher's recovery. "Your friends here haven't left your side, despite numerous instructions to do so and to return to their training."

"How long was I out?"

"Only a couple of hours," Lem chimed in, touching a finger still laced with ooze to his tongue. He instantly gagged.

"You missed one hell of a show," Lorrelli added, swatting Lem in the back of the head for being such an idiot.

Asher looked at her questioningly, and then to his arm, running his fingers over the spot where the creature's talons had dug in. His skin was smooth. There wasn't even a scar.

"You don't seem to have any lasting effects from the attack," the Cleric said, somewhat perplexed, "but if you start to feel unwell at all, even in the slightest, be sure to seek me out immediately. Now, clean yourself up and get back to training, all of you, before the legate blames me for your absence."

Cleric Riffenbon promptly turned and walked out of the room, leaving behind row upon row of oversized copper pipes, all firmly cut into the base of several augalyptus trees extending up into the ceiling.

"I don't know about you two, but I've had an absolutely brilliant first day," Lem grinned at Asher.

"You really are such a bell end," Lorrelli shook her head. "Time and place."

"It's alright," Asher winced as the two of them helped dig him out of the sticky sap that clung to his body. "Now would someone please tell me what the hell happened?" After Asher scraped the remaining sap from his skin, he donned some fresh clothes and the trio left the rejuvenation chamber.

Lem and Lorrelli deliberately took their time getting to their next training session in order to fill Asher in on everything he'd missed. Lem dutifully retold his version of events, re-enacting the part when Tribarion Roolta had swooped into the room and shattered the umbraghaam with her sword and forced the Mortis Skulk's soul back into a new carcerion. His exaggerated embellishments and over-the-top actions were hilarious enough that even Lorrelli was laughing at his impression of Finneus Slink.

By the time they'd reached their next training session they were arrived horribly late, but they didn't care. The instruction was already near completion when they stepped through the arched threshold of Mantlecrest's armoury.

Apprentices were grouped in pairs around a series of unlit forges that were lined up neatly in rows.

A morbidly obese man stood next to a training dummy at the front of the room and ushered them to find a free forge with a wobbly wave of his arm. The loose skin under his upper arm jiggled with the action, causing an outbreak of sniggers and smirks across the room with each wiggle.

The armoury was adorned with all manner of dangerous weapons, although all of them seemed to be missing something, either from the face of their blades or on their hilts, which were roughly the size of an auger. Everything from swords and shields to chains and staves hung from the walls, whilst more delicate weaponry adorned a series of tall armour racks scattered around the edges of the room.

The trio went and stood behind one of the free forges at the back of the room. Quickly looking around at all the weaponry, Asher noticed the distinctive lack of any sort of firearm or projectile weapon. He couldn't help but consider their noticeable absence as somewhat strange. Thinking back, Asher couldn't remember having seen a single gun since long before his escape from Egypt, despite the numerous near-death encounters he'd managed to survive since his discovery.

"Why aren't there any guns?"

"Guns?" Lem smirked, doing little to hide his surprise at the ludicrous question. "You're joking, right?"

"You see me laughing?" Asher sniped back, quickly growing tired of their constant quips about his ignorance.

"Suppose not," Lem's snigger vanished. "There are no guns, 'cause all guns do are fire bullets, you spoon."

"What?" Asher looked at him strangely, not quite understanding what he was implying with the particularly obvious statement. "You trying to tell me you can stop bullets?"

"Stop? No," Lem raised an eyebrow somewhat comically. "Well, not me, obviously, but, yes, if it came down to it, most of them could," he waved a hand casually at the rest of the apprentices before continuing.

"From what I've heard, it's not even that hard; but we can't just go stopping bullets with a wave of a hand, now can we? We'd give ourselves away for sure. Besides, it's much easier to cause a firing mechanism to fail, or deflect a bullet's trajectory."

"One of the first things we learn as children is how to protect ourselves against detection and capture in The Blind," Lorrelli interjected, stopping Lem's rant before it broke into full swing.

"So you can stop bullets?" Asher asked incredulously as the fat instructor mumbled something at the front of the room.

"It's not bullets you have to worry about down here," Lem said quietly. "Look around you. Haven't you wondered why everyone's in armour?"

"Yes, but to be honest, I was wondering more about all the

medieval weapons," Asher admitted.

"Battle mantles, Asher, not medieval weapons," Lem whispered. "Big difference."

"Most human weapons were initially modelled after ours, Asher, before they went tech-crazy, anyway. Think about it: all throughout history, humans—especially their rulers—have some sort of jewelled weapon or two. The church, monarchs, dictators, they've all got them. Although, admittedly, not so much anymore. Now their wives and mistresses wear the jewels around their neck unless they're a gardcore hangster." Lem crossed his arms and struck a ridiculous pose with fingers crossed on each hand for added effect.

Despite Lem's offbeat sense of humour, Asher sat back in his chair and realised that everything his friend was saying, weirdly, made sense. "Okay, so what's with all these weapons, then?" Asher nodded at the excess of armaments haphazardly strung up on the walls and armour racks around the room.

"Those?" Lem asked looking around nonchalantly. "They're the battle mantles of past apprentices."

"Don't they need them anymore?" Asher asked innocently, his eyes drawn to an iron trident with a twisted golden handle.

A few nearby apprentices laughed at the remark, causing the obese master at the front of the room to peer over the rims of his spectacles. Misunderstanding the reason for their laughter, he became flustered and rapped his flailed mace hard against the training dummy's chest.

A large thunderous crack rumbled across the room, causing some of the apprentices to baulk and straighten up as battle mantles around them rattled and clinked together.

"Mantle artistry is no laughing matter. You must find the precise elements that are best attuned to your auger and bloodline. Imbue inferior alternatives or, worse yet, the wrong elements all together, and the effectiveness and strength of your blood callings will be dampened as a result."

"It's not like you can dampen mine any further," Lem

muttered under his breath, twirling his colourless auger between his fingers.

Lorrelli couldn't help but sigh. She was getting sick of Lem's constant mood swings. "We've got less than 10 minutes left, so unless you've enlisted in Physiaugal Defence training, we're done for the day." She raised her eyebrows at him, but he said nothing in response. "Good, now stop moaning, you're beginning to get on my nerves."

"Fine," Lem said in a dour tone as Asher retrieved his schedule tablet from his pocket and looked at it. He scanned down to his current training session.

4.00pm Mantle Artistry—Mantlecrest Armoury—Master Hadly McGoven
5.10pm Private Instruction—Praelior Arena

"Lorrelli, didn't you just say that this is our last training session for the day?"

"Yep, we've got the entire afternoon and night off."

"But I've got another session scheduled after this." Asher showed her the card in his hands.

"Private instruction… that's weird. I've never heard of private instruction for a first-year apprentice, especially not on the first day, and certainly not after everything you've just been through."

"Five PM? Karma's a bifty shitch, huh?" Lem blurted out, his mood lightening slightly. "Looks like you're going to miss out on the Hopralas match; not that our view will be any better, mind you."

"What's a Hoprala?" Asher raised his eyebrows and shook his head at Lem.

"Hopralas," Lem corrected, "only the best praccing team in the UA League. Every year on the first day of Mantlecrest's intake, the elder apprentices challenge them in a mock game of Utor Alea."

"The rest of the first-years are going to the observatory to watch it from afar," Lem murmured under his breath, fidgeting with the colourless auger in his hands.

The fat master at the front of the room slammed his mace against the dummy again, sending another thunder crack across the room, effectively silencing their conversation. "Six elements in total are needed to complete a mantle; seven, if you wish to imbue your auger within a battle mantle. It will be your job to discover and imbue each element within your mantle during your apprenticeship.

"Each element will be linked to your alignment in some way or another, allowing your auger to harness the power of your blood more efficiently and effectively."

Lem was about to say something clever, but one stern look from Lorrelli instantly made him change his mind.

An apprentice with short brown hair from the front of the room called out, "how will we know what elements will be best attuned to our augers?"

"Apprentice Gullybore, you needn't worry about what to look for, in most cases your auger will do the hard work for you. Usually, it will light up quite brightly when it has come into contact with a suitable element. It might be contained within a brush, a cup, a stone, a flower, a drop of liquid, the skin of an animal, practically anything. Once discovered, you'll need to obtain a sample of the element in its pure form: its true essence."

An apprentice nearer the front of the room looked confused. "True essence?"

"Simply bring the item to your alignment master if you are able. They'll take you to see Ermalt Dopplebock in his Mantle Emporium. He'll be able to extract any element's true essence from almost anything, and then imbue it in your mantle." His eyes scanned the room to see if there were any further questions.

There weren't.

"Well then, I believe that's as good a note as any to end on. Good luck in your search. Next time I will explain the different ways your auger interacts with your mantle."

As everyone filed out of the armoury, a quarter headed off in the direction of Mantlecrest's main gates. Another quarter headed towards the Munitio Pavilion for Physiaugal Defence training. The rest headed up the nearest stairwell towards the observatory to watch the Utor Alea match.

"Lorrelli, you coming to watch the elder apprentices get obliterated?" Lem asked in a gesture of goodwill, obviously attempting to make up for his sour disposition earlier.

She shook her head at him, still a little annoyed and somewhat glad for some time apart from both of them.

"Not this time, I'm going to check out the Spiretop Gardens. My sister told me they were pretty righteous. You good to get to the Praelior Arena, Asher?"

"I'll be fine," Asher said rubbing his hand over his auger. "I'll catch up with you two later."

Lem didn't even wave goodbye as he sauntered off to join a group already heading to the observatory.

Lorrelli wished Asher luck before quickly disappearing in the opposite direction, auger outstretched as it guided her way.

Asher had just about gotten used to being surrounded by people when he found himself alone. He touched his auger to his schedule tablet and felt it gently warm his hand. Following the directions of his auger, he navigated his way through a series of corridors and stairwells towards the arena's forecourt.

Much to his surprise, just before he approached the entrance to the arena he saw Morreby Fitch disappear into a doorway down the hall. Figuring he had a couple of minutes to spare, he carefully approached the black iron door Morreby had vanished behind. He tried to open it, but it was firmly locked. He waved his auger at the secureaug lock, but nothing happened.

The door wouldn't budge.

Putting his ear to the door, he thought he heard muffled voices, but could not make out who they belonged to or what they were saying. A muffled high-pitched wail and a soft rumble crept through the suppression of the heavy iron door, but only silence followed thereafter. A brief sense of suspicion spread through Asher's mind, but after waiting in silence for a few minutes with his ear against the iron, it faded away.

Closely examining the door, he could see no distinguishing features apart from some heavy iron rivets. Stepping back, he noticed a single inscription etched in stone above the doorway. *Surio Letifer.* He committed the name to memory and stepped away when he heard a soft thump land against the door. Looking down, he saw a tiny trickle of blood working its way between the cracks in the stone underneath it.

Gingerly touching it with his index finger, he rubbed it together with his thumb and middle fingers.

It was still warm.

His suspicion surrounding Morreby Fitch grew a great deal larger in the back of his mind. After a few more minutes of inactivity, Asher resigned himself to the fact he wouldn't be able to learn anything more about what she was up to from behind a locked door and decided to head back to the entrance to the Praelior Arena.

Taking a deep breath, he waved his auger at the enormous secureaug lock and stepped inside as the door swung open. A few seconds later, it closed behind him in whisper silence, the lock re-engaging with a soft clunk no louder than a finger click.

Asher anxiously stepped forward a few paces onto the sandy floor and looked around. He was in a small dark corridor leading to the wide open floor of the arena.

The tunnel was gloomy, but the arena was well-lit and, from what little he could see, mostly empty. In fact, the entire space was completely devoid of anything of note, the exception being a few broken columns that rose awkwardly out of a raised stone platform in the arena's centre.

A woman in resplendent gilded armour stood on the platform, sword sheathed in a scabbard by her side. She cradled something too small to distinguish properly in her hands. Asher apprehensively took a few steps forward, each step bringing him closer to the bright light filtering in from the arena. Nearing the end of the corridor, he slowed his approach.

Asher stopped in his tracks as an enormous creature popped into existence in the arena's centre. The beast's sudden appearance and epic size took Asher completely by surprise. He could do little else but marvel at the sheer enormity of the living behemoth that had just materialised before him. The creature's legs were as big as any tree trunk he'd ever seen and completely obscured the view of the tribarion.

Stepping to the side of the tunnel, Asher crept forward, hoping to catch a glimpse of the giant's head high atop its gargantuan body. It had its back turned to him but, as Asher drew closer, he saw its boulder-like head jerk to one side and shudder. Two cavernous holes in the back of the creature's neck sucked in vast amounts of air, as if trying to catch hold of a fine scent eluding its reach.

Slowly, the enormous head turned, dragging its shoulders and torso around with it. It took only seconds before a magnificent multitude of eyes came into view. Though the beast was a good hundred yards away, Asher saw his reflection mirrored back at him in each of the behemoth's many irises as they contracted in rapid succession.

The next thing Asher knew, his knees were knocked out from under him and his body was thrown to the floor. He clamped his hands over his ears as a deafening noise bellowed through his eardrums, a thousand times louder than any foghorn or air-raid siren. Asher's eyes blinked open, but his vision shook violently as the behemoth's massive legs landed a second time.

It had already covered two-thirds of the gap between them with only two steps. It had Asher's frail frame firmly in its sights as it stretched out a massive claylike hand towards him.

An earth-shattering roar howled through Asher's ears as three enormous club-sized fingers opened towards him, yearning to snatch their prize.

CHAPTER 24

FIRST EDICT MASTERY

Asher scrambled backwards in desperation as the creature's thunderous howls numbed his mind. His hands frantically scratched at the loose ground behind him as his feet kicked wildly at the floor, spraying sand in every direction.

But it was not enough.

The creature's hand was only ten feet away, and closing fast. Asher watched the multitude of eyes refocus and gaze down at him between the gaps of its mammoth fingers, each one wider than the width of Asher's torso. With nowhere to run, Asher closed his eyes and threw his hands over his face, waiting for the inevitable.

Asher didn't believe his own ears when the ear-splitting bellowing ceased. It was not until he realised the ground had stopped shaking and quiet had descended over the arena that he lowered his arm and reopened his eyes. Anxiously, he peered out, his heart still furiously pumping in his chest.

"What the...?" Asher exhaled breathlessly. The creature had vanished, leaving the vast open space of the arena empty. He rose to his feet and brushed the sand from his clothes before edging towards the tunnel's entrance, pivoting his head to take in the far reaches of the vast arena.

The only living thing he could see was the tribarion who stood in the same resolute pose on the same elevated stone platform as before. Asher hesitantly stepped out into the open, his neck craning in all directions for a sign of the colossus whose monstrous hand had been no more than few feet from his face mere moments ago.

Asher could not comprehend how the immense structure had been squeezed into the underbelly of Mantlecrest. A rugged terrain of clay, dirt, grass, mud, water, sand and stone covered the arena's massive expanse. A high stone wall rose up around its edges, encasing the arena floor like a prison yard. Tier upon tier of stone seats extended beyond the wall all the way to the roof, which was bespeckled with dazzling lights that sparkled against its curved black dome.

Enormous banners of varying colours hung lazily over the high walls of the arena, swaying back and forth as if caught in a gentle breeze, even though the air around them was still. Each banner had a massive Mantlecrest logo neatly embroidered in the centre, whilst the Mantlecrest motto repeated in stone between the banners around the entirety of the arena's edge: Elucidatus Introrsus, Expertis.

Enlighten within, without.

Asher remembered the translation as he searched for alternative entrances to the arena floor. He could only see the one he had just entered through, but the shimmer of four enormous vertistrands were visible high up in the spectator stands. The tribarion stood silently about fifty metres away, patiently watching Asher's anxious approach across the expanse.

Swallowing his trepidation, Asher crossed the sprawling terrain, hurriedly shuffling his feet across mounds of dirt and patches of grass until he was only ten feet from the tribarion's gilded greaves. She'd freed her sword from its scabbard and rested the tip elegantly in a groove in the stone next to her foot. Her other hand was firmly positioned on her hip.

Whatever she'd been playing with in her hands was now nowhere to be seen. "Come, Apprentice Bloom, it is time to begin your training in earnest."

Asher just stared at her, lost for words, before he awkwardly thrust an arm behind him and pointed to where he'd seen the behemoth. "What the hell was that thing?"

"That, you were not meant to see."

"That's not an answer." Asher stood his ground. "What was it and where is it now?"

The tribarion inspected the obstinate youth before her, silently measuring his resolve in the back of her mind as her eyes scrutinised him.

"The Cruaar Nation has long kept all manner of creatures hidden from human eyes. The acropall you saw is no exception, though you might know it better by the names given to it by human mythology: giant, titan, or leviathan, to name a few."

"Okay," Asher paused and nervously glanced around the arena once more. "So where did it go?"

"You assume much to think that it was ever here at all."

"I saw it with my own eyes."

"Eyes can lie, Apprentice Bloom. You, of all people, should know that."

Asher instantly raised his auger to his head and searched the arena again, this time with his divine eye.

Everything looked normal.

Nothing seemed out of place.

"Fool the eye and the mind will follow. An impossible feat made easy, by means of an edurus herald." She removed a small metallic ellipse from within her armour and exposed it for less than a second before stashing it away again.

Asher barely caught sight of its rune-etched features before the flat steel of the tribarion's sword filled his vision, her blade levelled at his face.

"Now let us begin your instruction." She lowered her sword for a moment and tapped its tip on the stone platform twice.

Asher felt the sandy ground rumble and tremor beneath his feet. Giant slabs of stone rose upwards out of the sand, growing out of the earth like oversized mushrooms, until he stood eye to eye with the tribarion.

"From this moment on, consider this platform your entire world. Fall from it, and suffer the consequences. Understand?"

Asher nodded, but his curiosity about the acropall did not diminish. "The acropall, where did it go?"

"Enough," the powerful tribarion snapped. She stepped

forward and levelled her sword at Asher's throat.

Asher felt the cold press of its tip press against his jugular.

"I am here to instruct you in the blood arts of Vita, not to satiate your curiosity."

Asher nodded in compliance, but not because his curiosity had been satisfied; he did so because of the cool bite of steel against his neck, as the tribarion dragged the tip of her sword over his throat.

"Mastering the space around you is the first rule of combat. Only blood callings suitable to the size and space of your environment will be of use when defending yourself."

Asher returned the woman's gaze, refusing to say anything against the off chance her sword nicked a vein in his neck.

"Between your mantle, your auger and the blood in your veins, you have the ability to defend against almost any attack. Few can boast such a claim."

Asher tried to look down at his auger, but she raised the tip of her sword, catching it underneath his chin and lifting it back up. She took a moment and stared deep into his eyes.

Asher's ingrained scepticism was poorly hidden by his wide irises and dilated pupils.

"Doubt has no place in combat. The Vita bloodline dwarfs all others in both strength and power. Not even the necrotic corruption of Decisus Umbra can penetrate the defences of a true Vita Master, or withstand an attack from one."

"I'm not a master," Asher wheezed.

"But you are Vita-born and, as such, will always be a threat and a target in their eyes."

"They're not gone, are they? There's more out there."

The tribarion lowered the tip of her sword to the ground between her feet and placed both hands on the hilt, covering the large emerald auger flecked with blemishes of gold at its edges.

"It would seem so. Before the attack on you, we believed the Mortis Skulk had been eradicated; but the truth is we may never know how many escaped and now live in secret amid The Blind."

Her expression grew serious as she slowly circled Asher and used the tip of her sword to correct his form as she did so. "I understand you are able to call upon your blood without invocation." She raised her eyebrows and waited for his response, slapping his legs lightly with the flat of her sword to correct his stance.

"Invocation?"

"Without words."

"I guess."

"I also understand that whenever you've called upon your blood, you've only done so reactively, when under direct assault."

Asher nodded in agreement as she slapped his back with the flat of her sword, correcting the angle of his shoulders in the process.

"You have strong instincts, but instincts alone are not enough to master the blood arts of Vita. Fortunately, your ability to call upon your blood, without invocation, steers you towards First Edict mastery."

Asher's blank face betrayed his ignorance of the term.

"Arm yourself with knowledge if you wish to survive the passing of years. Combined with wisdom, the two can be deadlier than steel and blood combined, if leveraged correctly. You would do well to enhance both." She paused, eyeballing Asher's form for further fault.

It took a moment, but Asher finally realised she was waiting for him to respond. "What's First Edict mastery?"

She curtly nodded her approval and turned to face a nearby column a short distance away. "There are two ways a Cruaar can call upon their blood. The first requires a vocal incantation, and is the tool of those only capable of Second Edict Mastery. Yet it will serve as the building block from which you will hone your craft." She levelled her sword at a nearby stone column sticking out of the arena floor. "Occumbo." The column cracked sharply at its base and toppled to the ground.

"Now you," she said, and pointed to another column opposite

Asher.

He dutifully held out his palm and faced his auger at the column. "Occumbo."

A sharp burning sensation shuddered up his arm and a heavy coat of dust shook itself free of the column, but the obstinate block of stone refused to fall.

Tribarion Roolta waved her sword at the column, before swatting the underside of his arm forcing him to lift it higher.

"Again."

Asher tried a second time, but with no improvement on his first attempt.

She nodded at him to continue. "Cruaar whose blood arts rely on Second Edict Mastery have no choice but to voice incantation with every drop of blood spent. They cannot will their auger to action with thought alone. You, however, have already proved yourself capable of such a feat." She held the flat of her sword against his chest, delaying the repeated attempts of his poorly executed blood callings.

"Repeating an incantation alone will not see stone toppled before your feet. You must will the action with your mind. Again."

Asher drew in a deep breath, paused and ignored the dull pain shooting up his arm. Focusing his mind on the task at hand, he visualised a jagged crack appearing, splitting the stone and him watching the broken remnants falling to the floor.

"Occumbo."

Another invisible force sped across the arena floor, shuddering as it hit the base of the column. A large crack splintered halfway across the rough exterior of the stone.

Asher let out a brief smile and tried again. It took two more attempts, but soon enough the column lay in toppled ruin on the arena floor.

"An adequate display of ability, but poorly executed." The tribarion reached out with her sword, holding its tip under Asher's chin as she lifted it upwards, forcing his mouth shut.

"First Edict mastery, on the other hand, forgoes the need of such primitive words and requires naught but willpower alone. Not all Cruaar are capable of such a feat. Fickle minds, weak alignments, impure bloodlines and a host of other reasons weaken their resolve. Again, this time mouth shut."

Asher raised his hand at a third column and tried to visualise it falling in his mind.

Nothing happened.

Tribarion Roolta nodded at him to try again, but each time Asher produced the same result.

"Try to visualise the invocation in your mind as you will the column to topple."

Asher tried again and again until, slowly but surely, the column cracked and broke apart, a little bit more with each attempt. He had no idea how much time had passed, Tribarion Roolta had said very little until the third column finally hit the ground with a dull thud. Asher lowered his aching arm, thoroughly exhausted.

"Congratulations, you've just bested your first inanimate object. How the Skulk will tremble in their boots."

Asher stood hunched over with hands on hips, panting. His tunic was completely drenched in sweat, but a broad smile was plastered across his face. He gave her an exhausted thumbs-up in acknowledgement.

"Now let's see how you fare against a slightly more sentient opponent." Tribarion Roolta turned away from him and retrieved something tucked away inside her armour. A moment later, a large square stone in front of her sank into the ground with a low rumble, revealing a large hollow chamber.

An awkward-looking creature with two long spindly legs, a short round body and a thin horn-tipped tail hopped out of the hole. It scratched at the stone platform with its oddly shaped feet, licking the cool stone slabs with an elongated green tongue from its oversized mouth.

Asher took a step back in surprise, every aspect of the creature looked drastically out of proportion.

Tribarion Roolta remained as stoic as ever. She deftly replaced the metallic ellipse beneath her breastplate without Asher even noticing. "This pitiful creature is a mawblink. It is as far from dangerous as a common garden-variety three-toed sloth. However, if provoked, it will defend itself. Now, again." She pointed her sword at the oddly shaped creature, inviting Asher to attack.

Asher adopted the correct pose the tribarion had taught him and raised his hand, levelling his auger at the mawblink's legs.

It tilted its head, four large eyes blinking back at him in unison as a bemused look of curiosity spread across its face. Its floppy green tongue hung loosely from the corner of its mouth, a long elastic band of saliva drooling to the ground.

"Occumbo."

Asher felt himself whispering the word as he released a large burst of energy that knocked the creature clean off its feet. It tumbled head over heels across the platform, but somehow landed upright, stamping its awkwardly long legs hard against the ground at its mistreatment.

It let loose a whinny growl and spat a large gob of sticky saliva at Asher. The gelatinous projectile hit Asher in the face, completely covering his mouth and eyes. The next thing Asher felt was a dull heavy blunt object collide with his chest and the sensation of weightlessness as he flew backwards through the air and off the platform, until he finally landed heavily amidst the sand and dirt of the arena floor.

The air expelled from his lungs in a rush, allowing the bitter saliva covering his face to seep into his mouth. He gasped for breath as he wiped the spit from his face with his sleeve and repeatedly spat it from his mouth.

Gathering himself up out of the dirt and sand of the arena floor, he rose to his feet, only to buckle at his knees as he was struck hard again by something from behind. Asher reached down and felt large red welts forming on the back of his legs. He heard Tribarion Roolta's unapologetic voice call out from the platform above.

"I warned you about leaving the platform."

Clearing the rest of the spit from his eyes, he scrambled back on to the elevated stone ledge as fast as he could and skirted around the mawblink, being careful to watch his footing against the platform's edges this time.

"Allow an opponent to silence you and you'll remain at their mercy until your tongue finds voice again. Forgo invocation altogether, and silence matters not."

"No talking, got it." Asher said bitterly, wiping the last globule of spit from his face and flicking it to the ground.

"Precisely. Think of it as a learning aid only. First Edict Mastery will exact a greater toll of blood from your body, but will generate a much greater and more effective blood calling in return."

Tribarion Roolta made Asher continue until he was able to topple the mawblink without uttering a word. She signalled the end of training by sheathing her sword and dismissing him from her side.

Asher left the arena nursing a series of welts and bruises, but a slim glimmer of excitement had settled deep in his heart. Despite everything he'd been through, the thrill of unleashing his blood through his auger was an intoxicating feeling, and he was only just getting started.

"Bring it on."

CHAPTER 25

LIFE INSIDE

Asher's day-to-day life in Mantlecrest blurred into a monotony of daily training sessions. Each left him battered and bruised, yet still he remained as wide-eyed as ever, keen to learn as much as he could with every passing moment. Before he knew it, a month had passed, making the memory of his life prior to Mantlecrest seem like a distant memory that somehow didn't feel real.

He received little news of the outside world, but what did reach him hardly seemed relevant anymore. He had received no news from Braak, nor any whisperings or rumours, and the fact he hadn't played greatly on his mind.

The Undergall Testament proved to be a great source of intelligence and gave him a small, albeit heavily censored, insight into the Cruaar Nation as a whole. Its history stretched back far beyond what Asher could have ever imagined, although much of what he learnt within Mantlecrest had amazed him, and he hadn't even stepped foot beyond its walls and into Undergall's vast sprawling mass.

Each day, during his instructions, he learnt more and more of what his blood was capable. His off-time was mostly spent learning as much as he could about the Cruaar Nation and the more common items of knowledge the other apprentices took for granted.

He'd managed to attend all but one of Master Welticrum's training sessions, failing to decipher only one of his clues about where the next location would be but, then again, most apprentices had missed at least one training session already, so he was not alone.

Apart from the occasional slur in the hallways, or a passing debased comment from an older apprentice, most of those inside

Mantlecrest had assumed an attitude of indifference towards him, for which he was surprisingly thankful. This was mostly because the tribune had taken a special dislike to him, plaguing him constantly in the halls with bitter looks of disgust and verbal insults that Asher had no choice but to endure.

Luckily, most of the other elder apprentices spent much of their time outside Mantlecrest, so he rarely saw them, apart from the occasional sighting during the evening meals and as they passed by his door after curfew.

Whilst the sight of Asher in the corridors of Mantlecrest became commonplace, coming by new friends wasn't exactly easy. Although, on the plus side, after the events within the Catacomb Cathedral, the majority of apprentices had stopped looking at him like an outcast, even if they still distrusted the black scar staining his auger.

In his travels between training sessions, Asher had discovered more of the strange glowing symbols hidden in the outbreaks of creeping green mould. The blighted fungi had continued to spread into the lower levels of the Mantlecrest's corridors, despite everyone's best attempts to disperse it.

Seeing as he was the only one that could see the symbols, he'd decided to keep the secret to himself, even from Lem and Lorrelli, at least until he could properly identify it: but so far all his attempts to do so had proven of little use.

Asher's suspicions of Morreby Fitch still lingered. Often, he would follow her through Mantlecrest's corridors and stairwells, and she'd always end up in the room marked Surio Letifer. Unfortunately, despite his best efforts, he hadn't been able to turn up any information about the words, nor had he been able to discern what was in the room or who she was meeting. Eventually, he had given up following her, content enough to hold onto his suspicions and watch her from afar, ensuring he gave her a wide berth at all times.

Lem had the most trouble out of anyone inside the academy. Several months in, he still couldn't master even the smallest of blood callings. The fact was beginning to wear on him, and Asher suspected his friend was heavily depressed, though he never admitted as much. His jokes became fewer and further apart, and he was distancing himself more and more from the Lorrelli and Asher.

Wandering off in his free time, he would come back more distressed and temperamental than ever.

Asher and Lorrelli had gotten used to his mood swings, especially as they had become more frequent, yet they were still as unpredictable as ever. He had even developed a weird tic, and was forever licking the front of his teeth or chewing his bottom lip during training.

Every now and then during conversation, two of their augers would flare up during conversation for no apparent reason, whilst the third remained lifeless and blank, much to their ongoing confusion.

Their training was relentless. Day after day it continued and, for Asher, well into the night with little reprieve; but his skills were growing at an alarming rate. He had now mastered a number of blood callings and his control over his auger was at a point where it did not hurt to use it. He still felt the pang of its bite, but it no longer bothered him.

All in all, life continued as usual, or at least what passed as usual within Mantlecrest. Each day blended into the next with little change. It was not until the day Asher woke to Lem's annoyed muttering that things changed, and changed for the worse.

Lem noisily opening a large crate in the corner of the room, a more-common-than-not scowl of annoyance plastered across his face.

CHAPTER 26

CAUGHT OUT IN A LIE

"It's from my step-father," Lem mumbled at Asher after noticing he had woken up. He read the delivery docket, "straight from his office at Craftpaw Industries."

"Go on, then, what is it?" Lorrelli asked, rubbing the sleep from her eyes as Lem removed a long steel stand and circular podium from the box. Following the instructions closely, he assembled the device and stepped back to inspect his work. "No way."

"What?" Lorrelli yawned, clutching her sheets around her for warmth as she rose out of her rack.

"It's one of the new promensi tables," Lem whispered, surprised. "These haven't even hit the stores yet."

"What does it do?" Asher asked sleepily.

"You know how sand projection tables work?"

"Basically," Lorrelli nodded, joining the pair at the promensi table.

Asher's frightening introduction to the council had been forever etched in his memory. Watching the echo of Braak's auger play out was nearly impossible to forget.

"Well, this is the next-gen equivalent. Fidget says it's been in the pipeline at Craftpaw for ages."

"Who's Fidget?" Lorrelli asked.

"My step-dad. He said it allows live communication across great distances through a new type of augineered semi-solid sand." Lem scratched his head as a light blinked from within a large opaque pearl on the side of the table-top. "That's weird."

Lem waved his auger at the pearl before stuffing it and his apprentice mantle out of sight, deep inside his tunic.

The semi-solid liquid that filled the low dome bubbled and

churned, rising through the glass and forming various shapes on its surface, one much taller than the rest. Within seconds, a small figure stood a foot above the top of the dome, waiting for something further to happen. A shrill whirring sound echoed around the room and a bright light surged upwards from the dome's base. It spread through the semi-solid substance, solidifying it into some form of flexible glass.

A small replica of a man was left on the table's surface, free to walk and interact with its surroundings. The amount of detail the liquid substance infused into the figure was extraordinary.

Asher could even make out wrinkles on the tiny man's face. Asher quickly realised he was looking at a miniature replica of Lem's step-father who stood in his office at Craftpaw Industries.

"And, presto… There you are, my son."

"I'm not your son," Lem stated bitterly, it was clear he had little to no respect for his step-father.

Fidget ignored the comment. "As you can probably guess, I've managed to be the first on the allocation list for the new promensi tables. At your mother's request, I managed to get one allocated to you." The small figure moved its head from side to side as if it was looking about their room.

"You must be Lorrelli Wittlearch, which would make you the rather infamous Asher Bloom. Well met to the both of you. I'm Flavink Erda, this shabby excuse for an apprentice's father—"

"Step-father," Lem rudely interrupted.

"But everyone just calls me Fidget," the man finished, ignoring Lem as though it was second nature to do so.

"Can he see us?" Asher whispered, awkwardly waving at the small man on the table whose hands were busy tinkering with a small augineered device Asher had never seen before.

"Well, of course I can. Brilliant little contraption, isn't it? It captures so much detail. For pity's sake, Lem, do tuck your tunic in, you look a mess." The small glass replica of Lem's step-father waved a dismissive hand at his step-son as a look of disappointment crossed his face. "I thought you of all people might be somewhat impressed by my latest augineered device, but obviously some Cruaar are easier to impress than others."

"You made this?" Lorrelli raised her eyebrows in astonishment. She had no idea Lem's step-father was so brilliant.

Lem, on the other hand, defiantly untucked more of his tunic, ensuring his step-father saw the gesture.

"Yes, well most of it, anyway. I was the head augineer on this project, as well as a few others I can't talk about. I did have a small amount of trouble with the connection side of things at first; damn near lost my eyebrows."

Asher and Lorrelli chuckled with Fidget as Lem shook his head, not buying into his step-father's charms.

"How is the old Cresticle, anyway? It's been years."

"Good," Lem blurted out before either of his friends had the chance to answer.

Asher and Lorrelli narrowed their eyes at him, but Fidget's excited voice didn't allow them to dwell on the issue. "Oh, you'll never guess what happened last night. You'll undoubtedly read all about it today in the Undergall Testament, but you might as well get the news hot off the sand." Fidget paused and looked over his miniature shoulder, checking to ensure he was alone. "Craftpaw's security system was breached for the first time ever, last night."

"Craftpaw was broken into?" Lem repeated in disbelief. He may not have liked or respected his step-father, but his respect for Craftpaw and its security was unbreakable. "How is that even possible?"

"We're still trying to figure that part out. The whole place is in an uproar today, secureaugs everywhere, tearing the place apart looking for answers." A loud bang echoed somewhere behind Fidget, but the small figure ignored it as if it was not the first one he had heard.

"Nothing to worry about," he said as he saw their concerned faces, "only a minimum security wing was breached and nothing was stolen; but even that's quite a feat, I assure you."

"So who was it?" Asher whispered, leaning in closer to the

table.

"No idea, there was no sign of them this morning, just trace remnants of some black sand. It's almost as if they vanished into thin air, as if that were possible." Fidget chuckled to himself at the notion.

"It's probably just some rogue augineer wanting to prove their worth to old Craftpaw. Attempts are made all the time to crack our systems, but this's been the first one to ever actually succeed." Fidget turned his head, hearing something behind him that the trio didn't.

"Right, security is here. I'm off like an oyster but, before I forget. Lemule, your messages home have practically ceased and your mother has been in a dither of worry. Hopefully, the promensi table should make the process a little easier to check in."

"Great," Lem muttered under his breath as Asher and Lorrelli sniggered.

"Right, then, chins up and all that."

With a sharp pop the semi-solid liquid inside the figurine lost its shape, splashed back down inside the dome and settled back into its lifeless state.

"Can you believe it?" Lem whispered, disbelief still evident across his face.

"I know," Lorrelli said, trying hard to hold back a laugh desperately trying to get out.

"I can't believe someone managed to break into Craftpaw Industries," Lem said, mortified.

"Oh, not that." Lorrelli tried her best to contain the urge to laugh, but still a slight snigger managed to force its way past her lips.

"What?" Lem demanded gruffly.

"Nothing, Lemule!" Both Lorrelli and Asher grinned before bursting into a fit of laughter.

"It's Bedlem, not Lemule, Lemule is just a dumb nickname step-dad gave me," Lem snorted defensively.

Both Lorrelli's and Asher's auger flared to life the moment Lem had finished speaking.

"There they go again," Lorrelli said trying hard to control her laughter, holding her auger up and watching green flares of light flicker and swirl around inside.

"Wait a minute… Lemule, where did you grow up again?" Asher asked, doing his very best to keep a straight face.

"Bedlem or Lem. Never Lemule," Lem warned, "and I grew up in Undergall. What's that got to do with anything?"

"Tell me you're from Oakrim," Asher instructed, forcing himself not to laugh as he closely watched the auger in his palm.

"But I'm not."

"Just do it."

"Asher, what are doing?" Lorrelli asked, thoroughly confused.

"Fine, I'm from Oakrim." Asher and Lorrelli's augers instantly flared up with light again.

"You're lying," Asher murmured to himself.

"No, I'm not. You know I'm from Undergall. What the prac are you playing at?" Lem snapped, his patience threadbare, a single wisecrack away from breaking point.

"No, my auger flares up when you're lying. Lorrelli's, too. Lorrelli lie about something, anything."

"Err okay, my father's a tribarion," Lorrelli offered. Lem and Asher's augers instantly flared to life with a brief flash of light. "Wow, you're right, how weird."

"Don't you get it?" Asher asked. Lem and Lorrelli stared back at him with wide dumbfounded eyes. Clearly they didn't.

"Think back to what the legate said to us, after the Ceremony of Alignment." Asher attempted to impersonate Legate Seville's stuck-up voice. "Whatever drew you three together, your trust in each other will see you stay that way." He waited for them to realise what he was getting at. They didn't.

"The veritusk bind. It stops us from lying to each other."

"I think you're right, Asher." Lorrelli agreed. "You realise what this means?"

"What?" Lem asked.

"Lem's real name is Lemule," she blurted out and fell to the floor laughing.

Asher couldn't help himself and fell on his bed laughing, only to catch a glimpse of Lem's back as he stormed out of the room.

"I better go after him," Asher sniggered, pulling himself together. "See you on Mess Hill for breakfast?"

"No," she promptly declined. "I have to get to the Spiretop Gardens before training."

"You've been spending a lot of time up there lately; anything I should know about?"

"No," she said sharply, instantly raising Asher's suspicions about her activities even further. "It's nothing, though I think I might be closing in on finding my first mantle element."

Asher's question left Lorrelli a little flustered, but his auger didn't flare up at her explanation, so he decided to let the matter go. "Need any help?"

"No, you better go find Lemule and calm him down," she sniggered. "Probably best we don't tell anyone else about his real name. He's having a rough enough time as it is and I don't think I'll be able to stand him if he gets any moodier."

Asher nodded his agreement and left the room.

Lorrelli waited until his footsteps had receded down the corridor before fishing something out of the trunk at the end of her bed and heading to the Spiretop Gardens. She took her time getting there, being extra careful to make sure she wasn't followed. Hurrying past a group of elder apprentices that were largely ignoring her, she climbed the last set of stairs to one of the garden's lesser-known entrances.

Waving her auger at the trunk of a large oak jutting out of the end of an otherwise dead-end hallway, she whispered a command under her breath. The trunk groaned loudly as its bark warped and wood twisted apart, revealing a small dark hollow that extended upwards inside the tree.

Stepping inside, she put a leg up on a knob and hoisted herself up. Her arms and knees scraped against the bark as she clawed and climbed her way up the narrow hollow. She finally emerged through another hollow in the trunk on all fours and found herself surrounded by all manner of strange plants and dense foliage.

Spiretop Gardens actually sat on the top of one of Mantlecrest's larger annexes: not a spire as its name indicated. A series of old stone towers loomed overhead like watchful guardians, but the garden itself was deserted.

Lorrelli found herself alone and smiled; it was what she intended all along. She hurried past a large bed of native flowers that had blossomed into a delightful cascade of colour, before navigating through a dense cluster of hanging vines overgrowing the lower branches of an enormous angel oak. Luckily, the guardians above were all still asleep this early in the morning.

She brushed the vines sticky residue off her tunic as she pushed forward, navigating her way through a thick cluster of bamboo shoots. Emerging on the other side of them, she nimbly ducked underneath a large rock formation and finally reached a hidden grove. It was nestled deep within the garden that she'd come to know all too well in recent weeks.

Quickly removing something from her tunic, she rested the item inside a sunken knot of an old gnarled carob tree. It stood alone in the centre of the small clearing, its solitude undisturbed except for the girl who patiently waited at its base.

Asher was halfway to Mess Hill when he spied the slim figure of Morreby Fitch disappearing down a stairwell heading towards the arena. Still determined to find out what she was up to and who she was meeting with, Asher followed her. Being careful to keep his distance, he had gotten quite good at tailing her without her knowledge. He'd made it a habit to duck inside doorways and hide behind corners in order to avoid detection from her frequent glances over her shoulder.

Morreby descended another two flights of stairs and traversed the length of a disused corridor, when she heard a distant scrape that sounded like a muffled footstep. She spun around and peered behind her, but saw nothing. Her beady eyes scanned the corridor a few moments more but, hearing nothing, she turned away and walked off muttering to herself.

Asher breathed a sigh of relief and stealthily followed, ducking into an alcove and hiding from view, watching from within the darkness as Morreby approached a heavy door he'd never seen before. A large sign had been nailed to its face.

ENTRY TO UNDERCELLARS
STRICTLY PROHIBITED
UNTIL FURTHER NOTICE

Morreby took no notice of the sign and retrieved something from a bag slung over her shoulder, waved it at the secureaug lock and disappeared inside.

Asher sprinted down the length of the corridor and caught the door with his fingertips before it closed behind her. If it were not for the years Asher had spent on the street, Morreby would have probably heard the footsteps rush to the door, but Asher was as silent as the creep of coming dawn. He slipped inside the doorway and let the door close shut with a loud clang to avoid arousing her suspicion.

Asher waited and listened intently before attempting to continue his pursuit. He heard nothing, but Morreby's fresh footprints were clear in the layers of settled dust, which made tracking her relatively easy. As Asher followed Morreby's trail deeper into the Undercellars of Mantlecrest, he noticed large patches of creeping mould had begun to overgrow the walls and roof of the corridors. The further he descended, the more the mould became a prominent fixture, until he finally reached a point where only small patches of stone were still visible under the soft green muck.

Morreby's footprints vanished as the dusty stone floor was

replaced by living bed of green and yellow mould. It had taken root over the corridor's walls, floor and roof as far as Asher could see.

Slowing his pace, Asher peered closely at the mould-covered floor. His eyes narrowed, searching for squashed growth where Morreby had crushed the delicate living carpet Undergall. His progress was slow. Between the severe lack of light, the soft squelch of his own footsteps and the ever-growing distance between auglights, following her trail at speed became almost impossible.

A little further along the passageway, large sections of mould had been burned and scarred black. Someone had obviously tried to burn away the creeping menace, but had evidently found little success. Fresh outbreaks of mould had even started to regrow over the charred remnants, even thicker than before.

Every so often, Asher raised his auger to his head to search the walls for hidden symbols, but the mould was far too dense to see anything clearly. He rounded a corner and found himself in a narrow bent hallway, the distance between auglights now so great he could barely see the walls around him.

An auglight shone up ahead, illuminating the curve of the wall, but its light did not extend near as far as Asher would have liked. Taking an awkward step forward, he felt a crunch beneath his foot a moment too late to be able to readjust his weight. Looking down, he couldn't see anything beneath his foot, so he gingerly reached down with his hands and let his fingers wrap around the thing on which he had stepped.

It felt soft and hairy and warm to the touch. Whatever it was had died recently, but not by his clumsy footsteps. Raising it up against the light of the distant auglight, he saw the gaunt silhouette of a rat or, rather, the freshly killed corpse of a rat, swaying back and forth from its tail in his hands. He groaned with disgust and threw the carcass away behind him. Its bony corpse squelched against the mould as it landed.

"Who's there?" a loud voice called out.

Asher froze. It didn't belong to Morreby. He silently cursed himself for his foolishness and frantically looked around for a hiding place. He saw none, only the mould-covered curved wall and darkness.

A bright light appeared from around the corner behind him. The silhouette of a large man shone against the wall as it approached, the light bouncing and jerking his shadow this way and that like a marionette doll.

Before Asher could even contemplate running, the bright gleam of an auglight rounded the corner and blinded him to the man who wielded it.

"Apprentice Bloom, is that you?"

Asher peered out from behind his raised hand and squinted at the man's silhouette.

Mason Gobbler dropped the auglight, affixed to the end of a short pole, from his shoulder to the ground and stood at the end of the corridor eyeing off Asher suspiciously. "What in all of Mastonon are you doing down here? You know this area is off limits."

"Sorry, Master, I took a wrong turn and got lost down here," Asher lied.

"It's Mason," Mason corrected, "and you're about as convincing as I am tall. Yet it is fortunate our paths have crossed nonetheless. The Overseer asked me to personally deliver this to you." Mason reached into his tunic and withdrew a small figurine with a metallic base, handing it to Asher.

The small sculpture of a gavrin stared up at Asher blankly. It looked similar to the pyxis Raglan had left him, but it was a much more modern variant than the rudimentary wooden ibis that Raglan had obviously carved himself.

Mason leaned in close to Asher and spoke in voice no louder than a whisper. "Listen to it somewhere safe and share it only with those you trust." His tone turned deadly serious. "No-one else! Understand?"

Asher met his stare and saw the man's seriousness. He nodded his understanding, but said nothing.

"Now, unless you're prepared to tell me what you're really doing down here, you'd best return upstairs to corridors dryer than these."

Asher maintained his silence and shook his head. Mason nodded unimpressed and motioned for him to follow. He swiftly led Asher through a maze of winding corridors and turns until, finally, they reached the entrance to the Undercellars. Opening the door, they stepped through, but Mason made sure to lock the door behind him, mumbling something to himself about upgrading the secureaug lock on the Undercellars door.

Asher muttered his thanks to Mason and left, Gobbler's watchful gaze following him as he sped off. Asher nimbly ascended a flight of stairs and ducked into the nearest empty room he could find. He commanded the pyxis to life and listened to the message twice before stuffing it back into his tunic pocket.

Ensuring the way was clear, he snuck out of the room like an alley cat and sprinted all the way to his first training session. He did not stop until he was standing snugly between a still-annoyed Lem and a strangely bemused Lorrelli. Morreby Fitch had already arrived and stood three rows ahead of Asher, looking painfully innocent of all wrongdoing.

Asher leaned in close to Lorrelli and Lem, ensuring his eyes were glued to Morreby Fitch.

"We need to talk," his voice barely registered above a whisper. "Braak sends word from The Blind."

CHAPTER 27

GUARDIANS OF THE FALLEN

Mistress Penny's Basic Augestry training was ordinarily the one time and place that Asher could count on Lem's temperamental attitude being skewed towards the positive, but after he'd whispered his news about Braak, Lem's outward demeanour was anything but uplifting.

Lem and Lorrelli had only heard stories of the warder that had saved Asher's life, but this was the first time he'd made contact since. Asher had sternly refused to talk any more about the matter until their training had finished, despite Lem's constant whispers in his ear theorising about what it might be.

Instead, Asher kept a close watch on Morreby, refusing to let her out of his sight, even for a second. His friends thought his newfound interest in Morreby Fitch disturbing, but felt it best to keep their mouths shut until he had the chance to explain what was going on.

When Mistress Penny finally dismissed them, the trio hung back from the rest of the apprentices as they headed off down a stairwell. Asher grabbed Lorrelli by the arm and ducked into a nearby corridor, heading back towards their racks. Lem and Lorrelli tried to pry answers from him along the way, but Asher refused to say a word until they were safely within their room and the secureaug lock had been engaged.

"You mind telling us what the praccing hell is going on?" Lem demanded abruptly. "What's with all the doak and clagger?"

"I have something important you both need to hear," Asher replied, fishing something out of his tunic pocket. Revealing the pyxis, he engaged its recorded message and sat it down on his trunk. The tiny pewter gavrin rose to its feet and turned in a circle before Braak's voice spilled out from its miniscule metallic throat.

Braak's tone sounded cautious and concerned, as though he'd recorded the message in secret, away from prying ears.

"Asher, my apologies for not contacting you sooner. I was ordered by the Elder Council to return with a team to investigate the scene of our attack without delay, but I do not trust those they sent with me.

"One man in particular keeps asking after you. He rarely leaves my side and watches me constantly. I fear he hides his true motive behind the false pretence of this investigation. I managed to smuggle this pyxis to a trusted friend, so hopefully it finds you. Heed my warning: be wary of anyone that uses or mentions the name Farrenk. He is not to be trusted.

"As for my investigation, I've found little to no evidence of our attacker. Nor have I found any sign of Raglan. The trail has gone cold, for now. I'm sorry."

Braak's voice lowered to a whisper, his tone becoming more agitated with every passing second. "Something doesn't sit right in all this, but one thing is sure. Someone went to great lengths to cover up what happened to us in Aswan. Much more than our attack has been tainted by some form of augmented projection and they have not been easy to unmask.

"From what I have managed to piece together, I do not believe that you, or I, were the initial targets of the Mortis Skulk, but were unfortunate bystanders in the wrong place at the wrong time. I cannot prove it, but it's almost like the cultist that attacked us was searching for something or someone else entirely. What or who, I cannot say."

A distinct whistling sound and muffled voices echoed faintly as Braak's speech quickened. It was clear he had underestimated the time needed to safely make the recording. "You must be on guard. Assume the worst of everyone, especially those acting out of character around you. We have no way of knowing how deep this cover-up goes, or who is involved. Whatever we face, you are not alone, but neither are they. You must be careful.

"I have a friend keeping tabs on you in Mantlecrest, but I, more than anyone else, know what you've been through. Remember, every cut and bruise you take, I take also, so be careful and stay safe. I will contact you again when I know what's going on. Braak out."

"Prac me, he knows how to dampen the mood doesn't he?" Lem murmured solemnly as the severity of Braak's warning sunk in.

"Conspiracies and cover-ups aside, if the Mortis Skulk weren't after you, what were they after?" Lorrelli pondered out loud.

"More importantly, who's Braak's contact in Mantlecrest?" Lem added concisely. "It'd be good to know who we can trust."

"I have no idea," Asher's expression was blank, "but there are a few things I haven't told you."

Asher told them everything he'd been holding back. The rite of bonded blood; Raglan's true name and origin; Gibraltair's conversation in the Fall of Foreguard; the Elder Council mandate; the acropall in the arena; the door marked by the name Surio Letifer; the symbols in the mould as well as all of his suspicions surrounding Morreby Fitch, especially her actions in the Undercellars.

Lem and Lorrelli sat back and listened intently to everything Asher had to say, their astonishment growing with every detail. Not once did either of their auger's light up during his explanation. Asher was telling the truth about everything, which made everything he said all the more alarming.

Thinking back, none of them could recall any other apprentice's acting suspiciously, but they all agreed Morreby was definitely worthy of investigation. After listening to Braak's warning once more to see if they had missed anything, the trio briefly prioritised what was more important: investigating the symbol in the mould, or Morreby Fitch. Ten minutes of careful deliberation later and a unanimous decision was reached.

"So we're agreed. We need to find out why Morreby was creeping about the Undercellars and who she's meeting in the room marked by 'Surio Letifer'"

Lorrelli was about to reveal a secret of her own when her eye caught the latest story breaking on the Undergall Testament. She grabbed the glass tablet from the foot of her bed and read, urgently, a large frown slowly spreading across her face. "Gibraltair's in Undergall."

"What?" Lem and Asher said, almost in unison.

A large image of Gibraltair sat prominently featured above the latest breaking story. As usual, he was ridiculously overdressed in all his bespoke finery. He pompously stood at the crest of a grand stairwell with one arm resting gracefully on the balustrade, with the other firmly clutched around the shaft of his cane. He had a self-important smile on show for everyone to see beneath his tinted glasses. An oversized heading preceded the main article.

PRIVVYBELL TOLLS FOR TRUTH:
FOREGUARD'S SECRETS LAID BARE

Asher waved his auger over the black pearl to engage the audio and listened as a clear voice narrated the article.

"Gibraltair may have the Cruaar Nation readying their augers in protest upon his return from yet another unauthorised augiological expedition, this time venturing deep beneath the abhorrent black sands of war and into the Fall of Foreguard.

"In his usual flamboyant style, the famed augiologist dismissed public outrage, declaring his latest discoveries will stand as a testament to the Cruaar Nation's limitless resilience against oppression.

"This he promises and more when his all-new exhibition, Guardians of the Fallen, opens in Undergall. However, his exhibition may be delayed longer than expected, the council announcing its impending review of his unauthorised excursion and so-called discoveries mere moments ago. In the meantime, Gibraltair humbly submitted to remaining in Undergall, with restricted access to the city, until all the council's questions are satisfied. Grand Chancellor Valderook Wrakburn had this to say."

The voice in the recording changed with a loud crackle into that of the Chancellor's. "Gibraltair Privvybell Reine's unauthorised incursion into Foreguard borders on treason and will be investigated in full. He will remain a guest of the council, with restricted access to Undergall, until such a time as his trespasses and crimes have been dealt with." Another crackle spluttered as the voice changed back to the previous narrator.

"Never one to shy away from council persecution of his unauthorised excursions, Gibraltair firmly stated this in a public address."

Gibraltair's voice warbled through the tablet loud and clear, his speech strong and articulate. "I stand resolute in my belief that Undergall's most honourable council will clear me of whatever pending charges they can throw at me, and readily legitimise my latest augiological expedition. I have every confidence that my voluntary internment as their guest will be brief, though I must thank the council for their continuing warmth and hospitality," Gibraltair's voice faded away with an insolent laugh.

The narrator returned. "Whether the council will keep to Gibraltair's expeditious schedule is yet to be seen. Upon his release, however, he has made it perfectly clear that a celebration of his vindication is in order at none other than Undergall's more notorious beacon of ill repute, The Swaying Tribarion.

"While the grand opening of Gibraltair's exhibition may still be months away, undoubtedly, the hype he has already stirred up through his blatant disregard for authority in the pursuit of augiologically significant artefacts will see the demand for tickets skyrocket when they finally go on sale. Deriat Ungeltread reporting."

Asher and Lorrelli sat in silence, soaking it all in, but Lem was too disappointed to remain quiet.

"Guardians of the Fallen," he said again, rereading the title of

Gibraltair's exhibit. "Looks like you were right about the constructs after all, Lorrelli. I guess even the Vitalsior Heart is out of Gibraltair's reach."

"Don't bet on it. Constructs alone wouldn't warrant this much council attention. I think there's more going on than what's being reported. Who knows, maybe he'll even visit Mantlecrest while he's here."

"You think?" Lem perked up. "That'd be sweet."

"We can deal with Gibraltair later," Asher said, snatching the tablet away from Lem and throwing it behind him on the bed. "We need to work out what Morreby Fitch is up to."

"Whoa, easy soldier," Lem raised his eyebrows at Asher.

"Sorry, but the sooner we discover what she's up to, the better. Let's start with the room marked by the name Surio Letifer, someone has to know something about it. Maybe, if we knew what the words meant, we could discover a way in or, at least, work out what Morreby's doing in there."

The other two nodded their heads in agreement, Lem somewhat begrudgingly, then the trio formulated a plan of how best to tail Morreby and begin making discrete enquiries about the name Surio Letifer.

Pretty soon a week had passed and, despite their best efforts at surveillance, reconnaissance and research, they were no closer to finding anything further about the name Surio Letifer or the room beyond it. Nor had they seen anyone else enter or leave the chamber, but they had all heard the muffled voice through the heavy door at one point or another.

Whomever Morreby was meeting with inside the room obviously had another means of entrance. The most logical explanation was that the room had its own vertistrand. It was the only thing that could explain why they had never seen anyone else entering or leaving.

Asher had almost given up hope of ever getting access to the room until, one day, he arrived a few minutes early before his private training sessions to see Mason Gobbler disengaging the lock to the room with a wave of his auger.

Asher discretely hurried over to Mason's side and followed him inside the room, hypothesizing a theory about what might be causing the mould. Mason patiently heard him out before dismissing his theory and prattling on with his own suspicions about the underlying cause of the blighted outbreaks.

As Mason scanned the walls for more occurrences of mould, Asher took the opportunity to study the room as best he could, soaking up every minute detail.

At first glance, it appeared to be a relatively ordinary room of average size, with no obvious remarkable features. One thing Asher instantly noticed was the inherent lack of a vertistrand, which both puzzled and troubled him.

The only notable fixtures in the room were two small arched alcoves set in opposing walls and an empty stone ceremonial font in the room's centre. Its sculptured bowl was bone dry and free of any distinguishing features, as was the exterior of the font. Concentric circular pavers extended outwards from its base in a wide circle, before the regular square stonework resumed and continued to the far corners of the room.

"You don't know who Surio Letifer was, do you Master Gobbler?" Asher asked innocently as he lazily scratched his head, unable to fathom how Morreby's accomplice was accessing the room.

"Hmm, what that's now?" Gobbler mumbled under his breath, wiping a finger along the inside of the font, before inspecting a fine film of white dust and a few short grey hairs that stuck on the tip of his finger.

"Surio Letifer," Asher repeated casually, trying not to arouse the peculiar man's suspicion.

"Sorry, sprout, never heard of him; what makes you ask?" Mason frowned, a troubled expression crossing his face as he wiped the dirty finger on his jacket leaving a small white smear of dust on the fabric.

"It's above the door outside."

"Humph," Mason grumbled as Asher's continued persistence broke through his concentration, shaking away the disturbing thought lingering in his mind.

"Never really noticed. Wouldn't be too concerned in any case, most of these rooms are named after all sorts of weird and wonderful hooligans and olden-day heroes, amongst other things more nefarious in nature."

"So it might not be a name?"

"Might be," a twinge in Mason's eye betrayed his own annoyance at his momentary slip, "but then, it just as easily might not. Right, then, no outbreaks here. Come on, then, off with you." The small man hurriedly ushered Asher out of the room, muttering something about talking to the legate about the blasted mould situation getting out of hand.

Asher was so excited to tell the others about his revelation he never saw the suspicious scowl lining the small man's features as he watched Asher depart. Gobbler locked the door behind him and tapped a small square object in his tunic pocket just to check it was still safe.

It was many few hours and many fresh bruises later, courtesy of training with Tribarion Roolta in the Praelior Arena, before an exhausted but exhilarated Asher burst into his racks to find Lorrelli studying a selection of older-looking tablets on her bed.

Lem, however, was nowhere to be seen.

"Where's Lem?" Asher asked.

"Off trailing Morreby. Again. We might be wrong about her, she hasn't been anywhere near the Undercellars, or the entrance to the Undercellars, since we started tailing her."

"Maybe she knows we're on to her."

"Not likely. We've been using the tricks you taught us. Lem even managed to follow Mistress Penny the other day for a whole hour without her knowing. Which, to be honest, is a little creepy, but the fact remains Morreby's none the wiser."

"Maybe she's found another way in?" Asher scratched his chin, thinking out loud.

"Perhaps, but the only time she's been out of our sight is when she's in the room marked Surio Letifer, or in her racks after curfew."

"She could be sneaking out," Asher countered.

"No, we ruled that out already. Lem's become good chums with her roommate, Apprentice Uller, and he says Morreby sleeps like a baby from sundown to sun-up every night, without even so much as a whisper."

"Hmm," Asher puzzled, trying to reason everything out in his head. "I was going to wait for Lem, but this is too important. I think I may know why we haven't been able to find any information about the name Surio Letifer." Asher quickly explained what he saw inside the room and his conversation with Mason Gobbler.

"So if Surio Letifer isn't a name, then what is it?" Lorrelli pondered, a perplexed look on her face.

"I'm not sure," Asher said, "but I know where we need to start looking."

CHAPTER 28

QUERELUS BARKS AND WORMWOOD VINDICAT

Asher and Lorrelli gazed out over the city from Mess Hill whilst they waited for Lem to arrive. Asher refused to explain any more until Lem had joined them, leaving Lorrelli completely in the dark about Asher's idea.

Apprentices sprawled out over the hill like ants going this way and that. Most keep to themselves, but Asher still caught the occasional glare as they glanced in his direction.

When they saw Morreby enter through the double arched doors and on to the hill, Lem emerged moments later. He looked as downcast and dejected, as usual: head down, mumbling to himself with a finger in his mouth rubbing his teeth.

Morreby, on the other hand, looked visibly exhausted and even more drained than usual.

Lem didn't even wait for Morreby to sit down before passing her as though she didn't exist and crossing the lawn. He wasn't more than two steps past her when a loud tone chimed above them. The enormous statues perched atop the large stone columns came alive readying their coarse throats for an announcement.

Tribune DeGrulz stood at attention with his hands behind his back beneath the statues, waiting for all eyes to focus on him. His deep voice bellowed down over the grassy mound silencing all remaining whispers.

"Attention! Legate Seville has an announcement that concerns you all, so listen up." High above the tribune, an enormous statue of a ferocious stone beast sprang into action. Powerful stone arms flailed through the air and hammered clenched claws against its chest one after the other, the legate's voice bellowing from its mouth.

"Apprentices. As we have yet to stem the spread of the creeping mould from the Undercellars, I hereby throw down a gauntlet of opportunity to you all. Any apprentice that discovers a way to slow the spread of the mould—stop it, or kill it entirely—will be rewarded with a once-in-a-lifetime opportunity.

"It is well known that Mantlecrest has a long and proud history in producing the very best Utor Alea augletes. Considering that the UA Seven Seal Championship is nearly upon us, I have personally organised with the Grand Chancellor that the first match will be held here, inside our very own Praelior Arena."

A slew of nearby apprentices exclaimed their excitement in a volley of hoots and hollers. Riotous applause and wild cheers quickly flooded over the hill as everyone else joined in the celebration.

"Should any of you be clever enough to discover a cure for the mould that plagues your hallowed halls, you'll not only watch the Undergall Hopralas crush the Hollow's Rest Rajas, but do so rubbing shoulders with the elite of Undergall, as an honoured guest in the Custodian's Box."

"Righteous," Lorrelli smiled, her excitement equal to everyone else's as another round of raucous cheers reverberated out over the hill.

"I have also just been informed that a special guest will be stranding in one of his latest discoveries specifically for the interference round. I speak of none other the infamous augiologist Gibraltair Reine, who was just this past hour cleared of all council charges. A self-admitted devout Utor Alea fan, he will be watching the tournament from within Mantlecrest's Custodian's Box. Good luck, apprentices, and remember: to the victor go the spoils." Legate Seville's announcement ended with another loud chime and the statue resumed its frozen resolute pose atop the column.

A hive of excited chatter broke out over the hill as everyone started sharing ideas about how best to tackle the mould. A group of apprentices rushed off the hill in search of the nearest mould outbreak, many more following after realising where they had gone.

Though Asher didn't quite understand what the big deal was with Utor Alea, it was evident the prize on offer was too great for any apprentice to ignore.

As usual, Morreby remained seated by herself, all too often casting disapproving and disturbing glances in their direction. Asher knew there was something dreadfully wrong with the girl, he just didn't know what it was.

Lem slammed down on the grass next to Lorrelli with a loud huff. He was just as excited as everyone else about the legate's challenge. So great was his excitement, Asher couldn't get a word in edgeways and had to wait until the end of dinner to properly explain his idea.

After almost everyone had left Mess Hill and headed off to their racks, Asher dragged Lem and Lorrelli to one side and made sure they were away from all prying ears before sharing his idea.

Lorrelli instantly became lost deep in her own thoughts after hearing it, whilst Lem just stared at him, a dumbfounded expression on his face.

"You can't be serious?"

"Why not?" Asher asked. "If the answer is anywhere, it's most likely there."

"Well, sure," Lem blurted out, trying hard to maintain the relatively low volume of his voice. "But come on, seriously. Do you even know how big that place is? How long it'd take to search? We'd have to look through hundreds, thousands of records, not that we know how or anything… and that's only if we could break in, which we can't." Lem made his obstinate agitation at the ridiculousness of Asher's plan blatantly obvious.

"We're only first-year apprentices, Asher. We can't even leave Mantlecrest, let alone just go and raid the Annals of History. You're mad, that's what you are, a laccing proonatic."

"They don't just let anyone go and access the Annals. We'd have a better shot of slapping the legate in the face and getting away with it," Lorrelli agreed unhelpfully.

"Who said anything about we?" Asher replied calmly.

"You got someone else in mind in that vast circle of friends of yours?" Lem scoffed holding up his hands around him. "Look around you, spoon. We're it."

"Hmm, let me think," Asher said coyly, someone already firmly in mind, deciding to let them arrive at the realisation of what he intended on their own. "Who do we know that already has access to the Annals and just happens to be an old friend of your father?"

Seconds passed before Lorrelli's head swilled around, as she realised what he was inferring. "Welticrum!"

"Precisely," Asher clicked his fingers together, pointing at her.

"We've already asked him, Lem countered. "He didn't know anything."

"Not personally, but the Annals might."

"I don't know, Asher, Welticrum is odd at the best of times," Lem argued.

"Come on, Lem, who better? Your father trusted him enough to look out for you; besides, he's the La Tête Auglorian of the Annals," Asher mimicked Welticrum's thick French accent in an attempt to appeal to Lem's lighter side. "He'd probably even know where to start looking. He's perfect."

"Okay," Lorrelli said quietly. "Assuming the Annals holds the key to the Surio Letifer mystery. The real question is how do we ask him to research it without raising any suspicion?"

"What do you mean?" Asher asked.

"We don't know what Surio Letifer means. What if it's something horrible, or forbidden, and he reports us to the legate, Lobrolo, or worse yet the council?"

"Good point," Lem said gruffly throwing the problem back at Asher.

"I hardly think something horrible or forbidden would be

etched above a door in Mantlecrest," Asher downplayed her fears.

"I'm sorry, did you forget about the Catacomb Cathedral that's loaded to the gills with skulls, bones and the carcasses of rotting dead Cruaar?" Lem jeered.

"Not to mention that horrible floating sea of blood," Lorrelli added, a shiver running down her spine at the memory of gazing up into the murky depths of the Tutela Sky.

"Or, hang on, how about the skulk cultist that nearly killed you," Lem said bitterly, "or did you forget about that little chestnut?"

"Yeah, alright," Asher conceded, "just keep your foul mood swings to a minimum, would you? They're not helping," Asher spat at Lem, sick of never knowing what mood Lem was going to be in at any minute. "What's going on with you, anyway?"

"It's nothing," Lem lied.

Lorrelli looked at Asher as their augers simultaneously flared up, but they both knew it was probably not a good idea not to push the subject any further.

"Asher, the reality is that some of the things that are forbidden now may not have been ages ago," Lorrelli rubbed her hands on her legs for warmth, bringing the conversation back on track. "You know, when the words were first etched above the door. We have to be smart about this and cover ourselves. Remember Braak's warning."

"Fair point," Asher agreed, quietly racking his brain for ideas. Surprisingly enough it was Lem who had the first good idea, which consequently also seemed to lift him out of his grim slump. "Gibraltair!"

"Not now, Lem." Asher said dismissively, expecting another miserable outburst from his friend.

"Swoon after your hero some other time," Lorrelli agreed, also fed up with Lem and his ridiculous obsession with the augiologist.

"What? No, listen. Gibraltair, as in we get Gibraltair to ask the question for us at the Utor Alea match. Welticrum is bound to be in the Custodian's Box for sure, he is practically one step away from becoming one, anyway. All we have to do is plant the idea in Gibraltair's head. If he's anything like Asher says he is, his curiosity will do the rest."

"Lem, you're a genius," Asher grinned and slapped his friend hard on the arm, apologising for his previous attack. "It wouldn't be strange at all for a famous augiologist to ask Welticrum to research something in the Annals of History."

Lem couldn't help but let loose a wide grin, clearly enjoying his moment of clarity.

"I think you're forgetting one small detail," Lorrelli interjected sharply. "In order to plant this brilliant seed in the first place, we'd need to get inside the Custodian's Box and there's that little problem of the creeping mould to deal with first."

"She's right," Asher said, thinking hard about the problem at hand. "Well, at the very least, we're one step in front of everyone else."

Lorrelli looked at him perplexed. "How do you figure?"

"We know about the symbols and we know whatever is causing the mould is strongest in the Undercellars. That's more info than anyone else has," Asher pointed out.

"Except maybe Morreby," Lem exhaled, trying to think. "But we still don't know anything about the symbol and it's not like we can go around asking about it, either, unless we want people to start catching on, or get suspicious."

"Okay, so who do we ask about a symbol surrounded by mould?" Asher paced about the room, lost deep in thought.

"Maybe we don't need to ask about the symbol," Lorrelli grabbed Lem's arm and squeezed. "Maybe we just need to ask about the mould."

"That's hardly thinking outside the box, Lorrelli." Lem replied. "Besides, who would we ask that hasn't already been asked by every apprentice in Mantlecrest?"

"Not who. What."

"Well that's just plain gibberish." Lem threw his hands up in the air. "Am I the only one here not bippin flonkers?"

"Trust me on this," Lorrelli tried to explain, "you both know how much time I've been spending in the Spiretop Gardens?"

Both Lem and Asher nodded in agreement.

"Well I haven't been up there alone. I've been talking with something."

"Something?" Asher repeated suspiciously.

"It's probably better if you see it for yourself. If we hurry we can get there before curfew comes into effect." Lorrelli was already hurrying towards the exit before Asher and Lem had a chance to argue. "Come on."

The trio promptly left Mess Hill and hurried through a series of hallways, stairwells and corridors, trying hard to avoid all unnecessary contact with other apprentices as they went. Apart from having to wait for an elder apprentice to finish smoking a chillskin pipe and discretely blow the resulting sweet-smelling smoke out a nearby window, they reached the secret entrance to the Spiretop Gardens without incident.

Lorrelli approached the large tree trunk protruding through the wall of what was an otherwise empty dead-end corridor and waved her auger at it, whispering an invocation under her breath.

Asher made sure to listen closely, despite her hushed tones.

"Arguo Ascendo."

The bark of the tree groaned and shuddered before slowly twisting and folding in on itself. A gaping hole emerged in its trunk, which revealed a tight passageway just big enough for them to squeeze inside one at a time.

"This is the only entrance to the gardens that works after curfew. My sister told me about it. She discovered it when she was an apprentice here," Lorrelli whispered, as she squeezed through the gap and awkwardly clambered upwards.

"Family secrets of hidden dark hollows… great," Lem muttered as he stepped inside the hole and followed her up, swearing and muttering under his breath the entire time.

Asher followed after Lem's feet had disappeared. He had only just climbed up after him when the tree groaned again and twisted shut behind him, plunging the tight space into darkness. With nowhere else to go, he climbed up blindly after Lem, trying his best to ignore the intermittent showers of dirt, bark and dust that his clumsy footwork dislodged from the walls of the tree.

When all three finally emerged topside, they found themselves crawling out of the enormous roots of a massive tree towering over Spiretop Gardens.

The central auglight of the city had dimmed, allowing a simulated night to descend over the city far below. All around them, the trees, leaves, plants and vines glittered and shone amidst the darkness with a sort of enigmatically beautiful iridescent light. Ferns, flowers and insects let off a kaleidoscope of pale blues, vivid yellows and vibrant reds, casting beautiful shadows in every direction as their light danced on the weird and wonderful vegetation thriving in the garden.

Lorrelli plucked a nearby seed pod that radiated with an unnaturally blue iridescence and used its luminance to light their way.

Asher had never seen anything like the garden in his life. Its natural beauty and dazzling charms were spellbinding. "Lorrelli, why haven't you told us about this place? It's amazing." Asher reached out and touched a nearby plant. The oversized leaves changed from red to yellow around each of his fingertips as they gently touched its surface.

"It's complicated," Lorrelli deflected as she pushed past the vines engulfing the angel oak's lower branches. A dark shape hissed and scratched the air at them from above.

Lem could just make out a pair of yellow eyes peering down at him. "Err, Lorrelli." Lem stopped moving and peered up anxiously.

Lorrelli removed a slab of uncooked meat from her bag and threw it up into the branches above. The eyes vanished for a second before reappearing one branch lower. The sounds of teeth gnawing into the meat echoed from above.

"It's an orilla. I'm pretty sure it guards the hidden grove. Took me ages to figure out what it eats."

"Flesh, Lorrelli, it eats flesh. Yet you don't find that the least bit disconcerting." Lem swallowed hard, staying as far away from the bobbing eyes as he possibly could.

Asher arched his head back to look at the pale gold eyes, which nimbly shifted from branch to branch in the darkness above. "What's an orilla?"

"Imagine large tree monkeys, but uglier and nocturnal. They only live in and around the trunks of elder angel oaks. I call that one Chucka," Lorrelli said with a smirk.

"Why?" Lem asked loudly, swearing as his foot accidentally caught on one of the tree's giant roots on the ground.

"Stick around long enough and you'll find out." Lorrelli laughed as she crept forward, prying apart the bamboo shoots standing in her way.

"Ow!" Lem cried out as something unexpectedly collided with the back of his head. His sharp cry echoed out around the garden, disrupting its serenity. Wild animal noises echoed back a warning from the underbrush nearby.

"Shh, we're trying not to attract attention, remember?" Lorrelli whispered angrily at him.

Lem looked down and picked up a small iridescent seed pod from the ground. "Praccing ape threw it at me," Lem said, thoroughly annoyed, glaring up at the yellow eyes. He could've sworn they were silently laughing at him. He hurled the seed pod back up at the eyes, but they nimbly dodged out of the way and hissed back at him.

"Come on, Lem, probably best not to get on Chucka's bad side," Asher sniggered and followed Lorrelli through the cluster of crowded bamboo shoots.

"Chucka. Very funny, Lorrelli," Lem muttered, begrudgingly following his friends and leaving his newfound nemesis lurking somewhere in the darkness behind.

After pushing their way through the small bamboo forest and ducking under a rocky outcrop, they emerged in Lorrelli's secret grove. She stopped and turned to face them, her demeanour turning deadly serious. "You two have to shut up until it comes out and say nothing when it does. Not one sound, understand?" After Asher and Lem reluctantly agreed, Lorrelli reached into her tunic and pulled out a small vial of liquid.

"What's that?" Lem whispered, pointing at the vial, breaking the promise he made mere seconds ago.

Lorrelli silenced him by holding a finger to her lips before tiptoeing forward and placing the container within a large knot of an old gnarled carob tree.

"Come on, Lorrelli, no secrets anymore." Lem placed a hand on her shoulder and raised his eyebrows at her, awaiting an explanation.

"Fine. It's Wormwood Vindicat. Now shut up."

Lem's chin nearly hit the floor when he heard what the liquid was, his voice snapping into urgency and possibly even more serious than Lorrelli's. "How in praccing hell did you get a vial of Wormwood Vindicat inside Mantlecrest? You know what they'll do to you... hell, what they'll do to us, if they catch us with it?"

"No-one knows I have it."

"What's Wormwood Vindicat?" Asher held up his hands to settle the two, not understanding what all the fuss was about.

Lorrelli ignored the question and continued to stare at the knot in the tree.

"What? You don't think Asher has a right to know you've been sneaking around with the poison that the Mortis Skulk used to corrupt the victims they turned? Praccing hell, Lorrelli, how could you be so stupid?"

"It's only poisonous if polluted with their blood." Lorrelli fumed at him through clenched teeth. "This is nothing more than an alcoholic tonic. So unless you actually want us to get caught, make some more noise. Otherwise, shut the hell up and wait. I'm doing this for all of us, remember?"

Asher placed a hand on Lem's arm and willed him to be quiet with his eyes.

It was against every instinct in Lem's body to remain silent after seeing the Wormwood Vindicat, but he begrudgingly obliged for Asher's sake.

Insects faintly chirped and somewhere a trickle of water dripped into a much larger pool, but nothing else disturbed the serenity of the garden. Minutes passed as Lorrelli waited patiently, her eyes glued to the knot in the tree.

The small vial of liquid had not moved an inch, leaving Lem particularly annoyed as he silently fumed at the back of Lorrelli's head.

Asher, on the other hand, enjoyed the grove's tranquillity and serenity. Letting his eyes wander, he took in its natural beauty and wondered how such a place could exist within a city trapped beneath the earth.

A small still pool lay in one corner of the grove, mirroring a cascade of iridescent lights from the flickering insects hovering above it. A small grassy knoll lay opposite, bordered by a row of bushes, all filled with lush wild flowers half of which had not yet bloomed.

Every now and then a mysterious sound would echo in the distance and carry over the garden, disrupting its eerie silence, but Asher couldn't place its source, or the creature that had made it.

After fifteen minutes had passed, Lem's impatience got the better of him and he turned to leave, noisily making his way back to the passageway under the rocky outcrop, mumbling as he went. "This is ridiculous, we may not be able to lie to each other, but not telling us about the Wormwood Vindicat is the same thing, Lorrelli. I'm outta here."

Asher turned, attempting to stop him, but a raspy voice stopped them both in their tracks.

"Impatient. Noisy."

Asher and Lem turned around to see a creature protruding from within the knot in the tree. A small body, made entirely of bark and sap, slowly twisted out of the knot of the carob tree. Its entire form was no bigger than Asher's torso, but as its face emerged, a heavy frown and perturbed nature could have equalled Lem's dour disposition at its worst.

The carob tree didn't seem to be any happier about the creature's emergence, either, audibly groaning as the creature of bark moved this way and that. One long, thick branch extended out from one side of its body, like a knotted bark-covered arm. A charred black stump scarred the place where a similar branch should've been on the other side, but it wasn't noticeably absent. The small creature reached out and wrapped the tip of its branch around the vial of Wormwood Vindicat.

"Vindicat. Have?"

"As promised," Lorrelli bowed her head. The small wooden creature looked at the trio with large knotted eyes. Clumsily, it knocked the top off the vial and dribbled a small amount of the liquid into the hole that served as its mouth, and then spat it on the ground, narrowly missing Asher's feet.

"Hey!" Asher snapped back at him, barely dodging the creature's rank smelling spittle.

"Ergh. Mawblink piss. Never swallow first taste."

Lorrelli held up her hands at Asher ordering him to be silent as the creature took another swig, the wrinkles on his face easing a little after he had swallowed.

"Drink second. Better."

Asher and Lem both peered curiously at the wooden creature. Neither could tell where his body began and where the tree ended, or whether they were even two separate entities.

"Harbinger, want what?" The creature spoke with a thick gnarled accent that warbled and resonated from deep within the trunk of the tree.

Asher had trouble following his words, everything he said seemed back to front and the key elements needed to make sense of his sentences were missing.

"Prum, this is Lem and Asher. Lem, Asher, this is Prum. He's a querelus bark. He's the one that's been helping me find my mantle's first element."

"What's a querelus bark?" Asher stepped a little closer and inspected the tiny wooden creature. In return, Prum eyed off Asher in an equally nosey fashion.

"Denied," Prum coughed rudely. "Harbinger liar. Clear terms. Element swap Vindicat. Strangers none. Surprises none. Agreement break. Deal break. Unacceptable. Forget never. Again never. Go!"

"Wait," Lorrelli called out, but it was too late. With an audible wooden groan, Prum disappeared back within the knot of the tree, taking the Vindicat with him.

Lem scowled as he set off again. "Nice plan, Lorrelli. Liquor-up a disgruntled strip of bark with poison and ask for its help. You two are both as bent as each other."

Lorrelli spun around, her face fuming with rage. "How many times did I tell you two to shut it? Now he's gone and so is any chance of finding my first element. What the hell is your problem anyway, Lemule?"

"Lemule," he repeated dejectedly, the sound of his own name only stirring his anger further. "My problem is that you're so praccing worried about finding your first mantle element, you're sneaking around with a banned Mortis Skulk poison. Behind our backs, I might add. Meanwhile, Asher's so praccing caught up in trying to unravel a conspiracy that probably doesn't even exist that it's never crossed either of your minds that I might be dealing with slightly bigger and more realistic problems."

"Lem—"

Lem cut Asher off with a wave of his hand. "Forget, for a moment, I was the only apprentice that's failed to be aligned since the Overseer. Ignore the fact I'm unable to perform even the simplest of blood callings. Or that I'm not only the worst apprentice in Mantlecrest, if not the history of Mantlecrest. How about the fact that I'll be facing exile or the chop if my auger fails to be aligned during the second round? Which I'll be attending alone, thank you very much."

"I'm…" Lorrelli tried to interject, but Lem shut her down.

"You know what's worse? The only thing I'll have to show for my time here is a praccing flask of whirlpool clarity. No blood callings, no alignment, no future, just two self-righteous, selfish spoons for friends and this nearly empty praccing flask of booze."

"Nearly empty?" Asher repeated, eyeing off the flask of whirlpool clarity Lem held in his hands. He had obviously decanted the liquid into the flask some time ago, ditching the original horn that held the liquid and had been indulging in it ever since.

"At least I can get drunk and numb the pain a bit before the axe falls. Praccing hell, and Fidget wonders why I haven't contacted home in months. Like he even knows the half of it." Lem collapsed to his knees in a sorrow-filled heap and unscrewed the top of the flask. A pungent and alluring scent spilled out across the garden.

"Aren't you being a bit dramatic?" Asher asked bluntly, clearly not understanding the origin of Lem's frustration and anger.

"Asher!" Lorrelli said horrified, silencing him from saying anything else to exacerbate the situation with a strong look.

Asher still didn't know what he'd said that was so bad.

"Dramatic? I face exile or the chop, and that's the support I get from my so-called friends? A bit dramatic? Prac you Asher. Prac you!"

Taking a swig of the liquid inside the flask, he angrily got up on his feet ready to storm away. He swallowed the sweet alcoholic liquid and let it slide down his throat as he fought back tears. He put a finger in his mouth and rubbed his teeth: a necessary action to rid them of the furry feeling the elixir left after swallowing.

Asher and Lorrelli looked at each other solemnly. Both had been well aware Lem's mood swings had been getting progressively worse. Neither of them, however, had any idea that he'd been carrying so much weight on his shoulders, nor that he'd been tucking into so much of the whirlpool clarity.

All those times they'd caught him wiping his teeth, he'd been drinking the stuff. Asher instantly felt sorry for him and was about to apologise when a familiar voice resounded behind them.

"Clarity. Whirlpool?" Prum re-emerged from his hiding place within the tree and licked his wooden lips with a strip of bark at the prospect of a sip of the delicious distilled alcohol. "Say earlier, not?"

A cooling stillness washed over Lem's body as the whirlpool clarity took effect. He knew full well what the elixir would do, but he had never taken as bigger gulp as this before. The effect was instantaneous. Lem felt his emotions magnify and swell, but his mind became clear with a distinctive clarity he'd never known before. Struggling to maintain the balance between his emotions and his actions, Lem spun around and marched back over to the tree, deciding to vent his pent-up anger and frustration on the rather obnoxious querelus bark lodged in its centre. Waving the flask just out of Prum's reach, Lem's mind was razor sharp.

"Oh, so now we have your attention? What happened to deal break. Unacceptable. Forget never. Again never?" Lem's emotions spilled out in an avalanche as he used Prum's words against him.

"Prum forgive. Hasty maybe." Prum's branchlike arm reached out for the flask, but Lem held it beyond its reach, kicking the base of the tree for added effect.

Lorrelli tried to calm him down, but Lem was too riled up to hear her, brushing her off as he would an insect.

"Oh, you want this do you?" Lem jiggled the flask in front of the tree, watching Prum's eyes. They were glued to it like a mawblink in auglights. "Okay then, let's make a deal then you oversized block of kindling. You're going to give Lorrelli her first mantle element like you promised."

Prum's eyes narrowed, apprehension and desire tormenting his features as he switched his gaze between the visibly fuming

Lem and the flask. Agonising over the decision, he grumbled loudly, highly perturbed at being manipulated in such a way. Lem waited, impatiently tapping his finger on the side of the flask and blowing over the opening, letting the pungent scent of the beverage waft on the airwaves before Prum's face.

"Fine! Deal agree. Prum agree." The tiny wooden creature barked at him. A look of disgust crossed Prum's face as he convulsed, his tiny body shuddering as he coughed something up from deep within the trunk of the tree.

His small frame shuddered as a tiny green seed pod with a hard outer shell emerged in the hole that served as his mouth. Spluttering violently, he spat the pod from his lips and into Lem's outstretched hand. It was covered in a white gooey sap from the tree and was sticky to the touch. Gurgling to clear his throat, Prum gasped for breath and demanded the flask in payment, extending his branch outwards.

"Deal made. Clarity give."

"Not yet. Next you are going to tell us everything you know about the creeping mould spreading from the Undercellars and how to stop it."

"Swindle made. Deal break," Prum angrily snapped at him. "Nothing get." He noisily tried to withdraw from the scene, his tiny body wrestling back into the knot of the tree, but Lem didn't miss a beat.

"Pity, then all this will go to waste." Lem poured a tiny stream of liquid from the flask, spilling its cool contents on the roots of the tree. Prum was back in a flash, flailing his arm in the air, begging Lem to stop.

"Roots waste! Prum tell."

Lorrelli and Asher stood back, amazed at Lem's ability to negotiate and blackmail a barely comprehensible querelus bark.

Prum looked furious, but was powerless to his own desire to get his hands on the whirlpool clarity.

"How do we stop the mould?" Lem demanded again, his tone more resolute than ever.

If querelus barks could sweat, then Prum looked like he had been in a sauna, bathing in his own clammy disposition. He thrashed about angrily, clearly fighting some internal battle before coming clean about what he knew.

"Natural not. Blood old. Sageroot."

"Sageroot. Is that some form of plant?"

"Plant not. Cruaar."

The name stuck a chord with Lorrelli. "Sageroot as in Belkraen Sageroot, patriarch of the Natura bloodline?"

"Sageroot same."

"That doesn't help us! How do we stop it?" Lem asked again, teetering the liquid inside the flask a little closer to the opening.

"Stop. Prum tell. Sageroot blood. Descendant same. Find augefact. Curse undone. Sageroot for Vindicat. Now drink. Give Prum."

Lem looked at Asher and Lorrelli before offering the flask to Prum.

"Wait," Asher stopped him, retrieved his schedule tablet and quickly scratched out the symbol he'd seen within the outbreaks of mould. "Do you recognise this?"

Prum took a good look at the symbol, his large sap-filled eyes glistening widely for a second, but he shook his head and raised his voice in anger.

"Seen not. Deal made. Clarity give."

Lem took a small swig from the flask before dropping it above Prum's outstretched branch and watched as the wooden creature snatched it. By the sounds of the swish of liquid in the flask it was almost empty. Lem stuck a finger in his mouth and rubbed it over his teeth, scratching away the furry residue the whirlpool clarity left in its wake.

Asher finally understood that Lem was hooked on the stuff.

Prum sneered a wooden scowl at them and disappeared back within the knot of the tree, flask in tow.

Lem turned around and handed Lorrelli the seed pod as magnified emotions once again swelled in his chest, his mind filling with a host of unsettling, but clear-headed, thoughts.

"Lem, I don't know what to say." Lorrelli stammered, completely amazed at what had just happened. "Thank you," she whispered earnestly as she gazed down at her auger. It was ablaze with life, rippling with vibrant undercurrents of emerald as it fed off the energy of the seed pod in her hand.

"Don't sweat it," Lem stopped her, "I should have told you both, but the whirlpool clarity gave me a release from all this." He swung his auger back and forth at his surroundings, "from Mantlecrest."

"It magnified everything I'd been feeling inside, but my mind... my mind was perfectly clear. I've never thought so clearly in all my life." He touched a finger to his temple and rubbed it in a circular motion. "Everything just clicked."

"Whatever it was, it was amazing." Asher slapped him on the back to congratulate him. "Not only did you help Lorrelli get her first mantle element, but you may have helped us solve the mould problem as well. Not bad for someone that can't even call on the power his blood."

"I suppose so," Lem smiled to himself and felt the pent-up feeling of uselessness momentarily ease from his mind.

"So now all we need to do is find an augefact made by a Sageroot, or a descendant of one. Shouldn't be too hard, right?" Asher laughed, even though he had absolutely no idea what an augefact was.

"Tomorrow, Asher, after we've slept. It's been a long day," Lem yawned, attempting to rub the tiredness from his eyes. "I need to sleep."

"Agreed," Lorrelli said as she led them from the secret grove, fondling her newfound seed pod like a precious gem.

After leaving the garden the same way they came in, the trio tiptoed back downstairs, avoiding several elder apprentices on their nightly patrol. They only narrowly missed an encounter with Tribune DeGrulz by quickly ducking inside an unused training room. They listened to him as he marched past, mumbling something about the legate to himself, until his voice faded down the corridor. When they finally reached their racks, they slipped inside, engaged the secureaug lock and tumbled into their respective beds, exhausted.

"So I just have one question," Asher whispered, staring at his auger, watching the black scar slowly sway and move inside his gem. "What's an augefact?"

"Go to sleep," Lem and Lorrelli snapped in unison, rolling over and drawing the sheets up over their heads, firmly ignoring him.

CHAPTER 29

LYING TO A LEGATE

The next morning Asher woke early, long before Lem and Lorrelli showed any inclination of stirring. After 10 minutes of tossing and turning, his body still refused to fall back to sleep, so he decided to take a walk to clear his over-stimulated mind.

He silently got dressed and headed out the door towards the rooftop observatory to sit and gaze over Undergall. There he would ponder his newest dilemma: where to find a Sageroot augefact or, better yet, a living Sageroot descendant.

A gust of fresh air hit him in the face as he stepped out onto the rooftop observatory. The temperature was perfect—not too hot, not too cold, just right—like it always was. How exactly, Asher couldn't quite understand, but like everything else around him, he assumed there was some sort of auger-powered device behind it.

A soft breeze wafted over his skin as he took a seat on the edge of the parapet. He let his legs dangle over the lip of the mammoth drop and gazed out at the majestic view. A replicated dawn had just ignited from deep within the central auglight high above, repelling the fading shadows blanketing the city and its bloodstained cobblestone streets below.

Asher let his gaze wander towards Mastonon Commons and the massive square dominating the city centre, taking time to let its detail sink in. A large statue of a single man stood proudly in the central square. Asher couldn't quite make out who it was from this distance, but he noticed the statue had changed position from the last time he had seen it, assuming a new pose as though it had grown bored of the old one.

"I see I'm not the only one who likes the solitude of the waking hours."

The voice took Asher completely by surprise. He hadn't heard any footsteps echoing from the stairwell indicating someone was behind him. Spinning around, he saw the rigid frame of Legate Seville standing by the observatory doorway, casually drinking in the view.

She calmly approached the parapet, a few paces from where Asher sat. Her taut leather tunic creaked softly as she assumed a restful, but guarded, position next to him.

"I'm sorry, Legate. I didn't know you'd be up here."

"Stay yourself, Apprentice." She held up her hand to stop him from getting up. "I'd not willingly deny someone the enjoyment of such a grand sight without good cause." She let her eyes wander out over the city as she took in the morning light of the simulated dawn.

Asher watched in silence as the legate closed her eyes, basking in the city's serene tranquillity. Her brow twitched and flickered involuntarily, as thoughts far beyond Asher's reach flashed somewhere within her mind.

Her hair was pulled back in a tight knot on her head. It was held in place by no fewer than six long silver pins that pierced a large iron clasp and stuck up in the air like a peacock's tail.

Asher couldn't work out where she kept her auger, but he suspected it might be buried somewhere beneath the knot of hair. There was no noticeable bulge under her clothes and she carried no visible weapon, chain or any other battle mantle he could see. There was only a single pouch attached to her waist, which he assumed contained a volume of sand, much like every other adult Cruaar he'd come into contact with, which left only the oversized hairpin and clasp.

"Being up here sometimes reminds me of my home."

Asher thought he detected a twinge of anguish in her voice, but her face was unreadable.

"It was beautiful, perched in a hidden valley high in the mountains, far away from here, picturesque and serene all year round. Winter would see snow up to your waist, while summer

313

would see it melt into crystal streams of vitality." She inhaled deeply and sighed. "I do miss the sun. Auglights are poor substitute. They lack the warmth that natural light imparts on the skin."

Asher glanced down at his own hand and realised she was right. Whilst the temperature was warm, the warmth did not increase as the central auglight slowly grew brighter overhead. When he turned his head back to look at her, she had a calm, but firm, expression on her face.

"But enough of my beleaguered memories, how are you finding Mantlecrest, Apprentice Bloom?"

"It's amazing..." Asher started.

"But," she raised her eyebrows inquisitively.

"Everything here is so foreign but, even so, it makes more sense than my life in The Blind ever did."

"And yet you still feel out of place?"

Asher nodded his agreement silently and looked down, instantly leaning back, shifting his weight away from the massive drop beneath his dangling feet.

"Your sheltered life in The Blind did you no favours for what you face now and what is yet to come. Nor will that wretched blight on your auger offer you any reprieve from the judgement of the world's past evils."

Asher glanced at the black swaying scar set within the heart of his auger and wondered how such a small blemish could cause so much distrust in those around him.

"We must play the hand dealt to us, but whether you do so honestly, or stack the deck in your favour, is entirely up to you." She raised her arm and gingerly touched her fingertips to her temple as if thinking of something else entirely.

"I suppose," Asher agreed, albeit completely bewildered by her confusing metaphor.

"Do you know what I see when I look over this city?" the legate said as she took a seat next to Asher and let her legs dangle over the edge of the parapet.

Asher shook his head, leaned forward and poked his head over the wall. The drop beneath his toes made his sense of balance reel with vertigo, but the legate showed no ounce of fear or discomfort whatsoever.

"I see a living ruin. A breeding ground of distrust, borne of manipulated fear. The carefree days the Cruaar Nation knew before the Rebellion are gone and are unlikely to return. You cannot get a proper sense of the futility that infests the streets within these walls, but once outside, in the city…" She switched her gaze to Asher: the alarm and suspicion on his face was evident. "You and your friends have been careful, but not nearly careful enough. Now is not a time to be reckless. Act on what you must, but know, I see all."

Asher's heart skipped a beat.

"I am duty bound as legate to ask the manner in which Apprentice Wittlearch smuggled a vial of Wormwood Vindicat into Mantlecrest. I am prepared to forgive her the transgression, but if and only if you first tell me what she was doing with it in the Spiretop Gardens."

The ultimatum sent Asher's mind reeling. He did well to hide his panicking emotions, maintaining a confused look on his face as he desperately tried to figure out how she could possibly know about the Wormwood Vindicat.

"She smuggled what?" he asked, feigning ignorance.

The legate inhaled a deep breath and pierced Asher with her intense gaze. She had deep blue eyes, one laced with tinges of gold, the other with radiant flecks of emerald. Her nostrils flared as she exhaled a deep sigh of disappointment and placed a hand heavily on Asher's shoulder, forcefully holding him in place on the edge of the parapet and pushing his weight forward.

"Never make the mistake of lying to me again."

Asher gulped back his fear as the view of the fall rushed up at him. He didn't have a choice. The legate saw through his attempt at deception like it was made of glass and he didn't want to find out what she was capable of if he lied to her again. Silently drawing in breath, Asher rallied together the courage necessary to speak. His voice was barely more than a whisper. "She needed it to get her first mantle element."

"Interesting," the legate weighed the answer over in her head. "Was the entire vial used to procure the element?"

Asher nodded.

"And is that all she needed it for?"

Asher nodded again in silence, hoping she wouldn't be able to detect his deception. After what seemed like an eternity, she released her gaze and turned her head to once more look out over the city.

"Half-truths are naught but half lies disguised, Apprentice."

Asher felt the sweat roll down his temple as her grip on his shoulder intensified. He felt her slowly forcing his weight forward towards the edge of the parapet.

"Okay, okay. We were looking for a cure to the creeping mould," Asher quickly blurted out.

She smiled, only for a second, no longer, but the answer was enough for her to release his shoulder. "Honesty, at last, but I'm curious. Impropriety aside, was the risk worth the reward?"

"We don't know yet," Asher replied as he swung his legs back over the safe side of the parapet and stood up, relieved to have both feet on solid ground again.

The legate seemed happy enough with the answer, even though her deadpan expression would never betray as much.

"I hope so. Consider this pass a one-time-only offer. I will not overlook such transgressions again," she said as she briskly walked towards the stairwell, the creaking of her leather tunic fading into obscurity as she left the rooftop and disappeared from view.

Asher breathed a heavy sigh of relief. He decided to wait a few more minutes before returning to his rack, just in case, but the urge to tell the others what had just happened was overwhelming.

When Asher finally burst through the door, Lem was putting on his tunic. Lorrelli had just woken up and was startled by

Asher's rushed entrance. Asher slammed the door shut and locked it behind him before proceeding to tell them of his altercation with the legate.

"I told you the Wormwood Vindicat would lead to no end of trouble," Lem said bitterly after Asher had finished.

"How did she found out about it?" Lorrelli blurted out, "I didn't tell anyone. Not a soul."

"Well, neither did I," Lem added quickly, shifting the blame off his own shoulders.

"How did you smuggle it in here in the first place? Maybe she caught your source," Asher offered.

"I didn't smuggle anything, I found it here."

"What?" both Asher and Lem blurted out in unison.

"Prum demanded a vial of it in exchange for my first mantle element. He told me there was a secret stash somewhere within Mantlecrest. An old apprentice used to bring it to him, so I started searching for it."

"How?" Asher enquired.

"The same way we find out where our training rooms are every day. With my auger," Lorrelli answered.

"But what did you use as a reference point?" Lem asked, dumbfounded that a stash of Wormwood Vindicat had been hidden within Mantlecrest all this time.

"This," Lorrelli dug around in her trunk and retrieved a small piece of ribbon with an embossed wax seal stamped on it. A small crest sat in the centre of the seal, but time had worn away at the wax impression, leaving it completely unrecognisable.

"Prum said he snatched it from one of the old apprentice ages ago. It led me to the spot where I found the vial of Wormwood Vindicat."

"Let's just forget the whole thing," Lem snorted as he sat down on his bed. "You've got your element and prac only knows how, but we got away with it."

"There's something more to this than just Vindicat," Asher said as he took the ribbon from Lorrelli and looked at it closely.

"I have a hunch."

"There isn't a grand conspiracy behind every single thing, Asher," Lem said bluntly.

"Was there anything else where you found it?" Asher directed the question at Lorrelli, ignoring Lem's comment entirely.

"No, just the vial. It was hidden behind a lose stone in a disused corridor upstairs."

A sly smirk flashed in the corner of Asher's mouth for a split-second as he looked down at the unrecognisable wax seal.

"Show me."

CHAPTER 30

SAGEROOT MARKS THE SPOT

Lem begrudgingly followed his friends upstairs, with Lorrelli leading the way towards the vial's original hiding spot. When they arrived at the entrance to the deserted corridor, Asher instructed Lem to stand guard to ensure no-one would interrupt them.

Lem sullenly agreed.

Lorrelli had already pried loose the stone she'd mentioned earlier, when Asher joined her halfway down the corridor. She placed it on the ground with a dull thud. A small amount of dirt fell from its rear face as its full weight came to rest.

Stepping away, she exposed the hollow recess in the wall for Asher to inspect. Sure enough, the space was empty, but far bigger than Asher expected. Dust had settled in and taken root over the years, encrusting the recessed base of the hidden hollow. A small round indentation of dust had built up around where the vial had previously lay, but the rest of the hiding spot had no signs of anything else previously hidden there. "Why hide only one vial in a space this big? It doesn't make sense."

"Maybe someone else knew about the stash and pinched the rest," Lorrelli offered without much faith in her answer.

"And leave one behind? Doubtful. Besides, see how the dust has built up around where the vial was. It hasn't been disturbed in years."

"Psst! Hey, you two," Lem called out in a hushed whisper from down the hall. He stood nodding his head and pointing at the back of the stone Lorrelli had just removed from the wall. The dislodged dirt had partially uncovered some sort of etching. "That stone. There, on its back, there's something there."

Asher waved his understanding back at Lem, directing him to

resume his watch. He pushed the heavy stone farther away from the wall with his foot to get a better vantage point on the wall closest to Lem.

Sure enough, the top corner of a small crest was visible behind a layer of grit and grime. He wiped away the residue blocking the remainder of the imprint and tilted the stone upwards so he could see it clearly.

"Is that the same crest as the one on the ribbon?" Asher asked Lorrelli.

She quickly removed the ribbon from her tunic and held it against the stone for comparison. "Maybe, but the one on the ribbon is really worn. It's hard to be sure," Lorrelli said quietly before beaming an enormous smile, "but it doesn't matter."

"Why's that?"

"Because that's the seal of Belkraen Sageroot: the patriarch of the Natura bloodline. I'd know it anywhere."

The ornate etching of an elder tree stared back at them. The seal sat as clear as day in the face of the stone. Its roots extended far into the earth, with a large book perched high within its topmost branches.

Asher looked up at Lorrelli with hope in his eyes. "Are you certain?"

"My mother has a mural of it in her study, Natura fanatic, and all. Which means the wax-seal on the ribbon probably belonged to a Sageroot, as well, seeing as it led us here. Look, there's even some initials at the bottom." Lorrelli peered closer at the engraving and inspected the lettering.

A.F.S.

"Okay, so if S stands for Sageroot, what do A and F stand for?" Asher pondered.

"No idea."

"Okay, so now what? All we have is a dirty old ribbon and one empty hiding place of one A.F. Sageroot. We're still no closer to finding a Sageroot augefact, or his praccing descendant," Lem hissed at them over their shoulders. Their interest in the engraving had blinded them to his stealthy approach from the end of the corridor, though his annoyance at the entire situation was still painfully evident.

"Can't we use the ribbon as a reference point to lead us to a descendant?""

"Augers can't lead you to people. Only things or places, it's got something to do with living auger interference," Lorrelli shot him down. "Even trying to find an augefact would be a stretch."

"Why?" Asher asked, inspecting the crest closer for any clues. "What's the problem with an augefact?"

"Augefacts are imbued with a fragment of flesh or bone from their creator," Lem answered unapologetically.

"That's revolting." Asher's face contorted.

"It's also why we can't find one via our auger navigation trick, because augers can't focus on flesh or bone," Lorrelli said, scratching the side of her face, puzzled as to what to do next.

"Even if it's dead tissue?" Asher's face lit up hopefully.

"No, augefacts are usually only made out of desperation and serve a single purpose. They can't be broken, damaged or destroyed while a descendant of the bloodline lives on and are mostly impossible to find once hidden," Lorrelli folded her arms and tried to think.

"Great, so now we just go around and ask if anyone knows of any Sageroot augefacts?" Lem quipped sourly.

All three of them stood silently within the corridor: Lorrelli and Asher thinking, Lem smouldering in irritation. No-one had any idea what sort of augefact they should be looking for, nor had they even heard of a Sageroot augefact, let alone one that might be hidden somewhere within Mantlecrest.

"So we're back to square one, then," Asher exhaled in defeat, looking back at the cavity. "But why hide it here, of all places?" Asher asked, gazing into the hiding space.

Raising his hand to his head to check the area thoroughly with his divine eye, he received only a second feeling of disappointment when it revealed nothing out of the ordinary.

"Why hide what here?" a loud voice echoed down the corridor at them, causing the trio to spin around and face their inquisitor.

A hulking silhouette with a large white T on the front of his tunic and a heavy gauntleted fist stared back at them. His face was immersed in shadow, but his eyes burned a brilliant blue in the darkness. Even with half his features lost in the shadows, the tribune was a menacing figure and not to be trifled with.

"Nothing, Tribune DeGrulz," Lem said quickly, addressing the man by his name and title, showing him the proper level of respect he demanded of them.

Asher sensed a familiar warmth radiating from his auger as it sparked to life in his palm, revealing Lem's lie. He instinctively stuffed it inside his pocket to hide it from view.

"You're lying," the tribune growled, marching down the corridor towards them. "What are you hiding?"

"Nothing, we swear." Lorrelli answered, backing away from the loose stone on the floor and covering the cavity in the wall with her body.

Asher's auger flared up again as he and Lem also backed up against the wall, one on either side of Lorrelli. Asher instantly realised his auger was not the only one that would betray them. He nervously glanced at Lorrelli and then at Lem.

Lorrelli's auger was hidden beneath her tunic, but Lem's hung loosely around his neck in plain view for all to see. It glimmered with a dull grey sheen as small sparks danced and twirled inside it. To the untrained eye, it was barely more than a twinkle, but to the tribune, it might as well have been a spotlight.

"I warned you about disrespecting me," the tribune's gauntlet swayed back and forth as he approached. The metal shimmering as it caught the light. As he got closer, the gauntlet looked even more jagged and brutal than Asher remembered.

"Now, I will ask you one more time. Hide what where?"

Asher spoke first, but he didn't even get two words out before he felt the air rushing from his lungs. Doubling over in pain, he collapsed to the ground, gasping for air. He hadn't even seen the tribune's gauntlet move before it slammed into his gut.

"Let's try this again," the tribune said calmly, placing a hand on Lorrelli's shoulder. Slowly and purposefully, he clenched his fingers, digging them deep into the flesh between the joint of her shoulder and her arm. She squealed and her legs buckled.

"And remember, no lies."

Lem looked at Asher on the ground, he could barely breathe let alone speak, and Lorrelli's face was contorting with agony under the grip of the tribune's gauntlet.

"Whirlpool clarity!" Lem blurted out. "I found a stash of it here, but it's all gone now, I used it to get high."

The tribune leaned in close, pressing his face against Lem's. He held it there and locked eyes with the apprentice, all the while deepening his grip in Lorrelli's shoulder. Finally, he sniffed.

"Yes, you reek of it. Fool."

He released his debilitating hold over Lorrelli and she dropped to the floor, nursing her shoulder. The tribune spun Lem around and patted him down, making sure he didn't have any more of the elixir. Satisfied with his search, he turned his attention to the cavity in the wall, seeing nothing but an empty space.

He pointed a gauntleted finger at the gaping hole and muttered, "If I find out you're lying to me and have more whirlpool clarity stashed somewhere, next time I won't be as gentle." He slammed his fist as hard as he could into Lem's kidneys, and left the trio crumpled in a heap, nursing their wounds. He marched off back the way he had come and disappeared, until the only noises were the sounds of their moans.

It took a minute or so before any of them were back on their feet. Lorrelli was first, then Asher, but he still couldn't breathe properly. Lem, on the other hand, was coughing and spluttering like someone dying from lung cancer.

Asher tried to haul him up but he could only get him as far as the cavity in the wall, before Lem's lungs gave out.

He coughed and spluttered and expelled a large breath of air into the cavity, spraying built-up dust everywhere, including his own face, which just exacerbated his beleaguered attempts to breathe.

"Lem... look," Asher gasped, letting go of his friend as he noticed the faintest of straight lines appear in the gathered dust within the cavity.

"Prac me," Lem cursed in pain as his knees smashed against the stone floor.

"What's that?" Lorrelli asked, ignoring Lem's plight as she peered into the cavity, her hand still nursing the shoulder where the tribune had manhandled her.

Asher gently blew away the remainder of loose dust, causing more of the choking grey cloud to spray outwards. He coughed and waved his hand in front of his face to disperse it before leaning in and examining the base of hidden cavity.

A large smile crept over his face when he saw four exposed lines in the encrusted dust. Together, they made up the shape of a small rectangle.

"Asher, you were right," Lorrelli winced, "there was something else hidden here."

"Once perhaps, but this box was removed a long time ago," Asher whispered, tracing the outline of dust with his fingers.

"So we're looking for a box. Marvellous," Lem gasped as he struggled to push himself upright. "I can't tell you what a relief that is to my kidneys. Now can we go already?"

"A box is something our augers can find, right?" A brief flash of excitement sparked across Asher's face.

"Assuming it's still within Mantlecrest," Lorrelli said, "but it'll have to wait until after training."

She kicked away the dirt and dust they had deposited on the floor as Asher replaced the stone into the hollow recess in the wall, both hurriedly doing as much as humanly possible to cover all traces that anyone had been in the disused corridor.

Lem was only capable of leaning against the wall with his head arched upwards, both hands on his sides, but even that looked painful.

The next eight hours of training were painstakingly brutal. Lorrelli and Asher wanted nothing more than to go exploring to uncover the hiding place of the missing box, but could not do so without arousing suspicion for their mysterious absence from training. Nor did they want to incur any more anger from the tribune; they were all still sore from the last time.

Lem, on the other hand, wanted nothing more than to go back to his rack and sulk. His foul mood had only worsened over the course of the day.

Asher wasn't sure if his mood was deteriorating because he didn't have any whirlpool clarity left, or whether it was the residual effects of withdrawal running through his body as it attempted to readapt to normality.

Morreby Fitch kept casting them peculiar looks during training, almost as though she knew they were up to something, but couldn't determine what it was.

Asher couldn't help but return the judgemental stare each time he caught her untrusting eyes leering in his direction.

When their last training session finally ended, Asher looked at his schedule tablet and sighed heavily. He still had his private tutoring session with Tribarion Roolta to go. Lem and Lorrelli, however, were free to pursue and discover the hiding place of the box. Asher made them both swear that if they found it, they would wait until he was there before opening it.

Lorrelli loyally promised and eagerly headed off, auger outstretched, dragging a disgruntled Lem behind her.

Asher descended towards the Praelior Arena, his mind abuzz with thoughts of everything except where he was going. He was too preoccupied to notice someone was following him, realising his error only when he felt a hand land on his shoulder. He spun around with auger raised, to find the pale face of Morreby Fitch looking back at him.

"Why have you been watching me?" she demanded in a soft but menacing voice.

"I don't know what you are talking about," Asher lied.

"I've seen you and your two cronies following me."

Asher looked her up and down, noticing for the first time her petite features. She was undeniably pretty, though she made no effort whatsoever to let anyone around her know as much. Jet black hair cascaded down around her shoulders, lining a face flecked with light freckles that complimented her fair skin. Her big brown eyes were almost lost behind the narrowed untrusting slits in her eyelids that deepened her frown.

"You of all people should know how hard it is for someone from The Blind to adapt here. Just leave me the hell alone."

She stormed past him in a huff and Asher got a strange tingling sensation in the back of his mind that something was not quite right about the girl. As she walked away, he could have sworn he saw a bulge move inside the rucksack casually hanging over her shoulder. Raising his auger to his head in hopes to catch her out, he saw nothing out of the ordinary, so he simply watched her disappear around the corner before continuing downstairs to the Praelior arena.

Sure enough, as he passed the door marked Surio Letifer he heard muffled voices, but could not make out what they were saying. Just as he was about to leave, he heard a muffled scream from behind the door.

It didn't sound human, but like it belonged to a small animal.

Pressing his ears against the door, he listened intently, but all sounds from inside had lapsed back into silence. He waited a few minutes but heard nothing more. Whatever had happened was over, the culprits responsible hidden behind the locked door.

"What the hell are you up to, Morreby?" he asked himself silently as he shuffled off towards the arena's entrance. When he finally walked onto the pitch of the arena, its entire floor had been transformed into a sea of white sand. Grabbing a fistful of it and letting it run through his fingers, he noticed it was finer than any sand he had seen before and completely unblemished. It was pristine, like fresh fallen snow. Gazing beyond his hand, he surveyed the arena.

A single 10-foot-high pyramid had been erected, whilst the foundations of two more had been laid equidistance from each other opposite it. All three surrounded a small well with a two-foot-high circular wall positioned in the arena's centre.

"Apprentice Bloom, you're late." Tribarion Roolta's voice rang out from the base of the nearest pyramid not yet fully constructed.

"What's all this?" Asher called out back at her.

"The arena is being prepared for the upcoming Utor Alea match. Ignore the fixtures. They'll serve little purpose for today's training."

"Which is?"

"A test. I have taught you most of what I am able until you find your first mantle element. So consider this as an all-encompassing test of everything you've learnt. Overcome the challenges I've set and I'll advance your training to a more advanced level: one worthy of your abilities. Fail, and see your blood stain the sand where it falls."

"Great," Asher said bitterly under his breath.

A mawblink popped into view above one of the unfinished pyramids in an explosion of sand. An infestation of small green creatures rained down from an invisible hole above the second foundation whilst, atop the finished pyramid, a male gavrin appeared out of thin air and howled loudly.

Asher took a deep breath and steadied himself.

"You test starts now, Apprentice," Tribarion Roolta's voice echoed around the arena, but somehow she had disappeared from view.

Asher hadn't even seen her leave.

"Begin."

Several floors up, Lem dutifully followed Lorrelli and her outstretched auger, trying hard not to look too far out of place when they passed other apprentices in the hall; but his glum features were hard to miss. They finally found themselves at the entrance to Mess Hill.

"Seriously, the secret hiding place of Sageroot's augefact is on Mess Hill?" Lem dubiously scoffed.

"Hidden in plain sight, I guess." Lorrelli replied, looking around nervously. "Act casual, we're not the only ones here."

A few older apprentices were practicing blood callings on the lawn, paying no attention whatsoever to the two first-year apprentices passing through the entrance arch.

"Casually now," Lem mocked Lorrelli as she slowly waved her auger in a 180-degree arc as inconspicuously as possible.

It blazed brightly when pointed at the top of the hill. She started climbing the banks of the steep incline towards its crest.

Lem awkwardly slipped and rolled down its banks a number of times as he attempted to follow, causing the apprentices on the lower levels to stop what they were doing so they could laugh and jeer at him.

"Real casual," Lorrelli snapped at Lem, shaking her head as he finally reached the top.

"Shut up."

Lorrelli waited until Lem had composed himself before holding out her auger and continuing her search. She followed the steep crest of the hill towards a series of towering columns that held the gargantuan statues aloft. Passing the first three columns, they reached the fourth and stopped. The statue on its top sat 10-feet high and depicted a large monkey-like creature clinging to a tree trunk.

Lorrelli walked around the column and moved her auger up and down methodically. It shone radiantly regardless of where she pointed. Scratching her head, she glanced up again at the statue towering over them. "Well would you look at that," Lorrelli said, startled. "I never noticed it before."

"Noticed what?"

"The statue, it's an orilla," she murmured.

"So that's what they look like. Ugly praccers, aren't they?"

Lorrelli jabbed him in the ribs for continuing to use the word she hated so much in such a casual manner.

"So where's the box, then?" he grunted, rubbing his ribs.

"Hang on," Lorrelli shushed him and walked around the base of the statue a second time, slower this time, watching the brightness of her auger subtly change depending on where she aimed it. Completing her inspection, she positioned her auger at the point where it shone the brightest and looked at Lem with a frown. "We've got a big problem."

"How big?"

"Oh, about 10-feet high and three tonnes thick."

Lem looked down at her auger and back at the base of the enormous column. "You got to be praccing kidding, right?"

Lorrelli shook her head and jabbed him in the ribs again, unwilling to allow him to get away with such vulgar language.

"I told you. Hidden in plain sight."

It was well after dark when Asher finally emerged on Mess Hill after a harrowing ordeal in the Praelior Arena. His muscles ached and his outer extremities were laced with a plethora of small cuts and bruises. He staggered over to Lem and Lorrelli and slouched down on the grass. Lorrelli was the first to notice the various injuries lining Asher's exposed skin.

"Asher, what happened?"

"The usual: tribarions, mawblinks, gavrins and the like," Asher moaned as he painfully sat upright to accept a plate of food. Strangely enough, Lem and Lorrelli's augers didn't flare up at his explanation.

"What the hell does Roolta put you through in the arena, anyway? You look bloody awful."

"No worse than your ugly mug," Asher grinned, before wincing and rubbing away some lingering pain in his right arm.

"No, you actually look bloody and awful." Lem wiped away a large section of blood on a napkin and held it up for Asher to see.

"She knows you're a first-year, right?" Lorrelli said looking down at Asher's battered body.

"Would it make any difference if she didn't?"

"I suppose not," Lorrelli leaned in close to his ear and lowered her voice, "but we've got some good news. We found it. We found the box."

Asher's energy levels instantly perked up. "Well, where is it?"

"Well, we kind of hit a small snafu," Lem interjected, a forlorn smirk spreading across his face.

"Snafu?" Asher repeated, raising his eyebrows, waiting for a better explanation.

"We found another etching of the Sageroot crest, complete with initials and all," Lorrelli offered, trying to keep an optimistic mindset.

"That's great. Where is it?" Asher asked, his eyes flitting back and forth between the two.

Lem tilted his head towards the top of the hill and nodded.

Asher's eyes followed Lem's gaze up the hill, but didn't quite understand where he was looking. "I don't understand."

"It's err… under the statue of the orilla," Lorrelli whispered faintly. "Underneath the column; under the statue, to be precise."

Asher looked at the row of statues, but had no idea what an orilla actually looked like.

"Fourth from the left," Lem coughed loudly.

Asher's eyes shot to the fourth statue of the hideous-looking monkey-like creature and wondered why he'd never paid any attention to it before.

"That's an orilla? They really are ugly, aren't they?"

"Asher meet snafu. Snafu, Asher." For the first time in ages Lem's levity actually worked to lighten the mood.

"I take it we can't just dig it out?"

"The foundations extend to the rear wall. We couldn't even

work out how someone buried it in the first place."

"Nothing is ever easy, is it?" Asher sighed and scanned the hill. It was filled with apprentices of every age but, as usual, most were keeping away from them. Morreby Fitch was watching them from a distance, and kept stealing glances at the top of the hill where Asher had been staring.

"Well there isn't much we can do now. Finish your meal and we'll head back to our racks so we can talk in private." Asher pushed away his plate, he didn't have an appetite for anything. Painfully rising to his feet, the trio made their way towards the exit. Their trip back to their racks was slow and uneventful. Once safely inside the security and comfort of their room, Asher sat on the bed, took off his shoes, and spoke softly.

"I think I know how to take care of the statue, but you're not going to like it."

"What a surprise." Lem rolled his eyes.

"I'll need time alone on Mess Hill in the dead of night, well after curfew."

"What do you want us to do?" Lorrelli rubbed her hands, all too eager to join in on Asher's mayhem.

Lem exhaled deeply and frowned, acknowledging his reluctant involvement.

"What I've got in mind is going to be loud. Really loud. So I'll need a distraction." Asher looked at the pair of them, one after the other, to gauge their reactions.

"A big one."

CHAPTER 31

UPROOTING AN AUGEFACT

"Is everyone set? You know what you have to do?" Asher's gaze flicked from Lem to Lorrelli and back again. It had taken two weeks to work out a diversion big enough that would allow Asher enough time on Mess Hill to retrieve the box from under the statue without interruption.

Day and night they dredged every single memory from the depths of Lem's subconscious about what he knew of Mantlecrest's secureaug system. Lem had only briefly seen the plans for the system upgrade in his step-father's study, but one memory led to another, and another. Each time they uncovered a new recollection, they recreated the section of Mantlecrest in miniature via the promensi table, studying it in depth before disregarding it and plumbing Lem's memories anew.

Recreating the plans from Lem's memory had not been easy, but the effects of the whirlpool clarity left his mind sharp as a tack, enhancing his memories and his ability to recall the smallest detail. Asher put his newfound ability down to the prolonged exposure of the elixir. By the end of the week, they were all exhausted, Lem more than anyone, but eventually they found a crux in the system they could use to their advantage.

It took another two days for Lem to fully recover from the invasive intrusion into his mind. When he awoke from a, almost-comatose slumber, Lorrelli and Asher had already settled on a plan; they just needed to convince Lem to agree to one key part.

Upon hearing it, he instantly and obstinately refused. It took no end of persuasion to even get him to consider what they were asking, but it wasn't exactly a routine request.

Another week passed before they got Lem to agree that the plan would theoretically work. It took another week again to strategise what needed to happen to make the far-fetched scheme a reality. Another week was lost learning the elder apprentices' routines after curfew by way of a series of exhausting reconnaissance excursions in the dead of night.

Tribune DeGrulz posed the biggest threat to the plan. Ever since their encounter, he had taken a special dislike to the trio and routinely threatened and intimidated them when he passed them in the halls. Worse yet, he had no set routine after curfew and would often wander throughout Mantlecrest at random. He had almost caught them out after curfew twice already, but both times they'd been able to hide at the last second.

They all knew if the tribune didn't take the bait and investigate Lem's distraction, Asher's actions on Mess Hill would surely see an end to his apprenticeship at Mantlecrest. It was a risk Asher was willing to take, so the others had no choice but to agree.

When they'd finally figured out the best time of night to act, with the least chance of interruption, they agreed on a date and anxiously waited. Lem was still visibly hesitant, despite having agreed to do his part, but if he still had any objections or doubts, he did not share them.

"Okay, we better try and get some sleep," Asher whispered, but knew in his heart it was unlikely any of them would. It was midnight, but still far too early to attempt something as brazen as what their plan involved. They needed to wait another four hours, until the very last of the elder apprentices had retired for the night, leaving a mere half-hour gap until the first masters arrived for morning training.

It was a small window of opportunity, but it was their best and only shot. The Utor Alea match was only five days away and they didn't even know if the box would contain an augefact, or just another piece of the Sageroot jigsaw puzzle they were slowly piecing together.

Time ticked by slowly and Asher slipped into a restless slumber, constantly forcing his eyes awake time and time again. He heard similar movements from Lem and Lorrelli. It was clear no-one was likely to get any sleep this night. When Asher did finally drift off, he was midway through an incoherent dream when he was rudely shaken awake by Lem. "It's time."

Blinking his eyes awake, Asher threw off his sheets and clambered off his mattress. He was already fully dressed, as were Lem and Lorrelli.

Lorrelli peered outside their door. They'd left it unlocked and slightly ajar the entire night to remove any chance the sound of opening it would carry into the hall and wake anyone in neighbouring rooms.

They had decided to forgo the luxury of shoes, wearing only their socks in order to tread silently against the cold pavers of Mantlecrest's stone floors. Without a sound, they crept outside into the hall and headed to the nearest stairwell. The auglights were at their lowest setting, little more than a dull glimmer, leaving the halls and corridors blanketed in early morning gloom.

When they reached the stairs, Asher offered a good-luck nod to Lem and Lorrelli as they set off up the stairwell. He waited a few seconds, then headed towards Mess Hill, silently hoping lady luck was on his side. He made his way through the eerily quiet corridors of Mantlecrest, stopping whenever he heard the slightest hint of an out-of-place sound. After what seemed like hours, but was actually only minutes, Asher found himself staring at the enormous double-door entrance to Mess Hill.

The doors had been left open, as usual.

Peering through the opening, he couldn't see much of the hill itself. It, like the city beneath it, was immersed in darkness. Even the streets of the city were illuminated only by the faint pinprick of auglights shining through windows on the cobbles of the streets. The central auglight's simulated dawn was still an hour away from bathing the city in its unnatural radiance.

Asher wasted no time. He crept out onto the lawn and around the corner of the entrance's archway, and hugged the wall as best he could. After he'd managed to scramble to the top of the steep hill where the bases of the statues rested, he stopped and listened.

A cocoon of silence blanketed the hill. Asher was certain no-one was any the wiser to his presence.

Keeping low to the ground, he crept along the crest of the hill towards the first of the large stone columns. Reaching it, he nervously disappeared behind the column, vanishing into the darkness. His shadow emerged a moment later and disappeared again, nimbly ducking behind the second column.

Asher was about to shimmy along to the third when he caught a shadow of movement at the bottom of the hill out of the corner of his eye. Instinctively, his body froze in place, hidden behind the giant column, eyes glued on the panoramic view of the hill and beyond in nervous anticipation. He slowed his breath to a standstill as he waited. Then the shadow moved again. Alarm bells chimed in his mind. He was definitely not alone.

Lem and Lorrelli finally reached the stairwell leading to the rooftop observatory. It had taken them roughly 20 minutes after they'd left Asher's side to arrive here, and they were running heavily behind schedule.

An elder apprentice had fallen asleep in a rocking chair with his feet up against the wall, effectively blocking a passageway they had planned to take to get to the roof. They were forced to backtrack and take a different route. When they finally climbed the high stairwell and reached the observatory rooftop, the door was shut but, thankfully, not locked.

Lem gently pushed down on the door's heavy latch and forced the heavy bulk of the door open. Stepping through the doorway and out into the cool fresh air, he motioned for Lorrelli to follow.

"I'm not sure about this," Lem said fearfully as he approached the observatory's ledge.

"The theory's sound," Lorrelli reassured him. "We triple-checked it, remember?"

"Theory's all well and good, but it doesn't mean shack jit in reality." Lem peered over the edge of the crenelated parapet and closed his eyes, immediately taking a step back. He was sweating heavily and his knees were trembling. "Oh, prac! That's a long way down."

Lorrelli ignored his use of the word she hated and tried to get him to focus. "Listen to me. You're going to be fine. Have you got it somewhere safe?"

Lem nodded and tapped his tunic pocket, putting a hand inside moments after, just to be sure.

"And do you remember your story for afterwards?"

Lem nodded again, but his body refused to stop shaking.

"I'm ready to step in if you can't do it. Just say the word."

"I hate you guys for this. Asher should be the one up here, I don't even care what Surio Letifer means."

"You know you've got the best chances of pulling this off," Lorrelli reassured him. "Besides, we're counting on you and we're out of time. It's now or never."

Lem shakily climbed up on to the parapet wall and chanced another look below. He'd never told the others he'd always been petrified of heights, but he doubted it would do any good telling Lorrelli now. He took a deep breath, closed his eyes and tried to muster up enough courage to do what needed to be done, but his body wouldn't budge. His legs were frozen in place. Fear gripped every inch of his body. "Lorrelli, I... I... can't."

"It's alright, Lem." Lorrelli reassured him, placing a hand gently on the small of his back. "I'll do it."

Lem's visibly trembling head nodded his relief.

Lorrelli could feel Lem's fear, his skin quivering against her hand. She closed her eyes and momentarily focused on the sensation of Lem's thundering heartbeat she felt through her fingertips. "Forgive me," she whispered. She didn't know whether he heard her. With one strong push she shoved him off the ledge, sending Lem plummeting down into the vast emptiness below, his terrified screams trailing after him as he fell.

Asher's body was rooted to the spot. His cautiousness had just saved his hide. Silently, he watched and waited for the shadowy form of Tribune DeGrulz to finish his unplanned patrol of Mess Hill. Asher was frozen to the spot, fervently hoping Lem's distraction would kick into gear soon. Minutes passed and nothing except the sounds of the tribune's heavy footsteps met Asher's ears, one solemn footstep after another as he traversed the entire length of Mess Hill and back again.

Asher rearranged his handhold on the large stone column to peer out a little farther in order to better track the tribune's position. He made the mistake of underestimating how much holding his body in place would make him sweat. His clammy fingers slipped on the surface of the column and he lost his balance, falling to his knees. The material on his pants scratched against the coarse stone like sandpaper. Whilst the sound was barely even as loud as a whisper, it rang out like an avalanche over the quiet stillness of the hill.

Tribune DeGrulz stopped in his tracks and swung around, peering up at the row of columns looming high above Mess Hill's crest.

Asher warily made sure he was out of sight, but silently cursed his own stupidity.

The tribune took a few steps forward towards the steep incline of the hill, his untrusting gaze trying to pierce the darkness engulfing the wall behind the columns. Raising his large-fisted gauntlet in the air above him, he peered into the darkness.

His lips remained welded firmly shut, ears listening for anything that would give away the location of whatever was hidden in the darkness. A brilliant white light ignited within his palm and slowly levitated higher above him, illuminating the hill and everything on it.

Reaching a height directly in line with the base of the columns, it slid sideways, branding the sharp shadows of the columns and everything behind them on the far wall for all to see.

In a few shorts seconds Asher's shadow would be exposed and there was nothing he could do to stop it. He closed his eyes and prayed for a miracle. The light inched ever closer, forcing

Asher behind the last vestige of cover before his shadow would become visible on the wall behind him or he would be forced out into the open.

The light was mere inches away from exposing his shadow, when it faltered and stopped. Asher nearly jumped out of his skin when a deafening siren wailed around him. The tribune spun on his heels and turned his gaze on Mess Hill's entrance, then switched his attention to the rooftop observatory. Auglights were flashing on an off everywhere as the alarm intensified.

He cast one more glance over his shoulder at the columns and cursed loudly before sprinting away. His lumbering gait was heavy on the ground, leaving deep imprints on the soft lawn long after he'd vanished through the large open double doors.

Asher mouthed a silent thank you as he watched him leave. Quickly turning his attention to the fourth column that held the ugly statue of the orilla aloft, Asher approached its base, looked for the small symbol and raised his auger. He didn't have long. Soon Mantlecrest would be swarming with alarmed masters, concerned elder apprentices and startled first-years.

He cleared his mind of everything, everything but a single word. *Occumbo*. He repeated it over in his mind, focusing every ounce of concentration at the giant base of the enormous column, willing it to topple.

Asher felt his auger bite blood and burn against the scarred skin of his palm. The wide stone base of the column trembled, sending shivers up the massive stone monolith. The unyielding stone column was much bigger than the one he'd bested in the arena, but the principle was the same.

The bigger it is, the harder it falls.

Concentrating all his energy, he focused on the word, repeating it again and again in his mind, visualising the stone crackling and buckling. Seconds stretched into moments and moments into minutes as he stared at the Sageroot-etched emblem, desperately willing the column to shatter and fall.

A single crack, no bigger than his little finger, appeared in the corner of the giant square column which sent a small chunk of stone down the grassy hill below. Asher smiled and redoubled his efforts, forcing more blood into his auger. A spider web of cracks splintered across the columns base. It groaned loudly as more fissures splintered through its core, dislodging additional chunks of stone, some as thick as Asher's wrist.

Asher slashed the air in front of him viciously with his hand, tearing chunks of stone from the ever-widening hole in the rear side of the column. A massive section of the column gave way and fell to the ground. The column's inner core was exposed and its structural integrity began to falter.

Teetering on the edge of destruction, the weakened column only needed one more final assault before its own weight would ensure its undoing. Asher braced his auger with his free hand and, with one final momentous effort, dragged it hard to the right. *Occumbo!*

The thought tore an enormous chunk of stone from the already enlarged hole in the column's middle. The statue's last vestige of resistance against Asher's attack broke underneath the strain of its own growing momentum and it agonisingly submitted to gravity's unforgiving vengeance. High above Asher's head, the statue toppled forward and fell from its perch. It slammed down on the steep slope of the hill, picking up speed as the column's foundations tore away from the ground with a sickening groan. Asher exhaled triumphantly.

He'd done it.

The sound of the monstrous statue crashing down the hill tore at Asher's eardrums. He clamped his hands over his ears and backed away, watching intently as the enormous column followed suit. The column landed with an enormous dull boom before its momentum saw it thunder and roll down the steep slope. It barrelled over itself, sending massive chunks of stone flying in every direction as it broke apart against the unrelenting earth. It obliterated everything in its path, leaving a trail of shattered masonry and splintered fragments of timber in its wake as it crashed through heavy dining tables.

The statue of the orilla had long since been reduced to a mess of fractured rubble. The once-magnificent stone carving was now little more than fractured rubble, smashed beyond repair.

Asher wasted no time. He dropped to his knees and pawed at the newly exposed patch of dirt with his bare hands like an animal. He desperately tore at the compressed earth, searching for any sign of the box.

Time was running out. Soon someone would come to investigate the thundering noise and discover the strewn wreckage of what remained on Mess Hill. He only hoped Lem's distraction would buy him a few extra minutes. He was going to need to find the box and get out undetected. Ripping his fingers through the ground, he realised the box wasn't there. Asher stared at distressed earth in dismay.

"It has to be here. It just has to."

A loud thud resounded over the hill as the column came to rest, stopping against the large stone outlook in the middle of Mess Hill. Something in Asher's mind clicked and, without blinking, he threw himself forward, sliding down the steep grassy incline in the direction of the fallen column. Scrambling to his feet halfway down the slope, he sprinted across to where the base of the column had come to rest, dodging a multitude of ruined debris as he went.

Reaching the large square base of the column, Asher saw a small rectangle groove in its centre. Grabbing a large chunk of stone with a pointed edge, he smashed it hard against the rectangle. The stone crumbled away after a few well-placed hits and Asher found what he had been hunting.

A small wooden box.

It had not seen air in centuries. He snatched it from its rocky prison and made for the exit. He was only a few feet away from the massive entrance archway when he heard loud voices coming towards him from the corridor just beyond the open doors. He frantically looked around.

There was nowhere to go and even fewer places to hide.

The huge bulk of Master McGoven and the tiny frame of Mason Gobbler emerged through the entrance to Mess Hill. McGovern's enormous flabby folds around his chin wobbled as his jaw dropped at the sight of the destruction before him. He awkwardly shuffled forward, throwing his massive arms up in dismay.

Mason was gobsmacked as well when he saw the raw destruction that had been unleashed upon the lawn. Their wild disbelief and shock allowed Asher just enough time to nimbly duck behind them and disappear out into the corridors of Mantlecrest, the loud wail of the alarm masking the noise of his escape. He left Mess Hill with no-one any the wiser to his presence as he sprinted for his life, vanishing like a shadow into the darkness within Mantlecrest's maze of corridors.

Lorrelli frantically paced about their room in a dither of worry, chewing her fingernails anxiously. She'd stayed on the parapet long enough to watch Lem vanish into darkness, praying like crazy to her ancestor's the siren would sound. When it died, she breathed a sigh of relief and hurtled back down the stairwell.

She only narrowly missed the tribune's bulky frame by a second. He lurched past the doorway she'd ducked into after hearing his heavy footsteps pounding up the stairs below her. He rushed past without as much as a passing glance. Quickly retreating to their racks, she'd only just closed the door to her room when she heard a tremendous crash and felt the roof shake above her. The next 20 minutes had been a nightmare of frightened screams and terrified chatter of the startled apprentices from the hall just behind the closed door to her room. When Asher silently slipped inside the room, she threw her arms around him and exhaled a big sigh of relief.

"It's pandemonium out there. There are people everywhere. We've stirred up a hornet's nest," Asher smiled proudly. "Is Lem okay?"

"I don't know, I..." she stammered awkwardly releasing him from her grasp, "I had to push him."

"You did what?" Asher looked at her astonished. "That wasn't part of the plan."

"The plan changed. There was no way I was throwing myself off the roof. So? Tell me already; did you find it?" Lorrelli asked excitedly, the need to justify her actions paramount in her mind.

Asher smiled and nodded.

"Where is it?"

"There were too many people in the halls, I had to stash it."

"Where?"

"Where do you think?" Asher said as he held up Sageroot's ribbon. "Worked for a couple hundred years, I figure it's good for another couple of days."

"Brilliant. Was the augefact inside?"

"I don't know," Asher shrugged his shoulders. "It was locked."

"You're kidding me. After all that." Lorrelli heard some loud footsteps approaching the door. "Quick, clean that dirt off yourself."

Asher hurriedly did so, throwing his dirty tunic and pants in his trunk. He speedily put on fresh ones, but forgot all about changing his socks.

A loud knock at the door silenced both of them.

"Asher, your hands," Lorrelli whispered.

Asher looked down and saw his hands had been stained brown from the dirt. He stuffed them behind his back as the door swung open. The towering body of Tribune DeGrulz stood on the other side, his face seething with a controlled rage. He looked at the two younger apprentices who were already fully dressed in everything but their shoes.

"Legate Seville has requested your presence."

Lorrelli pointed to herself in mock surprise to draw the attention away from Asher and his dirt-covered socks.

"Both of you. Now!"

CHAPTER 32

THE AGGRAVATION OF DUMB LUCK

The tribune marched them out of the room before either had a chance to put on shoes.

Asher was very mindful his socks were still covered in dirt but, then again, so were his hands, so there wasn't much he could do to hide the fact without blatantly incriminating himself.

Luckily, the tribune's pace was too quick for him to take any real notice of the underside of Asher's socks. He led them to the nearest secluded vertistrand and threw a pinch of sand at its mirrored face.

"Why does the legate want to see us?" Asher demanded, unwilling to step through the glimmer of the vertistrand without more information.

The tribune said nothing. His stern features were as staunch as ever, but his hand was clenched in a loose fist at his side.

Asher nervously glanced down the massive iron gauntlet enveloping his right arm: sure enough, it was clenched into a fist as well. Both Asher and Lorrelli had been on the receiving end of the tribune's wrath once before and it had not been a pleasant experience. He thought about standing his ground and repeating the question but, in the end, he didn't get time to decide whether it would be a good idea. As soon as the mirrored face of the vertistrand focused, he and Lorrelli were roughly pushed through its glimmering face.

Legate Seville sat quietly behind a large wooden desk, patiently waiting for the arrival of the tribune and his guests. She was not surprised when Asher and Lorrelli stumbled through the shimmering face of the vertistrand, nor was she sympathetic. Instead, she remained silent behind her desk, the same unreadable expression on her face, as always. With a nod of her head, she silently thanked the tribune for his service when he emerged after Asher and Lorrelli. Tapping a finger on the desk's red mahogany surface, she waited for the apprentices to approach of their own accord.

DeGrulz offered a quick bow of his head in acknowledgement and marched past the apprentices, nimbly stepping to the side of the desk and assuming a relaxed stance to await further orders.

Asher shuffled over to one of two chairs in front of the legate's desk and sat down, being sure to tuck his feet out of sight and keep his hands wedged deep within his pockets.

Lorrelli sat down in the other chair and obediently waited for the legate to speak, her visible trepidation evident on an all-too anxious brow.

"Asher, Lorrelli, a grave occurrence has seen the need for me to summon you both. Apprentice Bruwell…" she carefully examined their faces. Her eyes slowly shifted from Lorrelli to Asher, meticulously gauging each of their expressions. "Apprentice Bruwell has attempted to commit suicide by jumping off the observatory tower."

Asher and Lorrelli's eyes flew open in mock surprise. They proceeded to barrage the legate with questions, frantically speaking over the top of each other as they had rehearsed many times in their racks.

"Is he alright?"

"Where is he?"

"What happened?"

"Can we see him?"

"Is he alive?"

"He lives." The legate held up her hands, effectively silencing them. "His fall was broken by the secureaug catchment system installed for precisely such an occasion. He's recovering in the rejuvenation chamber under watchful eye of Cleric Riffenbon. "He'll report back after he's outlined the underlying psychological causes that may have led him to take such a drastic action."

Asher and Lorrelli let out genuine sighs of relief on hearing the news and settled back in their chairs a little easier, knowing for sure Lem was fine and had survived the fall.

"You are both close with Apprentice Bruwell. Do either of you know of any ongoing problems that may have led him to this?"

Asher and Lorrelli hesitated before answering, doing their best to make it look as if they were thinking hard about the question.

The legate prompted them further. "Was he under any undue pressure because of his failure to be aligned?"

"He was having a pretty hard time with it, sure, but he didn't like to talk about it much," Lorrelli said quietly, placing a hand over her heart to make it look like she was calming herself down.

"He was having problems mustering even the smallest of blood callings. He hadn't contacted home in a long time. I'm not even sure if they knew about, you know…" Asher trailed off, channelling the inner sadness he felt for his loss of Raglan into the explanation he'd rehearsed many times in his head.

The legate picked up a glass tablet that had started flashing with a vivid blue light, and examined it.

"From his preliminary reports…" she read the Cleric's diagnosis carefully, "he appears to have had a prolonged exposure to a very specific neve toxin, more commonly found in high-end, exotic elixirs from the Quaridaan basin."

Asher and Lorrelli looked at her blankly.

"It has many names, but perhaps you would know it best as whirlpool clarity." She raised her eyebrows at them and awaited an answer.

Asher swallowed hard and Lorrelli nervously twisted a braid of her hair, but neither said anything.

"The drug creates a chemical imbalance in the body that separates body from mind in order to give the imbiber moments of pristine clarity. Unfortunately, without a mind to keep a body in check, prolonged exposure to such separation leads to an unstable imbalance of emotions, which would explain his mood swings and the emotional distress you described, if he was indeed hooked on the drug."

She swung her gaze at both of them. Their eyes were downcast and refused to meet hers, implying their complicit knowledge of Lem's addiction. "I thought as much. I've contacted his parents. His step-father is already on his way to Mantlecrest to collect him as we speak."

"Collect him?" Lorrelli stammered surprised.

"Can we see him?" Asher butted in.

"Lem will be taking some time away from Mantlecrest to reconcile his actions under watchful eyes, until such a time as he is mentally competent to return. Lobrolo Altier is with him as we speak. He has a unique viewpoint on such matters and has taken a vested interest in Apprentice Bruwell's future."

The surprise branded across Asher's and Lorrelli's faces betrayed the fact they clearly weren't prepared for this. At the very worst, they thought Lem would've had to spend a couple of days in the rejuvenation chamber until he cleared whatever psychological and auganic test they threw at him. Neither of them could have imagined the Overseer of Undergall would get involved.

Asher silently hoped Lem was strong enough to hold up under the pressure and keep his mouth shut. "How long will he be gone for?"

"That remains unclear. Lobrolo wants to keep this between us. If anyone asks about his absence, tell them he's away because of a family tragedy. Fortunately, another major incident last night will suffice to fool everyone else about what set off the alarm…" She cast a quick glance at the tribune momentarily.

He gave the slightest shake of his head in response.

Asher and Lorrelli watched the subtle interaction closely, before returning a blank look of misunderstanding.

"The siren that undoubtedly woke you up."

"How could it not? It was deafening," Asher looked at Lorrelli, a spark of fear evident in his eyes. It was obvious the legate knew more than she was letting on.

The legate narrowed her eyes at the two apprentices, reaching beneath the desk and pulling open one of its drawers.

"Deafening, indeed," she whispered, refusing to let up her gaze for even the slightest of moments. "Record a message on this pyxis and I will see that Apprentice Bruwell gets it before he departs." Legate Seville rose from her seat and placed a small carving of an orilla before them.

Immediately, both of their eyes flickered with fleeting moment of alarm. The same thought ran rife throughout both their minds, but neither had any idea how she could possibly know. There was no way she'd randomly chosen a figurine of an orilla by coincidence. "I assume you know how these work, especially you, Apprentice Bloom."

Her words haunted Asher. *How much did she know? Did she know about Braak's message? If so, how?* Asher's mind ran riot with questions as the legate stood, tapped the tribune on the shoulder and exited onto the balcony.

He obediently followed her out like a trained lapdog.

Asher was sure they were still within earshot even though they had their backs turned and were speaking softly to one another. He shook his head at Lorrelli who was looking at him with violent alarm in her eyes.

Asher took the opportunity to remove his socks and stuffed them deep into his pants pockets, immediately feeling the cold sting of the floor on the soles of his feet.

Lorrelli picked up the pyxis tapped it to her auger, thought of Lem and spoke in a hushed voice. The legate's words had her nerves shot to pieces, which probably aided her in giving the best rendition of a terrified and worried, albeit relieved, voice she could muster. She was extra careful not to mention anything that could incriminate them.

"Lem, we heard what happened. We're just both so glad you're safe. I'm sorry I pushed you so hard to do better."

Asher stifled an involuntary smirk at her choice of words and took the pyxis from her, keeping his hands low behind the desk, obscured from the legate's and tribune's view. After a brief warm-hearted message he finished with, "we'll look forward to sharing a box of treats with you when you return."

Asher handed the pyxis back to Lorrelli who tapped the base with her auger and placed it back on the desk, just as Legate Seville and Tribune DeGrulz walked back into the room.

"Unless you two have any further questions, you'd better head to the Auxilia Amphitheatre and get some breakfast."

Lorrelli was about to get up when Asher hastily spoke to cover her movement and lapse in concentration. "You mean Mess Hill, don't you? Breakfast is always on Mess Hill." For a split second Asher was certain the legate had raised her eyebrow but, when he looked again, her expressionless gaze had returned.

"Forgive me. I forgot the tribune collected you from your racks. The aforementioned incident has rendered Mess Hill inoperable for the time being," she paused, allowing Asher and Lorrelli time enough to stand.

Asher's did so awkwardly, hands still firmly wedged inside his pockets, but at least this time the bulge of his socks and the dirt on his hands were out of sight.

"But you wouldn't know anything about that, would you?" The legate's question was cold and unforgiving.

Asher couldn't tell if the remark was harmless, or whether she was waiting for them to incriminate themselves under the pressure of their own guilt. Regardless, they both shook their heads and Asher felt the sting of his auger flare up his arm. Thankfully, Lorrelli's was tucked inside her tunic and out of sight, so no-one was any wiser to their lie.

The legate closed her eyes for a moment and nodded. "Of course not, but, before you go," she held out a hand towards them. Asher and Lorrelli tensed up, unsure of what she was going to say or ask. "Congratulations on your unorthodox acquisition of your first mantle element, Apprentice Wittlearch. Have you had a chance to extract its true essence yet?"

Lorrelli shook her head.

"I'll have Master McGovern find some time to escort you into Undergall to Dopplebock's Emporium so you can imbue it within your mantle."

Lorrelli nervously smiled and nodded her thanks before the tribune escorted them back towards the vertistrand, activated it and ushered them through.

The only sounds filtering through the room as they left were the footsteps of the tribune's boots, alongside the faint patter of Asher's bare feet against the stone floor.

Legate Seville's austere features never left her face as she watched them depart. If Asher or Lorrelli had dared to glance back, they would've seen the wild distrust hiding beneath the surface of her eyes.

When Asher and Lorrelli returned to their racks, it was obvious someone had already searched the room thoroughly. Lem's trunk was empty, all unessential belongings piled neatly on his bed. Asher checked his own trunk and, sure enough, things had been moved around inside.

Lorrelli closed the door and locked it with a wave of her auger.

"You too?" Asher asked as Lorrelli inspected her trunk.

She nodded, turning her focus to Lem's bed. Asher was about to say something else when Lorrelli stopped him and methodically waved her auger over every inch of the room whispering, "detego," every few seconds until she was satisfied and promptly sat down on her bed.

"What was that?" Asher asked suspiciously, scrunching his eyebrows together.

"I had to make sure there were no listening devices in here," Lorrelli replied.

"You might have to teach me that. I think our lives are about to get a lot more difficult."

"Lem will be fine, Asher," Lorrelli whispered reassuringly, "he's stronger than he looks."

"I'll tell him you said that." It was the first time Asher ever heard her pay him a compliment.

"I'm counting on it. I'll need all the help I can get to stop him from killing me for pushing him off the roof."

Asher smiled, but he couldn't help but mentally revisit the disconcerting conversation they had just had with the legate. "Tell me I'm paranoid, but the legate sounded like she knew we were involved with Mess Hill, right?"

"I don't know what to think, but she definitely knows more than she's letting on," Lorrelli said as a worried frown crossed descended on her face. "But, to be honest, I'm a little more concerned about what we're going to find inside that box."

"I've been thinking about that, too," Asher agreed and paced about the room. "In any case, we won't be able to find out for a while until everything dies down. Doing anything after curfew is out of the question, which means we have to play it cool and find somewhere private. Somewhere that will give us enough time to work out how to open the box during regular training hours."

"Without drawing any unwanted attention," Lorrelli added before lapsing into deep thought. A few seconds later, a sly smile broke out over her face and she snapped her fingers. "We could always take a leaf out of Sageroot's playbook."

"What do you mean?" Asher shook his head, not following what she was getting at.

"We hide in plain sight: the Auxilia Amphitheatre."

"That won't work. It'll be full of apprentices at every meal now, thanks to us."

"But the ceremonial well chamber isn't and it—"

"Adjoins the Auxilia Amphitheatre," Asher cut her off excitedly. "But it's always locked, isn't it?"

"Yes, but that's the best part. Due to the historic importance of the well-shaft, it was never upgraded with a secureaug lock. It still has a traditional key-sprung lock. I remember Lem prattling on about it during his security breakdown. And don't worry about the key; I have that covered," she smiled proudly.

"Lorrelli you're—"

"A genius? Righteous? All of the above? I know."

Lorrelli had lost the entire afternoon visiting Ermalt Dopplebock to imbue her mantle with her first element. When she returned, a fine auburn vine had wrapped itself partway around the exterior of her auger, completely replacing one section of the silver fixtures that had previously held her auger in place. Almost immediately, she noticed a significant enhancement of her abilities to call forth and control Natura-specific blood callings, much to her utter delight.

It had taken another two days for her to find the right moment to slip away upstairs, undetected, to get Sageroot's box just before the evening meal.

Asher didn't have the time to get it himself. He was too busy with his private instruction in the Praelior Arena, and the tribune always had a constant eye on him.

They both agreed going after the box at all was a risky move, but they only had two days before the Utor Alea tournament. They needed time to work out how to open the box and then to figure out how to use the augefact, if it was even inside.

They were rapidly running out of time.

Lorrelli ran upstairs and grabbed the box from its hiding place, and stashed it in the bottom of her rucksack, before returning downstairs for dinner. She casually joined a group of apprentices heading to the Auxilia Amphitheatre and arrived to see Asher eating alone at the side of the room. Small tufts of the creeping mould had spread across the floor, which had many apprentices trying to destroy them with various blood callings in vain attempts to win the highly coveted prize offered by the legate.

They waited for the room to fill up and decided to act only when the room was at its busiest. Asher loosened the drawstring on his rucksack beneath his feet and let it fall to the floor. Leaving the bag behind, they stood up and made their way towards the locked door that led to the well-shaft.

An apprentice with fair hair and freckles shrieked out in surprise as a small green furry creature hopped up onto her lap and split into two smaller identical creatures, leaving a slimy smear on her pants.

She reactively struck them both from her lap, casting them down into the tiers of startled Apprentices below, and shrieked again when the gelatinous ooze spread to her fingers.

Many of the older apprentices were already laughing loudly, considering the prank hilarious until soon there were twenty, then forty, then eighty, then hundreds of the tiny lawnkins bounding about aimlessly and multiplying unchecked, unleashing widespread pandemonium across the amphitheatre.

Apprentices everywhere called forth various blood powers to deal with the nuisance, some more effectively than others, as the pandemic infestation spread and grew in size.

"Foris rototo," Lorrelli whispered at the lock of the ceremonial well chamber door, turning over the lock's internal mechanism. Making sure no-one was watching, they slipped inside and closed the door behind them.

The well chamber was deserted, as was the adjacent observation gallery. Lorrelli used the same blood calling to lock the door behind them, before complimenting Asher on his distraction with a devious smile.

"Did you see Gullybore's face? She positively freaked when that lawnkin doubled on her lap."

Asher smiled briefly, allowing himself one quick laugh, before removing the box from Lorrelli's rucksack. He turned it over in his hands, inspecting every surface and groove for a sign of how to open it. "Well, there's no visible lock, lid or opening I can see." He passed it to Lorrelli. "You want to try that open-lock thingy you just did on the door?"

"That's only for key-sprung locks, but I know another I can try," Lorrelli replied and held her auger over the top of the box. "Arca dissere!"

The moment the words left her lips, Lorrelli's entire body was violently flung backwards across the room by an enormous invisible force. The box dropped harmlessly to the ground, undamaged. There wasn't even as much as a scratch on its surface.

Asher ran to her side. "Are you alright?"

"My ego's a bit bruised," Lorrelli sat up groggily and rubbed the back of her head, "but otherwise I'm fine. It must have some sort of augmented protection around it."

"So how do we open it?" Asher asked, pulling her to her feet.

"It beats the hell out of me. No pun intended." Lorrelli limped across the room. "Let's have a better look at the damn thing."

"A better look," Asher repeated as he raised his auger to his head and looked again. Instantly a brilliant green emblem of the Sageroot family crest appeared on the box's lid. "That's more like it," he whispered, explaining what he saw. Turning the box over in his hands, he saw nothing on the bottom or each of the four sides. Nothing looked out of the ordinary until he reached the last face of the box.

A small circular green ring sat in the middle of the box's surface, its circumference extending exactly halfway above and below the middle of the box. It was no more than a coin's width in size and had no distinctive markings whatsoever.

Lorrelli thought for a minute upon hearing Asher's description and retrieved something from her bag. She handed the ribbon she'd used to find the box's original hiding place to Asher.

"Try this."

Asher tilted the box upwards so the green ring was facing the ceiling and overlayed the back of the ribbon over it.

Nothing happened.

He shook his head and gave it back to Lorrelli. She thought for a moment and then delicately peeled the wax seal off the ribbon and handed it back to Asher.

"Worth a shot, right?"

He placed the back of the seal against the ring and instantly the red wax was engulfed in a warm emerald light, slowly reforming its mould into an exact replica of the Sageroot family crest. The box coughed up a deluge of dust as it cracked open with a pop. Asher turned it back upright and excitedly lifted the lid. Inside was a large wooden carving of an eagle's foot, neatly placed next to a vial of liquid on a bed of soft teal-coloured satin. The wood looked like it had been burned black, but it was smooth and clean to the touch.

"Is that…?"

"Wormwood Vindicat, yeah." Lorrelli ignored the vial of liquid and, instead, picked up the surprisingly heavy carving with her hands and examined it closely.

A small hollow hole ran down the centre of the leg above the extended claws. It looked roughly the same size in diameter as the vial. Four bright white talons protruded like curved ivory daggers on the tip of each toe, a vivid contrast against the charred burned black of the wood.

"It looks like the talons have been carved from bone," she said, handing it to Asher and swapping it for the box. "It's an augefact alright. So now what?"

"I guess we try it out on some mould," Asher said as he held out the augefact at a patch of mould that had crept under the door. Nothing happened.

"Maybe scratch it with the claws," Lorrelli suggested optimistically.

Asher did so, but the mould remained unchanged: resilient as ever. "Maybe it needs an invocation," Asher thought out loud.

"No, from what I understand, augefacts don't need invocations. It might need a catalyst, though," Lorrelli countered, opening the vial of Wormwood Vindicat and sliding it into the augefact's opening.

A drop of the liquid spilled on the back of her hand as she did so. She immediately wiped it on her pants, eager to get the unnaturally viscous liquid off her skin. The augefact, however, relished the liquid's touch, immediately springing the charred black eagle's claw to life in Asher's hands. Its toes flexed and stretched, shaking off years of debilitating immobility.

Asher tentatively kneeled down and held the augefact over a patch of clammy mould. The mould instantly bubbled and evaporated from its obstinate hold on the floor, vaporising into a fine green mist before vanishing entirely into thin air. Asher withdrew the vial from the augefact and replaced the lid, but where a victorious smile should have stood across his face, instead there was only a heavy frown.

"What's wrong? We did it; the mould's gone," Lorrelli's excited smile lessened as she saw the disturbed expression on Asher's face.

"It's gone and I'd love to say we've got some mould to destroy and a prize to collect, but this augefact's useless."

"What do you mean? It works perfectly."

"We can't be caught with Wormwood Vindicat again, let alone an augefact powered by the stuff." As soon as the words left his mouth, an enormous cheer erupted from the room next door.

Asher stuffed the claw inside his tunic and Lorrelli roughly stuffed the box back into her rucksack. Carefully, they both snuck back into the Auxilia Amphitheatre, but no-one was watching them. Everyone was vibrantly celebrating in the middle of the room. A fourth-year apprentice was being thrown up and down on his friend's shoulders and everyone in the room was chanting his name.

"Stemproles. Stemproles. Stemproles."

"What's going on?" Asher asked the nearest apprentice. The short, stocky boy didn't even so much as look them before answering.

"Stemproles just worked out how to kill the mould."

"What?" Asher and Lorrelli said in disbelief.

"Don't ask me how, he was attacking the lawnkin and then, poof, mould gone. Watch he's about to do it again."

Asher turned to Lorrelli with an alarmed look on his face, before running up to one of the amphitheatre's higher tiers to get a better view. Sure enough, Stemproles stood with arms outstretched, auger ablaze with luminous green slivers of light around his neck. His face betrayed his intense concentration focused toward a patch of mould near the edge of the crowd's feet. Without even so much as saying a word, the mould burst into a fiery black flame and receded back into the cracks within the floor.

The room erupted once more with insatiable applause and celebration. Raucous chants and hollering followed Stemproles as he left the amphitheatre and made his way towards the nearest vertistrand to find the closest master. A host of apprentices followed him out, still cheering and clapping.

"Well that's just great." Lorrelli said glumly. "The Utor Alca match is two days away and now we've got no way of getting into the Custodian's Box. What the hell do we do now?"

Asher slumped down into his seat deflated, the talons of the augefact digging into his sides as if karmically taunting him.

"I have no idea."

CHAPTER 33

THE INSINCERITY OF CIVILITY

Over the next two days, Lorrelli and Asher racked their brains for ideas, each trying to figure out a way to get inside the Custodian's Box for the Utor Alea game, but neither could come up with anything remotely plausible. The match was only an hour away and a growing din of excited cheers was already echoing throughout the hallways all around Mantlecrest.

"Come on, Asher, we might as well catch the match, even if we can't get inside the Custodian's Box. We'll find another way to figure out the Letifer mystery and expose Morreby." Lorrelli pulled Asher off his bed and out the door. "Besides, you've never seen Utor Alea before. The Seven Seal matches are breathtaking."

Asher and Lorrelli made their way towards the arena when they were caught up in a bustling crowd of apprentices all heading in the opposite direction, towards the Auxilia Amphitheatre.

"Where's everybody going?" Lorrelli called out to a dark-haired girl hurrying past them across the hall.

"Gibraltair is touring Mantlecrest before the match," Apprentice Percotty shouted back at them, before scampering off.

Lorrelli grabbed Asher by the arm excitedly as an idea struck her. "Gibraltair's the guest of honour at the match today."

"So what?"

"So he'll be in the Custodian's Box."

"And?"

"So maybe he'll recognise you and invite you to join him. Come on." Lorrelli knew it was a desperate stretch, but they had no alternative and anything was worth a shot at this point. They

357

quickly followed the group of apprentices, blending in to the back of the pack.

When they finally arrived in the corridor just outside the amphitheatre, their way was blocked by a horde of excited apprentices, each overly excited to catch a glimpse of the famous augiologist. They were so eager that their jostling bodies had become jammed together within the confined space of the narrow hall, forming an impassable blockade.

Asher and Lorrelli tried to push through the crowd, but it was no use, the apprentices were too tightly packed together for either of them to make any headway.

"Say the Shroud's Truth will you, please?" a younger apprentice eagerly begged Gibraltair at the front of the crowd.

Gibraltair held up his hands to quieten the screams and calls of the apprentices, waiting for everyone to settle.

Only after they had done so, he recited a passage that Asher instantly recognised. He had heard him recount it once before.

"Very well. I am, after all, but a humble servant to you all this day." Gibraltair paused and adopted an elegant orator's pose, raising his voice so it would carry to the far reaches of the corridor. "To Vita true, I leave to you, the fate of our nation. Behold at first, a father's thirst, and life for our salvation."

The apprentices in the narrow hall erupted into a series of cheers simultaneously.

"Such a grand response from those so important to Undergall's future makes me proud to return to these hallowed halls for a second time."

"A second time, Reine, when was the first?" The legate questioningly looked at the finely dressed man, who had clearly purchased a new outfit for the occasion.

"Please, my dear legate, call me Bell," Gibraltair politely ignored her question, extending his hand to her courteously in a gesture of goodwill.

Legate Seville bowed her head slightly, but did not take his hand. "Well, if you'll follow me, Bell, we've a little time before the match is due to commence. Perhaps you'd like to look out over the city from our newly refurbished lookout on Mess Hill. I have a surprise in store."

"Devilishly intriguing and beguilingly beautiful, dear legate, your ability to subjugate my senses is uncanny. Lead on." Gibraltair smiled falsely, gazing at her austere features with wary eyes from behind the tinted lenses of his peculiar glasses.

"Mess Hill!" Lorrelli exclaimed excitedly, yanking down hard on Asher's arm. "Come on, we can beat them there."

Before Asher had the chance to argue, Lorrelli had already set off at a run in the opposite direction from the teeming mass surrounding Gibraltair.

Asher followed, speeding after her towards Mess Hill. He had absolutely no idea what they would do or say when they got there, but he became too caught up in the moment to stop Lorrelli and ask about the plan.

Asher was panting heavily by the time they reached the double arched doors of Mess Hill. He heard the cheers of the crowd echo through the nearby corridors grow louder just as he and Lorrelli stepped out onto the lawn.

Dusk was a few short minutes away from showering the entire city in simulated night once more. Out of breath and gasping for air, they sprinted across the lawn towards the newly constructed lookout.

"We've got to make it look like a chance encounter to avoid the legate's suspicion," Lorrelli gasped as she ran.

Asher only nodded in response as he ran after her, taking in the newly resurfaced terrain of the refurbished hill. The steep slope of the hill that had previously towered over the dining tables was gone. A new rock-solid three-tier-high retaining wall had replaced it.

The top of each had been inlaid with a hundred small stone gargoyles, each gazing out over Mess Hill and the city below. Several new enormous stone columns had been added to those on the hill's crest, including one to replace the column he had destroyed. All of their tops were empty, noticeably devoid of any type of statue, but new stone arches had been added, firmly securing the columns to the back wall.

Asher's legs came to a stop just as a large crowd spilled out on to Mess Hill through its oversized entrance arch. Gibraltair and the legate were walking briskly in the lead.

Asher and Lorrelli waited patiently, trying to look as natural as possible, each of them secretly dying to hunch over and gasp for air. They purposely faced away from the approaching horde, instead choosing to gaze out innocently over the city.

Legate Seville said very little to Gibraltair as they crossed the lawn, but her watchful gaze did not leave the finely dressed man for a second. So much so, she failed to notice the two apprentices gazing out over the city as they leaned against the new lookout's stone balustrade.

"What do you think of the newly refurbished overlook of Undergall?" the legate asked Gibraltair over the rumbling din of the crowd.

"Quite pleasant," he answered quickly, clearly unimpressed, "but I'd be more interested in hearing about any clues as to who might have destroyed the old one."

The legate's demeanour darkened for a second as Gibraltair's statement hit home, which seemed only to delight the augiologist further. It was obvious he took great pleasure in catching people, especially those in a position of power, off guard with nothing more than a cleverly timed quip. Sensing her displeasure, he pushed the matter further. "Little escapes my attention when rogues season the pot with mystery, especially when it scalds the hand that stirs it."

"We're investigating a number of leads," she said sternly, abruptly ending the conversation in its tracks.

"Speaking of roguish mystery, who else should I spy against this wondrous backdrop, but the very individual that has the entire Cruaar Nation abuzz with villainous rumour? Master Bloom, had I known your ailment was so intriguing, I would've held your attention longer in the bowels of the great sandy beast upon our first meeting."

Asher remained silent, but politely turned around to face the man, bowing his head slightly in a display of subservience before the legate.

"You've met before?" the legate's eyebrows rose sharply, betraying her immediate suspicion at the remark and her surprise at seeing Asher standing before her.

"Oh, Asher and I share much more than our notorious levels of infamy. It would seem fate has intertwined our paths much more than even I first anticipated. Why else would we both be standing at this exact place at this exact time?"

Lorrelli shot a quick glance at Asher and buried a sly smile behind her hand.

"Only fools mistake happenstance for the hand of fate. News of your arrival has long been commonplace within these walls. Such a meeting can hardly be attributed to chance," Legate Seville stated sternly, suspiciously eyeing off Asher and Lorrelli, not quite fully aware how they came to be standing in front of her, or what they hoped to gain from the encounter.

"Nonsense." Gibraltair scoffed. "Chance is but an enigma, fallen victim to fate's lengthy shadow."

Lorrelli stepped in front of Asher and stuck out her hand in an offer of greeting to the augiologist.

Without saying a word, he swatted away her hand and pushed past her until his arm was wrapped around Asher's shoulders. "Had I known you'd be the cause of so much irritation for the council, I'd have not let you escape so easily the first time." Gibraltair smiled as he noticed the slight twinge of annoyance playing across the legate's brow. "And indeed those much closer to home."

"I never meant to…" Asher tried to play coy, not wishing to further anger the legate, especially after their last meeting.

"Intent aside, I'd be a fool not to indulge the motive of fate, and a bigger one to release you again before I've had a chance to unravel the intolerable enigma that surrounds you."

"I can't go to the match, first-years are not allowed," Asher goaded him, pushing him to defy the legate so he was free of any blame for what was about to happen.

"Nonsense," Gibraltair tapped Asher's chest reassuringly while beaming an enormously cheeky smile at the legate.

Asher couldn't believe the man's arrogance, but silently praised him for it. "After all, you are my guest."

The legate was about to object when Gibraltair looked at her and smiled cunningly. "I trust that, as an honoured patron of Mantlecrest, I will not be denied such a trivial request."

Despite her uncanny ability to mask her emotions, the legate was visibly unimpressed with the augiologist's method of coercion, but she was duty bound by her position as legate to grant the man whatever he wished, at least until the Utor Alea match had concluded. After a few tense seconds, she dutifully agreed and bowed her head, her eyes never leaving Asher's face. "Whatever you wish, Reine."

As if on cue, a wave of disbelief washed over the faces of the gathered apprentices as a number of jaws dropped in unison. Asher could feel their indignant outrage at his uncommonly good fortune. The privilege of watching Utor Alea from the Custodian's Box would undoubtedly see much more hatred and animosity thrown his way, but all Asher could do to stop himself from smiling was focus on the tight grip of Lorrelli's hand on his arm.

"Now as much as I enjoy the embrace of this fair city's delights upon my eyes," he said sharply, "you promised me a surprise, dear legate, and I'll wager young Master Bloom's appearance was not the surprise you had in mind."

Asher could tell the legate was not happy about Asher's sudden invitation and inclusion within the Custodian's Box, but she could hardly fault him for the impulsive will of an eccentric augiologist. She tore her gaze away from them and back to Gibraltair, who stood waiting patiently for her response.

"As a lover of all things augiological, perhaps you will appreciate Mantlecrest's newest additions. These acquisitions come at great personal expense, but I think you'll agree, will add an unmatched level of security to the grounds."

"Your words tantalise, but in which direction should I direct my gaze," Gibraltair's lips lingered on the last word as he stared back at the legate, smiling widely.

"They are here already. Though do not feel bad if you remain blind to them." The legate smiled back at him, turning her back on the city as she stared up at the row of now statue-less columns high above them.

"Allow me to introduce Mantlecrest's newest guardians." She held up her hand towards the tops of the empty columns and waited for darkness to descend over the crest of the hill. "A night-watch of caliors, trained by none other than Allma Ohery."

The crowd of apprentices turned and looked up at the immense stone pylons, but many were left scratching their heads in confusion as they saw nothing. A few recognised the name and turned to look at the central auglight before looking back at the pylons, but most looked completely bewildered.

Gibraltair hit a switch on the side of his glasses and instantly let loose a giddy smile. "Magnificent is too poor a word."

It was a few moments before the last glimmer of radiance from the central auglight disappeared, blanketing the hill in darkness. The crowd of apprentices clapped and cheered, oohing and aahing up at the creatures materialising above the empty columns as their naturally evolved camouflage faded, their existence slowly revealed to the world below as the darkness of simulated night embraced their perches.

Six large black-snouted beasts sat atop the empty columns, flapping their enormous bone-crested, opaque wings. They snapped their jaws loudly together between sharp twin tusks, before wailing a sickening collective screech at the awe-struck figures far below.

Two immediately took flight and climbed high above

Mantlecrest, flapping their enormous wings sparingly as they soared ever higher. The rest remained in place, perched on the columns, preening their rough leathery skin with long tongues as muscular hair-covered tails coiled tightly around the masonry below.

Legate Seville lowered her hand and raised her voice to properly address the gathered crowd. "Invisible during daylight while they slumber, the nocturnal night-watch of caliors will provide the perfect guardians for Mantlecrest's grounds during nightfall, protecting us from vandalism and attack, both inside and outside our walls." She shot a quick judgemental glance at Asher and Lorrelli as she finished.

Asher couldn't help but inadvertently gulp.

"Come now, you'll all have plenty of time to admire these magnificent creatures long into the future but, as for now, Utor Alea beckons."

"Indeed, dear legate, I have been looking forward to shaking the Chancellor's hand personally." He leaned forward so only Asher, Lorrelli and the legate could hear. "Nothing quite like rubbing in the stink after a good acquittal."

Legate Seville smiled back at him, but Asher could tell the smile was delivered only out of formality. It oozed of false graciousness and an underlying dislike of the man before her. "Unfortunately, the Chancellor will not be attending the match, nor will I. He's been called away on important business, but I will see you to the Custodian's Box before I depart."

The look of disappointment and annoyance spreading across Gibraltair's face was instantly evident, leading Asher to believe that Gibraltair had counted on meeting the Chancellor for reasons other than he previously let on.

"I hope you be able to enjoy the visual treasure of Utor Alea without us," Legate Seville said insincerely, ever so slightly bowing her head at Gibraltair as she rose up a hand towards the exit.

Asher sensed a shared and understood uneasiness between the

two, but could not put his finger on why it existed. He shot Lorrelli a last, slightly anxious look of reassurance, before falling in behind the legate and Gibraltair.

Lorrelli returned a quick thumbs-up as she lost sight of him behind the backs of the cheering crowd surging after the famed augiologist.

"Don't forget…" she cried out, but her reminder was drowned out by the raucous noise of the crowd.

CHAPTER 34

MOLIORS, FULCIORS & ARX BASTIONS

Asher hadn't had a chance to say anything to Gibraltair on the way to the arena. He could barely hear himself think over the cheers and adoration of the fanatical apprentices surrounding them. Besides, he didn't dare risk attempting to strike up a conversation whilst the legate was still within earshot.

Gibraltair seemed unfazed by all the attention, and humbly waved his appreciation back at the swarming mass who were cheering and chanting his name over and over again.

It wasn't until the legate activated a vertistrand and invited Gibraltair, Asher and the tribune to enter, that Asher found himself free of her untrusting gaze.

Asher emerged in a small room with the perfect viewing angle over the entire arena. He was promptly ushered forward by the tribune and forced into a seat next to Apprentice Stemproles. Stemproles tersely ignored him and turned away, leaving Asher alone and free to marvel at the spectacle before him.

The arena looked and felt five times bigger than Asher remembered. He couldn't be sure whether it was just his new perspective over things, or whether it had been augitecturally enhanced to accommodate the growing throng of Utor Alea fans lining every square inch of the spectator stands.

The arena was awash with Cruaar, not only from Undergall, but also the far reaches of the Cruaar Nation. The sheer size of the crowd far outweighed the relatively small number of apprentices at Mantlecrest.

Asher could only guess at the number of people in attendance, but it would have been close to 40,000, if not more. Most of the spectators were wearing one of two coloured sashed over their tunics: the red and white of the Undergall Hopralas or the blue and yellow of the Hollow's Rest Rajas.

Stemproles shot Asher a look of disdain from the neighbouring seat. He seemed hell-bent on ensuring no-one would mistake them as anything more than acquaintances. He even went as far as to stand up and join in on a conversation already underway on the other side of the box to avoid the remote possibility of any interaction between them.

The more Asher thought about it, most of the members in attendance within the Custodian's Box appeared to be taking great pains to avoid him, maintaining a wide berth around him at all times.

Asher had nearly forgotten he was still considered an outcast beyond the walls of Mantlecrest. The judgemental disapproving looks cast his way from random spectators around the stands, as well as those from inside the Custodian's box, reminded Asher only too well he was not a welcome sight.

Looking around the tiered seats of the Custodian's Box, he tried to think of a way to get closer to Gibraltair without raising any suspicion. Unfortunately, the augiologist was firmly engaged in conversation with several elderly, affluent-looking gentlemen to his left. Getting the information he wanted was going to be harder the he thought, despite his undeniable good fortune.

Master Rousso tipped his hat towards Asher upon seeing him, before returning to his conversation with two strikingly attractive ladies. Both were more beautiful than anyone else in the room, though Asher suspected they knew as much. Despite their conversation with Master Rousso, their attention was firmly fixated on Gibraltair's striking form a few feet away.

Asher returned a shy smile briefly before glancing around to see if he recognised anyone else in attendance. He didn't, except for the tribune, who was watching him silently from the rear of the box. He appeared to be patiently waiting for Asher to slip up, just so that he could remove him, preferably by force by the look of his eyes.

Asher gulped down his nervousness and turned his gaze towards the arena floor, taking in the grand spectacle that had been erected on the arena's rugged terrain he'd come to know. He'd spilled much of his own crimson blood on the sands under the somewhat barbaric tutelage of Tribarion Roolta. It felt strange to gaze down at the arena, far removed from the coarse feeling of its rough grit under his feet.

Asher decided to move closer to the front of the box, to a space not yet occupied by the elite of Undergall, and marvelled at what had been constructed on the arena's pitch. Three enormous pyramids, each topped with a small round glass dome, had been erected at an equal distance from a circular four-foot-high stone well. A bright silver liquid sat calmly in its centre, undisturbed by the wild emotions charging around the spectator stands.

The entire crowd erupted in vibrant cacophony of cheers as two teams marched out on to the arena's sandy pitch. Each fan cheered on their favourite players with a series of catcalls, team chants and raucous applause.

The players from both the Undergall Hopralas and the Hollow's Rest Rajas were a fierce assortment of armour-clad warriors. Some looked no older than eighteen, whilst others could have passed for forty, at a glance. Each player held up a single armoured gauntlet, much like the tribune's, in a salute to the crowd as they spread out, assuming their positions on the unnaturally white sand.

All sported some kind of weapon, all of them different, though Asher had long since learnt to identify a battle mantle. The glimmer of an auger on a weapon's blade, shaft, or hilt somehow always managed to catch the light, even at this distance. Some players let their battle mantles hang loosely from their waist, others had theirs strapped tightly to their backs, whilst the rest had theirs unsheathed, wielding them expertly within tightly clenched fists.

Asher tried to keep his mind focused on the task at hand and looked again at Gibraltair. He was busy shaking hands with the diminutive Mason Gobbler at the rear of the box in a private conversation. Their words were lost in whispers, almost as if the subject matter was pointedly unsuited for the common ear. Their conversation lasted only a moment before Asher's eyes were drawn back to the grand spectacle unfolding on the arena floor. He felt his blood warm in his veins and his heart beat a little faster in his chest as he took in the spectacle, watching the Utor Alean auglets of each team charge up the crowd.

"I take it by th' look of a stunned mullet strapped tae yer tiny wee dial, that ye've no' witnessed th' majesty of th' greatest game on Earth?" A large man approached the banister next to Asher and placed two powerful hands on it to support his bulky frame. Leaning forward until his large paunch was firmly pressed against the low guardrail, he spoke with a deep guttural highland accent which made him incredibly difficult for Asher to understand at first.

"Err, no. I guess not," Asher responded quietly as he looked up at the man's wild bushy face. Dark green eyes, set under a thunderous growth of thick, messy eyebrows, peered down at him in surprise. The man's moustache overgrew his mouth by a full inch, the corners hanging down past his exposed chin until everything became somehow messily tied together into one long, olive-tinged braid.

Funnily enough, despite the untamed mane on the man's face, his head, cheeks and chin were clean shaven. Although his chin looked more scarred than shaven, as if a part of it had been cut off and it was no longer possible for him to grow hair there.

His scalp sported a dark-green tattoo completely foreign to Asher. Parts of the design looked as though they'd been specifically inked over a series of large scars stretching down the length of the man's head and neck. It was almost as if the tattoo itself was holding his scalp together.

"Aye, ye poor wee blighter. Well, 'en, I'd be remiss in my duties not tae impart tae ye some of my worldly wisdom in th' matter, an' explain tae ye th' rules." He dramatically swept his hand out over the arena floor, nearly hitting the top of Asher's head in the process.

"Utor Alea is a brilliant contest of risk, tempered only by th' addition of strategy, ability an' opportunity, where advantage must be seized with an iron fist." He bent his arm and stuck up one finger in the air. "It's not a game fer loners, or glory-seekin' pretenders. So if ye fancy yerself a hero, laddie, ye'd best stick tae bloodline bouts."

Asher didn't understand half of what the man was saying, but didn't get a chance to clarify anything before the man swung his powerful arm towards the nearest pyramid. Scars lashed his exposed forearm, cruelly hewn into his skin from weapons and torments unknown. The sheer number of the cuts, burns and lacerations covering his skin made it hard to tell if any of it was the skin he was born with, or whether it was all just a mess of scar tissue.

"Two teams take th' field; five Alean augletes a piece. Three fulciors stalk th' terraces; one prime an' two bowers, right an' left. A lone molior roams th' void, an' finally an arx bastion protects th' palmabore."

Asher looked at each of the players as the bushy faced man pointed them out. Each of the fulciors seemed to be wearing a lighter form of armour than the molior who was, in turn, wearing lighter armour again than the full plate-mail encasing the arx bastion's bulky frame in augmented steel.

Though the moliors' armour was different to the fulciors', they were instantly identifiable by a long colourful sash extending upwards from their waist, slung over one shoulder and strapped down on their backs by a large gleaming buckle on their belt. The arx bastion, on the other hand, wore strong heavy gauntlets, gilded with a luminous foreign substance pulsating with energy as they flexed their armoured fingers.

Asher was about to ask about the difference between the three types of players on the field when the overbearing man heartily slapped a hand down on his shoulder and continued his explanation.

"Th' goal of Utor Alea is simple. Defeat yer opponents by strikin' th' palmabore with th' alea as many times as possible. Each successful alea that strikes th' palmabore's silvery depths lands a point for yer–"

"What's an alea?" Asher interrupted.

"What's an alea, he asks? Just th' greatest invention old Craftpaw's ever produced." The man slapped his hands and rubbed them together vigorously. "No bigger than yer tiny wee fist, an alea empowers its bearer with th' strength, speed, agility an' blood callings of a warrior five times their–"

A cane flashed past Asher's face from his right until its tip was positioned underneath the bottom of the burly man's plaited moustache that hung down to his chest. With a deft flick, the cane sent the man's mass of hair flying up into his face, cutting him off mid-sentence.

"I certainly hope PromMcKoll doesn't bore you to death before the sands have been paid their crimson toll. You must forgive his untamed enthusiasm; not all Cruaar share the same love of this antediluvian debauchery as this overgrown shag-pile."

"Well we can't all be privy tae th' rivetin' stories leant tae us by an unduly notorious career in augiology, now, can we, Gibblesticks?" PromMcKoll retorted, a large smile forming underneath the mountain of olive-tinged facial hair. PromMcKoll playfully swatted away Gibraltair's cane and Asher leaned back as the two shook hands across him in the manner of age-old friends. "Now shut yer dainty wee painted chops while I explain th' finer aspects of Utor Alea tae th' lad."

"Hurry it up, then, you disgruntled highland cow, I would have words with him, preferably before your garbled accent sees him tear off his own ears."

"Pipe down ye sook of a scullery-pished pillow-crumb," PromMcKoll smirked boisterously, swatting a hand at Gibraltair's face.

"Listen well, Asher. It's not often you'll receive sober

commentary from the greatest arx bastion to have ever lived. Normally, he'd need a belly full of Bonswoon Revelry for the pleasure, and I use the term 'pleasure' in its loosest possible sense."

"Aye, aye, ye have me there," PromMcKoll laughed heartily. "Now simmer down ye muckled puff-drop."

Asher decided it was probably best he just give up on trying to decipher PromMcKoll's strange highland insults, trying, instead, to focus on his explanation of the game unfolding in the arena below.

Gibraltair slipped Asher a sly wink behind tinted glasses and sat down next to him, content enough to engage the two beautiful women that had just positioned themselves to his right.

Asher couldn't believe his luck. Gibraltair was within his reach, which meant so too was finally deciphering what Surio Letifer meant and getting the answers he desperately desired.

"Now, where were we?" PromMcKoll muttered beneath his enormous moustache, trying to find his train of thought once more.

"Right, if ye consider th' team as a single man, then th' fulciors are its arms an' legs. They provide support, stability an' position tae attack. This allows th' molior, th' man's weapon, tae strike when opportunity arises. However, a strong offence is naught without an equally strong defence, which is where th' arx bastion comes in. Let's call him th' man's shield. He alone can ward off enemy attacks an' protect th' man from damage." The man looked down at Asher and winked. "Most important player on th' team, if ye ask me."

"An unbiased explanation would be superlative, Prommy, old boy," Gibraltair chimed in loudly not bothering to turn around. "If it's not too much trouble to get an honest word past that bearded travesty."

"Don't blame me coz th' Hopralas rejected yer feather-soft body, Prettybell." He held up his hand and whispered to Asher, "not once, but twice."

Either Gibraltair chose not to hear the remark, or his mind was focused on other matters. In any case, he did not dignify the insult with response.

"Where were we? Ahh, yes, th' palmabore." PromMcKoll pointed at the silver depths of the well in the centre of the arena. "Th' point of vulnerability an enemy will seek tae wound."

Asher was a little puzzled by the man's strange way of explaining things, but said nothing, instead, trying to decipher PromMcKoll's foreign accent between his back-and-forth insult match with Gibraltair as best he could.

A loud series of horns sounded across the arena and both teams' arx bastions walked and placed their hands on edges of the palmabore. Asher leaned forward a little further against the guard rail to get a better view.

"Are ye ready fer a spot of mayhem, laddie?" PromMcKoll asked excitedly, a crazed twinkle sparkling in the back of his eyes.

Asher broke his gaze from the excitement on the arena floor and glanced up at the enormous man's overgrown, bushy features.

"Ye'd better be."

CHAPTER 35

UTOR ALEA

The legate's voice echoed around the arena, but she was nowhere to be seen. Asher looked up and listened to her words ring out from the mouths of a hundred stone statues, each perched on a ledge just below the roof that ran around the circumference of the arena.

Each statue was different in appearance, but all were roughly the same size. They sat equidistance from one another, mouths agape, looming over the arena and spectator grandstands like an army of nesting monsters.

"Cruaar of Undergall and beyond, I welcome you all to the Praelior Arena for the first match of the Seven Seal Tournament. Tonight, the Undergall Hopralas will be pitted against the might of the Hollow's Rest Rajas."

As each team was announced, two raucous cheers went up as the supporters of each side tried to outdo the other's vocal barrage.

The legate waited for the crowd's emphatic support to die down, before continuing her address. "To mark this momentous occasion, Augiologist Gibraltair Reine has kindly provided a most exotic addition for the interference round, which I will let him introduce when the time comes. I would ask you all to please raise your augers in salute to the Alean augletes that stand before you and show them honour them they rightly deserve."

The crowd roared and jumped to their feet, hollering and screaming their support for their beloved teams. A series of team-specific chants broke out across the arena as groups of Hopralas fans challenged Rajas' fans in competitive rivalry.

The uproar continued to echo in waves as more of the crowd got into the celebratory mood, when a momentary flicker of warped light flashed mere inches in front of Asher's face. He hesitantly reached out to where he'd seen the shimmer until his fingers were stopped by an invisible barrier.

"Ye've a keen eye, laddie. What ye feel against yer wee digits is th' second best ting tae ever come through Craftpaw's golden gates: th' Retego." PromMcKoll reached out with his own hand and flicked a finger at the invisible barrier, sending ripples of distorted light outwards in every direction.

"Tis th' only ting that keeps everythin' in th' arena, in th' arena. Arguably, a necessary evil, considerin' th' unfortunate accidents of th' past, but an evil not without its perks." He waved his auger at the barrier and a much larger translucent image of the two arx bastions magnified instantly against the invisible surface of the shield.

"Better than being on the sand itself, one might say," Gibraltair quipped.

Asher slowly moved his head around the projected transparent image, amazed at the level of detail he could see of the magnified Alean augletes.

PromMcKoll dismissed the enhancement with a wave of his hand and leaned in close to Asher, nodding at the players on the field. "Watch closely now. When both teams draw their weapons an' submit tae th' lawlessness of th' arena, war will break upon th' sands."

"Lawlessness and war," Asher repeated to himself in a whisper, not understanding the man's meaning.

The three fulciors of each team faced off against one another, a rival pair on top of each of the three pyramids. Muscular hands unsheathed battle mantles until a variety of pikes, swords, war-hammers, maces, chains, shields and spears were being held aloft, pointed skyward in tribute to the crowd: a signification the augletes were ready.

No two battle mantles were the same, each one unique to its owner, as was the auger embedded in each weapon. Every gem had a slightly different shape and colour that glinted as it caught the light.

Asher narrowed his eyes and focused on the closest player on the arena floor. He waved his hand at the Retego, but nothing happened. Looking at PromMcKoll, the burly man showed him how to properly command the light-bending device.

A magnified image of the female auglete popped up in front of him. Her auger had been embedded in the shaft of a spear, but Asher's eyes were more interested in the myriad of strange shapes and colourful objects that encased and surrounded the gemstone. Asher counted six distinct components: each had a different colour, and all looked as if they had somehow grown out of the spear's shaft to lock the gemstone in place.

Asher looked down at his own hand, unfurled his fingers and wondered what his mantle would look like once he'd found all six of his elements. A less-than-subtle grunt from PromMcKoll indicated it was probably better to keep his auger hidden for the time being, so Asher forced his hand deep into his pocket and waved away the magnified image in front of him.

The two moliors on the arena floor thrust their battle mantles up in the air, leaving the two arx bastions as the last on the field to draw their weapons. They stood opposite each other on either side of the palmabore, each with their gilded, shimmering gauntlets laid flat on the low wall of the palmabore's well. In unison, they raised their awe-inspiring battle mantles from their sides, lifted them high above their heads and simultaneously plunged them downwards, submersing their tips into the palmabore's silvery depths.

A deafening rumble vibrated around the arena floor and spread throughout the stands, causing a fresh bout of cheering and excitement from the crowd.

Two large glowing balls of white-hot energy were released from the glass domes on top of the nearest two pyramids. The game was afoot. A sea of red-and-white-clad supporters jumped to their feet, erupting in savage approval as two of the Hopralas' fulciors emerged with aleas held firmly in gauntleted fist after a brief scuffle with their opponents. Bounding down the sides of the pyramids, they rushed headlong onto the pitch, their opposing augletes in hot pursuit.

"See how th' alea changes colour when a team holds possession. It helps tae identify who's who when things git messy in th' scrap heap later on."

Asher's eyes inspected the glowing energy balls, held tightly in each player's gauntlets, with a little more attention. Sure enough, they'd turned a bright red to signify Hopralas' possession.

"When an auglete holds possession of an alea, it imparts its energy tae them, augmentin' their natural abilities. Basically allowin' them tae run faster, jump higher, hit harder an' dodge more effectively."

In the few seconds it had taken for the alea bearers to descend the side of the pyramid, it was obvious both were pulling away from their pursuers.

"Be mindful, each alea only has three charges before its energy is depleted, so ye must keep count if ye want tae keep up with th' game. Attack another player an' lose a charge. Defend against an attack an' lose another. Revive a fallen teammate an' lose all three. Ye can pass th' alea tae a teammate without penalty but, if intercepted, all three charges reset."

PromMcKoll grabbed the top of Asher's head and twisted it towards the nearest pyramid. "When all three charges are spent, th' alea will disappear an' respawn above one of th' stone terraces at random, fully charged. So it becomes th' job of th' molior an' remaining fulciors tae attack and defend th' charged alea bearers as best they can."

"What do you mean 'revive a fallen teammate'?"

The words had barely left Asher's lips before the Hopralas' molior obliterated one of the opposing fulciors with a devastating hammer throw. The hammer collided with the man's breastplate in the centre, knocking him clean off his feet, slamming his body into the sand. The Hopralas' molior quickly retrieved his hammer as he leaped over the fallen fulcior and resumed his escort duties.

"Utor Alea is a blood-sport, laddie, full contact an' entirely lawless… to a degree," PromMcKoll stared down at the concerned look on Asher's face. "Don't fret yer daft wee head, though, th' arena's sands are augmented to assist in th' healin' process; but sands or not sands, a blow like that will still belt th' badger out of ye."

Asher cringed and instinctively clutched a hand over his chest, imagining how much it would hurt being hit like that.

"That bein' said, if these Alean auglets are worth their ruddy custard, it'll take a much greater love-tap than that tae lay 'em out." He fully exposed the scars on his arm by pulling back his sleeve up his arm. "Trust me, I should know."

The paths of the two charged Hopralas' fulciors and their escort guardians converged and the auglets merged together like a wolf pack, running as one in a wide circle around the palmabore. The Hopralas' molior covered the rear, whilst the remaining uncharged fulcior ran at the vanguard of the attack, leaving the two charged Hopralas' fulciors running side by side in-between.

One of the charged fulciors launched high over the head of his teammate in the lead and struck the earth hard with his heavy mace. The ground shuddered before him and a powerful shock wave steamrolled through the sand at an oncoming enemy molior and fulcior.

The Rajas' fulcior took the blast of energy front on, but the molior nimbly ducked out of its way and responded in kind, sending a volley of blue energy hurtling back at the now kneeling Hopralas' fulcior.

Reacting purely on instinct, the kneeling Hopralas' fulcior managed to muster a defence in the very last second before the attack landed, dispersing the violent blue energy attack harmlessly against a shimmering red shield.

"Argh, the dang eejit! He's down tae his last charge, he'll never score now."

"Why not?" Asher asked, unable to look away from the action

on the pitch.

"Coz fulciors an' moliors cannae physically attack th' opposition's arx bastion, an' in return, an arx bastion cannae attack an opposing auglete unless they step inside th' palmabore's strike zone."

"Strike zone?" Asher repeated, thoroughly confused.

"Ye'll know when they cross it. Ye need only watch th' sands."

Asher watched on in awe as both of the Hopralas alea bearers circled the palmabore, waiting for just the right moment to launch their respective attacks. As they did, the Hopralas' arx bastion launched a bloodthirsty attack on his rival as he leaped over the palmabore.

The sheer audacity of the move forced his opponent into a defensive position and diverted his attention from the circling Hopralas wolf pack.

"Aye, he's a clever wee runt, that one."

"I thought you said they couldn't attack the arx bastion."

"They cannae," he said nodding his head at the circling wolf pack. "Only arx bastions can batter one another, be it tae distract their opponent, or tae settle, or start, a blood grudge."

Taking advantage of the diversion created by their arx bastion, the attacking Hopralas wolf pack split in two, with two augletes veering off in different directions as they diverted from their circular orbit of the palmabore. One team of two was immediately set upon by three members of the opposition, and a fierce hand-to-hand scrap broke out.

A wayward lance savagely swept at the heels of one of the advancing Hopralas, knocking him to the ground, but not before he swung his massive flailed mace at the face of his attacker. The man only narrowly deflected the pulverising blow by twisting away at the last second; the barbed spikes of the mace collided heavily against his armoured pauldrons.

The charged Hopralas' fulcior nimbly dodged a backhanded assault and stooped low to haul his fallen teammate up from the floor, but the momentary loss of momentum cost him dearly. He did not see the sweeping arc of a heavy Rajas' battle-staff until it was too late. A large red flash exploded from his side as a tremendous force collided against the armour protecting his rib cage. A sickening crack echoed out across the sand as he was sent sprawling across the ground, lungs gasping for air as a single charge was drained from the alea in his hand.

The fighting between the warring augletes intensified with every second that passed. Thundering collisions of metal and grunts of exhausted exertion roared upwards from the arena floor as the pristine white sand was paid its toll of blood. Just when the fracas in the middle of the arena had transformed into a frenzy of clashing battle mantles, two Hopralas somehow broke free of the melee and dashed out into the open, an alea pulsating wildly in one of their hands for all to see.

Simultaneously, on the other side of the palmabore, the other Hopralas alea bearer had just launched himself off an opposing player's back and high into the air with a sensational gravity-defying leap. His actions, magnified by the pulsating red alea encased inside his gauntleted fist, propelled him to unnatural heights and granted him a unique opportunity to strike at the palmabore.

With perfect aim, he swung his arm and catapulted the alea at the palmabore's glistening silver surface. On the opposite side of the well, the second Hopralas alea bearer ducked under a decapitating sword swipe and was now madly dashing towards the palmabore. The sand under his feet erupted into a chaotic dance, vibrating and bouncing off the ground as a high-pitched whine spread outwards. Within a split second, an energised circle of shuddering white sand had turned a brilliant shade of red, engulfing the area surrounding the palmabore.

"There's yer strike zone, laddie," PromMcKoll chuckled, enlarging the image of the palmabore in front of Asher on the Retego just as the second alea bearer whipped the pulsating red alea forward and threw it towards the palmabore's exposed surface.

The crowd jumped to their feet as both energy balls shot towards the silvery liquid surface.

The Rajas' arx bastion saw the sand erupt beneath his feet and nimbly ducked to the side of an incoming uppercut from his rival and spun around, surveying the scene in an instant. He didn't have time to think, only to react. He launched towards the palmabore's low wall and, with a sturdy thrust of his right leg, propelled himself upwards. With gilded gauntlet outstretched, his bulk rocketed upwards, effortlessly plucking the fiery alea from mid-air as it sped downwards.

There was no time to celebrate his achievement.

He turned his head to look for the other alea, but it was too late. He felt the cold barbs of a savage whip coil around his leg moments before the Hopralas' arx bastion brutally yanked down on it, viciously tugging his body back down to the sandy floor.

The arx bastion's plate armour did little to protect him as his chest smashed against the edge of the palmabore's low wall. He was sent sprawling on the ground as an intense agony exploded in his midriff. As the air exploded from his lungs, he caught a glimpse of a shimmering red object splash down into the silvery surface of the well. Hopralas fans everywhere roared in approval, blowing horns loudly all around the arena in a bout of manic celebration.

"Bah, 'twas lucky, if th' Rajas lad had any real skill he would've never been goaded in tae a scrap tae begin with." PromMcKoll smiled down at Asher underneath his bushy moustache and raised his eyebrows.

At least, Asher thought he was smiling.

"Seein' as someone's scored, th' game gets a tad bit more interestin'."

Asher couldn't imagine how the game could get more interesting than it already was, but watched on eagerly, nonetheless. Looking around the arena, a multitude of magnified windows were popping up and disappearing all around the arena as Cruaar everywhere waved their augers at the Retego, bringing up various vantage points over the action below and dismissing them just as fast.

PromMcKoll continued his ramblings, although Asher was beginning to get the sense his continued explanation was not simply for Asher's benefit. The oversized man had a love of the game that was unrivalled by anyone in the Custodian's box, perhaps even the arena.

"Coz th' Rajas' arx bastion caught an alea, he's able tae choose where it gets respawned from. However, coz th' Hopralas managed tae score, their molior can call out a land mount that'll greatly enhance his mobility. Not tae mention his offensife an' defensife capabilities on th' field."

Asher watched the magnified close-up on the Retego as a large saddled beast bounded into view. It emerged at speed from a darkened doorway that blinked into existence on the side of one of the large pyramids. He instantly recognised the dirty black-and-red spots of the female gavrin as it hurdled on to the arena's pitch, its savage gait scattering sand behind it as it sped towards the Hopralas' molior.

Both aleas had already respawned and had been quickly snapped up by the time the Hopralas' molior had mounted the lumbering beast. Each team now shared equal possession: one alea apiece.

"As th' Rajas hav'nae scored, their team stands at a decided disadvantage, so it'll be interestin' tae see if they've got any cunnin' up their flappin' wee kilts."

Members of both teams squared up against one another at different locations in the arena. Each tested their opponent as a seasoned warrior would, striking and retreating again and again, searching for weakness. A number of one-on-one scuffles broke out, breaking apart moments later as each team sought an advantage to attack the alea bearers.

"Th' pinch-wik'd eejit, he's fallen fer a blood grudge," PromMcKoll said as he slapped the balustrade and waved a hand at the Retego.

An enlarged image of the two arx bastions immediately popped up before Asher's eyes. Both were locked in a fierce battle with each other, seemingly ignorant of everything else around them, leaving the Hopralas' arx bastion completely blind to the oncoming attack being launched behind him by one of the Rajas' fulciors.

"Don't take th' bait, ye stoatin' bofin git!"

The mounted Hopralas' molior managed to pin one of the opposition under the gavrin's massive paws as it ferociously headbutted another player out of the way with its impenetrable bone-encrusted skull.

The Hopralas' molior desperately tried to lay his hands on the charged Hollow's Rest fulcior, urging his mount forward, but the Rajas' fulcior was ready for him. He lithely sidestepped the beast and unleashed an attack of his own. The devastating force of the uppercut caught the Hopralas' molior under the chin and lifted him clean out of the saddle, his head snapped back, sending a plume of blood arcing from his mouth as his body careened backwards through the air.

The Rajas' fulcior quickly jumped in the saddle of the gavrin and spurred the savage beast towards the unprotected palmabore, rocketing the pulsating blue alea at its wide-open silvery surface.

"Score one for the Rajas," Gibraltair said snidely, calmly goading PromMcKoll as he watched the events unfold on the Retego's magnified viewing window.

"Min' yer tongue, yer dust-fiddlin' guttersnipe," PromMcKoll mumbled back at him, his eyes not once leaving the field.

The Rajas' fulcior rode the gavrin to a safe spot on the field before dismounting and slapping it rudely on the hindquarters, sending it off to find its master. He held up a gauntleted fist high in the air in salute to the audience.

A small section of the crowd roared at the man's heroic actions, applauding him with a standing ovation from the spectator stands. A second beast bounded into the arena and across the sands as the Rajas' molior called forth his mount. It paused only long enough to allow the man to jump onto its leather saddle before thundering off in the direction of the newly respawned alea.

Asher waved his auger at the Retego to get a better look at what could only be described as a hairless bear with smooth leathery skin and enormous white antlers that were unnaturally bent back over the sides of its head. It had shoulders like sculpted body armour.

"A conquered extrokka, now there's something you don't see every day." Gibraltair's eyes lit up.

"Probably not up tae yer usual standard of beastie, I'm sure," PromMcKoll snorted.

"Scoff all you like, you bushel-faced broom handle. Just wait till you see the exotic delight I have in store to run interference." Gibraltair smiled smugly.

But PromMcKoll paid him no mind and, instead, hurled abusive advice at the players in the arena.

Moments later, the Hopralas were again on the offensive. Asher watched on closely as the Hopralas' arx bastion retaliated against the Rajas' arx bastion for his oversight, delivering a punishing backhand followed by a debilitating kick to the chest. The brutality of the blows knocked the Rajas' arx bastion to the ground, just as a charged Hopralas' fulcior approached the strike zone. The Rajas' arx bastion clutched at his face as his nose erupted with blood and the wind rushed from his lungs, allowing an unchallenged approach to the palmabore for the opposition.

The Hopralas' fulcior casually ran up, ignoring the red sand dancing at his feet, and dropped the fiery red alea into the well's silvery depths. He flashed one cheeky grin to the crowd and raised his battle mantle in salute, before taking off again, heading for the nearest pyramid.

Asher exhaled excitedly, it was an amazing game to watch, even if he abhorred the bloodshed. Letting his gaze wander away from the arena's floor, he found PromMcKoll distracted with the spectacle below and decided it was a perfect time to engage

Gibraltair. "You said you wanted to talk to me."

"Hmm," Gibraltair mumbled, his attention firmly focused on the bloodshed on the pitch below.

"Earlier, you said you would have words with me."

"Oh, yes, and so I would, dear boy, but I fear prying ears may prove privy to such conversation in an open forum such as this. No offence intended to the insufferable pismires that surround us." Gibraltair causally glanced over his shoulder and waved his hand flippantly at the man sitting behind them. "Oh, Renky, I didn't see you there."

With everything going on around him, Asher hadn't noticed the man at all. His name instantly struck Asher as vaguely familiar, but he couldn't place it.

"None taken, Privvybell," the man replied snidely. "Unlike the rest of the council, I actually enjoy attending such feudal displays. I find tongues loosen much more readily when the mind is distracted by the more debase viewing of unbridled brutality."

"Do you now?" Gibraltair disregarded the remark, doing his very best to ignore him.

"Pipe down, ye intolerable dun' sniffers, show some respect," PromMcKoll frowned at the both of them, before waving his auger at the Retego to better see what was happening on the far side of the field.

A tremendous blow from the charged Hopralas' molior sent one of the Rajas' fulciors tumbling backwards, blood spraying from his mouth in a violent crimson plume as he fell. The crowd cheered at the spectacle as blood rained down on the sands.

"Will you be unveiling the giant constructs you found in Foreguard at your exhibition?" Asher whispered under his breath as he leaned in close to Gibraltair.

The augiologist turned his head ever so slightly towards Asher and chanced a glance behind him, ensuring their eavesdropper was not listening.

"Amongst other, more exotic masterpieces…"

"Why so mysterious, Privvybell, do speak up," Renky said

blatantly over their shoulders. "Not afraid of being seen conspiring with one bearing the taint, are you?"

"If insight was your trade, you gormless buffoon, you'd ill afford a cup with which to beg," Gibraltair chastised the man in no uncertain terms whilst scratching his ear with the middle finger of his right hand.

Renky's lip twinged at the insult, but he buried the reaction beneath an insincere smile. "Come now, even you must be hesitant to align yourself with… the disease that's been inflicted on these halls like an infection on open wound."

Asher knew the man was talking about him, and his voice made Asher's insides squirm. He instinctively made sure his auger was out of sight and sunk a little lower in his seat.

Gibraltair casually placed a reassuring hand over Asher's to calm his visibly rattled nerves before flicking his wrist in the air at the man as if he was shooing away an insect. "Manners cost nothing, and yet you lack them in quantities unfathomable. What an unfortunate set of traits you'll be passing down through your bloodline, if indeed you are lucky enough to breed. Need I remind you a private conversation between friends remains just that: private!"

"Friends, is it?" the man said suspiciously before easing back into his seat.

Gibraltair ignored him and tilted his head closer to Asher. "I do so loathe insufferable council whelps."

"Deal with them a lot?" Asher smiled weakly at Gibraltair, but Renky's words had rattled him.

"Lately, yes. Usually, no. Ordinarily, my path steers me clear of the more obtuse stains on society, unless, I seek permission to plunder the Annals. Strictly for research purposes, of course."

"You can gain access to the Annals?" Asher's face lit up for a moment as the conversation looked like it was turning in his favour.

"Not anymore, I'm afraid. After the last unauthorised excursion the council has…" he searched for the best way to put things, "rancorously withdrawn my access, forcing me to muse in the company of drunkards and despots amid the motley tiers of the Swaying Tribarion." Gibraltair repressed an urge to shudder.

"Their loss. The Annals are such a dreadfully dreary place. I swear I used to soil a suit-coat on every visit, purely from dust alone." Gibraltair dusted off a patch of invisible dirt from his shoulder with a white-gloved hand and tapped his nose, lowering his voice to a whisper. "Though I still have my sources inside, should the need arise."

He sat back in his chair and scratched his chin with the hilt of his cane, pondering something in the back of his mind as he watched Asher from behind the tinted lenses of his glasses. "However, I do find myself wondering what your interest is in the Annals, dear boy."

"Well, now that you ask, there is something no-one in Mantlecrest has been able to explain."

"A conundrum that does not leave the mind perplexed is an enigma not worth solving. Pray tell, what is it that has set your curiosity on edge?"

"It's probably nothing. Forget I mentioned it," Asher answered bashfully, hoping to fully entice Gibraltair's enigmatic curiosity.

"Tell me no and I shall but scream for more." He waved his hand over on itself in circular fashion and brought it up behind the ear closest to Asher, awaiting an answer.

Asher allowed himself a single smirk before leaning in close and whispering. "Do the words Surio Letifer mean anything to you?"

Gibraltair frowned for a moment before a look of deep contemplation crossed his face. Before he had a chance to answer, the spectators in the Custodian's Box and the stands erupted as one.

Asher was grabbed hard by PromMcKoll's large hands and drawn up from his seat and pushed hard against the balustrade.

"Watch closely, laddie. Yer missin' th' best bits."

Asher said nothing, instead, casting his eyes out over the blood-stained sands of the arena floor.

"Th' Rajas are a man down, DeGrulz just pulverised a player with a three-hit combination of utter obliteration. Did ye not see?"

"Did you say DeGrulz?" Asher's eyes analysed the field, half expecting to see the tribune's hulking form gazing back up at him.

"Aye, Byron DeGrulz, the Hopralas' molior." PromMcKoll glanced downed at Asher's surprised face. "Recognise th' name, do ye? Aye, as well ye should, great up'n'comin' auglete. Fresh out of these very hallowed halls, naught but two years ago. Devastatin' offence."

Asher briefly nodded his understanding and realised PromMcKoll was unaware that Byron's younger brother was the current Tribune of Mantlecrest. Asher glanced over his shoulder, past the unsettlingly inquisitorial eyes of the man that had questioned Gibraltair earlier, and saw Tribune DeGrulz standing against the wall at the rear of the Custodian's Box proudly watching his brother's actions on the field.

The man sitting behind Asher turned and followed his gaze until he too noticed the tribune's stoic form against the back wall. Asher instinctively dodged his glare and turned back to face the front. The man's interest in him was deeply unsettling, and Asher had no desire to find out what drove it.

"There they go again," PromMcKoll bellowed, swinging Asher back around to watch the action. The Undergall Hopralas rallied against their weakened opposition, seized the advantage of the over-extended frame of the Rajas' arx bastion and landed their third alea in the palmabore's glistening depths.

"Three goals fer any team means their molior can call upon a winged beastie an' pass on that wee land mount tae his prime fulcior."

"But more importantly, the interference round begins," Gibraltair smiled to himself eagerly, elegantly rising from his seat in anticipation.

Before he'd even finished his sentence an enormous calior swooped down from the roof and Byron DeGrulz handed over the reins of his spotted gavrin to his prime fulcior. Clambering on top of the calior's mounted saddle, he dug his heels into its flank and flew high above, circling the arena in a series of swoops and dives.

"Interference round?" Asher repeated as he marvelled at DeGrulz's meticulous aerobatics on the back of the fierce-looking calior.

"Don't ask me. Ask Prettybell. It'll be his wee diabolical runt doin' th' interferin'."

"Runt? Hardly. Diabolical? Definitely." Gibraltair held the tip of his cane to his mouth and exhaled over his auger before touching it to the Retego. A single ripple spread outwards over the Retego's translucent surface, warbling Gibraltair's voice all around the arena and over the roar of the crowd.

"Utor Aleans. Today, I, Gibraltair Privvybell Reine, promised you a spectacle the likes of which you've never seen. A visual treat to surpass all others that have come before. My offering is beyond rare, it's the last of its kind. Found purely by chance during my latest expedition deep within the fetid bowels of Foreguard." He patiently waited for the crowd to fall silent at the mention of Foreguard. It was obvious many in attendance still remembered the horrors that had befallen the city during the rebellion.

"I battled this particular beast for a full day and night after I carelessly woke it from its slumber, but time is irrelevant when dancing with death. Natura, Scienta, Mortis and Vita patriots of the Cruaar Nation, allow me to introduce one of Foreguard's last gifts, a creature the world thought extinct…"

Gibraltair's actions were becoming more animated with every word. He jumped onto his chair and stood before the arena, the perfect orator, captivating his audience one by one until all eyes in the arena were upon him.

"A beast that instils terror in all who stand before it. A true horror of the wasteland plains. The ultimate harbinger of death. Behold…" Gibraltair gazed out over the mesmerised faces of the crowd. His words had left them spellbound. They were putty in the palm of his hand. He paused to drink in the awe of the moment, relishing in their suspended wonder.

"A Quaridaan leviathan!"

CHAPTER 36

IN DEATH LIES TRUTH

The crowd was hit by a wave of silent disbelief. Every face had the same expression of shock as the one next to them. Even the players on the field stopped their relentless hand-to-hand war on one another, backing away and anxiously looking around for any sign of the mythical beast.

A distinctive rumble ruminated throughout the arena as a large section of sand sunk into the floor between two of the enormous stone pillars. Mounds of dirt and sand gave way as a hidden stone slab withdrew under the earth, revealing a large subterranean chamber immersed in darkness.

An ear-splitting wail engulfed the stadium, bringing a few players to their knees until they were able to produce the necessary blood callings to protect themselves from the beast's debilitating shriek.

The Retego filtered the beast's devastating war cry, protecting the spectators sheltered behind it from the wail's incapacitating effects, but it did little to muffle the deafening noise assaulting Asher's eardrums.

Asher clasped his hands over his ears and cringed, watching on as best he could until the deafening scream echoing through his head subsided. After a few seconds, the demoralising screech died down and a large beaked snout emerged from the darkness. Large jaws, twice as wide as any man, snapped at the air with a loud cracking sound as the rest of the beast's enormous head inched into view.

A large beak sat in the centre of four backwards-spiked horns. Each stretched away from the creature's snout like a living grappling hook. The topmost horn was by far the largest, splitting into a fork over the beast's brow, both ends jutting up into the air

THE FRAILTY OF PERCEPTION

like ivory tipped lances.

Four shiny black eyes sat in pairs on either side of the high-ridged central tusk, all sunk deep within protective sockets of bone. Each eye colourlessly tracked a different pitiful-looking auglete as they skirted around the beast on the sands.

Two muscular, yet short, scaled arms clawed at the edge of the pit, hauling a gargantuan reptile-like body out of the hole and into the light. Most of the scales on its back were a dull shade of black or grey, though those on its underside glistened an almost-blinding pearl white as they caught the light.

Its massively thick legs dragged it forward another step, causing the nearest Alean augletes to back away cautiously, none game enough to engage the leviathan on their own.

"Th' raw power that the aleas exude makes them irresistible tae all manner of beasties. They're drawn tae it like moths tae an auglight. Regardless of who holds it."

"Hence the term 'interference round'," Gibraltair said coldly, watching his magnificent beast crawl forward onto the sands.

"I dinnae envy these augletes right now. 'Tis now a fatal game, worthy of heroes."

The leviathan launched the remainder of its body from the alcove, but the exposed head didn't move, instead, another identical head flew out of the darkness, followed by a long snake-like body.

The Alean augletes from both teams scattered away from it.

When the beast's entire body finally cleared the dark subterranean chamber, Asher saw the Quaridaan leviathan in all its ferocious majesty.

The second head was connected to the first by way of an elongated body, completely covered in scales, except for a large continuous tuft of thick brown fur running down its spine from head to head.

PromMcKoll enhanced the view of the beast on the Retego just as the second head landed in the arena, narrowly missing the Rajas' fulcior. By the time it landed, the leviathan's first head was already sailing through the air towards another target.

A third alea was catapulted skywards in a high arc from the top of an unmanned pyramid. Both teams burst back into action and darted this way and that across the arena. Most giving the leviathan as wide a berth as possible, leaving only a single fulcior from each team to engage and distract the ferocious beast from interfering as best they could.

Just after the final alea was released, a foot-thick silver column rose from within the palmabore's rippling depths until it towered at least ten feet over the two arx bastions squaring off beneath it. A second later saw the silvery liquid drained from the well as a hard metallic platform raised until it was level with the well's low walls.

"Durin' th' interference round, th' palmabore is closed an' th' utor raised. Both teams now have ten minutes tae either land as many aleas as possible tae th' utor's pinnacle. Alternatively, they can combine all three aleas an' hold th' utor's base against any an' all attacks. But once combined, aleas cannae be split, so timin' an' strategy are crucial."

Asher turned to his right to look at Gibraltair who was busy clapping and smiling to himself as he watched on in awe at the leviathan's raw strength, speed and guile when engaging opponents in the arena. Asher was about to follow up his line of questioning when one of PromMcKoll's enormous hands turned his head back to look at the arena floor.

"If a team can maintain charged contact between th' combined aleas an' th' utor's base fer a full minute, th' game is won by Utor Alea. If not, after ten minutes, two points are awarded tae each team per alea held an' th' match is judged on points."

Asher found it hard to focus on the PromMcKoll's explanation and the events in the arena, when all he wanted was to follow up his question with Gibraltair. The augiologist's earlier reaction had betrayed an inkling of knowledge about the term Surio Letifer. Asher desperately needed to know what it was to confirm whether his suspicions about Morreby Fitch were justified.

Meanwhile, on the arena floor, the action was fast-paced and violent. The two arx bastions, who were no longer required to guard the palmabore's silvery depths, relieved their exhausted teammates and engaged the snapping jaws of the terrifying leviathan with a series of brutal attacks.

Each man's armour shone like jewels against the bloodstained sand as they skirted around the beast's enormous heads in opposite directions. Though they were enemies on the field, they moved and struck the leviathan in unison. Every few seconds, they readjusted their positions to keep the monster's attention engaged and its stretched body fully extended.

The leviathan's thick leathery hide became a mottled mess of bloody wounds as the two arx bastions battered it from both ends with a series of well-aimed slashes, thrusts and jabs. The monster bucked and broke free of its attackers momentarily, lashing out at the charged Hopralas' fulciors the moment one stepped within reach.

The arena was organised chaos at its best. Each team haphazardly circled, dodged and charged after one another across the open expanse of the sands, all the while ducking and weaving around the gigantic beast.

Some rode high on the back of mounted beasts, both in the air and on the ground, where others had nothing but their own two feet to carry them. All of them fervently tried to land their respective aleas on the topmost section of the utor's pinnacle without getting injured in the process.

The Hopralas managed to land two aleas relatively easily, mostly due to their continued air superiority, granted to them by DeGrulz who swooped and glided over the sands on the back of his winged calior.

The Rajas finally managed to land a third point, releasing a large mechanaug gargoyle that swooped down from the rafters and plucked up the Rajas' molior from the sands. Now both teams were equally matched on the ground and the air above. As the battle intensified, so too did the raw devastation the enraged leviathan unleashed upon anyone careless enough to step within striking distance.

"Magnificent, isn't he?" Gibraltair marvelled as his pet violently thrashed this way and that, randomly launching itself after new foes in savage leaps as it continued to wreak utter havoc, interfering with everyone in its path.

"Aye, 'tis a grand spectacle for the ages, I'll give ye that."

DeGrulz's calior swooped down from the sky, seemingly out of nowhere, and skimmed over the arena floor, bowling over a Rajas' fulcior in his path and deftly stealing his alea in the process.

The crowd roared in approval of the daring move.

Flying low to the ground, he ducked and swerved over the scaly back of the leviathan, gathering a second alea from his teammate before banking to the left and climbing skywards once more over the centre of the palmabore.

A blinding red flash momentarily dazed Asher. Blinking away the lingering glare, he watched as DeGrulz came back into view, riding high on the back of his almighty calior. The alea he held in his extended gauntlet was now twice as bright as before.

"He's combined two aleas, the darin' wee carpetbagger." PromMcKoll gripped the bannister and leaned forward in giddy anticipation of the battle to come.

"Calm yourself, you feisty old toilet brush. There's no way he'd risk Utor Alea with my leviathan in the ring."

"Aye, but th' lad's got a pair of unpredictable brass knockers, so he just might." PromMcKoll refocused the Retego to a close-up of DeGrulz's face. "Dinnae tell me ye cannae see th' glint of madness in his eye."

"You looked like you were going to say something before," Asher interrupted, directing the question at Gibraltair, but was unable to take his eyes off DeGrulz's daring feats that had the entire crowd mesmerised.

"Hmm… oh, yes, your conundrum. I too find myself

perplexed. You've stumbled across quite the pickle of an enigma."

The Hopralas' arx bastion levelled an enemy fulcior with a savage kick, shoulder-barging another into the path of the Quaridaan leviathan, allowing his teammate to steal the third and final alea. All the members of the Hopralas converged on the raised utor.

"They're goin' fer it!" PromMcKoll shouted, hitting the bannister with a heavy open-handed slap.

"Perplexed?" Asher repeated, trying to pry more information out of Gibraltair.

"Yes, you're right," Gibraltair misunderstood Asher's repetition and promptly changed his description. "Flummoxed, is perhaps a better word."

In a daring testament to the man's courage and skill, DeGrulz leaped from the back of his calior high above the arena floor and fell through the air like a missile, plummeting headfirst towards the bloodstained sands, a large bright-red ball clenched within the iron grip of his gauntlet.

The last remaining charged Hopralas' fulcior launched his alea skywards at him as DeGrulz nosedived towards the ground. He caught it a split-second before his body collided with the earth in a savage eruption of dust, grit and sand. A thunderous boom echoed around the arena as a devastating shock wave exploded outwards from the point of impact, knocking every auglete to the ground, which forced the Rajas' molior off the back of his mechanaug gargoyle. It even managed to send the leviathan slithering backwards over itself in the sand, both heads thrashing about wildly under the pressure of the force.

Despite the protection of the Retego, Asher's ears were still ringing as an enormous red flare billowed up from DeGrulz's newly made crater.

"Go ye wee terror!" PromMcKoll ignored his lingering deafness and cheered wildly at the bold move, louder than anyone else in the Custodian's Box.

"Can ye believe th' stones on him?" he said loudly, overcompensating for the dull ringing in his ears as he excitedly slapped Asher on the shoulder.

Leaning away from PromMcKoll's overbearing excitement, Asher pressed Gibraltair for a better explanation. "Why flummoxed?"

"Because, it would be remiss to overstate one's knowledge if unaware of a truth's entirety."

"So have you heard the term or not?" Asher said bluntly, demanding a proper answer. He was rapidly becoming sick to death of the augiologist's pompous declarations.

When the dust from the explosion in the arena had settled, DeGrulz was already standing on the well's low wall, one hand firmly placed on the utor, the other ablaze with the pulsating wild energy of three combined aleas. The remaining Hopralas auglets had gathered around him in a wide circle. All readying themselves for the savage onslaught about to rain down upon them like a firestorm from hell.

"I told ye that wee boyo had some brass nuggets," PromMcKoll cheered boisterously.

"Yes and no," Gibraltair replied, his eyes remained firmly fixed on the events unfolding in the arena.

"Well, what then?"

Fifteen seconds on the countdown timer had passed and DeGrulz's hand was still firmly planted on the utor's base. So far the savagery of the Rajas attacks had been heroically thwarted by the extraordinary defence of the Hopralas' fulciors and arx bastion. Even the unmanned calior harassed the Rajas' molior in the sky, preventing him and his mechanaug gargoyle from launching a proper attack.

"The term 'Surio' remains a quandary without answer." Gibraltair clapped his hands with giddy excitement as his leviathan slithered away from the fierce onslaught in the centre of the arena towards one of the pyramids.

"Halfway home, laddie, stay th' course. Defence, Hopralas!"

PromMcKoll shouted through the Retego.

Asher knew PromMcKoll's words failed to reach anyone except those around him. "So you know what Letifer means, then?" Asher persisted.

"Logic alone would infer as much," Gibraltair said quite calmly, not feeling the need to explain his response any further.

The leviathan edged up on to the topmost face of the pyramid closest to the exposed Utor and coiled its torso tightly together.

Even Gibraltair gasped when it launched its massive bulk off the side of the pyramid, propelling one of its enormous horned heads high above the sands. Its elongated body catapulted through the air in a venomous arc towards the irresistible beacon of light pulsating before all four of its eyes.

It crashed heavily, halfway between the pyramid and the exposed Utor. Its massive claws sunk into the earth, talons digging heavily into dirt and sand. Tensing up its core, it whiplashed its rear head forward, viciously sideswiping three unsuspecting auglets before propelling one of its gaping maws towards the Alea in DeGrulz's outstretched hand. Its four-pronged beaked snout was agape, horns bent back over its head as it soared through the air, rapidly bearing down on the Hopralas' Molior.

"Well, what is it?" Asher wasn't watching the match. He was busy staring intently at Gibraltair, demanding answers.

"Look out, laddie!" PromMcKoll bellowed at DeGrulz.

It was no use. He had become distracted and was facing the opposite direction. The leviathan's razor-sharp beak closed in over his extended arm and bit down sharply, severing it clean from his shoulder in one bite.

DeGrulz felt the beast's coarse tongue scrape over his severed stump as it swallowed everything from his elbow down: gauntlet, arm, hand and the combined Aleas alike. A split-second later, he felt its massive horned snout smashed into his armoured side, instantly crushing part of his rib cage and piercing several internal organs with fragments of shattered bone.

DeGrulz eyes went wide with shock as his lungs struggled to breathe, but the leviathan wasn't done. Its second head was already swinging around the Utor, taking out another two players and wrapping around the pillar like a coiled spring. DeGrulz's was trapped between its scaly bulk, his back hard up against the metal Utor: a veritable ragdoll in its clutches.

With a sudden jolt, the leviathan jerked its coiled body high up the Utor, hauling DeGrulz's limp figure even farther out of reach of his teammates. DeGrulz felt his breastplate buckle and the last remaining unbroken bones in his chest snap as the beast constricted and crushed the life out of him. A sickening triumphant wail filled his ears as his world slowly went black.

Asher turned to see the very last wisp of life ebb away from DeGrulz's lips on an enhanced view on the Retego.

"Bravo, bravo." Gibraltair clapped lightly along with the majority of elders in the Custodian's Box. "You couldn't ask for a better finale."

Asher couldn't believe his eyes. A man had just died, savagely torn apart in the most horrific of ways, but the crowd saw only entertainment. Everywhere he looked, the crowd was clapping, cheering, hooting and hollering as the lifeless body of DeGrulz was pinned against the Utor beneath the body of the beast. Blood continued to spew from his severed limb as his body crumpled beneath the pressure of the leviathan's constriction.

No-one was appalled, nor were they even surprised at the murderous turn of events. Even PromMcKoll clapped and whistled through his bushy moustache in a morbid salute of respect at DeGrulz's death.

Asher peered around the Custodian's Box. The elite of Undergall were clapping and smiling as they would a successful musical performance, albeit in a more refined manner than the spectators in the stands. The seat behind Asher was empty. Renky, the man that had been so interested in him, was gone.

The tribune. Asher's mind clicked into gear and sent his eyes searching amidst the rear of the box where he had last seen him standing. The tribune was not clapping, nor was he cheering. He stood silently, like a gargoyle carved in stone. A powerless fury welled behind his eyes as his fingers dug deep into the soft fabric of the chair in front of him. He could do nothing but watch on helplessly as his brother died.

Few in the Custodian's Box would have known of the connection between the tribune and the corpse of the Alean auglete pinned against the utor in the middle of the Arena. Most in the box paid him no notice, although two men gave him consolatory nods before turning back to their conversations.

Asher knew how the tribune must have felt, even if Bison was adept at hiding his emotions. He had lost Raglan much in the same manner and had been helpless to do anything about it. The emotion of losing someone so close came flooding back, Asher couldn't help but chastise everyone around him for callously cheering the man's death. "Why are you cheering?" Asher blurted out at the remainder of the room. "A man just died."

Everyone in the box turned to look at Asher, but said nothing, instead, shooting scornful looks his way as if he was stealing honour away from the auglete's death by chastising them.

"Steady on, lad," PromMcKoll growled in warning, pulling Asher to his side, shielding him from view from the rest of the perturbed patrons of the custodian's box. "'Twas a good death, worthy of any Alean auglete. His blood honours th' sands."

A surprised look came over Gibraltair's face as he listened to Asher's outrage, as if a revelation had just dawned on him.

"But, he's dead," Asher stammered, looking at both of them for support or, short of that, the slightest hint of empathy.

None came.

Asher glanced at the tribune. He had murder in his eyes and was staring directly at Asher. A single tear escaped from the corner of his eye, before he turned and marched out of the Custodian's box before anyone else saw it. Asher watched him disappear through the vertistrand, when Gibraltair's hand touched him on the shoulder and drew his attention back to the augiologist.

He caught a glimpse of someone else leave through the vertistrand as he turned around, but couldn't see their face, only heavy leather boots stretching up to the knee as they disappeared through the shimmering face of the strand.

"Oh, you poor wet-eyed waif," Gibraltair's voice was dry and condescending. "No-one's told you, have they?" Gibraltair couldn't help but stifle a laugh, utterly delighted in Asher's obliviousness. "How positively medieval to be cocooned in such ignorance. How is it even possible you don't already know?"

"Know what?" Asher fumed.

"Dear boy, where do you think you are?" Gibraltair waved his cane around the arena.

"What do you mean?"

"Mantlecrest. You've been an apprentice here for how many months, and yet you're still denser than that gemstone buried in your palm."

"So explain it to me, then," Asher lost his temper. "What don't I know?"

"Asher, Mantlecrest is a gladiaugal facility."

"It's... a what?" Asher said, clearly not understanding the term.

"Since the reform, Mantlecrest's sole purpose has been to train apprentice Cruaar in the gladiaugal art of war. It is a recruitment facility, Asher, to replenish and supply the militaristic arm of the Cruaar nation with soldiers, to fight and die for the greater Cruaar cause."

"You mean," Asher stammered, unable to believe what he was hearing, "like gladiators?"

"No, no, no. Gladiators were but slaves trained for slaughter, gladiaugal warders, bireems, tribarions and sentinaugs are proud and honourable warriors. The Cruaar armed forces, if you will," Gibraltair couldn't help but chuckle, "but let's just call them what they are, shall we: the council's private army."

Gibraltair placed a calming hand on Asher's shoulder and

raised an eyebrow behind his tinted lenses as everyone else in the Custodian's Box moved away from them, content to cast them scornful looks from afar.

"You poor, ignorant child. Are you so blind to the death that surrounds you in these so-called hallowed halls? Were you not, yourself, attacked by a Skulk cultist in the very chamber where the dead are left to rot?"

"I…"

"Death infects the entrails of this arterial construct like a disease, metastasising its blight upon the living without cure or end." Gibraltair pulled at Asher's tunic to illustrate the point. "Where did you think all the bodies came from? The Guillotine Rebellion?" Gibraltair couldn't help but release a brief incredulous smirk. "The war has been over for decades and yet the bodies below are fresh."

"But…" Asher stammered.

"Everything around you reeks of death and yet you remain blindly ignorant to the truth. Even the conundrum you seek answers to reeks to high hell of what you choose not to see."

"What?" Asher murmured, his mind still reeling from everything Gibraltair had just said.

"Letifer." Gibraltair let the word hang in the air and suspiciously gazed around the Custodian's Box, before leaning in close to Asher's ear. "Simply put, it is a rather archaic term…"

It instantly became obvious to Asher that Gibraltair delighted in every single second he was able to keep those around him locked in a state of abject suspense, even if it meant prolonging their agonising ignorance.

Cupping one hand to his mouth to shield his words from prying ears, Asher felt the soft exhale of Gibraltair's breath as the augiologist finally whispered an explanation to him, one painful word at a time.

"For one who deals in death."

PART IV

THE LOSS OF TWO

"Whenever knowledge is unleashed
Without wisdom to hold it in check
Disaster and ruin will surely ride in its wake."

Belkraen Sageroot
Patriarch, Natura bloodline
Natura family annals
Date unknown

CHAPTER 37

THE LEGACY OF PRZRA LAXO

The end of the Utor Alea match was a blur to Asher. Somehow, he managed to blindly stumble back to his rack in a daze. The devastating revelation Gibraltair had all too happily unleashed was one he'd failed to recognise, but it had been right in front of his very eyes the entire time.

He didn't understand how he could've been so blind to the truth. The more he thought about it, the more it made sense. Memories he'd otherwise pushed to the back of his mind, or discarded as unimportant, came flooding back. He recalled all the ghastly things he'd seen since he'd arrived at Mantlecrest and, worse yet, they all fit together in one big sordid tapestry. He'd dismissed them all without question in order to savour his new life, no matter how tarnished it really was; but now he saw the awful truth revealed. He had willingly offered himself to the Cruaar war machine to do with as they saw fit.

How could I have been this naive? Raglan taught me better than this, to be smarter than this... or was this what Raglan wanted all along?

Asher's mind was numb, and yet still it spun a thousand different thoughts and questions over and over again. The things people had said. The dreadful images he'd seen. The morbid conversations he'd overheard. Somehow, everything fit together into one big nightmarish web, every fibre and thread interwoven together by death's hand.

The door to their racks burst open and Lorrelli sauntered in, waving a Hopralas pennant in her hand, a huge smile on her face. Her grin vanished when she saw Asher's grim expression. She shut the door behind her and came to sit next to him on the bed.

"Asher, what's wrong?"

"Why didn't you tell me?" Asher asked meekly.

"Tell you what?"

"About Mantlecrest. About everything!" He threw his hands up in the air around him. "Why didn't you tell me Mantlecrest was a Gladiaugal facility? That we're all nothing more than the future draft? That we were being trained to kill and become skulk fodder?"

"Asher…" she stumbled over her words. "It's… it's not like that."

"Then what's it like, Lorrelli? You going to tell me these so-called hallowed halls aren't soaked in blood and dead apprentices?" Asher's voice went up an octave in frustration.

"With everything you've been through, we just thought you knew." Lorrelli could only gaze at him through sorrow-filled eyes.

"I knew?" Asher said dejectedly. "How could I have possibly known?" Asher stared at her, hardening his features as she spelled it out for him.

"'Cause you've fought the Mortis Skulk three times now and you're still alive to talk about it. 'Cause every day you've had private training sessions with a First Order Tribarion who left you battered, bloody and bruised. Honestly, what did you think she was training you for?"

Asher's gaze sunk to the floor, his mind unable to process what he knew was the honest truth.

"You even agreed to an insane plan for Lem to fake a suicide attempt as a diversion so you could dig up an augefact."

"I…" Asher's voice failed him.

"You embraced the true nature of Mantlecrest more than any other first-year apprentice. Hell, even you refer to this room as racks."

"So?"

"Racks, Asher, short for barracks. Our barracks."

"But…"

"Everyone knows what Mantlecrest has become, especially after the old legate was murdered five years ago. The only reason this place still exists is because Lobrolo insisted Mantlecrest was a keystone of Undergall, vital to the city's very survival. The Chancellor wanted to close it down. Lobrolo had to promise he could reform it into something useful, just to keep the doors open."

"No, no!" Asher shook his head from side to side, looking at her with disbelief plastered across his brow. "How is that possible? This place thrives off death; how can one death change anything?"

"Mantlecrest never used to be like this. It was a haven for scholars, builders and augineers, and it was one of the greatest in the Cruaar Nation. But the rebellion changed everything. Mantlecrest was no exception. Horrific things happened here that can never be undone."

"But why would Lobrolo care so much about this place?" Asher threw his hands up in the air.

"Because of the old legate's murder, Asher. Everyone outside has been talking about it for years."

"Yeah? Well, you mind filling me in. I haven't exactly been outside these walls and not many people want to talk to me at the best of times," Asher replied brusquely, a cross look descending on his face.

"Sorry, I forget sometimes," Lorrelli apologised, "but we're in this together, remember? So stop taking all your misplaced anger out on me!" Lorrelli snapped back at him and sat on her bed in a huff.

"Sorry… I," Asher clearly wasn't prepared for her reaction and calmed down a little, his anger and frustration at his own stupidity slightly lessening. "This is all just a bit of a shock. I'm not angry at you. I didn't mean to—"

She waved her hand, fishing out the Undergall Testament from under a nearby pillow. She quickly searched for a previous article and handed it to Asher.

The grizzly portrait of two men stared up at him. A considerably older and balder man sat on the left. His greying side-burns extended all the way down his cheeks, separated only by a large and shaved, dimpled chin. Next to him on the right, the face of a much younger man, with dark features and piercing blue eyes, gazed out from the tablet's surface.

"It was before my time here, I was only nine when it all happened. The old legate was found murdered in his office. As the story goes, Finneus Slink arrived at the grizzly scene to find Przra Laxo, an elder apprentice at the time, standing over Legate Altier's body.

"Przra's hands and tunic were covered in the legate's blood, but before Slink could catch him, he disappeared through the vertistrand with the legate's auger, never to be seen again. The council's been hunting him ever since."

"Did you say Altier?" Asher whispered.

"Yeah, Haalbar Altier, the Overseer's… Lobrolo's brother."

"Lobrolo's brother," Asher repeated, stunned.

"Lobrolo only assumed the position of Legate at Mantlecrest after his brother's death, long before he took on the role of Overseer. His one vow was to keep his brother's legacy alive.

"I never knew Haalbar, but everyone in the Cruaar Nation was devastated when the news of his murder broke. Apparently he was one of the last true heroes of the Cruaar Nation. My mother said he was a pillar of sanity during the madness of the Rebellion. He was even one of the six tyrant-slayers that defeated Cerebule after Shyloft Pracca betrayed him in MaiSchloss."

"But how does an apprentice manage to murder a legate?"

"No-one knows for sure. Rumour was that Przra unearthed an ancient blood curse somewhere within Mantlecrest and unleashed it on Haalbar."

"Is that even possible?" Asher raised his eyebrows in disbelief and rubbed his neck with a worried hand.

Lorrelli could only shrug her shoulders at him.

"If a legate can be killed in such a way, what does that mean for the rest of us? Are we likely to die in here as well?"

"Oh, no, Lobrolo set up strict safeguards to ensure all apprentices survive until their prospect year. For instance, masters are never allowed to inflict mortal wounds on their apprentices—"

"Till their prospect year?"

"It's, err, complicated," Lorrelli hesitated, obviously struggling to find the right words.

"Well, uncomplicate it."

"Sometimes blood feuds develop between elder apprentices, and they have the right to challenge one another to Exsili Neco."

Asher's eyebrows rose even farther as the expectation of a follow-up explanation set in.

"A ritualistic blood duel with only two outcomes: death or exile. They call them bloodline bouts these days, but it's the same thing."

"I can't believe this," Asher's head dropped into his hands, with his elbows propped up on his knees.

"It sounds worse than it is. It rarely happens anymore."

"Rarely happens? What about all those bodies in the Catacomb Cathedral?"

Lorrelli didn't have an answer for him. Instead, she decided it was as good a time as any to change the subject. "Did you at least ask Gibraltair about Surio Letifer?"

"Yeah," Asher said glumly as yet another reminder of death crept into the back of his mind.

"Well, what did he say?"

Before he could answer, a blinking light distracted him from the corner of the room. The opaque pearl on the front of Lem's promensi was flashing at them.

"Lem," Lorrelli said hurriedly and quickly waved her auger at it.

The liquefied sand on the table's surface vibrated until it had worked itself into a frenzy. It quickly transformed into the shape of a seated miniature figure sitting in a room furnished with all manner of strange looking contraptions, none of which Asher recognised. As the sand hardened into its semi-flexible state, Asher recognised Lem's unusually happy face peering back at him.

"'Bout time you two got in touch. What is this: out of sight out of praccing mind?"

"Lem, it's good to see you," Asher smiled grimly.

"Sure it is. I'm good enough to push off a roof, but not good enough to hit up the sands and check in," Lem's confrontational attitude made Asher laugh, but Lorrelli looked away.

"I'm sorry, Lem, I had to. I'm glad you're alright… you are alright, aren't you?" Lorrelli asked quietly, her eyes laden with a deep-seated guilt.

"You owe me a new set of pants. But, all in all, despite the grand inquisition and aftermath that followed, it's been pretty dull on my end. Just a lot of worrying from my mother. By the way, I'll never forgive either of you for making me miss the Utor Alea match, either. A Quaridaan leviathan. I mean, come on." Lem's tiny figure looked around the room nervously before continuing.

"Everyone's out of the house for the next hour, so you've got until then to tell me everything. Only then will I tell you my news and, trust me, you're gonna want to hear it."

Asher and Lorrelli spent the better part of 45 minutes filling in Lem on everything that had happened since Lorrelli had pushed him off the rooftop. Asher spent the majority of the time talking, whilst Lorrelli sheepishly added bits here and there to fill in the parts Asher missed. She was obviously trying to tread lightly around Lem, but he didn't seem to mind as much as she did, butting in time and time again to clarify certain events. When everyone was on the same page, Lem focused his attention on Asher and lowered his tone.

"I can't believe you got to meet PromMcKoll! He's a living legend, but the stories about him will have to wait. Tell me more about the man that was so interested in you and Gibraltair; what was his name again?" Lem asked curiously.

"Renky, but I think that's just what Gibraltair called him on purpose to insult him," Asher replied, trying to remember every detail about the encounter.

"It does sound familiar," Lorrelli agreed with Asher's previous curiosity about the man's name. "What else do you remember about him?"

"Not much, except his boots: big, black and leather, all the way up to his knees. Oh, and his demeanour. It was very inquisitorial, almost like he was trying to catch Gibraltair out in a lie. But somehow I got the feeling he was just as interested in me."

"Interested in you? I thought you said he never spoke to you directly."

"He didn't, but not because he didn't want to. For some reason he wouldn't, or couldn't, talk to me directly, like he was under orders not to."

"Wait a minute, so you got the feeling he was interested in you," Lem repeated and tapped a finger on his knee, "and Gibraltair called him Renky, right?"

"If there's one thing my obsession with Gibraltair has taught me, it's that Gibraltair loves labelling those around him with pet names, especially when he can use the actual names of those he despises to demean them." Lem looked about both of them heavily waiting for them to make the connection.

"I'm not following," Lorrelli shook her head.

"Renky, as in Far-renk-y. As in Farrenk, the man Braak warned you about!" Lem spelled it out for them.

"What?" Asher and Lorrelli spat out in unison.

"I can't be sure, but given his interest in you, it stands to reason, right? How much did he overhear of your conversation with Gibraltair?" Lem asked.

"I'm not sure." Asher sat back and thought for a moment. "I don't know how long he was sitting behind us. He could've heard everything."

"Well there's prac all we can do about it now, but now at least you know what he looks like. I'll do some digging on my end and see what I can find out about him, but you've got to be more careful," Lem warned them both, before a large smile reappeared on his face. "Now who wants to hear my news?"

"Go on, already," Lorrelli urged him.

"Braak contacted me."

"What?" Asher and Lorrelli exclaimed in unison.

"He said it was too dangerous to communicate with you both, via pyxis, in case it was intercepted by the wrong hands. He gave me a message to pass on via the promensi tables." Lem scratched his head as if confused. "It's strange. I don't know how he even knew we had them."

"The message, Lem," Asher said with urgency.

"Oh, right. Well, basically, in his ongoing search for Raglan and the Mortis Skulk that attacked you, he's discovered a few things. He didn't go into much detail, but he thinks something big is going to go down in Undergall, and soon. For some reason, he thinks that someone in Mantlecrest is involved."

"Morreby Fitch! It's got to be." Lorrelli glanced quickly at Asher, but he offered no response.

"He didn't know who it was, but he's organised a safe house for us in Black Ingot Warrens. I have the directions."

"Black Ingot Warrens?" Asher flinched, "how does that help us? We're stuck in here."

"Not just you, I'm due back in roughly three weeks and Braak thinks whatever's going down will happen by month's end, his words. He's got a weird way of talking, by the way. In any case, you two have to find a way out of Mantlecrest. Especially if everything turns to hell in a handbasket, 'cause there's no way in hoody blell I'm going over that praccing roof twice."

"Is that it?" Asher said in disbelief, already trying to formulate a plan to escape Mantlecrest.

"Yeah, that's everything. But if you do find a way out, be praccing sure to keep it a secret. I mean it. Trust no-one. I'll do what I can to find out everything I can about whatever Surio is in the meantime." The loud sound of a door opening somewhere behind Lem's tiny figure put an abrupt end to their communication, "I gotta go."

"Speak soon," Lorrelli replied, but the connection had already been severed on Lem's end. Lem's miniature form spilled back down on the table in a splash of liquefied sand, leaving Asher and Lorrelli looking at each other anxiously.

"How do you escape from somewhere as secure as Mantlecrest?" Asher's eyes narrowed, a deathly serious glint setting in the corners of his eyes.

"More importantly, escape from what?" Lorrelli added nervously, her tone equally as serious.

Asher clenched his fingers around his auger and felt the cool touch of the gem's surface ignite as he mindlessly channelled a small trickle of blood into it.

"It's not the what that worries me. It's the who."

CHAPTER 38

THE DISMAY OF DREAD REBORN

Braak's warning had deeply unsettled Asher, perhaps even more so than the carnage he'd witnessed in the arena and the revelations about Mantlecrest that had followed.

After watching the tribune's brother die a horrific death for the Cruaar Nation's amusement, Asher knew he no longer wanted to be anywhere near Mantlecrest, let alone locked inside its harrowed halls. Regardless, he had little choice but to push such thoughts to the back of his mind until he found a way to escape. If Braak had found a conspiracy pointing at someone inside Mantlecrest, then the grave fears he had for Asher's life meant he feared for his own survival, as well.

Whatever the reason, something was definitely amiss within Mantlecrest: something far worse than the brutal death of an Alean auglete in the arena, or being a recruit for the council's private army, perhaps even worse than whatever Morreby Fitch was meddling with in the room marked Surio Letifer.

Asher got up and paced back and forth between their racks. The mindless repetitive action helped him clear his mind, allowing him to focus and develop clear, concise and logical thoughts.

"Okay, forget about the 'why' and the 'who' for a minute. Let's focus on the 'how'. How do we escape Mantlecrest?" He stretched out a hand at Lorrelli, "come on, think. What do we do first?"

"Rule out the obvious?" she guessed.

"Yes, good, okay. What about the main gate? Can we escape though it?"

"No chance, it's guarded around the clock by mechanaug

sentinels. Besides, it's fitted with a secureaug lock, and we don't have access."

"Okay, okay, what about emergency exits?" Asher countered.

"Same problem."

Asher thought for a moment, scratching his chin. It was still smooth to the touch. "Can't we 'strand out?"

"I haven't been trained to command the sands yet, have you?"

Asher regretfully shook his head. "Besides, we don't have any shifting sand. And going over the wall isn't an option," Asher mumbled to himself, sparing a quick thought towards Lem's predicament outside the walls.

"Especially with the legate's caliors patrolling the skies," Lorrelli was only too quick to readily agree with him. "They freak me out."

"Okay, so what about under the walls, then?"

"What do you mean?" Lorrelli tilted her head and looked at him quizzically, not quite understanding what he was getting at.

"Undergall is the oldest of all Cruaar cities, right? It must be riddled with tunnels and passageways that no-one knows about."

"No-one except a historian with a penchant for this place," Lorrelli grinned as an idea popped into her head.

"Welticrum!" Asher exclaimed excitedly, looking around for his schedule stone. "When is his next training session?"

Lorrelli was one step ahead of him, already scanning her training times on her own schedule stone. "Not for another week."

"Okay, do we at least know where it is?" Asher asked, peering over her shoulder. Welticrum's riddles were a nuisance at the best of times, but lately they had been getting harder and harder to decipher.

"No, I still haven't figured out his clue, yet." Lorrelli quoted Welticrum's riddle from her lesson card, word for word. "Find me where earth and air summit in heated embrace."

It took them the better part of a week to figure out Welticrum was referring to the boiler room that harnessed one of the larger geothermal vents, deep within the bowels of Mantlecrest's maze-like corridors.

When the time came for their instruction, they found the stone floor leading up to and around the room was warm to the touch: hot, even. Asher assumed the heat came from the constant supply of geothermic vapour he could see seeping through cracks in the mortar beneath his feet. He and Lorrelli had slipped out of their previous training session early in order to arrive before anyone else and get some time alone with Welticrum.

As they followed the extensive network of copper pipes running along the roof of the corridors, Asher wondered why he'd never paid them any notice before. He then realised there was a lot inside Mantlecrest he'd previously overlooked.

Thinking back, there had been large pipes of all shapes and sizes running through every room and hall inside Mantlecrest. There were even pipes in their own racks, yet he'd all but dismissed them as functionless: decorative trappings of yesteryear. Only now was it obvious they were redirecting steam from the boiler room and keeping Mantlecrest warm all year round. He pushed the thought from his mind as a few of the copper pipes merged together overhead into a much larger pipe. Within each corridor, more pipes converged and ran parallel until the walls and ceiling were lost behind them entirely.

When they finally arrived in Mantlecrest's central boiler room, a deluge of enormous copper pipes covered the ceiling, intertwined around one another in an endless series of 90-degree bends and junction boxes. Each pipe connected to a series of oversized and upside-down spherical boilers securely fastened to the floor; at least, Asher thought they were boilers. He didn't actually know what they were.

A thick clammy layer of steam unnaturally blanketed the floor, but luckily it was flat: unwilling to rise above their ankles or part, it obscured the warm stonework beneath their feet in an ominous moist fog. One step at a time, they cautiously waded through the low steam-bank and into the room. After rounding the first of the massive upturned copper cauldrons, Asher realised they were not alone.

A small figure was waiting patiently in the far corner, her hand hovering over the surface of a cauldron's tarnished green copper dome, basking in the oppressive heat as it washed over her skin. Her small frame was partially engulfed by the knee-high geothermal fog. A geyser of steam spat up into the air between them, shielding her features from view; but Asher already knew who it was.

Morreby's dark, alert eyes watched him as the steam fell away.

As Asher got closer, Morreby was almost unrecognisable. Her hair was damp and clung to the sides of her face. Her brow was lined with sweat, and her unnaturally thin visage made her look even more ghoulish than ever. As usual, she said nothing to them, content to watch them from across the room with untrusting eyes.

Judging from the heavy frown on Asher's brow, Lorrelli knew his patience with Morreby's unsettling stares was at an end.

Asher marched over to her, clenching his fingers into a fist around his auger.

"Asher, what are you doing?"

Lorrelli's words fell on deaf ears as Asher trudged forward, his legs cutting a swathe through the low-lying blanket of steam. "I know what you've been up to Fitch, and you're not going to get away with it," he lied.

Morreby seemed somewhat taken aback by the accusation. Retreating backwards a step away from Asher, her voice was little more than a whisper and sounded tired. "What?"

"I don't know how you've managed to fool the legate, but you don't fool me," Asher persisted, venomously pointing a finger at her neck.

"You don't know what you're talking about." Morreby took another step back to avoid contact with Asher's finger.

"I know everything, Letifer," Asher knew he was clutching at straws as he spat the words at her, but he had little else to go on.

Pressing forward with his bluff and threats, he advanced even closer, using everything he knew as a weapon to get her to incriminate herself.

"I know you've been creeping around the Undercellars; or did you think your secret wouldn't get out, death dealer?"

Morreby stopped retreating.

Her eyes narrowed and her demeanour soured at Asher's words. "Stop while you can." She stepped forward to move past Asher, but he blocked her with his body and forced her back against one of the large copper cauldrons. "Only fools and heroes seek out new enemies, and you're no hero, Asher Bloom." She moved her hand beneath her tunic and latched on to something, clenching it in her fist.

"It doesn't take a hero to expose you and whoever you're working for."

"Working for?" Morreby's eyebrows tightened for a moment, but her response was interrupted by the loud tapping of Welticrum's cane as he entered the room. "I hope I'm not interrupting something."

Five more apprentices followed him in, wading into the steam cloud noisily, allowing Morreby the perfect opportunity to distance herself from Asher.

"No, sir," Asher replied, glaring intensely at Morreby as she edged away from him.

"Good. Then let us begin."

The majority of Welticrum's training was lost on Asher as he impertinently scowled at Morreby for the next hour, despite Lorrelli's best efforts to persuade him to let it go.

Morreby, on the other hand, didn't give Asher a second thought, not looking at him even so much as once, which infuriated him all the more.

Asher did not get a chance to get Welticrum alone until the training session had ended. Despite his dark mood, he dared not risk asking the old man anything until all of the other apprentices had left the room, especially Morreby Fitch and her nonchalant attitude. As Welticrum turned to leave, Asher placed a hand on his shoulder, his voice lower than a whisper amidst the mass of copper pipes and cauldrons.

"Master Welticrum, I was wondering if you could help me."

The old man slowly turned around, a gentle expression gracing his tired features.

"I have some questions about Mantlecrest during the Rebellion."

Lorrelli said nothing, but her raised eyebrows betrayed her shared curiosity on the subject.

"A lover of history, as well, are we, Apprenti Bloom? Très bien." Welticrum's eyes glinted with intrigue as he recognised a similar thirst for knowledge. "Alas, the pursuit of enlightenment often begins with a journey back in time."

Asher frowned on hearing Welticrum's cryptic statement, sensing the man had long since mastered the art of steeping his words with layer upon layer of hidden truth.

"I know the city suffered during the Rebellion," Asher chose his words carefully, "but what about Mantlecrest?"

"Oui, Mantlecrest suffered equally under the Rebellion's tyrannical yoke. It was a merciless time for everyone, apprentice and master Cruaar alike. Even I sought refuge inside these walls during the darker days, and one or two other safe houses, mind you."

"Was Mantlecrest ever locked down completely from the city?"

"Oui. At the height of the Rebellion, Legate Altier, Haalbar Altier that is, sealed the doors and cut off all access to Undergall and the council. It was the only way he could ensure the safety of the apprentices from the treacherous horrors outside. His open defiance of council edict made him a target, but Haalbar was nothing if not the keenest strategist I've ever met."

"So how did he get away with it? Defying the council and shutting out the world?"

"Twofold. He had long held the ear of the Overseer, and by

personally vouching for every soul inside these walls, the council could not refute his governance over Mantlecrest. Laws are laws, after all, even in times of war, and without the Overseer to overrule the legate, Haalbar Altier stayed the war from ever passing through Mantlecrest's grand gates. You see, even at the very worst of times, he remained steadfastly loyal to those under his charge: his apprentices…" A sad expression slowly eroded away the old man's smile. "Much to his own detriment, in the end."

Asher wanted to ask more about what Welticrum meant, but if he was going to get the answers he wanted, he had to redirect the conversation back on track. "So no-one ever escaped, or travelled to the city while Mantlecrest was in lockdown?"

"Haalbar's trust was not easily gained during the Rebellion. He and the Overseer at the time created a secret network of tunnels that allowed passage into the city to smuggle information and pass supplies back and forth. He would not even share its location with his own brother, Lobrolo."

"I never knew that," Lorrelli said, surprised she had never heard about the tunnels before.

"It was not common knowledge then, nor is it now. Only those he trusted knew of the tunnels, even after the Rebellion, and all swore a blood oath never to reveal their existence while Haalbar lived. Yet many Mortis Skulk agents still tried to force, bribe and blackmail their way inside Mantlecrest during the Rebellion."

"Did any ever actually break in?" Asher interrupted, wiping a thick film of sweat from his brow.

"Not to my knowledge. However, corruption has many guises, and treachery is nothing if not cunning."

"What do you mean?"

"You're talking about Przra Laxo, aren't you?" Lorrelli asked in a whisper, fearful that mentioning his name too loudly may incur some age-old wrath from the halls surrounding them.

Welticrum nodded solemnly, the same sad expression washing

over his heavily wrinkled face a second time in as many minutes.

"These tunnels, do they still exist?"

"Goodness, no. All the tunnels were found by Craftpaw's augineers and demolished during the secureaug system upgrade two years ago."

Both Asher and Lorrelli's shoulders sank in unison.

"But there's a chance the augineers missed a tunnel, right?" Asher tried to keep their hopes of escape alive in light of the dim news.

"Highly unlikely. Although…" Welticrum's wrinkled features paused as a thought flashed through his mind.

"Yes?" Asher pleaded.

"There was a record in the Annals I came across once as a junior auglorian. Only once, mind you. It alluded to a secret passageway from Mantlecrest to the Forgotten Gardens that's never been discovered."

"Really?" Lorrelli exclaimed excitedly.

"When I showed Haalbar, even he was shocked to learn of its existence; but he believed it was forged by none other than Vitalsior himself during Mantlecrest's construction. However, deciphering the truth amidst one man's mad ramblings is a fool's errand.

"After all, history is recorded by those with the means to record, and too often are those poor souls cursed by leaders with their own agendas, bias and gullibility. This, of course, leads to embellishments, omissions, redactions or, worse yet, outright lies, all of which mask the truth behind layers and layers of falsehood." Welticrum winked at them and rapped his cane on the ground for dramatic effect, thoroughly enjoying the conversation.

"In any case, all of Haalbar's old tunnels were located in the Undercellars, which I am sorry to say are still under lock and key, so there'll be no playing augiologist for either of you anytime soon."

"But I thought Stemproles cured the mould," Lorrelli said

tilting her head in confusion.

"As did we all, but his was only a temporary solution. The mould quickly grew back over the areas that he cleared, even stronger than before in certain places. Master Gobbler is investigating further. Now, off with you, before they come seeking my wrinkled old scalp for your tardiness."

Asher and Lorrelli trudged through the wafting steam blanketing the floor of the boiler room and stepped into the relatively cool stillness of the corridor outside. They did not hear the faint sounds of footsteps disappearing down a nearby passageway over their own disappointed chatter.

The next two weeks passed by in a flash. Each day saw the two brainstorming ideas about how they could possibly get down into the Undercellars. Then, once inside, how to go about looking for one of Haalbar Altier's lost tunnels or, against all odds, find Vitalsior's secret passageway.

They were on the way to dinner one evening when a large commotion resounded through the corridors from the direction of Mess Hill. As they approached the arched entrance, a number of worried-looking apprentices hurried past them towards the growing din. Asher glanced at Lorrelli for a split second before taking off after them. By the time they arrived on Mess Hill, close to half of Mantlecrest's apprentices had gathered on the lawn, all of them staring down at the city.

They approached another pair of first-year apprentices, Harriette Gullybore and Haylan Uller, who were busy talking in hushed whispers to one other. Meanwhile, countless other apprentices had their arms raised, all of them pointing at Mastonon Commons.

"What's going on?" Lorrelli asked, gazing out in the direction they were pointing, unable to see what was causing the commotion.

"Someone's desecrated the Mastonon's statue in the Commons," Haylan answered her.

Asher couldn't help but notice the distinctive, lingering quiver of fear in the corner of his eye. "What do you mean 'desecrated'?" Asher asked, squinting his eyes as he tried to get a better look at the statue. It was no use: it was too far away to see clearly. Glancing around the hill, he saw a number of apprentices holding up the glass tablet of the Undergall Testament and peering through it, including Harriette Gullybore.

"The Mortis Skulk have penetrated the city's defences. They've defiled the statue as proof. See for yourself." She handed the pane of glass to Asher.

Asher held it up in front of his face like everyone else, but saw nothing different.

Lorrelli quickly waved her auger at it. "Aspio Retego."

The transparent glass instantly shimmered in Asher's hands, quickly magnifying objects in the distance to tenfold their normal size. He focused on a close-up of a building as clearly as if he was standing in front of it. He repositioned his arms and centred the tablet on Mastonon Commons.

A large crowd had gathered around the statue but were being held back by a circle of armed bireems. Five tribarions stood watchful guard behind them, close to the base of the sculpture, all of them keeping their distance from the billowing black shadow engulfing the bulk of the statue.

It looked exactly like the nightmarish blood veil that the cultist that attacked Asher had hidden within, first in The Blind and again in the Catacomb Cathedral. The statue's arms were transfixed, both outstretched upwards to the sky. They seemed to be clutching something, but even with the intense magnification Asher couldn't make out what it was. "How do you make it bigger?" he asked Lorrelli, "I can't see what it's holding."

"It's a baby," Haylan answered his question for him.

"I don't get it," Lorrelli said to no-one in particular. "Why would someone desecrate the statue to show the Mortis Skulk holding a baby?"

"It's a message," Harriette replied, her eyes wide with fear.

"A message?" Lorrelli repeated, shaking her head and staring back at her expectantly, waiting for a better explanation of what she meant.

"What message?" Asher pressed.

Harriette's face was a mixture of distressed emotions, her mind barely able to comprehend what her mouth was about to say. Luckily, she didn't have to say the words.

Haylan said them for her. Meekly, he turned his head towards them, eyes glistening as he said what everyone around them was dreading.

"The Mortis Skulk have been reborn."

CHAPTER 39

RED SCAR INVASION

Before Haylan's words properly registered, a loud series of chimes resonated around the hill. Everyone turned around and gazed at the hundred small gargoyles springing to life, high atop their respective terraces.

"Apprentices, the Grand Chancellor's elite guards have locked down the city and will be upon the grounds in minutes. Do not approach them or interfere with their investigation in any way. If confronted, wait until a master is present before answering any questions. Now return to your racks and await further instruction," the legate's voice boomed across the lawn from a hundred animated gaping mouths. "Go. Now!"

A multitude of conversations erupted on Mess Hill, some in hushed whispers between friends, others much louder and meant for all those around to hear. A flurry of movement accompanied the growing noise as apprentices flocked towards the exit in droves. Distinctive voices propagated wild rumours amidst the crowd, which spread like a storm front through the minds of those apprentices too frightened to think clearly.

"I can't believe the Chancellor's unleashing the Red Scars on the city." Asher heard a high-pitched female voice mutter in disbelief.

"Screw the city, that loco pendejo is ordering them inside Mantlecrest. Doesn't the legate trust her own apprentices?" another deep grumbling voice with a Hispanic twinge called out in reply.

"Not with piss-ants like you hiding tacos everywhere, Hefenall," someone laughed back at him. His laughter was soon joined by those around him as the joke hit home, but it was cut short by the much deeper and commanding voice of Tribune

DeGrulz as he barked orders at them.

"Hold your tongues and get to your racks. Now!"

The crowd on the hill moved a little faster. Though his commands did little to stop the flow of conversation, his orders had served to stifle it to a series of whispers.

"What are Red Scars?" Asher asked the others, handing back the clear glass tablet to Harriette as they hurried towards the exit.

"The Grand Chancellor's elite guard, personally selected from the strongest tribarions," Harriette answered in a whisper, stuffing the Undergall testament inside her tunic.

"Supreme inquisitors, more like," Haylan interjected. "The Grand Chancellor uses them to root out and terminate Skulk conspirators."

"Terminate, as in kill?" Asher asked with eyes wide, but he already knew the answer.

"They're the most dangerous of bloodhounds," Lorrelli agreed under her breath. "They're attuned to the scent of all known Mortis Skulk devices and materials. If they find one that's been recently augmented by a blood calling, they can trace it back to the traitor who used it."

"If they suspect you of Mortis Skulk collaboration, or the outlawed practice of Decisus Umbra, they'll haul you away for interrogation," Harriette's voice was audibly trembling at the prospect.

"If you have anything to hide…" Haylan looked at them anxiously, "don't! 'Cause they'll find it."

"The Scarlet Commander and the Half-brute hauled my grandfather away during the rebellion. My father never saw him again," Harriette whispered softly as a twinge of sadness crept over her face.

"The Scarlet Commander?" Asher repeated, the name meant nothing to him.

"A monstrosity of a man and the commander of the Red Scar Guard during the Rebellion," Haylan's response was laced with fear.

"The Harbinger of Hearts," a momentary shudder ran through Harriette's body. "Twice as wide as anyone you've ever laid eyes on, and half again as tall."

"And the Half-brute?"

"His offsider," Haylan whispered. "A horrid lying weasel with only one arm and half a hand on it, hence the name. He was the Scarlet Commander's spymaster. He saw what people tried to hide and heard the whispers people thought were secret."

"He was never far from the Scarlet Commander's side during the war. My grandmother said it was almost as if he lived in his master's shadow," Harriette interjected.

"It was rumoured that no-one knew the Scarlet Commander's true identity, except for the Half-brute and the Elder Council," Haylan whispered, his passage off the hill slowed considerably by the horde of apprentices blocking the large arched entrance.

"How? Surely people would recognise him," Asher said in disbelief.

"No, the Scarlet Commander always wore a black face mask to hide his true identity," Harriette ran a finger down her face, "marred with a scarlet scar stretching from hairline to chin over his left cheek," she quickly drew a second line across her face, "and another across his eyes."

"The Scarlet Commander and the Half-brute were the perfect combination. The Commander was the most brutal and unforgiving of all Red Scars, with limitless strength, ferocity and speed. While the Half-brute was the most cunning, deceptive and brilliant subterfuge agent you could imagine, feeding the commander an unending feast of suspects and traitors to devour," Haylan whispered under his breath, glancing nervously around the hill.

"They should have called them the Scarlet Reaper," Harriette hissed, "because the Scarlet Commander was death, and the Half-brute was his scythe."

"But no-one's seen either of them since the end of the Rebellion—" Haylan continued, but was interrupted when

Harriette pulled heavily on his tunic.

"Come on. We gotta go."

"Wait," Asher called after them, but it was no use. The two rushed off, hurriedly disappearing in the crowd. A worrying thought flashed in the back of Asher's mind, making him instinctively grab Lorrelli's arm.

Lorrelli looked at him curiously as their paced slowed. The majority of the other apprentices had already disappeared out the exit, with more leaving with every passing second. Tribune DeGrulz watched on dutifully from the rear of the crowd as the apprentices departed. Unbeknownst to Asher, his gaze sought them out and lingered for longer than usual, eyes narrowing as he noticed their movement had slowed.

"Asher, come on, we've got to get to our racks," Lorrelli dragged him off the hill after noticing the tribune gazing down at them.

"We've got bigger problems than the tribune right now," Asher whispered back at her, a grave expression on his face.

"What?"

"The augefact," Asher whispered.

"It's hidden, it'll be safe." Lorrelli pleaded pulling at his arm again. "Come on."

Asher intensified his grip on her arm to stop her from leaving.

"Lorrelli, the Wormwood Vindicat, it's stashed next to the augefact. If the Red Scars are attuned like everyone says, they'll pick up its scent in seconds and trace it back to us."

A fierce panicked realisation flooded over Lorrelli's face as Asher word's hit home. "Oh, no! But, Asher, there's no time. They'll be on the grounds any second. Besides, where would we hide it?"

"We have to try. Do you really think we'll be able to hold out against a Red Scar interrogation?" Asher took a step forward, still tightly holding on to her arm.

Lorrelli remained motionless, but her face grimaced at the prospect of being caught with the substance.

"Where are we going?" She reluctantly buckled to Asher's unwavering logic, as Asher quickened the pace, setting off at a run as soon as they were out of sight of the tribune.

"Somewhere that's already doused in the stuff. It'll throw them off the scent." Lorrelli threw him a confused glance mid stride.

"We've got to get the box to Prum."

By the time Asher and Lorrelli had retrieved the box from its hiding place, Mantlecrest's halls and corridors were empty of all sounds except the faint echo of their footsteps slapping the cold stone as they ran.

It had taken them about 10 minutes to reach the secret entrance to the Spiretop Gardens. It took another couple of minutes to climb up the hollow trunk, then five more to reach the angel oak, pass under it and weave through the bamboo forest. When they finally ducked under the rocky outcrop and found themselves in Prum's secret grove, they both ran to the old carob tree and pounded on its trunk.

"Prum, are you there?" Lorrelli cupped her hands and called out into the knot in the tree. There was no response. They waited nervously for a couple of seconds before pounding again.

"We've got more Vindicat. Prum, get the hell out here," Asher shouted, hammering hard on the tree's trunk. The tree moaned and a small branch emerged from the knot. Prum's diminutive form crawled out a moment later, a dirty look on his face.

"Want what?" his scratchy voice snapped at them.

"We need you to hide something for us," Lorrelli answered in a soothing voice.

"What hide? Get what?"

"Hide this." Asher held up the box for him to see. "We can give you more Vindicat when it's safe."

"When safe?" Prum eyed him off warily.

"After the Red Scars have left," Asher answered brashly.

"Prum want now," the disgruntled bark-encrusted creature

said indignantly.

"We don't have time for this," Asher snapped.

"Prum, we need you to hide it now, they'll be here any minute," Lorrelli pleaded.

"Care not. Deal not." Prum attempted to disappear back within the knot.

"Prum if we get caught with this box we can never come back. We can never bring you nice things to drink," said Lorrelli.

Prum slowed his retreat momentarily, allowing Lorrelli time to pounce on his indecision. "When was the last time someone brought you a drink?"

Prum stopped in his tracks completely and begrudgingly looked back at both of them. "Wait short. Promise Prum."

"We promise," Asher and Lorrelli hastily agreed.

"Agree then. Prum hide."

Asher held out the box and watched as Prum disappeared with it deep inside the trunk of the tree.

"Come on, we've got to go," he grabbed her hand and led her from the grove, ducking back under the rocky outcrop and through the bamboo forest towards the massive trunk of the angel oak. Just before they had cleared the last of its branches a loud voice stopped them in their tracks.

"Apprentice Bloom, we meet again. How unfortunate for you," a tall, menacing voice said threateningly as he emerged from behind a nearby tree trunk, pushing some foliage out of his way as he approached, callously breaking the plant's stem in the process.

Asher instantly recognised the man, although this time he was not casually sitting behind him in the Custodian's Box in plain clothes. Instead, Farrenk stood a mere few feet away from Asher's heels, dressed to the nines in full elite guard regalia.

Farrenk's uniformed figure was both an impressive and intimidating sight. The heavy black leather armour encasing his body clashed heavily against the soft greens and browns of the garden. He wore a long-tailed jacket that hung from his shoulders to his knees. The leather itself was completely black, with not even the faintest sliver of light reflected from its surface.

A single jagged red scar ran up his right side and disappeared into his armpit, whilst a high collar extended around his neck and over the lower part of his face, hiding his chin and devious smile from view. His hair had been slicked down back over his head and his stance was deep and purposeful, probably because of the effort required to move the black, heavy ironclad boots extending up the entire length of his shins.

Asher couldn't spot his auger or battle mantle anywhere, and figured the man must've had it hidden somewhere beneath his heavy leather coat.

Farrenk slowly pulled down his collar so Asher could see his triumphant sneer. "Imagine my surprise, that while pursuing the vile scent of a malicious Skulk concoction, I find you."

Skirting around them, he stalked over to the edge of the angel oak's hanging vines and made a single slashing motion at them with a finger. The severed strands instantly fell to the floor in a heap, as a low growl emanated from the branches above Asher and Lorrelli's heads. Farrenk ignored the noise, his wild eyes brutishly fixating on Asher instead.

"I suppose you can offer a plausible explanation for your presence here, especially when Mantlecrest is under lockdown by order of the Grand Chancellor?" Farrenk advanced a single step towards them.

Asher and Lorrelli nervously looked at each other, but said nothing.

"Silence, in my eyes, is an admission of guilt," Farrenk took another step forward and raised one of his arms, pulling back the sleeve with his hand. A long two-pronged blade, split down the centre like a deadly tuning fork, was strapped to the inside of his forearm.

"With all due respect, all apprenti were ordered not to talk to the elite guard without a master present." Welticrum's voice rang out from somewhere behind Farrenk, which caused one eye to unnaturally spin 180 degrees in his head, the other never wavering from its fierce gaze on Asher and Lorrelli.

"Is that so, Master Rousso? Well it is fortunate you're here then, now these two malefactors have no reason to hide answer from question. So I will ask again. What are you doing up here?"

With a deep frown setting in over his brow, he lowered his arm, letting his sleeve cover the long needle-thin blade once more.

Before Asher or Lorrelli could answer, Welticrum's voice chimed in again. "Had you the patience, or the humility to wait for my poor old bones on the stairs, I could've told you to expect them. They've been so kind as to offer to feed my pet to save me the exhausting task of doing so myself. I fear they must've missed the lockdown announcement as there are no announcers in the gardens." Welticrum walked past Farrenk's menacing frame and stood behind the two, protectively placing a hand on each of their shoulders.

"A convenient story, though I do not see any pet or, for that matter, any food." Farrenk smiled venomously, the prospect of catching out two apprentices and a master in a lie made his mouth water in anticipation.

"Your lack of perception is disturbing, but not as much as the fact that you wield the authority of an elite guard, yet you only possess the wisdom of a fool," Welticrum baited him calmly.

"Mind your tongue, should you wish to keep it, old man." Farrenk took a menacing step forward.

"Ignorance and threats, is that the measure of your power? Your answer sits before your very eyes, yet you refuse to see it. You need only look to the base of the tree to find the food, and skyward to see my pet. Had you the sense to simply listen to your surroundings, instead of verbally berating and accusing these two of maleficence, you'd hear him growling at you even now as you waste air drawing breath."

Farrenk glanced at the enormous trunk of the angel oak. There were, indeed, two small baskets filled with raw meat nestled within its oversized roots. Farrenk's eyes trailed upwards, following the angel oak's trunk to its topmost branches until they finally locked with a set of fierce eyes glowering down at him.

A deep frown came across his face as he returned his gaze towards the trio. Farrenk took a step towards the baskets of meat. The glowing eyes above jumped down a couple of branches and a threatening screech sounded at the Red Scar's invasion of its territory.

"Mind your step," Welticrum calmly warned him. "Orilla's are viciously territorial, especially when it comes to food."

Farrenk glanced up at the menacing eyes above and stopped in his tracks a few feet away from the baskets of meat. "Perhaps I was mistaken."

"If only a simple mistake was your only downfall. Asher, Lorrelli, take this and go to your racks. Do not tarry." Welticrum pushed them forward, pressing a large ribbon with the legate's seal proudly emblazoned on the front into Lorrelli's hand. "Any problems with their ilk," he nodded at Farrenk, "show them the pass, but do not stop."

Asher nodded, casually raised his hand to scratch his head, chancing a glance in the direction of the baskets. They vanished before his eyes, but he said nothing, instead grabbing Lorrelli by the hand and running from the garden all the way back to their racks. They passed several more Red Scars in the halls, but had no problem passing them once he displayed the legate's seal. Neither of them was game to speak until they were safely locked inside with secureaug lock firmly engaged.

"Asher, that Red Scar knew you. Who was he?"

"That was Farrenk. The one Braak warned us about, but I didn't know he was a Red Scar."

"Farrenk? Are you kidding? That's all we need, a Red Scar that wants your head." Lorrelli's face was visibly concerned as she slumped down on her bed, exhausted.

"You think he was there for me?"

"Come on, Asher, wake up. First, Braak warned you about

him when he was investigating The Blind where he found you. Then Farrenk turns up at the Utor Alea match and sits behind you, listening in on your conversation with Gibraltair. Now he just so happens to find us in the Spiretop Gardens minutes after he's permitted entry into Mantlecrest.

"Either he's been ordered to find something to incriminate you with, which means the Chancellor himself is after you, or you've done something to really piss him off. Either way, we've got a Red Scar on our heels and he's out for blood. Your blood."

"Well, at least we know there's one person on our side," Asher sat down on his own bed, exhausted, explaining Welticrum's projected illusion in the gardens. "Welticrum was willing to lie to a Red Scar to help us; that's got to count for something."

"But why?" Lorrelli thought out loud. "It doesn't make any sense. He promised Lem's father to look out for Lem, not us. Lem's not even here."

"We can figure that out later," Asher said as something caught his attention at the foot of his bed. "You're going to want to see this." Asher picked up the Undergall Testament from his bed and held up the two main headlines for Lorrelli to see. The first sat above a large picture of the hoodwinked statue in Mastonon commons.

MASTONON COMMONS DESECRATED

It was not the main article that grabbed Lorrelli's attention: it was the second headline that was much more terrifying.

RED SCARS TRACE TRAITORS TO MANTLECREST

Lorrelli waved her auger over the tablet to engage the audio.

The voice of Overseer Altier crackled against the quiet of the room. "Mastonon Commons has fallen victim to a most unsettling prank. Do not misinterpret this callous hoax as anything other than what it is. The Mortis Skulk are no closer to returning than they were a decade ago. Regardless, the Chancellor has taken swift action to bring the culprits to justice and has dispatched his own elite guards to deal with the matter."

The audio track stalled for a second.

"I have just been informed that the elite guards have tracked the culprits responsible for the defilement of the statue in Mastonon Commons to the walls surrounding Mantlecrest. Overseer Altier had this to say."

"There is no evidence as yet to support any notion that anyone inside Mantlecrest was involved, or that Mantlecrest has been compromised in any way. Until such a time as the matter has been investigated properly, I ask you all to remain calm and not to fall prey to this senseless fear-mongering." Lobrolo's unwavering voice sounded more resolute than ever.

"Staunch unyielding words of reassurance from Overseer Altier today, as yet another unexplained Skulk-related incident rocks the three cities…"

The voice trailed off as Lorrelli silenced the audio. "Did you hear that?" she asked, biting her lip, "they tracked the culprits back to the walls surrounding Mantlecrest."

"So what?"

"Remember what Braak said? Someone in Mantlecrest may be involved in whatever's going on. It's obvious that the council thinks so, too. Why else would Red Scars be scouring Mantlecrest and everything in it for clues?" Lorrelli sat on her bed and tried to reason out who the culprit might be, when Asher's voice broke her concentration.

"Whatever the reason, there's no way we'll be able to search for an escape with the Red Scars stalking the halls. We'll have to wait it out until something changes, but when it does I know where we have to start looking."

"Where?" Lorrelli wiped back her single plait over her ear and twisted its end nervously, somehow knowing what Asher was going to say before he said it.

"The Undercellars."

CHAPTER 40

BLACKMAILED ALLEGIANCE

Three days had passed since the Red Scar occupation of Mantlecrest. It was a glum and depressive time for all apprentices, regardless of their year, rank, bloodline or title. After completing their final training session each day, the vast majority of apprentices would retreat immediately to their racks. Only a few were brave enough to spend their free time under the watchful eye of the Red Scar Guards.

The masters and apprentices alike were still unsure about the Red Scars' true purpose within Mantlecrest. There had been no word of any kind of discovery of the culprit who desecrated the statue in Mastonon commons. In fact, the Red Scars spoke very little, unless they were taking away someone for questioning, and even then it was only ever two words.

"Follow me."

No-one had been brave enough to talk about their experience after questioning, or perhaps they had been instructed not to, Asher couldn't be sure. In any case, the only news Asher and Lorrelli received was from the various rumours floating around the halls, and whatever information he could pry out of Welticrum. But the old man had been uncharacteristically tight-lipped since his altercation with Farrenk in the Spiretop Gardens.

Lorrelli checked the Undergall Testament on the hour every hour, but still it shed no light on whether the Red Scars had found anything inside Mantlecrest, traitor or culprit alike. Fortunately, as far as they could tell, Farrenk had disappeared.

Where exactly, Asher could only guess, but they hadn't had once sighting of him since that night in the gardens, and the other Red Scars had left them well enough alone.

Asher and Lorrelli had to assume the augefact was still safe, though they dared not visit Prum to check on it. On the fourth night of the Red Scars' occupation, a loud knock reverberated on the door of their racks. Asher anxiously looked at Lorrelli before crossing the floor and disengaging the secureaug lock. Expecting one of the Red Scars to be on the other side, Asher opened it three inches and peered out, firmly wedging his foot behind the door to stop anyone from barging in.

Lorrelli stood nervously behind him and peered through the crack. Neither of them expected to see the diminutive frame of Morreby Fitch on the other side, her pale face more gaunt than ever as it stared back at them. Her cheeks were sunken. Her skin tone had turned a ghastly grey hue, whilst her body was thin and frail. But it was her eyes that truly betrayed how ill she really was: thick discoloured bags hung under them like sagging tea bags. A sickness was waging war against her and, by the looks of things, it was wining.

"Let me in," she pleaded with a voice so faint it was barely above a whisper.

"Not on your life," Asher snapped back at her.

"Please," she persisted.

Asher noticed her pale trembling fingers clutching the strap of her rucksack in a vice-like grip. "Let me in, or I'll turn you and your Wormwood Vindicat over to the Red Scars."

Asher couldn't contain his own surprise at her barb but, despite his astonishment, he recognised a threat when he heard one. Flinging open the door, he grabbed Morreby by the shoulder, pulled her inside and threw her to the floor.

Lorrelli immediately jumped on top of her, her hands firmly locking down Morreby's wrists, pinning her to the ground by her sides.

Asher popped his head outside the door and quickly made sure no-one had seen or heard anything. Satisfied no-one had, he closed the door and locked it behind him. Spinning on his heels, he reached down and grabbed Morreby by the throat with one hand and exposed his auger inches above her face with the other.

She was too weak to even attempt to fight back.

"You've got some nerve to threaten us!"

"I had no choice," Morreby wheezed at him through the choke hold, the pressure from his hand impeding her ability to breathe or speak properly.

"So you thought blackmailing us would save you?" Asher flared his auger at her, spilling a bright stream of light in her eyes.

She closed them and winced in discomfort, but did not cry out.

Lorrelli stared down at the girl's waist when she felt something brush against her leg from inside Morreby's rucksack. "Asher…"

"How do you about the Vindicat?" Asher demanded.

"I know you keep it in a wooden box," Morreby gasped. "The same wooden box you've hidden from the Red Scars."

"Asher, you really need to look at this," Lorrelli's whispered.

"How do you know about the box?" Asher moved his auger even closer to Morreby's face.

"I saw it."

A long, hairy leg emerged from the top of Morreby's rucksack.

Lorrelli shrieked and pushed Asher off Morreby, jumping clear just in time to see a hideously hirsute creature emerge from the bag's opening.

"What the…" Asher backed away from the mess of hairy legs clawing their way out from the discarded backpack.

"What the hell is that?" Lorrelli picked up where Asher left off, pointing her auger at the repulsive hairy creature.

"It won't hurt you," Morreby croaked, rubbing her throat as she gathered herself up off the floor. She carefully put the creature back inside her bag, one spindly leg at a time. "If you'll let me explain, I think we can make a deal."

"What kind of deal?" Asher asked warily.

"One which sees both our secrets kept safe from the Red Scars," Morreby wheezed.

Taking a seat on Lem's empty bed, Lorrelli and Asher sat

opposite Morreby on another bed, each warily eyeing off the girl and the moving bulge in her knapsack.

"If we're going to agree to anything, you've got a lot of questions to answer, no objections."

Morreby nodded her head silently.

"First, what is that thing?" Lorrelli commanded.

"It's a fannim."

"Never heard of it," Asher retorted, unwilling to give Morreby an inch with which to work.

"Hardly surprising, did you even know what Red Scars were until they were on the grounds, hunting you?" Morreby scowled back at him.

"How did you?" Asher narrowed his eyes trying to work out how she could have known such a fact.

"You think you're careful, but you're sloppy at shielding your conversations when around large groups."

"You've been spying on us," Asher spat the accusation at her.

"Only after you started spying on me," she snapped, picking up on their surprise. "Lem's not as subtle as he thinks."

"Fine, but how did you know about the box?"

"I saw the outline of it in your rucksack in the Auxilia Amphitheatre. I guessed the rest; your reaction merely confirmed it." She weakly brushed off her tunic with a hand. "Aren't you more curious about how I knew what was inside?"

"I'm curious about a lot of things," Asher snorted.

"Well, go on then," Lorrelli folded her arms, waiting for an answer.

"I have the fannim to thank for that," she tapped her backpack, forcing Asher's and Lorrelli's gazes down on the moving bulge in the bag. "It's an extremely rare creature, with even rarer blood. Its blood is so rare, the Red Scars are attuned to its scent, as am I, from having used it for so long now, which is also how I know your box had Vindicat in it."

"How?" Asher didn't see the link.

"Because when distilled, fannim blood is used to refine

Wormwood Vindicat," Morreby grimly smirked at both of them.

"That's why Farrenk was so quick to the Spiretop Garden."
Asher shot Lorrelli a look, but she immediately realised her slip.

"So that's where you hid it," Morreby wheezed.

"Hang on, if the Red Scars are attuned to fannim blood, why haven't they found you and your pet yet?" Asher asked.

"They are under the assumption that fannims are extinct. Therefore, they have only attuned themselves to the scent of their blood, not the creatures themselves. So as long as he remains uninjured, I'm safe." Morreby placed a hand over the knapsack protectively.

"If it's so dangerous, why do you keep it around? I can think of much better pets," Lorrelli's voice was laced with an audible layer of contempt for Morreby.

"It's personal, and it's not a pet."

"Not good enough, you promised us answers," Asher raised his auger at her again.

Morreby held up her hand to stop him and gritted her teeth. Sharing her secrets was obviously hard for her. "Fine. I need it to do something in a certain part of Mantlecrest."

"Which part?" Asher said knowing full well what the answer would be.

"The Undercellars."

"I knew it. I knew you were up to something down there," Asher exclaimed victoriously.

"You don't understand. It's not what you think." A hurt look came over Morreby's pale face.

"What is it, then? Explain it to me," Asher spat the question at her, his tolerance for Morreby's lies growing thin.

"It's because of my mother."

"Your mother's in the Undercellars," Asher snorted at the preposterousness of the remark.

"My mother's dead," Morreby snapped.

"What?" Lorrelli instantly felt a connection to the girl that she'd never felt before.

A single tear appeared in the corner of Morreby's left eye. She wiped it away before it spilled down her cheek.

"There were complications with my birth. The augwife told her there was no way both of us would live through the delivery. So my mother channelled her life into mine. She sacrificed her life so I might live."

"So you've got a—"

"Yes," Morreby cut her off not wanting to hear the word.

"A what?" Asher asked unabashedly, unable to make the same connection.

"Any birth that results in maternal death creates a…" Lorrelli trailed off, ashamed at her prior attitude towards and treatment of Morreby.

"A remorauger. A life-leech parasitic connection between an auger and its host… me," Morreby said sadly, allowing time for the revelation to sink in.

Asher looked at the two of them and shook his head, not understanding.

"What does that mean?" Asher asked hesitantly, leaning away from Morreby.

"My… my auger's killing me."

"Letifer," Asher whispered to himself, finally understanding what she was trying to tell them. "So you don't deal in death, but your auger," he corrected himself, "your remorauger does?"

Morreby nodded solemnly. "You're the first two people other than my father that knows. The augwife died shortly after my birth."

Lorrelli didn't say anything, knowing full well the implications of Morreby's condition.

Asher however, was more confused than ever. "Not even the legate? What's so bad about being born a death dealer, other than the obvious?"

"Don't call me that," Morreby scowled at him and shook her head intensely. "And especially not the legate."

"Asher, those with remoraugers were the first Cruaar targeted by the Mortis Skulk," Lorrelli explained, "they were the perfect recruits, misunderstood and ostracised for a fault not their own. Under Cerebule's rule, they were given free rein to drain anyone they pleased."

"What do you mean 'drain'?"

"We need to drain the life force of others in order to survive," Morreby said quietly.

"You kill to survive?" Asher said horrified, standing up and backing away from Morreby.

"No. I've never killed anyone, maybe a couple of rats but only when I have no other choice. I mostly drain animals and plants to survive."

"Animals and plants?"

"Remember when Stemproles killed the mould in the Auxilia Amphitheatre?"

Asher and Lorrelli had not forgotten that little set back.

"He had nothing to do with it. I drained the life from the mould by accident when I was trying to drain some of the lawnkins you two let loose. It just so happened to coincide at the exact moment Stemproles enacted a blood calling at the mould. Unfortunately, everyone saw the mould vanish, and I couldn't let my secret get out."

"That's why it grew back. He's not a true descendant at all!" Asher looked at Lorrelli, both making the same connection.

Morreby looked them both strangely. "Descendant?"

"Never mind. What has any of that got to do with the Undercellars?"

"Draining mould isn't enough to sustain my remorauger's hunger. Ever since the Red Scars arrived, I haven't been able to satisfy its cravings, so it's been draining me, draining my life force, ever since."

"Your auger's draining you?" Lorrelli said, surprised.

"Everyone thinks we're monsters and drain others because we're sick, or that we're natural born killers. The truth is we're slaves."

"Slaves?" Asher and Lorrelli said together in surprise.

"Remoraugers are as much parasitic as they are symbiotic. They constantly leech away our life force if not satisfied by other means. Which is why I look like–"

"Death," Asher blurted out, rudely interrupting her.

"Asher," Lorrelli snapped at him.

Morreby ignored him. She'd obviously dealt with worse insults than whatever he could throw at her. "Normally, I can satisfy its cravings by draining the rats I find in the Undercellars, but ever since the Red Scars entered Mantlecrest I haven't been able to feed its thirst," Morreby grimaced weakly.

"Why not?" Lorrelli asked, with genuine compassion.

"Because I need to amplify whatever I drain in order to keep the damn thing's thirst at bay."

"What do you mean 'amplify'?" Asher asked.

She looked down at the bulge in her bag. "Fannim blood has more than one use."

"And you can't use its blood because the Red Scars are attuned to it," Lorrelli deduced.

Morreby nodded solemnly.

Lorrelli finally recognised Morreby's dire situation. It literally was life or death. "So how long until?" she asked.

"Roughly four days, maybe five, until my auger consumes enough of my life force that my problem won't matter anymore," Morreby said with a relieved look on her face, as though a great burden had been lifted off her shoulders. "Which gives you three days until I tell the guards about the nasty secret that you've hidden in Spiretop Gardens."

"If you tell them, we'll out you as a death dealer," Asher threatened defensively.

"If I can't supplement its hunger I'll be dead anyway, so I've got nothing to lose," Morreby said, an emotionless stare blanketing her gaunt face. "You, however, are not as lucky."

"So you're blackmailing us?" Asher exhaled slowly.

"You only have yourself to blame. Had you nothing to hide,

you'd be free and clear, but you're not, so here we are."

Asher knew she was right, but couldn't bring himself to acknowledge it openly.

"So what is it you want from us?" Lorrelli asked, not sure whether she should hate the girl sitting weakly in front of her, or whether she should be impressed by her boldness.

"I overheard you talking to Master Rousso about the old legate's tunnels. I know you're looking for a way out of Mantlecrest."

"I thought I heard footsteps," Lorrelli whispered to herself.

"I want in. I never chose to come here, I need to get out and disappear before my secret gets out. So like it or not, from now on, we're a team," Morreby exhaled and slumped down farther on the bed.

"We're a what?" Asher blurted out in disgust.

"You heard me," she wheezed back at him, "and you two are going to find me something large enough to drain before my remorauger kills me."

"Anything else?" Asher laughed incredulously.

"That's all for now," Morreby's scratchy voice wheezed at them. "Now what do you need from me?"

"What?" Lorrelli and Asher asked in surprise.

"We're a team, right? Besides, it's in my best interests to help you succeed."

"Fine," Asher didn't like the position the gaunt-faced girl had blackmailed them into, but he saw little choice in the matter. "How were you getting into the Undercellars?"

Morreby pulled out her auger from beneath her tunic.

It was a small gem, smaller than any other auger Asher had ever seen, its colour resembled day-old blood left to rot under the midday sun: a bleak mottled brown.

Lorrelli took one look at her auger and couldn't help but blurt out, "It's brown. Why is it brown?"

"Because my blood's drying up and it's starving."

"Who cares," Asher interrupted rudely. "Answer the question.

How were you getting down there?"

"You mean after you got caught down there, practically forcing Gobbler to upgrade the secureaug lock and consequently negated my access?" Morreby said bitterly.

"Asher, her auger..." Lorrelli whispered forcefully trying to get Asher to take notice.

"Whose side are you on, Lorrelli? She's blackmailing us."

"We don't have time for this," Morreby said sternly. "My father told me there were special places throughout the Cruaar Nation created as safe havens for those with my condition. His research nearly got him arrested by the Tribarion Cohort, but he learnt of a room within Mantlecrest created by someone like me, a man named Surio."

"Surio Letifer," Asher exclaimed finally understanding the mystery that had plagued him for months.

"When I saw the door marked Surio Letifer, I knew I'd found his sanctuary. To anyone else, it appears as just a normal room, but if I use the ceremonial font to drain a life force, it reveals a stairwell to the Undercellars."

Morreby removed a chunk of mould from her bag, "I can drain this to open the stairwell, but I have no idea where to start looking for a tunnel entrance down there, everything's covered in mould and there's too much for me to drain, not that it would do any good without the fannim's blood to amplify it."

"We can take care of the mould, but not while the Red Scars are here."

"I'll assume you'll tell me how later, but first you need to find me something big enough with a pulse I can drain, but small enough that it won't put up too much of a fight," Morreby groaned, looking weaker than ever.

All three of them thought long and hard, but in the end it was Asher that proposed a solution.

"Does anyone know how to use an edurus herald?"

CHAPTER 41

THE MYTH OF WEYGLO MORTIMA

Neither Morreby nor Lorrelli had even heard of an edurus herald, let alone had any idea how to use one. That fact didn't even deter Asher for a moment. He started formulating a plan about how to get his hands on the one Tribarion Roolta used inside the Praelior Arena, after which he could figure out how to use it to summon a creature for Morreby to drain.

Two more days passed as they anxiously waited for Asher's next private training session to come around. Even in that short time, Morreby's condition had deteriorated tenfold, leaving her weakened body clinging to life by a thread. The mould they'd discretely collected from the various corridors did little to slow the decay plaguing her vital organs as her remorauger slowly fed on her waning life force.

The next morning, Asher and Lorrelli were awoken when the door to their room was abruptly flung open. It clanged loudly and shuddered as it slammed against the wall, flooding the darkness of their racks with an abrasive intrusion of light. Asher and Lorrelli held up theirs hands and squinted against the onslaught, but couldn't identify the silhouette standing in the doorway.

As their eyesight slowly adjusted, the silhouette's features took shape. An enormously cheeky smile beamed down at them both, which promptly transformed into an unsettling frown as his gaze caught sight of the crumpled form of Morreby Fitch in a disturbed wheezing sleep in the corner bed.

"Seriously? I'm gone for less than a month and you're already sleeping with the enemy." Walking into the room, he threw his rucksack on the floor, kicked the door closed behind him and waved a hand at the nearest auglight. It sprang to life and slowly warmed the room with light. "Literally sleeping with the enemy. I was right, the world has gone to hell in a handbasket."

"Lem!" Lorrelli yelled as she climbed out of bed and threw her arms around him, actually glad to see him alive and well.

"Get off," Lem struggled against her embrace, punching her lightly in the shoulder. "I'm still pissed at you!"

"Fair enough." Lorrelli winced, but couldn't help but smile back at him.

Asher blinked his eyes fully awake and jumped out of bed to heartily slap Lem on the back.

"Alright, alright, enough of all that. Now will someone please tell me what the prac is going on round here? Bloody Red Scars in the halls, caliors circling the skies and you two napping with the Fitch. What's she doing here? And what's wrong with her?" he belted off the questions one after the other in rapid succession, demanding answers from his two friends.

Morreby's inability to satisfy her remorauger's hunger had left her weaker than ever. She opened her eyes and painfully drew herself up on her elbows.

"She's a death dealer," Asher started, but Morreby voiced her objection to the term by coughing angrily.

"But her remorauger's draining her," Lorrelli added.

"So she blackmailed us," Asher said.

"'Cause she knows about the Vindicat," Lorrelli said. "It's a long story."

"It's good to have you back." Asher grabbed Lem by the shoulder and tousled his hair.

"I bet," Lem said uneasily as he sat on the foot of his bed, casting Asher and Lorrelli incredulous looks. "I think you two had better fill me in on what exactly is going on."

Lorrelli and Asher spent the next hour filling Lem in on everything that had happened in his absence, being careful to leave out all mention of the augefact and the symbols in the mould in front of Morreby. Morreby added in parts where she could to help the story along, but it was obvious even that was a strain in her weakened state.

Lem listened to everything, mostly in silence, before summarising it back to them to make sure he understood the position they were in. "So, basically, she's got us bent over a barrel and you want to steal an edurus herald to summon something for her to drain."

"Borrow, not steal," Asher corrected, "but, yeah."

"I take it no-one here actually knows how to use an edurus herald?" Lem inquired. All three of them shook their heads.

"So, basically, your plan is to wing it and hope for the best?" Lem asked.

Asher and Lorrelli nodded in agreement.

"Well. Good to see that my being thrown off a roof hasn't perverted your moral compass at all," he said as a coy smirk appeared in the corner of his mouth.

"You're taking this rather well," Asher said suspiciously.

"Not really, I just haven't told you my news yet."

"Your news?" Morreby wheezed at Lem from the corner.

"Well, you want the good news or the bad news first?"

"Good news," Lorrelli replied optimistically.

"I know where to get my first mantle elements," Lem smiled confidently.

"Elements, plural? As in, more than one?" Lorrelli chirped, making sure she didn't mishear him.

"Yep."

"That's great, where?" Lorrelli asked.

"Well that brings me to the bad news."

Asher, Morreby and Lorrelli raised their eyebrows at him.

"I know who A.F.S. is."

"What? Who?" Asher and Lorrelli said in unison.

Morreby looked at the three of them with a confused expression on her face.

"Alvah Firenze Sageroot, third daughter of Belkraen Sageroot–"

"Lem, that's fantastic, but how is that bad news?" Asher

butted in, unable to control his excitement at the news.

"'Cause she's a disciple of Weyglo Mortima," Lem lowered his voice.

Asher had never heard the name, but it was obvious everyone else in the room had, judging by the disparaging expressions on their faces. "Who's Weyglo Mortima?"

"I thought he was a myth," Lorrelli ignored Asher's question.

"Weyglo's no myth," Morreby coughed loudly. "Just because his name was stricken from the Annals by his father, doesn't make him any less real."

"Who's his father?" Asher tried to make sense of what he was hearing.

Annoyed by his interruptions for clarification, Morreby coughed a response at Asher. "Weyglo Mortima was the illegitimate son of Vitalsior, the patriarch of your precious bloodline. You know, the man that disappeared without a trace five thousand years ago after going mad and lopping off his fingers and toes."

Silence descended over the room whilst Morreby retold Weyglo Mortima's fable as quickly and succinctly as she could, struggling to do so between bouts of coughing and wheezing gasps for air. "After Vitalsior betrayed and murdered the Chromfaddar Warhost, the truce between the two races was broken. When the Warhost's wife, a Chromfaddar priestess, learnt of Vitalsior's betrayal, she vowed revenge.

"She sought out Vitalsior's bride-to-be in secret, murdered her and assumed her form. So powerful was her projected illusion, she fooled Vitalsior's own eyes and tricked the old fool into marrying her. She lured him to bed, disappearing into the night after the deed was done, never to be seen again by his eyes.

"A baby was born in secret sometime later, but the birth was tainted by his mother's insatiable hatred and lust for vengeance, leaving the child horribly disfigured, with blood as black as night." Morreby coughed violently, a spatter of brown blood staining the whites of her teeth as a result, but she was determined to continue.

"The baby was named for the Chromfaddar god of betrayal, Weyglo, and was a half-Cruaar and half-Chromfaddar abomination, though no-one except his mother knew his true lineage. She raised him and taught him everything she knew, instilling her hatred of the Cruaar deep inside his black-blooded heart.

"Legend tells that she died some twenty years after his birth, but demanded a dying wish from her son on her deathbed: to make Vitalsior suffer as she had." Morreby convulsed and coughed violently, clutching the sheets of her bed over her mouth. She wiped away a small smear of blood from her lips before continuing.

"Cruel and devious like his mother before him, Weyglo used his unique set of half-Cruaar half-Chromfaddar blood-traits to mask his true form. He went on to sire the first of the Mortis bloodline, forever corrupting his father's legacy and ensuring for all time that Mortis would forever shadow Vita."

Asher sat quietly for a moment letting the Weyglo's fable sink in before trying to work out what any of it had to do with Alvah and the Sageroot augefact. "I don't get it, how could you possibly know Alvah's connected with Weyglo?" Asher stared at Lem, curious eyes begging for answers.

"There's a reason why no-one could identify the symbol you can see with your divine eye, Asher," Lem said bluntly, not caring whether Morreby knew about the symbol.

Morreby narrowed her eyes at the remark but said nothing. After retelling Weyglo's Fable it took her last remaining ounce of energy just to keep her eyes open and remain lucid.

"Why's that?" Asher asked.

"Because no-one's seen it in a couple of thousand years," Lem produced a single piece of parchment from his tunic and dropped it gently in Asher's upturned hands.

The frail scrap of paper was impossibly old and looked like it would fall apart at any moment if mistreated. Asher gently unfolded it and gazed down at the stained surface. A lone image sat squarely in the middle. It had been carefully scorched onto the paper in the most precise manner, varying levels of burns providing different shades and textures, which lent the image a sense of depth.

As Asher looked a little closer at the faded image, he saw a woman standing next to the base of a large column. Asher couldn't be sure, but she appeared to be holding a baby orilla in her arms, wrapped tightly in a shawl.

"Don't ask me where I got it, but that's Alvah Sageroot on the day she donated the statue she had personally commissioned for Mantlecrest, thousands of years ago," Lem explained.

"So what?" Morreby croaked weakly.

"Look at her right leg," Lem pointed to the bottom of the image.

Asher's eyes raced to her leg, but where a foot should have extended out of the bottom of her skirt, there was only a hard metal stub.

Lorrelli sat next to Asher to look at the image.

"I figure that's what she used to create the…" Lem shot a distrustful look Morreby's way.

"It's all right, she might as well know," Asher reassured him. "We're all in this together now."

"To create the augefact," Lem whispered still not completely willing to trust the frail, dark-haired girl staring at him intently from across the room.

"Now look at the pin on her chest," Lem said casually.

All three stared intently at the tiny pin in the image but couldn't see it clearly.

Lorrelli grabbed a blank tablet of the Undergall Testament on the bed next to her and held it over the parchment.

"Aspio Retego."

The image magnified tenfold, making the pin on Alvah's chest instantly clearer. A small symbol sat in its centre for all to see.

"That's the same symbol I've been seeing," Asher exclaimed

excitedly. "Lem, how in the world did you find this?"

"It's probably better if you don't know," a defensive expression washed over Lem's face.

"Okay," Asher said suspiciously. "So what's the significance of the pin?"

"I can't be certain, but I think the pin was a symbol of allegiance to Weyglo," Lem said.

"How can you possibly know that?" Asher asked.

"Someone on the outside's been helping me. He's been studying this stuff for years. Don't ask me who, 'cause I can't tell you. But he's the one that found the parchment in the first place, after I told him about the symbol," Lem said.

"You just happened to find someone that knows more about Weyglo Mortima than anyone else in existence," Asher scoffed and raised his eyebrows in disbelief.

Lem looked at his feet bashfully. "He found me, actually."

"I suppose he's also who told you where you'd find your two mantle elements," Lorrelli laughed.

"Yes, actually," Lem said.

"Who is he?" Morreby coughed.

"I can't tell you, I swore a blood oath I wouldn't."

"Lem, you didn't…" Lorrelli trailed off.

"Just praccing drop it, alright? We needed answers and I got them. It's done," Lem's harsh response to the question killed all other conversation.

Everyone except Morreby left the room to attend their first training session of the day. Her fragile state left her too weak to walk, let alone train, so they made a plan to return for her and hide her in Surio's Sanctuary later until they had the edurus herald.

The day's various training sessions dragged by, but Asher finally found himself on familiar sands with Tribarion Roolta. As always she stood in her usual stoic position in the centre of the arena. After an hour of gruelling training, mostly conducted in silence, Asher was left as battered and bruised as always. The armour-clad First Order Tribarion watched on in silence, motionless in the centre of the arena as Asher's blood rained down on the sands time and time again.

Sensing the training session was nearing an end, Asher seized the opportunity and approached her. "Tribarion Roolta," he paused, "I need a favour."

"I didn't realise I owed you as much, Apprentice Bloom," she replied curtly.

"I wish to hone my blood callings further in your absence. I need the edurus herald so I can summon creatures to practice against."

"Either you're a fool, or you think me one," Tribarion Roolta laughed unapologetically.

"I only want to train further."

"Then find your first mantle element, like I instructed you to do months ago," she barked at him and frowned. "Besides, even if I was to ignore the Red Scar Guards stalking Mantlecrest's halls, there's another problem with your request that you've severely overlooked."

Asher cursed silently. He'd expected this kind of objection, but had hoped the tribarion would cut him a break. "And what's that?"

The tribarion's head snapped to her left as if responding to an alarm, but Asher couldn't hear or see anything that would warrant such a pronounced deviation in her attention.

"Well, could you at least summon me a mawblink before you depart so I may continue training for another hour or so?" he asked a little louder this time, trying to regain her attention.

She drew her sword from her scabbard and adopted a battle stance, waving her free hand and barking orders at invisible figures around her. "They're here. To arms! Secure the strands!"

"Tribarion?" Asher said nervously and took a step back.

"Warders to the streets, safeguard the bunkers," she ordered invisible troops, before marching forward, stepping towards the edge of the raised stone platform. With sword clenched firmly in hand, she shouted commands at unseen allies as she stepped off the stone platform. She did not fall, nor did she even so much as drop an inch. Each foot landed on a platform of air, but she did not stop. She was an entire foot off the ground and gaining speed, her resplendent armour and long sword glinting in the light.

"Bireems, defend the Augestry. Tribarions with me, we will tear this Skulk scourge asunder." Her sword charged to life in her hands, rippling with power as she sliced open a gash on her forearm and allowed her gold-tinged blood to leak over the blade's surface. It hardened into a glimmering augmented covering of gold.

"Protect Hollow's Rest."

Asher looked around, but could not see or hear anything. "I don't understand. You're in Mantlecrest. We're in Undergall." He held up his hands around him as her fierce gaze swung around to face him.

"I haven't been in Undergall since our first instruction." Tribarion Roolta barked as her body flickered and faded. Soon all that was left of her was a ghostlike spectre floating above the sands of the arena as it marched forward and disappeared. She cast one lasting glance back at him.

"Secure yourself Apprentice, and take arms."

Asher couldn't believe his eyes as the armour-clad tribarion disappeared entirely, her ghostly voice whispering back at him over the sands like a message from the grave. "We are at war!"

"Tribarion wait, the Mawblink," Asher called out, but it was too late. She was gone.

He didn't waste a second as he sprinted from the arena, heels scattering sand until they finally hit the firm hold of stone. Asher burst through the arena's entrance and hurtled down the corridor towards Surio's Sanctuary. Skidding to a halt in front of its heavy door, he desperately hammered on its surface.

It opened an inch, then stopped, Lem's eyes peering out cautiously before Asher violently pushed past him, a wild look on his face as he slammed the door closed behind him.

"Hollow's Rest is under attack."

"What?" Lorrelli said in a bout of surprise.

Lem said nothing, but his expression betrayed his surprise.

Asher quickly explained what happened and what the tribarion had said before she had disappeared.

"Did you get the Herald?" Morreby asked weakly, her feeble frame propped up against the wall like a ragdoll.

"No, she disappeared. She said she hasn't been in Undergall in months. I don't understand."

"That's it, then," Morreby leaned her head back against the wall.

"Oh, no you don't, you're not dying on me yet. Tribarion Roolta didn't know how widespread the attack was and you're my only way into the Undercellars and out of this wretched place. I'm going to find you something to drain if it kills me." Lem, Lorrelli and Morreby looked at Asher, nervously awaiting his instructions. "Lem, with me, Lorrelli, you stay here and look after Morreby. We'll be back shortly."

"Where are you going?" Morreby asked.

"We're going to get the augefact and then we're getting out of here. All of us."

CHAPTER 42

SPIRETOP SKIRMISH

Together, Asher and Lem sprinted through Mantlecrest's hallways, stairwells and corridors towards the Spiretop Garden. All the Red Scars had mysteriously vanished, leaving Mantlecrest's corridors unusually vacant.

Asher slowed to a casual, inconspicuous walk when they stumbled across a group of elder apprentices outside one of the larger training rooms. Luckily, they were too busy huddled around a tablet of the Undergall Testament to pay them any attention. The latest breaking news of the attack in Hollow's Rest was being read loudly through the tablet's crisp audio track.

Tribune DeGrulz stood in the middle of the group. Glancing up at them, he eyed them off warily as they passed, all the while listening intently to the report as it warbled out of the tablet.

Asher and Lem heard a snippet of the report as they passed.

"…Nation is at war. The Chancellor ratified a vote mere moments ago, recalling every able-bodied tribarion, bireem and warder back to the three cities to ensure the unprovoked Skulk attack on Hollow's Rest will remain an isolated encounter.

"The Chancellor's elite guards are already investigating the breach in security and have ordered a nationwide lockdown until the scale of the threat can be properly ascertained…"

Asher and Lem desperately wanted to hear more about what had happened, but the tribune's gaze was unsettling and they had a mission to accomplish. Once they had moved passed the elder apprentices and were out of sight, they sprinted again, rushing up the last few stairwells towards the Spiretop Gardens.

"The attack must be what Braak warned us about. We have to get out of Mantlecrest and get to the safe house before it's too late," Asher shouted over his shoulder as he ran.

"At least the Red Scars are gone," Lem shouted back, trying hard to look on the bright side. "What are we going to do about Morreby? She'll die if she doesn't drain something soon, and then we're stuck."

"I'm working on it."

They emerged from the secret passage to the Spiretop Gardens in a rush. Simulated night had descended on the city and the ethereal glow of insects and plants shone and sparkled around them in the darkness. Together, they rushed under the branches of the angel oak. Ignoring the low growl of the orilla in the branches above, they pushed their way through the bamboo forest and ducked underneath the rocky outcrop until they finally reached the secret grove.

A loud screech echoed out high in the skies above, but they didn't have time to stop and gape upwards to see what made it. Asher hammered his fist hard on the trunk of Prum's hole, noticing the scorched marks and rough divots in the wood where it had been hit repeatedly with a heavy object.

"Prum, come out, we need the box."

After 10 seconds, Prum crawled out of the tree knot, dried sap staining his bark below a series of savage wounds. He looked weaker than ever and his tiny body was laced with deep cuts, a ghastly yellow sap still weeping from the wounds.

"Prum, what happened to you?"

"Scar Red. Torture much."

"Prum, I'm so sorry. I never thought..." Asher's mind flashed with fear. "Oh no! The box, Prum, tell me you didn't give them the box."

"Box safe. Nothing give. Vindicat now."

"It's inside the box. Give it to me and I'll give you some."

In agony, Prum disappeared for a second and then spat the box out from the hole, crawling weakly out after it.

Asher caught it roughly and said a silent prayer, thanking whoever was listening that it was safe.

"Vindicat!" Prum demanded.

Withdrawing the small wax seal from his tunic, Asher pressed it into the ring on the side of the box. It cracked ajar, releasing a small puff of dust. Asher lifted the lid to fetch the vial of Vindicat to reward Prum when a horrendous ear-splitting wail sung out across the gardens.

Lem and Asher dropped what they were carrying to hold their hands over their ears, sinking to their knees under the severity of the incapacitating screech. The box fell to the ground, its contents spilling out onto the lawn.

Asher craned his neck to see where the wail was coming from, only to find it echoing from Prum's sap-filled mouth. As the wailing subsided, Prum hurled abuse at them across the grove in a series of high-pitched shrieks.

"Vile. Hurters. Fiends. Villains."

Asher and Lem got back to their feet. Asher picked up the augefact and vial of Vindicat in his hands. "Shut up, Prum, someone's going to hear you." Asher tried to calm him down, but the querelus bark was enraged.

"Evilness. Wicked. Tricksters. Sageroot savages."

"What?" Asher asked not understanding.

"Prum's arm. Butcher. Hatchet. Defiler."

Asher looked to the augefact and back to Prum, his eyes instantly locking on the deformed blackened stump where Prum's other arm should've sat, understanding why Prum was so upset. Alvah Sageroot had made the augefact out of Prum's arm. She'd been the one bringing him the Vindicat all those years ago.

"Prum, I'm sorry, I didn't know."

"Asher," Lem whispered.

"Wretched. Wicked. Horrible. Traitor!" Prum's wails deafened all other noise in the grove.

"I can make this right," Asher screamed at the Querulous Bark over his ear-splitting cries.

Lem grabbed Asher's arm and spun him around. The menacing eyes of 10 ferocious orillas had materialised behind them in the darkness of the grove, each beast snarling ferociously.

Asher immediately realised that the orillas had been guarding Alvah's secret all this time. This was the grove where she'd created the augefact after tricking Prum and tearing off his arm-like branch. She'd put the orillas here as a final defence to stop anyone finding out about the horrors of what she'd done.

"What now?" Lem whispered unable to move.

Asher gulped down his fear and slipped off the cap of the vial of Wormwood Vindicat and dropped a couple of drops within the augefacts central hole. Instantly, the claw awakened, sparking the stationary pack of orillas to life, causing them to writhe and jump about in a fury. He pointed the augefact at them and they reluctantly calmed down, instinctively yielding obedience to the augefact, though many still bared their fangs and hissed at the two of them.

"Stick close to me," Asher instructed Lem as he made his way through the darkness, the savage pack of orillas parting around them as they edged out of the grove. Prum's wails ceased as his small abused body disappeared back within his tree.

"That can't be good," Lem whispered under his breath, trying hard not to anger the pack of orillas any further.

With the still-wriggling augefact outstretched, they emerged from under the rocky outcrop and through the bamboo forest, underneath the massive branches of the angel oak. The savage pack of orillas remained hot on their heels, bounding into the branches of the angel oak above them and racing forward to block their escape.

"How long does that thing last for, anyway?" Lem whispered anxiously, looking at the writhing talons of the augefact in Asher's hands.

"No idea." No sooner than Asher had finished muttering the words, the augefact stopped moving as if on cue.

"Prac," Lem swore under his breath.

"Run!" Asher screamed, augefact in one hand, vial of Vindicat in the other. There was no time to reload the liquid into the augefact; the orillas would be on them in seconds.

Lem didn't need to be told twice, his legs already moving faster than they ever had before. They burst out from under the enormous sprawl of the angel oak's branches at full pelt, the guttural violent snarls echoed out around them spurring them on all the more. An explosive gust of wind knocked them both to the ground as the giant body of a calior swooped down in front of them, buffeting them with its enormous wings.

It landed with a tremendous thump of its tail, its clawed feet scratching at the earth as enormous wings extended out on either side of its body. Bellowing an aggressive howl, the colossal beast flapped its opaque leathery wings back and forth, and snapped its jaws at them, barraging them with a torrent of air laced with the scent of its foul-smelling breath.

The pack of orillas hissed back at it ferociously, standing their ground and violently shaking the foliage and branches around them, making the entire garden seem alive and threatening.

Asher and Lem were trapped.

Asher clambered up to his knees and stared at the huge winged beast in front of him with eyes panicked with fear. Then his body froze, his limbs locking up as raw unbridled terror engulfed his consciousness.

"Praccing hell, Asher. Move!" Lem roared at the top of his lungs, just as the savage ivory tusks of the calior charged at them both. Lem pushed Asher's body aside at the very last moment before the immense bulk of the calior slammed headfirst into the pack of snarling orillas behind them.

Claws and fangs lashed out violently in every direction as the orillas battled against their new aggressor. More orillas rained down from the trees above the beast's wings, each seemingly larger and more vicious than the last.

The calior managed to shake off three of the orillas from its shoulders, but not before their razor-sharp fangs bit deep into its exposed flesh. The calior's powerful tail thrashed about viciously, knocking several more orillas to the floor. Spinning around, its claws dug into the ground and it viciously twisted its entire body

90 degrees, sending its tail crashing into the chest of a slightly smaller orilla which, in turn, sent it flying over Asher's and Lem's heads.

The orillas fought ferociously, pummelling their much larger opponent with a constant assault of teeth and claws. Wave after wave attacked and retreated, scaling back up the angel oak's trunk and scurrying along its branches before launching themselves back into the skirmish once more. They rained down on top of the calior's exposed head, back and wings, savagely thrashing at its hide with their claws.

The calior's wails echoed around the garden as it became overwhelmed by the sheer number of aggressors. It was almost about to collapse under the weight of orillas on its back when a second calior, larger and fiercer than the one already engaged in battle, joined the battle. Swooping down from on high, it snatched an orilla in each claw before closing its jaws over another's head, decapitating it and hurling the bloody mess towards the rest of its marauding brethren.

Asher remained transfixed on the ground, unable to act. Eyes wide with fear as the spectacle of death unfolded mere metres from his feet.

"Asher, let's go!" Lem yelled, and pulled Asher to his feet, forcing movement back into his limbs. "Snap the prac out of it. Wake up!"

Together, they ran as fast as they could, ducking in between the bulk of the two enraged caliors. Lem punched one orilla square in the face as it came at them out of nowhere, sending it sprawling backwards into the brush, just as Asher vaulted over the thrashing tail of the second calior.

The two sprinted through the brush, keen to disappear long before anyone learnt they were the catalyst responsible for sparking a primal war to life on Mantlecrest's rooftop. Primeval screams echoed all around them and foliage slapped at their faces as they rushed, stumbled and staggered their way towards the garden's hidden exit.

Lem swore loudly as he tripped over something behind Asher, scooping it up and slinging it over his shoulder as he ran, whilst Asher held on to the augefact and the vial of Vindicat for dear life. The two of them disappeared down through the hollow tree and into the safety of Mantlecrest's stone corridors.

"Remind me never to offer to help you again," Lem mumbled at Asher as he stuffed the small body of the unconscious orilla slung over his shoulder into the rucksack he'd left by the entrance.

Asher stuffed the augefact and the vial of Vindicat safely inside his tunic, when he caught Lem smiling down at his bag with a wicked grin on his face.

"Morreby's going to love you, Chucka."

The two of them made sure the hallway was clear before carefully heading back downstairs to Surio's Sanctuary.

Mantlecrest was abuzz with movement. The cacophony of commotion from the rooftop had everyone on alert as they mistook the calior and orilla battle for another Mortis Skulk attack. Asher wasn't about to stop to correct them. Trying to be as inconspicuous as possible, he averted his eyes from the lingering gazes of the other apprentices as he and Lem painstakingly navigated back through Mantlecrest's many hallways and stairwells. When they finally reached Surio's Sanctuary, they banged heavily on the door three times.

Lorrelli opened it an inch, a grim look on her face.

"You're just in time; she's gotten worse."

Morreby was lying limply on the floor, struggling to cling to her own consciousness. Her back was propped up against the ceremonial font, but her head drooped lazily to the side. Her eyes were the only things still registering the world around her, the slow determined blink of her eyelids letting the others know she was still conscious.

Lem quickly unfurled his rucksack and emptied the orilla's unconscious body on top of the ceremonial font. The small body of the orilla engulfed the stone bowl, its limbs overflowing, dangling limply over the edges.

Lorrelli and Asher picked Morreby up off the ground and held her up between them, facing the font.

"Oh, no you don't. Nobody's dying on me today," Asher groaned as he fished out her auger from around her neck and slapped it hard in Morreby's hand, trying to instil some life in her.

They waited for Morreby to drain the orilla, but she did nothing. Her head just lolled lifelessly from side to side.

"She's too weak," Lorrelli said.

"Sod that," Lem said harshly, grabbing a pin from within his tunic and pricking one of the orilla's paws. It didn't move. It was still out cold. Grabbing Morreby's hand, he held her remorauger underneath the wound. Squeezing the orilla's skin together, a single drop of blood oozed out of its leathery paw and hung on its skin. Without hesitation, he smeared the blood on the surface of Morreby's brown auger.

The effect was instantaneous.

The auger ignited with the taste of blood and pulsated with energy, revitalised. It drank deeply, drawing more blood from the small pinprick. At first, it was barely more than a trickle of blood, but soon small lacerations appeared all over the orilla's body, spewing its thick orange blood into the basin of the font.

Morreby slowly raised her head, her body regaining some of its lost strength as the orilla's life force reignited energy throughout her limbs. As her muscles slowly came back under her control, she lifted her arm out of Lem's grasp. After a minute, she was standing upright unsupported. The pallid colour of her skin slowly grew darker as colour flowed back into her cheeks. After three minutes, she was back to full strength, standing as strong as ever. She severed the drain her remorauger held over the orilla's bloody body.

"Cutting it a bit close, weren't you?" she whispered, pulling the orilla's body to the floor and dragging it to the side of the room. Before anyone could respond, a low rumble reverberated up from the floor. Moments later, the pool of blood filling the ceremonial font's basin bubbled, emitting a low distorted voice.

"Come forth, young Letifer, don't be shy. A remorauger's hunger need not see you cry. Surio's Sanctuary provides life and more. Now drink deep your thirst in the Mantle's core."

"Not much of a poet, was he?" Lem scoffed.

As each word resounded around the small chamber, they became emblazoned on the circular stones surrounding the ceremonial font. One by one, each etched stone sank down deep into the floor, creating a series of circular steps, until a spiralled stone stairwell had consumed the centre of the room around the ceremonial font.

"Well come on, then," Morreby said forcefully, fully reinvigorated now that her remorauger's hunger had been satiated. "Let's get the hell out here."

CHAPTER 43

WHAT LIES BENEATH

With renewed purposed, the newly formed band of unlikely companions descended down the spiral stairwell into the Undercellars, Morreby in the lead, all too eager to escape the prison-like clutches of Mantlecrest. The farther they descended around the narrow winding staircase, the more the air grew stale. With every step they took, the walls became increasingly claustrophobic and, pretty soon, all light from the auglights in the room above vanished amidst the stairwell's oppressive darkness.

"Did anyone bring an auglight?"

"I've got a couple." Lorrelli reached into her bag and withdrew two. She passed one forward to Morreby and one back to Lem.

They had gone down four floors when the stairwell unexpectedly opened out into a long corridor extending away into darkness. Their auglights shone brightly in their hands but did little to unmask the darkness clinging to the walls, roof and floor. Morreby swung hers to the nearest wall, revealing to the others that it wasn't darkness at all. It was mould. It had overgrown the Undercellars in a living tapestry of blossoming fungal spores.

"If I remember correctly, the mould was thickest much further in, but how will we know what we're looking for?" Morreby whispered.

"Hopefully, I'll be able to see it." Asher raised his hand to his head and peered down the corridor. It was no use. Even his divine eye couldn't pierce through the thick augmented layer of mould. Withdrawing the augefact, he held up the vial of Wormwood Vindicat to the light. It was a little over half full.

"I don't want to waste it until we're closer to whatever the mould's hiding down here."

"It's hiding everything," Lorrelli said unhelpfully, scraping a finger on the wall, collecting a small clump of damp asparagus-coloured moss with her finger.

"Follow me, I'll show you where the mould was thickest." Morreby resumed the lead and set off, her feet squelching softly with each step.

"I don't suppose anyone's considered the fact that perhaps it's not wise to mess with something Weyglo Mortima and Alvah Sageroot took such extreme measures to hide."

Nobody answered, although Lorrelli's concern did raise doubt in all their minds.

After a few minutes of cautious headway through several indistinct mould-covered corridors, Asher decided to feed the augefact a few drops of Vindicat and search the walls for signs of any symbols.

The effect was instantaneous.

The second the augefact's claws wriggled to life, every square inch of mould around them evaporated in a puff of greenish-yellow haze, leaving behind the cold grey chiselled masonry of Mantlecrest's Undercellars.

"Whoa," Morreby exclaimed in surprise as the spongy growth under her feet vanished.

"Anything?" Lorrelli asked Asher as he scanned the walls for any sign of the symbols.

Asher kneeled down to check closer to the floor and saw two small symbols about a foot apart from each other. "This way." Asher took the lead, the revitalised augefact outstretched in front of him, obliterating all traces of the mould within range.

"If you've got mould, there's nothing quite like Sageroot's secret mould killer, made with real Sageroot," Lem said in a mock announcer's voice.

Lorrelli sniggered at the remark, but Morreby just looked at him darkly.

"You really are a bell-end. You know that, right?"

"Hardly fitting words for the brave hero that saved your life," Lem winked at her in the darkness.

"Idiotic child, more like." Morreby shook her head at him.

It was clear to Asher that Lem had suffered no lasting emotional side effects of his prolonged exposure to whirlpool clarity. His weird sense of humour had returned in full force.

"The symbols are getting higher," Asher interrupted, cutting off their conversation, just as the Wormwood Vindicat wore off on the augefact and it became lifeless in his hand once more. Almost instantly, the mould grew back over the walls and floors it had just cleared at an unnatural rate.

"We must be getting close, look how fast it's growing back."

Morreby put her hand on the wall and watched mould grow back around it. The shape of her hand print remained on the wall for only seconds before it disappeared beneath the thick algae-like mould.

Asher dribbled a few more drops of Vindicat into the augefact and set off again, quickening his pace. After a few more narrow halls and several corners later, the passageway stopped entirely. Asher had led them to a dead end.

"Now what?" Lorrelli said, looking around. The corridor opened up into a small semi-circular alcove, with a single flat wall sitting directly opposite them, which cut the alcove's perfectly round exterior in half.

Asher said nothing, opting instead to inspect the wall with auger raised to his head. A single symbol, much larger than any other he'd seen, stood halfway between the floor and the ceiling in the centre of the wall. The augefact stopped wriggling in Asher's hand, depleting the source of Vindicat inside its core.

Asher and the others took a step back as a flood of green mould spewed forth from the symbol's centre, enveloping the walls in a tidal wave of unoppressed growth.

"Well safe to say, whatever Alvah was hiding, I'm pretty sure it's behind this wall," Asher said softly.

"You think?" Lem scoffed.

"Or on the wall." Morreby chimed in.

"Great, so how do we get at it?" Lem inspected the wall. He saw nothing but mould. "Whatever it is."

"First problem first, how do we get rid of the mould once and for all?" Lorrelli asked, trying to think out the problem logically.

"It's got to be something to do with the augefact," Lem stated. "Obviously."

Asher quietly checked the vial of Wormwood Vindicat, it was nearly empty. It only had a few more drops left in it. Slowly, he poured the remaining liquid into its centre. Once again, the mould vanished as the augefact's talons sprang to life. Asher checked every inch of the wall with auger pressed against his temple, but couldn't for the see any sign of a clue. "I don't know," Asher turned around looking for help. "I can't see anything."

"It's alright, Asher, it was a long shot, anyway," Lem said in support, stepping forward. As he did so his foot tripped over a small round stone, slightly higher than the other flagstones around it.

Asher bent down and wriggled the stone out of its fixture revealing a deep black hole about the diameter of his forearm.

Morreby shone an auglight over it, but the darkness within the hole consumed all the light.

Handing Lorrelli the augefact, Asher pulled back the sleeve of his left arm and prepared to stick his hand down into the hole.

"Am I the only one that thinks sticking your hand down a dark hole in the middle of the Undercellars is probably a bad idea?" Lem's attempt at levity did little to ease the tension in the air.

Asher ignored him and plunged his arm deep inside the hole. His fingers connected with a small orb-like stone with four large grooves cut into the side of it. "There's something down here, but I can't get a grip."

"Asher don't…" Morreby flinched.

"My fingers are too thick," Asher exhaled in frustration. "They don't fit in the grooves."

"I don't think they were cut with fingers in mind," Lorrelli said, looking down at the sharp still-wriggling talons of the augefact.

Asher quickly removed his arm from the hole grabbed the augefact and carefully inserted it into the hole, trying to align the talons with the grooves as best he could. "Here goes nothing."

As soon as he felt the talons connect with the small orb, the augefact twisted around and jerked out of his grip, clasping its sharp talons into the orb's grooves. The symbol blazed to life on the wall, burning brightly within the stone. The scratchy voice of an old woman echoed up from the hole in the floor.

"Weyglo's will be done."

"Hah, I knew it," Lem exclaimed smugly, briefly glancing at the others. They were all too busy staring intently at the wall in front of them.

"The symbol, I can see it now," Lorrelli said, watching as the glowing symbol grew bold and bright in front of her. They all took a couple of cautious steps back.

Unbeknownst to the four apprentices deep in the Undercellars of Mantlecrest, small symbols were igniting all over Mantlecrest, scorching the stones around them as they burned away all traces of the mould with a fiery black flame.

After the mould had been banished back to whatever dark recesses it came from, the symbols disappeared entirely, leaving nothing but scorch marks on the walls.

If it were not for a few pairs of watchful eyes, the phenomenon might have gone unnoticed, but the sudden burst of black flames raised the suspicion of more than one person high in the corridors above.

Asher, Lem, Lorrelli and Morreby watched as the enormous symbol flared brightly for a few seconds before shrinking to a diminutive size on the wall and flickering out of sight.

"Now what?" Morreby asked.

Asher looked at the wall again, raising his hand to his head. This time he saw a golden message appear on the surface of the wall in flowing handwritten text. To his surprise, the same symbol that had just burned so brightly remained in the centre of the wall, an inscription surrounding it. He briefly described to the others what he saw when his voice trailed off.

"What is it, Asher?" Lem asked, looking blankly at the wall Asher was gazing at so intently and seeing nothing but stone.

"It's an inscription."

"What inscription?" Morreby squinted her eyes at the wall in an attempt to see what Asher was talking about. She couldn't.

"I've seen this before. Listen."

Asher read out the inscription word for word as Morreby grabbed her schedule stone and waved her auger over its surface. Lem and Lorrelli watched on over her shoulder as each word became emblazoned on the tablet's surface.

> In hallowed halls slumbers shattered mind,
> Sensing six, not seven, gifts of life entwined,
> Across plains and seas and mountains steep,
> Ill-gotten ilk my heart does naught but weep.
> Seek me out not for false desire,
> Erred pursuit swells only black blood's ire,
> Shield gilded virtue against last dark,
> Trust first in blood and hope and heart.

"Where in the seven hells of prac could you have possibly seen that before?" Lem shot him a bewildered look.

Asher turned to face them, a perplexed look of confusion covering his face. "In Ancestor's Hall, when I was first brought to Undergall."

"Where specifically?"

"On the pillar underneath Vitalsi…"

"You don't think…" Lorrelli said. "Surely not."

"I bet it is," Lem's smile doubled in size as he excitedly slapped Asher on the back.

"What are you jabbering on about?" Morreby demanded, intent on knowing to what Lem and Lorrelli were alluding.

"Asher's just discovered Vitalsior's secret passageway, the one that's never been found," Lem's beaming smile could have lit up the room, as he tousled Asher's hair enthusiastically. "Asher, you may have just found the resting place of Vitalsior himself. Maybe even the Vitalsior heart."

"Let's not get ahead of ourselves," Asher motioned for calm. "What I've found is a wall with a riddle on it."

"No, you giant spoon. You've found the doorway: the gateway to Vitalsior's secrets. We just have to work out how to open it." Lem ran his hands over the stone wall searching for a hidden lever or anything he could use as a clue.

"So that's what Alvah was hiding," Lorrelli said in amazement.

"That doesn't make any sense," Morreby said, looking down at the tablet.

"What doesn't?" Lem asked curtly.

"Assuming that your source is correct about Alvah Sageroot being Weyglo Mortima's disciple, then why would she hide Vitalsior's secret hideaway?"

"Maybe she was hiding it for Weyglo, so no-one else found it," Asher offered.

"But the mould's only been here recently. Alvah's been dead for thousands of years."

"Who gives a prying flac? Let's just work out how to open the sucker up." Lem was quickly growing impatient with Morreby's line of pragmatic reasoning as he ran his hands over the wall, searching for anything that might provide a clue.

"I think you're looking in the wrong place," Lorrelli said to Lem as she took the tablet from Morreby. She pointed at the first line of the poem. "I think this is the key to opening it."

In hallowed halls slumbers shattered mind,

"I've heard a thousand people refer to Mantlecrest's hallowed halls before," Lorrelli murmured, trying to decipher the problematic riddle.

"And slumbers shattered mind could mean to wait…" Morreby said quietly, "or die. So maybe all this was meant to be found after his death."

"Okay, so what about the next line, then?" Asher asked, staring at the writing on the wall.

Sensing six, not seven, gifts of life entwined,

"I have no idea," Lem said trying to think what gifts of life could possibly mean.

"Forget that part, look at the next lines," Morreby said hastily reading on.

Across plains and seas and mountains steep,
Ill-gotten ilk my heart does naught but weep.

"Ill-gotten ilk my heart does naught but weep," Morreby repeated slowly, looking at them expectantly with eyebrows raised, waiting for them to clue on to what she was thinking. After a few silent seconds, it was obvious they had no idea what she was on about.

"Ill-gotten ilk. Ilk means kind, family, kin." She looked at them again. Their faces remained as blank as ever. Morreby sighed heavily, "ill-gotten, as in being tricked into fathering a child with the wife of your enemy." Morreby frowned and explained, "he's talking about Weyglo. He has to be."

Everyone finally nodded in understanding.

Asher skipped to the next two lines of the verse.

Seek me out not for false desire,
Erred pursuit swells only black blood's ire,

"Not for false desire," Asher repeated. "Maybe Vitalsior created this place and hid it from Weyglo."

"Well he didn't do a very good job on that front. Alvah found it, which means that Weyglo at least knew about it," Morreby said cautiously, looking at the blank wall in front of her.

"Black blood's ire. That could mean Weyglo's anger, or bloodline, maybe…" Asher thought out loud. "So if Vitalsior knew Weyglo would find this place, maybe he made it in such a way that Weyglo would never be able to get inside."

"Prac, if his own son couldn't get in, what chance do we have?" Lem punched the wall and instantly regretted doing so, waving his newly bruised knuckles in the air as pain spread throughout his hand.

"What does sensing six, not seven, gifts of life entwined mean?" Morreby puzzled over a previous line, but Asher was too busy analysing the last two lines on the wall.

Shield gilded virtue against last dark,
Trust first in blood and hope and heart.

"What's gilded virtue?" Asher asked the others.

This time Lorrelli answered. "Maybe it means only the Vita bloodline can open it. You're a Vita, Asher, try opening it with a blood calling."

Lem waited for her to finish before shaking his head in disagreement, earnestly surprised that none of the others had heard the term before. "Gilded virtue is what Vitalsior called his blood." Everyone looked at him in surprise. "What? I like history. You should be thanking me for that titbit."

"So basically whatever's behind this wall, it won't open for anyone that doesn't have his blood," Asher exhaled despondently, staring blankly at the wall.

"Maybe a descendant could open it," Lorrelli offered, "like the mould and Sageroot augefact?"

"But Weyglo was his direct descendent," Lem argued.

"But he was also born with black blood of Mortis, not Vita's gilded virtue," Morreby interjected.

"That must be why he could never open it," Lorrelli said, "and why Alvah hid it from everyone else."

"That still doesn't explain why the mould has only recently shown up." Morreby's astute observation caused silence to fall over the small alcove as each of them pondered a possible explanation. Ten seconds passed and the silence continued, until it was finally broken by a loud pretentious voice echoing out of the darkness behind them.

"Why is it no-one ever looks beyond the obvious? Your assumption that the mould is only a recent occurrence is inherently flawed. In truth, it's existed for far longer than you give it credit. Months, years, half a decade in fact, if you want to be precise."

All four of them spun around, augers raised, ready to defend themselves against the unseen owner of the voice.

"Hardly a welcome to warm the heart, but at least you're not treating such a blatantly ill-prepared incursion into Vitalsior's vault lightly."

Gibraltair Privvybell Reine was as nonchalant as always, as he gracefully emerged from the darkness in a plush white tunic, complete with all the trimmings one would expect to find in a ballroom, not deep within Mantlecrest's Undercellars. The outfit was damp from head to toe, some metallic fastenings still glistening under the flicker of their auglights.

"Gibraltair, what are you doing here?" Asher asked flabbergasted, failing to hide his wide-eyed surprise.

Lem, on the other hand, was speechless, mouth agape, never before being so close of his childhood hero.

"Come, come, my intrepid interlopers. Did you really think I would miss out on the greatest augiological find of the millennia?"

"But how did you—" Lorrelli began, but Gibraltair cut her off with a wave of her hand.

"Augiologists never ask how. How, is best left to uninspired auglorians who chronicle such things within dusty halls in the Annals, young Miss...?"

"Lorrelli," she blushed as he tenderly bowed before her and kissed the back of her hand gently.

"I believe I may have underestimate your usefulness, the last time I almost met you," he smiled at her warmly, remembering that he did in fact snub her on Mess Hill, "my apologies."

"How did you get into Mantlecrest when Mantlecrest is under lockdown?" Morreby demanded as she inspected the man closely, noticing the dampness of his clothes. "And why are you wet?"

Gibraltair sighed and shot a disparaging look Morreby's way, rapping his cane on the floor and irradiating the clothes on his back with a surge of heat, drying them off entirely.

"Concern yourself with the when, where and who, followed closely by the what and the why. The how will always inexplicably reveal itself," he bowed one hand towards her, "as it already has, hence my presence here, Mademoiselle...?" Gibraltair let the word hang in the air, forcing her to answer.

"Fitch," Morreby snarled back at him, content only enough to give him her last name. She remained unmoved by Gibraltair's charms. "And you didn't answer my questions."

Gibraltair ignored her for a second time and stepped past her raised auger. Approaching the wall, he flicked a switch on the side of his glasses and marvelled at the sight before him. "This day is indeed fortuitous, but I fear we must hasten our endeavours in this moistened crypt before the unbridled wrath of a certain Red Scar ruins this party for all involved."

"The Red Scars have withdrawn from Mantlecrest to deal with the Hollow's Rest attack," Lem said anxiously, glancing over his shoulder briefly at the dark corridor behind them.

"Not all Red Scars are compelled to wear the uniform if better served by another. Young Master...?"

"Lem, I mean Bedlem, Bedlem Bruwell," Lem giddily beamed back at him.

Asher and Lorrelli's augers flared brightly as Lem lied about his name, Morreby's eyes narrowing as Gibraltair made a point of shaking Lem's hand.

Farrenk's cunning smile flashed in the back of Asher's mind at the mention of Red Scars, but he shook it from his mind.

"The Red Scars will be drawn to the Wormwood Vindicat," Lorrelli whispered worriedly. "Sageroot's augefact is covered in the stuff; it'll lead them right to us."

"Sageroot's augefact," Gibraltair repeated, "so that's how they hid it. It seems you have the makings of an augiologist yet, Master Bloom. No wonder Gobbler couldn't dispense with the mould, Sageroot's a powerful bloodline. I wonder if that's what he used..." Gibraltair mumbled to himself before trailing off and becoming lost in his own thoughts.

"So let's work out how to open the door already and get the hell out of here."

"Quite right, Master Bloom, if you would be so kind," Gibraltair bowed and dramatically waved his hand toward the wall.

Asher's eyes flared in surprise at the man's notion. "What? I don't know how to open it."

"And yet it must be you, Vita to Vita, blood to blood, and all that. Vitalsior always had a soft spot for his own gilded kinsman."

"Apart from Weyglo," Morreby said quietly.

The slightest turn of Gibraltair's head betrayed the fact he'd heard her, but he chose not to dignify the comment with a response.

"Give it a go, Asher," Lem gave him an encouraging nudge forward.

Gibraltair slyly cast him a tip of his hat for his encouragement, causing Lem to blush.

Asher looked at Lorrelli and Morreby to seek their advice.

Lorrelli half turned her hands up as if to say why not.

Morreby merely shook her head slowly from side to side, warning against such an action.

"Okay," Asher said, hesitantly placing his trust in Gibraltair's hands. "Stand back."

"Asher, wait! What about Weyglo's symb—" Morreby tried to speak up, but Gibraltair loudly shushed her, drowning out her cautionary cries.

Asher stepped back from the wall and raised his auger at its centre, allowing the others to retreat back into the rear passageway.

Gibraltair was seemed unfazed in regards to his safety and simply took one step to Asher's side.

"What do I do?" Asher asked Gibraltair, looking for some sort of guidance.

"Your actions matter not, only the blood in your veins."

Asher didn't know any other blood callings he could use to open things other than the one Lorrelli had taught him, so he figured, why not. Levelling his auger at the wall in question, he took a deep breath and exhaled, thinking of two words and willing the wall to open in the back of his mind.

Foris dissere.

Asher felt the familiar sting of his auger as it bit blood and welcomed the warm tingle of energy coursing through his veins. He was, however, unprepared for the recoil of raw power the symbol unleashed back at him.

His entire arm immediately became rigid, stuck out in front of him like a wayward lance, auger locked in an unseen embrace with the symbol on the wall. Struggling as he might, his arm wouldn't budge, nor could he lower his auger, or even close his fingers around it. Whatever he had unleashed, now held him prisoner in his own body.

"I can't move." Asher wheezed, struggling against his trancelike imprisonment.

Lem and Lorrelli rushed to his aid, but Gibraltair stopped them in their tracks with a swat of his cane, holding it against their chests as he shook his head at them and repeated his earlier idiom. "The how will always inexplicably reveal itself."

A shimmering darkness spewed forth from the symbol on the centre of the wall and quickly grew in size, covering the stones with a thick black ooze that randomly flared with garish streaks of purple light.

Asher heard a deep guttural chanting inside his mind, but could not understand its words, or block its unwanted intrusion. The cacophony of voices in his head increased with every inch the devilish ooze expanded across the flat surface of the wall. The noise quickly became unbearable, building to a deafening crescendo barraging his every thought, pushing Asher's sanity to breaking point.

Just when he felt his consciousness about to slip away from him entirely, a dark ethereal substance jettisoned from the wall and funnelled inside Asher's outstretched auger. Asher felt the cold clammy substance congeal inside his auger and seep into his bloodstream. Somewhere behind him, he heard his friends call out his name, but their voices seemed distant and their words died before his mind could make sense of them.

Asher watched as the ooze drained completely from the wall. The chanting inside his head reached a crescendo as the last of the thick gelatinous jet stream disappeared inside his auger. The next thing he knew, a colossal force had collided with his chest.

The impact released the wall's hold over him and violently hurled his body backwards through the air like a ragdoll. Asher smashed into his friends with such force that it knocked them all to the ground.

Gibraltair somehow sensed the impending backlash and stepped nimbly aside. He callously brushed some dust off his otherwise unmarred white coat and watched as Asher's body hurtled backwards into his friends. Casually raising one eyebrow, he looked as if he was contemplating a hefty decision in his mind as everyone else collapsed to the floor.

"What did you do?" Lorrelli screamed at Gibraltair as she regained her footing and stood over Asher's dazed body. "Asher, are you alright?"

Asher slowly nodded his head and blinked away his surprise. "I really have to learn a better way of opening things."

Gibraltair said nothing, remaining as silent as ever, gazing down at Asher with a perplexed look on his face as if half expecting something else to happen.

The others pulled themselves to their feet and were in the process of helping Asher up when the muscles in his arm cramped and seized up. Gripping his auger with his free hand, he howled and doubled over in agony.

"Asher," Lem cried out, catching his friend's collapsing body.

"What's happening to him?" Morreby's shrill voice rang out over Asher's pain-filled screams as she watched an ink-black substance ooze out of his auger and creep around the rim of his golden mantle. She tried to raise her own auger above Asher's to help when Gibraltair's hand lashed out and stopped her.

"There's no need for any of that."

"Let me go!" Morreby struggled weakly against Gibraltair's unrelenting and surprisingly powerful grip.

Asher screamed in agony, gripping his wrist hard with his uninjured hand until his knuckles turned white. His golden auger pulsated violently as it regurgitated the black ooze, most of it dribbling onto the floor and disintegrating on impact.

"Help him!" Lem demanded, looking desperately at Gibraltair.

Lorrelli roughly grabbed Lem by his tunic sleeve and held him back. "Wait, I've seen this before."

"Seen what?" Lem shouted frantically, feeling completely powerless to help his friend.

"Just wait a second."

"Lorrelli, what the prac are you talking about, look at him, he doesn't have a second." Lem pleaded with her, watching Asher, his friend, writhing in agony on the floor.

Asher fought back another urge to scream, gritted his teeth together and locked his jaw shut, as lashings of pain ripped through his hand and up his arm.

His fingers were a deformed mangled claw, black smoke and

ooze still seeping from his auger, though in much less quantities than before. Just when he thought he was about to pass out from the agony, every ounce of pain vanished. Asher's screams stopped and he blinked away his surprise, tentatively flexing his hand.

"It's alright," he stammered as he stood upright. "I'm... I'm fine."

He and everyone else around him looked down at his auger. It sat as golden as ever, the same single black jagged streak running down its centre as it always had. The only noticeable difference was that now one half of his golden mantle was lined with fine black etchings of a language Asher had never seen before.

Gibraltair marvelled at the spectacle in silence, his mind reverting back to a conversation he'd had some months ago. Whatever was spoken that day, he chose not to share with the rest of the group, content in the knowledge the man had been right all along.

"What the prac was that? And what's that on his mantle?" Lem barked at Gibraltair, channelling his rage at the man he held responsible for what'd just happened.

Gibraltair didn't have an answer for him, neither did Asher and Morreby, but Lorrelli did.

"Don't ask me how," Lorrelli spoke slowly and deliberately, "but Asher just got his first mantle element."

"My first what?" Asher asked.

"Look at your auger, it's been imbued," Lorrelli said quickly holding up her own mantle for comparison next to his. "Dopplebock extracted the essence of the seed pod for me and imbued it in my mantle. I've never heard of an auger extracting and imbuing its own element before, but yours just did."

"Aren't Vita mantles supposed to attract elements of life, not whatever dark secret Weyglo bonded to this wall?" Morreby pondered out loud, a disquieting expression settling on her face.

"Poppycock! An auger craves what it craves," Gibraltair dismissed the severity of what he'd just witnessed with a click of his fingers.

Asher glanced at his friends frightened faces one after the other. He could tell by the apprehensive expressions that everyone, including Gibraltair, knew Morreby was right. Still a little groggy, he stared at the wall and slowly raised his auger to his head to see if anything had changed. Vitalsior's golden riddle was still as clear as ever, but Weyglo's symbol had vanished entirely.

"The symbol, it's gone," Asher croaked and massaged away the stiffness from his jaw.

"Well, of course it is. Though, I'll admit, it seems gaining your trust poses a much more difficult affair. Now, shall we breach this outer barbican and press on?"

Asher was about to answer when a fierce roar bellowed in the distance behind them, echoing and magnifying off the walls throughout the maze of passageways in the Undercellars.

"What was that?" Chills ran down Lorrelli's spine as each echo reverberated in her ears.

"That, my dear, is the sound of bought time. An advantage that slips further through our fingers the longer we stand idle without action. So let us delay no further and crack open a bit of hidden treasure," Gibraltair said.

"Err, how?" Lem asked eagerly without any idea how to proceed.

Gibraltair's expression immediately changed to one of a perturbed look of annoyance. "Not how, Master Bedlam. Never how. This time all we need is who," Gibraltair smiled and put his hand inside his tunic to retrieve something.

"Who?" Morreby repeated, equally as confused as everyone else by the man's odd vernacular.

"Precisely."

"What are you talking about?" Lorrelli said trying to decipher the augiologist's baffling reasoning.

"What indeed, young inquisitors." Gibraltair twisted his cane back and forth between his thumb and forefinger. "What, begotten from the blood of who."

"He's doing my head in," Morreby exclaimed abrasively, "and he still hasn't explained how he got here, or why his clothes are wet?"

Another sickening roar echoed around them, much closer this time, followed closely by the distinct sounds of battle.

Ignoring the noise that set everyone else's nerves on edge, Gibraltair drowned both the roar and Morreby's suspicions simultaneously by reading out two lines of Vitalsior's riddle for all to hear.

"Shield gilded virtue against last dark. Trust only in blood and hope and heart."

Morreby, who'd instinctively hidden the inscription on her tablet at Gibraltair's surprise arrival, frowned heavily at the augiologist. She was definitely sure he'd not seen her tablet, which could only mean one thing. "How did you?"

"Not all of us are plagued by an insufferable blindness to our surroundings, Miss Fitch." Gibraltair shot her a dark look for asking 'how' one too many times and promptly withdrew a small glass vial containing a tiny amount of golden liquid inside.

"What's that?" Lem's eyes lit up when he caught sight of the luminous shimmering substance in the vial.

"This, ladies and gentlemen of the hour, is the last known remnants of an unspoiled bloodline…" Gibraltair carefully dribbled a single drop of the golden liquid onto the surface of his auger, "otherwise known as gilded virtue."

"Vitalsior's blood?" Lem exclaimed, utterly astonished. "How in Nac's prame did you get Vitalsior's blood?"

Gibraltair ignored the question and adopted an elegant fencing pose. With arm outstretched, he held his cane upside down like a crude foil, hilt and auger wavering in the air as he faced off against the wall, readying himself for what was to come.

"Incedo incruentatae vitalis."

Gibraltair's voice sung out around the small space as a threadbare puff of golden mist exploded from the surface of his auger. The fine gilded vapour landed on the wall, where the residue quickly set and formed a distinctive pattern. Letters, then words took shape and burned brightly before their eyes.

Another ferocious and terrifying roar reverberated down the corridor, rumbling ever closer as the sounds of battle increased. The war raging in the corridors behind them was getting closer, leaving the four apprentices more concerned than ever.

But Gibraltair only had eyes on the task at hand. He waited until the gilded residue had set within every curve and arc of the words of Vitalsior's riddle before lunging forward, striking his auger into centre of the inscription against the surface of the cold unyielding stone.

"Arguo carmen!"

The impact of his cane and blood calling made a single word from each line illuminate 10 times more brightly than the others. The rest of the riddle dimmed, before all 10 lines of the inscription melted away entirely, disappearing into the centre of the stonework, leaving behind only one word from each line on the wall.

Asher read them from top to bottom out loud, though everyone could see the words clearly themselves. "In six and heart seek blood's last hope."

"And so your secrets are laid bare to me at long last, old boy." Gibraltair smiled smugly to himself.

"How did you know how to do that?" Lorrelli asked, completely in awe of the augiologist.

"The pursuit of Vitalsior's mysteries has been a lifelong passion. I've consumed every ounce of knowledge he left behind, as well as every word, every rumour and every fable every written thing about him. Do you know what a lifetime in the man's shadow has enabled me to see?" Gibraltair looked at Lorrelli as if expecting her to know what he was about to say. When she didn't answer, he slowly raised his glasses to his forehead and exposed his eyes to them. Where pupil and iris should have been, there was only a thick film of cloudy white haze.

Asher had never seen the man's eyes before, he'd always kept them hidden behind the tint of thick lenses, but it was instantly obvious that without his glasses Gibraltair was completely blind. A devious smile spread across the augiologist's face as a lone word escaped his lips.

"Everything."

Lem gulped back his momentary surprise at the realisation that his lifelong hero was blind. He quickly looked away, re-reading the remaining words on the wall in his mind so as not to stare at the man's milky-white eyes.

"What does it mean?" Asher asked.

Gibraltair once again ignored the question as the sounds of feet slapping against the cold cobblestones and the unmistakable distinctive creak of leather met his ears. The terrifying roar of an enormous beast and the sounds of battle had long since subsided, leaving only one conclusion in Gibraltair's mind: whoever was approaching was coming at speed and with furious intent. "It seems our bought time has run short."

Gibraltair quickly stepped to the wall and dribbled another drop of Vitalsior's gilded virtue on the surface of his auger. Raising it to his lips, he recited the remaining words on the wall in order, exhaling his warm breath over the wet smear of blood.

"In six and heart seek blood's last hope."

The entire room rumbled and shook. The floor shuddered violently as the curved walls of the small antechamber revolved. A deafening grinding noise grated against their ears as the entrance to the corridor behind them became smaller and smaller. The hope of turning back now, disappearing inch by inch.

Gibraltair stepped up to the rapidly closing gap just in time to see the silhouette of a single person sprinting towards the rapidly closing gap. The corners of his mouth twinged upwards at the enraged face of the legate as she furiously rushed down the corridor.

Her hair was no longer pulled back in a tight bun, but hung loosely, flapping in the breeze in her wake. Her pearl hair clasp, with the silver peacock needles, was no longer pinned behind her head, but clenched firmly in her hand, dangerously swinging back and forth by her side as she ran. In the blink of an eye, she whipped her hand up and unleashed a powerful blood calling at him. It landed a split-second too late, rebounding harmlessly as it struck Vitalsior's augmented bastion.

The gap between them was now fully closed. The walls had fully revolved 180 degrees and ground to a stubborn halt. A musty cobweb-covered stairwell now lay in front of them. The stairs fell away in a straight line until they became lost to the looming dark that had engulfed them for a millennia or more.

Ignoring the furious pounding and frustrated muffled screams on the other side of the wall, Gibraltair flicked a switch on the side of his glasses. He rapped his cane on the floor enthusiastically and glanced at the four distrusting, frightened and confused faces staring back at him.

"I applaud your hesitation to ally your trust in me. After all, trust is something that must be earned, never given. The choice of who to trust, however…" Gibraltair nodded his head towards the muffled thumping behind them, "is another concern entirely. Though, I do hope this small trinket, might help tip the balance in my favour." He fished something out of his pocket and flicked it through the air towards Asher.

Asher instinctively caught it in his hand and slowly unfurled his fingers. His eyes immediately locked on to the small metallic object lying outstretched in his palm.

"What is it?" Lem asked bluntly.

Asher turned the small copper band over in his hand, but he already knew what it was long before he saw its silver face. He was the only one out of his friends that recognised it.

The others simply stared down at the ring. A small brown polished pebble sat in its centre, whilst seven raised lines extended away from the stone. Their gaze switched to Asher's perplexed face, awaiting an explanation.

"It's Braak's ring. He was wearing it when I met him. It was only thing he had left of his father."

"His father?" Lorrelli echoed.

"I'm glad to see the meaning is not lost on you." Gibraltair smiled and watched as Asher slipped the ring on his index finger for safekeeping.

"Hopefully, proof of Braak's trust in me is enough for the opportunity for me to earn yours." Gibraltair turned and headed down the dusty stone stairwell, his voice trailing behind him as he went. "Now, let us embark into history and discover everything it has to hide."

CHAPTER 44

THE VITALSIOR FOLLIES

"Not so fast." Morreby ran in front of Gibraltair and raised her auger at him suspiciously. "I thought you said that Red Scars were after us? That was the legate in the hall. I saw her."

Dull thuds echoed through the augmented stone wall that stood between them and the legate.

"And I remain certain that they are." Gibraltair attempted to move forward towards the dusty stairwell, unbothered by her question.

Morreby jumped in front of him and blocked his passage again, further straining the uneasy tension between the two.

"Morreby, what are you doing?" Lem frowned at her. "He's own our side. Braak gave him his ring, for prac's sake."

"I don't know who Braak is, but," she pointed at Gibraltair, "he'd better start explaining himself or we're going to have a problem." Morreby's shrill voice did not add an ounce of menace to her threat.

A demeaning smile broke out across Gibraltair's face, betraying his amusement at Morreby's taunts.

"Morreby, Braak saved me in the Blind. We are bound in blood. He would never give up his father's ring if it wasn't important," Asher attempted to reason with her.

"Listen to your friends, Morreby. I think you'll find your allegiance is somewhat misplaced. After all, to side with those, who for generations have sought only imprisonment and death for your kind, seems a tad unwise."

"What do you mean my 'kind'?" Morreby tilted her head, narrowing her eyes warily at the remark.

"Death dealers, Letifers, who else?"

Morreby's shocked expression revealed her surprise at

Gibraltair's astute observation. Gibraltair's mocking expression of pity did not help things.

"Oh, come now, you don't possess the necessary cunning to keep a remorauger like yours hidden from my eyes, blind as they might be. My dealings in the less-than-reputable underbelly of the Cruaar Nation has seen me cross paths with several of your kind. Much to their benefit," his hand instinctively patted something he'd stashed inside his tunic for safekeeping, "or mine, at the very least."

Morreby didn't know how to react, so she simply remained transfixed opposite him, her remorauger raised.

"Are you telling us that the legate is a murderer?" Asher interrupted, his mind slowly processing what Gibraltair was actually implying.

"I never thought it true, but it seems I was wrong. Ignorance truly is bliss." Gibraltair frowned at them, displaying his disappointment at their overwhelming obliviousness. "Then again, she has managed to fool everyone else in the Cruaar Nation, so perhaps you are not to blame.

"After all, too few Cruaar question the motives of their beloved Grand Chancellor. Fewer still are willing to brave the wrath of the Red Scars in the pursuit of the truth. I, however, do not share a kinship with such cumbersome notions." Gibraltair seemed to be talking more for his own benefit than theirs, cognitively reasoning out their ignorance to what he considered the obvious.

"What truth?" Lorrelli snapped.

"It seems it is once again left up to me to be the igniter of enlightenment, but I shall not spell it out for you. Uncover the truth, as I did, with logic and reason, only then will you know where the legate's allegiance stands. Perhaps then you'll not only allow, but join me, in plumbing the depths of the old boy's surreptitiousness." He swung his cane sharply at Lorrelli. "Did you not think it strange the Grand Chancellor himself appointed the legate instead of Lobrolo?"

She didn't answer. Neither did anyone else.

Gibraltair sighed and struck the tip of his cane on the floor. "It is common knowledge that a retiring legate can name their successor, yet Lobrolo Altier's choice was ignored for a nameless young upstart, hand-picked by the Chancellor."

Swatting Morreby out of the way, Gibraltair strolled past her down the darkened steps, continuing his explanation as he went.

Asher and the others had little choice but to follow him, listening to Gibraltair's voice echo back at them.

"Needless to say that unusual turn of events piqued my curiosity. The truth is she's not quite as nameless as everyone has been led to believe. Legate Seville is but her current title. It's her former appellation that's far more interesting…" His descent down the stairs hastened, moving further away from the relentless thumping against the augmented barrier. Two words echoed up from his white coat tails, "and insidious."

"Well what was it?" Asher asked, hurrying after him.

Gibraltair promptly waved a finger back and forth in the air at the question over his shoulder. "Enlightenment without insight is but the delusion of intellect." Gibraltair gently scratched his chin with the handle of his cane. "Perhaps, though, if you were to learn her first name, you'd be better able to guess her prior designation."

"So what's so special about her name, then?" Morreby's patience was quickly fading with Gibraltair's incessant and pompous musings.

"Names are but labels we bind to our conscious for the purpose of identity. Her name, however, was bound to something far more sinister," he stopped in his tracks and spun round to face them. Raising his voice he let his tongue hang on the word as it slipped past his lips. "Fear!"

"What do you mean 'fear'?" Lorrelli asked.

"If you could only grasp the complexities of why all is not what it appears to be within these hallowed halls, you would understand why your precious legate cannot be trusted. Especially by your kind." He glanced at Morreby as he twisting his cane back and forth between his fingers.

"Well, what's her first name, for prac's sake?" Lem demanded, exhausted by Gibraltair's enigmatic explanation.

Gibraltair's cane stopped abruptly mid-twirl. He tilted his head to one side and gauged each of their faces to ensure he had their undivided attention. "Scarlet, dear boy. Her first name is Scarlet."

It took a second before anyone said anything.

Asher looked around at the others, but it was Lem's mind that first made the link.

"What? Like the Scarlet Commander?" he said in ridicule.

"Precisely like the Scarlet Commander." Gibraltair touched a finger to his nose.

"But that doesn't make any sense," Lorrelli dismissed the idea, "everyone knows the Scarlet Commander was a man."

"More than a man, he was a giant of man by all accounts." Morreby seconded.

"And what better camouflage for a woman than that of a man's body? Especially one twice her size?"

"So you're saying Legate Seville is secretly a man?" Lem's face contorted at the idea.

"Hardly." Gibraltair chuckled. "I assure you, what you see of her today is real enough, to a point, but Asher knows only too well how easily it is for your own eyes to lie.

"The art of deception needs only someone cunning enough to prey on our consciousness's inherent desire to believe. Then a lie can so easily become truth. And yet behind every lie, no matter how small, there remains the deceiver: the masker of what is real and what is false, one whose actions corrupt the truth we see and use it to poison it with a lie."

"You talk of the necrotic arts?" Lorrelli nervously glanced at Asher.

"I talk of deception. I talk of devotion. I talk of the blood arts that time and time again have bent lies into truth and twisted myth into legend."

"Come on now, think! Who never left the Scarlet Commander's side during the rebellion? Who lived in the man's shadow? Who fed him all his dark little secrets?"

"The Half-brute," Morreby whispered.

"Yes, Miss Fitch, the Half-brute, a man so named for his true birthright, not for the one dealt to him by maimed appearance. A guise he lent himself so others thought him a cripple. Half human, half Chromfaddar, all brute. Who better than a man with one arm to pull the wool over your eyes and avoid suspicion of the act?"

"The Half-brute was a Chromfaddar?" Lem repeated.

"Only by half," Gibraltair twirled his cane again. "Once I discovered the Scarlet Commander's true identity, I spent years unearthing the fate of the Half-brute, the master deceiver, but all traces of him vanished after the Rebellion. Whether she killed him," he nodded in the direction of the dull sounds of pounding coming from atop the stairs, "or he merely adopted the visage of someone else entirely, I cannot say, but as he knew her true nature and all of her secrets, my bet is that his blood has long since left his veins."

The distant thumping against the wall at the top of the stairs seemed to grow louder in Asher's mind. Turning around, he peered back up into the darkness and found everyone else was doing exactly same.

"Who would've thought a name could hold so much power over a person, but the past is a hard thing to escape, harder still to bury. And to think, all this time, the most bloodthirsty and infamous Red Scar of all has sat atop Mantlecrest's proverbial throne.

"How the Cruaar Nation would revolt if it knew the truth. But, finally, her sordid secret is unmasked and you know the truth," Gibraltair smiled deviously. "But now that you know the truth, the question is: will you be able to look at her the same?"

Silence descended over them in the dark corridor, disturbed only by the faint thudding drifting down the stairwell. Gibraltair's face was alive with excitement, thrilled at finally being able to unburden his discovery and shatter their perception of the revered Legate Seville. Asher's eyes flittered from face to face, looking at each of his friends in turn. The reality had sunk in on all their faces but one: Lem just looked more confused than ever.

He kept trying to form a thought in his mind and say something, only to close his mouth a second after he opened it. Until, eventually, his eyebrows shot up and his voice cut through the silence.

"But if she was the Scarlet Commander, she must've first been a tribarion, right? But tribarions forgo their first name when they take the oath and swear allegiance to the Cohort." His eyes shot a questioning look at Gibraltair, the man had still not won his trust. "So how did you discover hers?"

Gibraltair's expression instantly perked up at Lem's interest in his accomplishment.

"Very good, young Master, you are correct in your deductions. The revelation was not easily ascertained, I assure you. Far from it. I paid a heavy price for the privilege of such knowledge." Gibraltair turned his head away so the apprentices could not see his brow furrow at the memory of a distant and torturous memory. "Needless to say, the price paid has allowed me to see the truth, especially where it has been purposely shielded from view."

For some reason, Asher could not help but think Gibraltair didn't quite believe his own words.

"One such insight was a restricted record of the ancestral bloodlines of all tribarions, including whether they hold mastery over First or Second Edicts, their most prevalent blood affinity but, most importantly, their first name prior to induction in the Cohort."

A glimmer of understanding twinkled in their eyes as Lem took a step closer to being convinced of Gibraltair's claim.

"So that's how the legate knew about the Vindicat the first time," Lorrelli stammered, trying to make sense of everything that'd happened in the past.

"If she was a tribarion and a Red Scar, then she's…" Asher reasoned.

"She's praccing well attuned to it," Lem finished his sentence. Turning around, Gibraltair was on the move again, descending downwards, two stairs at a time.

"But if she's so attuned to it, then why wasn't she on to us sooner in the Undercellars when we were dosing Sageroot's augefact with the stuff?" Morreby's question betrayed her lingering suspicion of the augiologist that, so far, she'd managed to hide, as she reluctantly followed him deeper into Vitalsior's vault.

"Bought time, naturally, or in layman's terms, the Quaridaan leviathan I released moments before joining you. Hard to chase the scent of skulkery when a devilish two-headed mountainous viper stands in your way," Gibraltair smirked unapologetically.

"Hang on," a confused expression hung over Asher's face, "the Rebellion was fifty years ago, she can't have been the Scarlet Commander. She's too young."

Gibraltair let loose a merry chuckle and continued on until the silence behind him made him realise that Asher was deadly serious. "Oh, dear boy, your ongoing ignorance stands testament to your inability to see past the truth of the matter." He turned and placed a patronising hand on Asher's shoulder. "Every Red Scar is handpicked from the very best of the Tribarion Cohort."

"So what?"

"The what, Master Bloom, is that tribarions hold mastery over three blood affinities, Scienta, Natura and… Vita." He said the last word with enhanced emphasis.

Asher looked at him blankly, not understanding what he was trying to get at.

Gibraltair suspiciously turned his head towards Asher's three friends. All three instinctively averted his gaze.

"Gutless to the last, so much for loyalty amongst thieves. I can't even imagine how you've survived this long when even those closest to you withhold secrets of such import."

"What secrets?" Asher looked nervously at his friends, but none would meet his gaze.

Gibraltair leaned forward and whispered in Asher's ear.

"The simple truth about that gilded blood of yours."

"What truth?"

"To gain mastery over the Vita bloodline is to align one's body with the timeless echoes of life eternal."

"Life eternal," Asher repeated, not understanding what Gibraltair was getting at.

"Life eternal, the prolongment of death. Tribarions know this only too well, the very weakest among them live at least two hundred years, if they are not brought down in battle first."

"Two hundred years, so the legate could have been the Scarlet Commander," Asher exclaimed in reluctant acceptance.

"Unequivocally so, yet you still overlook the most pivotal keystone of this puzzle's arch." Gibraltair bent down and lowered his face close to Asher's. "If tribarions live for two hundred years or more with only an inkling of the Vita bloodline in their veins, how long do you think a true gold-blooded Vita-born lives for?"

Asher's mind shot back to something Lem had said ages ago. *Vitalsior was rumoured to have lived for over five thousand years.* A slow realisation flooded over Asher's face as he realised what Gibraltair was trying to get him to realise.

"And understanding is ascertained at last," Gibraltair patted Asher gently on the shoulder and nodded his head. "Should you master your blessed bloodline, you'll outlive us all, Asher Bloom."

Asher looked around at his friends again, but they still refused to meet his gaze. Something was wrong, there was more they weren't telling him: something far worse than life eternal. "What aren't you telling me?"

"What, dear boy? The 'what' boils down to this: nothing is without cost in this life, least of all the act of defying death."

"Enough!" Lem snapped. "He doesn't need to hear this."

"Like hell I don't," Asher demanded sternly, silencing Lem and his objection. "What cost?"

"Time is the enemy of all things, especially a mind."

"Stop it. You don't know that," Lorrelli interrupted, breaking her silence as Gibraltair taunted Asher with glimpses of the truth.

"Oh, but I do. I've seen firsthand the madness that takes root within a mind blessed by longevity, yet corrupted by the merciless ravages of time."

"Cut it out," Lem snapped at the man.

"You think that by shielding him from the truth he would not find out when the voices come calling?" Gibraltair snapped at Lem, before sharply turning back to Asher, his speech quickening to drive the point home. "Did you not think it strange that there are so few Vox Vita within the Cruaar Nation? Surely you must have noticed you were the only Vita-born within these walls."

Asher had often wondered just that, but had dismissed the thought based on the belief they'd all been hunted down during the Guillotine Rebellion.

"The Mortis Skulk targeted and killed them because they were the biggest threat."

"Ah, but that is only half the tale." Gibraltair snatched Asher's hand in his own and squeezed. The pressure of the man's grip on his skin forced blood into his auger. "Your mind has only just tasted the first of many pains to come, but soon it will discover the madness that lurks beneath the surface."

"Let him go," Morreby feebly tried to break Gibraltair's hold over Asher, but the augiologist's grip was as hard as iron.

His expression turned dangerous as he spun around to face her. She reluctantly retreated, still fielding a venomous glare on her face. "If you weren't friend enough to tell him the truth, do not stop those who will."

His head swung back around to face Asher. "Many Vitas were killed at the hands of Skulk cultists, but many more at the whim of the council after they'd turned to join Cerebule's legions. But do you know why? Why so many Vitas betrayed their own kind to side with the Mortis Skulk? The real reason, not the one the council would have you believe?"

Asher shook his head, just wanting the pain in his hand to stop.

"Because they would've done just about anything to rid themselves from the insanity that comes with the gift of life eternal. Cerebule simply promised them a cure."

"A cure to what? What insanity?"

Gibraltair sliced a thin gash across Asher's arm with a sharp barb on the side of his cane. "To the curse your bloodline bears. To the inevitability of madness. Insanity eternal, a wretched gift, etched in your very blood." His fingers floated down and pointed at the bleeding gash on Asher's arm, inspecting the blood trickling from the wound. It was dark crimson.

"Your blood has not yet undergone its metamorphosis, but when it does you'll hear the voices soon enough and then it's only a matter of time." Gibraltair shot one last look at the other apprentices before releasing Asher's arm. Without another word, he turned and walked off down into the darkness, leaving the four apprentices to deal with the turbulent aftermath of Asher's awakening to the truth.

"Is it true?" Asher turned and asked his friends.

Lem and Lorrelli said nothing.

"He's trying to get inside your head, Asher. You can't trust him," Morreby answered.

"Why not? Braak trusts him, and right now he seems like the only one I can trust. Besides, you can lie to me, they can't." Asher stepped closer to Lem and Lorrelli. "Is it true?"

"What do you mean 'they can't lie to you'?" Morreby interjected, her curiosity rattled by Asher's words.

Asher ignored her.

"Asher, we wanted to tell you, but you already had so much to worry about. We didn't want to burden you," Lorrelli said.

"Nothing's set in stone, Asher, heaps have mastered the Vita bloodline without going nuts… mad… prac! You know what I mean," Lem stumbled over his words just as Asher's auger fired to life with an all too familiar sensation.

Lem was lying.

"Well, maybe not heaps, but High Cleric Pluwarie is one of the strongest and most powerful Vitas alive today, and he's not mad, not even a little."

This time Asher's auger remained lifeless. The black scar swayed peacefully amidst the golden centre of the gem. "You should've told me."

"We're sorry, Asher," Lorrelli apologised as Lem put a hand on his shoulder, but Asher shrugged it off.

"You've got a veritusk bind on you, don't you?" Morreby said, staring at the three of them.

"How did you…" Lem looked at her quizzically.

"Who put it there?" Morreby cut him off.

"Why does it matter?" Lorrelli snapped back at her rudeness.

"Who?" Morreby insisted.

"The legate did, on our first day here. Why?"

"Then she knows. She knows everything," Morreby said under her breath as a demoralising realisation of fear swept across her features. "We need to go. Like it or not, Gibraltair's our only way out of here now." The thought of Gibraltair being their only option demoralised her more than anything else she had heard. She did not trust the man one bit, but she found herself running down the stairwell after him nonetheless.

The rest of them bolted down after Morreby and found her standing next to Gibraltair in front of a massive iron door shimmering with augmented power in the low hue of the auglights. The top of the door disappeared high into the ceiling. There was no way to tell how high it actually extended.

Gibraltair consciously ignored their noisy approach as they came to stand behind him. His eyes were busy inspecting foreign inscriptions carved into the door's heavy metallic frame.

"The old boy does not part with his secrets lightly," Gibraltair said to himself, thinking hard on what he'd just read.

Asher decided to take the opportunity to ask him something that had been nagging him since he'd first shown up in the Undercellars. "So how did you find Vitalsior's blood, anyway?"

"Hmmm?" Gibraltair mumbled as he ran his fingers over the inscriptions on the door's frame. "What, you didn't actually think I was actually searching for my ancestor's long lost construct within Foreguard, did you? Although that discovery did prove somewhat fortuitous. Saved me a lot of digging."

He tapped his fingers over a particular inscription. The corners of his eyes cringed together as he pondered something, searching his idea for flaws. "As it turns out, Vitalsior once had his own construct of sorts."

"What do you mean?"

"Before the council's wretched lapdog put an end to my legitimate investigation within the more forgotten of Annals, I stumbled across an obscure reference to the Vitalsior follies. It was hidden deep within a rather disturbing entry, depicting a particularly invasive study of a madman's mind. A mind that had succumbed to the blood madness of Vita."

"Vitalsior follies?" Lorrelli repeated, catching up to the man.

"Are you my echo? Yes folliessssss," Gibraltair pursed his tongue and extended the word into an audible hiss to drive the point home. "It seems everyone is under the misunderstanding that the lecherous old fool cut off his fingers and his toes in a bout of madness. As it turns out, he was a darn sight more cunning and a lot less insane than the Cruaar Nation has been led to believe."

"What do you mean?" Asher asked, his mind flicking back to a similar story Lobrolo had told him in Ancestor's Hall.

"What indeed, Master Bloom. I found it strange there was only one mention of the follies in the Annals entirety."

"Why is that strange?" Lem asked, not entirely following Gibraltair's train of thought.

"Because one does not simply cut off a finger or toe in each city before disappearing without reason, mad or otherwise. Why not two toes in Undergall, and four fingers in the Shell of Symphony? No, it did not make sense."

"For once in your life, just answer the question. How did you get the blood?" Morreby snapped at the man harshly, trying to cut short his story.

"Always 'how' with you, isn't it, Miss Fitch?" Gibraltair sneered irately. "How? How? How?" He flicked a switch on his glasses and shifted his focus from the door to Morreby. "Allow me to expedite your understanding by tapping into my vast reservoir of knowledge: knowledge that has taken me a lifetime to learn and has already saved all your lives once already this day." He swatted his cane into a gloved hand and tightly clenched his fist. "Do any of you know where an augefact gets its name?"

They all looked at one another blankly. No-one had ever really questioned the origins of the word.

"It is a word we repurposed from the human term artefact, which promptly begs the question, do you know what an artefact is?"

"An ancient tool," Lorrelli answered.

"An object produced or shaped by hand, especially a tool, weapon, or ornament of archaeological or historical interest, to be a little more precise," he corrected her, flicking his cane up into his armpit as he stood with legs apart, facing them all. "Now, I already know that you are aware an augefact contains its creator's flesh or bone, so combine the two trains of thought and…" His raised his eyebrows at them, sincerely hoping he wouldn't have to explain how the two correlated.

"Vitalsior made an augefact?" Asher's eyes went wide with surprise.

"By the sounds of things he made more than one," Lorrelli corrected.

"Indeed." Gibraltair nodded his approval at her statement.

"I've never heard of any Vitalsior augefacts, no-one has," Lem rebutted the idea confidently.

"That's because he created them long before humans ever

came up with the term 'artefact'."

"So what?" Morreby said, not seeing what this had to do with anything.

Gibraltair pinched his brow between his fingers in frustration. "No artefact, no augefact, merely gifts of life. So even though I hate to state the obvious and loathe quoting a posthumously adored augmad," he waved his hand flippantly towards her, "a rose by any other name, Miss Fitch."

"Holy prac!" Lem exclaimed, completely spellbound by what he'd just heard.

"You see, there was never any other mention of his fingers and toes other than their absence, because as far as I know, the old boy created six augefacts, or gifts of life, as he liked to call them, installing them in secret within the seven cities and no-one was ever any the wiser."

"I can't believe this," Morreby's vocal scepticism echoed back from the heavy door.

"And yet the Vitalsior follies exist despite your disbelief," Gibraltair snarled at her. His growing dislike for the small death-dealer was beginning to become more obvious in the way he spoke to her.

"But why follies?" Lem asked.

"What better way to hide your gifts than let the world think you mad? Nobody searches for something that doesn't exist, especially if the only person that knew it existed was a madman."

"So that's what you were doing in the Fall of Foreguard..." Asher asked quietly.

"Looking for a Vitalsior augefact," Lorrelli finished his train of thought.

"Vitalsior's gift of life," Lem corrected, eyes alight with excitement.

"Funny you should put it like that, because the fall in Foreguard is exactly where I found one of the old boy's gifts."

"Don't you mean the Fall of Foreguard?" Morreby smiled to herself at catching Gibraltair's apparent slip of the tongue.

"I do not misspeak," Gibraltair barked at her, quickly running out of patience with the girl's incessant distrust. "The common misconception that the Fall of Foreguard refers to the city's demise is as flawed as that auger of yours. The Fall of Foreguard was named as such for the ever-flowing waterfall that made existence within that barren wasteland possible. A gift of life, if you will."

"An augefact can't be a waterfall." Morreby rebutted the very notion of the idea.

"But it can be the augmented font from which it stems," Gibraltair snapped back, "which is what took me months to excavate deep within the fetid bowels of that wretched place. When I finally unearthed it, it was still bubbling away with life-giving water. Even after decades of entombment beneath the decrepit black sands of war."

"You found it?" Lem's eyes lit up.

"Of course I found it," Gibraltair said arrogantly. "Where else would I be able to extract Vita's Virtue that I used to penetrate this infuriating vault. Pity I had to destroy the augefact to do so."

"You destroyed a Vitalsior augefact," Lem clasped his hands over his head in dismay.

"As you destroyed Sageroot's augefact," Gibraltair snapped, and turned once more to face the door standing before them. "Double standards are so unbecoming Master Bruwell. Now, if I've explained the course of my actions to your satisfaction, I'll need your auger if we hope to bypass this particular inner bastion and breach said ark."

"What ark?" Lorrelli asked.

Gibraltair ignored her and turned his head at Lem, awaiting his reply.

"My auger?" Lem asked, his mind still stumbling over Gibraltair's revelations.

"Should you wish to proceed, the inscriptions clearly states," Gibraltair pointed at each word of the inscription with his cane, translating the ancient text as he went, "only an unblemished heart unlocks vaulted ark."

"What's that supposed to mean?" Asher asked.

"Interpret it not as you would, but as the mind that first scratched groove into steel."

"So think like Vitalsior?" Lorrelli clarified.

"Precisely."

"Everyone referred to his auger as his heart," Lem said under his breath.

"And, again, we reach an understanding." Gibraltair looked back at the door. "Only an unblemished auger will unlock vaulted ark. A rather simple defensive mechanism, I'll admit, but also a particularly ingenious one."

"Why's that?" Lem asked confused.

"I highly doubt anyone intelligent enough to discover and, indeed, venture this far into the old boy's clandestine crypt would do so in the company of an unaligned Cruaar. Thereby, they would remain trapped at this impasse and would be unable to retreat through the revolving wall above. Henceforth, entombing said unfortunate souls in this wretched catacomb forever."

Lem gulped at the prospect.

"I must say it is fortunate we all find ourselves here together. Without me, you would have never made it past the outer bastion, but without you I would not have made it past the inner. I knew fate's shadow was cast over us for a reason, Asher Bloom, I'm just thankful I was clever enough to listen." Gibraltair stepped away from the door and motioned for Lem to approach.

Lem glanced nervously at the others. They had little choice.

He anxiously stepped towards the massive iron door.

Morreby leaned towards Asher, close enough that only he would be able to hear what she had to say. "If there is a Vitalsior augefact down here, we can't let him get his hands on it."

Asher twisted Braak's ring on his index finger, his mind registering the serious glint of distrust in her eyes as she looked darkly at Gibraltair.

"I don't like our chances of getting out alive if he does."

CHAPTER 45

VITALSIOR'S VAULTED ARK

The faint thumping against the wall at the top of the stairs had long since subsided, replaced, instead, by an eerie quiet, interrupted only by the sounds of their uneasy feet scraping against the stone floor.

By Asher's reckoning, their downward passage had led them far below even the lowest sewer of Undergall. Surprisingly, the floor and walls were dry and warm to the touch: not moist or damp as he expected. The more he thought about it, the temperature had been steadily rising with every step of their descent, and it was obvious everyone was sweating.

Gibraltair didn't seem to mind the heat, but every couple of seconds he flicked a switch on the side of his glasses to clear them from the damp haze fogging up the lenses.

Asher raised his auger to his head and inspected the giant iron door with his divine eye. He ignored the dull lingering pain in his arm and hand, and examined it in depth, half expecting to see some form of trap, symbol or hidden inscription jump out at him from its surface.

None did.

The enormous blockade was as simple as it looked. In fact, except for the occasional shimmer of augmented power that lay dormant on its surface, everything about the massive metal wall seemed normal.

"So what can we expect to find down here?" Lorrelli asked Gibraltair.

"The Vitalsior heart," Lem offered meekly, trying to ease the tension.

"We should be so lucky." Gibraltair placed a hand on Lem's shoulder. "I'm afraid that despite my substantial knowledge and extensive research, I haven't the foggiest what lies beyond yonder wall. The only person that's ever seen this place has been gone a very long time."

Lem went red with a mixture of anxiety and excitement as he felt Gibraltair's hand land on his shoulder. Even the smallest of actions from the famed augiologist still had a profound effect on him.

"Our journey's continuance rests solely on your shoulders, Master Bruwell."

"Okay..." Lem's excitement at being the focus of Gibraltair's attention momentarily overpowered the growing concern for his own safety. He squared off against the massive iron barricade in front of him. "Err, what do I do?"

Gibraltair frowned briefly, not willing to openly admit he was not quite sure himself. "A simple problem often demands a simple solution. Try touching your auger to its surface–"

"Be careful," Morreby muttered, cutting short Gibraltair's offered advice.

Lem glanced back at Asher over his shoulder.

Asher curtly nodded, he was obviously still a little bitter about his friend's omission of his bloodline's curse.

Lem took a step closer to the wall: it was now within his reach. He unclasped his apprentice mantle from around his neck and gazed down at his colourless auger. He would never have imagined his failure to be aligned would turn out to be such a fortunate, life-saving occurrence. Slowly, he extended it towards the door.

Turning his head away from the massive iron blockade, Lem closed his eyes. He turned his body to the side and used his free hand to awkwardly cover his crotch. He couldn't help but think something horrible was about to happen. Ever so softly, he tapped his auger against the surface of the door. The gentle rap was as light as the touch of a pencil, yet it echoed around the room like the beat of a drum, growing softer with every reverberation.

Lem opened his eyes and peered around.

Nothing had happened.

The door stood as resolute and unyielding as ever. Quickly removing his hand from his crotch, Lem turned around to face the others, hands extended upwards by his side.

"Well, that didn't work."

"Anticlimactic as ever, Master Bruwell, I agree." Gibraltair's obvious disappointment in Lem made his idoliser's shoulders visibly sink.

"Hold it against the wall, maybe it needs some time to release the lock," Lorrelli encouraged him.

"What lock?" Lem mumbled dejectedly.

"Whatever is locking it in place."

Lem nodded and faced off against the door again, this time a little less excited than before. He raised his hand and rapped his auger against the cold metal again, a little harder this time, holding it in place against the surface of the metal. Seconds passed as the echo sung out, rebounding off the walls and unpleasantly into their ears. Lem pivoted his waist and turned his head to look at the others, keeping his auger firmly pressed against the surface of the door.

"Now wh—"

Before he could finish his sentence a single spark of light flashed inside his auger and jagged cracks of light appeared on the surface of the iron barricade. Each crack splintered and split again and again until a spider web of lightning-scarred streaks covered the iron door's surface. Lem stumbled back a step, his expression a mixture of awe and fear.

"Marvellous to the last. Who would've thought? A shatterweb seal, still intact after all this time." Gibraltair slapped his hand on Lem's back in approval, causing a wide smile to break out across Lem's face as the young man blushed.

"What's a shatterweb seal?" Asher asked, watching shards of light crack and splinter outwards from the centre of the web.

Gibraltair sighed loudly and explained as succinctly as his

wearying patience would allow. "Imagine a spider web rolled flat to no thicker than an atom, yet ten times stronger than steel, especially when set upon by the wrong auger, but, if set upon by the right auger, ten times more fragile than glass." Gibraltair pointed to the edges of the shatterweb slowly disappearing from view, steadily merging back together into one unified invisible shield.

"It's the perfect security measure, really, practically invisible to the untrained eye, but infinitely deadly if opened incorrectly, or by force. The shatterweb crack you see before you is a warning, another hit from the wrong auger would see the entire wall explode in our faces, but Lem's auger should be just peachy." Gibraltair patted Lem on the shoulder, a large smile on his face as he encouraged the apprentice to repeat his actions. "Well, what are you waiting for? Hit it again."

Lem didn't blush this time, Gibraltair's words only served to renew the trepidation and fear running through his veins. "And get a wall exploding in my face if you're wrong? Prac that. You hit it!"

"Very well," Gibraltair sighed exhaustedly, grabbing Lem's hand. Before anyone could object to his actions, Gibraltair grabbed Lem's arm and swung it high above the Apprentice's head and brought it down hard against the surface, directly in the middle of the ominous shatterweb cracks.

The distinctive clank of Lem's auger reverberated around them 10 times louder than the noise that preceded it. The sound rumbled off the walls and ceiling as though a massive gong had been struck. The shimmering cracks of light on the wall splintered and fractured one after the other. A thousand shards broke free from the barricade's surface and fell in a heap on the floor, disintegrating into oblivion a moment later.

"Trust, once earned, can be a wonderful virtue," Gibraltair smiled to himself just before a deafening rumble engulfed the room. The stones in the walls and roof vibrated fiercely in the wake of the auger-made thunder, raining a deluge of dust down around the group. The thunderous reverberations and tremors originated somewhere high above them, as something triggered and released the massive iron stronghold from its locking embrace.

Inch by inch, the top of the iron door edged away from the ceiling and the roar of heavy iron chains tore through the group's ears as the barricade picked up speed and fell forwards. It tore away from the anchors that had held it in place for millennia and showered them in a hazy orange glow as the gap between the wall and door widened. The light consumed the darkness and the feeble glow of their auglights simultaneously.

As the massive iron wall's rigid iron face roared away from them, they realised the giant barrier wasn't a door or a barricade at all. It was the bottom section of an enormous drawbridge.

With every passing second, more of it fell away and came into view. Asher marvelled at its sheer magnitude. As it dropped past a 45-degree angle, Asher saw his first glimpse of the massive chains responsible for the thunderous roar tearing through his eardrums. Mammoth iron rungs, as thick as Asher's torso, tore away from an unseen wall high above his head.

With a thunderous boom, the drawbridge collided with the earth, its roaring chains finally coming to a stop. The resulting force of the impact shook the walls around the group and the floor beneath them. Everyone's knees buckled as the shuddering spread uncontrollably up their legs, just as a wave of intense heat hit them in the face.

Lem's shivering, petrified silhouette standing in front of the ominous glow was the only thing blocking Asher's view of the enormous, phosphorescent cave beyond. Its roof was illuminated by a million pinpricks of iridescent blue light. The light covered a thousand hardened lavacicles stretching down from the cavern's craggy ceiling, threatening to fall at any moment.

Stepping forward, Asher realised only the base of the drawbridge was made of the hard-forged iron, whilst three quarters of its length comprised of enormous wooden beams:

many of which were rotten, probably from the vapour-clouds of water-rich steam wafting upwards from below.

Lem slowly opened his eyes and marvelled at what he saw. The length of the drawbridge stretched away in front of him across a vast chasm that dropped away at least 100 feet to either side. All around the enormous cavern hundreds of tiny streams of lava trickled and fell from cracks in the roof, small pockets of steam left wafting in their wake. A few small splotches of lava had already landed on the vast wooden stem of the drawbridge during its descent, melting small holes and divots in the decaying wood in a fierce spatter of smoke and fire.

Veins pumping with adrenaline and face lined with sweat, Lem stepped forward onto the drawbridge. Unable to stop himself, he approached the nearest edge and anxiously leaned forward to peer into the depths below.

He immediately regretted his decision.

At the bottom of the gorge, a violent mass of gurgling lava bubbled and churned like an enormous cauldron of stew, sending up wild plumes of hot air. Far ahead of Lem, the two enormous chains converged at the end of the massive drawbridge. The end of the enormous structure was locked into place against a prehistoric stone platform that rose up out of the lava bed below like a precarious beanstalk.

Farther still, beyond the central stone landing, three narrow craggy paths extended away like gnarled fingers and stretched across to the far side of the abyss. Each was balanced on top of a series of haphazard stone columns, made up of hundreds of different boulders perilously and impossibly stacked on top of one another. The three paths looked as though they were only seconds away from collapsing into the lava below.

On the far side of the chasm where the three paths converged, an enormous cylindrical shaft extended all the way from the lava bed to the cavernous roof. A small recessed alcove lay directly opposite from the group, but much of its detail was engulfed by the intense light threatening to blind anyone who looked directly at it for too long.

"Nothing to it, eh?" Asher patted Lem on the back as the others cautiously stepped out onto the iron base of the drawbridge alongside their friend.

Lem jumped back from the edge of the drawbridge in fright when he felt a hand land on his back. "Praccing hell. Are you trying to scare me to death?"

"Pretty righteous trick for someone with less blood callings than your average doorstop," Lorrelli teased as she came to stand on Lem's other side.

Gibraltair, however, did not stop for pleasantries. Instead, he marched past them and out across the smouldering wooden section of the drawbridge. He nimbly bounced from beam to beam, ducking and weaving between the falling streams of lava responsible for a number of small fires breaking out on the drawbridge's oversized length.

"Tarry not for wonder's sake. Only the promise of flames awaits those who linger," his voice echoed back at them.

Lem, Lorrelli and Asher glanced at one another briefly before another large splat of lava dropped heavily a short distance in front of them, igniting a large fire in the middle of the drawbridge.

Lorrelli didn't waste any time and started retracing Gibraltair's route across the drawbridge as best she could.

Asher quickly followed, giving the falling globules of red hot lava a wide berth as he went.

As each missile of lava landed, the impact sent clusters of smaller lava droplets scattering in every direction, sparking more pockets of fire as the liquid fed on the timber beams. Soon hundreds of plumes of black smoke were visible, rising and converging into a thin ash cloud high in the vast cavernous roof.

Lem was hesitant to move at first, but did not want to be left behind.

Gibraltair had already reached the central platform and stood with his back to them, his cane by his side. His focus was transfixed by something within the glowing alcove on the opposite side of the gorge. The drawbridge creaked and groaned under their combined weight and the growing mass of lava burning holes in its centre.

Lorrelli and Asher were already most of the way across the drawbridge, which was now dangerously ablaze.

Lem, however, had fallen behind due to his fear of heights, which slowed his pace in navigating across the burning bridge. Caution and dread overwhelmed his nerves as chilling memories of his previous plunge off the observatory tower filled his thoughts. His mind was so intently focused on each nervous step forward that he was completely oblivious to the fact Morreby hadn't taken a single step forward.

Everyone was.

Her frail body stood rooted to the spot in the antechamber, unable to move. It wasn't even Lem that eventually noticed her absence, but Lorrelli, who'd spun around once she'd stepped off the drawbridge and reached the relative safety of the central platform.

"Morreby, what are you doing? Come on, hurry up! The bridge won't hold much longer," her faint voice called out across the chasm.

Morreby didn't hear Lorrelli's cry, but Lem did. It was enough to make him turn around on the bridge and stare in her direction.

"Move it, Fitch. Don't make me come back there to get you!"

Lem's harsh words broke through her daze, but fear had her in its grips. Her terrified eyes looked back at him and she shook her head.

Lem looked towards the others for guidance.

Asher was already heading back, when Lem shouted at him and waved him forward with his arms. "Go. Go. I'll get her!" he shouted and angrily spun around, and picked his way back between the fires towards the drawbridge's iron base. "Don't worry about it. Lem'll take care of it. He loves dodging lava to rescue a praccing death dealer," he mumbled under his breath, narrowly avoiding a falling globule of lava that exploded like a fiery cluster bomb two feet to his left.

The flames around his feet were already ankle high and rising fast: some flames were already as high as his knees and thighs. With a little less caution in his movements, Lem quickly navigated his way back across to the cool iron base and into the antechamber, where he firmly grabbed Morreby by the hand.

"Time to go, you baft dint."

She resisted, stammering a weak response, "I'm not good with heights."

"You're joking, right? You'll suck the life out of a rat, but heights are too much? You're unbelievable. I got pushed off a praccing rooftop and even I can do this, so let's go." Lem pulled on her arm again, harder this time, turning his head back towards the bridge. Morreby resisted and struggled against him. Without looking back, he yanked on her arm, forcing her forward a few steps.

"I can't," she muttered, peering over the sides of the drawbridge and down into deep recesses of the fiery gorge. The sight that met her eyes only increased the level of terror in her mind.

"You're running out of time," Asher's voice floated towards them over the flames, but he wasn't sure if his friends heard him or not.

"Isn't there anything you can do?" Lorrelli tugged on Gibraltair's sleeve.

"Hmmm," Gibraltair turned around, his train of thought broken. He looked across the burning drawbridge and heaved a loud sigh to no-one in particular, raising his cane at the flames. "Why does no-one ever heed instruction?"

Gibraltair waved the tip of his cane in an intricate pattern at the growing flames on the drawbridge. The spot of lava he aimed at instantly exploded into a blazing fireball, raising the level of the flames a foot higher than they were before, obscuring Lem and Morreby from view. "Augmented lava," Gibraltair said, perplexed. "Well that's a first."

"What did you do? They'll be trapped over there," Asher shouted at him trying to look over the engorged flames.

"Well it's hardly my fault the old boy augmented the entire lava bed. Your friends had better hasten their resolve. Time is their enemy now."

"They can't hear us," Asher declared, trying again to shout out across the hiss and crackle of the flames.

"Then I hope they've developed an instinct for self-preservation." Gibraltair said, unhelpfully, gazing across the flames at the two figures, their forms flickering behind the oppressive waves of fire.

"Damn you, Fitch, move…" Lem yanked on her hand, but trailed off as he looked back at the terrified girl. But it was not Morreby his eyes focused on. Instead, they narrowed on the stairwell behind her. A pair of white leather-clad boots was coming into view: one purposeful step at a time.

Alarm spread across Lem's face as he raised a hand and pointed behind Morreby, but her eyes were frozen on the gaping chasm beneath the iron base of the drawbridge. Using his free hand, Lem grabbed Morreby by the chin and forcefully turned her head to look at the figure descending down the stairs.

"Morreby, run!"

Morreby's fear of heights evaporated in an instant as her senses registered a new and more terrifying threat. The sight of the legate's unmistakable white leather outfit descending down the stairs sent fresh chills up her spine. Even without her infamous Red Scar mask, the mere knowledge of the atrocities inflicted upon death dealers by the Scarlet Commander during the Rebellion was more than enough to free Morreby's legs from their petrified state.

Lem and Morreby desperately scrambled to get away from her in the only direction they could: forward. With their legs pumping, they dashed along the iron section of the drawbridge, flying headlong towards treacherous flames.

"Stop right there," the legate's voice bellowed across the chasm as she marched forward.

"Prac that!" Lem shouted as he and Morreby burst through a narrow gap amidst the first pillars of flame on the drawbridge's wooden section. Smoke choked their lungs and the overbearing heat licked at their skin. Sweat and perspiration dripped into their eyes, making it increasingly difficult to see where it was safe to step. There were only a few planks of wood not yet fully ablaze beneath their feet, and even they were becoming structurally unsound.

They were about halfway across the bridge when Morreby's scream tore through Lem's ears. He turned his head to see the grim figure of the legate advancing with battle mantle raised, marching through the flames, completely indifferent to the domineering heat.

For the first time since Lem had first laid eyes on the legate, her hair hung down loosely around her shoulders. The peacock tails of silver spikes that usually held the tightly wrapped bun behind her head in place were now firmly interlocked between her fingers. Each silver spike penetrated a round glass orb and converged into a long silver spike, its tip pointed directly at Morreby's back.

A wild whiplash of air hit Lem in the back of the head, and sent Morreby stumbling forward. Lem caught her at the last minute, moments before she was about to collapse into a large pillar of fire. The blow knocked the air out of her lungs and dazed her mind into unconsciousness.

Lem desperately dragged her dead weight away from the fire and slowly struggled backwards across the drawbridge. He could see the legate marching steadily towards them, her silhouette flickering and wavering in the tyrannical heat.

The burden of Morreby's weight made movement difficult for Lem, especially when trying to navigate safely through the fire at a speed fast enough to get away from the advancing Scarlet Commander.

"Stay away from us," he desperately cried out, knowing there was nothing he could do to stop her advance.

The legate whipped the point of her thin silver stake up into the air above his head. A large globule of falling lava exploded above their heads, showering Lem and Morreby in an intense shock wave of heat. Lem instinctively covered his head with one arm and fell backwards onto a patch of wood that was devoid of lava and flames. Morreby fell on top of him, her unconscious weight pinning him against the timber.

"Be quiet! This will all be over soon," the legate ordered, slowing her approach through the flames as if the lava-fuelled inferno was inconsequential. Her eyes narrowed as she tried to pierce the flickering orange-and-red fiery pillars raging upwards before her. "Where is he?"

"Who?" Lem screamed back at her, the thought of Asher flashing briefly in his mind.

"You know perfectly well who."

"Leave him alone!" he threatened. "We know who you really are; we'll expose you." Lem's taunt redirected her somewhat surprised gaze down upon his pathetic form. The legate quickly regarded and dismissed the pair of apprentices, awkwardly slumped over each other before her. There was no way either posed any threat to her.

"You would expose me?" Her face glazed over for the briefest of seconds as distant memories flashed through her mind. A realisation made the tiniest smile surface in the corner of her mouth. "So… you think me your enemy."

A flash of blue light exploded violently against her chest, cutting her off mid-sentence. Completely taken by surprise, the legate's rigid form stumbled backwards a few steps into a surging pillar of flame.

Lem arched his neck back to see where the attack had come from, only to hear Gibraltair's voice resonating out beyond the hiss and spit of the raging fire.

"They think you much more than that, dear legate."

CHAPTER 46

THE BLOODLUST OF BATTLE

Lem arched his head backwards to see an inverted view of Gibraltair's white coat, now marred with soot and ash, marching forward through the flames, the tip of his cane squarely pointed at the legate's chest.

The augiologist came to a stop next to Lem's head and lowered his cane to the floor. Its tip gently brushed against Morreby's back just as the last of her strength finally gave out.

The legate's eyes blazed with controlled rage at Gibraltair's attack; she was not used to being taken by surprise. The sight of Gibraltair's arrogant smile, flickering amidst a fierce orange glow from the rising flames, only served to fuel her desire to retaliate. Her eyes twitched as her fingertips bled into her auger. Her mind conjuring a deadly image of the blood calling she was about to unleash.

She felt her blood surge and magnify in her palm as her auger pulsated with violent green bursts. With a flick of her wrist, she hurled one of her most lethal blood callings at Gibraltair. The attack was as savage as it was instantaneous. She'd used it many times before, against much stronger opponents, and all had fallen before her, sooner or later.

Gibraltair was no exception.

He barely managed to defend against the blow in time, deflecting its energy downwards. The resulting impact snapped a timber slat beneath his left foot, sending him stumbling backwards through the flames, off balance and exposed.

Lem watched in horror as the legate advanced, unleashing another vicious battery of destruction against Gibraltair, briefly losing track of the man as he retreated farther and farther into the rising inferno. Morreby's unconscious weight had him pinned against the drawbridge, as the writhing flames inched closer to them. Smoke choked his lungs until he found it impossible to draw in breath without his throat burning. He coughed violently, struggling to suck down clean air as the burning soot and ash flooded his lungs. His eyes were clogged with bitter tears, which clouded his vision with a blurry haze.

Straining to free himself from underneath Morreby's unconscious body, he was surprised to see a hand reach down over his head and grip his shoulder reassuringly. He swung his head around and saw Asher kneeling down behind him.

"You can hug your girlfriend later. We gotta go."

Even though he could barely breathe, Lem couldn't help but cough up a smile.

Asher rolled Morreby off Lem and helped him up off the wooden beams. Together, they slung Morreby over their shoulders and turned away from the advancing form of the furious legate.

"Take her and go. I will deal with this charlatan," Gibraltair barked at them over the furious hiss and spit of the flames. He lashed his cane savagely upwards, deflecting another vicious blood calling as he too advanced across the drawbridge.

Asher glanced back over his shoulder to see Gibraltair's rippling outline disappear amidst the blinding heat of the raging inferno.

"You're no match for her," Lem spluttered after him, his lungs still burning from the despotic heat.

"Come on, Lem, leave it," Asher yelled at his friend, Morreby still slumped between them, heels dragging limply on the floor as they hauled her towards safety.

Gibraltair retaliated against the legate's onslaught against him with a series of vicious blood callings. The air above the drawbridge was laced with blinding blue arcs of light as he hurled attack after attack at the legate.

She deflected each attack effortlessly with a swipe of her auger and assumed a defensive battle stance opposite him.

Asher and Lem struggled to find solid footing on the treacherous drawbridge. Between the falling lava and the ever-growing pillars of flames closing in around them on all sides, they dragged Morreby as best they could, but her clothes were already singed, some parts were even alight.

When they finally stumbled off the drawbridge and onto the safety of the stone platform, they collapsed in a heap, exhausted. Asher and Lem coughed and spluttered as they wiped tears from their eyes and patted down their singed clothing, leaving Lorrelli to tend to Morreby.

Gibraltair had long since waved his auger at the disappearing apprentices as they fled, sending a wall of flame soaring skyward, obscuring the teenagers from the legate's view altogether.

The legate watched them disappear behind a barricade of fire and ash and couldn't help but smile. She only had eyes for Gibraltair and she had him right where she wanted him. "Lies and deceit won't help you down here, Bell. I see you for what you really are but, then again, I always did. Didn't I?"

The legate's eyes narrowed as she taunted the man, pressing him to make a mistake she could take advantage of. She slowly withdrew one of the silver pins from the glass orb in a smooth motion and clutched it venomously at her side. Without blinking, she pointedly flicked her wrist. The silver pin became flaccid. Flicking it again, it dramatically multiplied in width and length. With one more flick, a long silver whip with a sharp barbed tail was coiled on the burning wooden beams by her feet.

"I have dreamed of this reckoning for an age," Gibraltair sneered, fanning the flames between them ever higher with a wave of his cane, further obscuring himself from view. "Twice you have stolen something precious from me, but now I shall return the favour."

The legate brought the hilt of her whip up around her head and lashed its barbarous tail through the searing fire towards where she'd seen him last. Its serrated teeth tore through the air, razor-sharp metallic fangs hungry to taste the man's flesh.

Gibraltair didn't flinch. He didn't move a muscle. He waited until the last second before swatting away the glistening barbed fangs with a simple swipe of his cane. An enormous crackle of energy exploded as the two weapons met, lacing the air with vicious streaks of light as the legate's whip was sent sprawling harmlessly to one side.

"Twice you say, yet I recall only the once," the legate called out, taunting him again, trying to get him to reveal his position. Gibraltair's face twinged with a glimmer of loss, but his lust for vengeance surged and heaved inside his veins.

"For all your worth, you remain naive to the realities that you cauterised into existence. I suppose I should thank you, really. I would not be the man I am today, were it not for you."

The legate waivered as the augiologist's unexpected response sunk in.

"Had you not orphaned me in the Rebellion, I would have never sought out your true identity in the Annals and, in turn, stumbled on my true calling." Gibraltair taunted and waved his cane at the pillars of fire, parting them momentarily so she could see him clearly. He lowered his glasses with his free hand and gazed in her direction with his milky-white eyes.

"The feat was not without cost, but I'd pay it again gladly, just to hear you burn." Raising his glasses, he commanded the flames to converge once again and unleashed an offensive burst of energy at her with a savage uppercut of his cane.

The legate deflected the blast and countered with a powerful crack of her whip that exploded in a shower of green sparks next to his head. The resulting thunderclap burst an ear drum and nearly sent him sprawling off one side of the drawbridge as his equilibrium and sense of balance was shattered.

"All this to avenge the death of two Skulk spies?" she smiled at him callously. Her eyes were alight with intensity, blood drunk with the coming promise of unleashing her pent-up rage and brutality against Gibraltair.

"They were innocent!" Gibraltair could barely hear her over the ringing in his ear. Her attack had left him completely deaf in his left ear. He could feel a trickle of blood dripping from his earlobe onto his neck. Desperately, he hurled another fierce burst of savage blue energy towards her feet, splintering the timber planks beneath her into a thousand tiny shards, but she was too quick for him.

Nimbly retreating back into the flames, she withdrew another needle from the glass orb and twisted it into her hair. A brilliant golden liquid burst forth from the head of the pin, washing over her head and shoulders as it weaved into an exotic shimmering cloak that caught the flames. Within seconds, her entire body was camouflaged amidst the fiery pillars and she disappeared from sight.

Gibraltair flicked several switches on the side of his glasses, but it was no good. The legate was gone: a ghost amidst the flames. A whip lashed out at him from nowhere again and again, each time from a different direction to confuse and beguile him.

He desperately deflected each blow at the very last second as they hurtled towards him, but he was under attack from all sides and still reeling with vertigo. He wildly returned a few savage bursts of blue light at random, frantically seeking out a target amidst the roaring inferno.

"You disappoint me, Bell. You're pathetic, like your parents before you." Withdrawing another two silver needles from her orb. She flung them out into the abyss, one on either side of the drawbridge, as a menacing smile crept into the corners of her mouth.

Two small silver birds of prey formed from the falling pins she'd discarded, hot air filling their wings as they took flight, spiralling underneath their prey on scorching hot airwaves far below the burning expanse above. As their speed increased, their feathers changed colour. Jet black wings stretched out from their sides as their chests and heads turned a brilliant scarlet. A razor-sharp black beak grew on their heads as long silver talons extended from their feet.

"Show yourself!" Gibraltair bellowed into the raging flames, flicking a combination of switches on his glasses as he searched the inferno for any sign of his attacker.

Locking on to the sound of Gibraltair's voice, the birds climbed high into the cavern's roof above him, metallic talons and deadly beaks primed to strike unsuspecting flesh.

"Or do you fear to face me."

The legate smiled wickedly beneath her fiery cloak, every second advancing a step closer to the traitor she would soon dispatch from this world. Using an old trick she'd found useful during the Rebellion, she magnified her voice and threw it into the flames to disorientate and confuse her prey.

"How it must hurt, to have waited so long for vengeance, only to fail so miserably."

The legate's voice echoed behind Gibraltair, causing him to spin around and wildly lash out at a pillar of flame.

"All that time spent thinking. What you would say to me."

This time her voice sounded like it was right next to his right ear. Again, he spun and swiped at thin air.

The legate smiled, watching her prey flail about harmlessly. "How you would enact your revenge."

Her voice whispered at him from two sides, front and back. Gibraltair didn't know where to look or which direction to strike. He held his cane out before him, madly changing stances as each word landed.

"How it would feel to kill me."

The voice came at him from behind him and rushed past his ears. Gibraltair twirled in an awkward dance of death, striking the air desperately around him.

"I am a little underwhelmed with your efforts but, then again, I expect no less from the offspring of two traitors. What were their names again: Pentora and Agama?"

Gibraltair's face cringed as she deliberately got their names wrong. He could take no more. Holding his cane upright before his face, he focused his mind on a single thought. One by one the flames around him lifted off the burning timbers and hovered in the air, inching upwards as they levitated higher and higher.

As each lick of flame rose above the smouldering charred wood, small wisps of fire shot through the air and disappeared inside the exposed tip of his cane. A large circular patch of black-and-brown smouldering timber was exposed, revealing everything around him. Yet still he could not lay eyes on the legate.

"At least they put up a fight before I bled their veins into the streets."

Her voice came at him again, this time from dying embers beneath his feet. The insult to his parents' memory was too much for Gibraltair. He lashed out like a wild animal, unleashing a series of vicious attacks, thrashing the edges of the fire. Blue arcs of untamed energy shot out in every direction in the vain hope of unearthing the legate's position. His rage made him oblivious to everything except his immediate surroundings. He did not see the blur of motion strike downwards from the sky, but he felt cruel talons slice open his chest.

He caught a glimpse of fluttering black wings, but by that time the pain of his skin being ripped apart had set in. Before he even had time to recover from the first attack, another attack blindsided him. Silver talons slashed through his heavy coat, rending a savage gash across his shoulder blades as metal claws tore through his flesh and scraped across his bones.

The brutality of the twin attacks brought Gibraltair to his knees, leaving him writhing in agony. His once-brilliant white coat was now a mess of torn rags, stained with fresh blue-tinged blood and charred ash.

Again, the scarlet nightmares swooped to attack, but despite his agony Gibraltair was ready for them; they couldn't hide from him like the legate could. He waited until the last moment before unleashing the full wrath of the pent-up flames stored in the shaft of his cane. With blinding accuracy, he focused the blast directly into the face of an oncoming bird as it plummeted towards his face, silver talons outstretched.

The amplified firestorm hit the bird full in the face, incinerating it in midair until all that was left was a splattering of liquefied metal on one of the drawbridge's heavy chains. Just as Gibraltair lowered his cane, the second bird of prey hit him from behind. Gibraltair cried out in agony as the bird's silver beak bit into his flesh, its vicious talons slicing open a gash on the rear of his thigh. He lifted his head back and roared at the burning flames as the winged menace disappeared back into the searing inferno in a flurry of feathers.

"Come out and face me, damn you!"

An enormous pillar of flame steadily advanced into the clearing and blazed unnaturally a few feet in front of him. It stood twice as wide as a man and half again as high. Gibraltair watched it approach from bent and bloody knees as a gap emerged in the flaming pillar, revealing the tortured face of a long-forgotten foe.

A black leather mask with a single scarlet scar ran down one cheek, whilst another blemish stretched across two large black eyes, both of which stared down at the augiologist pitifully.

"Very well, traitor." The Scarlet Commander's voice was one of pure malevolence, deep, raspy and booming. "If you cannot outrun your past, then relive it and die."

The pillar of fire split down the middle, revealing the rest of the Scarlet Commander's overwhelming bulk. Black boots stretched high over his calf, whilst a thick black leather jacket hung down to his knees. His tunic was stitched with fragments of bone and pulsated with blood that refused to drip or fall. His back and sides were wreathed in fire like a demon straight from the underworld: a demon of Gibraltair's past that had haunted him for a lifetime.

"How?" Gibraltair stammered, the words choking in his throat.

"You look surprised. Did you honestly think I needed that whelp of a Half-brute to project this visage?"

With one hand locked onto his cane for support, Gibraltair's eyes widened with fear. He reached behind his back with his free hand, fingers fumbling to retrieve an object stashed under his fire-ravaged coat.

The Scarlet Commander took a menacing step forward and cracked his whip to one side of the fumbling augiologist. Chunks of seared timber split away and danced in the air like acrobats, which sent embers soaring into the air.

"War is my birthright, this facade, merely a tool fashioned for me by the Half-brute while I honed my own ability to control what I wanted the world to see." He took another step forward and cracked his whip again, this time on the opposite side of him.

More wood splintered and erupted from the burning drawbridge, showering his world in a cascade of fiery sparks.

"This form freed me. It allowed me to do what was necessary. To cleanse this earth of the necrotic scourge, once and for all. As I will cleanse you from it, traitor."

With his strength rapidly withering, Gibraltair sliced his cane up at the towering Scarlet Commander.

The giant of a man deflected the blow with a wave of his hand, sending the resulting blast shooting up wildly towards one of the drawbridge's massive iron chains hanging high above them both.

The force split a giant chain link in two, leaving only one side of the link to carry the full load of the chain's weight. The massive iron link immediately buckled and stretched, but did not fall.

Now on all fours, hand still clutching the hilt of the cane against the charred timber, Gibraltair's broken body aimed his cane towards the severed chain link. Using the last of his strength, he channelled a silent blood calling to hold it in place and stop it from falling.

"I have seen inside your quisling mind," the Scarlet Commander's voice echoed through the air, "I have seen your guilt."

Gibraltair was nothing more than a pitiful wreck in the eyes of his attacker. Beads of sweat ran down the augiologist's agonised face as his chest heaved with exhaustion. He was already dead, he just didn't know it yet.

"Your treachery shames the blood in your veins." The Scarlet Commander's voice boomed as the splatter of falling lava spread more clumps of molten rock across the only section of the drawbridge not yet aflame.

Embers ignited, bursting into a fresh inferno as the two faced off against each other.

The Scarlet Commander inhaled a deep breath through his mask, completely unfazed by the smoke and haze, as though he was breathing the cleanest air on Earth. His fiery cloak and hood billowed with fire. With back and shoulders ablaze, he looked down in disgust towards the feeble man cowering before him on his hands and knees.

Gibraltair wasn't even able to muster the strength to face death on his own two feet.

The Scarlet Commander did not bother getting closer. Even at this distance, Gibraltair was as good as dead.

The black-and-red bird of prey swooped down from above and landed gracefully on the Scarlet Commander's shoulder. Its beady eyes fixated on the blood seeping from Gibraltair's open wounds as it leaked all over his torn clothing, staining it dark crimson with tinges of blue.

The Scarlet Commander repositioned his feet upon the splintered and charred timber beams, preparing to deliver the final coup de grâce, a venomous sneer forming behind his mask. He lashed his whip out once more, this time it landed just before Gibraltair's knees.

Gibraltair felt the wood buckle and rip apart beneath his skin, but still he did not yield.

"All Skulk conspirators deserved death for their treachery. Do you honestly think you were the only one orphaned by my hand?"

The Scarlet Commander's twisted sense of righteousness only served to heighten Gibraltair's anger. "Conspirators!" Gibraltair spat the word back in disgust, a mouthful of blood landing on a pile of molten lava busy melting a groove into a nearby timber slat. "They were augineers, simple builders and inventors."

"Your quest for vengeance has blinded you to the truth," the towering giant ridiculed him. "It matters not. No-one, orphaned bastard or otherwise, has ever uncovered my true identity and lived to tell the tale," he taunted cruelly. "And you, traitor, are no exception."

"You talk too much, wretch," Gibraltair sneered at the visage through blood-spattered teeth and closed his eyes. He only had one shot if he hoped to survive the encounter, but he needed his opponent to believe it was already over. Focusing intently on what he had to do, his fingers fumbled over the small device behind his back and depressed a small button on its surface, engaging the mechanism. It silently came to life, vibrating in his fingertips as its internal elements whirred and turned.

The Scarlet Commander raised his auger, levelling his remaining silver spike directly at Gibraltair's face, delighting in the thrill of impending victory.

Gibraltair agonisingly pulled himself up on his haunches and dragged his cane across the burning embers and up his thigh, locking it into place against his hip.

"I may be blind," he gazed up through ash-smudged glasses, making sure he would be able to witness the moment when the Scarlett Commander would realise he'd played directly into his hands, "but I alone have seen how this will end."

The small bird on his shoulder took flight as the Scarlet Commander's lashed out in rage at the Gibraltair's open defiance. The towering giant hurled a powerful barrage of blood callings at the augiologist with a series of savage slashes of the silver spike. Each one exploded destructively in a storm of raw elemental power against Gibraltair's chest.

Gibraltair felt no pain.

Nor did his body sway or move an inch. Gibraltair remained an immovable statue as each attack savagely tried to rip a vicious hole in his chest and pierce his heart. He kneeled on his haunches, face agonised with pain, body covered in blood, but he would not yield.

The device in his hand behind his back glowed and swelled, absorbing the vicious elemental rage exploding against his torso. Gibraltair's face contorted into a sadistic smile as a thin rivulet of blood spilled from his lips and dribbled down his chin.

The Scarlet Commander roared in furious anger, streaking the air with a rift of light as his whip's barbarous metal fangs hurtled towards Gibraltair.

Gibraltair defended against the onslaught at the very last second. He caught the whip with the shaft of his cane and watched it entangle on its own treacherous barbs. The sudden movement of his cane dislodged Gibraltair's augmented hold over the massive chain link above, shattering the damaged iron and sending its remnants spiralling into the abyss below.

The Scarlet Commander's head swung upwards as he heard the metal shatter. Gravity had already taken hold over the drawbridge's iron chains, both ends of the mammoth chain groaned loudly as they careened down towards the men below.

With one arm strapped to the hilt of his whip, which was still ensnared on Gibraltair's cane, he had no choice but to strike out upwards with the only free hand he had available: the one clutching his auger.

Gibraltair watched the events unfold in slow motion, exactly as he had hoped they would. The bird of prey took flight and climbed high into the air and out of the path of the giant falling chain. The Scarlet Commander turned away from him to focus on the destruction of the falling chain roaring down towards them, leaving the augiologist the smallest of windows to press his attack.

It was the only opening he needed.

He whipped his hand around and hurled the small orb,

releasing the depressed button on its face and engaging the device's secondary function. It visibly trembled and shook as it hurtled through the air.

High above the burning drawbridge, the scarlet bird of prey tracked the path of the orb as it left Gibraltair hands. Without pause, it reacted, letting instinct guide its actions. Folding its wings into its sides, the bird dived headlong towards the orb's tiny outline. Its slender black body flexing shiny metallic talons as it raced downwards, zipping through gusts of scorching air.

The Scarlet Commander had only just finished deflecting the fall of one of the gargantuan chains, repelling it away from the drawbridge and back towards the far wall of the cavern, when he saw a flash of light in the corner of his eye.

Only when he turned back to face Gibraltair did he see the orb hurtling towards him. The Scarlet Commander tried to take a step back and desperately swung his auger around to deflect the orb, but it was already too late.

The bird of prey swooped down and caught the orb in its outstretched talons, snatching it out of the way just as the Scarlet Commander released a deflective blood calling. Lashings of golden light shot out at the orb but missed, harmlessly whizzing over the bird's head as it broke off its suicidal descent with a flurry of its wings. The small bird tried to climb, but the weight of the orb in its claws was too heavy. It was only able to hover. The orb pulsated with energy, dangerously suspended inches above a large patch of lava that was busy melting through the drawbridge's thick timber slats.

The Scarlet Commander's eyes darted forward, refocusing on the augiologist.

Gibraltair stood upright like a revenant of revenge. The tip of his cane was firmly pointing at the lava pool beneath the bird's furiously flapping wings. Gibraltair's bloody face contorted into a victorious smile for an instant, before it transformed into a venomous sneer.

The Scarlet Commander almost thought he saw Gibraltair

mouth, "prac you!" as a blue shard of energy erupted from the augiologist's cane. It shredded the air with an arc of cobalt light as it raced forward and struck the lava's surface.

The visage of the Scarlet Commander flickered momentarily as the world slowed to a standstill. He helplessly watched the fiery liquid erupt upwards in a geyser of molten death, engulfing the bird and the mechanaug orb caught in its claws.

In that moment, both Legate Seville and the Scarlet Commander were as one, and both were powerless to act. The Scarlet Commander vanished as the legate quietly closed her eyes and waited for the inevitable.

The corners of her lips quivered into a strange smirk as she felt the heat of a thousand suns assault her flesh. Even her mastery over the Vita bloodline couldn't save her from the intolerable destruction that swept over her. It blasted her body backwards into oblivion as the molten lava tore through her skin, melting ligament from flesh and muscle from bone.

Then she was gone.

CHAPTER 47

A SHROUDED SECRET

Mere seconds had passed since Asher and Lem had escaped from the burning drawbridge and the legate's fury. Still collapsed in a heap on the relative safety of the central stone platform, they gathered their breath and collected themselves, all the while gazing back at the towering inferno on the burning drawbridge, but neither could see past the flames.

Thick black plumes of smoke billowed upwards, converging high above them in the cavernous roof like a surging storm front. Flashes of light streaked through the swollen clouds of smoke as large chunks of molten lava rained down from the roof of the cavern. The radiant orange glow looked strangely beautiful as the lava chunks thundered past, plummeting into the abyss below.

Turning his gaze back to the burning drawbridge, it was hard for Asher to see anything other than the rising flames engulfing its wooden section. Peering into the flames, he thought he saw a faint arc of blue light lace the air, then another, and another, until a war of light erupted amidst the flames.

Rising to his feet, Asher moved to the side of the platform to get a better view of the drawbridge's length, but he still only saw flames. Gibraltair and the legate were nowhere to be seen. A scarlet chested bird appeared from the chasm, then a second, their black wings and silver talons swooping in and out of the fire at foes unseen.

Turning his attention to Morreby, it was clear she was still unconscious. Her breath grew short and was becoming weaker by the second. Lorrelli had tried every restorative blood calling she knew in an attempt to wake her, but none had worked. The blow Morreby had suffered at the hands of the legate, combined with the drain of her auger, had left her an inch from death's door.

Asher's head swung around as a massive crack echoed out from one of the giant chains suspended above the drawbridge. Shards of metal splintered into the air as one of the links ripped apart, splitting the chain in two. A sickening snap tore through the cavern as the lower half of the chain ripped a dozen wooden beams from the burning drawbridge like twigs off a branch.

Asher put an arm up to cover his face from the flying debris but, just as he did, a sickening explosion detonated in the centre of the firestorm, expanding outwards in a savage ball of wrath.

The resulting shock wave knocked Asher and Lem off their feet and sent them sprawling backwards across the stone platform, scrabbling for a handhold on the smooth stone with their bare fingers.

Lorrelli tried to shield Morreby's body with her own, but even her feeble attempts were little protection from the burning debris and powerful gusts of burning hot air assaulting them.

None of them were prepared for the deluge of heat and anger washing over them, least of all the man at the centre of the blast.

Gibraltair's body flew backwards through the flames like a discarded toy soldier, hurtling towards them in a deadly barrel roll. He landed hard on the splintered end of the drawbridge and rolled, a large wooden shaft protruding from his rib cage and another from his leg. His white outfit was now almost entirely black, charred beyond recognition. Some sections were still on fire, whilst other parts had been melted into his flesh. All of the exposed skin on his back was covered in horrendous burns; even his scalp and the sides of his face had not escaped the savage kiss of the furnace.

Asher and Lem peeled themselves off the ground and rushed to Gibraltair's side, extinguishing the remaining flames on his clothes with their naked hands, but clumps of scorched hair continue to sizzle and smoke. When Asher finally turned Gibraltair over to look at his face, he heard Lem gag in revulsion. Asher's stomach was a little stronger, but even he had to fight the urge to do the same.

"Nothing to it," Gibraltair gurgled, blood dribbling from his mouth. Half his face was just gone, his muscles burned beyond repair. The once-handsome man was striking no longer, his broken body now hideously disfigured.

Asher glanced back at the drawbridge. The majority of it had been destroyed, a gaping chasm now separating its two halves. The mighty timber beams that had stretched across the gap now lay in smouldering ruins, completely obliterated in the blast. Even the solid iron base had been warped and bent.

"What happened? Where is the legate?" Asher asked hesitantly, trying to figure out how to help Gibraltair up without hurting him.

"Turned the old boy against her…" he coughed. "Augmented lava," he moaned loudly as he tried unsuccessfully to sit upright. "Packs a hell of a punch." A thin rivulet of blood dribbled down his chin from the side of his mouth. "Underestimated the effects a little." He spat out mouthful of blood and laughed hysterically.

"Morreby's not doing so good over here."

Lorrelli's voice broke through Gibraltair's maniacal laughter, forcing him to roll his head in her direction.

Lorrelli was worriedly twirling the end of her braid as Morreby's head sagged unconsciously in her lap.

"Neither is he. Prac, what do we do now?" Lem asked quickly, wiping a layer of soot off Gibraltair's forehead.

Gibraltair tried to gurgle something through a mouthful of blood, but it was indistinguishable.

"What?" Asher asked, tilting Gibraltair's head even more until he was able to spit and clear his throat. The man was growing visibly weaker and paler by the second. His wounds were haemorrhaging blood everywhere and nothing they could do was helping. "What are you trying to say?"

"Gift of life…" Gibraltair slurred, weakly extending a charred arm and pointing towards the glowing alcove that lay across the fiery chasm. "The augefact."

Asher, Lorrelli and Lem followed the direction of his finger and gazed at the three craggy paths extending away haphazardly across the chasm. At this distance, they looked more ominous than ever.

"What are we waiting for, then?" Lem rose to his feet and walked towards them.

"Wait," Gibraltair gurgled, before fishing out a hipflask from his jacket pocket and taking a swig. The cool liquid inside momentarily numbed his pain and the feeling in his mouth. Replacing the hipflask, he proceeded to pull out a heavily dented metallic case from his breast pocket with a burned hand. He was only able to mumble out a reply, his voice heavy with a lisp as the elixir took effect and a gentle numbness spread across his tongue. "Parthingth three."

"What did he say?" Lem stopped in his tracks and pointed at what Gibraltair held in his hands. "What's that?"

"I think he said 'passings three'," Asher replied, reinterpreting Gibraltair's answer as he took the metallic case from the man's charred fingers and gingerly opened it. Inside was a scrap of torn material, older than any other Asher had ever seen. He turned it over in his hands and carefully unfolded it. A heavily faded message had been scrawled in some form of golden-hued liquid on the material's surface. "Gibraltair, what is this?"

Lem's eyes lit up like the moon, instantly recognising the scrap of cloth for what it truly was.

Gibraltair leaned forward with all his strength and mumbled at Asher through beleaguered breaths. "Thekond haff… of the throud."

"What Shroud?" Lem said fiercely, knowing full well what Gibraltair was about to say.

"Thalvathon…" Gibraltair collapsed back against the ground as his burned lungs coughed and spluttered, gasping for clean air.

Astonishment and disbelief surged through Lem as he gazed down at the crumpled piece of material in Asher's hands. Tenderly lifting the material from Asher's palm, Lem let his gaze wander over its surface with eyes wider than an owl's.

"You've got to be praccing kidding me." Lem was beside himself. "What the hell do you mean 'second half'?"

Gibraltair didn't answer him. Instead, he rolled over on his side away from them, exhaling a short gasp of relief as his weight shifted and eased the agony coursing through his back. Lem and Asher were too busy staring at the second half of the shroud to pay any real attention to his actions or his moans. Lorrelli, on the other hand, was too busy worrying over an unconscious Morreby to offer him any sympathy.

Gibraltair weakly clutched at his cane with trembling fingers, mumbling something inaudible between hard-fought gasps for air. A fine golden aura emerged from his auger and radiated over his body, slowly easing the pain from the most severe burns and cauterising his numerous open wounds. His tortured flame-scarred patches of mutilated skin slowly softened in colour as they were replaced by scar-tissue, all of which was still agonisingly sore.

The golden aura only lasted a few seconds, but it left Gibraltair with enough strength to sit upright and afforded him the full use of his voice again. But his body remained far from healed. He was wrought with pain and teetering over death's doorstep like a terminal patient too stubborn to die. Despite the agony he must have felt, Gibraltair managed to half-drag, half-crawl his way across to Morreby's side.

She was slumped on the floor, unconscious, her head propped up in Lorrelli's lap. Gibraltair gently opened one of her eyelids with a burned finger and gazed into her pupil, leaving a smear of blood on her eyebrow in the process. A lucid yet paralysed retina of fear and anger stared back at him. Resting his cane on her torso, he turned his head to face the others and released her eyelid, pushing it closed to help ease her suffering.

"How is she?" Lorrelli whimpered.

"She doesn't have long," Gibraltair wheezed, his voice coarse and his body still in need of rest and recovery.

"Can't you heal her?" Lem pleaded.

"Not without knowing what foul malady the legate cursed her with." Gibraltair cleared his throat, his voice regaining a little bit of strength back. "Whatever it is, she'll die if you don't do something."

"Us? We can't help her, you have to," Lorrelli begged, stroking Morreby's cheeks with her hands.

"I can only stabilise her, but I'll need your augers to neutralise the drain of her remorauger. I'm too weak to keep the damage at bay myself. The only thing powerful enough to reverse whatever the legate did is the old boy's augefact." He nodded his head towards the alcove glowing brightly across the abyss. "She need his blood."

"We can't just leave you our augers. You look worse than she does, besides, what if we need them," Lem said defiantly, gazing down at Gibraltair's wretched body, partly in revulsion.

"She'll die without them!" Gibraltair's snapped, his chest heaving with effort as he shifted his weight upwards. "Use the Shroud, cross the abyss and bring her back the augefact, or watch her die, it's your choice."

Lem and Lorrelli glanced nervously at each other, weighing up the other's obvious reluctance to relinquish what he was requesting.

"Your augers will give her an aura of life to cling to and prolong death's hand from reaching her," Gibraltair added.

Lorrelli closed her eyes and reluctantly held out her auger.

Gibraltair gently took it and placed it in Morreby's right palm, wrapping her fingers around it firmly.

Lem begrudgingly did so, too, placing his auger in Morreby's other hand and closing her cold fingers into a fist. "Hope it's more use to you than it was for me," he whispered in her ear.

"Good. Now go!" Gibraltair weakly waved them away, his voice struggling to make any noise whatsoever.

Asher didn't wait, gently taking the shroud back from Lem, he pulled Lorrelli to her feet and marched to the edge of the central platform.

"Here we go again," Lem muttered at Asher.

Asher delicately unfolded and examined the ancient material in his hands.

"Well, go on, then, what's it say?"

"No idea," Asher replied as he inspected the faded passage. Most of what was once scrawled on it was now illegible, degraded by the ravages of time. Some words were missing altogether, whilst others resembled a faded collection of scratches and brush strokes. Regardless, whatever the original passage had said, its full meaning had been lost to the ages.

"So much for Vitalsior's last message. No wonder Gibraltair never told anyone about the second half of the shroud. There's nothing to tell," Lorrelli sighed in vain, peering over Asher's shoulder at the missing sections of text as she tried to decode what was left.

"But maybe there is," Asher countered as he raised his hand to the side of his head. Instantly, the passage became as clear as day, the particles of gilded blood shining before his eyes as if the passage had been written an hour ago.

"Well?" Lorrelli twirled the end of her braid, waiting nervously for Asher to answer.

"Anything?" Lem's tone was far less confident.

"Not anything…" Asher said slowly. "Everything."

Quickly reading the passage his divine eye revealed, Asher read it aloud to his friends. "Best passings three, do so cautiously, tread light with nimble grace. First rains the swarm, then Aduro's arm. Leaving last to tempered life deface."

"What the hell is that supposed to mean?" Lorrelli snapped.

"It's blindingly obvious, really," Lem frowned.

Asher and Lorrelli just looked at him.

"Vitalsior's a massive poss tot that's going to get us all killed."

"You waste time. Time she does not have," Gibraltair's scratchy voice called out at them.

Asher turned round and saw Morreby suffering from a series of erratic convulsions.

"Okay, everyone pick a path. Stay alert. Stay safe," Asher commanded.

"Safe?" Lem raised his eyebrows comically as he peered out over the edge of the platform and down into the abyss. The sight made his head spin.

Asher and Lorrelli were already each facing two of the three treacherous stone pathways. Each path arched out over the chasm away from them, winding over and under one another like a twisted creeping vine.

Ahead of them, fiery clumps of lava whizzed down through the ash cloud like liquid lances of napalm. A flash of light and the sound of rushing wind accompanied each deluge as they rocketed downwards, some missing the stone pathways by mere inches. Hardened pockets of molten rock were scattered over the surface of each path, leaving traces of where the lava had unsuccessfully tried to assault the tempered stone.

"I'll take the right," Lem said as he stepped away from them, casting one last sly glance in their direction. "Whatever happens… well, you know." Before either could reply, he selflessly took a single step out onto the right path.

"I guess I'll take the middle, then," Lorrelli shrugged, feigning a wry, albeit slightly terrified smile as she tenderly tested her weight on the first uneven stone of the middle path.

Asher shot one last look at Gibraltair and Morreby. Her right leg convulsed in a spasm as if on cue. He gritted his teeth and took a resolute step out onto the narrow ledge of the left path, his arms outstretched for balance.

"Here's goes nothing."

CHAPTER 48

PASSINGS THREE

Lem exhaled and stared ahead. His fear of heights crept up the back of his throat despite his numerous attempts to swallow it down. Refusing to let his gaze wander off the path and into the cavernous abyss dropping away on either side of his feet, he focused on his balance and edged forward, one careful step at a time.

"Tread light, with nimble grace," Lorrelli said loudly in an effort to reassure her friends.

But Asher knew deep down it was more for her own benefit than theirs. Her face and features hid it well, but fear still glistened in abundance in the corner of her eyes.

High above them, out of sight beyond the growing ash cloud on the cavern's malformed roof, large globules of magma oozed through timeworn cracks and dislodged, plunging downwards like molten lances into the abyss below.

Asher could feel their heat on his skin as the nearer streams of lava hurtled past him. He imagined the lava would have emitted a much more severe heat, but he pushed the thought to the back of his mind and pressed on. Mindful of his foot placement before putting his weight on the treacherous narrow path, he edged forward. He narrowly missed getting hit by a trickle of falling lava that glanced off the pathway half a metre in front of him.

Seconds later, he heard a loud splat echo behind him. Glancing over his shoulder, he saw a much larger patch of molten liquid oozing over the pathway where he had been standing a moment ago.

Beads of sweat ran steadily down the sides of his face. His clothes were already soaked with perspiration and felt heavy, sticking to his body like an unwanted second skin. Asher jerked his foot up as he felt something give way beneath it. Shifting his weight, he repositioned his foot elsewhere and watched a section of solid stone break apart and fall away into the void.

"Tread light, with nimble grace," he swallowed, repeating Lorrelli's words to invoke vigilance.

Steadily, the trio advanced along their individual paths at a cautious pace, edging out across the expansive gorge one step at a time. The treacherous ledges Undergall were little more than a half a metre wide and the brittle stone trembled and shuddered dangerously with each footstep.

Lem nearly lost his balance twice as large chunks of stone lurched and fell away into the abyss.

Lorrelli's path wasn't any safer: she scrambled forward as her entire pathway disappeared inches behind her heels, leaving nothing but a gaping void, with no possibility of retreat.

On the far side of the cavern the towering inferno continued to grow, engulfing whatever was left of the wooden drawbridge, but the trio was barely more than a third of the way across the abyss. Large black plumes of smoke billowed high into the cavern and hung above their heads, massing like a storm front poised to unleash its fury. It was so dense it even obscured the iridescent blue twilight that had sparkled so clearly on the cavernous roof before the legate's intrusion.

Asher nervously glanced up at the flashes of orange light that streaked through the swelling ash cloud like a hailstorm of hellish daggers. Somehow, amidst all the danger, excitement and fear rushing through his mind, he couldn't help but be reminded of Raglan's fireworks. Losing himself for a moment in the memory, a heavy bout of coughing eventually snapped him out it.

Lorrelli's path was higher up than Asher's and Lem's higher again. The lowest layers of smoke had already worked their way down to Lem's shoulders.

Though Asher's view was fast becoming blurred and clouded by the haze, he watched Lem double over and cough wildly.

Lorrelli tried to cover her mouth and nose in an attempt to

suck in clean air when the smoke hit her, but it had already worked its way into her nostrils, permeated down her throat and settled inside her lungs.

Asher had to act. Within seconds the lower levels of the ash cloud would hit his face. Aiming his auger at his nose, he focused his mind on a single word.

Anoksium.

Asher's mouth and nose instantly clamped shut, only to reopen with a thin translucent veil that blocked out all the choking ash and smoke. He found himself breathing a little easier, but the blood calling did little to stop the smoke creeping into his eyes. Ignoring the optical irritation, he pointed his auger at his friend's faces and summoned the blood calling again for both of them.

Lorrelli, who saw what he was trying to do, nodded her permission and steadied herself for the effects of Asher's blood calling.

Lem, however, was in a world of his own and too busy coughing to focus on the actions of his friends. He nearly lost his balance on the ledge when his nostrils and mouth clamped shut. Steadying himself, he swung his head around to look at his friends through the murky haze.

Asher's auger was still ablaze with golden light aimed directly at his face.

"Whad dah prak? Mu tryn do kull me?" Lem could barely speak through the thick veil covering his mouth and nose. Hearing his own nasal outburst, he drew in a deep breath of fresh air and realised what Asher had done, instantly offered a sheepish look of apology. "How'bout som' warn'n nuct tme?"

The blood calling had worked a little too well. Asher couldn't help but smirk at Lem's muffled words as he reset the veil over his friend's mouth and nose. "Better?"

"Much."

Asher nodded and gave his friends a quick smile of reassurance, then returned his attention to the precarious pathway beneath him, carefully edging forward another few paces. *First rains the swarm.* He still hadn't deciphered what the unusual phrase was referring to. A multitude of possibilities flickered through his mind and not a single one eased his apprehension.

Glancing around in the murky haze, he couldn't see anything resembling a swarm. As far as he could tell, the only thing raining inside the gigantic cavern was the intermittent lances of molten lava, but Asher wasn't aware of any way lava could swarm. Swallowing his trepidation, he pressed on, trying to be as mindful as possible of his surroundings.

Looking to his right, he noticed Lorrelli's path. It had been completely out of reach since they left the central platform, but he could now see it would converge with his own a short distance ahead. Whilst the base of her path was at the same level as Asher's chest, soon only a metre would separate them. He didn't know why, but somehow the thought comforted him.

"If you care for your friend's life, I'd hasten your resolve!" Gibraltair's scratchy voice echoed out behind them in the haze.

Glancing back over his shoulder, Asher could no longer see the augiologist through the sinking ash cloud, nor could he see Morreby or the central stone platform. Even so, somehow, he still felt the man's milky-white eyes upon him, watching his every step, despite his blindness and the impenetrable haze of smoke and ash between them.

Dusting a worrying amount of black soot off his arms in order to wipe his eyes with his sleeve, Asher realised his vision was growing increasingly limited. He could no longer see more than a couple of metres around him in any direction. Lem was almost entirely out of view: only the bottom of his legs were visible.

"Get down!"

Lem's voice rang out above Asher and echoed throughout the cavern. He instinctively dropped to his knees and held on to each side of the brittle ledge with both hands, his head tilted skyward, searching for danger.

He couldn't see anything through the smoke.

Lorrelli wasn't as fast. She didn't have the same combat instincts, or reaction times that had been drilled into Asher time and time again by Tribarion Roolta in the Arena. She continued to stand, worriedly looking up at Lem. Even though she could only see as high as his waist, it was enough to witness his torso twist this way and that as his feet madly shuffled ever closer to the edge of the path.

"Lem what is it?" she frighteningly yelped up at him.

"Praccing hell, Lorrelli, get down!" Lem's voice bellowed down at her as his chest hit the stone ledge.

But it was too late.

Their eyes met, but only a second before Lorrelli's gaze was distracted by the first glimpse of the swarm. A thousand creatures, each no bigger than the tip of her little finger, swarmed around Lem. Their blue iridescent bodies shone like beacons through the greyish haze of the ever-growing ash cloud.

A loud droning hum invaded Lorrelli's eardrums as countless insect-sized wings flapped a hundred times a second. They converged on her in a wave, her vision blurring into a miasma of flashing lustrous blue light as the swarm whizzed around her in a thousand different directions.

Lorrelli flailed her arms wildly, twisting her torso in a desperate attempt to fend off her miniscule attackers. She felt the first pinprick as a miniature barbed stinger stung the back of her hand, and the second on the back of her neck, but then there were too many to count. Every futile swipe she made at the swarm only further incited their onslaught. Hastening their attacks, the swarm ducked and weaved around Lorrelli's erratic and ineffective attempts to defend herself and stung her again.

Her legs buckled and her muscles cramped as the microscopic venom unleashed in each sting built to dangerous levels inside her bloodstream. Wild pains raced throughout her body from every angle as her limbs contorted uncontrollably. Within a minute, the toxin in her bloodstream had overwhelmed her nervous system, shutting down her control over the muscles in her legs and arms.

Desperately trying to control her balance, Lorrelli took a step forward towards the centre of the path, thrusting her leg downwards in a thunderous stomp. It was a stomp the brittle stone ledge could ill afford.

The resultant force made the entire stone shelf shudder, the tremors spreading to the support pillar of haphazardly stacked stones extending down into the lava bed below. A number of small stones that had previously wedged larger, more pivotal boulders in place were now free from their enslavement and fell away below, bouncing off other larger boulders into the abyss.

Lorrelli's left leg went completely numb and dragged beneath her. Then Lorrelli vanished.

Asher could no longer see her behind the mask of a thousand kaleidoscopic blue lights as the swarm surged over him. Asher winced in pain as he felt the sting of the first barb pierce his skin. Moments later, he felt a second barb pierce his flesh, then a third and then he lost count.

Whilst each sting was sharp and bit into his flesh like a needle, the pain was fleeting. He could feel his body faltering as the venom built and grew inside his veins, slowly working its way into his central nervous system.

One by one, the venom shut down control of his limbs. As each creature enacted its wrath upon Asher's exposed skin, his mind became a tormented haze, unable to focus amidst the assault of a thousand pin-sized stab wounds. He desperately flipped onto his back as his muscles contorted, yet still the swarm found fresh flesh to puncture. A single ear-shattering scream, louder than any other he'd heard, broke through the sea of chaos in his mind.

"Lorrelli."

Asher turned his head to the side and tried to look towards her, but he couldn't see anything past the blinding haze of smoke and the whirlwind of blue lights.

"Asher, do something! Anything!"

When Asher heard Lem's wounded voice call out from somewhere across the enormous chamber, something snapped inside him. His instincts took over and his mind shut out the pain. Gazing up blankly past the whizzing specs of blue light and into the dark ash cloud, a thought popped into the back of his mind. Using the last of his strength, he forced his contorted muscles of his arm upwards, raising his auger up at the swarm's fury.

The swarm pounced on his exposed flesh with its razor-sharp stingers, but it didn't matter. Asher felt his blood surge into his auger and release through it before he even knew what he was doing. He felt the dull lashings of pain pulse through his palm as he instinctively channelled a blood calling.

At first nothing happened, then a shrill whizz and a sharp bang exploded somewhere above him, followed by another and another, until the decrepit black cloud of ash was ablaze with a dazzling kaleidoscope of colours. A hundred blue lights blinked out of existence as a pocket of the swarm was sapped into unconsciousness. The loud droning hum faltered and eased as a large number of the swarm fell out of the sky and plummeted down into the gaping maw. As more loud whizzes and bangs exploded amidst the ash cloud, the sky above Asher's head became a pockmarked display of disappearing blue lights and violent bursts of colour.

Asher's mind swam in a daze of toxin-infused nausea as he aimed his hand towards where he'd last seen Lorrelli and painstakingly funnelled several more bursts of blood into his auger. Moments later, another series of detonations laced the air with colour.

Whatever was left of the remaining swarm was already in full retreat in the face of the new and overwhelming threat. Their luminous blue bodies disappeared into the obscurity of the grey ash cloud engulfing the cavern's roof as they fled skywards to safety.

Asher could feel the integrity of the craggy path beneath him weaken with every explosive shockwave he released from his auger.

Far below him, two enormous boulders, stacked precariously atop each other, dislodged from a support pillar and fell away, collapsing a large section of the pathway behind him into the abyss.

Asher feverishly scrambled back from the rapidly collapsing bridge like a wounded animal, desperately trying to escape the certain death rushing towards him. The toxin in his system made his limbs numb and slow to respond, encumbering even the most basic of movements. Asher's eyes went wide with fear. He forgot all about the stinging pain from his wounds as the path beneath his feet gave way and disappeared. His hands gripped the side of the stone pathway at his waist and he closed his eyes, bracing himself for the inevitable. He felt his feet give way as the stone fell out from under them.

Seconds passed before he opened his eyes again and looked down at his feet. The path underneath his torso had held strong, but only just: his feet were dangling over the edge. He let his aching muscles relax and breathed a heavy sigh of relief and laughed hysterically. Clawing his way back upwards on the path until his feet were touching stone again, he rolled his head in Lorrelli's direction.

He saw her instantly, but could barely recognise her.

Her face was pockmarked with red sores and bleeding from a multitude of miniscule punctures. Asher knew he probably looked exactly the same, but his looks were the last thing on his mind.

Lorrelli was in trouble.

She looked visibly weak and more frail than he had ever seen her. The swarm had sapped her strength and impeded her ability to control her own body, yet somehow she was still upright. Through puffy blood red eyes Asher caught her gaze for a brief moment, before her consciousness gave out and her eyes rolled back into her head. As if in slow motion, Asher watched her body fall backwards away from him.

"Lorrelli!" Asher screamed as he tried to scramble to his feet, but his sluggish body was slow to respond. Asher willed his limbs to action, fighting back against the toxin's debilitating paralysis, but they refused to obey. Asher could only watch on in terror as Lorrelli's head arched back and her arms swayed upwards limply in front of her.

He felt helpless.

He couldn't get to her in time.

Lorrelli was going to fall.

Her legs went limp, crashing her body down hard against the craggy stone pathway. Her head smacked against the stone with a sickening crack, knocking whatever was left of her beleaguered consciousness into oblivion. One leg bounced back upwards and down again, swinging dangerously out over the edge. Its momentum pulled at her waist, until it too was treacherously close to the brink.

Asher had only managed to turn over onto his chest, but Lorrelli was already about to roll off her path and fall. Nothing he could do would allow him to get to her in time. Tears welled up in his eyes as he scrambled to his feet and awkwardly lumbered towards the closest point between their paths.

Just as he reached the edge of her path, her helpless body slipped out of reach. He desperately threw out a hand to grab her, but he was too late.

She was already gone.

Asher watched in horror as Lorrelli's face disappeared from view, a solitary arm trailing after her like the mast of a sinking ship.

"Lorrelli, please, no," Asher gasped, forcing his eyes shut. He couldn't bear to watch her fall. His eyelids had barely even closed, when an enormous thump echoed in front of his face. A loud groan was followed a split-second later by the sound of rock breaking apart nearby. Reopening his eyes, Asher was met with the image of Lem's legs sprawled out across Lorrelli's pathway directly in front of his face. One arm clung to the edge nearest Asher, whilst his torso hung out over the far precipice, his other hand latched on to Lorrelli's hand like a vice. His exposed skin was pockmarked, swollen and bleeding profusely from the swarm's relentless attack.

Lem strained every muscle in his body, but he could only just support her weight. There was no way he would be able to pull her up, the swarm's attack had weakened him and she was far too heavy. Even now he could feel the swarm's toxin swimming through his veins and slowing his movements, but his grip on Lorrelli's limp wrist was unbreakable.

"Praccing hell, Lorrelli, wake up. Wake up!"

Lorrelli's limp body dangled beneath Lem like an oversized pendulum; the features on her unconscious face were expressionless, almost serene. Between the blow to her head and the venom surging through her veins, there was no chance she'd be waking any time soon, but Lem was getting tired. His grip on the stone pathway was faltering, a finger slipping from its grip as the venom in his bloodstream trickled into his heart and major arteries.

"Lorrelli, wake up, please wake up!" Lem shouted at her, desperately pleading with her to help save her own life. Another finger slipped from its hold as Lem strained to pull her up.

It was no use. He didn't have the strength. He was losing her.

"Lorrelli!"

Lem heard a sudden scrabbling noise behind him, before he felt a pair of hands roughly grab at the back of his tunic and steady him. Asher reached over Lem's body and grabbed Lorrelli. Together, they slowly and agonisingly pulled her upwards until all three were sprawled out on the stone ledge.

Lem and Asher collapsed, panting heavily, whilst Lorrelli lay limply between them, unconscious and utterly oblivious to everything that had just happened.

"Thanks." It was all Lem could wheeze out. His body was overcome; his strength was gone.

"Don't mention it," Asher exhaled breathlessly, as a low rumble and grinding noise emanated from somewhere beneath all of them.

"Asher?"

"We're too heavy," Asher whispered at Lem as the stone pathway shuddered and jerked downwards violently. Both of them felt the reverberations of the support column as large boulders broke free of their holdings and fell away into the abyss.

"Get up. This whole thing is going to collapse. Get up!" Lem tried to jump to his feet, but his actions were still slow and sluggish.

Asher's reaction time was only slightly better, but together they struggled to their feet and hauled Lorrelli up between them, slinging her arms over their shoulders, Lem in the lead.

The grinding was getting louder by the second, forcing them to move along the path faster than they would have liked. Lem scanned ahead as best he could, but the ash cloud had gotten worse and his eyes were covered in smoke and soot. Wiping them clear with a sleeve, he leaned his head out over the edge and saw Asher's original pathway. It was running alongside their own, but was still too far away to jump to.

"We got to keep moving," he wheezed at Asher, urging him on. Shuffling forward another few steps, the duo moved in bursts, not trusting the shuddering pathway under their heels. Lorrelli's dead weight did not make movement easy, but somehow they managed.

Lem narrowed his eyes and peered into the smoky haze, finally finding what they desperately needed: an escape.

"Up ahead. The paths merge," he shouted over the low villainous rumble of collapsing stone. A few feet ahead Asher's original pathway converged to within a foot of separation from their own crumbling ledge.

"Well, what are you waiting for?" Asher's exhausted face stared back at him with both eyebrows raised. "Go!"

CHAPTER 49

THE ARM THAT BURNS

Suspended high above the fiery abyss, on a brittle bridge of narrow stone, lost amidst the ash cloud, a series of ominous grinding sounds filled Asher's ears with an imminent sense of dread. Even though he couldn't see more than five feet past his outstretched hand, he could hear everything around him.

He heard heavy boulders far below him grate against one another, desperately trying to tear free from their entrapment within the tenuous grasp of the support pillars. He heard Lem's beleaguered breath coming out in gasps and Lorrelli's unconscious shallow breaths.

Every loud crack and disastrous rumble only reassured Asher that another pivotal piece of the rock formation's precarious support structure had failed. The trio's path was little more than a house of cards, pushed to breaking point, inching towards utter ruination.

He felt every shudder and jolt of the collapsing support column reverberate up through his feet and into his bones as it buckled and broke apart Undergall. The stress their combined weight added to the already overloaded stone bridge didn't help things. Nor did the frantic movements of their feet: a necessity to help compensate for Lorrelli's dead weight.

Asher and Lem had each of Lorrelli's arms slung over their respective shoulders, supporting her like a marionette, but the narrow width of the path made it impossible for them to walk side-by-side, forcing them to shuffle sideways, with Lem in the lead.

The pathway lurched forward and dropped down a foot with a tremendous crack. Asher heard a series of loud bangs as boulders crashed into and bounced off other support columns, until even they were out of earshot.

Lem swore loudly as their balance shifted. His knees buckled as the majority of Lorrelli's unconscious weight lurched forward on his shoulders. He desperately pushed back against her, compensating for the dramatic shift, halting their movement entirely.

"Give us a praccing break already," Lem grunted, as Lorrelli's head swayed limply between them, a trickle of blood running down her neck.

Asher was too busy ensuring his feet were in the centre of the path to respond to Lem's frustration. One wrong step, from either of them, would mean certain death for all of them. The path lurched forward again as more of its foundations fell away beneath it. A massive section of the pathway disappeared behind them, vanishing with a loud rumble into the gaping void.

Asher glanced over his shoulder, eyes widening in fear as he watched the pathway disintegrate. "Not the best time to ask for a break!" Asher shouted back at Lem as he pushed against Lorrelli to urge him forward.

Redoubling his efforts, Lem hauled Lorrelli's slumped frame closer to the safety of the intersecting ledges. He was only a few feet away from where they'd be able to hoist her to safety when a deep rumble groaned somewhere beneath their feet. The vibrations that followed saw the pathway erratically jerk left and drop another two feet.

Lem's smile faded as he watched the of Asher's original pathway ledge rise in front of him. It was at the height of his thighs, then his waist, until it was as high as his chest. Lem wasn't going to wait until it was above his head. Desperately, he reached out and grabbed the ledge. "You got her?" he called back, before shifting Lorrelli's weight back onto Asher's shoulder.

Asher nodded and braced Lorrelli's body as best he could, but the added weight quickly reminded him how much the swarm's toxin had exhausted him.

Lem awkwardly shimmied up onto the safety of the

intersecting ledge, frantically scrambling with his arms in order to pull up his uncooperative legs. Finally, his body rolled over the lip and disappeared. Almost instantaneously, his face re-emerged and his hand reached out, grabbing Lorrelli's tunic. He yanked her towards him, taking the majority of her weight.

Asher tried to help as much as he could, but quickly noticed Lem was doing most of the work.

The strength and determination required to haul Lorrelli's unconscious weight upwards should have been near impossible for the weakened duo, but Lem didn't once complain or appear to struggle. Despite his wiry build and irritable demeanour, Lem had an untold reserve of physical and mental strength.

Lem had almost completely pulled Lorrelli's torso over the lip of the ledge when another tremendous groan lurched Asher forward and sent him sprawling. Asher's knees went out from under him as a key section of the support pillar disintegrated, dropping the pathway another three feet, which left Lorrelli's legs dangling in the air. The gap between Asher and the safety of his original stone pathway looming overhead was now insurmountable. A ragged assortment of boulders stacked perilously on top of each other in no apparent order was all that was keeping his friends aloft.

Most of the oversized rocks were worn. Many of them were weakened by the centuries of constant exposure to a barrage of steam that had invaded every crack, breaking down their grip on one another from the inside out.

A single boulder sat amongst the multitude of stones in the precariously stacked rock formation, which was larger by half than any other Asher could see from his view just underneath the main body of the stone ledge above. A massive diagonal crack stretched across its face from side to side. Smaller fragments of stone had already splintered and fallen away from the crack's edge. Each tiny movement from above saw more fragments dislodge. It was already structurally unsound. There was no way it would support the combined weight of the trio.

Lem disappeared for a moment behind the path to ensure Lorrelli's unconscious body was safely positioned atop the precarious stone bluff.

Asher swallowed his fear and calmed his nerves, but he knew when he saw his friend again it would be for the last time. Lem's face reappeared moments later as he leaned out over the edge, stretching a hand down towards Asher. As he rose to his feet, Asher gazed up at Lem with sorrow in his eyes and unapologetically shook his head.

"Asher, come on!" Lem thrust his hand down at his friend again and wiped his eyes clear of smoke-filled tears. The ground rumbled and shook violently beneath Asher's feet.

It was now or never. He had to act.

Asher shot a desperate look at the pathway behind him. More of it was disappearing by the second. Its jagged crumbling end hung over the precipice like the leprotic remains of a once-mighty limb. Large chunks of stone tore away from its disfigured stump with each shudder. It was only a matter of time before the entire pathway collapsed to the fiery depths below and took Asher with it. He bravely glanced up at Lem one last time, a fierce determination already set in his eyes.

Even to Lem it was clear: Asher's mind was made up. "Don't you dare," Lem growled at him, but there was no anger in his voice, only poorly restrained sadness.

"Keep her safe," Asher whispered softly as he searched for something within his friend's eyes. An enormous crash from the collapsing pathway deafened him, broke their locked gaze and forced Asher to turn and hurry away along the collapsing path as fast as his legs would carry him.

"Asher!" Lem called out after him, his hand left grasping in the void, but finding nothing but air.

Asher never heard Lem's cry over the destructive grinding of stones smashing against one another. Thunderous cracks echoed like gunfire as the surface of the path split apart beneath Asher's feet. Small stone chips sprayed against his legs, but they were instantly lost within the ash cloud enveloping everything around him.

Asher was exhausted. His legs were sluggish and felt sodden as they clumsily tried to navigate the disintegrating pathway. Even though it had been minutes since the swarm's assault, the venom's debilitating effects had only partially subsided. His arms had become a little more responsive, but the venom had left his balance severely compromised. Each violent tremor threatened to send him reeling off the pathway and into oblivion, yet somehow every time he managed to regain his composure at the last second and press on.

Chancing a glance behind him, Asher saw only a gaping void, the last fragments of the pathway crumbling into non-existence mere inches from his heels. The demoralising sight spiked a surge of adrenaline in his heart. He pushed his legs harder than ever, forcing them to comply with his demands as he scrambled headlong into the billowing mist. Half blinded by the heavy smoke billowing into his eyes, Asher dropped down on all fours and trusted his hands and feet to find solid footing where his eyes could not.

His situation had rapidly become desperate. There was no way he'd be able to maintain any sort of speed in this stance. His eyes blindly scanned everything in front of him, frantically searching for an escape. Before him lay the crumbling pathway, which was riddled with cracks and splinters: some fine, others frighteningly large. Its distressed surface was intermittently illuminated with a dull orange glow as lances of lava whizzed down past his face on both sides.

Asher figured he must've been at least two-thirds of the way across the gorge by now, although there was no way to be sure. The only thing he could see clearly through the smoke was a growing sense of despair and lost hope. He couldn't even suppress the looming dread settling in his mind. Even his subconscious was telling him he was probably going to die, but there was nothing else he could do. He buried down the feeling by focusing his thoughts on the image of his friends: Lorrelli, Lem, Morreby and, to a certain extent, Gibraltair. They were all relying on him. He needed to succeed.

He needed to survive.

His hands were bloody and sore. Every time he found a new handhold, his auger pushed and rubbed against the bones in his hand. Asher didn't even flinch at the pain, instead, he embraced it. It kept him focused. His head darted upwards as a blurry black shape emerged through the haze ahead of him. Standing upright, Asher estimated it must have been a foot or two above his head, at the very least. He wouldn't have seen it at all if it weren't for the bright orange glow of lava that had just landed on top of the shape and dribbled over its side.

Just when Asher thought hope was at hand, his foot caught on a splintering shard of stone. He'd become distracted and wasn't prepared for it. His momentum carried his body forward as his legs gave out beneath him. Asher's chest hit the stone path with a heavy thud, knocking the wind from his lungs. The resultant force was enough to break an entire section of the pathway free ahead of him. Asher found himself atop a seesaw of rock as the path's face rose sharply to a 30-degree slant and pivoted, twisting around clockwise on its axis. He clung on to the sides of the rotating stone bluff as it teetered on top of a support pillar like some kind of terrifying carnival ride.

This is bad. Real bad.

Asher was in trouble, more so now than ever before, and there was no-one that could save him this time. When his legs slid down the rock ledge, his weight increased the angle of the seesaw's slant: first to 35, then 40 degrees.

Asher desperately tightened his grip on the ledge's jagged edge with his hands and feet. He shredded the skin on his fingers until he felt his body slow to a precarious stop. The souls of his feet were mere inches from oblivion. Silently gasping, he wanted to thank the stars, but there was no time. If the seesaw slipped past 45 degrees, it would tip over itself, and Asher would die.

He had no choice.

He had to climb back up to counterbalance the teetering stone shelf. Digging his feet into the craggy edges, he vaulted upwards, one handhold after the other. Small fragments of rock crumbled under his rough grip and the clumsy scrabbling of his feet, but with every metre he gained, the giant seesaw tipped back towards the horizontal.

When he'd finally reached the tipping point, he was utterly exhausted and saturated with sweat, but he wasn't done yet. Using his own weight to counterbalance the stone ledge towards a new equilibrium, he steadied the unbalanced pivoting stone pathway until it lay flat and unmoving. Asher perched in the middle of the pathway and peered out into the murky haze, searching for a way off the infernal ledge.

Other than the intermittent flares of orange light from the falling lava piercing the gloom, he couldn't see anything. Even his divine eye yielded nothing through the ash and smoke. The ledge he'd seen had to be somewhere close by, but Asher had no way of knowing how far the stony shelf had rotated or in what direction to look.

A loud grinding noise berated his ears as the seesaw's base scraped against the support pillar's topmost boulder like 10-tonne sandpaper. Asher gave it 10 seconds at best until the entire stone bluff collapsed in a shower of rubble. Drawing in a deep breath to calm his pounding heart, he curled up his feet under his body and leaned back, once again allowing the ledge to shift under his weight. One end of the stone seesaw pivoted upwards with an almighty groan.

Asher exhaled, steadying his nerves against what he had to do as the ledge approached the right angle, when the entire stone shelf lurched to his right and twisted around 30 degrees on its axis. Asher was out of time. It was now or never.

He launched himself up the unsteady incline, feet madly scrambling along the crumbling stone shelf. He didn't have far to go, but the dramatic shift had pushed the pathway's incline to far steeper than he would have liked. In his exhausted state, it was near to impossible to scale the slope at speed.

The stone shelf moaned and shuddered violently with every footstep, nearly throwing the exhausted teen. Asher launched himself off the end of the massive stone shelf, just as it split in two with a loud crack. An almighty groan filled the air as the beleaguered support pillar finally gave way underneath the seesaw and toppled into the abyss in an avalanche of boulders and rubble.

High above all the crumbling debris, Asher's momentum carried him through the void, his arms flailing wildly as he desperately sought out any sign of the shadowy ledge through the haze. There was nothing, only the endless haze.

Then his upwards momentum turned and he began to fall. His mind went blank as his body became weightless, just before gravity grabbed hold and yanked him downwards. Asher couldn't help himself. He screamed.

His terrified voice had barely left his lips when he felt a sharp crunch against his chest. The next thing he knew, the air exploded from his lungs and his eyes burst open.

Breathless and disorientated, he watched the flat stone surface rush up towards him, seconds before his face smashed into it. He'd seriously misjudged how far away the ledge was when he'd launched into the void. His right cheek ultimately paid the price as it slammed down against the smooth surface of the stone with a loud thud.

The impact left Asher winded, his lungs breathlessly crying out for air as his upper torso was sprawled dangerously across the rock face. His legs dangled over the edge of the path, and his face hurt like hell. He smiled again. Against all odds, he was alive.

Just as the pain from the impact registered across his bruised face, the smooth stone surface, now smeared with his blood, blurred and rushed away from him. Asher's hands and fingers frantically grasped at the smooth surface as he slid backwards, desperately searching for a handhold: a crack, a crevice, anything he could hold on to.

There was nothing.

Asher felt his waist slip over the edge, followed immediately by his torso. With a final effort he threw one arm over the lip of the rock face and jerked his body to a dramatic stop, shoulders and face now the only thing above the ledge, his lower half dangling in the void. As he struggled to find a proper handhold and call upon the strength necessary to pull himself up onto the ledge, a thought came out of nowhere in the back of his mind.

First rains the swarm, then Aduro's arm.

With everything that had happened he'd completely forgotten about the second line on the shroud. He strained with all his might, trying desperately to pull himself up, but only managed to lock his other arm over the edge. An enormous blur of orange light above him caught his attention as it rushed down, enveloping the ashen cloud of black smoke like a tidal wave.

A waterfall of golden lava exploded in the distance. It splattered heavily as it landed, scattering small droplets of searing magma in every direction, a few feet away from his arm. Asher's eyes crystallised with fear as he glared up into the ash cloud. Violent bursts of golden magma cascaded down around him like deadly rain as more lava spewed forth through the glowing haze. One small globule of lava splashed against the stone and exploded next to Asher's left arm, spraying his skin with several specks of scorching lava.

Asher snatched his hand away from the ledge and wailed in agony as the droplets melted his flesh. Tears of agony, ash and smoke stung his eyes as he felt the searing lava chew through his muscles until it scorched bone. There was only one thing Asher could do to avoid being burned alive by the intensifying downpour of molten rock.

He let go.

CHAPTER 50

A GIFT OF LIFE

Asher's body shifted to a state of perpetual weightlessness as he released his grip on the path's crumbling edge. Had he waited another second, the downpour of molten rock would've engulfed him in a tidal wave of scorching death.

His life now hinged on a single moment. He had one chance to stop himself plummeting into the fiery depths of hell and only one arm with which to do it. The other arm was tightly clutched at his side, enveloped in agony, small droplets of lava still assaulting his skin, muscle and bone.

A hundred tiny creases of the ledge's craggy underside whizzed past as gravity yanked Asher downwards. All of the folds were too small for a handhold.

Blinded with pain and ash, his watery eyes searched the craggy underbelly of the pathway for anything large enough to grab on to: anything that would support his weight and shield him from the volcanic deluge about to unleash a tidal wave of brimstone on his head.

A dark shape flashed between two uneven rock shelves. Asher couldn't be sure what it was, but he was out of time: another second and the underside of the ledge would be out of reach. His uninjured arm shot out like a coiled snake striking its prey. His auger pulsated in his palm, radiating a golden light at the craggy surface as his fingers frantically searched for a handhold. At first only smooth stone met his fingertips, with nothing he'd be able to hold on to.

Asher's heart skipped a beat.

Then his fingers caught on the lip of a jagged crevice, a small life-saving fracture in the rock. It wasn't much, but he felt the muscles in his hand lock into place just as his arm reached its full extension. For a moment he thought everything would be alright, that he might actually survive, then a sharp pain tore through his right shoulder.

It felt like someone had impaled him with a hot poker as it spread up his arm, then down his side and chest. The sudden jolt nearly dislocated his shoulder with a violent snap as his full body weight came crashing to a thunderous halt in mid-air.

Despite the torture, Asher's arm held firm, his fingers locked around the lip of the fracture. His body swung beneath the underside of the stone pathway. He dangled with nothing but the cavernous abyss and fiery fire pit echoing below him.

Asher wanted to smile at cheating death one more time, but his face was contorted with too much pain to manage anything more than a grimace. His scarred body hung in the void like a discarded toy soldier. Asher didn't care that his arm burned, his shoulder reeled with pain, or that he could barely see through his smoke-clogged watery eyes.

He was alive.

The thought hit him just as a massive deluge of lava surged over the sides of the pathway above, drowning out everything on either side of him in a torrent of molten death. Asher had never felt such an oppressive heat in all his life. A waterfall of igneous wrath cascaded down around him, barraging the exposed skin of his face, arms and hands with scorching hot gusts of air.

Asher peered around his newly formed free-flowing molten prison. Where there had once only been a blinding ashen haze of smoke, there now stood a surreal orange glow, which illuminated every cranny of the craggy underside of the pathway above his head. A few metres in front of him, every sinuous detail of each boulder, rock and pebble of the precariously stacked support pillar lay exposed.

Despite enjoying his newfound clarity of vision, Asher found it hard to do anything other than hold on for dear life with his one good arm. Every inch of his body was racked with exhaustion, whilst the rest was drowning in agony.

Amidst it all he felt the familiar dull throb in his palm as blood funnelled into his auger, but for the life of him he couldn't explain why. He was far too weak and exhausted to call on his blood. It was taking all his strength and concentration just to maintain his grip and not succumb to the horrendous smell of melting flesh drifting up from his arm.

Casting his eyes down, his head reeled at the echoing abyss looming below his feet. Either side of the enormous drop was entombed by flowing curtains of lava that disappeared into the fiery hellhole below. The sight was sickening.

Asher had to look away before vertigo set in. He desperately looked for anything else on which to focus. His eyes landed on his arm, still clutched against his chest, his knuckles as white as snow as his fingers gripped the edges of his tunic in agony. He noticed several patches of fresh pink scars pockmarking the skin of his wounded arm.

"What the...?" Asher couldn't believe his own eyes. He'd been too preoccupied with everything going on to notice that his skin was actively healing itself from the damage the lava droplets had wreaked. The cauterised holes that had sent his mind reeling with agony moments before now only throbbed dully.

Absolutely amazed, Asher released his torturous grip and extended his arm to inspect the freshly healed scar-tissue. "No way," he whispered, unable to comprehend how his body had managed to heal itself from its debilitating wounds.

Gingerly, he stretched out his fingers and flexed his forearm. The agonising pain had subsided. Now only a dull throb echoed beneath each scar.

He craned his neck upwards at the underside of the rock's face and searched for another handhold. It was surprisingly easy to find in the disquieting glow of the lava. Slowly reaching up with his freshly scarred arm, he latched onto it and let it take his weight. A sharp pain shot down his arm, but his muscles held.

Growing more confident by the second, he forced aside the pain and found another handhold, then another, slowly swinging himself towards the bulk of the nearest support pillar. Working his way along the underside of the rock face, he swung between the curtains of molten fire like a wounded orangutan and found himself with both feet firmly planted on an extruding boulder of the support pillar.

For the first time since he had entered the enormous cavern, Asher breathed a little easier, an exhausted smirk creeping into the corners of his mouth. Despite everything, he was still alive. His face beaded with sweat. His limbs ached to the point of collapse. His auger dully throbbed in his palm and his arm sported a fresh batch of new scars. He was stuck underneath a prison of molten rock, suspended high above a gorge of lava with no visible escape, but he was still alive.

He couldn't help but smile, but the seriousness of his predicament soon sunk in again. The impenetrable waterfall of molten rock on either side of him showed no sign of abating and there was no visible way out.

"Now what?" Asher asked himself, cautiously attempting to peer around the edges of the large boulder in front of him. Reaching out with his right hand, he secured another handhold much closer to the wall of liquid flames. Ignoring the furnace punishing his exposed skin with blasts of igneous heat, he leaned a little closer to the molten deluge.

Peering his head out as much as he dared, he squinted his eyes against the inferno and tried to discern if there was a large enough gap between the falling river's monotonous flow and the pillar for him to squeeze past.

There wasn't.

The lava's inflammatory kiss missed the side of the pillar by mere inches, making it impossible for all but a butterfly to squeeze past. He leaned back and cast his eyes down, hoping to see a gap somewhere beneath his feet.

There was none.

If anything, the haphazardly stacked boulders making up the support pillar only got bigger the farther down his eyes travelled, their edges disappearing into the lava's gut with a splash. Moving back to his original position, he edged his way closer to the left-hand side of the pillar, reaching out with his freshly scarred arm for a better handhold.

As Asher's left hand edged closer to the cascading torrent of magma, he felt the all too familiar sting of his auger igniting in his right palm. Asher's eyes winced in discomfort as the dull sensation shot up his arm, once again fuelling blood into its core.

After nearly a year of attempting to master the power of his blood, he was all too used to the dull sensation in his arm. He did not, however, expect the sensation to leap across his chest and into his heart. He felt a raw power surge through his veins and propel down his arm, leaving his entire upper torso and extremities tingling with wild lashings of power.

Asher had no idea what was happening, so he clung to the pillar with both hands. His right hand remained close to his body, whilst he stretched out his left and latched onto a rocky handhold. It was close enough to the downpour of molten rock that the hairs on the back of his hand and lower arm first wilted then melted away.

He waited with clenched teeth as the dull throbbing sensation splintered through the muscles of his left forearm. Inch by inch, the feeling crept down his arm until it had reached the first of the fresh scars now marring his skin.

Asher's eyes widened as, one by one, the scars ignited to life with a burst of golden brilliance. The flare of colour subsided almost instantaneously but left his scars glowing radiantly like a luminescent tattoo. The glow was barely visible at first, little more than a weak discolouration irradiating his scarred skin, as though the tissue beneath was radioactive.

Asher extended his arm until his hand was only a few inches away from the lava's teeming wall to better examine the phenomenon. The scarred flesh once again surged to life, illuminating with a fiery golden brilliance until a fierce glow had enveloped his forearm.

At first, Asher didn't notice the absence of the ever-present orange glow behind his outstretched hand, but as his eyes refocused on the waterfall of lava he noticed a small gap had appeared. It was as if something was diverting the lava's flow. Peering through the tiny hole, he saw the thick cloud of black ash polluting the air of the cavernous void beyond his infernal prison.

Repositioning his hand closer to the edge of the support pillar, he leaned closer to get a better vantage point, but the gap disappeared. The flowing molten curtain returned once more into an unbroken wall of liquefied death.

The glow over his arm and beneath his scars also dimmed. Asher's gaze switched between the impenetrable wall of lava and his glowing scars as a spark of recognition registered in his mind. He edged his hand back towards the waterfall lava, inching his palm closer to its surface.

His scars blazed back to life, their glow a feverishly bright golden hue; but, strangely, he felt no heat from the lava whatsoever, despite it being inches from his fingers. Another small gap appeared, directly in front of his arm, as the lava's flow was diverted once more.

"What the…" Asher said in awe as he waved his hand from side to side at the fiery wall. The gap in the lava moved with it, following the direction of his hand precisely, creating a small moving rift in the flow of lava.

He concentrated and willed his body to funnel more blood into his auger. The dull ache lingering in his hand magnified into a constricting ache and ignited a brutal burning sensation in the skin around his glowing scars. Clenching his jaw to help bury the discomfort, he forced more of his blood into his auger until the size of the rift doubled.

A gap the size of a small child stared back at him, but still it was not big enough. He pointed his hand above his head, where the lava washed over the edge of the stone shelf above, and willed even more blood into his auger. The igneous downpour was wrenched apart, splitting the curtain of fire to reveal something that brought a triumphant smile to Asher's face.

As he gazed down at the smooth stone lying beyond the lava's reach, Asher realised it was his original pathway staring back at him. It remained untouched by the lava's infernal rage. He didn't stop to consider his odds of making the jump. He couldn't wait. He could feel himself growing weaker with every drop of blood he forced from his veins into his auger. Remembering to keep his auger aimed at the lava high above his head, Asher drew in a single breath, bent his knees and launched himself off the pillar towards the narrow gap.

Flames licked at his clothes as they brushed against the lava, but Asher sailed through the gap with arms outstretched towards the safety of his original stone pathway. His feet skidded to a stop unsteadily, which left him overbalanced. He slipped and promptly fell sidewards, landing heavily on his hip.

He'd made it.

He picked himself up and dusted off his tunic, turning his head away from the molten waterfall to gaze out into the abyss.

The black smoke that had been remarkably absent from his precarious position underneath the lava's twin falls was now all he could see. His mind instantly reverted to Lem and Lorrelli as his eyes welled up with tears from the hazy cloud. Asher had no idea whether they were alive.

"Lem?" he shouted out into the cloud of smoke. "Lorrelli?"

Only the monotonous downpour of the fiery deluge met his ears. He tried again, but heard no reply. Asher, instead, looked at his feet. The glow of the nearby falling lava made it easy to make out the path he was standing on, but little else.

Its crumbling remnants had broken away behind him, leaving only one direction in which to travel: towards a brilliant starburst of light shining through the blackened smoke cloud like an ominous spotlight.

Asher was about to take a step forward, but then stopped in his tracks. Reaching into his tunic pocket, he retrieved the second half of the shroud from its metal casing. After everything that had just happened, he needed to know what would come next. He read each word of Vitalsior's riddle from start to finish. Much of it made a lot more sense than it had before, but the last line remained as much an enigma as ever.

Best passings three, do so cautiously, tread light with nimble grace. First rains the swarm, then Aduro's arm. Leaving last to tempered life deface. Putting the shroud away safely in his pocket, Asher repeated the last line, trying to unravel its mysteries. "Leaving last to tempered life deface."

Asher had no idea what it meant but, then again, he had absolutely no idea what the other warnings had meant until it had been too late. With no alternative available, he carefully worked his way along the path, half expecting yet another trap to spring at any moment.

The menacing starburst of light that emanated through the ash cloud grew larger and brighter with every step. Asher came to a stop only when both of his feet had left the narrow stone pathway and were firmly planted on solid ground.

Asher had finally reached the outer landing surrounding the large stone tower. It stretched high above him, disappearing into the ash and smoke like an enormous elevator shaft. So precise was the craftsmanship of each stone, it was impossible to see where one ended and the next began, leaving the entire facade of the tower as smooth as glass.

A single iron door, at least double his height, rose up ominously before him. Asher gazed up at the final defensive barrier of Vitalsior's vaulted ark in awe, his mind filled with trepidation. In its centre, an enormous intricately cut crystal beamed prismatic shards of light like a colossal eye of a god. Each ray shining through the crystal's translucent face was blinding, but fractured, as though someone was holding up a broken kaleidoscope to the sun.

The shifting lances of light and the heavy ash cloud made it difficult to make out any of the other details of the spire. But as far as Asher could tell, it looked as if the entire area had been untouched by human hands for at least a millennia. There was no handle on the door, no lock and no visible sign of how to open it.

Asher wondered if it was a door at all. Taking a few nervous paces forward, he held up his hand across to shield his eyes from the blinding radiance. Swallowing his trepidation, he warily placed the fingertips on the surface of the metal beneath the enormous jewel. It was ice cold to the touch, as if the entire surface had been snap-frozen. Its coolness seemed ludicrous to Asher, given the sheer amount of heat, steam and smoke radiating throughout the cavernous void. He tried pushing on the door.

It didn't budge.

It didn't even make a sound.

Asher pushed again, harder this time, with both hands, palms flat on the surface. "Oh, come on," Asher shouted in frustration, slamming a clenched fist against the metal. Backing away from the door, he gave himself a second to think. The shroud's last line immediately popped into his head again. *Leaving last to tempered life deface.* He looked at the door, then at his scar-burned arm, then down at his golden auger, complete with black-scar taint. Somehow he knew they all fitted together.

They had to.

Morreby's life hung in the balance.

He just didn't understand how they worked in unison.

Raising both arms in front of him, auger-adored palm outstretched, he closed his eyes and concentrated his thoughts on opening the door. He blocked out the familiar sensation of blood coursing through his veins and into his auger's core, but he could not block out the barrage of light shining into his face. It burned through his eyelids and bored down into his eyes, searing his retinas. He frowned harder and clamped his eyes shut as hard as he could, but no matter what he did he couldn't block out the light. It burrowed past his defences and delved into his mind, commanding him from inside his own head with authoritative tone of a voice beyond age.

You have come far, but your journey ends here.

The voice bored into Asher's skull and permeated every thought. Each word numbed his mind as it landed, draining away his control over his actions with a debilitating effect. The more Asher tried to fight against the voice—or the light, he couldn't be sure which—the more its incapacitating influence over him increased.

The voice spoke again, louder this time, a deep arrogance echoing through its words. It churned Asher's thoughts into a frenzy, until he could no longer focus his mind on a single idea.

Your blood is strong, but your mind is weak. Your thoughts betray you, fallen kinsman.

The accusation struck home like a hammer. Asher cried out in agony and threw his head this way and that, hands clutching his temples in a desperate attempt to throw the voice out of his mind.

"I just want to save her!" Asher screamed, but he wasn't even sure if he had said so out loud or just in his mind. Crossing the abyss had drained his body of precious blood and energy, leaving him exhausted beyond measure, and his mind even more so.

You lie!

Each word of the voice inside his head felt like a gong had been struck, ringing inside his cerebral cortex and sapping away his sanity. Asher felt more and more of his consciousness slip away as it succumbed to the voice's power over him.

If you are the last of my lineage, then my gifts were for naught.

The impact of the voice's words brought Asher to his knees. His hands dropped to his sides, palms still open towards the door. He felt the light intensify even further and wash over him like a drug, engulfing his mind and body in a sea of insanity. The core of Asher's auger swirled and churned, gorging itself upon his blood of its own accord, as the light seized control of his body. Asher felt his mind slip away, but forced his lips and tongue to whisper a last message before he lost control completely.

"I won't let them die for me!" Asher's voice echoed in the gloom with an undercurrent of looming despair.

The light faltered for a moment as if dissecting Asher's thoughts for deception or betrayal. Asher's life ebbed away as he kneeled on the floor. His body hunched over itself as the last traces of his consciousness waited for the voice to destroy his mind forever. As his world turned to black, the thought of his friends crept into Asher's subconscious. Lem and Lorrelli flashed across his mind, their faces as clear as when they'd first met moments before the alignment ceremony.

Morreby's face and frail body convulsing in the centre of the cavern flickered past, until the memory of Braak's hulking body battling a demon in the night outshone her. That image was also lost, as an image of Raglan leaping on the back of the Mortis Skulk replaced it: Raglan sacrificing his own life so that Asher might live.

The memory of losing Raglan brought a raging ferocity to life inside Asher's mind that made his blood surge inside his veins, renewing life to his limbs. Asher opened his eyes and stared directly into the faltering godlike eye.

Truth sits well in your heart, but life is fleeting. My gift will bring only death in your hands.

"It's the only thing that can save her," Asher pleaded.

So you say, but villainy easily corrupts a heart with pure intent. May the tormenting memories of those you doom, steel you against such a fate.

The crystal surged with power, magnifying in strength and brilliance until its lances of light pierced across the entire cavern, obliterating the ash cloud that permeated the void, rendering the air fresh once more. In a blinding flash, the light and the voice were gone.

The heavy iron door stood ajar, the enormous crystal in its centre gone. Whether it had been destroyed or had simply vanished, Asher didn't know, but he was finally face to face with what he'd been seeking. With heavy legs and a tired mind, Asher dragged himself to his feet and stepped forward, pushing past the large iron door and disappearing into the interior of the giant spire.

At first he didn't quite know what he was looking at, but then his mind shook off its sluggish daze and processed what he was looking at. The tower itself was hollow, the high glass-like chimneystack exterior served only as a support structure for a massive pipeline extending upwards from the bowels of the lava pit beneath him that disappeared high into the tower's roof above. The pipe was twice as wide as Asher's shoulders, and was comprised of an augmented metal as thick as his chest.

It rumbled loudly in the small space.

Directly before him a large portal of tempered glass had been fitted into the pipe. A small, shiny metal plate had been embedded in its exterior, facing outwards. Asher blinked furiously, shielding his eyes from the rapid movement of molten lava, as tonnes of it were pumped upwards towards underbelly of the city above.

A single golden orb vibrated in the middle of the metal plate, releasing a low-pitched humming noise as it went about its work as though it had a life of its own. It quivered and shuddered with every surge of the lava, sending wave upon wave of the molten rock hurtling upwards.

"A gift of life," Asher mumbled as he finally realised what he was looking at, then his mind flickered back to Morreby. There was no time to admire the magnificence of his discovery.

He had to save her.

It was the only reason the voice had let him live.

He gingerly approached the metal plate and reached out with both hands, wrapping each one around the outside of the orb. His auger flared to life within his palm once it made contact, but only for a second. The metal was surprisingly cool to the touch.

He tried to pull the orb out from the pillar, but it wouldn't budge. It throbbed in his hands, pulsating with life, but it wasn't going anywhere easily. He tried twisting it right.

Nothing.

Then left.

The orb sprang free and twisted, unlocked from its position

with ease. He continued to twist it until it stopped, then carefully pulled on it again. This time it came away from the metallic plate freely. He slowly withdrew a sceptre-like probe from the hole, some sections still covered with trace elements of lava, until finally the probe was free of the pipe and lava altogether.

Asher held it down and shook it. The last remaining lava droplets came away freely, leaving the metal pristinely clean. As the last globule of lava fell to the floor, the gilded sceptre ceased its monotonous humming and Asher felt the vibrations stop.

The glowing orange light behind the pipeline's glass instantly faded a little. Peering closer, Asher realised the lava was no longer being sucked up from the fiery depths and pumped upwards; in fact, it was now quite the opposite. Tonnes of molten rock stuck inside the pipeline instantly changed direction and fell, lights flaring and fading as it rocketed downwards, picking up speed with every second until Asher could only make out a blur of orange and black.

The entire cavern rumbled and shook as though two tectonic plates had just collided in its centre. Asher took a step back and held the sceptre to his chest, fear spreading across his trembling face as the realisation of what he'd just done struck home. Retreating back a few paces from the shuddering pipeline, he couldn't bear to watch it drain completely; instead, he spun around, the gilded sceptre still locked against his chest within trembling fingers.

Throwing his head back, he called out a message and listened to the echo of his voice as it disappeared up into the darkened hollow of the tower. Whether it was a message for the voice, or a reassurance for himself, he couldn't be certain. The only thing he could be certain of was that he didn't believe his own words.

"You're wrong about me!"

CHAPTER 51

SCARS THAT BIND

When Asher re-emerged into the cavern via the tower's doorway, it was instantly obvious the noxious black cloud of ash was gone. The air was fresh, without so much as a hint of the lingering smoke that had stung his eyes earlier and made it impossible to see properly.

The torrential downpour of lava that had imprisoned him underneath the rocky shelf had also vanished, as had the rest of the lava that had rained down intermittently from the cavernous ceiling. Without the ash and magma, the echoing void before him and chasm below felt even more immense and unnerving.

Removing the augmented veil from his mouth and nose, Asher breathed in deeply, letting fresh air fill his lungs, but he instantly felt lightheaded. He paused to steady himself against the wall of the tower, but knew his body was far beyond the limits of exhaustion. The trauma he'd suffered during his ordeal across the chasm, combined with the ravages the voice had wreaked upon his mind, had left Asher shattered beyond measure. Every action was a challenge, every thought a struggle.

Asher gazed out across the shattered remnants of the three paths he and his friends had used to cross the gorge. Somehow, against all odds, one path had survived the devastation. Large sections of its surface were still smouldering with the pooled remnants of lava that had settled on its surface, but the path itself was intact.

Its stony arm stretched out across the void in a long unbroken arc that towered over the shattered remnants of the other two paths. A fragmented series of half-collapsed pillars and fragmented rocky plateaus that stuck up from the gurgling lava bed like broken arrows on a battlefield were now the only reminder that three paths had once perched high above the abyss.

Asher scanned the debris for signs of his friends. It took a few seconds as he ducked and leaned to get a better vantage point, but when he saw two distant figures huddled together on one of the rocky plateaus, an enormous sensation of relief washed over him.

They were alive.

The path had collapsed on either side, stranding them on a precarious, solitary stone bluff in the middle of the abyss. But they were safe. Asher waved his arms at them wildly, frantically calling their names. Even that small effort was almost too much for him. His own voice set off a dull ringing in his ears, making his insides reel as a wave of nausea hit him, but Asher didn't care. He was overjoyed.

When Lem finally caught sight of Asher, he flashed his friend an enormous grin and pointed him out to the now-conscious but visibly groggy Lorrelli.

Asher held the golden sceptre high above his head so they could see it clearly. Their distant cheers told him they understood, but their enthusiasm was short-lived. Lem shouted something at him, pointing wildly at the central platform like a madman.

Asher's ears were still ringing too loudly to hear what Lem was saying, but he didn't need to. Their frantic gestures sparked a momentary forgotten fear back to life.

Morreby.

Asher's eyes shot towards where Lem was pointing, but the arc of the path in front of him obscured the central platform from view. He didn't particularly want to cross back over the pathway: he felt dizzy and nauseated. His balance was shot and every thought hurt; but, ultimately, he knew he had no other choice. He felt responsible for Morreby. He had to do the right thing. He had to prove the voice it was wrong.

He had to save her.

Asher turned away from his friends and hesitantly approached the last remaining pathway that stretched out over the chasm like a gnarled finger. Much of its surface was still glowing with a thin coat of lava that had settled within depressions, some still oozing down the slope.

Gulping back his trepidation, Asher steadied himself. He wedged the golden sceptre firmly between his tunic and belt, making sure it was secure before setting out on the path. His pace was slow and cautious. He had come too far to let poor balance and careless footing ruin everything now. He held out his left hand as he approached the section covered in lava and concentrated his thoughts as he did before.

The familiar stinging sensation surged up his arm, through his chest and down his other arm, just as he expected it to. Light sparked underneath his scars and he set about clearing the lava off the edges of the narrow stone ledge with a methodical wave of his left hand. With arm outstretched, Asher climbed the slope, treading carefully as he cleared the path of lava. When he had almost reached its crest, he caught sight of Morreby's unconscious body.

Gibraltair was kneeling over her, head upon hers, a strange expression on his face set amidst the burned flesh and charred ash that marred his face and scalp. Asher desperately wanted to see more, but trying to focus on anything so far away made his mind reel with pain, which increased his vertigo tenfold.

Asher saw colours and shapes better than individual features, but the sight of Morreby's ghost-white skin stopped him dead in his tracks. Gibraltair's cane lay flat on her chest as it had before, but it did not rise or fall as it should have, which could only mean one thing.

She wasn't breathing.

"Hurry, Asher, she's fading."

A cry to Asher's right broke his concentration. Turning his head, he saw Lem and Lorrelli staring back at him helplessly. "Lem, Lorrelli," Asher whispered as he wondered how he could save them.

"Don't worry about us. Get her the augefact for prac's sake. Go!" Lem's words snapped Asher back into focus and forced his legs into action.

Climbing the rest of the ridge, Asher noticed a blur of movement as Gibraltair's head turned towards him.

"Asher," Gibraltair's voice was coarse, his throat weak as he shielded a sickening cough behind a hand. "Did you get it?" he gasped through haggard breaths, moments before his beleaguered gaze locked on to the golden sceptre tucked inside Asher's belt. "You did, didn't you? Miraculous… Quickly, bring it here." Gibraltair's body convulsed as he coughed up a mouthful of blood. "She doesn't have much time."

Asher nodded and continued to clear large patches of lava at his feet.

Behind tinted glasses, Gibraltair frowned as he watched Asher divert the augmented lava off the sides of the path with a simple wave of his hand.

When Asher's feet finally stepped onto the central platform, he hurried over to Morreby's side. She lay as still as death itself, her cheeks devoid of all colour. "Is she…" Asher couldn't bring himself to finish the question as he slumped down next to her.

"Death lurks," Gibraltair wheezed heavily, "but will not claim her," Gibraltair nodded his head towards the golden sceptre tucked into Asher's belt, "thanks to you."

"Tell me what to do." Asher withdrew the augefact and held it firmly in two hands.

"A gift of life," Gibraltair mumbled, his voice clearing a little as a mixture of excitement, greed and wonder came across his face. A scar-burned smile emerged as he marvelled at the augefact. "Imbued with the flesh and bone of the old boy himself."

"Tell me how to save her!" Asher demanded, snapping Gibraltair from his ramblings.

"I can save her, but I'm too weak," Gibraltair struggled to raise a few inches, exposing his mottled flesh for Asher to see.

"You must heal me first." The words fell from his mouth in a rush as a new wave of pain exploded all over his body.

"Can't you heal yourself?" Asher blurted out, "Morreby's dying."

"No!" he snapped breathlessly, his nostrils flaring with anger and desperation. "The lava was augmented by the augefact, only it can undo the savagery it has caused."

He opened up his tattered tunic, and exposed his lava-scarred chest to show Asher the true extent of his injuries. Skin peeled away from muscle as he pulled at the fabric. Lava had melted his skin into the weave of fabric until the two were one.

Gibraltair's face contorted as he stifled an agonising scream. Much of his flesh had been burned black. Every movement unleashed a fresh wave of agony across his nervous system, spurring his pain receptors into revolt.

Asher leaned away from Gibraltair. He too understood the pain of the lava's kiss. He had felt the mutilating bite as it melted through his flesh; yet, for some reason, he could not bring himself to trust enough to give him the augefact.

"Her death is assured unless you can save her," Gibraltair barked, his voice more gravelly than ever. "Can you?"

Asher stood up and took a step away from the man, forcing an almost instantaneous emotional retraction from Gibraltair as a sorrowful expression crossed the augiologist's face.

"Forgive me," Gibraltair moaned, lowering his arm, "the pain is unbearable."

"I know." Asher involuntarily ran his fingers over the scars on his left arm.

"Aduro's arm," Gibraltair whispered with an intake of breath as he caught sight of the scars. But the phrase was inaudible to Asher.

Morreby's body convulsed, her limbs uncontrollably trembling like an electric current was being forced through her body.

She was going into shock.

Gibraltair weakly placed his hand over his cane, his auger

flaring with blue light. His actions eased the convulsions somewhat, but a slight tremor remained, just under her skin. "I cannot save her without your help." He grimly turned his head up and took off his glasses to let Asher stare through the augiologist's opaque pools of blindness and peer into his soul. "You have to trust me, Asher."

Asher had no choice.

Every inch of his being fought against the trust Gibraltair was asking for, but he had no idea how to save Morreby without him. "Okay. But first promise me you'll save her."

"I swear it." Gibraltair's milky-white eyes stared back at Asher with a blind sense of necessity. The augiologist let his gaze linger a second longer before replacing his glasses. "Now, aim the augefact at me and hold your auger against it."

Asher did as he was instructed, but he couldn't help his eyes wandering off to gaze at Morreby's unconscious body. It had resumed its deathly still state.

"Repeat after me, Salus Reddo," Gibraltair wheezed. "The augefact will do the rest."

"Salus…" Asher began, but his words trailed off as a shiver rain through Morreby's body, making it shake uncontrollably.

"Concentrate," Gibraltair coughed, blood spattering his teeth and lips. "Salus Reddo."

"Salos Redo," Asher murmured, mispronouncing the words accidentally as he gazed forlornly at Morreby's frail body. Somehow the image of her like this made it impossible for him to focus on anything else clearly.

"Do you want her to die?" Gibraltair shouted at him, breaking Asher's gaze. Gibraltair's face was a mask of anger, agitation and desperation, all horrendously burned beyond measure.

"No."

"Then focus." Gibraltair was becoming increasingly agitated. "Salus Reddo."

"Salus red … reddo," Asher stammered.

"Concentrate!" Gibraltair grabbed hold of his cane, the action sent a small shockwave of air billowing past Asher's face, freeing the youth's mind of the daze plaguing it.

"Salus Reddo. Salus Reddo. Salus Reddo!" Asher's voice rose in intensity with each reiteration of the incantation. The augefact whirred to life in his hands, the golden metal vibrating and growing warmer against his skin. When the metal had almost become too hot to hold, Asher felt a bone-jarring sensation shoot up his arm. It was hot and cold at the same time. It made his muscles quiver and his skin tingle, then burn. It was unlike any else he'd ever experienced.

A shimmering ripple unleashed from the sceptre's tip and shot through the air. Gibraltair moaned with discomfort as it hit his chest and washed over his body, the ripples distorting as they swirled over his burned flesh. A soft golden light appeared, glistening above his skin like a godly aura. One by one, each wound healed, healthy tissue replacing scar-burned flesh as the augefact rejuvenated Gibraltair's muscles and skin.

Charred flakes of burned skin fell to the floor as new strands of hair sprouted from his scorched scalp. Within seconds, Gibraltair's luscious locks had regrown over his temple where the lava's kiss had just before left only charred skin and exposed sections of his skull. The disfigured horror Gibraltair had been moments before, was now a distant memory. The man's former good looks had become vaguely recognisable again.

Just as the last section of his newly regrown skin had almost returned into Gibraltair's regular complexion, a searing pain exploded the right side of Asher's rib cage, which sent his body into an involuntary spasm. The ferocity of the assault tore up Asher's side like the slash of a blade. He uncontrollably wrenched the sceptre away from Gibraltair as his arm contorted in pain, but not before a small amount of the agony lapping at his subconscious was discharged down into his auger and magnified through the augefact.

A wild arc of energy laced the air and struck Gibraltair square in the jaw, rending a huge gash in his newly healed facial muscles from hairline to chin in the sceptre's wake. The savage burst of energy severed his glasses in two as it slashed through the augiologist's facial muscles, leaving Gibraltair wailing in pain, hands clutching his face as a torrent of blue-tinged blood gushed from the wound.

"Lower the weapon and step away," a distinctive, yet unforgettable, voice boomed from across the chasm on the other side of the destroyed drawbridge.

Asher recognised the voice immediately and dreaded hearing it because he knew who it belonged to. Gritting his teeth against the ache of his throbbing rib cage, he turned to face his attacker.

Asher's eyes narrowed as his worst fears were confirmed. A figure dressed in the unmistakable black leather of the Red Scar Guard stood across the abyss in battle stance, auger aimed directly at Asher. A snide face with cruel features malevolently sneered back at him across the void. The face had been forever burned into Asher's memory.

He would have known it anywhere.

It was the face of Farrenk.

CHAPTER 52

TRUST AND SENTIMENT

Asher could almost feel the man's scathing arrogance bearing down upon him from across the chasm.

Farrenk lowered his twin-bladed battle mantle as he summarily dismissed Asher and the pitiful bleeding body of Gibraltair as plausible threats. Instead, he aimed his battle mantle at what was left of the shattered charred timber stumps protruding from the drawbridge's iron base. The wood splintered loudly as fresh saplings emerged and rapidly grew in branches as they interwove amongst one another for strength. Again and again they split, new shoots emerging on the trunks of older ones, all of them growing, stretching and expanding across the gaping chasm.

"Asher, the augefact," Gibraltair's whispered at him, through blind eyes strewn with blood. "Quickly!"

Asher heard the urgency and desperation in the augiologist's voice, but he hesitated, a lasting dread inside him warning him not to relinquish the augefact.

"Mine is the voice of the Chancellor and you will obey." Farrenk stepped out onto the first tangled branches without fear. His auger remained aimed at the vanguard of the tangled regrowth, while his feet were unnaturally steadfast on the gridlock of tangled wood beneath him. "Relinquish the weapon."

"It's not a weapon," Asher cried out.

"The wound it rends begs to differ." Farrenk's tone was unyielding and betrayed no ounce of leniency as his eyes glanced towards Gibraltair's bloody face. "Put it down and step away from the traitor Reine."

"Traitor?" Asher repeated under his breath, the accusation came as a shock to him.

"Do not trust him, Asher," Gibraltair's voice trembled as a

fresh stream of blood haemorrhaged his neck. "The Red Scars are trained to deceive and beguile you."

"The traitor Reine is wanted for sedition, subversion and treasonous acts, in addition to the murder of Legate Seville," Farrenk's voice grew even louder, booming across the cavern as he edged ever closer on his mangled wooden bridge.

How does he know about the legate? Asher asked himself silently, trying to make sense of the accusations. *He wasn't down here. He didn't see her die. There's no way he could possibly know.* "The legate's not dead," Asher lied, in a weak attempt to stall for time.

"The dead are incapable of lying, unlike traitors and their collaborators," Gibraltair's tone instantly became more menacing. "And unless you surrender that weapon, I'll personally see to it that you'll be tried as his accomplice."

"But she was trying to kill us."

"Kill you?" His eyes flicked to Gibraltair, "did he tell you that? It is no surprise, really. Every word born from a traitor's lips is laced with treachery and lies. Are you so blind you cannot see the truth that kneels so bloody before you?"

"He's lying, Asher. Give me the augefact. There is still time to save her," Gibraltair pleaded, thrusting out an open hand towards Asher.

"You're lying!" Asher spat at Farrenk, hurling the accusation at the Red Scar.

Farrenk withdrew a large pearl-like object from his tunic and held it out for Asher to see, sneering at his insolence. "I alone have seen the echoes of her auger. They were... excruciating, but enlightening."

Asher recognised the pearl orb instantly. It was unmistakable.

"She was trying to save you, all of you..." his words trailed off as his gaze transfixed on Gibraltair's bloodied face. He openly smiled as the large gash sent fresh spurts of blood streaming down the augiologist's face. "From him."

"He's lying, they all lie. They'll twist any truth and manipulate you. You were there, Asher, you saw what she did. Don't let him corrupt your mind, your memories. He'll kill us all and bury the truth down here."

"Silence, traitor!" Farrenk flicked a burst of blue energy from the tip of his twin-pronged blade at the augiologist.

Gibraltair never saw it coming.

It hit him square in the side, knocking him to the floor. His body crumpled over in a heap across Morreby's legs as his lungs slowly asphyxiated. The only upside of the attack was that now he had his back to Farrenk. Gibraltair grabbed his cane with murderous intent and readied himself. Blind, bloody and broken as he was, he was not going down without a fight.

"Legate Seville was the Scarlet Commander," Asher spat at Farrenk, squaring off against the Red Scar Guard, trying to muster up all the courage he possessed. "Of course you'd lie to protect your master."

"Enough!" Farrenk spat the word from his mouth, spittle landing on the branches at his feet. "I serve only one master, boy: the Chancellor. And by his power my word is law. Defy me and you defy the Cruaar Nation. Now step away from the traitor and surrender the weapon."

Farrenk was now halfway across the echoing gorge and getting closer by the second. Asher glanced down at the sceptre, then at Morreby, then at Gibraltair, and finally back at Farrenk. He didn't know who to believe, who to trust. He was confused and frightened that no matter what choice he made, it would be the wrong one.

"Last chance!" Farrenk's voice bellowed across the gap.

Asher held out the sceptre in front of him, silently hoping the right decision would come to him if he stared long enough at it.

"Asher, please," Gibraltair croaked at him.

"I need it to save her," Asher whispered under his breath, his face transforming into a look of pure defiance as he levelled his gaze at the Red Scar.

Farrenk didn't laugh. He was well trained to recognised rebellious behaviour from even the tiniest of mannerisms, but

Asher's expression had practically screamed his betrayal at him. He couldn't help but smile callously. Soon it wouldn't matter.

The bridge had regrown to two-thirds of its original length. It was still too great a distance for Farrenk to jump across unaided, but soon enough he'd have the weapon, the traitor and Asher within arm's reach. He just needed to stall for time. "Save her? Save her from what?" Farrenk bellowed and shook his head from side to side in disbelief. "There's nothing wrong with her."

"What?" Asher's defiance faltered, his decision wavering whilst his eyes raced to Morreby as the Red Scar's words tumbled through his mind.

Farrenk seized full advantage of Asher's hesitation and pressed him further, his eyes glistening with cunning amidst the perpetual orange glow radiating up from the lava bed far below. "Ask yourself, who are you saving her from? Do you even know what's making her sick? I just told you the legate was trying to save her, but where has his auger been throughout all this?"

The memory of Gibraltair's cane on Morreby's chest flashed before Asher's eyes. He turned his head and looked again to confirm the man's accusation. Sure enough, Gibraltair was still slumped over Morreby's body, one hand clutching his cane in a trembling fist, auger intermittently pulsing with blue light.

"Asher, it's the only thing keeping her alive." Gibraltair's blind eyes glanced up feebly in the direction of Asher's voice as blood streamed down his face.

Morreby's face was gaunt and devoid of colour. To Asher, she looked dead already.

"The augefact, before it's too late," Gibraltair rasped and held out his free hand.

Farrenk smiled again as he saw the indecision in Asher's eyes. "He's the one lying, Asher. Tricking you. Manipulating you," Farrenk called out, taking a few more steps closer to the edge of the precipice, making sure to raise his voice for added effect. "He's the one making her sick!"

"Asher, please, you must trust me." Gibraltair's milky eyes

gazed up into space, searching the expansive darkness, pleading for Asher's trust.

Asher's eyes flicked to Morreby, then to Gibraltair, then back at Farrenk. He needed to act. He was out of time.

He needed to make a decision, but he had no idea who to trust. He had no idea who was telling the truth and who was lying. He didn't trust either of them: not Gibraltair and certainly not Farrenk. Not even his divine eye would help him see through their lies. All he cared about was saving Morreby.

Two choices tumbled around inside his head: trust Gibraltair and save his sick friend, or trust Farrenk and believe that Gibraltair was the one making Morreby sick. Either way, he lost the possession of the augefact and possibly Morreby's life in the process. Asher blinked twice and made a decision, hoping like hell it was the right one. Slowly he turned to face Farrenk.

"It's not a weapon, it's an augefact."

Farrenk's face went pale for a moment as Asher's words hit home. His eyes narrowed and the corners of his mouth cringed as Asher raised the augefact towards him, outstretched not in violence, but as an offer.

"Asher, no! You mustn't," Gibraltair begged.

"Quiet, traitor," Farrenk snapped, silencing the augiologist with a demented gaze. Farrenk's smile grew on his face like a waxing crescent moon and grew larger as he realised he'd done it. He'd convinced the boy to see the light. The traitor, the augefact and Asher were about to become his. He raised an open hand towards Asher, waiting for the branches to close the remainder of the gap between them.

"It's Vitalsior's gift of life," Asher continued, his auger defiantly blazing to life within his palm. Asher felt the familiar warmth as he funnelled what little spare blood he had left into the gemstone's core. He purposefully kept his arm hidden behind his leg, safe from Farrenk's view.

But the Red Scar only had eyes for the augefact. He never saw it coming.

"And I need it to save her." Asher whispered, just loud enough for Farrenk to hear, before swinging the augefact towards Gibraltair and raising his other hand up, palm out, auger ablaze with golden light.

Farrenk swung his own two-pronged battle mantle up to defend himself a moment too late. He felt his feet go out from under him as Asher's blood calling struck him across the knees. The mass of timber branches at his feet instantly ceased their advance as the cavern went deathly quiet.

It wasn't a very powerful attack, but it had given Asher the time he needed to move across to Gibraltair's side and step between him and Farrenk.

Gripping his battle mantle in both hands, a disquieting grimace crept across Farrenk's face as he stood back up. Adopting an aggressive battle stance, he aimed his mantle's bladed fangs at Asher. "Now both your fates are sealed."

Asher took a deep breath and prepared to defend himself. He had no idea if he was making the right decision, but there was no turning back now. He held out the sceptre behind him towards Gibraltair, never taking his eyes off Farrenk for a moment. "Promise me you'll save her!" Asher yelled at Gibraltair.

Gibraltair reached out blindly and grabbed at the air around the sceptre, his milky eyes ablaze with desire as his fingers awkwardly wrapped around the augefact's gilded metallic shaft.

Asher's grip held firm, refusing to release the sceptre until he heard the words. "Promise me!" Asher screamed at him.

"I swear it on my life." Blood gushed from Gibraltair's face with his hands no longer able to help close the wound.

Asher released the end of the sceptre and felt a spark of energy leave his fingertips, race down the metal and surge into Gibraltair's hand. The smile that graced the augiologist's face as he wrapped his fingers around the sceptre was instantaneous.

"Die, traitors!" Farrenk bellowed as he channelled a savage blood calling through his battle mantle and unleashed it in an attempt to interrupt the handover.

The ferocity of the blast was brutal, but Asher's battle instincts managed to deflect it before it struck home. Farrenk didn't stop at just one attack, though. He was relentless, launching brutal onslaught after savage assault at the damaged duo.

Asher lost sight of Gibraltair as he called upon his blood, funnelling it into his auger time and time again to deflect each of Farrenk's savage attacks moments just before they landed. Despite the fact he was holding out against the devastating barrage, Asher felt his strength draining, his blood levels waned closer and closer to empty as each defence drained more of the precious liquid from his body. Soon he'd have no energy or blood left to fight back.

Then Farrenk would have them both, augefact and all.

"Gibraltair!" Asher screamed in desperation over his shoulder, unable to glance in the man's direction lest one of Farrenk's attacks land and annihilate him. Asher was left on the verge of collapse, yet still he held his ground against the Red Scar's insatiable fury. Tribarion Roolta had taught him well, but there were always limits to what a body could endure.

"Damn you, fool!" Farrenk's voice boomed across the gap as his eyes refocused on the figure standing behind Asher.

Gibraltair's lean figure stood tall behind Asher, Vitalsior's golden augefact in one hand, cane menacingly clutched in the other. The blood had been washed clean from his face and the gash that had stretched from hairline to chin had healed. A solitary long scar was all that remained of the wound.

"You've doomed us all." Farrenk's comment struck Asher like a hammer as the man whipped his battle mantle up in a vicious arc, launching one final attack at the boy who had just defied him.

Asher felt his neck snap backwards as Farrenk's attack broke through the last of his defences, his body finally succumbing to the drain.

His auger spluttered out.

It had consumed the very last drop of blood it could without killing its host. Asher became weightless as an explosive jolt sent him flying backwards into space. His eyelids closed involuntarily, shutting out the world as Asher's body careened through the air, his mind waiting for the inevitable painful collision with the ground. Piece by piece, his consciousness came to terms with the pain rippling through his tormented limbs. It felt as though death itself was clawing its way through his veins and towards his heart like a venomous poison.

Pitting his mind against his withering body, he frantically tried to fight back against the tidal wave of darkness threatening to consume him, and forced his eyes open. Even that minor action was a gargantuan effort. After what seemed like an eternity, a rift appeared between his eyelids, spilling light into his fractured mind. The world was a blur. Bile surged up his throat, but there was nothing he could do about it. He couldn't even swallow.

Then, all of a sudden, everything stopped.

His weightlessness came to an end as his body crashed down against the stone. His head, however, was spared the same callous fate: it landed against something soft and cushioned the impact which, in turn, saved his mind from being blasted into nothingness.

A vicious barrage of light whiplashed the air above him as Farrenk and Gibraltair traded blows with each other, both men pitting the might of their skill, training and bloodline in a ferocious battle to the death. From the angle where his head lay, Asher could vaguely see the twirl and sway of Farrenk's battle mantle in the distance as it spun and sliced the air with the precision of a seasoned assassin. Each flick and twist sent a new volley of riotous blood callings hurtling above Asher's head, but none of them were aimed at him.

Asher felt a trickle of strength return to his limbs, but he couldn't explain where from. With all the grace of a headless snake, he flopped his arm around above his head, fingers fumbling for something. He blinked his eyes several times, attempting to clear the stupor drowning out his ability to think clearly and twisted his head, catching sight of Morreby's blank emotionless face.

Her eyes were closed.

He felt gusts of wind batter his cheek and hair as another series of devastating lights flashed above. Asher couldn't see where they were landing, or who was winning the battle raging on around him. He was stuck in the middle, his role in this feud over. His fingers awkwardly fumbled around Morreby's waist, his hand blindly searching for hers. When he finally found it, he tried to squeeze it tight, but his grip was little lighter than a feather and far too weak to rouse her. He looked at her face again hoping to get some sort of a response: any kind of indication she was alive.

There was none.

There was only the chilling stillness of her features. Then he realised her features weren't the only thing that was still. The barrage of wind thundering overhead had ceased, the air around him quietening as the terrifying sounds of battle disappeared. The two-man war being waged between Gibraltair and Farrenk was over.

Still, Morreby had not yet blinked or moved.

Asher struggled to lift his head off Morreby's legs, only to see Farrenk slumped over in a bloody heap upon the tangled branches across the chasm. His battle mantle lay a few feet away from him, firmly wedged in a gap between two branches, inarguably out of reach.

The black leather of his uniform was torn and ripped, the lone red scar on his side almost unrecognisable. His body was awash with plasma, flowing from several fierce gashes on his torso, half of which ran as deep as the bone.

He had lost.

Gibraltair had won.

Asher breathed a sigh of relief and let his head fall back onto Morreby's legs.

"Thank you, Asher. I doubt I would've been able to best that brute without the old boy's augefact."

Asher tilted his head back and stared up at Gibraltair's face.

The wound that had stretched from hairline to chin was gone, a long narrow scar now the only proof the wound had ever existed.

Gibraltair's victorious smirk was as clear as day, despite the fact his glasses were broken and his eyes remained blinded by a milky haze.

"Morreby?" Asher croaked weakly, his eyes struggling to focus on Gibraltair's tall figure.

"She's fine for now. Unconscious, but fine."

"So," Asher blinked his eyes and exhaled a deep sigh of relief, "it's over?"

"Almost."

Gibraltair became much clearer amidst the blur of Asher's eyes when he kneeled down on his haunches and gently placed a hand on Asher's shoulder. Asher could do nothing else but watch on weakly as Gibraltair raised the Vitalsior's golden sceptre to the side of his own temple and whisper something under his breath.

The milky opaque cloud hanging over his retinas like a fog slowly started to clear. The thick off-white film withdrew from the centre of his eyes to the sides and revealed the most dazzling azure irises Asher had ever seen.

Gibraltair's retinas quivered as his pupils contracted, reacting to the first natural light they'd seen in an age. The image of Asher's pale face slowly registering in his mind.

"It's nice to finally put a face to a name, with my own eyes," Gibraltair blinked repeatedly and tilted his head, stopping momentarily to take in the majesty of the cavern. He glanced once at Farrenk's bloody body across the abyss, then turned his attention back to Asher, the smile vacant from his face.

"I'm truly sorry that I'm unable to repay your kindness, Asher," he vigorously rubbed the side of his face and pinched his brow together between his fingers, frowning heavily, "or your trust."

"What?" Asher stammered weakly.

"Trust, that is not earned, but coerced, will inevitably always betray the one who placed it." Gibraltair reached down and twisted the ring on Asher's index finger hard enough to ensure that Asher felt every movement. "A trinket is easily forged and inherently worthless, unless... Unless, it can prey on sentiment in order to leverage trust. Then it becomes invaluable, priceless."

Fear gripped Asher's heart and his breath froze in his throat as he realised what Gibraltair was saying.

"Ultimately, you were undone because you betrayed your instincts and sided trust with sentiment."

"So you're a... a..." Asher stammered, unable to get the words out.

"What? A traitor?" Gibraltair cut him off sharply. "Hardly! I'm merely a man, searching for something unjustly stolen from him." He tapped a finger repeatedly against the side of his temple. "Unfortunately for you, my success comes with a price attached. But, we all have our debts to pay, don't we, Asher Bloom?" He raised his eyebrows and opened his eyes wide as he stood up. "And I never leave a debt unsettled."

Asher's heart sank.

He had made the wrong choice. What was worse, he was powerless to do anything about it. He gasped for breath and rolled his head towards Gibraltair as the man walked around his body, Vitalsior's sceptre causally slung over one shoulder.

"Who owns your debt?" Asher coughed. "The Mortis Skulk?"

Gibraltair allowed himself a mild chuckle at the remark, tapping his cane on the ground in enjoyment at Asher's delusions.

"Wake up, Asher, don't be blind to the realities at hand. They are but pawns, smoke and mirrors, used to prey on age-old fears in order to hide a much greater game."

Asher felt utterly betrayed. The augiologist had tricked him and manipulated him every step of the way and he'd fallen for it.

"Don't you see?" He held the sceptre out in front of him. "This is but a piece of the puzzle. A puzzle that the man to whom my debt is owed has pieced together bit by bit, all of his life."

"Who?" Asher's words dried up in his mouth.

"Tsk, tsk, tsk." Gibraltair shook a finger back and forth in the air. "That would take all the fun out of things." He looked Asher up and down, a strange expression on his face as though he was trying to figure out something in the back of his mind. "I don't know how, or why, but somehow you fit into his master plan. Which is where my debt comes into play, and we find ourselves full circle, back to your inability to see things as they truly are."

"What do you mean?" Asher choked out as the fear sitting in his heart jumped into his throat.

"One interesting fact I came to learn about the old boy's gifts of life, from my experience with the last one, is that much like the human's precious understanding of physics, one action must have an equal and opposite reaction."

Asher tried to swallow back his fear, but he could feel his entire body trembling.

Gibraltair could see it too.

"Balance in all things, Master Bloom. Betrayal and trust. Truth and lies. Victory and failure. Life and death. You cured me of my burns and for that I will afford you the same kindness." He briefly glanced in Farrenk's direction. The man's bloody body was sprawled across the tangled branches, barely alive and struggling for breath.

"Besides, I have another much worthy recipient in mind which, unfortunately, leaves the issue of my sight, or blindness as the case may be." He spun the sceptre over itself in his hands. "If it were up to me, I'd happily unleash such a pox upon Miss Fitch, nasty little death dealer that she is."

Asher's eyes worriedly shot across to Morreby's face as Gibraltair prodded her harshly with the tip of his cane several times to ensure she was truly unconscious. She didn't blink. There wasn't even the slightest twitch in her eye as the blunt tip of his cane stabbed at her flesh.

"Alas, he…" Gibraltair noticed he'd lost Asher's attention. He brazenly clicked his fingers three times loudly in front of the boy's face to regain it. "He insisted it must be you, such is the partial payment of my debt."

"Who did?" Asher's mind was in a panic. He was powerless to stop Gibraltair from doing anything he wanted to do to him.

"In time, Asher, you'll understand. You'll see the truth," he tilted his head to the side condescendingly. "But, then again, perhaps not."

Asher turned his head frantically from side to side, searching for any avenue of escape. There was none. He squeezed Morreby's hand as tight as his exhausted limbs would allow, but she didn't budge. Gibraltair lowered the tip of the sceptre down to the side of Asher's head and touched it gently to his temple. Asher heard the augefact whir to life and vibrate against his head.

"Lights out," Gibraltair's voice echoed down at him as Asher screamed in terror, total panic tearing through his consciousness.

With terrified eyes, he turned to look at Gibraltair and watched the man's face disappear behind a milky-white sheen of nothingness. An off-white sea shifted and swarmed over his eyes, which left nothing behind but the blur of shadows and the intermittent, unrecognisable flicker of light.

Almost as soon as it began, it was over. Asher felt the cool touch of the sceptre lift from his temple as Gibraltair raised it up, flipped it over once in his hand and slung the head back over his shoulder. He felt strange and disorientated. He felt like a part of him had been stolen.

He lay on the cold stone, head resting on Morreby's legs, blindly looking up into space. His eyes remained open, unblinking amidst the orange glow filtering throughout the cavern, unreactive to any small movement around him, an impenetrable fog enveloping his world.

"So that's what I looked like." Gibraltair's shoulders and head quivered in revulsion at the sight of Asher's milky eyes. "Consider this a parting gift."

Asher felt something light and small land on his chest. With trembling fingers he awkwardly fumbled over his chest where it landed, picked it up and slowly worked his fingers over its edges.

Judging from its shape, it was a small glass vial, identical to the one Gibraltair had stored Vitalsior's gilded virtue in, but there was no way Asher could know what was inside without his eyesight. He let it fall back on his chest and dropped his hand back to his side, exhausted.

"You should look after your gifts more carefully, but then, that is your prerogative, I suppose. I'll be back to deal with Miss Fitch and your friends after I deliver a well-earned blistering end to a particularly forgettable council whelp."

Asher heard his footsteps move away and the creak and splintering sounds of wood being bent and twisted under the augiologist's yoke as he continued to regrow the branch bridge. Asher couldn't move, even though he wanted to. The warning the voice had left in his mind echoed through his thoughts as he gazed out into an eternity of nothingness.

My gift will bring only death in your hands.

The voice had been right. Asher had brought death to everyone around him and he could only imagine how many countless more would die, now that Gibraltair had control of the augefact. Asher's consciousness was about to slip into an endless despair at the thought of what he'd done, when he felt Morreby's fingers gently squeeze his hand.

Morreby.

Asher was about to say her name, when he heard her mutter a calming shush in his ear. She squeezed his hand one more time in reassurance, before unlocking her fingers from his and moving her legs, carefully lowering his head to the floor.

"Stay down," Morreby warned him in a voice no louder than a whisper.

Asher wanted to say something. He wanted to stop her from doing something crazy, but he couldn't move his limbs. He couldn't even lift his head. He was powerless. He heard the creak and groan of the tangled branches cease, followed by heavy footsteps and the rough tap of a cane tip against the wood as

Gibraltair took his first steps upon the newly completed and fully regrown drawbridge.

Asher could hear Morreby's shallow breaths and the soft jingle of delicate chains unravelling from somewhere nearby. She was up to something, but he had no idea what it was. After a few moments, the loud footsteps on the wooden branches stopped and Asher heard a distant gurgling voice break the silence.

"The elite guard are but moments away. You'll never escape alive." Farrenk's voice was audibly laced with pain, but resolute in its defiance against the man standing over him.

"Oh, but I will." Gibraltair flippantly mocked the bloody man at his feet. "But not before I bestow on you a final gift."

Farrenk's terrified screams and excruciating wails tore through the confines of the cavern and pierced Asher's eardrums like a horn of war. Each torturous cry was magnified tenfold inside his head as if an orchestra of agony was playing just for him. Even from where he was, the smell of burning flesh invaded his nostrils, as the sounds of torture pulled at the very fibre of his humanity.

He couldn't block them out, his lack of sight only served to amplify his other senses to the horrors that Gibraltair was unleashing on Farrenk. Amidst it all, Asher felt a small weight lift off his chest and the cold press of glass against his lips. A gentle voice whispered a warning down at him.

"Don't let the drain take you."

Asher felt a single drop of cool refreshing liquid slide over his lips and hit his tongue. It fizzed and bubbled in his mouth, sending small shockwaves of energy rippling down his throat. The sensation spread throughout his entire body, speeding along his veins and overloading his senses until the dull opaque cloud over his eyes was lost to an inky black nightmare filled with demented screams.

Just before Asher lost consciousness, he thought he heard a savage beast-like howl amidst the torturous wails. Then all sounds faded away and Asher's mind finally succumbed to exhaustion.

CHAPTER 53

DEBTS TO PAY

When Asher finally regained consciousness, he had no idea how long he'd been out. He hesitantly opened his eyes, only to be reminded of the all-too-demoralising reality awaiting him.

He was completely and utterly blind.

It all seemed surreal, like a nightmare he desperately needed to wake from, but he knew it was no dream. He felt the pressure of a strange gelatinous substance half crawling, half flowing over his skin. Somehow it felt oddly familiar. Pulling his hands up through its sticky substance, his fingers broke free of its hold over him. His hands soon followed, then both his forearms.

Raising both hands to his face, he desperately rubbed at his eyes, hoping to wipe clear the demoralising white haze washing over them like a snowstorm. As he did so a distinctive smell wafted into his nasal passage and he finally realised why the strange oozy substance felt so familiar. It was augalyptus sap. He'd recovered in it before, after the Mortis Skulk had attacked him in the Catacomb Cathedral.

The sensation of being immersed within the restorative sap wasn't unpleasant, despite its clammy hold over the rest of his body, he actually felt more refreshed than he had in a long time. However, the sap's rejuvenating powers had done little to alleviate his blindness. More than that, the sap made his eyes itch like crazy, so he rubbed them even harder with balled-up fists.

"Easy, lad, that won't do anyone any good, least of all your peepers. Leave them be, they've been through enough."

A low voice rumbled to Asher's left as he felt a pair of enormous hands gently close over his own, pulling them away from his face. The grip was firm but gentle at the same time. The hands lowered Asher's and released them squarely by the youth's side, leaving them to float on top of the soothing augalyptus sap. The man's voice sounded vaguely familiar, but without a face to put next to the voice, Asher could not identify who it was trying to comfort him. "Who's there?"

"A friend," the man's voice was deep and powerful.

The voice also had a soothing and empathetic tone that made Asher feel safe.

"I see you've managed to put the mantle I had crafted for you to good use."

The man turned Asher's palm over, exposing Asher's mantle to the light. The gelatinous sap refused to stick to the gilded mantle surrounding his auger and slid off, leaving the metal clean and smooth. Asher had no way of seeing the concerned frown that crossed the man's brow as he gazed down at the black etchings on the surface of Asher's otherwise pristine mantle.

"Overseer Altier, is that you?"

"Aye, lad," the man squeezed his hand tenderly, "but I think you've earned the right to call me by my first name. Lobrolo will do just fine."

As Asher's other senses gradually returned to him, he heard the actions of those around him much more clearly. He heard Lobrolo reach back and run one of his giant hands through his hair, roughly scratching at his ageing scalp as he did so.

"It would seem that trouble has a knack for seeking you out. Perhaps I was wrong not to keep a closer eye on you."

His words made Asher instantly uneasy and he reactively withdrew his auger and mantle from the man's hand.

"Easy now, you're safe. We're alone."

Alone. The word raced through Asher's mind. *But that must mean…*

"My friends? Where's Morreby? Lem? Lorrelli?" the words tumbled from Asher's mouth in a rush. His overwhelming concern for his friends was emotionally plastered across his face for all to see.

"Alive and well. All three of them. Safe and sound in the next room. And you are not the only one devoted to your friends; they haven't left your side in three days. I had to order them out so they could get some rest."

Asher breathed a sigh of relief. They'd made it out of the cavern. They'd escaped and were safe.

Wait, three days? The words were an unwelcome echo, repeating in Asher's mind. "I was out for three days?" The news of his extended absence from consciousness snapped Asher's mind from its sluggish daze. He stretched his legs and wriggled his toes underneath the restorative augalyptus sap to make sure the lower half of his body still worked. As far as he could tell, everything was fine. Sore, but fine. Everything apart from his eyesight. With a little effort he managed to half push, half pull himself out of the sap and into a sitting position in the large copper pipe. "Where am I?"

"One of Mantlecrest's rejuvenation chambers, but you already knew that. It's a far cry from Vitalsior's vaulted ark where we found you, I might add."

Asher's mind immediately snapped back to the last thing he could remember before he blacked out. "The augefact! He's got the augefact—"

"I know," Lobrolo attempted to calm Asher's alarm with a gentle squeeze on his forearm.

"You don't understand. Gibraltair's got the augefact. I gave it to him."

"What's done is done."

"It's my fault," Asher shook his head adamantly, refusing to listen, as he struggled to lift the rest of his body out from the suction the augalyptus sap had over him. Even that small exertion exhausted him.

Lobrolo placed a hand on Asher's shoulder and gently pushed him back into a relaxed sitting position, despite Asher's continued resistance.

"Let me go, I have to stop him."

"He's gone, Asher. Dust in the wind, but the fault is not

yours. You mustn't blame yourself. The traitor Reine fooled us all." Lobrolo watched Asher slump back into his pillowed backrest as he let the news sink in.

"We've already begun backtracking his every move in the last six months via his auger. It has shown us a great deal." Lobrolo reached down and gripped Asher's hand in reassurance.

"Like what?" Asher asked dejectedly.

"Like the tunnel he used to infiltrate Mantlecrest, for one. It was the oldest I've ever seen and not on any known Mantlecrest schematic. It led from the bottom of a small pool in the Forgotten Gardens, near the outer wall, directly into a small corridor hidden behind a series of false walls in the Undercellars. We know enough to start our investigation. Do not fear, he has the entire might of the Cruaar Nation hunting him now. We'll find him and recover the augefact. It's only a matter of time."

Asher didn't hear most of what the Overseer's had said. His own guilt had deafened him beyond reason. "But I gave it to him," Asher's demoralised voice rebounded back at him off the walls of the small room. "I handed it to him. Now hundreds will die, just like the voice said they would."

"What voice, Asher?" Lobrolo asked, frowning heavily, deeply concerned by Asher's remark.

"It knew this was going to happen. Somehow it knew, but I refused to believe it."

Lobrolo quietly regarded Asher's agitated features. The teen's face was a mask of remorse, burdened with shame and guilt at the memory of what he had done. He took a moment to ponder whether it was worthwhile pushing the issue of the voice. After a few seconds of silent contemplation, he decided against it, opting instead to help alleviate some of Asher's guilt. "A wrong decision made for the right reasons will always plague an honest heart. Besides, if Seville had shared her concerns about Gibraltair, the decision would have never been yours to make."

"Don't you mean the Scarlet Commander?" Asher said bitterly, waiting for a confirmation from the Overseer. Even though he couldn't see the expression passing over Lobrolo's face, the Overseer's silence confirmed that Gibraltair had at least been telling the truth about the legate's true identity. "You knew. All this time. You knew?"

"Aye. I knew." Lobrolo leaned back in his armchair and interlocked all of his fingers. The chair's wooden supports groaned audibly as his weight shifted. "But, believe me, I was as disturbed as you, if not more so, when the Chancellor appointed her to govern over my hallowed halls. Especially because I knew the truth of her turbulent past–"

"Turbulent past? You knew who she was. What she was. What she did during the rebellion," Asher's words were cold and unforgiving, even though he himself had not witnessed the monstrosities he was accusing her of committing. "How many people did she murder? How could you leave her here? Alone? With us?"

Lobrolo patiently waited for Asher to finish venting his anger and frustration before answering. "I remember all too well the darkness and the hatred that the Rebellion instilled. I witnessed firsthand the atrocities that good men committed in the name of righteousness, under the guise of justice. Inhuman and immoral acts legalised by misguided council mandates in a feeble attempt to end the bloodshed." Lobrolo sighed deeply as he rubbed a measure of tiredness away from his eyes. "We all have our demons, Asher. Scarlet Seville more than anyone."

Asher's frown did not change or lessen at Lobrolo's explanation. So the Overseer tried a different approach. "Lem and Lorrelli told me of the veritusk bind the legate placed on all of you on your first day in Mantlecrest. Do you remember?"

"The Scarlet Commander placed on us," Asher snapped, correcting him as memories came flooding into his mind. He remembered the way his auger used to flare up every time he caught his friends lying, or every time Lem overembellished a story so much that fact was bent into falsehood.

"The veritusk bind has a simple purpose. It creates an

unbreakable bond of truth between whoever is bound by it, unmasking all forms of spoken deception, lies and untruth for all to see, but you probably knew that much already."

Asher nodded, confirming the man's assumption, but still unsure what he was building to.

"A lesser-known fact about the veritusk bind, however, is that once a lie has broken the bond, a connection is established between those bound and the bond's arbiter.

"Arbiter?"

"The person who first established the bond," Lobrolo waited for Asher to process this information.

"So the legate—"

"Yes, Asher, she knew each and every blood calling you summoned since the bond was first broken."

"Everything?" Asher's face drained of colour as he thought of every illegal act they'd done since his arrival at Mantlecrest.

The legate had seen it all.

She'd seen him uprooting Sageroot's augefact, destroying Mess Hill, the Wormwood Vindicat, their battle with the orillas, Braak's warning, Morreby's pet fannim, the four of them breaching Vitalsior's vault… everything.

"I don't understand. If she knew everything we'd done then why didn't she stop us? Why didn't she help us?"

"The Scarlet Commander amassed an army of enemies within the Cruaar Nation during the Rebellion, though none bar Gibraltair ever learnt her true identity beyond the mask. Her name was stricken from the Annals to protect her identity, or at least, so we thought.

"She was, and has always been, the right hand of the Chancellor, but the Rebellion is over and has been for decades. Where people once saw the Chancellor as a grand liberator, a freedom fighter that fought for peace and justice amid anarchy, the harsh mandates he has enacted under his rule have since distorted and warped the people's perception of him.

"The Scarlet Commander's unwavering allegiance to him only

helped the transition of the public's perception from liberator to overlord, pushing it ever closer to the brink of tyrant. A perception he despises more than anything else in this world, or the next, and one someone in his position cannot afford."

"What's any of that got to do with Scarlet Commander and Mantlecrest?"

"The Chancellor hoped by making the Scarlet Commander disappear he'd be able to change the hearts and minds of the Cruaar Nation. Scarlet, however, was still far too valuable an asset to dismiss entirely and far too loyal to ever fully abandon.

"He needed her somewhere close, somewhere he could keep an eye on her. Somewhere he could control her. A place he could bury the horrors and memories of the Scarlet Commander once and for all. Much to my own surprise, he had worked out how to accomplish the feat in one swift stroke and in plain sight, under the noses of everyone involved.

"Mantlecrest was the key, but first he needed me out of the way. So he offered me the position of Overseer, promising me a seat on the Elder Council in High Cleric Pluwarie's absence, on the proviso he got to pick my replacement." Lobrolo's deep sigh conveyed his heavy remorse at his own naivety.

"I was foolish enough to think I'd earned what was being offered to me and that I would finally be in a position to make a difference. So, naturally, I accepted the deal, never imagining in my wildest dreams he'd be mad enough to insert the Scarlet Commander in my stead. By the time I realised what he his plans were, it was too late. He'd played us both for fools, using her loyalty and my naive ambition to keep us both in check."

"Fools?" Asher whispered confused, "I don't understand."

"Seville voiced her initial objections, loudly, I might add, believing full well she'd earned the right to stand at his side as the Scarlet Commander and help him rule with an iron fist. But times have changed since the Rebellion and he no longer needed an enforcer, so he threatened to expose her if she refused the role.

"I can only assume she turned her back on your antics because she thought she could uncover Gibraltair's treachery and expose it to the Chancellor, escape her imprisonment in the place and return to her rightful place by his side."

"So she used me, used us, as bait?"

"Yes and no. The legate trusted no-one except the Chancellor, but even he betrayed her in the end."

The sounds of Lobrolo's fingers scratching against the stubble on his chin filtered in through Asher's ears as the man continued his explanation.

"Which is also probably why she never shared her suspicions about Gibraltair's treachery until she had proof. The two have shared a somewhat antagonistic history."

"So they did know each other?"

"In a way…" Lobrolo peered into the murky haze floating atop Asher's eyes, hoping Asher might somehow return his gaze.

He didn't. He couldn't.

Lobrolo chose his next words carefully. "It was the Scarlet Commander that caught Gibraltair in the forbidden Annals. She interrogated him for weeks, torturing him and holding him at the brink of death in order to find out what he was searching for, but he never told her. He never uttered a word. He just stared back at her, unblinking, silent as the dawn.

"When she realised she'd never break him, she punished him instead, taking from him the very thing he used to defy and antagonise her. His eyes."

"So she was the one…" Asher's words dried up in his mouth as he gently raised his fingers to his own temple.

"Yes, Asher, she stole his sight," Lobrolo leaned forward and placed a comforting hand on Asher's shoulder. "A curse that you now unjustly bear."

Asher sat in silence, unsure of what to say, listening to Lobrolo's chair creak as his heavy bulk rose up from the timber's worn frame.

"Now you're awake, I have another matter to attend to, but I will return."

Asher heard Lobrolo's heavy footsteps walk to the edge of the room and open a door. It creaked loudly on a pair of hinges in desperate need of a good oiling.

"Wait," he cried out, "I have so many questions."

Lobrolo briefly glanced back at Asher's milky-white eyes, allowing himself one last glance at the troubling sight of his auger before he departed. The waving black scar in its centre stared back at him hauntingly as it always had. More disturbing still were the black etchings set into the gilded mantle surrounding it.

"As do I, Asher. We all do."

With that Lobrolo was gone.

The next thing Asher heard was the sound of running feet and the excited cries of his friend's voices.

"Asher, you're okay!" Lorrelli's voice was the first to reach his ears, moments before he felt her hand clamp down around his own.

Asher smiled at the sound of her voice, but before he could respond, Lem's sarcastic voice was already harping away at him. "About time you woke up. They've put us through the roody blinger because of all your praccing adventures. Not that they weren't worth it, mind you."

Asher shook his head in confusion, having absolutely no idea what Lem was talking about.

"Put your hand down you fool, he can't see your mantle," Morreby snapped sharply and swatted away Lem's hand.

"Oh, right," Lem muttered sheepishly, lowering his arm and placing the mantle in Asher's upturned palm.

One part felt cold and metallic to Asher's touch, whilst another was rough and prickly. "Lem, you found your mantle elements, but how?"

"Not only that, my auger has been aligned, too." Lem said happily.

"Here we go again." Morreby sighed. "He hasn't shut up about it ever since he got back from Dopplebock's."

"Hey, don't be jealous of Mantlecrest's next best bireem,"

Lem defended himself. "You wouldn't believe it, Asher. Apparently, my elements were these two mibbering guppets all along. Beats me how I didn't see it before, but Lobrolo picked it like a rotten nose. All it took was a lock of their hair and old Dopplebock sorted me out in minutes." Lem snapped his fingers loudly. "Now I'm calling forth blood callings left, right and centre. You should see me go." Lem instantly realised his slip and fell silent.

"Nice one, Lemule," Morreby said disapprovingly, shaking her head at him.

Asher could almost hear Lem's stoic frown at the mention of his real name.

"Call me whatever you want," Lem smiled arrogantly, "as long as you stick bireem in front of it."

"It's alright," Asher said solemnly as the smile faded from his face. "I'm blind, you don't have to sugar coat it. It's not your fault."

"Well, is anyone going to tell him, or should I?" Lorrelli interrupted, trying her best to change the subject.

"Tell me what?" Asher asked.

"Braak's back," Lem blurted out.

"Braak!" Asher exclaimed excitedly. "Where is he?"

"In the next room, Lobrolo just went to check on him," Lorrelli said softly.

"Take me to him." Asher tried again to rise out of the clammy augalyptus sap, which made his head spin.

"Asher, stop. You're going to hurt yourself," Lorrelli scolded as she placed a restraining hand on his shoulder to steady him.

"No, I have to speak with him." Asher said again, determined to clear his head of its lingering wooziness.

"Slow down, Asher."

Asher spun his head to look in the direction of Lem's voice, but saw only a swirling haze. "He's not going anywhere."

"What do you mean?"

"You're such a bell-end," Morreby snapped at Lem. "He

601

doesn't know."

"Know what?" Asher demanded loudly.

Lorrelli ran her fingers along his forearm, her fingertips pausing over each of his lava-burned scars. "The rite of bonded blood, Asher, remember? Braak went through everything you did, but he didn't have your blood's natural healing powers."

"What happened to him?" Asher stammered, trying to push himself to his feet against their restraint but collapsed with exhaustion seconds later.

Lem quickly ducked under one of Asher's arm and took the majority of his weight, instructing Morreby to do the same under the other.

"When are you going to learn you don't have to do everything by yourself," Lem groaned as he and Morreby hauled Asher out of the sap and dragged him to his feet. With the majority of his weight suspended between them, they slowly guided him towards the doorway.

"Braak's been on death's doorstep for days, ever since–" Lorrelli stopped herself short, eyes watching on helplessly as Asher's feet struggled to hold even the smallest amount of his own weight.

"Ever since what?" Asher's groaned as his concern intensified.

"Since a tribarion carried him through the vertistrand into the council's chambers," Morreby curtly interjected, telling Asher the unpleasant news nobody else wanted to share. Lem shook his head at her in warning, but she merely raised her eyebrows at him and nodded her head at Asher. "He was unconscious and covered in blood. One of his arms was melted through to the bone and he'd succumbed to the drain. He's been in a coma ever since."

"I need to see him," Asher demanded.

"Asher, you can't–" Lem stopped himself short, silently cursing his own stupidity when he realised what he'd just said. "I mean–"

"Just take me to him!"

CHAPTER 54

A SEVERED END

Asher struggled to find his feet. His muscles were still extremely weak, despite three days of recuperation within the restorative augalyptus sap.

Everything hurt.

Without Lem and Morreby bracing his weight, he could not have made the small journey to the door himself, step by painstaking step. Asher saw nothing as they entered the adjacent room, but somehow he knew Braak was close by, even if the man was unconscious.

The ever-so-slight rise and fall of Braak's chest as his lungs mechanically drew in air was inaudible to everyone except him, but Asher's sense of hearing had been heightened in the absence of optical stimuli.

Unbeknownst to Asher, however, Braak's condition was being closely monitored by Cleric Riffenbon, who'd kept a close eye on both of them over the last few days.

The man was deeply engaged in a hushed conversation with the Overseer at the foot of Braak's copper pipe, which promptly ended as he spied the four apprentices enter the room. He was almost about to chastise them from dragging Asher out of his rejuvenation chamber when Lobrolo shook his head and motioned for them to approach.

The Overseer waited patiently in silence, concern wrinkling in the corners of his eyes as he watched Asher cross the room with the help of his friends. His austere expression made it almost impossible to glean any information in regards to what he thought about the outlook of Braak's recovery. Asher couldn't see it anyway and everyone else had already feared the worst, though none dared say as much out loud.

When Asher finally reached the foot of Braak's rejuvenation chamber, he could sense the presence of another man in the room. None of the other apprentices recognised him, but judging by the evident scowl branded across his face, the man unequivocally recognised Asher.

Gilded armour encased powerful shoulders and a muscular torso, both of which remained locked in a tense, folded-arm embrace as he leaned back against the wall. He had one foot firmly wedged against the wall behind him, which kept his body rigid. With every puff of smoke he drew from his ebony pipe, his scowl deepened a little more and his teeth ground against one another a little louder than before. The tribarion gave no outward indication if he knew Asher was blind, though by all outward appearances, it probably wouldn't have changed anything.

His blazing emerald eyes offered Asher no ounce of comfort or compassion, nor did his unforgiving glare that pierced the awkward silence of the room with invisible barbs of blame. There was a dire hatred burning in his heart and it was only aimed at one person: Asher. Despite all this, Tribarion Opspray stood in silence and exhaled a lung's worth of smoke at Asher as he approached. It spread through the air above Braak's head.

Surprisingly, it smelled fresh and reinvigorating, unlike any other tobacco smoke Asher had ever encountered. The effect was pleasantly uplifting, which was a stark contrast to the man's outwardly chilling carriage.

He said nothing as the three apprentices guided Asher around the edge of the copper pipe to Braak's side. Lowering Asher against the edge of the pipe until his weight was balanced, Lem and Morreby took a step back and watched him slowly run his hands through the augalyptus sap until his fingers found Braak's chest.

Asher instinctively reached across Braak's body until he found Braak's remaining hand. Running his fingers over his protector's unmoving scarred skin, Asher dug around in the sap until he felt the touch of cool metal against his fingertips.

Underneath the soothing sap, Braak's father's ring was still firmly positioned on his index finger as it always had been. Asher silently cursed his own stupidity and slowly withdrew his hand, returning it to Braak's torso. He felt the man's chest rise and fall weakly between shallow breaths. His fingers felt along the man's scarred rib cage to his left shoulder and then down his arm, where it abruptly ended at his elbow. It had been strapped with what felt like a coarse bandage, wrapped tightly around the stump where his forearm should've been.

"Braak?" Asher said weakly, with tears in his eyes. He had no idea what to say, or who to say it to. He simply blurted out the first question that came to mind. "Where's the rest of his arm?"

"Gone!" A vicious voice barked back at him. "But perhaps you can explain to me why I had to listen to him scream as his flesh melted away to the bone? Why I had to cradle him in my arms after he collapsed with wounds all over his body? Why I had to watch with my own eyes as some hellish storm robbed him of his arm? No? Then perhaps you can you tell me why none of my restorative blood callings had any effect? Or why he continued to fade in my arms until he succumbed to the drain?" The man's raw emotions spilled out in a torrent of unchecked anger. His unwavering loyalty and devotion to Braak was matched only by his hatred and loathing of the person he held responsible.

"He tried to tell me something before whatever devilry you unleashed stole him from this world, but he never got the chance. I alone carried him to Undergall. I alone felt his life slip through my fingers, only to deliver him to the council, who had me bring him here. To you, of all people." The Tribarion's tone was unforgiving and without remorse as he spat the words at Asher.

"Do you want to know what his last words were, boy? Do you?" The tribarion pushed himself off the wall and leaned in close.

Asher could feel his breath on his neck.

"Tell Asher—"

"Tribarion," Lobrolo said, sternly cutting off the man.

"Tell Asher what? Huh?" he continued. "Perhaps you could tell me seeing as he wasn't able to."

"I... I..." Asher stammered, unable to find the words to answer the man.

"Hold your tongue," Lobrolo snapped, momentarily silencing the tribarion.

Tribarion Opspray scowled at Lobrolo and took a step back, resting a heavy hand on the handle of the golden chain hanging from his belt. "Pray he lives, boy," he muttered under his breath, "or I'll speed you to his fate."

"Enough!" Lobrolo's voice boomed and resonated around the room. "Control yourself, Tribarion. You know full well Asher is no more to blame than you or I for Braak's condition."

"Like prac he's not," the tribarion swore defiantly, as his eyes shot daggers at Asher and Lobrolo.

"You'll keep a civil tongue, Opspray, or find solace continuing your vigil outside." Lobrolo's ultimatum was resolute.

"I'll not be in the same room as the tainted prac that rendered my friend a cripple on death's doorstep," Opspray spat back as he marched past the Overseer and out of the room, slamming the door behind him.

Asher fought hard to keep the tears from his eyes, as Lorrelli and Lem helped him to a chair next to Braak's bed.

"Never mind him. There is nothing worse than to be powerless to help when those you care for need it most." The Overseer turned his head and motioned the Cleric forward. "Tell them what you just told me."

The Cleric nodded and set aside the augineered device he was using to monitor Braak's vitals. "Warder Saada clings to life, but barely. He needs to wake before his mind is forever lost to the drain, but his body is far too fragile to endure any physical treatment that could possibly save him. The augalyptus sap is the only thing keeping him with us."

"What can we do?" Lem asked bravely, his forlorn features betraying the dismay behind his outspoken bravado.

"You? Nothing," the Cleric replied, "Asher, however–"

"I'll do it," Asher blurted out blindly. "Anything."

The Cleric paused and glanced at Lobrolo.

The old man gave a single nod in reply, giving his permission for the Cleric to continue.

"Because you two are joined by the rite of bonded blood, what happens to you happens to Braak. I can attempt to heal his mind through yours and bring him back from the brink. But there are risks."

"I don't care. Do it. Do whatever you have to, just bring him back," Asher said.

"Very well, but first your condition must be as close to Braak's as possible if what I am planning to do is to work." The Cleric carefully scooped away some sap covering Braak's torso and rounded the rejuvenation chamber, readying his auger. "Lobrolo will help mitigate the damage to your mind during the procedure, but there will be pain and we must work quickly. Braak grows weaker with every minute that passes."

"Asher, you can't," Lorrelli pleaded, "you're still so weak. You might die."

"There are risks, yes, but without you I fear Braak will not live past the dawn," the Cleric added.

"No-one else is dying for me." Asher's words were succinct, forceful to the point where they almost silenced his friend's objections and concerns.

"Asher," Morreby tried to argue.

"No!" Asher snapped. "Braak is only like this because of me. We both live, or we both die, it's that simple." He thought back to something Gibraltair said to him and whispered the man's words back at his friends to drive the point home. "We all have debts to pay."

"So be it," Lobrolo whispered, "Morreby, I'll need your remorauger."

"What?" Morreby exclaimed in surprise.

"Why?" Lorrelli immediately seconded Morreby's confusion.

"Only Morreby's remorauger has the natural ability to leech away Asher's life force without killing him."

Morreby glanced at Asher with a lingering dread in her heart, before hesitantly removing her apprentice mantle and handing it to Lobrolo.

Asher was about to say something when he felt himself being guided towards a nook in the roots of Braak's augalyptus tree. The next thing he felt was a finger pressed on his chin until he opened his mouth. The urge to gag erupted in his throat as he felt a large globule of a sticky, sweet-smelling liquid hit his tongue. He felt Lobrolo's large fingers hold his jaws shut as his right hand wrapped around Asher's auger and slowly raised it until the gemstone was touching his right temple.

"This will be unpleasant."

Asher couldn't help but think Lobrolo was somewhat understating the effects when he felt the cool surface of Morreby's remorauger lightly press against his left temple. A scorching sensation rippled across his head, rebounding back and forth across his mind between the two augers.

Asher watched the milky haze swirl and churn as intermittent flashes of light breached through the fog, penetrating its unyielding hold over his eyes. Another brilliant flare surged across his vision and made Asher's eyelids involuntarily tremble as Lobrolo's face pierced the blinding sea and rushed towards him, mouth agape as if bellowing. But Asher heard nothing but his own screams.

Lobrolo's face broke apart as it raced towards him, disintegrating into a chaotic burst of wild particles. Each atom danced about madly as they swarmed over his face, funnelling into his eyes, nose and ears. Asher felt the elements dredge through the base of his consciousness, uprooting the very fabric of his mind and propelling it out of his body. Seconds later, but what felt like an eternity to Asher, his world slowly came back into view.

His blindness was gone.

He found himself back in Vitalsior's vaulted ark, staring up at the craggy lavacicles hanging down from the roof high above him in the cavernous void. Asher tried to blink his eyes, but they would not respond.

They were not his to control.

He desperately wanted to turn his head, but he couldn't. He had no control whatsoever over his own body. He could only watch and wait. Slowly, his view of the cavern's roof changed. Whomever was in control of the body that his mind currently resided in slowly rolled their head to one side. Asher gasped, or at least wanted to gasp, when he caught sight of himself lying on the ground, too weak to move.

"Morreby," Asher heard his own voice call out weakly. A soft shush echoed back at him from lips he couldn't see, but somehow Asher felt them move as they mouthed the sound. Lobrolo's voice echoed out through the forgotten recesses of his mind.

"You're experiencing the past as Morreby remembers it, through the echoes of her auger. This will answer some of the questions you desperately seek but, more importantly, it will distract your mind from the agony your body is about to endure."

Agony? Asher called back at him subconsciously, at least he thought he did, but he heard no response. He heard Morreby's voice whispered a warning at the memory of his semi-conscious body.

"Stay down."

Asher's view over the scene jerked and swayed as Morreby rose to her feet, eyes carefully tracking Gibraltair as he walked towards the tangled drawbridge, cane raised at the stunted expanse of mangled branches extending precariously across the abyss.

Asher heard loud groans and creaks of splitting timber as Gibraltair resumed the construction of the living bridge spanning the void. The sounds drowned out all other ambient noise in the cavern, allowing Morreby to scramble to her knees and check on

Asher.

Asher heard her gasp as she looked into his milky-white eyes for the first time. He didn't blame her. Gazing down at his own face, he saw the cloudy white haze floating over his pupils like smoke trapped behind glass. His view changed as it swung up and down over his body. He watched her hands run over his limbs, checking them for wounds.

Finding none, her hands came to rest on a small glass vial that had been discarded on his chest. She held it up to her face to examine it. The ambient orange glow of the cavern caused the golden liquid inside to glisten as it caught the light.

"A single drop of Vitalsior's blood," Lobrolo's voice echoed. "The only reason you're still alive."

Another more-distant and wounded voice interrupted Lobrolo, distracting Morreby's focus on Asher and causing her head to turn back towards Gibraltair.

"The elite guard are but moments away. You'll never escape alive."

Farrenk's voice was faint but audible from across the bridge. Morreby's head shot in his direction just in time to see Gibraltair flip the man over on his back with a flick of his cane.

"Oh, but I will. But not before I bestow on you a final gift."

Morreby kneeled low and huddled over Asher, watching on as Farrenk defiantly stared up at the augiologist standing over him. Gibraltair smiled victoriously as he lowered the tip of the golden sceptre to Farrenk's chest. His smile rapidly transformed into a deformed scowl as Asher heard Farrenk start to scream. Morreby tore her head away from the sight and focused on Asher.

Asher watched on helplessly as his body convulsed, shivering uncontrollably as the screams tore through his mind. Morreby's unflinching fingers quickly unfastened the top of the vial and pressed its opening against his lips.

"Don't let the drain take you."

The glimmering drop of blood rolled down the side of the glass, over his lips, and finally landed on Asher's tongue.

The effect was instantaneous.

An involuntary shiver swept across his face as his mind lapsed into unconsciousness. A ferocious howl ripped through the cavern, which reverberated off the enormous walls of the abyss and momentarily drowned out Farrenk's screams.

Asher's vision blurred and spun again as Morreby whipped her head in the direction of the noise, just in time to see the giant body of a saddled gavrin bound through the opening of the antechamber on the far side of the tangled drawbridges.

It leaped onto the iron base of the drawbridge and paused. Its large boned crown and savage fangs glinted in the orange light as its claws scratched against the heavy metal branches. A lone figure straddled the beast's back, but he was too far away to make out any real detail other than the fact he rode high in the saddle with both feet pressing down hard on the stirrups.

The sheer bulk of the rider made it too big to be a woman, but the rider's face was hidden beneath the deep hood of a heavy black cloak which enveloped his upper body. His purpose was unmistakable.

He'd come for Gibraltair.

Broad shoulders and a powerfully muscular arm gripped the reins tethered to large circlets on either side of the alpha gavrin's gaping maw. With a flick of his wrist, he spurred the beast forward, simultaneously digging his heels into its flanks. The rider and his mount ferociously charged forward across the iron base of the drawbridge.

The beast leaped onto the rebuilt timber branches with murderous intent and landed heavily on its haunches, never missing a step. Despite the patchwork of holes between the latticework of branches beneath its feet, the gavrin gained speed as it flew across the makeshift bridge. Every hammering thud of the beast's massive paws brought it one step closer to its prize as it recklessly charged across the ravine, lumbering like mounted death towards Gibraltair.

Asher's vision blurred and fragmented, transforming the world into wisps of smoke and figureless demons as his mind was shredded in agony. A searing pain tore through his subconscious as the reality of the real world invaded the frail echo of Morreby's auger.

Focus your thoughts, Asher. Distract your mind from the torment.

Lobrolo's voice thundered through Asher's head, carving a path through the anguish laying siege against his consciousness.

Braak's survival depends on you.

Lobrolo's words granted Asher momentary control over his fractured mind. He struggled to focus his thoughts on the events he was bearing witness to, forcing his subconscious to obey his conscious will.

Piece by piece, the cavernous abyss came back into focus. First, the smooth stone floor reformed out of the haze underneath him, then his own body beneath him and the cavern's mighty walls until, finally, the tangled branch drawbridge, Gibraltair, Farrenk and the rider came back into view.

Gibraltair had turned to face the new threat, temporarily ignoring the wails of the dying man lying crippled at his feet. He tried to raise his cane at the thundering bulk of the alpha gavrin bearing down on him, only to find a burned, blistered and skeletal hand latched onto its shaft in a death grip.

Gibraltair glared down at Farrenk's scorched face, rage swelling behind his eyes. Without a moment's hesitation he sent a shockwave down through his cane, severing Farrenk's tattered claw from his body at the shoulder.

Farrenk didn't cry out.

He didn't make a sound as his flesh and bone were separated. He didn't even blink when he felt the sinew, muscle and bone disintegrate beneath his shoulder. He merely smiled at his towering tormentor. Farrenk's maniacal half-melted face chilled Gibraltair to the depths of his soul, especially in the split-second it took him to realise what the man's brief delay had cost him.

A furious panic washed over Gibraltair as he desperately spun around and lifted his cane, managing only to ram its tip into the beast's exposed chest a breath before its jaws sank into his flesh and its bulk slammed into his body.

A massive hole exploded in the gavrin's flank as it steamrolled over the top of Gibraltair. It careened into him at full speed, brutally snapping several of his bones as its momentum pummelled the augiologist into the cruel knots of the twisted branches beneath them.

The rider jumped clear of its mount mid-assault, just as the alpha gavrin realised its death was imminent. The huge beast tumbled over itself several times before coming to a stop against the mangled wood.

With its last shred of breath, it howled one last agonising scream before its veins bled dry, one last gurgle of blood gushing from the hole in its chest where its heart used to be.

Gibraltair's broken body lay quivering on the wooden mess of branches as he struggled to breathe. The brutal collision had caught him unawares and his body had paid the price. Several of his ribs were broken, as was his left arm. A large gash had appeared on one thigh, whilst his other calf had been pierced by a thick branch that had torn off and stuck through him like an arrow. The top half of his cane lay a few short feet away, well out of reach. The bottom half was nowhere to be seen. His auger glinted in the light, but remained lifeless and dull. Gibraltair's eyes frantically searched the tangled mess of branches before him, desperately hunting for something he had lost.

The broad-shouldered rider, however, had regained his footing quickly. A life-saving roll at the last minute had saved him from breaking any bones, but had also left him winded. He paused to gather air in his lungs before stumbling forward and breaking into a shambling run towards Gibraltair.

Gibraltair's face was a mixture of rage and desperation as his eyes locked on to what he had been seeking. Frantically, he dragged his broken body along the mangled web of branches, as blood gushed from his wounds with every movement. He sadistically glanced and glared at the silhouette of the rapidly approaching cloaked rider. His attacker's hooded head and broad shoulders were just visible over the imposing bulk of the gavrin's carcass as the man charged towards him.

"Stop him." Farrenk's voice scratched its way out of his scorched throat and echoed across the abyss.

Morreby's head jerked around sharply, leaving Asher desperately willing her to refocus her attention on the cloaked rider. After making sure Asher was okay, she obliged his wish, moving closer to the edge of the central platform to get a better vantage point of the battle.

The rider was quick and agile. His legs were weapons beneath him, the balls of his feet pummelling the mangled branches as he raced across the ravine, a heavy black cloak billowing in his wake. He was roughly eight feet away from Gibraltair and showed no signs of slowing. The only obstacle between him and his prey was the mountainous carcass of the dead alpha gavrin. He used it as a launching board to propel himself up and into the air at Gibraltair.

"Finish him, Tribune!" Farrenk's garbled voice cackled out. The man's cloak caught the wind, exposing his torso and the massive iron gauntlet he had raised above his head like a blacksmith's hammer. His fingers were locked into place like a savage iron claw, all of them eagerly waiting to deliver the killing blow on Gibraltair's broken body.

A bloodthirsty roar reverberated from his lungs as the tribune hurtled through the air. His auger radiated with power and pulsated a violent blue as he fed it with every ounce of anger and vengeance he had, funnelling all of it into his blood and through his auger's core.

Gibraltair had only just managed to wrap his fingers around the handle of the Vitalsior's augefact when the tribune's gauntleted claw smashed into his chest and pummelled him against the ground. Before Gibraltair even knew what hit him the tribune's hand jerked upwards. Gibraltair felt five heavy armoured fingers wrapped around his throat, as the tribune's armoured elbow collided with the augiologist's sternum, breaking his collarbone in the process.

The tribune's momentum sent the two men somersaulting backwards over each other, locked together in a deathly embrace. Vitalsior's golden augefact was somehow caught between their two entangled bodies.

Asher's vision swayed and shuddered again, sending his world into a nightmare of nauseating pain. The tumbling figures melted away into a sea of suffering as an inhuman agony was unleashed upon Asher's consciousness. His mind reeled as his thoughts blurred and became fragmented, unrecognisable. He tried desperately to focus on the scene before him, but it was beyond reach as violent shockwaves threatened to tear his sanity asunder.

Straining against the torment, he summoned his last ounce of energy and repressed the pain, burying it deep inside his fading subconscious, until the cavernous interior of Vitalsior's vault jolted back into focus. The mindless haze parted in a rush as his vision returned, jerking from side to side erratically as Morreby sprinted towards the edge of the platform.

Asher watched on helplessly as the tribune hauled his prey over the edge with one final blood-curdling cry. His iron grip on Gibraltair's throat never ceased, even after their bodies fell from the tangled mess of branches. Gibraltair's terrified screams pierced the air as the two dropped away into the abyss, bodies interlocked as they hurtled towards certain death.

Asher lost sight of them as they disappeared behind the lip of a rocky plateau, until Morreby's body skidded to a stop and she threw her head over the edge, peering down into the ravine.

Against the fiery backdrop of the cavern's enormous lava bed, two silhouettes spun and twisted in the air, still wrestling with each other as they plunged towards the gates of hell far below. DeGrulz's powerful gauntleted hand was still latched onto Gibraltair's throat, almost as if the tribune was determined to personally deliver the traitor to death's door. Gibraltair tried to hit him repeatedly with the golden sceptre, but the tribune's hold on him was unbreakable.

Asher gasped as he caught sight of a black ripple in the air somewhere beneath the two men and the above the relentless churning of the lava bed far below. At first he thought his eyes were playing tricks on him but, in an instant, the very fabric of time and space tore apart until a rift of black particles swarmed beneath the two falling figures. A swirling black vortex materialised in its wake, whirling and whipping the air around it with the force of a hurricane as it grew in size.

Morreby's hair flapped violently about her face as vicious gusts of wind shot upwards as the vortex intensified.

Asher's eyes refocused on the tiny figures of Gibraltair and the tribune as both men plummeted helplessly. They pierced the core of the spinning black scar and were momentarily lost amidst the unearthly maelstrom. Then neither man was visible amongst the explosion of black particles that displaced their bodies.

Far below Asher and Morreby, the bodies of the two men dematerialised into an extended trail of suspended black sand. When their bodies had completely evaporated into a waterfall of black particles, each microscopic speck was sucked upwards into the spatial breach. Both men's tortured screams lingered in the void long after all physical traces of them had vanished through the malignant black hole.

When the last remnants of black sand had disappeared through the void, Vitalsior's golden augefact was the only solid thing that hadn't dematerialised. It too vanished through the core of the churning black void before it violently imploded on itself.

Morreby retracted her head from the edge and Asher's linked hearing was dulled as an enormous boom tore through the cavern. Asher felt its raw power wash over Morreby's body as a fine spray of black sand rained down on her exposed skin. He felt the urge to be sick as his reality inverted and spun away from him. Asher's vision transformed into a sickening haze as his consciousness was ripped from the echoes of Morreby's auger and brutally plunged back into his own body.

He blinked his eyes repeatedly, but his vision was gone. He was blind again. He rubbed at his eyes, desperately trying to focus on anything other than the dense impenetrable fog that had stolen the world from his sight.

As his mind slowly adjusted to his surroundings a series of deafening terrified screams tore through his eardrums. They were so intense and laced with torturous suffering that they almost broke his hold over his twisted sense of sanity. Asher clamped down his hands over his ears in an attempt to block out the terrifying sound, but it did little to muffle the chaos of agony.

He then realised the screams were his own.

CHAPTER 55

HOPE AND DESPAIR

As his own terrified screams subsided, Asher found himself gasping loudly, his ravaged lungs crying out for air. His head swam and body shivered uncontrollably: both were racked with pain. Before he could make sense of anything around him, Asher's gasps were silenced as a soothing gelatinous substance filtered into his mouth, which coated his throat and pooled in his lungs.

Asher felt like he was drowning.

He could no longer breathe properly, every attempt resulted in a horrid gurgling noise that filtered into his ears, until he choked on a diluted mixture of augalyptus sap and his own blood. A massive hand landed heavily on his back, forcing his chest to contract and convulse, sending a sickening amount of bloody, sticky liquid up his throat and out his mouth.

"Asher."

Lorrelli's trembling voice penetrated Asher's ears.

Lem and Morreby also whispered his name, but they too were incapable of finding any further words.

Lobrolo held up a hand, motioning for silence, as he channelled a restorative blood calling through his auger.

Asher felt a warm tingling sensation spread across his chest. Somehow, it eased the pain racking his body and soothed his tortured nervous system, until his breathing returned to normal. Lobrolo was tempted to wait a few more minutes for Asher's body to adjust to the healing process, but the teenager's mind was far too impatient to wait for his ailing organs to catch up.

"Braak?" Asher's throat convulsed, spraying a small amount of blood from his mouth.

"He needs time, Asher, we'll know soon enough."

Lobrolo's words did little to reassure Asher about the chances of Braak's recovery. Asher's shoulders sank in dismay as a tremor passed through his heart and made his chest spasm. He gritted his teeth and shut his eyes, determined to not give in whilst Braak was still drawing breath. When the pain had subsided, he reopened his eyes, but the world remained lost behind a swirling white snowstorm.

"Gibraltair. The tribune. What happened to them? Where did they go?" Asher moaned weakly, collapsing into the roots of Braak's augalyptus tree in a heap, utterly exhausted.

Lobrolo waited for Asher's breathing to become regular before answering. He hesitantly lifted Asher's right eyelid to check something, but lowered it a second later and sighed heavily. Leaning over the old man's enormous shoulder, the other apprentices saw only a forlorn murky haze swimming over Asher's retinas.

Asher saw nothing.

"The truth is, I don't know. No-one does." Lobrolo briefly stole a glance at Cleric Riffenbon and raised an eyebrow, awaiting an answer to an unspoken question.

The Cleric paused, hovering his auger gently over Braak's temple before mimicking Lobrolo's actions on Asher, gently raising Braak's right eyelid with a finger, searching for any sign of recognition.

He returned Lobrolo's gaze and shook his head silently from side to side. Lobrolo's frown deepened as he shifted his gaze back down at Asher. He wiped away some of the blood from the side of Asher's mouth with his sleeve.

"We've never seen anything like it, but it bears all the signs of the most insidious of blood arts."

"Decisus Umbra?" Morreby whispered under her breath.

"So Gibraltair's in league with the Mortis Skulk?" Lem said unsurprised. His respect and admiration of the augiologist had long since vanished, replaced instead with a deep-seated sense of resentment and loathing.

Lobrolo retrieved something from within his robes and turned it over in his hands. The solid silver hilt of Gibraltair's shattered cane was cool against his skin. A defunct blue gem lay embedded in its crown amongst a sea of runes, ornate fixtures and sculpted metallic mouldings.

Lem, Lorrelli and Morreby stared down at what was left of Gibraltair's cane. Each of them had seen it before but never as it looked right now. The blue gem was lifeless and dull. A jet black scar ran down its centre.

"The taint," Lorrelli whispered in horror, eyes locked onto the long steadfast band of black scarring the surface of the gemstone. She'd never actually seen an instance of the taint in person. None of the apprentices had.

"His treachery is undeniable," Lobrolo whispered in a resolute and unforgiving manner.

"Praccing hell, all this time," Lem muttered under his breath, infuriated by the ease at which Gibraltair was able to pull off his duplicity.

"We can now safely assume that the method of his disappearance from Vitalsior's vault was the same way his accomplice escaped from Craftpaw Industries some time ago."

Asher's body might've been tormented with pain, but his mind was ablaze. His deductive thought processes sprang to life as he recalled a conversation he'd had with Lem's step-father about the security breach at Craftpaw. There had been a sprinkling of black sand left on the floor after the break-in.

"So Gibraltair masterminded the break-in at Craftpaw?" Lorrelli butted in, unable to believe the arrogant augiologist capable of such a grand achievement.

Lobrolo turned his head ever so slightly in response to the remark. "There's no definitive proof of the connection, but it stands to reason given what we know now."

"But why break in to Craftpaw at all?" Lem interrupted. "I mean, nothing was stolen."

"Nothing was reported stolen," Lobrolo corrected him,

relaxing his auger from Asher's chest. Lobrolo leaned back into his chair and scratched his fingers across his stubbly chin as he spoke. "In truth, an experimental augineered device was stolen, but it wasn't yet operational. Gibraltair, or the person he was indebted to, must have somehow worked out how to complete its design. How, I do not know. Even Craftpaw himself couldn't finish it. Yet it's the only thing that can explain how Gibraltair was able to overpower the legate."

"What do you mean?" Asher croaked, wiping away another trickle of blood from his mouth.

Lobrolo glanced at each of the confused faces before him, forgetting for a moment they knew little of the world outside of Mantlecrest. "Scarlet Seville was one of the strongest tribarions the Cruaar Nation has ever produced. The Chancellor recognised her potential and personally expedited her training, granting her unrestricted access to the Annals.

"The knowledge she gained there increased her understanding and control over the blood arts tenfold. But, in the end, she became a victim of her own strength. Gibraltair's device allowed him to turn the power of her blood against her."

"What was it?" Morreby raised her eyebrows at the Overseer's solemn face. "The stolen device?"

"It was initially designed as a defensive aid for the Tribarion Cohort: a way to absorb and nullify offensive blood callings."

"Like a personal Retego?" Lorrelli's mind jumped back to the Utor Alea match she'd watched from the safety of the spectator stands earlier that year.

"Similar, I suppose," Lobrolo nodded, "but Gibraltair modified the device into something far more dangerous. Instead of nullifying the absorbed offensive energy, it absorbed it, allowing Gibraltair to unleash it in one, pent-up, magnified blast."

"How can you be so sure of all this?" Lorrelli asked timidly.

"Farrenk lives. Barely, but he lives. Finneus has held him at death's door for days now. He told us everything. The fleeting echoes of the legate's auger and what little information we've gleaned from Gibraltair's auger helped fill in the rest. However, many of his secrets remain hidden to us."

"Gibraltair would be unstoppable with that device," Lorrelli whispered, fear creeping up her spine at the mere thought.

"No," Lobrolo cut off her train of thought. "There was only one prototype of the device ever made, locked away inside one of Craftpaw's most secure dead-man vaults. Gibraltair's accomplice may have been able to break in, steal it, and modify it, but it would be impossible to recreate it."

"Why?"

"Because Craftpaw himself personally destroyed the augineered schematics—"

"And the only working prototype has been destroyed," Lem interrupted, finishing Lobrolo's sentence before he had the chance.

"Indeed. However, I believe the break-in had a secondary objective: to distract the council from properly investigating Gibraltair's incursion into Foreguard. The timing of the break-in and Gibraltair's return to Undergall are too close together to be sheer coincidence."

"So the robbery was a diversion?" Lorrelli asked in a whisper.

"Yes, except both diversion and theft were successful, which means Gibraltair has more than one accomplice."

"How so?" Morreby frowned.

"Because Gibraltair couldn't have possibly known about the prototype. It was developed in secret by Craftpaw himself alongside his most-trusted augineers."

"Wait… are you saying what I think you are?" Lem blurted out hastily.

"Yes," Lobrolo looked at him sternly, the austerity in his eyes conveying the seriousness of his accusation. "The only way Gibraltair's collaborators could have possibly known about the device is if the information was leaked from a high-level augineer. So yes, Master Bruwell, I believe beyond a shadow of a doubt that a traitor has embedded themselves within the upper echelons at Craftpaw."

Everyone except Asher gasped at the news, Lem loudest of all.

"Not only that, but for the thief to escape from Craftpaw in the same manner as Gibraltair from Vitalsior's Ark, their auger would be forever scarred with the taint. As would anyone's auger that desecrated the statue in Mastonon Commons. Gibraltair's auger was free of the taint after both events, so he is neither the thief, nor the desecrator, though I fear both acts may belong to a single culprit. Needless to say, Gibraltair's conspirators still lurk in the shadows, and at least one of them is marked by the taint."

Lem, Lorrelli and Morreby looked at each other gravely.

"You four must be extra vigilant. There's no way of knowing how far this conspiracy has spread its shadow, or how many collaborators have infiltrated our ranks and gained our trust."

A solemn silence settled over the room as Lobrolo's words sank in, but it did not last long.

"What about the Foreguard augefact, the one Gibraltair told us about?" Asher wheezed, oblivious to the dismay that had set within the faces of his friends.

"First Order Tribarion Karbosch was dispatched immediately after your rescue to uncover the site of the Foreguard augefact."

"And?" Lorrelli squeaked.

Lobrolo frowned deeply. The craggy timeworn wrinkles around the corners of his eyes were the only outward sign to betray his exhaustion. It wasn't obvious to anyone other than the Cleric, who knew how to look for such things, but the Overseer hadn't slept in days, perhaps weeks. Despite everything, it was almost as if Gibraltair's disappearance and theft of Vitalsior's augefact were mere tipping points of a much greater problem weighing heavily on his mind.

"The font you described was not an easy thing to find. Gibraltair covered his tracks well, collapsing the hidden chamber under a mountain of decrepit black sand. When Tribarion Karbosch finally excavated it, it was dry, with no sign of the augefact."

"So now he has two of Vitalsior's gifts of life," Asher exhaled angrily, blaming himself for everything that'd happened.

"Why are you telling us all of this?" Morreby asked suspiciously, unsure why the Overseer would confide so much in the three of them, especially after everything that had happened because of them.

"Because, after all you've been through, you deserve an explanation. And also, well, without the four of you we'd still be blind to Vitalsior's gifts of life, let alone the vile plot surrounding them. Despite how things stand now, you four are as much on the frontline of this fight as any of us."

"So what about the other gifts of life?" Morreby asked suspiciously.

"The very best auglorians are scouring the Annals as we speak for any reference of Vitalsior's gifts, but I fear Gibraltair may have long since disposed of any such records to cover his tracks."

"So you think he's still alive and after the others?" Lem asked, confirming their worst fears.

"Without question," Lobrolo said solemnly, "but now we know they exist, the entire Tribarion Cohort has been tasked to lock down the four fallen cities until the final five are discovered. We'll find them and Gibraltair before he can do any more harm."

"Unless he already has them." Asher murmured, slumping down even farther into the cushioned back of his chair, a defeated look on his features as his eyes stared out into a sea of nauseating nothingness. Although everyone else in the room assumed Asher was talking about Gibraltair, he wasn't. He was referring to someone far more sinister that had yet to reveal their identity.

Alas, he insisted it must be you. Gibraltair's words haunted Asher's thoughts, plaguing his mind with terrors. There was a much darker force behind the exterior facade of Gibraltair's treachery.

"There's still one thing I don't understand," Morreby's shrill voice filtered in through Asher's ears as clear as day. "How did the tribune come to be in Vitalsior's ark, riding a battle gavrin, no less?"

"Actually, I was wondering about that, too," Lorrelli seconded.

"Ah, yes, the tribune. His presence and disappearance inside Vitalsior's vault was one of the first answers Finneus drew out of the depths of Farrenk's mind." Lobrolo held his finger up in the air decisively. "You see, the two had grown quite close over the years. A friendship spawned from Finneus's relationship with the tribune's late brother, Byron. The loss of two such powerful friendships has hit Finneus hard."

"And what was his answer?" Morreby demanded, wanting to know for what the tribune had died.

"Farrenk admitted to recruiting the tribune—"

"Recruiting him for what?" Lem cut him off.

"Information and intelligence."

"He was a spy?" Lorrelli countered, leaving the accusatory question hanging in the air.

"A necessary evil in these untrustworthy times, it would seem." Lobrolo frowned.

"What do you mean 'a necessary evil'?" Lem asked bluntly, still unable to grasp the bigger picture. "Who was he spying on?"

"Who do you think, you idiot?" Morreby snapped at him. "Asher," she looked quickly at Lobrolo, "right?"

Lobrolo nodded curtly. "As Mason Gobbler was doing for me."

"Wait, what?" Lorrelli exclaimed, mouth agape.

"So let me get this straight," Lem held up his hands in the air, "Mason Gobbler was spying for you and the tribune was spying for Farrenk? Was anyone not spying on us?"

"Trust is not an easy thing to give in my position, especially considering the circumstances surrounding Asher, especially as I had to place him under Scarlet's governance. We all now know of her past. I needed eyes on both you and her, eyes I could trust.

"The mould that took root in these corridors after my

brother's murder provided the necessary cover story to position him with unrestricted access inside Mantlecrest. He's been watching over Asher and the two of you ever since. Miss Fitch, however, escaped his attention."

Lobrolo placed his hands over Asher's and ran a finger along his gilded mantle.

His words struck a chord with Lorrelli and she became lost in thought, her mind trying to piece together a series of seemingly random yet somehow interconnected clues.

"Mason has long been a trusted ally and friend. It was his idea to augment your mantle with an essence extracted from your own body. To think, all it took was a lock of your hair," Lobrolo explained.

"Since your brother's murder..." Lorrelli whispered to herself. "But if the mould's been there since his death, then that must mean..." She stopped herself short as a blinding realisation clicked in her head.

A glimmer of resolute understanding quivered in the corner of Lobrolo's eye as Lorrelli pieced together what had taken him five years to uncover. He silently nodded his head at her before confirming what she already knew. "I now know how Przra Laxo murdered my brother."

The room instantly fell silent, no-one really knowing what to say to the Overseer.

"How the same Decisus Umbra blood trap did not kill you, Asher, I do not yet fully understand, but were it not for Mason's foresight and nimble fingers, I doubt a regular apprentice mantle would have saved you from death as your mantle did."

After a few moments of silence, Lobrolo released Asher's hand and shook his head free of all thoughts concerning his brother's death. He cast another hopeful glance at the Cleric, holding his gaze until it was clear that Braak's prognosis had not changed. The warder showed no obvious signs of improvement. Lobrolo sighed, his mannerisms growing more disheartening by the minute, yet his voice remained as resolute as ever. "Now, where was I?"

"The tribune, Overseer," Morreby whispered in response.

Lobrolo rubbed the tiredness from his eyes with a heavy hand before continuing with what he'd deduced from Farrenk's confession. "Yes, the tribune. His recruitment starts and ends with Farrenk. Braak was right to warn you about him. He's the most dangerous kind of Elite Guard."

"Red Scar you mean," Lem corrected.

"Zealot would be a better word," Lobrolo recorrected. "One granted the autonomy to act, unchecked, under the Chancellor's authority. Farrenk's original assignment was to investigate the Mortis Skulk attack on Braak in The Blind, but it quickly transformed into an unhealthy obsession with the boy who had an auger for a hand. Asher."

"Why? What's Asher ever done?"

Asher smiled weakly in the direction of Lorrelli's voice at his friend's continuing loyalty in defence of his innocence, something even he had begun to question after everything that had happened.

"Whatever the reason that fuels Farrenk's obsession, he's devoted a great deal of time and effort towards finding definitive proof of Asher's involvement with the Mortis Skulk."

"What garbage, Asher's no Skulk," Lem said fiercely.

Lobrolo held up his hands to assuage their concern. "I know. Trust me, I'm on your side, or I would not be here. Yet despite Farrenk's cunning, he swore a blood oath to the Scarlet Commander during the Rebellion. All the Elite Guard did. He could not break his oath even though he did not know she was the Scarlet Commander and Seville refused the Elite…" He stopped himself short, adopting Lem's terminology when he caught sight of the boy's sharp frown. "Refused the Red Scars entry to Mantlecrest."

"But Farrenk was in the Custodian's Box long before all that," Asher interrupted.

"Unless…" Lobrolo explained, running his rough fingers over

his stubbled chin, "he could get higher orders from the Chancellor himself. Orders that were promptly given after Gibraltair publically announced his unauthorised excursion in Foreguard.

"I fear Farrenk used the guise of investigating Gibraltair to gain lawful access to the academy, in open defiance of the legate's instructions. After he was inside, it was a simple matter of recruiting an agent to keep him informed."

"But why DeGrulz?" Lorrelli could think of several other apprentices who would be better suited to inform on Asher.

"More importantly, how did he turn him?" Morreby asked, unable to fathom why the tribune would align himself to such a manipulative person.

"Farrenk targeted the tribune after witnessing his reaction to his brother's death during the Utor Alea match. From there, it wasn't a hard sell to manipulate the tribune into blaming his brother's death on Gibraltair. After all, it was Gibraltair's Quaridaan leviathan that dispatched him into the afterlife."

Asher's memory shot back to the image of the Custodian's Box. He'd seen the look Farrenk had given the tribune. He remembered the tribune leaving through the vertistrand after his brother's death and a pair of black leather boots promptly following: Farrenk's boots.

"Consumed by anger and torn apart by grief, the tribune was perfectly positioned, both emotionally and strategically, making him ripe for recruitment. He quickly succumbed to Farrenk's guile and manipulation, agreeing to spy on Asher in exchange for the promise of revenge."

"So that's why he was in the vault," Lem exclaimed, finally understanding how everything fitted together.

"To see vengeance done," Asher whispered.

"Misplaced grief, when transformed into vengeance and fuelled by rage, is as deadly as the sharpest sword," Lobrolo's tone was sombre as his mind dredged up repressed emotions he'd long since buried in a dark forgotten memory. His head jerked up and, without explanation, he rose to his feet.

A loud commotion reverberated through the closed doors from the outside corridor a few moments later.

"What now?" Lem said, startled by the Overseer's sudden change in demeanour.

"It's not over, is it?" Asher whispered to himself through shallow breaths. Either no-one heard him, or they didn't want to acknowledge his fears openly.

The sounds of heavy boots marching in unison filtered towards them, muffled by the closed door. The dull uniform thud of 10 pairs of boots grew louder with every step, sending ominous vibrations reverberating through the timber slats of the door. The creak of rolling wheels clattered over the uneven stone pavers and an inhuman rasping noise followed loudly behind them.

The sounds ceased, leaving those in the room waiting in a tense silence, until a pair of confrontational voices could be heard just beyond the door. Even though the conversation was muffled beyond coherency, Asher knew that nothing good was waiting for them on the other side of the door.

Lobrolo obviously shared his sentiments and was already preparing himself to intercept any unwelcome intruders. With fists clenched by his sides and fingers flexed around his dagger-like battle mantle, he flared his transparent auger to life as he readied himself for whatever was about to come through the door. The apprentices readied themselves in a similar manner, rallying behind him, augers clutched in trembling hands.

Asher tried to lift his arm in the direction of the door, but the effort made his head spin and his chest heave. His arm collapsed before it moved an inch off his lap. Weakly clenching his fist, he gritted his teeth and forced down the pain, thinking only of his friend and protector lying unconscious in the rejuvenation chamber next to him.

Braak, wake up. Please wake up. Asher silently pleaded with the man, desperately wanting to hear his voice one last time.

With a deafening boom, the door swung open as though it had been kicked from the other side. A contingent of Red Scar Guards promptly marched into the room, battle mantles held in readiness at their sides, augers ablaze with intensity.

Lobrolo quickly assessed the three men and two women that stood before him. The Red Scar Guards moved as one. They were all seasoned war veterans, well versed in the art of synchronised combat. Their combined bulk quickly blocked both exits as they fanned out across the room, a wall of black- and red-scarred leather blocking the cool grey of the stones behind them.

"Explain yourselves!" Lobrolo demanded.

None of them said a word in response, their resolve unwavering before the Overseer's demands. Austere faces simultaneously assessed the possible threats inside the room through unblinking eyes, as fingers tightened in readiness around respective battle mantles.

"Answer me. What is the meaning of this?" Lobrolo's voice deepened and became more guttural, more animalistic, as adrenaline surged through his veins.

"Justice..." a horrible raspy voice wheezed back at him from behind their ranks. Two of the centre Red Scars immediately parted, exposing a frail wounded creature awkwardly propped up in a wheelchair. It was wrapped from head-to-toe in white bandages, most of which had turned a dark crimson from being saturated with blood that had long-since dried.

It was immediately obvious the deformed monster in the chair had once been a man, but it was no longer. Its skin and underlying muscles had been horribly deformed, melted and mutilated by flame, leaving the figure as a living ghoul whose countenance was hard to stomach.

Only one of the thing's arms was visible, but its skin was completely covered in moistened bandages. The other arm was missing entirely, a bloody stump protruding from the living embodiment of mummification at its shoulder. A thin strip of skin was visible around the fiend's eyes. It was blistered and burned beyond recognition, but its eyes remained black diamonds, shinning amidst the red-scarred flesh, burning with malevolence.

Finneus Slink stood silently behind the ghoulish creature, a long plait of silver hair draped over his shoulder. His bone-encrusted mantle rested peacefully on the creature's bandaged shoulder, whilst his auger pulsated away in its centre, emitting a venomous purple haze that spilled down over the creature's chest and legs. Tribarion Opspray stood next to him, a begrudging smirk smeared across his face.

"You've no right to be here," Lobrolo threatened menacingly, "Finneus, we agreed, Farrenk would not step foot within these walls."

At the mention of the man's name, Lorrelli instantly convulsed and fought back the urge to vomit on the floor. She could not believe that anyone could survive the mutilation that Farrenk had endured.

The mutilated man's sadistic, distorted laugh gurgled across the room. A burned and blistered tongue lolled out of his mouth as he spoke, whilst his gravelly voice sent shivers down Asher's spine with each and every word. "Oh, but I do, Overseer. I have a warrant for Bloom's arrest."

"What?" Lem burst out.

"Preposterous." Lobrolo barked. "On what charge? On whose authority?"

Another disgusting laugh scratched its way across the man's horrendously charred vocal cords as one of the Red Scars produced a black tablet engraved with white writing. An official-looking insignia had been stamped onto a bed of black wax atop a slender red ribbon.

"The Chancellor, of course."

Lobrolo snatched the tablet and quickly scanned over the list of charges. "Assault and insurrection? Sedition! Collusion and acts of conspiracy?"

"Lobrolo?" Asher muttered.

The Overseer ignored his pleas.

"You're delusional, Farrenk. You've let your thirst for revenge poison your mind. You know this will never stick." Lobrolo's eyes burned with a seething rage at the evil grin that adorned what was left of Farrenk's bandaged, blistered face.

The man's scratchy breathing and laughter stopped as he painstakingly rose from his chair unaided. Loose bandages hung around him like long wilted leaves. Patches of black- and red-charred skin were visible in the gaps between his dressings. Each new movement caused his burned flesh to weep, sending a fresh wave of blood, puss and fluid seeping from his wounds. Farrenk straightened up as best he could, but his wounds kept his back bent, almost doubled-over, his missing arm noticeably absent from his side.

"An attack on an Elite Guard is an attack on the Chancellor himself…" Farrenk spat at Asher, as he narrowed his eyes fiercely at Lobrolo, exposing a horrifically deformed smile which, in turn, revealed the few teeth that remained in his mouth, "and I will see justice done." Using the last of his energy, he raised the only arm he had and pointed a skeletal finger at Asher. "Arrest him."

Morreby was quick to rush in front of Asher and raise her auger in his defence. Lobrolo nimbly stepped in front of her and forced her auger down with his hand.

"Not here. Not now."

"Lobrolo?" Asher asked again as he felt rough hands drag him to his feet. "Lem?"

"We can't just let them take him. We have to do something!" Lem cried out desperately as one of the guards pushed past him and removed Asher's apprentice mantle from his hand, shackling his arms together.

Retrieving something from his waist, the guard fixed a large augmented clamp over Asher's hand, encasing his auger in a numbing augmented bind.

Asher instantly lost feeling in the lower half of his arm.

"You're not just going to let them take him. Prac that." Lem raised his auger, but was instantly hit in the chest by a blast from the closest Red Scar Guards. His body crumpled against the wall as pain radiated through his body.

Lobrolo retaliated in the blink of an eye.

Moving faster than anything Morreby or Lorrelli had ever seen, he rammed the hilt of his dagger into the sternum of the nearest Red Scar, sending him flying backwards into the wall. Before the man's body hit the floor, Lobrolo had already dispatched another guard with a savage shoulder throw, hurling the man across the room.

With his massive fist, he uprooted the Red Scar responsible for the attack on Lem and hurled her at the wall and pinned the woman in a chokehold against the stonework. His nostrils flared with rage as one enormous hand closed around her throat, fingers tightening, crushing her windpipe whilst his dagger was firmly poised millimetres from another Red Scar's eye.

"Enough, Overseer! This is not a battle you can win with strength alone," Finneus warned.

The remaining Red Scar had positioned the tip of her battle mantle—a serrated rapier—against the back of the Overseer's muscular neck.

Finneus's warning snapped Lobrolo from his venomous rage, a breath before the Red Scar holding the rapier against his neck was forced to act.

Lobrolo slowly lowered his dagger and dropped the woman's barely conscious body to the floor. Subduing the anger that had momentarily escaped into his veins, he turned to face the three apprentices who stood transfixed with augers raised, trembling.

"Stand down, apprentices. Finneus is right. This battle will be fought and won elsewhere," he spat the words at Farrenk as he crossed the room. Leaning in close to Asher, he spoke so softly that only Asher could hear his words.

"This is not the end, lad. I promise. You are not alone in this."

Underneath a head wrapped in a swathe of blood-stained bandages, Farrenk's depraved smile widened as he finally realised his long-awaited goal.

Asher was his.

His mind filled with anticipation as he imagined what interrogation techniques he would use to force a confession from the traitorous Asher Bloom. Soon he would have all the proof he needed. "Take him!" Farrenk hissed through blistered lips at the Red Scars as they collected themselves off the floor.

His friends could only watch on helplessly as Asher was carried out of the room, slung between two Red Scar Guards, when a commanding voice sounded out.

"Wait!"

Everyone in the room turned to look at Cleric Riffenbon who, until this point, had remained completely silent and motionless. He was bent over the rejuvenation chamber, one hand gently placed on Braak's clean-shaven temple. A dull sheen of sweat on his ebony skin shone under the auglights as his eyelids flickered and opened for the first time since he'd collapsed. It was instantly apparent to everyone in the room that Braak shared Asher's blindness.

"Asher?" he croaked weakly, his voice no more than a whisper.

"Braak?" Asher called out, unable to see his friend as he struggled weakly against the Red Scars' hold over him.

"Enough! Take him away." Farrenk rasped before motioning for Finneus to wheel him out of the room. One by one, the guards peeled out of the room. With every ounce of energy left in his veins, Asher desperately tried to break free of his captors to get to Braak's side.

Despite Asher's resurgence of energy at the sound of Braak's voice, the two Red Scars restrained him with ease. They picked him up and half-carried, half-dragged him out of the chamber. It was not until they had passed through the doors and were nearly out of sight that Braak's weakened voice sung out again, much stronger and louder than before.

"Asher! I found him!"

Asher's heart stopped for a moment as Braak's words hit home. Long-forgotten memories flooded back into his mind. Even as rough hands hauled him away, a glimmer a hope ignited deep inside his heart as Braak's voice rebounded off the walls and into his ears.

"He's alive, Asher! Raglan's alive!"

TO BE CONTINUED...

THANKS FOR READING

To find out more about the author, the characters
and the upcoming books in the series,
head to the official website:

WWW.ASHERBLOOM.COM

Or share your thoughts with Joey directly:

www.facebook.com/asherbloom

twitter @authorjoeyraw

GLOSSARY

BLOOD AND AUGER TERMINOLOGY

blood calling: The act of converting blood into a physical exertion of power by way of a Cruaar's auger and mantle.

bloodline: The auganic nature of a Cruaar's blood, specifically relating to the alignment to one of the four bloodlines: Vita, Scienta, Natura, Mortis. Bloodlines are hereditary, however mutations can occur where a child bloodline is different to that of the parents.

Vita: The oldest and most superior of the four bloodlines, now extremely rare, which grants powers that link to all living things.

Mortis: The second oldest and most vile of the four bloodlines, a distortion of the Vita bloodline, which grants power over deathly blood arts and all things dead.

Natura: The third oldest bloodline, which grants power over all natural, existing elements in the world.

Scienta: The most recent and one of the more common bloodlines, which grants the power to interact with all things fashioned by men and Cruaar alike.

First Edict: The highest measure of strength of a Cruaar's bloodline and resultant control over their abilities. First Edict mastery allows the ability to produce a blood calling without a vocal invocation.

Second Edict: The lesser measure of strength of a Cruaar's bloodline. Second Edict mastery requires a vocal invocation to perform a blood calling.

Exsili Neco: A fight to the death or banishment, whichever comes first. It can be initiated by any Cruaar over the age of 18 within a city. Banishment from the resultant city is permanently in place for as long as the victor lives.

auger: A special gemstone that transmutes a Cruaar's blood into a physical manifestation of power.

augment/ed: When an object, person or place has been physically/mentally amplified by a blood calling.

augineer/ed: The process of developing a physical device or object through the manipulation of blood powers, or the reverse engineering of human technology to use in the creation of new auger-driven technology.

augefact: A rare augineered object imbued with a certain power, made only by a sacrifice of blood, flesh or bone by its creator.

Augestry: The official branch of the council, dedicated to the registry, census, monitoring and all other auger-related affairs within a city.

auganic: The alteration, manipulation and mutation of natural genetic organisms via specific blood callings.

augalyptus: An auganic organism that produces a highly effective rejuvenating sap, which is used quite often within the Cruaar Nation.

remorauger: A parasitic auger that constantly feeds on its host's bloodstream if not satisfied with a constant supply of external blood.

gladiaugal: The art of using blood callings in battle, both offensively and defensively, via the use of battle mantles.

physiaugal: The alteration, manipulation and mutation of a Cruaar's physical body, bloodstream and mental function by the continued exposure to blood callings.

the drain: A devastating and often fatal side effect of using too much of one's own blood at one time to produce blood callings. When a Cruaar's body is drained below the bare minimum blood requirements to resume brain function, the drain sets in.

death dealer: A term given to Cruaar whose birth results in the maternal death of their mother. Death dealers are further afflicted by a parasitic link between their remorauger and bloodline.

Chromfaddar: A race that were natural enemies of the Cruaar. They are now all but extinct, with the vast majority of survivors in hiding, where they use their natural ability of projected illusion to remain hidden in plain sight within the Cruaar Nation and The Blind.

Mortis Skulk: The name given to Cruaar cultists that followed Cerebule in necrotic blood practices and led the uprising that begat the Guillotine Rebellion.

blood-leech embrace: The deathly embrace of a Mortis Skulk cultist that has deployed a necrotic blood shroud. Blood is drained from a victim's body via physical contact until paralysis sets in and all blood has been drained. Once the blood-leech embrace is set in motion, the cultist converts the victim's blood into an umbraghaam (see below) to protect itself until the victim has perished.

umbraghaam: An augmented barrier of protection released by a cultist during a blood-leech embrace (see above), fuelled by the blood of the victim.

veritusk bind: A physiaugal unification that compels those it is placed upon to tell the truth, lest their lie be revealed by flashing auger.

AUGINEERED INVENTIONS & DEVICES TERMINOLOGY

mantle/battle mantle: An augineered device that focuses the power of a Cruaar's bloodline. Every auger is comprised of seven elements, each unique to a specific auger and a base mantle, which can be interchanged for a battle mantle (weaponised mantle) after the seventh element has been imbued.

auglight: An augineered device that creates an endless supply of light without releasing any heat.

vertistrand: An augineered device commanded by the use of shifting sands (see below) that connects to all other networked vertistrands and can transport matter from one vertistrand to another. Older models are not networked and have only a fixed connection with another vertistrand.

pyxis: An augineered device used to record a message and the voice of the recorder. Once a message has been created, a pyxis can only be accessed by the blood and auger of the specified recipient.

shifting sands: An auganic organism used to command a vertistrand, also used in augineered glass and stone (e.g. Undergall Testament and promensi table).

whirlpool clarity: An auganic tonic used by scholars to induce a physiaugal state that separates mind from emotion to achieve a higher clarity of thought and deductive reasoning.

Secureaug Defence System: A series of augineered systems from Craftpaw Industries designed to protect a structure from internal and external threats.

edurus herald: An augineered device that allows the physiaugal manifestation of the operator over vast distances.

promensi table: An augineered device that reconstructs and displays a miniature version of the user and their surroundings in precise detail and in real time via use of the shifting sands for communication across great distances.

construct: An ancient augineered semi-intelligent entity, imbued and bound to the direct bloodline of its creator. Only true descendants of the creator can wield control over a construct.

mechanaug: The latest in augineered devices, reverse augineered and adapted from human technology.

OTHER TERMINOLOGY

prac/cing: Now a common slur in the Cruaar Nation, prac originates from the shortened name of vile betrayer Shyloft Pracca.

TITLES AND PROFESSIONS TERMINOLOGY

prelate: A title given to those who spend their life in service to the Augestry of a city.

legate: The title given to the person responsible for the governance of Mantlecrest.

sentinaug: A military rank, given to those who serve as the first line of defence against human detection, as well as any and all human threats.

augwife: A female cleric trained in the physiaugal arts of the birthing process.

tribarion: A military rank given to those who have the ability to master three bloodlines to varying degrees of proficiency and swear their lives in service to the Tribarion Cohort.

First Order tribarion: The highest military rank attainable in the Tribarion Cohort.

bireem: A mid-tier rank given to those who serve their host cities as intelligence officers, internal protectors or as part of the city guard.

warder: The lowest military rank still in active duty, given to those who serve their host city as reconnaissance troops, scouts and foot soldiers.

augiologist: A title given to those who pursue the study of augiology (the ancient history of the Cruaar Nation) and the recovery/conservation of any and all lost augefacts, augineered devices, artworks, etc. (amongst other items of historical importance).

auglorian: A title given to those who dedicate their lives to the study the annals of history.

augisarry: A title given to those that are commanded with the task to report on human activity, deliver human breakthroughs in technology so that they may be re-augineered, cultivate relationships with human collaborators and to safeguard the secret of the Cruaar Nation. They're often guarded by sentinaugs.

auglete / Alean auglete: Trained in the arts of gladiaugal combat, an Alean auglete competes in Utor Alea for profit or glory. Over time, prolonged exposure to the Alea changes the physiaugal make-up of their bloodstream and creates abnormal mutations in their physical appearances.

augmad: A Cruaar that has disposed of their auger and mantle, and has chosen to live out their life in The Blind in a self-imposed banishment. As a result of the loss of their augers, over time, an augmad's bloodstream reverts back to an innate state and all blood powers are lost. Many Cruaar fled the Cruaar cities during the Guillotine Rebellion and now reside in The Blind as augmads under false identities.

Overseer: An appointed official, chosen by the chancellor to govern over a city's municipal needs. An Overseer holds no authority over the Red Scar Guards, but can command the Tribarion Cohort under times of extreme duress.

grand chancellor: A position and title that was created out of necessity during the Guillotine Rebellion. The title is largely honorific of the work done to stabilise the Cruaar Nation during its darkest times, however, the position grants the bearer command of the Red Scar Guard, as well as the ranking vote within the Elder Council and authority over all city officials.

Red Scar Guard: A highly trained regiment with absolute authority over the Cruaar Nation, chosen by the chancellor and handpicked from the very best of the Tribarion Cohort. Answerable only to the Elder Council and the grand chancellor.

tribune: A title given to the most promising apprentice that has proven to be the strongest candidate for selection for induction into the Tribarion Cohort. The tribune must have demonstrated mastery over the three bloodlines and must maintain an exemplary service record.

apprentice: A title given to adolescent Cruaar placed in the gladiaugal training care of Mantlecrest. Apprentices are placed into the academy before the Ceremony of Alignment to ensure their training can be contained and controlled.

UTOR ALEA TERMINOLOGY

fulcior: One of three lighter-armoured auglets on an Utor Alea team, primarily responsible for the capture of the alea on the terraces. The three fulciors (prime, right- and left-bower) provide support, interference and defence for the molior while he possesses the alea, or battles to reclaim it.

prime fulcior: The strongest of the three fulciors, usually found at the vanguard of the attack when a team holds possession on two or three aleas, the prime fulcior will carry the extra alea if it has not been merged. The prime fulcior is the only fulcior that is allowed to make use of the molior's ground mount once a flying mount is summoned onto the pitch.

right bower: The second strongest fulcior that positions himself closest to the palmabore at all times when attacking.

left bower: The third strongest fulcior that will position himself to the rear of the molior and other fulciors, hanging back to provide long-range support and defence.

molior: The molior is the second strongest player on the team, responsible for the majority of attacks and strikes against the palmabore. The molior is heavily armoured, wears a colourful sash over his shoulders, and can summon both ground and aerial mounts during the match after a certain amount of points have been scored.

arx bastion: Named after the hero Arx, who, during the rebellion, stormed a Skulk bastion single-handedly to bring to justice the cultist that murdered his son. Arx bastions are the most powerful of all combatants on the team. They have the heaviest armoured and are charged with the protection of the palmabore. They cannot be attacked by the fulcior or molior of the other team, only by the challenging arx bastion. They wear special charged gauntlets that lend them the power of one alea, granting them increased speed, strength, agility and dexterity to make them formidable defenders against the onslaught of attackers.

Undergall Hopralas: Undergall's Seven Seal Championship Utor Alea team, named after Abigallah Hopralas, the founder of the Utor Alea.

Hollow's Rest Rajas: Hollow's Rest Seven Seal Championship Utor Alea team, named after Tjindar Rajas, founder of Rajas Orphanage, which has housed and cared for thousands of orphans, orphaned by war and the rebellion.

palmabore: The liquid silver well that houses the unraised utor, named after Palm Abore, who invented a way to maintain silver in a permanent state of liquidation.

utor: The long flagpole-like object that is raised during the final stages of Utor Alea. If all three aleas are combined and held against the utor for a full minute, victory is automatically declared in favour of the team holding the aleas.

alea: An augineered device with three charges that temporarily physiaugally enhances the bearer with increased strength, speed, agility and dexterity. Multiple aleas can be combined together to create an even more powerful device, but cannot be split once combined. Once all three charges are spent, the alea is destroyed.

CREATURES TERMINOLOGY

acropall: A mountainous semi-intelligent race, long thought extinct by the Cruaar Nation, until a solitary pregnant female was found entombed in ice and revived. Now the endangered race is being slowly repopulated and kept under the close secretive watch of Allma Ohery, who keeps their true location a secret.

gavrin: A formerly-domesticated breed of hyena-like creatures unique to the arid desert plains of Foreguard. Now they remain savage predators, corrupted by the Mortis Skulk's necrotic arts. They hunt in packs and are usually led by a female of the species. The males are blind and mostly deaf, whilst the females are the stronger of the species with heightened senses and resistances.

mawblink: A common lake-dwelling amphibian with long legs and a short stout torso. It's harmless unless provoked, and even then, still mostly harmless.

calior: A hostile winged species capable of flight, first created by auganic augineers delving into the reverse engineering of the human science of genetic manipulation. The result was a half-bird, half-reptile beast that, whilst violent and often deadly, could be trained as the winged equivalent of an oversized guard dog.

the swarm: A cluster of auganically enhanced creatures capable of flight and rapid movement, specifically augineered by persons unknown to act as a defence system against intruders. Each creature carries a microscopic amount of neurotoxin that, when administered in large doses, causes paralysis to the central nervous system as well as all attached organs and appendages.

Quaridaan leviathan: A vicious and deadly species thought extinct, completely wild and untameable that was first found in the subterranean cave system near MaiSchloss. A reptilian creature with two heads, limitless strength and lightning sharp reflexes, these beasts were often hunted down for their scales, or for their ferocious fighting ability in the arena.

querelus bark: A rare and exotic species believed to the unexpected by-product of auganic experimentation on heavily forested areas. Graced with a sentient thought, querelus barks can hibernate for decades, and only shown themselves when in the presence of an undiluted Natura bloodline.

orilla: An auganic experiment gone wrong, orillas are descendants of gorillas, but somehow ended up less evolved than their genetic ancestors. Despite living as a close-knit family, orillas are largely cannibals, inbred, extremely territorial and prone to unprovoked acts of violence.

lawnkin: Small, green, furry and loveable, not to mention the most harmless of all auganically enhanced organisms, the only problem with lawnkins is their unpredictable and unstoppable asexual replication when not auganically castrated.

extrokka: Bred primarily for hunting purposes and their prize antlers, these bald bear-like creatures are near impossible to tame. They retain an instinctive savageness that can be linked back to the exotic mix of adrenal proteins found in the bone marrow of their antlers.

fannim: An extremely rare swamp-dwelling creature with a thick gelatinous blood that survives long after extraction and naturally mutates into an auganic catalyst that is highly effective in inducing physiaugal paralysis. Hunted by not only the Mortis Skulk but also the Tribarion Cohort and Red Scar Guard, fannim blood is now a highly valued commodity on the black market.

moonkite: A species of nocturnal birds with beautiful black, orange, blue and purple plumage. A large colony resides in Undergall's Forgotten Gardens.

wandering dark: A mindless creature born out of a physiaugal mutation that manifests in a perpetual necrotic blood veil. The mutation is permanent and occurs when a Mortis Skulk projects their blood for too long without the necessary strength to maintain the veil without succumbing to the drain. When the blood veil mutates, the mutated blood feeds upon the original host's body and mind until nothing is left, except for the haunting memories that terrorise and agonise the creature for the rest of its existence.

LOCATIONS

Undergall: The oldest surviving Cruaar city in existence. Housed inside a giant cave, deep underground, the city is illuminated by a multitude of auglights, including one giant central auglight that is kept in the roof of the cave.

The city is divided into five main areas: the Forgotten Gardens, Black Ingot Warrens, Mastonon Commons and Fathomdeep Lake (which sits below the Azuretop Falls).

Decimated by the Guillotine Rebellion, many have fled this city in search of a new start, however, the seat of the Cruaar Council remains. Their chambers are housed within Earthreach Spire, alongside the Augestry, Grand Auditorium, the Annals of History, the Legion of Auger Regulation, the Tribarion Cohort Core, Ancestor's Hall. Traitor's Reach sits below the spire and holds the deepest, darkest prison within the Cruaar Nation.

Mantlecrest is the second biggest institution within Undergall, and sits on a high hill overlooking the city. Sections of Mantlecrest include: the Praelior Arena, the Undercellars, Mess Hill, the Catacomb Cathedral, the rooftop observatory, legate's office, central boiler room, barracks, ceremonial well room, the armoury, Auxilia Amphitheatre, Spiretop Gardens and Vitalsior's vault.

Oakrim: The Cruaar Nation's newest and strongest city was purposely designed and built with defence in mind. The city itself is elevated and protected by three separate tiers: the outer is the shield wall, the middle is the side-mount, and the innermost is simply known as the bastion. The city is also home to Featherpeak Conservatory and Craftpaw Industries, the biggest manufacturer of augineer devices within the Cruaar Nation.

Hollow's Rest: The second oldest remaining Cruaar city, although it was created several thousand years after Undergall.

Now home to much of Undergall's population that fled the Guillotine Rebellion, it has becoming a thriving hub of prosperity and wealth within the Cruaar Nation. Home to the Havenhaus Institute, Borbas's Beastly Bazaar, amongst countless other attractions, Hollow's Rest has become the new hot spot for those who wish to forget the horrors of the rebellion.

(Cities that fell during the Guillotine Rebellion)

Foreguard: Now referred to as the 'Fall of Foreguard', it was one of the first cities to fall to the Mortis Skulk during the Guillotine Rebellion. Foreguard was once a mighty oasis amidst the desert sands. Now, however, the city lies in ruins, covered in a necrotic layer of corrupted black sand that has buried much of its original majesty.

MaiSchloss: Now referred to as 'The Geist of MaiSchloss'. This city was once a power-house of industry and was home to countless augineers, each who had sworn an oath to serve one of the five clans of House Geist: Angelika, Ganine, Prost, Dunkel and Cochrane. Whilst the Mortis Skulk never physically attacked the city, the devastation here was possibly the worst of any municipal. Through clever manipulation and deception, a few key cultists were able to turn the five houses against one another and systematically escalate the tension until the five clans of House Geist tore one another and the city apart.

Symphony: Now referred to as the 'The Shell of Symphony', this city was initially created as an experiment as a free-floating, underwater hub that could freely navigate the oceans of The Blind. Governance of this city has had a turbulent past and changed hands hundreds of times during its existence. Although initially popular with traders and auganic augineers, the city quickly fell victim to its own success and was targeted by smugglers, pirates, free agents, augassins and rogue sentinaugs.

With no clear system of government in place and no ties to any other city, the cities rule was always dictated by the strongest contender at the time, however, the reign of the cities rule never lasted longer than 10 years, except in the case of Shanty Octomuk (aka The Sunken Sabre) whose reign lasted close to 1,000 years.

The city fell when the current ruler of the city, Salacious Muck, was poisoned by the Mortis Skulk and subsequently went mad, ordering the destruction of three of the four main ballast shafts that kept the city's buoyancy in check. Although his orders were defied, he set about destroying the ballasts himself, and took down two before he was slain. His efforts crippled the city and sent it into a steep descent until it was lost at the bottom of the deep blue.

The Blind: Everything that sits outside the Cruaar Nation, namely the human realm, is known as The Blind. Named for the ignorance of their inhabitants to the existence of the Cruaar race, key leaders of The Blind are always kept in check, monitored and influenced by augisarries, whose sole responsibility is to safeguard the secrecy of the Cruaar Nation.

CAST OF CHARACTERS

Agnus Theo Matrickville: Scienta bloodline (First Edict, current patriarch of the Scienta bloodline). Exalted augineer and member of the Elder Council.

Allma Ohery: Unknown bloodline. Renowned trainer of exotic beasts at Borbas's Beastly Bazaar.

Asher Bloom: Vita bloodline (First Edict). Raised by Raglan (an augmad) in The Blind, Asher has a golden auger embedded in the skin of his right palm. It is marred by a mysterious black mark that no-one can identify. His origins and bloodline remain a mystery.

Ballah Stemproles: Natura bloodline. Fourth-year apprentice at Mantlecrest.

Bireem Myorn: Dual bloodline (First Edict). Guard in Earthreach Spire.

Bison DeGrulz: Trifold bloodline (First Edict). Tribune at Mantlecrest.

Braak Saada: Natura bloodline (Second Edict). Warder of Undergall.

Byron DeGrulz: Unknown bloodline. Older brother of Bison DeGrulz, molior of Undergall Hopralas.

Cerebule: Tainted bloodline (First Edict). Founder of the Mortis Skulk, leader of the Guillotine Rebellion, necrotic blood-arts cultist.

Deriat Ungeltread: Unknown bloodline. Reporter for the Undergall Testament.

Ermalt Dopplebock: Unknown bloodline. Owner of Ermalt Dopplebock's Mantle Emporium.

Farrenk: Unknown bloodline (First Edict). Investigator with a keen interest in Asher Bloom.

Finneus Slink: Mortis bloodline (First Edict). Member of the Elder Council, residing Master of Mortis at Mantlecrest.

Flavink Erda: Scienta bloodline (Second Edict). Chief design augineer at Craftpaw Industries. Lem's step-father.

Gibraltair Privvybell Reine: Scienta bloodline (First Edict). Famous augiologist and explorer of the fallen cities. Discovered famous artefacts the Horn of Goopler's Cradle and the Shroud of Salvation.

Hadly McGoven: Natura bloodline (Second Edict). Master of Natura at Mantlecrest.

Harriette Gullybore: Natura bloodline (Second Edict). First-year apprentice at Mantlecrest.

Haylan Uller: Natura bloodline (Second Edict). First-year apprentice at Mantlecrest.

Hediant Slew: Unknown bloodline. First-year apprentice at Mantlecrest.

Iradi Rydecky: Scienta bloodline (Second Edict). First-year apprentice at Mantlecrest.

Lady Venuvria Mosslay: Natura bloodline (First Edict, current matriarch of the Natura bloodline). Member of the Elder Council.

Legate Seville: Unknown bloodline (First Edict). Appointed Legate of Mantlecrest by the Grand Chancellor.

Lem Bruwell: Unknown bloodline (Second Edict). First-year apprentice at Mantlecrest.

Lobrolo Altier: Unknown bloodline (First Edict). Overseer of Undergall, brother of Haalbar Altier (deceased).

Lorrelli Wittlearch: Natura bloodline (Second Edict). First-year apprentice at Mantlecrest.

Mason Gobbler: Natura bloodline (Second Edict). Augmented flora specialist, sent to Mantlecrest to investigate the spread of the creeping mould.

Montrook Ignaroff: Unknown bloodline (First Edict). Arx bastion of the Undergall Hopralas.

Morreby Fitch: Unknown bloodline (Second Edict). First-year apprentice at Mantlecrest.

Padrian Percotty: Natura bloodline (First Edict). First-year apprentice at Mantlecrest.

Penveli Catterfract: Dual bloodline: Scienta, Natura (First Edict). Master of Scienta at Mantlecrest.

Prum: A querulous bark living in an old carob tree in the Spiretop Gardens above Mantlecrest.

Przra Laxo: Dual bloodline (First Edict). Former apprentice at Mantlecrest, alleged murderer of Haalbar Altier.

Raglan (Turag Landry): Natura bloodline (since abandoned). Augmad that raised Asher from infancy in The Blind.

Reignard Fillpot: Scienta bloodline (Second Edict). First-year apprentice at Mantlecrest.

Rodrillo Hefenall: Dual bloodline (Second Edict). Third-year apprentice at Mantlecrest.

Shyloft Pracca: Corrupted Vita bloodline (first edict). The vile betrayer, served as second in charge under Cerebule during the Guillotine Rebellion.

Tortle Pluwarie: Vita bloodline (First Edict, current patriarch of the Vita bloodline). High Cleric and Elder Council member.

Tribarion Karbosch: Trifold bloodline (First Edict). First Order Tribarion of Undergall.

Tribarion Opspray: Trifold bloodline mastery (First Edict). Former member of Symphony's Tribarion Cohort, now serving in the Oakrim Tribarion Cohort.

Tribarion Roolta: Trifold bloodline mastery (First Edict). First Order Tribarion of Oakrim.

Tyranus Ranpumk: Scienta bloodline (Second Edict). Custodian of Oakrim's Augestry, reverse engineered a human blood test to identify augers corrupted by the taint.

Valderook Wrakburn: Scienta bloodline (Second Edict). Grand Chancellor of the Elder Council and current commander of the

Red Scar Guard.

Wartle Mofarder: Dual bloodline (Second Edict). First-year apprentice at Mantlecrest.

Yitsa Riffenbon: Natura bloodline (First Edict). Cleric at Mantlecrest.

(Deceased historical characters)

Abigallah Hoprala: Unknown bloodline. Founder of Utor Alea.

Alvah Firenze Sageroot: Natura bloodline Second Edict. Daughter of Belkraen Sageroot, corrupted by Weyglo Mortima and the necrotic blood arts. Resting place unknown.

Belkraen Sageroot: Patriarch and founder of the Natura bloodline (First Edict). Founder of Oakrim.

Corryl Archentor Mastonon: Matriarch and founder of the Scienta Bloodline (First Edict). Founder of Foreguard and Symphony.

Haalbar Altier: Vita bloodline (First Edict). Former Legate of Mantlecrest, brother to Lobrolo Altier (murdered).

Herion Friatt Vitalsior: Patriarch and founder of the Vita Bloodline (First Edict). Founder of Undergall, Father of Weyglo Mortima, disappeared mysteriously. Resting place unknown.

Palm Abore: Scienta bloodline (Second Edict). Cruaar augineer that invented a way to maintain silver in its liquid state at room temperature.

Tjindar Raja: Natura bloodline (Second Edict). Deceased

founder of Rajas Orphanage in Hollow's Rest.

Tribarion Tetrom: Fallen tribarion whose bones were laid to rest in the Catacomb Cathedral.

Weyglo Mortima: Patriarch and founder of the Mortis bloodline (Second Edict). First practitioner of the necrotic blood arts, illegitimate son of Herion Friatt Vitalsior and a Chromfaddar priestess. Resting place unknown.

ABOUT THE AUTHOR

Joey started writing his first novel at the age of 21 in whatever time he could spare between full-time study at University and full-time work in the hospitality sector. However, the lure of travel soon overtook his creative desires, at least for a time, and although he did graduate university, he never finished his first novel.

After three years spent travelling all over the world, he returned home, started a publishing company and again, in whatever time he had leftover, began formulating ideas for a new personal project: an epic, contemporary fantasy that would eventually become *The Frailty of Perception*; Book 1 of *The Asher Bloom Chronicles*.

When Joey is not writing or editing his novels, dabbling in graphic design, illustration, and web design, you can find him either travelling the world or working full-time in other endeavours. But he does like to take time out to enjoy a few of the simple pleasures in life. The first and foremost being a glass of single-malt scotch, or if none can be found, a delicious craft beer. Though if you do encounter him in your travels it'll most likely be on a plane to a remote location, conversing with fellow travelers in a local bar, on a dive boat amidst the deep blue sea, or atop a mountain of fresh powder with a snowboard underfoot. However, he is never happier than when he is beside a warm fire, or a remote beach, with a good book in hand.